A Trinity of Ages

Michael Dennis

Published in 2017 by FeedARead.com Publishing

Copyright © Michael Dennis

First Edition

The author has asserted their moral right under the
Copyright, Designs and Patents Act, 1988, to be identified
as the author of this work.

All Rights reserved. No part of this publication may be reproduced, copied, stored in a retrieval system, or transmitted, in any form or by any means, without the prior written consent of the copyright holder, nor be otherwise circulated in any form of binding or cover other than that in which it is published and without a similar condition being imposed on the subsequent purchaser.

A CIP catalogue record for this title is available from the British Library.

Book covers in collaboration with Anne Owen and Alistair Bates

michaeljohndenniswriter.co.uk

CHAPTER ONE

Suddenly the bear was there again! Very close, and very annoyed about something. Big Nose supposed he would be if that 'something' had woken him from winter sleep. Or maybe he was just hungry, and here was more trouble for him. Then he saw it. They stood looking at each other, the beast pawing the snow and sending up a cloud of it, and making a lot of noise. It launched towards him. He reached into his bag, hurled a stone and missed, throwing himself behind a meagre oak as the giant charged past, well wide of him, grunting ferociously. Definitely sleepy! He grabbed another stone out of his pouch. It was a really handy one, prized that morning from the bed of the shallow, icy river below the camp. Big Nose could hear the beast lumbering about in the undergrowth, never far away. He was sure it was just collecting itself, soon to reappear, and maybe wider awake.

He was thankful the rhino's prints were going in another direction, and not towards the camp. But now it seemed he was still in trouble. The bear stumbling about in the forest had woken him moments after he had stopped and fallen asleep from sheer exhaustion (never a good idea). There had been moments when he doubted he would ever get back to the camp in the ever-deepening, stinging snow, weak from hunger and with the hip that had been bad for as long as he could remember and was getting worse with every moon that passed. And now that bear! He was worrying! Sooner or later he – or she – would be back!

Here and there, where there was a thinning of the trees, the freezing wind off the sea not far away had come through and blown some of the snow away so that it was less deep and he could quicken his pace just a little – as much as he could with his infirmity – until he ran into the inevitable drifts thrown around the next birches or stunted ashes as if to keep them warm! But despite the clearings it was not good country for proper hunting, not really, not for able-bodied men: too many trees for an organised hunt even in good weather! You had to go farther for good hunting country, towards the sea and the lagoons. But if you had to be on your own, then round here could be all right. Some straying baby deer popping out of nowhere and getting a big surprise might be just the answer. Might! But he was dreaming.

Something stirred behind him. He turned round. The bear was cruising back toward him across a clearing with what appeared to be even greater determination. The pain as he raised his arm and twisted his body to throw the stone he was holding was terrible. It connected, the blow to the head causing the animal to veer slightly, its huge body almost touching him as he leapt aside, before retreating out of sight and smell in an impressive but decreasing commotion of snorting and grunting and snapping of branches. Big Nose could only hope it might have deterred him.

He wiped his forehead with the sleeve of his mammoth-fur coat, pulled his lynx-fur cap more firmly down on his head and took stock, then stumbled on through the snow. Again and again the tops of the trees swayed as the freezing wind reached down, rushing through the dead birch leaves in the trees around him, making his eyes water and half blinding him with another wave of the swirling white stuff. It was getting dark now and he had only one decent stone left.

And what had he got for his solitary expedition, his risky attempt to find food for Curvy Lips nursing the baby – Curvy Lips! She with lips that curved like the rest of her; kind, hard-working, gentle Curvy Lips who loved him as though his bad hip did not exist? Or for her mother, Shining Leaf, who was now feeling her age and relying on him? Zilch!

He would be sorry to disappoint the old lady. They would have to rely on some leftovers from the rest of them. But there would be a fire... The others had not gone hunting today, and for good reasons, so why was *he* out here in the freezing cold? On the off chance – on the off chance that he might be lucky. It wasn't often he felt fit enough to run with the hunt, but he wanted to fend for himself and his family and went out by himself as often as he could, rain, snow or shine. Of course, the others thought he was mad, but he had long got used to their jibes. True, the others wouldn't leave them to starve, but he wasn't content to tend fires and scrape and sew skins all day with the women like any good cripple.

A very small movement caught his eye. He could hardly believe his luck. Of course, baby hares had to eat like everything else, and it was just what he was looking for. There were two of them there, not four man-lengths away, scrabbling around in the snow among the trees. There was nothing like hunger for accuracy of aim. The stone intended for daddy bear hit one of them like a mammoth colliding with a baby deer. Only one result possible: dead hare – almost, anyway. Hooray! He held up the quivering animal by its hind legs and killed it with a blow. Then he noticed – what luck! – that the other one was wandering around in a daze. This was caught easily enough, and a good whack with a boulder finished it off promptly. As he popped it into his deerskin pouch with the other one he thought he caught sounds of the bear again, and froze, but the faint sounds of parting branches and breaking twigs were clearly receding, although he could see nothing in the falling snow and the dusk. The bear's den might be near, though the bears were mostly encountered some distance up the river. This might be a loner. There were some. A wanderer. What chance would he have of avoiding those claws as long and thick as his fingers?

The camp could not be seen for the snow which was now falling thickly all the time, but two owls seemed to be guiding him, one to the right, one to the left. It gave him comfort and confidence.

When finally he came out of the trees and down to the river, and had struggled with his gear across its stony bed, despite the encouraging glow from the camp fire ahead he sprawled exhausted on its snowy bank, in pain from the bad hip but relieved to have made it once again. He would give himself a moment before tackling the slope towards the line of trees where the camp, and safety, were just beyond the brow.

He was roused almost immediately, however, by shouts from that direction. It seemed there was trouble. Hastening with difficulty up the final slope and reaching the top he encountered a scene of confusion; women running around screaming, children being hustled into the shelters, men with clubs. One of the men caught sight of him. It was Smooth Face. The young man was running towards him. That was never a good sign in itself. So-called because of his white skin and sparseness of beard, Smoothie was rarely a carrier of good news. He was certainly in good shape, Big Nose thought, running like that. But then, he did look after himself. No solitary ventures for him…

"Bad news, Big Nose". Big Nose was filled with foreboding. "I'm sorry, but it's Curvy Lips. A bear came."

Big-Nose later could not later remember exactly what happened after that. Curvy Lips's baby was being held by one of the women, and other women and one or two of the men were standing there in his shelter on the edge of the camp. One of the men – Strong, the toughest man, and after Giant Man (the headman) the tallest in the camp – was holding Curvy Lips in his arms. She was not a pretty sight with her neck broken and blood everywhere.

"I'm sorry," he said. "She just went out somewhere and the bear got her. We cornered it and speared it. It's dead."

Apparently, one of the women had come and helped him to his shelter, while other women had taken care of Curvy Lips's distraught mother, Shining Leaf.

And that was that. He remained alone with the body, here in the shelter which he had built where a hawthorn and elders had become intertwined and roofed it over with birch twigs and skins and Curvy Lips had skilfully padded the sides with evergreen fronds. Here at least was protection from the snow and some respite from the wind and cold, but sleep was impossible for him.

At first light the women came and prepared the body for burial and covered it in the red burial juice. They offered him food, but though hungry before, now he could eat nothing. Later, Giant Man and certain of the other men, including Strong and also Smooth Face (who was never far from Giant Man, but whom Big Nose could have done without on that day), walked with him as with great difficulty he carried the body to the pit in the forest. By custom, two of the women were allowed to accompany him, although he would have preferred not and he had no idea, later, who they had been. Meat, and certain things which the women judged Curvy-Lips would need, were carefully wrapped in a delicate skin and placed with the body. Digger, who's job it was to extend the pit as necessary and see to burials, piled soil on the body, and then when Giant Man gave the word they all returned.

The weather still being too bad for hunting, the men gathered in shelters chatting or playing games with stones, while others sharpened spear or axe heads. But the snow stopped in the middle of the day, and GM ordered the hearth to be prepared, saying they could roast the bear and eat it rather than just burn it to ash, even though it had killed Curvy Lips. Big Nose couldn't face the meat, and later, after the others had finished eating around the big fire in the clearing in the middle of the camp, he took one of the hares and cooked it on the hot stones around the edge.

"You could have done without that," a voice said while he was in the middle of his cooking. "Then you might have kept her." It was Slanty Face, so called because one side of it was higher than the other and somehow one eye looked one way and one the other. Everybody disliked him, but everybody envied his speed and skill at hunting. Evidently he was telling him he shouldn't have gone hunting on his own. He couldn't stop himself blabbering any more than he could stop himself running. Big Nose took no notice; he felt too angry with himself. And Curvy Lips, why had she gone out? She was impulsive, a bit careless. She might even have been going to look for him. How he wished he had not gone out. Now the women would look after the baby, and he wouldn't see much of her. Old Smooth Face hung about, too, making supposedly sympathetic but not particularly helpful remarks. He could never resist stirring things up.

Big Nose had already decided to take the cooked hare back to Shining Leaf's shelter and suggest she share it with him. They had always got on well, and she was grateful for the suggestion. Generally, though, she had always preferred to eat by herself in her shelter, which was in shrubbery close by his own, rather than with the other women, one of them bringing food to her before joining the others round the fire after the men. Big Nose reflected that if Slanty had said what he did in her presence she would have spat on the ground and told him to go and straighten his face.

She would not let him do the same with the other hare on the following day, saying he needed all of it himself, but Strong, the only person he could really call a friend in the camp, seeing him eating in his shelter on his own, brought food and came and joined him. Big Nose wished afterwards that his friend had not happened to mention the wound on the bear's head, which was very new, he said. It looked as if he'd been hit by a large stone. It was a remark that he knew he would never forget. He would like to have gained some consolation from the knowledge that at least the bear provided some food for the rest of them, but his heart was too heavy.

About three days after the death, Big Nose tried to run with the hunt. They had already been out on the last two days, since the snow had slackened and turned to sleet and it was not quite so cold, but he had not been able to run with them since that last, long day on his own in the snow because his hip and his back had hurt so much. They had not had great success. The chief now said they would head for the Long Lagoon. Although Big Nose had a sudden dread of leaving his little daughter – so precious a link with his cherished Curvy Lips cruelly snatched from him – he felt sure really that the women would let her come to no harm, and it comforted him to know that wise old Shining Leaf would be keeping an eye on things.

As usual, the strategy as the party followed the course of the river down to the lagoon was for four men – two on each flank – to run through the surrounding trees to flush out anything that might be there. Because of his bad hip, Big Nose was struggling to keep up with the main party. Unlike him, most of the men ran barefoot and with minimal deer-hide covering. The day began promisingly. The sun had barely risen when, not long after they joined the river, a huge buck suddenly crashed out of the undergrowth on the right-hand side, preceded and followed by the excited shouts of the beaters and then by the beaters themselves urging the terrified beast into the path of the main party. Nobody knew how Slanty Face could see straight when he was looking two ways at once, but as usual he was in the front of the main party and running like lightning across the uneven, snowy ground straight for the animal, aiming his spear, with Long Legs and others close by. It would have been a miracle if he had hit his target given that the deer was moving like a…well, like a deer, but if anyone could perform such a miracle, Big Nose thought, it was Slanty Face. Alas! Even he missed, and so did the others. Old spotty coat roared into the undergrowth on the other side and then, because it ran into the beaters on that side, almost immediately emerged again just in front of the second line of advance which included GM. Strong, just to GM's side, heaved a large rock at the buck's head. Only he could have hurled such a huge rock so accurately. The buck staggered for a second, and then the kind of the thing happened that Big Nose dreaded most. Staggering and bleeding, and hemmed in on all sides, it came towards him as he trailed behind the other men. In those few moments, for Big Nose time seemed to stand still and all his past life, his misfortunes, his difficulties and bad luck weighed him down. Everyone fell silent as he reached for a stone – surely another hit would slow the animal down so that they could beat it to death! But then as he turned to aim, a terrible pain low down in his back caused him to stumble and he fell to the ground. The beast saw its chance and almost touched him as it shot into the wood.

"You old woman!" GM yelled. "We put it there for you. A gift, and then you couldn't take it!" Slanty Face, too, was looking disgusted – insofar as one could tell.

"Anyone can slip," Strong said, drawing close to GM, his wide, strong face betraying an unusual concern. He did not often push himself forward..

"I s'pose you'll tell me it was a one-off slip," GM countered, "but he spends more time down on the ground than on his feet these days. We need people with legs. Let's get moving." Strong did not reply, and the party resumed its advance, walking now, being temporarily out of breath, and pinning ever more hope on a good day where the trees opened out nearer the sea.

Smooth Face approached the chief. "There's work needs doing in the camp, Giant Man," he suggested. "I mean, for Big Nose."

"Do you think the women would have him?" GM replied.

"Or he could try some fishing…"

But no more was said – then. By the lagoon the wind was strong, and freezing cold. Despite several alerts when animals were startled out of their hides on the scrubby, ice-strewn flats, nothing was taken all morning but a few seagulls caught in a seaweed net.

"It may have been the two geese I saw in an ash tree this morning," Giant Man said. "That must be why we have caught nothing. I hoped I was wrong about the geese." Big Nose knew that according to the chief, geese in an ash were always a bad sign. They belonged in the river. What would they be wanting to do there except shit on somebody, he would say. No-one doubted that Giant Man knew most of what there was to know, though that was not to say that there were things he could not explain, like where the spirit went after death. Naturally, that was something that concerned Big Nose greatly at the moment.

Hungry and disappointed, and with nothing for the fire that night, at noon it was decided by Giant Man that they would have to abandon the trip. Not surprisingly, the uphill homeward trail through the snow was dismal, with no-one really expecting any change in their fortunes. In the circumstances it was no surprise to Big Nose, who was very much aware that he had been foremost in ruining the expedition – having failed to distinguish himself by his agility at the lagoon any more than earlier in the day – that on the way home when they came near the place where the buck escaped Smooth Face said suddenly,

"Come to think of it, Giant Man, now I think *I* remember seeing those two geese that *you* saw this morning flying from an ash tree. It was here, where we missed that buck., wasn't it? "

"I expect it was," GM agreed. "Smooth Face, you are very observant. I think you must be right."

The others began to murmur among themselves as they went along. If anyone doubted Smooth Face's memory, they did not say so.

Lagging behind, Big Nose did not hear what GM said finally in a low voice, but he could make several guesses, and no-one but Strong came near him for the rest of the way home. He thought about how Smoothie never missed anything, and never missed getting a word in. GM always believed him but never seemed to notice that he rarely actually caught anything or did anything much at all. He had long since concluded that it must be that GM liked being flattered.

"Did you see the geese?" he asked Strong when only he was within hearing.

"I may have done."

"I mean when I slipped."

"No, but I wasn't looking. May have missed them."

"Smooth Face could have been making it up."

"Giant Man doesn't think so."

At any rate, nothing more was taken that day. It was always like that with GM, Big Nose thought to himself. The chief was always right. Giant Man saw many signs in subsequent weeks. Everybody was talking about them: a white dunnock (Smooth Face pointed that out), a plague of ducks, an orange moon... All were bad in one way or the other. Then others began to say they had dreamed terrible dreams, dreams of cold and starvation, failure in hunting...

A couple more outings and Big Nose gave up trying to follow the hunt. It was bad enough not being able to keep up, but bad as well not being able to run near-naked like the others because being older and slower he felt the cold all the more. Then there were the jibes and bad feelings caused by the suspicions put about by Smooth Face and others, and indeed the near-certainty that somehow he, Big Nose, was behind all the bad luck that came their way in hunting as in everything else.

Increasingly, Big Nose did not eat with the rest but went to his own shelter and ate anything – maybe a hare or a water bird – that he had been able to obtain in his own little forays in the woods or upstream and cook by the big fire. He felt bad about taking advantage of the others' rare successes, and anyway they were making it clear now that he was not welcome even if they did not actually refuse him food when he had had an unsuccessful day. Once, though, he managed with an uncanny skill that surprised everybody to hunt down a young deer that had been wounded by a bear, and club it to death. Because nobody would eat it, he and Shining Leaf fed well on it for several days, while she cut slices off it and hung them up to dry over the fire that the old women often lit just for themselves.

Amid jeers, he started regularly taking food he had cooked to Shining Leaf's shelter (where at other times many of the women would gather) and sharing it there with her. Said to have seen fifty winters, Strong called her the Camp Mother. The fact was, however, that she was ailing badly. Shining Leaf had never really got over her daughter's death, though she never blamed Big Nose for that or for anything else and by all accounts remained grateful for his kindness towards her and thus his faithfulness to her daughter's memory.

The women saw signs and portents, too, but Shining Leaf didn't have much belief in them. A crow landed in a tree where a woman was heavily pregnant and cawed itself hoarse. It was a sure sign of bad labour, the women said. The men were murmuring about Big Nose's bad influence, but Shining Leaf would have none of it:

"Fie on you all," she shouted – at least it would have been a shout if she had had much voice. "You believe anything. Leave the poor old crow out of it – and Big Nose!"

When the baby was stillborn, seemingly confirming the bird's prophetic powers, none of the women dared criticise Shining Leaf, but among themselves they began to blame Big Nose again, reckoning that he had begun to exert a bad influence on the old woman.

It was at about this time that Big Nose returned to his own place one night and was amazed to find a little meal of pigeon breast and hazelnuts and walnuts laid out on a tray of bark decorated with leaves and flowers. A woman's work, certainly, but he could not imagine what woman had had such thoughts for him. He said nothing to anyone about it.

As spring got under way, wind and rain set in. Several times it blew down or flooded their shelters, put out their fires and made them feel more miserable than when they had been frozen. In the middle of all that they found Shining Leaf dead on her reed mat one morning. It was as if the storm had come and taken her life away in the night. She was buried with more than the usual ceremony, with all the women contributing items of food and clothing, medicines and ornaments, and many of them insisting on going to the burial. It was made clear, however, that Big Nose should stay away for fear of a bad reaction from the spirits.

In the absence of Shining Leaf, his standing among the women went from bad to worse, with nothing now shielding him from their contempt for him. They even decided he should be kept away from his daughter and no longer allowed to play with her for fear of his bad influence. Shining Face, fed by one of the women in milk, was growing well and would soon be on her feet. All in all, things became very difficult for him to the extent that he thought he would have to leave his people and make his own way. Not many left a camp, especially on their own, but he knew that his father had been one of them. It was said that although he, too, had difficulty walking – even greater difficulty than he did himself – he had walked alone for two moons as a boy after his parents and almost everybody else in their settlement had been wiped out in a flood. He had been adopted by this people out of pity and had been content to work alongside the women. He had died many years ago, and Big Nose's mother even earlier, giving birth to him. The worst thing about leaving – if he did go – would be leaving Shining Face behind, surely never to see her again.

Big Nose did not even know what lay further inland, since they usually pitched camp not far from the sea. People spoke of endless forests and wide rivers, and perhaps another sea beyond, but nobody really knew. However, the weather was getting a bit warmer and soon there would be plenty of birds' eggs for the taking, on which he might survive even if he had little success in hunting. In any case, wasn't he a dab hand at getting fish out of the river with a piece of meat on a little antler hook dangled on a length of sinews? And that despite the jibes of those men going out for a day's hunting in good times who thought nothing could be worth catching without swank and sweat.

Big Nose told only one person of his thoughts: Strong.

"I wish I could help you *here,* make things better for you," Strong said, sitting in his shelter on a carved log seat, shaping his spear of yew with a sharp flint blade, "but I really have no power to do so. You see how we rely on GM. We have no-one else who knows everything."

"*Almost* everything", Big Nose said. Strong looked at him curiously, the dark countenance darker and more severe than usual. "He doesn't know where the spirits of dead people go."

"True," Strong agreed, grudgingly. "Nobody can know that."

"There are lots of things nobody knows, Strong, like what lies beyond the sea."

"You are grieving still," Strong said, sympathetically. "Do you think *she* is there, over the sea?"

"I don't know. She's not here, is she? Anyway, there's nothing for me here."

"I think they need me here; otherwise perhaps I'd go with you." Strong looked thoughtful. Then he got up slowly from his comfortable seat and went and took another of the yew stems leaning against the hazel twigs that made up the side of the shelter.

"Sure they need you," Big Nose agreed. "But I hope we shall always be friends."

"Of course. So will you go?"

"I'm not sure. Say nothing."

"In case you do, I'll make you one of my special spears," Strong said. "It's the least I can do for you. Do you know which way you will go?"

"They say there's another sea beyond where the sun sets in spring."

The other looked at him, but said nothing.

*   *   *

Each spring when the weather really warmed up, a kind of

celebration would take place in which, just before sundown, everybody in the camp except the children would ceremonially drink bark juice prepared by GM and mixed by him with the juice of certain berries. The chief would watch closely to make sure there were no defaulters. Things would happen that night that nobody ever spoke about afterwards, and indeed no discussion was ever allowed on the subject. Although the tribe often struck camp and moved on at about this time – and this was known to be Giant Man's intention now – it was never possible for at least a day after the ceremony owing to its effects. The weather being suddenly warm, though, Big Nose thought it might be possible for him to make an unnoticed departure very early in the morning. However, back in his own place he soon found himself in a half-world of alternating lucidity and fantasy and the disordered sounds of chasing in the undergrowth and screams and laughter coming from where the young, unattached women slept together. He hesitated to settle down to sleep for fear of oversleeping. It was a moonless night and pitch black, if far from silent, among the thickets of the camp.

The woman came to him almost imperceptibly as he leaned unsteadily against the side of his shelter...somebody beside him, a body touching his, the scent of a woman slowly almost without his realising it drawing him to herself, supporting, he might almost have said comforting, him. She was strong, but her manner was tender. Her breath, her hair smelled faintly of lilac. She held him firmly but lightly, and with the gentleness of an intimate friend, and against the screams and laughter in the distance her presence in the stillness and peace of the shelter were a solace that he had no desire to resist, her lips eventually finding his and her long hair rippling down his body, and her fingers gripping his shoulders from behind. He could not see her at all, but of one thing he was certain: that whoever she was this was nothing random, like everything going on around him, and that the woman had meant to come to him, and just him. Yet no woman had been near him since Curvy Lips had gone, and he could not imagine, thinking of all the women in the camp, who she might be.

She had shed most of what she had been wearing, leaving only the thin skins that women wear as undergarments. Now she was letting herself down onto the rushes strewn upon the ground, gently drawing him down beside her, undoing the thongs of hide that tied his tunic. Her breasts beneath the garment as she drew his hands firmly down her body were warm and, yes, welcoming. Nimbly she moved to kneel over him, still kissing him, moving on him, savouring him. Yet even now, something – some desire not to know, perhaps, or even some fear – prevented him from asking her who she was. Long since fully aroused he encouraged her, as she straddled him, to guide him, and she took him into herself powerfully, eagerly, and when the moment of ecstasy came, not even Curvy Lips had gripped him so tightly inside her or throbbed so long. When it was over it seemed she would never stop kissing him – a delight that he shared, and a gift that he returned, in full. Then as suddenly and silently, and as unexpectedly as she had come, she was gone. Not a word had been spoken.

Big Nose awoke only when the sun was well up, and it was quickly clear that it would be another day or two before camp was struck, for there was little movement around him. They must all be feeling like he was – weak at the knees and sick. He decided to postpone his departure until they were leaving and he could see which way they were heading. Then he would slip quietly away in another direction. It was only when he was about to go and sit by the river with his fishing line later in the morning, as much to revive and fortify himself as anything, that he noticed half hidden near where he had been lying the pieces of pigeon meat and nuts nicely presented upon a tray of bark. He would eat them when he returned if he felt well enough.

Fishing was never his only reason for being by the river. Everybody knew about the Spirit of the River, but most of them only appreciated its importance when it got angry – or when a bird that belonged to the river got up an ash tree where it should not be. For him the river was where he went when he needed strength, courage. Did it not become part of the mighty sea?

He had not been there long when Smooth Face approached, unheard, as if from nowhere. He had some disturbing news, delivered as usual with that mask of seriousness below which there lurked, Big Nose always felt, a certain mischievous pleasure.

"Big Nose, I have heard that Giant Man wishes to have you killed because you are a danger to us. I tried to stick up for you, but he was angry."

"Why should he be angry all of a sudden? What have I done now but keep myself to myself."

"I don't know, but I have never seen him so angry," Smooth Face said. "He got his spear – you know, the ceremonial one dyed in bear's blood and sharpened with the antler of a stag in rut – and slammed it into a tree. It only just missed Slanty Face who happened to be standing near."

"Who will do this, my friend?" Big Nose was trying to hide the tremor in his voice.

"There were volunteers, they say. I couldn't tell you more."

"Evidently you weren't one of them."

"Of course not!" Smooth Face said indignantly," and then, after a few moments, "Will you go?" A mere whisp of a man, Smooth Face was standing a few paces from him. fidgeting with his smart leopard skin and avoiding his eye as he waited for an answer..

"What do *you* think I should do, Smooth Face?"

"I should head upstream."

Big Nose stared at the water rippling over the pebbles in the river. The sun was shining and made the water sparkle brilliantly. A small bird was hopping about determinedly from rock to rock. There was something remarkably stupid about that man, he thought, if he expected him to take that advice. He would not follow the river at all. When he looked up, Smooth Face had vanished.

He started back immediately. He had caught no fish. That was a bit unfortunate, for in view of the great danger, if the unpredictable Smooth Face was to be even half believed – and he could take no chances – he must collect his belongings and hasten his departure. He did not fancy having his skull smashed by Digger (once or twice Giant Man, in a fit of temper, *had* ordered Digger to slay someone) – or for that matter having his body burned and his ashes taken and buried deep in the forest so that no trace of him remained. It was regrettable that he could not say goodbye to Strong. A first-class spear would also have been useful. Worst of all, he would not even be able to have a last glimpse of his little girl.

As he approached the edge of the trees he could hear raised voices. There seemed to be some argument. It sounded more serious than a bit of bad temper resulting from the hangover that generally followed the orgy. Several times he heard a woman scream. It wasn't one of those excited screams he had heard last night; it was something far less pleasant.

It was fortunate that his own shelter was on the edge of the settlement, and that he was able to enter it unseen – so far as he knew. Listening as he gathered his things together, it seemed that the commotion was coming from just one part of the camp, and that despite it many people were still asleep after the revelries. An improbable but frightening thought crossed his mind, which, although he dismissed it instantly, had the effect of making him move more quickly.

First he retrieved his mammoth fur (it had been his father's), two or three spare skins and his rhino hide boots. He fastened on the boots. Then he took a small deerskin pouch containing his most precious belongings and another into which he thrust what scraps of fresh and dried meat and other food he could lay his hands on, and tied these round his waist. Next he drew his mammoth fur round him and fastened on his large pouch loaded with axe heads and other essential tools. To this he would add a few stones as ammunition. Finally he slung his fire-making gear and the spare skins over his shoulder before quickly thrusting the morsels left for him on the bark tray into his mouth, gathering up his spear, pulling on his lynx-fur cap and sliding out of the shelter.

In bursts of sunshine and relative warmth, keeping at first to the trees on the higher ground he then crossed the river some distance upstream. Reflecting that at least there should be plenty of water about at this season he started up the opposite slope strewn with oaks and hawthorn and sometimes almost impenetrable long grasses. It was a place he had often come to so as to be alone. He wouldn't be hanging about here now, though, but would head straight for the low hills inland. So far he was on familiar ground. Soon it would be another story. Two hills ahead and he would be in the unknown. He was pondering this, and glancing behind him from time to time to check that no-one was coming after him, when suddenly, a movement among the trees ahead attracted his attention.

His hand went to his spear. At the same time he was searching the ground for stones. He did not want to encounter either man or beast at this moment, but simply to put as big a distance between himself and the camp as he could. If he had to choose, he would prefer animal to man. When a man emerged from the greenery holding two spears his first thought was that someone had seen him preparing to leave and that this was an interceptor sent under Giant Man's orders. He prepared to make a stand.

"I thought you would never come, you're so slow," the man shouted as he approached. It was Strong. He was smiling as much as

Strong ever could with those powerful but near-immovable features dark under his frowning forehead. "I saw you leave. I thought somehow that you would come this way, and I slipped round the back there..." He pointed to beyond the long, scrubby spur that Big Nose had followed, now on the opposite side of the river.

"Smooth Face saw me. He told me everything."

"Perhaps not everything. But if I were you I wouldn't trouble yourself about that, save to know that Smooth Face, as I'm sure you know already, is treacherous and not to be trusted. You must go quickly. But before I give you the spear I promised, I have to inform you that the beautiful Red Hair begged me to say to you that she wished to go with you. I discouraged her, but she was insistent. If you take my advice, you'll clear off. You can't be doing with her. Go now! I wont tell her which way you went."

So it *was* her! The beautiful Red Hair with the slim body and eyes that shone like the sun through leaves on a warm, summer morning. He whistled. Giant Man's Red Hair! – when she wasn't someone else's! Big Nose hesitated, but only for a moment.

Strong handed him the spear. It was magnificent. It was just the right weight and length, and he must have spent a long time shaping and sharpening it with his flints and deer antler. "And don't worry about the baby," he said, reading his thoughts, which were in turmoil. "She will be all right." Another moment, and his friend was gone, running in another direction to arrive at the camp from the other side.

Big Nose walked on, up the slopes that led inland, and away from his people and away from everything he knew. Like he frequently did, he fingered the ring of acorns strung round his neck with lynx's gut – a charm passed on to him by his father dying from a poisoned leg years ago. In spite of it, he did not rate his chances high, but for the moment the warmth and the onset of spring gave him hope, and he would certainly put Strong's gift to good use.

CHAPTER TWO

"Marcelle, will you stay behind a moment, please."

No-one minded staying behind for Miss Palmeson, but her sister would be waiting outside. Lenie got pretty cross when she didn't come out on time. "Lenie will be waiting for me, Miss Palmeson"

"It will only be a minute or two." Marcelle went up to her teacher's desk. "You were getting on fine with that card, Marcelle. Did you enjoy doing it?"

"Yes, thank you, Miss Palmeson."

"I am glad."

" But I wish I wasn't so slow."

"Never mind, you will be able to finish it next time." The teacher said nothing for a few moments. Marcelle had the feeling she was wanting to saying something else, and soon it came out: "By the way, Marcelle, that mark on your head where there's a little bruise. Does it hurt.?"

"No, Miss Palmeson, I was just getting out of bed when I fell a bit."

"You were hurrying, possibly…a bit late, maybe?" Teacher was smiling. She always did. She smiled back. "This morning, was it?"

"I can't quite remember," Marcelle replied, but then corrected herself: "Yes, I remember it was this morning. Please, Miss Palmeson, can I go now? Lenie gets very impatient."

The teacher did not seem in any hurry. She sat back in her chair, thoughtful for a moment, pencil tapping her lipsticky lips. How near, how real everything was then...the whiteboard with its words in colours explaining how to make funny birthday cards with bits that popped up...the wrinkles on the teacher's rosy cheeks, the grey bits in her dark hair. She must be pretty old, older than Mummy, much older. Mummy didn't have any wrinkles, and her hair was all brown... "All right," she said at length, getting up from her desk and coming round and putting a kindly arm around her shoulders as they moved towards the classroom door, "you can go home now. Be a bit more careful when you get up in the morning. What about getting up five minutes earlier?"

"And where the bloody hell have *you* been," her sister growled, when she got outside.

"Seeing Miss Palmeson."

"Chatting up Miss Palmeson? Nosey old bag. That's the worst of not getting married..."

Marcelle did not like the way Lenie talked about Miss Palmeson. She was really nice. But she did not try disagreeing with Lenie any more than she would have thought of disagreeing with Miss Palmeson, who had been telling them all about Sir Isaac Newton and Albert Einstein. Lenie knew everything that mattered. She *was* grown up, after all – twice her own age: sixteen and a half, and tall, and to make it all worse *she* was small for her age.

"I was asking Miss Palmeson something about 'levers'."

"About what?"

"Levers and sliders. Things that make words and pictures and things pop up in Christmas cards and whatnot."

"Good God, the things they stuff into little minds these days. You didn't have to explain about the marks on your head, then."

"She didn't ask me."

"Good." Lenie was shielding a cigarette against the cold wind as she tried to light it. It was April.

One of the nicest things about going home was that it was mostly downhill. First you went along Laburnum Road, then you went down the long, straight, steep hill of Sycamore Road. At the bottom (reached after crossing several roads that went straight across) if you turned right it was their road, Hawthorn Road. It, too, sloped down and had roads going straight across it. So everything was in squares, and all the houses were semi-detached and similar to each other, with little square gardens and hedges, but a little different as well.

Seeing the grandparents' Volvo parked outside seemed to make Lenie smoke all the harder – a thing Marcelle had often noticed. Entering the house, Lenie passed the open door of the sitting room with a brief "Hi!" and a waft of her cigarette arm, and went on into the kitchen. Marcelle paused by the door to hear Grandpa say,

"And here's number two! Looking very smart, Marcelle!" Marcelle liked the grey skirt and red jumper of the school uniform (introduced recently) because they made her feel the same as everybody else. "How did it go today?" Grandpa was her father's father.

"Fine!" she said, going in (she could hardly not go in). Instead of waiting for the inevitable question she said, "We were making birthday cards with pop-up names, and jokey cards with a little hole where a picture came in when you pulled something across. It was really fun, but I was a bit slow."

Grandma in one of her posh two-pieces and Grandpa all kitted out with his cherry waistcoat and his yellow tie and polished brown shoes were sitting in the plush brown-leather armchairs helping themselves to fish paste sandwiches and jam-roll sponge cake and tea from a trolley which opened out into a low table and was brought out on these occasions. "Really," Grandma said, "That sounds most interesting. And was your teacher pleased?"

"So pleased she had to stay behind and talk about it." Lenie had come back, having deposited her coat and a shopping bag in the kitchen and stubbed out her cigarette, probably having been told to by their mother since it sent Grandma into fits of coughing. She had perched on an arm of the large sofa and was glancing through the entertainment pages of the Evening Post. If there had been no-one else there Marcelle would love to have gone and sunk herself into the big sofa with its sponge-roll whirly patterns, its seats and cushions thick and soft enough to almost swallow her up, but she remained standing, as always, in the expectation that her mother would soon come in and order her out to do something for her or just make herself scarce. "Can't think what there is to talk much about with 'levers' and 'sliders'," Lenie concluded. "What bloody good is all that going to do her?"

Grandpa visibly winced at the expletive, but Grandma asked calmly what 'levers' and 'sliders' were.

"Must say it sounds pretty technical for primary level," Grandpa put in, and coughed significantly as if to emphasise it.

"Ask her," Lenie suggested, and Marcelle was launching into her own explanation only to be interrupted when Grandma noticed the large bruise on her forehead.

"My dear, what a nasty bruise! I hadn't noticed it. How did you get that? Did you bump into something?"

"Tell them how you fell out of bed," Lenie said before she could answer.

"I fell out of bed."

"That was very careless, wasn't it?" Grandpa said, with a short laugh and another cough.

"She's too much of a dreamer, that's her trouble. Sooner or later she'll dream herself under a corporation bus." Ida Weston had come in from the kitchen. Marcelle could not remember her mother ever sitting down – sitting down and talking to people, that is. She was always *up there,* very tall.

Grandma was not quite herself for a moment. "What a horrible thing!"

"She never thinks. You've got to look where you're going in this world. What was it that that Mr. Forster said about your numeracy?"

"That it seems not to be my strong point. And Mr. Jones says I appear to be short on literacy skills, but I don't understand what he means."

"I shouldn't think you do, then, you little blockhead."

"*What* was Miss Palmeson saying to you, Marcelle?" Lenie asked, lifting a piece of sponge cake off the tea tray " – about those levers and things, I mean."

"She was showing me how to do it a bit more quickly."

"She's not very good with her hands," her mother said. "Have you brought it home, Marcelle?" she asked, rummaging in the school bag that Marcelle had left on a chair.

"It wasn't good enough."

"Oh we would love to have seen it, Marcelle dear," Grandma said.

"Yes, of course we would love to have seen it, Marcelle," Grandpa repeated.

Marcelle did not think they really meant it. After all, she had never made anything much that looked right. There was always *something* wrong, and the card with a little head that was supposed to pop up and say "Mummy" was no exception. Grandma was always the same – "We would *love* to…" and always in the same voice. Grandpa and Grandma did not know anything about her, actually. It was not really their fault, because they hardly ever went over to see them at the comfortable bungalow in Culver so that you could talk to them properly. Mostly when they did go they would have to come home early because, as she had been told, Grandpa suffered with his nerves.

"So *you* had the day off, Lenie," Grandma said. Lenie had picked up the remaining piece of sponge cake on the tea tray and was eating it noisily.

Grandpa put on his serious face, his dark eyes fixing on Lenie and his mouth getting ready to say something.

"In-post training, " Lenie explained.

"For the teachers," Marcelle recognized her mother's sarcasm. Then, as Grandpa's face returned to normal her mother, still turning over the contents of her school bag, added, "You begin to wonder what they've been doing all these years, these teachers. Lenie doesn't want to go for teaching, do you Lenie?"

"Not likely. What? Face all them kids messing about? You've got to be joking."

"Very honourable profession," Grandma said, as nicely as only Grandma could, while stacking the used crockery neatly on the tray, and then, after fussing to gather up some stray crumbs on the carpet in her fingers, "You are sure I cannot help you with the washing up, Ida?"

"Don't bother yourself. Lenie will help me," her mother replied as she disappeared into the kitchen with the tea things. Marcelle was glad that for a moment she was not the centre of everybody's attention. Maybe she could disappear to a quiet corner and read 'Jancis Dimple's Friends'. Her reading wasn't all that bad. But it *was* only for a moment. "And Marcelle," her mother's voice rang out, "you did give Mr. Forster that money for the coach trip, didn't you? And did he give you a receipt?"

"I decided not to go."

"Why ever did you do that? You've been pestering me for days. Where's the money, then?"

"I decided I'd want to wee on the coach and they wouldn't stop."

"Of course they'd stop," Lenie said. "Anyway, that's not what you told me.".

"I am sure they would," Grandma was saying, and Grandpa was nodding unusually vigorously.

"That's not what you told me," Lenie repeated. "You said you were scared of going in the caves in Ravensdale."

"Where's the money?" her mother, back in the room again, repeated in that heavy voice of which only she, Marcelle, knew the full force. At least, Marcelle reckoned, Grandpa and Grandma being there would stop the blows raining down.

"I gave it to Timmy Roach."

"You bloody liar," Lenie exclaimed.

"Why did you do that, Marcelle dear?" It was Grandpa asking a question for once. He looked quite concerned, but there was no chance of answering as her mother finally collected herself after her astonishment:

"You what?" It was like an explosion. Behind the voice was that fixed, square look, as though staring into space.

"I gave it to him, to Timmy Roach. His parents have got no money."

"You never!" Lenie exclaimed.

"You'd have gone and got it off him if I'd told you."

"If he hadn't gone home I would 'ave."

"So we've got plenty of money, have we?" The heavy voice came again. "We just give five pound notes away, just like that, do we? And what makes you think, Marcelle, that those Roaches have no money, with a father that owns newsagents all over the place."

"Because he said so. I like 'im anyway, and nobody plays with him." Sometimes it was best to give the whole truth, loud and clear.

"He 'ad you there, Marcie," Lenie said. Her sister's tone had softened just a little.

"Now you just get upstairs and *I'll* give you summat!" It was Mother in full flight, now. Sure, it was going to hurt, but she supposed she had been stupid to give the money away. Lenie was probably right.

"Just a minute!" It was Grandpa. "Might we just ask Marcelle what put the idea in her head in the first place."

"Stay where you are, then, Marcelle. Grandpa wants to ask you a question, and let's hope he gets a good answer!"

Marcelle did not wait for the question. "The Reverend Baxter."

"Ah!" Grandpa's voice sounded full of understanding.

"Did he come to the school?" Grandma's voice was softer.

"Yes."

"I suppose he'd been giving them that Sermon on the Mount thing," Lenie interposed.

Everyone seemed to be waiting to see who would say something after that. It was Grandpa again.

"Yes, now of course that is pretty strong meat, that is, and should not be quoted without regard to the level of understanding of the listener."

Grandpa's words, whatever they meant, seemed to calm things down, but Marcelle felt there was something she should add: "He said we should help the poor *and weedy*," she explained.

A faint smile that crossed Grandma's face was obliterated by her mother's thunderous "Well I'll be..." which had no time to be completed before the front door was heard to open and her father in his neat and shiny dark suit, popped his head in the sitting room, his tall form slightly stooping, as though he was afraid to wake the house up. It was how he always came in from his travelling job. The thunder was replaced by the cross tone of voice that usually greeted her father, even when he had been away for days, as Marcelle knew he had this time (and she herself was so glad to see him): "Marcelle's been giving money away, Tom."

"Better that way round, at all events," he replied. Marcelle knew her father was thinking about a recent occasion when she had tried to lift a card of pens from a store in the town and been found out. The lady in the store had made her put it back and no more had been said. When somehow her father heard about it, it had been one of the few times when he was really angry with her. She had been thinking about it ever since.

"She gave her money for the Ravensdale outing to that Roach boy and lied to Lenie about it. Well aren't you going to tell her it's wrong, or she'll have no more idea about money than you have?"

"She just told *me* she was scared of going in the caves; that's all she told me." Lenie was always determined to get her word in.

"This means you won't be able to go on the trip, Marcelle," her father said.

"I know."

"Is that all you're going to say to her?" Her mother's voice was rising. Soon Grandpa would say something, for sure. "And you'd better go and read the latest threatening letter from 'Affordable'".

Marcelle knew that 'Affordable' was someone her father paid money to for the house.

"What about a little talk to Marcelle, Tom?" Grandpa said. "She's got the right attitude, at any rate. But welcome back to family life, son," he added.

"Right attitude!" Her mother spat out the words.

"Well could we leave this subject a moment," Grandpa said after her father had given Grandma a hug and gone to take his coat off, "because Grandma and I really wanted to talk about your future, Lenie.?" At this point her mother told her to go upstairs since this had nothing to do with her, and Grandpa continued, "Yes, we wanted to talk about what you are going to do when you leave school."

Disappearing up the stairs and out of earshot, Marcelle was determined not to miss the rest. She had found a good way of doing this. She and Lenie slept in the bedroom over the front room. Something she had read somewhere – she thought it was in a Jennings book – had given her the idea of taking out a bit of floorboard that she had managed to loosen in the walk-in wardrobe (which filled one side of the room) so that only the thickness of the plaster separated her from the sounds below. With the extra sound produced by a wineglass placed on the plaster (she kept it under the board) she could hear pretty well what everybody was saying as long as Jamie Pearson was not roaring up the road on his pop-pop bike. The only real hazard was if her mother came up the stairs, in which case it was out of the wardrobe and into bed very fast. Fortunately, she rarely went quietly anywhere. Often the best china in the tall cabinet in the sitting room could be heard rattling as a result. Lenie was no obstacle. She knew that if she split on Marcelle her sister could tell their mother about the crack in the plaster in the back of the walk-in wardrobe where it met the woodwork next door, through which Lenie had apparently seen things of absorbing interest going on in their mother's bedroom. It was when, occasionally, someone – a man – had come and stayed the night when her father was away. When he was at home her father slept in the little bedroom over the hall.

Grandpa was already in full swing by the time she got in the wardrobe. "A girl of your intelligence would do well to study and not drift into some dead-end job in one of those supermarkets." Somebody had to do those jobs, Marcelle thought. She would like to be a checkout assistant, actually, smiling at people and being nice to them, but Grandpa went on, "You don't have to follow all the rest. Let's see, what did you get? Four B's and two C's was it?"

"Yea, two 'B''s in Citizenship and Art, flamin' useless. Don't know how I got a 'B' in English. Don't know how I got that. Didn't do any work."

"And a 'B' in mathematics."

"That's easy peasy, that is."

"She's very good at that," Marcelle heard her mother say. "But that's just it: she's got brains but she's not..." and the next word she did not know at all. It wasn't 'intelligent' – she knew that. It sounded like 'intellect...something'. "Don't know why she wants to go on to sixth form. Best let her get earning some money – modelling or some such."

Lenie had said she knew their mum was doing some modelling herself. Her mum just called it an 'agency'. Grandpa cleared his throat. "I did suggest she could go for Art and Design."

"Too much like hard work," Lenie said, "and they all finish up spending their time in the locals and then on the dole or in rehab. Boring."

Marcelle didn't understand all that, but she could imagine Grandpa fiddling with the cuffs of his posh jacket and clearing his throat. Grandma would have that smile on her face that wasn't a smile, and next she would be saying, 'Grandpa only wants to help you, dear'. Her dad would have gone out to the kitchen to be out of the way. Anyway, he would always let Grandpa do the talking, especially when it came to Lenie.

"She's a lazy beggar, Henry," her mother said, "but Lenie has a will and a way with her when it's something she wants. I always said there's valuable material there."

"Remember Grandpa only wants to help you, dear," Grandma said. Then Grandpa said something about A-levels, university... Lessingham, Nochester..., arts degrees, and it was as if they were waiting for him to say something else. Then he said, "I want to make an investment (whatever that was) for you as soon as I can to supplement a grant when the time comes," and suddenly everybody started talking at once and becoming quite excited, and there was a string of words like 'prospexes' and 'sillybuses' and enquiries.

Soon Grandpa and Grandma left, and suddenly Mum was starting up the stairs and Marcelle was out of the wardrobe and into bed in one practised move. Lucky her mother made so much noise coming up the stairs!

"If only you had some nous like your sister," her mother said, "instead of being so stupid. Can't imagine you going to university like Lenie. Now come down and have your tea."

Her mood had improved remarkably, Marcelle thought as she sat eating her slice of pizza. She felt it was because Grandpa had said what he had said, whatever that was, although if there was one place she could not imagine Lenie going, it was to any university. Universities were full of serious people doing serious things. Wasn't it a bit dumb of Grandpa not to realise that?

The good mood did not last long enough to allow her to watch 'Sky Captain and the World of Tomorrow', even though her mother had admitted reluctantly that it was 'suitable'. Usually that meant there was nothing that Lenie would want to watch on the big new wide screen. Lenie had her own small-screen tele over her bed, where she could get the sound through earphones, but she preferred the wide screen in the sitting room and would sit watching it for long hours in the evening when she wasn't going out with Jamie.

Tonight, Jamie called at half-past six and they roared off to town on his Yamaha, but as soon as Emmerdale had finished, her mother sent her upstairs and said she wanted to hear nothing more from her. Did that mean 'ever', really? Marcelle wondered. No, of course not, but she wished her mother would not say it so often.

"A good night's sleep might put a bit of sense into your head. And no watching Lenie's tele!"

Her mother need not have warned her, Marcelle thought as she washed and cleaned her teeth. She was too scared of falling asleep in Lenie's bed and getting punched when she came home. She sat much longer than was necessary on the lavatory reading bits of Lenie's borrowed copy of 'Bliss' that she could understand, and then lay in bed awake a long time, thinking about universities and how she would never go there but that it would be nice if Lenie did, somehow, and she could have her bed with the tele. It seemed like the middle of the night when she was woken by the sound of raised voices below. She got out of bed very quietly and switched on the halogen torch that Lenie had given her for her eighth birthday. The clock over Lenie's bed said nine thirty. It was too early for her sister to be home. After a while it became clear that a row was building up between her parents. She crept into the wardrobe. The words were rising up with surprising clarity…

"Well did you read the bloody letter?"

"Of course I read it."

"So?"

"I'll pay it."

"What will you do? Sell the budgie?"

Surely they couldn't be going to sell Jimmy, Marcelle thought, and heaved a sigh of relief when her dad said,

"Don't be silly! Might have to cancel the Canaries, though. I haven't sent the money yet." For a moment she couldn't understand what the 'Canaries' were, but soon realised that they might be going to have to forget the Tenerife holiday. That didn't worry her much. They just left her and Lenie in some children's entertainment place or in the evenings with a baby sitter while they, as Lenie put it, "hit the town… some dodgy nightclub". Lenie said their father would always worry about them and come back early to make sure they were all right. She hadn't gone with them to Tenerife the last time. Said she would prefer to look after the house. She told Marcelle afterwards that she and Jamie had had a fantastic time, but her sister became very agitated when Marcelle happened to find a packet with 'Durex' written on it under Lenie's bed. Marcelle didn't know what it was, but she had to swear blind not to say anything about it. "Or we could sell the widescreen," her dad went on. "We'd get six hundred for it – it's nearly new. That would pay three months' instalments."

"Lenie would do her nut."

"She spends hours in front of the thing. She should be putting in hours studying. She's got the brains… if she wants to get to university, that is."

"Of course she doesn't want to go to university! She just wants to skive in sixth form. Anyway, a business management degree doesn't seem to have put *you* in the way of much money, does it?"

"That's a bit unfair. You wanted everything straight away. Now you still want it."

"I could have been managing a string of boutiques if you hadn't given up that first job. There was me thinking of you managing some prestigi-something (whatever that meant) catering business (whatever that meant) and I was having to take typing work." Then her mother said, "What a fool I was! And what was the next job, but something –

it was never quite clear to me what you were – something in a chain of retailers (another tricky word) where you stayed far too long and daren't sack anyone? No wonder the firm never went anywhere." Marcelle caught the drift. It was easy to hear. Her mother was spitting the words out: "You're too timid, Tom, in every way. But there's no point in going into all that again." There was a pause...

"On the contrary," Marcelle could hear her father say, "It seems we have to go through it all for the hundredth time. I remind you that it was not a case of 'not daring', but a case of valuing people. I don't give up on people easily." Marcelle didn't understand what her father said after that. He was angry, too. It was something about the 'catering business' again – the first job.

"And probably you made yourself so small they hardly knew you were there..." and then, a bit later, "You never understood *my* needs, Tom. Sometimes I ask myself if you're the same go-getter I married."

"I understood them all right," she could just hear her father say. "They were clear enough. You were spending the earth on furnishing our overpriced house in Wollaston. No wonder I had to get out and try and earn some more money."

"And even then we had to sell and lost money, and your father helped us out..." Now she understood what they were talking about. Lenie had explained about her father not earning enough money at his first job, not getting on with the manager and trying to study at the same time, and about the house at Wollaston and that they hadn't had enough money to pay for it. Lenie didn't have much sympathy for their father. That was partly because, as she had explained to her once, her (i.e. Lenie's) real father was someone else and their mum had only married her own father when Lenie was four. Lenie never knew her real father. She had told her other things: about how she still remembered her excitement when her mum and new dad moved into the house at Wollaston with its big, overgrown garden when she was six, with the sudden change to a bright new school from the dingy school in town. She remembered how exciting it was to go after school to the boutique with its perfumes and pretty clothes and get played with by the assistant. There were holidays at Sandbay-by-Filport where Pop and Nan lived (their mother's parents), going there in the new Mondeo, perfect days on the beach, getting ice creams from Mr. Pinelli, dragging nets through crab pools and going on the Caterpillar in the fairground when it was wet. There was no shouting in those days, Lenie said. Then there were plans to open more boutiques (with Grandpa Weston's help), but their mum became pregnant, the boutique – even the original one – came to nothing, and because of the money problems nothing, according to Lenie, was ever the same again. "And things have been going downhill ever since." her mother was saying. "Blame me, but if you imagine I'm foregoing my holiday, think again." Marcelle pictured her mother's face, searching, angry... Sometimes it was almost as if she was going to cry, but she never did. Her father would be calm, would not answer back, just run his hand over his face in the way he did, trying to think what to say, avoiding her gaze. Then her mother said, "What about this money he's going to give Lenie? We'll have to handle it, won't we? We can pay it back..."

"What? What are you talking about? That would be dishonest!"

"So bloody what!" Ida shouted, and then added, "And Lenie won't worry. Soon as she sees what amount of work she'd be doing at university..." It was at that point that Marcelle somehow managed to kick the bit of detached floorboard, so that it made a little noise above the sitting-room ceiling. "What was that?" she heard her mother exclaim. "Marcelle must be doing something." And before she could even think of getting out of the wardrobe her mother was clomping up the stairs and bursting into the bedroom.

Marcelle did not know whether to stay in the wardrobe, hope she would think she had gone to the lavatory and go and see, and hop into bed before she came back. The alternative was to be looking for something in the wardrobe.

Ida stayed in the room.

"I was looking for something," Marcelle said, coming out and trying to think of why she might be in there when she was supposed to be asleep.

"Oh you were, were you?" Her mother towered by the door.

"I suddenly couldn't remember where I had put my purse." Marcelle couldn't think of anything else that she might have lost. But suddenly it did not seem to have been a very good thing to mention. She was right.

"There's nothing in it, is there? You *are* a naughty girl today, Marcelle. So that's what made the noise I heard! Where is it, then?"

Marcelle remembered it was in her raincoat pocket downstairs. "It isn't here," she said, resignedly.

"What *were* you doing in there, Marcelle?"

31

"Nothing."

"We'll have to see, then," and with that her mother dived into the wardrobe, driving the clothes apart and throwing her arms about rather like she did when swimming in the sea on Tenerife, as if she didn't quite know where she was going but was determined to get somewhere. And there she was, thrashing about until her foot stepped on the piece of floorboard. "What's this ?" she exclaimed. Marcelle said nothing. Things could only go downhill, now, as her mother would say. "And what's this hole in the floor?" Now she was really cross.

That was *it*, she thought. "What hole?"

"Did you remove this board? And that's a wineglass there. You haven't been drinking, have you?"

Marcelle shook her head, and before her mother could bend down to pick up the glass the sound of her dad's voice rose up out of it with unexpected clarity, like that of nice Mr. Price the deputy headmaster shouting to try and keep them together when they were out on a school project.

"Keep your cool, Ida. That's enough for one day. And remember what we said!"

"Like hell one day!" her mother shouted back down, through the wardrobe, and then, coming out of the wardrobe she grabbed Marcelle by the arm, "You naughty girl," she thundered. She had that fixed look again that always meant the worst was about to happen, a look that was seeing and yet not seeing. "How long have you been listening in there? How many times?"

"I don't know."

"Days? weeks? How did you take the board up?"

"With Daddy's crowbar."

"I'll give you Daddy's crowbar. "You *bad* girl!" And now the hand that she knew must have been raised came down on the side of her face real hard, and then the same happened on the other side. The pain was great but had to be borne, as had the next onslaught which knocked her flying into the door and landed her in a heap on its inside so that her father, who she was vaguely aware had come running up the stairs, could not at first get in. When he did finally make it her mother punched him in the face.

"It's not you she takes after, is it?" she yelled as she went downstairs. "The naughty girl!"

Her dad just stood there for a moment, at the top of the stairs, hesitating, his tall form hiding her mother as she disappeared. For a moment she thought he was going to say something to her mother. Then, seeming not to be feeling anything from the clout she had given him he pulled her up, took her to the bathroom and bathed her face, then went to the medicine cupboard, got a tube of ointment and spread some where it was hurting. But already when she looked in the mirror she saw that the purple colour was appearing on her cheekbone and forehead.

"I'm sorry I didn't come up quickly enough," he said. He looked so sad, his black hair tumbling all over the place.

"It's my own fault," Marcelle whispered.

He went back to the bedroom with her. She got into bed, and he sat down on it. "I know it hurts, Marcie," he said, "but imagine something nice, the nicest thing you can, and you will get to sleep." He stayed with her awhile. Then he said, "Marcie, I'm sorry it's not very nice for you here. You must sometimes wish you lived somewhere else."

"Oh no, Daddy, I don't wish that!" And she smiled.

"It's not right you should get hurt."

"If it's not right, why don't you stop it happening?" She was still smiling, but there was a tear trying to come.

"It's hard to explain. I'm not very good at some things. Do you understand?"

"I think so," she replied. "Daddy, do you love me?" she asked as he tucked her up in bed.

"Yes," he replied.

"And Mummy?"

"Yes, and I love your mother."

"And Lenie?"

"Yes, and Lenie...and Jimmy." And he hugged her and kissed her goodnight.

Marcelle dreamed that Lenie had gone to university and that she was in her bed watching the television. But there was no sound from it, and somehow it did not matter because what she saw was part of her thoughts so that it did not need any explanation. She saw a wide-open land with a big river flowing towards her. On the other side of the river a steep slope rose up, full of trees, a bit like the ones did in Ravensdale, but more grandly. On *her* side, away from the thickets along the river's edge the land was flat and open to a great distance, covered with long, luscious grass taller than herself and just a scattering of trees. No houses, no signs of habitation, no path, no track.. There was an untouched look about everything, The sky was full of birds. "It's 'old'," she could hear her geography teacher Mr. Tattenhall saying, "but not 'old old'...say just forty thousand years, or maybe a hundred." No blazing volcanoes, no pterodactyls, not in a time before the land was shaped like it is now. And could that be a herd of rhinoceros in the farthest distance?...

And strangely, even the rhinos – if that is what they were –, like everything else there, made it not so much a place, a land, somewhere unimaginably far away from her as somewhere familiar, even if only in a second-hand sort of way, and, in a way, just for her.

Her attention suddenly became focussed on the river. She had not seen the man walking slowly towards her along the bank on her side. He was wearing a sort of apron of what she thought must be an animal skin, and carrying some furs over his shoulder. A pouch hung about his waist, by the sagging look of it containing stones. He had a spear. At first she thought he was hobbling because of a bad foot, but then she saw that he had trouble with his hip, like a friend of her father's up the road.

She wished she could see him more closely, and was astonished then to see the man come closer on the screen. He looked swarthy, and just a bit frightening. But as he came closer she thought he might not be as fierce as he looked, appearing so only because of his grim expression, long, long hair and big, tangled beard – and the fact that one eye was partially closed. His nose was incredibly large.

But now too she could see that he was very thin, and more heavily laden and moving even more slowly than she had thought at first. He had a big gash in his leg on the side opposite the damaged hip. He wore big boots all bound round with something, and he actually carried *two* spears, one in each hand. Walking with his head bowed he would sometimes pause, and with evident effort straighten up to look about him. Marcelle wondered how this man could survive alone in such a place, for she knew instinctively that he had come a long way, a very long way.

Out there in the plain the rhinos were moving along in the same direction as the man and coming just a little nearer, but then as the hunter, too, came closer, suddenly another movement caught Marcelle's eye. It was an animal – a deer or something – hiding in the shrubbery, hoping he would pass and not see her. From his angle, the man certainly could not see her – yet. Anyway, it seemed a forlorn hope that he might be able to spear it in the state he was in, though she guessed he needed the food badly. Certainly Mr. Tattenhall would say this hunter could make a fire to cook it on. She was sure of that.

The man saw it. It *was* a deer, a young one she thought. Everything happened in a flash. Now Marcelle could distinctly hear the snorting of the beast and the sound of its hooves as it made a dash for it. Suddenly the hunter became a different person. Throwing down most of the stuff he was carrying and breaking into a crab-like run, a spear poised in one hand and a large stone in the other, he moved faster than she would ever have thought he could. He did not run straight for the animal, but, guessing its next move, and then the next and the next, edged it towards the steep bank of the river. With a shout he lunged at it with the spear, but with a mighty effort the deer leaped on to a neighbouring bit of the bank that stuck out into the water. Quick as lightning the man, still holding the spear, raced round and was able to trap the animal where it stood almost completely surrounded by water, forcing it into the river. He tried to follow it along the bank as it leapt along with the fast-moving current, but in doing so he appeared to trip over some obstacle and, letting out a loud cry, plunged heavily off the bank and into the water himself, where he disappeared. The deer came ashore and made its escape into some trees.

The shout woke Marcelle. She thought it was her father calling her.

"Wake up, Marcie! You're dreaming." But it was Lenie's voice. "You've been having a nightmare. You sounded really worried. Better get up, or you'll be late. Christ! Your face is a mess. You can't go to school like that! I'll tell Mum."

"No, don't tell Mother."

"I must. You can't go like that or they'll be taking you away…"

CHAPTER THREE

Young Lexin Solberg 'came to' from a sort of daydream state and switched his computer to 'standby'. It had been very strange at first, having these trances, or whatever they were. There could not be actually anything *wrong* with his mind. He had had scans and genetic profiles, all that stuff, and everything was normal. The trances would coincide with a 'blip' in the picture or in the words on screen. Or a website would become overlaid by something else, sometimes subtly and almost imperceptibly, sometimes abruptly. But it was hard even for *him* to explain, with his thinking clarified and enhanced by somatic genetic modification and other changes. The images, the scenes, had come out of the blue, source and purpose unstated.

He sat there at his desk for a minute or two collecting himself. It was all rather remarkable, really. It had started when he was much younger and doing basic solar system. It was level two stuff, and he was about fourteen years old. They were into anthropology and studying early man, and there was this H6/442 camp among the trees (originally a 'sapiens sapiens' group before the days of dead accurate dating). It was all skull features, hunting reconstructions, mapping of the itineraries of local migrating groups, etc. etc. – all very interesting, but then suddenly it, or rather the picture in Lexin's personal monitor, was different. Best to quote his autodiary:

'Suddenly it was more than historical reconstruction – the widely used 'historics' – at any level, with their inevitable feeling or suggestion of predictability. There were all these ancients. Nothing odd about that except that they were all high as kites, and I kept on seeing this fellow with a bad hip; the man seemed to be a bit on his own, on the edge of things. It was quite clear what was going on in the camp, because I happened to move the cursor up a little and saw it clearly and completely naturally. It was not that there was anything particularly unusual about moving up the file in order to go back in time, or moving down to go forward in time. We do it in scene reconstruction, after all. The interesting thing was that it seemed the chief – it was easy enough to pick *him* out, a much taller man than the others – must have got all of them, men and women, to drink some kind of aphrodisiac. The result was that as dusk came they were all getting into each other's hay and deerskin beds and having a whale of a time. Moving the cursor *down* a little I became aware of another figure, a woman, emerging on the scene – part of the scene, and yet not part of it – and I began to associate her with the crippled man for some reason that I did not entirely understand until I realised both had vanished. It was like a pointer, and it all felt far removed from accurate scene reconstructions no matter how profound the analyses.

'Moving the cursor over perhaps weeks or months, I realised that if I was right in my suspicion this guy had been in fact only the last of many to succumb to her charms. It became apparent that she was quite promiscuous in normal times, having it off with many of the other men. Sound-recall in historical reconstruction is generally pretty arbitrary, but here it was unmistakeably real, catching every grunt, every word; they were really noisy about it. The man with the deformity did not figure at these times, but the chief did, often, and he turned out to be pretty violent. And lo and behold! When I moved to the very end of the file, i.e. just after the orgy, there he was, giving the poor woman a big hiding, knocking her about quite a bit, and there was a lot of noise then. She was a redhead, quite an eye-catcher! One could be forgiven for thinking that he might have been right jealous of that crippled fellow. I reckoned I would not like to have been in *his* place.'

'There were twenty-two of us in the class,' he had recorded, 'and nobody else had seen anything special. Funny, that. Another funny thing was that I didn't seem to have missed much in the class. It must have been all over very quickly. The supervising robot could not make anything of it when I told him afterwards'. And that was the end of it – of *that* episode.

Lexin stood up, momentarily taking in through the wall-high windows behind his computer station the distant domes and spires of the city suffused with late-afternoon light. Then, dressed in his customary three-quarter length trousers, tunic-style shirt (currently taken up under a sash), and sandals, he descended the wide spiral staircase from the office above his apartment high up in the back of the family residence – the home of Olaf Solberg, President of the Earth Society for the Advancement of Intragalactic Relations. Traversing the central hall he arrived in the main living space. Spring was beginning, and the city's invisible climate canopy was completely open, allowing an early-season warmth to percolate the air outside and, through the opened glass doors and the windows, into the house.

He crossed the living space, with its scatter of light-versatile rugs now in soft, warm colours, sinuous sofas inviting relaxation, intimate alcoves, and yet overall an airy spaciousness that owed more to cleverly conceived vistas of 'rooms beyond' than to the new, pseudo-transparency-producing materials that were really its only offering to modernism. Exiting the living space he stepped out on to the mosaic of Spanish tiles that formed a terrace above the downwards-cascading flowerbeds and beyond them the lawn, and in the distance, down the Hill of Lyra, the central part of Galaxy City. Being short in stature his elbows barely reached the top of the concrete wall of the balustrade as he stood looking down on the copious white flowers of the rock rose, dazzled by them and by the array of tulips and narcissi, and enjoying the rich scents of the lilac and the chalice vines.

"Was it a good day, then?" His elder sister was striding up from the lower gate in summery shorts and flowing, yet form-sensitive, astralon top – the beautiful Lenica who, unlike him with his short stature and dark, curly hair, had the tallness and colouring of her Norwegian father, the same keen but not unkindly blue eyes.

"Yes, very good," he said as she joined him in taking in the view. "Still working hard to absorb data on interstellar time discrepancy philosophies."

"I am afraid I am too down to earth."

"You will get there soon enough, but I tell you this, sis'," he announced, with mock pomposity, "None of us can begin to imagine the infinity of surprises awaiting us in this amazing universe of ours."

"Ah, you are so diligent, so hard-working, brother of mine," Lenica said, teasingly, "even when you pretend you are not. Seriously, are you sure you should not relax more? Just because we are enhanced, it does not mean that we cannot enjoy ourselves. Just look at the beautiful day. I took the afternoon off and saved the study sessions for tonight. A couple of taramils should do it."

"You should not lose sleep like that."

"Why not? We get biochemically reviewed. If anything is out of balance…"

"Yeah, yeah."

"*You* should relax. We had a great time at the pool. There were crowds there, loads of Normals…" Well, she would – he knew that – with her gorgeous figure and long blond eyelashes over limpid eyes flashing beneath her long blond hair. "…We were talking about the Mars terraforming business, and they were asking us whether we thought the Government was going to make any announcement about progress or otherwise in making contact with the Bods to obtain some much needed advice."

He knew the World Government in Canberra was being hard pressed to act on the proposal to divert a comet with its nitrogen load to make a buffer gas for the Red Planet, with certain elements in the media giving the Department of Solar System Development an increasingly rough ride. In its turn the DSSD was probing ever deeper into the reasons for lack of progress by the Society at the Mission Station in its efforts to get a direct response from the 'Bods'. This was a friendly-sounding name universally accepted for the entities, never yet seen, who had contacted Earth's people centuries before in a time of great crisis and given humanity a new lease of life.

"What did you say?"

"We do not know of any announcement," she replied as they went inside, "nor can we tell them anything they don't already know about progress in making contact, can we? But the Normals want to know these things." Lenica had taken an athletic leap into one of the invisible air cushions in the living space. These were very popular with guests, and their father took great delight in referring to their "Great leap into the unknown" (a double entente by which of course he also meant "into the Galaxy"). "One fellow – some idiot in a track suit whose breath suggested too many beer stops – said we ought to be able to solve those little problems ourselves and save the long-distance communications for when they were really necessary."

"Little problems! What does he reckon are the big problems?"

"Oh I don't know. Maybe by big problems he means if we were in some real bother again – in terms of the Earth's survival, I mean."

"Maybe we *should* spare the Bods out there the trouble," Lexin said, thoughtfully, going into the little bar recess. There are real dangers in trying to communicate through spacetime via the wormhole, as you know. Want a fruity drink?"

"Sure. A good long one," she replied.

"Anyway, Lenica," he went on, as she took several swigs of her Mediterranean on Ice ,"with not a sniff of an answer to any of our problems transmitted so far – I mean problems of... I don't know what... new crop creation, personal democratic value indices... and now this Mars business, perhaps it's best we leave it all alone for a bit. I have a hunch we are jumping the gun."

"Lexin, I must say you surprise me," Lenica said in that big-sister tone to which her otherwise mellifluous voice was apt to revert. "But hasn't the time come to try our utmost to take much greater advantage of their intragalactic overtures..."

"Darlings! This all sounds so serious. Now here is some *good* news." Felicitas Solberg, tall and dusky, had swept in in a generous, star-studded gown, and a breeze of her characteristic agarwood perfume, with that étalage and aplomb that the American-born daughter of a Russian princess and an Arab Sheikh might be expected to be able to achieve better than most. "That tutor of yours of whom I think so highly despite his inclination to lean too close to one..."

"Well simply make sure you are away when he next comes in person, then," the reclining Lenica suggested, interrupting her mother. "Anyway, it is time Lexin took things up with him off his own bat, face to face. He is a big boy, now."

Lexin barely registered his sister's aside. He was suspecting that Professor Tang (Beijing University) with whom he still had tutorials by holopresence, had failed to check a testosterone imbalance – a strange omission, he thought, in an expert in normal and enhanced behaviour. In enhanced humans the balance was genetically fine-tuned to the specialized lifestyle. There was, though, a certain inflated self-confidence about the Prof. Someone had even registered it in his volatile emissions.

"Could not possibly absent myself!" Felicitas declared. "The little professor is much too influential. And as I was about to say, and I am sure you will agree, Lenica," Felicitas took up again, turning towards her son, "he has his sights firmly set upon you." He was pouring her favourite long drink – a Manzanasco ('Manzo' for short), which was something that she had long ago latched onto from Chile or somewhere during an airship tour of South America with the local Societan Ladies branch. It was, she said, something invigorating (her word), and it tasted strongly of apples and apricots. She sat down and composed herself in her favourite tropical woven banana leaf armchair. Thus in a position of comfort she was able, she believed, to maintain 'the dignity of altitude and attitude' – erect, and a little Cleopatra-ish with her faintly slanted eyes and pointed nose – befitting her position and her seventy-five years.

"Upon *me! Has* he now?" Lexin said with that calm detachedness that he knew would annoy his mother. "Well that is interesting."

"He is from a long-enhanced family, you know" Felicitas added a little haughtily. "And we have a long way to go to the galactic heart, Lexin…"

"… where I fear only individuals like Tang – philosopher, psychologist, biologist, and I don't know what else – can lead the way," Lenica added.

"Lead us along the road to the most amazing future that mankind could ever have envisaged," Felicitas echoed in a dream-like tone – her enthusiastic mode.

"Some road!" He observed.

"Lexin!" Now his sister was really annoyed.

"Oh, I know him only too well. He is a good boy. Anyway, in this business you need to have a sense of humour. Thank God for a *bit* of humour in him."

"There is a difference between humour and being stupid," Lenica countered, "Of course he should relax, but so often I think he is only half serious about everything. It is important to catch the mood of the people. You know it has really captured the imagination, this comet diversion business…"

"The imagination of the press at any rate, I suppose," Lexin put in.

"...For a start," Lenica went on, ignoring the interruption, "it will be so visible. And you can understand it if the Normals are impatient about all the talking, and more talking, and nothing happening. And what of the precious text left behind for our guidance nearly four centuries ago? What has it produced, anyway?"

"Oh come, come, my daughter!" Felicitas exclaimed. "Plenty! Historical reconstruction, worldwide sub-surface transit, 12-hour working week, transformation of society...!"

"Yes, yes, but memories are short. I am talking about the *big* breakthrough to galactic participation, which is all the more reason to consolidate the knowledge we have gained, achieve proper direct communication despite the dangers, invoke help from out there as often as possible, form closer bonds, make friends. Are we not all in it together, floating specs in a vast, hostile environment? Only by co-operation..."

"You sound more like one of those early twenty-first century politicians every minute," Lexin interrupted: "communication, co-operation... It will be the pooling of resources next, then refinement of objectives, agreement of targets. Remember we are talking about the Galaxy here. We have no idea what is going on out there. And memories are short on the dangers of our work in general, dear sister, let alone the hazards of time crossing. Remember the disastrous ultralight metal domes on Mars, for instance? We have had a lot of trouble with ultralight metals. There is something in the physics that we have not grasped."

"How downbeat can you get!" Lenica exclaimed.

"Leave the boy be, Lenica," Felicitas said. Now it was the *gentle* Felicitas, daughter of gentle Grandpa Dubai. "He is doing very well. Do you imagine he does not understand how people feel, that he does not understand what is at stake?"

She ignored her mother's question and ploughed on with a determination unusual even for Lenica, who as P.A. to the Society's representative in the World Government and Assembly was admittedly concerned with promoting the Society's interests and image. "So what about that Professor *Malinovsky*? Here you are at twenty-five and far ahead of most of our contemporaries. Isn't it time for *you* two to have a tête-à-tête? He would not consider it inappropriate. He must know your standing among your peers. He thinks you have a great future. There are those who reckon the professor the physicist of the century.

Aged, shy and retiring he may be, but if anyone has found the elixir of life, it is surely that old boy with his smooth and rosy cheeks. What's more, they say if anyone can take us where in spatiotemporal terms the Bods want us to proceed, it is he. Find out what he really thinks has happened to snarl things up. You already know more than our father does. Father has devoted his life to the Society – to which our family has belonged for two hundred years, has it not?" Lenica stopped, seeing her brother was not giving her his full attention. "Tell him, Mother," she said, turning on her heel and going into the interior of the house, tossing back the last drop of her drink.

It was occurring to him that it had been in the white haired professor's cosmology classes that he had seen striking shots, such beautiful images of a certain young girl who was to figure so large in his daydreams – or whatever they were.

Following the episode in that prehistoric camp, no more blips had occurred for ages – for several years, in fact. But it was no longer those ancients when they started again. First it had been when he was in a class studying social affairs in modern-human populations in historical times, specifically in what you might call dysfunctional families, fortunately quite rare now.

'There came a moment,' he had recorded, 'when what I was hearing in the class and what I was seeing on my screen were two different things. Some families were being mood-monitored in holiday places. The commentator was going on about productivity in terms of personal optimism and spiritual creativity. The next moment, the only picture I was seeing was of two bored girls, one perhaps six or seven, the other an early teenager, being entertained by Charlie the Wonder Man in Tenerife: I guessed they were sisters. Date: the earliest years of the twenty-first century. You could see one of those old ferryboats through the windows occasionally and – blow me down – aircraft coming in to land. God, how they messed up the skies in those days! I've read enough about the environmental problems...the confusion, the contradictions. Anyway, nothing I did altered anything, There wasn't much to it, and in a minute it had all disappeared. It was almost as if no time in the present had elapsed at all. There seemed to be no connection with the other blips of long ago.'

That was only the beginning. After that, when blips came they always showed one of those two sisters, the younger one. Once it was in basic physical-biochemical interaction studies using biochemical pseudo-hologram sequences. 'Instead of holograms in my monitor revealing the body-wide biochemical effects of physical exertion in performing athletes, suddenly there she would be in her own holograms, getting a beating or a slapping from a shadowy female figure – presumably her mother. She was being quite knocked about. No question of it being any kind of demonstration any more.' Moving the time-sensitive cursor up, he was able to witness many similar episodes, starting very early in her life. Sometimes the indicators would tend to become hidden in favour of the more fully defined appearance of the girl herself during such violent episodes, a sturdy girl despite her sufferings, typically in the skirt, top and school-crested jumper of school uniforms of the epoch and clutching a school bag, but sometimes in other clothes around the house, or getting up or going to bed. He guessed she would have been around five or six years old at the beginning. A general steady decrease in the variation from the biochemical norms during violent episodes over time would confirm a degree of accustomisation. There was no sound. Eventually the holograms would merge back into demonstration ones. 'I don't know how I managed to follow the class' he had noted finally..

Another kind of episode came while he was doing some private study. 'I was revising some historical stuff about child abuse, and occasionally the solid text on the monitor would fade as from behind it there began to emerge the outlines of unhappy children. Then suddenly *that* girl emerged from the greyness, as sharp and definite as you like, a part of the picture and yet not quite part of it. She was being taken away from her home, and she didn't like that at all in spite of all the beatings that I had witnessed. This time I could hear her crying bitterly.'

Then came Malinovsky's cosmology class. The girl came out of nowhere. Slowly, out of the awesome, dazzling confusion of the Lagoon emission nebula in its infinity of colours, there emerged in his monitor the girl's starry, glittering image. Lexin knew his world classics. It was clearly a daring children's version of 'A Midsummer Night's Dream', and she was Titania, Queen of the Fairies, attired by an obviously gifted local mum in a diaphanous, many-layered silken costume. It was that moment when she is refusing to give her Indian page boy to Oberon. It was such a lovely image, and a surprising one in view of her earlier traumas. It was not just the deep-set dark eyes, the tendency towards a Mediterranean complexion: it was a composure, a sense of calm assurance that accompanied her gestures (there was no sound in this sequence), a 'presence' that owed absolutely nothing to stature or sylphic form, for the girl had neither...

The image lasted almost no time. More sequences followed in the cosmology and other classes – rapid sequences, sometimes perhaps more subliminal. They were of her among her friends at school, where she seemed to be everybody's friend and helper, and at a house where she was living with an elderly couple who must have been her grandparents. There, too, you saw the same serenity, the same loyalty, but also the same forthrightness, determination, occasionally even a flash of indignation. Lexin wondered whether he would ever know her name...

"You *are* very thoughtful today," his mother was saying, getting through her favourite drink at above-average speed, and when she was not actually holding her Russian antique glass, fiddling with her crocheted Arabic stole as if she could not quite get it to sit correctly on her shoulders. She did not miss much.

"Feeling tired. Reckon I should take a taramil or two like Lenica."

"You don't need those, Lexin. Lenica is so highly strung, you know. I fear she is not looking after herself. How she takes after Olaf!" There was a longer silence than was usual when his mother was about. The image of the girl came to him again...realisation of the way he had come to accept her appearances...how they had become in some way a part of his life..."Your father has been away two weeks. It is terribly difficult work," she went on.

"Yes, I know," he replied, suddenly aware of her renewed concern about her Olaf. He knew that his father, a physicist, travelled a great deal as President of the Society – a position he had held now for ten years – to major centres such as Beijing, Paris and Brasilia. This was in addition to his work at the Mission Station in the decipherment unit, where they were still routinely interpreting the text received from the Bods long ago, and in its wormhole and its experimental laboratories. "The comet business is very trying, but I think – I hope – people are more understanding about the problem than Lenica might imagine. There will always be hotheads who want to rush to get Mars atmospheric. I did not think it necessary to spell it out to Lenica yet again – if it is any indication of the urgency or otherwise of the problem – that in forty-five years of working on the relevant text where it concerns wormhole development we have not even built a reliable wormhole terminal yet – or at least not learnt how to receive messages as well as send them – never mind hobnobbing with the galactic deities. Only recently have we been able to *transmit* safely – though I should add that we do not know whether our cries for help hit target."

"Still, when you know there are Bods out there who have all the data..." Felicitas stopped herself. "They will manage to iron out the difficulties at the Station, though, I'm sure of that," she said, standing up and gazing for a moment at a large painting on one of the walls. It was a reduced reproduction of Goya's 'Maria Luisa, Queen of Spain, in Court Dress'. Lexin had the impression that through its aura of confident regality she was endeavouring to boost her own confidence, though it had to be said that his mother's appearance bore little resemblance (fortunately for her, in his opinion). She turned and faced him. "Tell me, Lexin, why is it proving so difficult?"

"I don't know. Nobody does. And nobody knows why, even though we have advanced in philosophy, linguistics, mathematics, psychology, physics – in all branches, in fact – sometimes we do not seem to be any nearer our ultimate objective, which is presumably to take our part in the galactic club, or whatever it is."

"Dangerous, too. People have died."

"Yes, in spite of our best efforts." It was true that mishaps were all too frequent in the outward transmission of signals, and even in testing and simulation work, never mind the complete lack of success in signal retrieval.

Felicitas came and put her arms around him, Felicitas daughter of gentle Grandfather Dubai again. "You will carry the torch one day, Lexin, won't you – or at least take a step towards it by getting yourself elected to the Conference – , if the Matriarchs should decide that by innate ability, family superiority and common consent you are the person – as seems more than likely?"

"You must not think I do not care about my responsibilities," he replied. Certainly it wasn't all honey being 'modified', and there were things that inevitably separated him and his like from the Normals: exclusion from politics, restriction to a Societan partner, the strange job of text decipherment and its application that while it might appear humdrum to the outsider was literally mind-blowing and – for himself at least, when he had done some of it – all consuming. Moreover, enhancement was designed only to further the work for galactic advance and conferred no guaranteed benefits in everyday living not available to Normals. Their work did, after all, imply a dedication, as enablers, to the advancement of all Earth's people together.

"But *do* you really care?"

"I hope so, but if I were offered a place in the Society Conference and I changed my mind, it would not be because I am afraid."

"Then because of what?" She paused. Still with her arms encircling him she leaned to one side a little, searching his face. "Is it to do with that girl, the one you first saw in that social affairs website you happened to log onto ages ago – and just occasionally have deigned to tell me about since? Has she bewitched you?" She pursed her lips at that.

He knew the compelling, yet not unkindly look. "It was not a website, Mother;" he said. "Not in the usual sense. It just came on the screen, and just as quickly went off. It has been the same every time. I told you." He had not dared tell his father about that (or, in fact, about any of his strange experiences), and had no more than briefly mentioned the girl and the pseudo-holograms to his mother. It was the same with the scenes of her different life away from her parents as they wove seamlessly in and out of the fabric of his own days. He hesitated to dwell on all that, and in fact kept it mostly to himself, since it would only confuse his mother more. He would not like to be having to try and convince her that he was not actively and personally seeking out this 'local' girl of long ago in some voyeuristic way in order to mitigate the occasional loneliness of his somewhat isolated existence. "Why would I want to abandon my calling to seek out a poor little girl living in a past age?" he asked, "a girl with a history of abuse that we have – thanks not least to the Bods – more or less overcome worldwide?"

"Maybe she was pretty."

"Mother, you malign me," he said, smiling, (for he knew she would never do that). Anyway, even if I were to tell you that at fourteen or so she was very pretty, you know that our affairs of the heart are between enhanced individuals. Anything else is dangerous, never mind frustrating to our very purpose."

"Well let us hear no more of her." Felicitas said it kindly. She kissed him on the forehead and went out onto the terrace. "Come out here," she called. "Let us enjoy what is left of this spring sunshine!"

* * *

Lexin was bracing himself, for there was more to tell her, more that he *wanted* to tell her, about the things to do with the girl that he had been seeing via his computer monitor during these last few days – and indeed that very morning. But it was not going to be easy to convince her. Certainly it would be counterproductive telling her explicitly about what had appeared at first to be just some blips from historical porno websites, websites of such a kind being rare nowadays. Sexual entertainment had over a long period become far more subtle in the way in which it played with the mind and body – and in most people's view neither exploited nor depraved anyone. This, with its mishmash, its surfeit of pink flesh titillatingly yet coldly shot from every angle was something truly from her day. But it was not quite what it seemed, for again and again it undeniably portrayed *her*. Or rather, it portrayed bits of her, though quite how he could be so certain he did not know. Young she certainly was…, *very* young. Perhaps it was the pure skin of a certain shade, the thick, dark hair – though her actual face was never seen as a whole –, the sturdy, shapely limbs…some other feature of her appearance or behaviour, perhaps, recognized in a split second or subliminally. And could it be that even in the fragmentation of her face and body, the bold intimacies, he sensed something at the same time yielding, compliant, yet also steadfast and *somehow in control. Was* there some inner quality that he could not know from outside but was given to him to know? "There are things I need to tell you, though," he said, joining his mother at one of the little tables, very twenty-second century, all galactic black with splodges of star clusters of various colours and Earth most dubiously at the centre.

"I am glad you discuss everything with me, Lexin. Even at your age there are things…"

"…Things you might find it hard to understand."

"How do you reach that conclusion? Have I not been married thirty years to the man with the most worries this side of the Galaxy?"

"It *is* about this girl. She must have returned home from living somewhere else, most likely her grandparents. She was there because she had been repeatedly beaten by her mother, as I told you. Without burdening you with the details, it seems that at fourteen or fifteen somebody back at home took to abusing her sexually. I feel sure it is not her father."

"Why not? There were plenty of those kinds of men. It is not completely eradicated in the world even now."

"It is rather hard to explain this, Mother, but I feel there is a sort of link between us so that there are times when I know the way she is thinking."

Felicitas gave him a long, thoughtful look with those searching, dark eyes. Then she smiled faintly, quizzically "I've heard of plenty of Normals getting hooked on historics. But we Societans are not Normals. We have this special task, this important task of reaching out into the Galaxy, making our contribution."

Didn't she know he *knew* that? "These are not made up, something fabricated. These are not historics. Nor are they old film. They are something real, something *now*."

"How can they be real if they were hundreds of years ago?"

"I don't know, but they are telling me something."

"Well I cannot pretend never to have heard of this sort of thing, either – paranormal phenomena, visions, 'experiences', and the like, but I don't quite see the connection with our cause. Lexin, when all that stuff arrived from a hundred and forty light-years out in the constellation Lyra, it was not for fun, was it? It was about something positive, forward looking, not dwelling on the past, not trying to recall what it is best to forget."

But the images had stuck in his mind. Their tantalizing intimacies did not stir him sexually, although he knew they might still excite some Normals, but affect him they did. He knew she had returned home to something terrible, and it was almost as though he were grieving for her lest he should never see her again, unless.... "Perhaps it is to bring us down to earth," he said, quietly. But he was talking to himself.

It was cooler, now, and while he had been engrossed in thought Felicitas had gone and fetched her cardigan. She had also summoned Robert and asked him to bring up some tea, which he had done with his usual alacrity, appearing at a respectful distance in his discreet waistcoat and breeches, black hair brushed neatly back. She did not hesitate, after he had disappeared, to take the opportunity of pointing out their indebtedness to their benefactors in Lyra for the amazing gift of the robots in a form resembling dynamic pseudo-holograms with solidity mimickers, and for Robert especially.

"What better than a superhuman butler and a down-to-earth cook?" she observed. "But if we cannot *change* anything back there…"

For a second or two Lexin was thinking about Veronica the cook, and how it was fortunate he was not a Normal – he would be so distracted… "Perhaps I can do just that," he said. "Perhaps I should."

"I don't see how we can mend historical problems. Learn from them, yes, but…" She paused, looked at him in puzzlement. "What exactly are you suggesting? Are you suggesting that these images you have seen, which thankfully you have not thought fit to show me – but perhaps you ought to – are relevant to you, to us, all of us…? Or is it something even more than that?"

She wasn't going to let this go; he could see that. "To answer your question, yes. I am convinced it is something even more than that."

She leaned forward, her left elbow in Orion and her right elbow somewhere between Pisces and Pegasus, her thick, black head of hair almost filling his vision and her perfume commandeering his olfactory senses. (It was not for chance reasons that with its undeniable power it had always been referred to by family and close friends alike as 'the Princess's favourite perfume'). She said, slowly,

"Let us get this straight, Lexin, because you are the only son I have and I love you very much and want you to do the right thing for my sake and Olaf's, for the family, for planet Earth and the Galaxy – and presumably the cosmos. In January 2072 the World Association of Radical Operatives finally said they trusted nobody, and least of all the press, and, after another year in which the rich of the world continued to bleed the poor, they precipitated Armageddon. Or it would have been the end of the world if a power beyond all our imaginings had not offered help, notably by removing the terrifying cloud of dust and radioactivity circling the Earth following the destruction of a large chunk of the USA. In doing this the Lyrians employed knowledge of which we had at that time not the remotest understanding.

"Are you saying, son, that the events which followed the deposition by the Lyrians, one week later, of genetic material in a bank in a certain city, together with a huge quantity of incredibly compressed text implanted in indestructible disks telling us how to deal further with the situation and then how to proceed gradually towards active participation in the Galactic Community…, are you telling me that all this requires amplification, even some kind of 'further unlocking' or 'facilitating' – I don't know how – by reference to a girl who lived four hundred and fifty years ago?"

"For some reason, yes."

She straightened up, then said quickly, "Better not tell your father this."

Robert suddenly appeared. "You asked me to tell you when Mr. Solberg was approaching, Mrs. Solberg. He was at the Meeting of the Avenues five minutes ago. He is on foot, as usual."

"Then he will be here in less than five minutes." Felicitas got up and went to the balustrade. "Please bring another pot of tea, Robert, and some titbits from the kitchen, and Lexin," she added after the robot had disappeared, "please get a sun bed out in the conservatory in case he needs to flop. Thank goodness neither you nor Robert is any more afraid of hard work than Olaf is, at any rate. I must say, though, that I am just a little envious of the ease with which our excellent Robert does everything, takes his decisions, knows what to say."

"It may be that we should be a bit more robotic, allow ourselves to…how can I put it…? allow ourselves to be guided," Lexin suggested when he returned.

"Isn't that what we *are* doing, Lexin?"

"I mean that it could be we are trying to do the impossible. Put another way, there could be something missing in the way we decipher the text."

"It is very highly skilled, isn't it, the deciphering job?"

"You have to be very dedicated… how can I put it? Receptive." He had done stints in the deciphering facility, under supervision, over a long period. Most Societans, in fact, received at least simulated decipherment experience, and the most promising students came to the facility, of which just a few later specialised in decipherment in various fields.

"Now what are you saying exactly: 'something missing'…?" she began, only to be interrupted by a shout from below and the sight of the tall, blond figure of Olaf lolloping up in his running shorts and singlet.

"Hello, hello," he was yelling. "Is Lexin there?" He was just below now, and starting up the steps. "Tell the little fellow he can stand ten feet tall, just like old Zhang" – a reference to C.F. Zhang's four goals in the Asia-versus-Africa intercontinental of the previous day. Olaf was into football in a big way, having played till he was seventy-five, and being frequently seen supporting the Galaxy City team at the Arturo Mendez Sports Complex, which also housed the International Stadium. Now his tall frame had leapt up the last three steps and, both Felicitas and Lexin having risen to greet him, he was giving Lexin a big hug followed by another for Felicitas. Lexin had to admire his father for sheer exuberance. "The good news for you, Lexin, is that you are indeed in the final three or four for election to the Conference in this region of Northern Eurasia as things stand at present." Lexin knew that only two out of the ten aspirants would be chosen by the delegates in the forthcoming election. He hoped they were not expecting too much of him, but in any case there was still a while to go before the election, and the Matriarchs made the final, definitive selection. "The Matriarchs have been very impressed with what they term your 'over-all grasp' of the various topics," Olaf continued with no lessening of the exuberance as he returned to Lexin and drew him to himself inz a one-armed hug, his clean-shaven chin and cheek filling Lexin's vision for a moment. "I should add that they still await the results on dimensional physics and galactic philosophy."

"I fear no-one knows too much about that," Lexin said "– about the philosophy, I mean."

"Admittedly it is difficult, Lexin," his father acknowledged, letting go of him and allowing his gaze to wander over the city. "Of course, we have to make certain assumptions…" He appeared to reflect for a moment, then he said, "It may be in the stuff we have not yet got into, yes? Be all that as it may," he added, suddenly looking tired, "I sometimes think it will take someone younger than me to continue this work; it's becoming more difficult, more taxing. Is it *just* my age?"

At a hundred years old, Olaf was the elder of two brothers. The younger brother and his family were Normals. Sverre Solberg was a big name in sportswear in Bergen and was constantly complaining jokingly to Olaf that with the sub-surface transit trains still no nearer than Oslo, the Lyrians hadn't done much for Norway's economy or for him. Olaf would suggest, tongue in cheek, that he should emigrate to somewhere civilised like the Austrian Alps. Unlike Sverre, who had broken with family tradition and not joined the Society, he had maintained it and had in fact remained in the same house that had been in the family for over two hundred years. The city, at the heart of the Society's activities, had always been a magnet for those aspiring to leadership in it, their paternal grandfather having also served for many years as President.

"Olaf, you should go and lie down for a bit," Felicitas said. "You must be whacked. Take the tray that Robert's brought and go and lie down in the conservatory. He has put the sun bed out for you."

"I cannot deny I am tired," he replied, and went briskly into the house, followed a few moments later by Felicitas at a more sedate pace.

Lexin went up to his own office, activated the personal activity synthesizer app of his computer and fed in his perceptions of the day.

He noted without too much concern a continuation of certain unusual mental and physical indices (biochemical balances, cognitive functions, self appraisal, etc.) that he had been noting for some time on those occasions when he had turned to his PAS – it must have been ever since *that girl* had first appeared on his screen. Her appearance on the scene had demanded investigation, some investigation at least of its importance for his well-being, his studies. As was often the case, the most recent news of her threw the unusual nature of his indices more starkly into focus. He was relieved to note that the over-all assessments of his 'well-being' were still satisfactory, and even improved when new data were added, suggesting that his extraordinary experiences were somehow important to him.

Relaxing his mind for a moment as he swung around in his comfy chair, letting his eyes rove around the scientific and historical tomes lining the opposite wall, the box files of favourite newspaper cuttings, the compendia of reflections, prayers and meditations, some annotated in his own hand..., he was pulled up in his ruminations by Felicitas on the intercom saying she wanted to talk to him – if convenient. Almost before Lexin had had time to answer she was ascending the staircase.

"You don't mind if I come in, do you, dear? I just wanted to say privately how pleased I am about your progress."

"Thank you, Mother. But won't you sit down?" He motioned her to one of the armchairs.

"No, I won't stop. It was just to say I am so proud of you, as is your father."

He was used to his mother's effusions. "We should all thank the Bods," he said – "if it were not so dangerous trying to make contact!"

She caught the irony, of course. "I suppose I could understand it if you wanted to opt out, but your father..."

"...Would be pretty cross, putting it mildly."

"Devastated."

"No question of it," Lexin said. "To opt out would be unthinkable."

"And the...*girl*..."

"She comes along with us. You remember I said that I seem to know what she is thinking sometimes. There is much more to tell you, actually. She is not somebody that I can put out of my mind just like that."

"I am sure I do not really understand...what that means," she said with unaccustomed hesitation.

"Never mind, I think I do," Lexin said, and his mother, after a final hug and a pause in which no words came, left with less than her usual flourish.

It had been occurring to Lexin to take his PAS much more seriously. It appeared to be fed all relevant data relating to brain and body as well as all data received from outside (e.g. multimedia, multicom, personal encounter...). It could be used only by its 'owner' and was able to be used audio-verbally if desired. He had really used it very little before the girl appeared for the first time. In fact, education on its use had been minimal, and he reckoned that that was a more or less universal experience among the enhanced population. He had heard his father refer to it occasionally, his friends rarely. When Felicitas had gone downstairs, he decided to use its facility for receiving or requesting information on future guidance. The result from the FG prompt was interesting but posed as many questions as it gave answers:

"Your external time-crossing concerns are legitimate but very unusual," it read. "Are you sure you wish to continue with them?" The answer could only be "Yes". "The reliability of your personal indices is outside the scope of our assessment as yet." Was this a stricture on the under-use of his PAS? "Are you really happy to continue to respond to unusual computer activity?" Another "Yes". The following message was reassuring: "Your doubts on the present approach to galactic advancement are unusual, but they are entirely understandable".

Questions about the precise purpose of his anomalous experiences were brushed politely but firmly aside.

Scrolling through the newspapers 'on screen' the following morning, Lexin saw that the progress of candidates aspiring to election to the Conference of the Earth Society for the Advancement of Intragalactic Relations was the subject of a press release by the Society. Frequent efforts had been made in recent years to publicize the Society's elections after a decades-long period of sparse achievement in comparison with the spectacular advances of earlier times. On this occasion the focus was on the Central Asia region, the local one. Lexin suspected his father's participation in this latest release, especially as his own son's write-up featured prominently in the day's papers. Olaf had warned him there was something coming. All the papers, that is, except one.

There was no doubt about his father's undying optimism about him, he had noted, as he came finally to the 'London Times', but on arriving at the press release about the candidates on page four he noticed a curious thing. At the beginning was a notice: "Continued from World News, p. 9", but on scrolling to page nine he could find no mention of the matter – and certainly not the account of himself, his "happy and celebrated family" in Galaxy City, his "brilliant success" in the School for Aspirants, and his "unprecedented rise in popular esteem" which led the press release in the other papers – any more than there was anything about him on page four, which continued with an account of the other aspirants. Tucked away at the bottom of page nine, however, his eye did come to rest on a curious story about a woman found wandering in a forest reserve in the Carpathian Mountains of Europe.

Glancing casually through the story, puzzled rather than annoyed by the omission of himself everywhere, including on page four, he was wondering what the big deal was about an old huntsman, a lone hunter, finding and rescuing this woman who had fled from a private community in the forest. At the same time it had to be said that such events were hardly an everyday occurrence in what might be regarded as more enlightened times. Details were sketchy, but it appeared that the woman had been enslaved by the community's leader and forced to flee after his death, and already now, when Lexin's eye closed on her photograph at the end of the text he knew even before he had closely examined it, and indeed almost before he looked at it, that although some years had passed it was that same redhead caught in glimpses in his anthropology studies.

Lexin fed his thoughts into his p.a. synthesizer once again, simultaneously transferring to it the whole page of 'The Times' containing the article. The result was flagged up as 'significant', but there was no further help. To get a better handle on his thoughts he tried questioning from various angles via his FG prompt and was advised simply, as if confirming earlier answers and his consequent positive assumptions, "Do not hesitate to use your PAS" and "Use your PAS for timeless access". That was very encouraging, a kind of authentication. Perhaps his fears for the hunter had been justified and he had had to flee too, long before. Any other thoughts on the story would be pure speculation. At any rate it appeared someone somewhere was anxious to update him about something more important than his electoral chances.

The rest of the morning was spent on some work for Professor Malinovsky. As he was finishing this a signal to his brain indicated an important message. Picking up his personal multicom, he received a terse circulation statement: "Nine dead in wormhole transmission and retrieval control; two engineers seriously injured," and he hurried downstairs.

CHAPTER FOUR

"So I have just two or three questions to ask you, Marcelle, the man in the wig explained. (He was counsel for the prosecution, the lady with her said. In other words he was 'on their side'). First, did your mother come in while the man was doing what he was doing?"

"Yes."

"Did she try to stop him?"

"Yes."

"How?"

"She said, 'Leave off 'er. Stop it! It's wrong, Larry.'"

"And did she try to pull him away?"

"Yes, but she couldn't." (She hadn't tried very hard.)

"Thank you, Marcelle, you have been very helpful."

Earlier, the other man dressed the same – but the lady said he was from the other side – had asked her whether she had told the man to stop what he was doing, and she had said she hadn't dared. He had asked her whether she had ever seen the man before and whether he had spoken to her before, and she had said 'yes' to both those questions, and 'no' when he asked her whether the same thing had happened before.

In his summing up the judge said he was satisfied that the evidence of the plaintiff (that was herself) given in the video recording made earlier, and in court, and her mother's and the forensic evidence, were sufficient. A defence on the grounds that the accused believed Marcelle to be sixteen and that her mother encouraged this belief could not be upheld. Ida Weston had denied that, and also Marcelle had told the defendant on an earlier occasion what class she was in at school. The judge said he was sorry to have had to bring the victim to the court in person, but sometimes an appearance, however short, was helpful.

Of course, the health visitor had been and said she would have to go back to her grandparents. So it was going to be the same thing all over again! Lenie had been right about her being taken away the first time all those years ago when she was eight. After a couple of days of being 'unwell' and off school, and they had tried to hide her cuts and bruises, and she had been back at school a day or two, a lady from the council and the doctor came to the house after school and looked at her and talked to her mother and father. It was not for the first time. Never before, however, had she been told she would have to be taken from her mum and dad for a while. She cried every night. Gone would be the bedroom where she slept with Lenie, the wine glass, Lenie's peep hole; gone was nearly everything else, even her school friends, for she would be going to a new school. Most of all she would miss her mother and her dad terribly, and Lenie who punched her, and even the budgie. In the few days before she left, her mother wouldn't speak about it, and her father just kept saying that she would be happier with her grandma and grandpa for a while.

And every night when she went to bed she had wondered whether she would dream again about that hunter in another time. She hoped so, because she wanted to know what happened to him, whether somehow he managed to save himself. It had all ended so quickly and she had seen no sign of him. That he should have survived seemed almost more important to her than anything else. But there were no dreams.

She had lived with Grandma and Grandpa until she was ten. Returning now, at fifteen, with Grandpa to the bungalow in the village a few miles outside the city where he and Grandma lived (she had already been living there again for several weeks) she remembered the judge had also said that in view of her age any defence on the grounds that the plaintiff did not discourage the defendant, or even supposing she had encouraged him, was irrelevant. Grandpa tried to explain the words, as if she didn't understand them anyway, and asked her whether she had encouraged Larry. No she had not, she said, and felt so angry. How could she have done? She knew what could happen, and she was frightened of that, but when it came to it she somehow trusted Larry to take precautions because he knew her mother. As it happened, her boyfriend said she was not likely to get pregnant because she had a period straight after. She didn't tell her grandpa all that.

The health visitor lady seemed a tad cross when she said she did not hate the man because he had not hurt her too much. Marcelle did not tell her that she had even quite liked him on occasions when he had just called at the house before. It was always when her father was away travelling. Her mother was always talking about "that shabby 'Western Retail Supplies'" where Pop had managed to get her father a travelling job (that had been after he had lost the other job where she said he "daren't sack anyone"). Occasionally, other men had called, and once or twice – like when she had been younger – Marcelle realised that someone was staying the night and had heard things going on in the next room, but she had never looked through the peep hole, though it was still there after Lenie had left home and she understood everything now.

She felt sure that it was because Larry liked her that her mum had been very angry with him on occasion. Once she had heard her mother shout, "If it's her you want, you just watch out or you'll get yourself had up and all of us in trouble!" Larry apparently owned a mail-order company, and her mother was working for him part-time.

Marcelle kept this to herself, as she did also the matter of Larry's 'photography', and those pictures of her in her knickers and bra (usually). If he liked to look at those pictures, so what?

"Your mum wouldn't mind," he had assured her when she had once just casually queried it. She thought it best to say nothing to be on the safe side. It was borne out when her mother did come in once and find him with his camera. All Marcelle heard her say, as Larry left explaining he had just had the idea he would try it out – it was a new one –, was,

"So I'm not good enough, eh, Larry? Ought to be ashamed of yourself. Don't you dare show her face!"

But she was sure he only wanted the pictures for himself.

Of course there were some not-so-good times. Lenie, who had

married Jamie at seventeen and had a baby already (and another had died) and who came over from her house on the council estate at Springbank quite often, explained that it was when their mother was having to do fill-in jobs between the modelling contracts that she really liked doing. Then her mother was miserable, and it was best to keep out of the way. There were rows, and doing her homework was often difficult. But it was when her father was at home that her mother's outbursts of temper were worst, like when she had brought two stray kittens home, and they made a mess all over the house but her dad had been in favour of keeping them.

By the time she was turned thirteen her mother would be out many evenings when her dad was away (which was usually), and it was then that once in a while she might return very late with a guest, when it was a case of making herself scarce and asking no questions. But by fourteen Marcelle had an occasional boyfriend, and there were discos and sometimes she would let a boy take her to the cinema if he would pay, because her papers money didn't stretch far, but she never invited anyone in. It was about this time, too, that Larry, she realised later, began to take an interest in her. Was he not gentle, hugged her, was kind like her father who was never here …? And if she had told somebody, anybody, about the photography…where would she have been then? Back in Culver. It was obvious!

At least she had had freedom, and now she had gone and lost it – and something else as well, unfortunately.

Although Grandpa was always very kind, memories of Culver were not happy from the very beginning. She had wanted to bring Jimmy the budgie's body on the bus from home to bury it in Grandpa's garden, and it had not been allowed.

"No, dear, I don't want you bringing it here, not even in a cut-down cereal packet wrapped in a newspaper and a polythene bag." That was Grandma, and when Marcelle had wanted Grandpa to take her in his car in her Oberon costume to show her mum after the last performance of the key-stage two play at the end of her next to last year at the primary school, it was not allowed either, because Grandma said it would have to go in a handicrafts exhibition in the village and might get spoiled. It was as if everything to do with home was best forgotten.

Now, back at Culver again it was ,"No, I don't think you should go on the bus to Lenie's to baby-sit while they go to the disco, especially when the new baby is not very well and there is a history of cot deaths in the family." Lenie had not gone to university of course. Naturally, Grandma and Grandpa were a bit upset about the investment, supposedly towards university fees, but at least it was being put to good use for baby clothes and toys (they hoped). "And what if the baby stops breathing?" Grandma said finally. Grandma was seventy years old and of slight build and (in the words of Marcelle's new boyfriend, Mark) always "with the same dissatisfied expression, and not very cooperative."

Another time, Marcelle asked, "For the future, Grandma, could I go to the first-aid course after school? I really want to do that. Then I could do resuscitation. And join the St. John's Ambulance when I'm old enough and help at the Newchurch marathon."

"We will have to see what is best, Marcelle," Grandma said as she laid the table nicely in the dining room overlooking the dull back garden, which in summer would be even more dull when beyond the neat rectangular lawn it sprouted row upon row of vegetables and the inevitable runner bean frame cutting off the view across the fields towards the woods and the canal.

"Or I could become a lifeguard on the beach, or I could be a nurse."

"We will have to see, Marcelle," Grandma said. "I'm not sure you shouldn't be considering staying on at school to get your A-levels. Grandpa thinks so, and he has had a lot of experience, you know."

One thing was certain: school or job, there was always going to be the boring bus ride into Newchurch. Marcelle wondered what "experience" meant. Was it conversing in the 'Rose and Crown'? Was it messing about with the car engine...? She supposed it was his work before he retired.

"Then you could go for a really good job," Grandpa said. He was in his shirt sleeves trying to un-stick the dodgy French window. "Look how well Mark has done." Oh yes, the tall, blonde, fair-skinned Mark in his well laundered jeans and T-shirt and discreet sneakers! The new boyfriend was seventeen. Yes, he was doing very well. He was about to take his A-levels, and he wanted to go into computers. Incidentally, Mark wasn't keen on Lenie and her bloke. Marcelle was sorry about that. She had always slotted in well with Lenie in a funny sort of way.

With Grandpa it was all about being safe. There was the refusal to let her go with a school friend and her family to an anti-hunting demonstration. She had sneaked out and gone, and that was the first time Grandpa had ever been really cross with her.

"But I don't want to be 'safe'", she protested.

"Well I want you to be," he replied.

Or was the word 'conventional'? It was even worse when she put all the money she had earned on her paper round in a week in a beggar's bowl in the city centre. Grandpa was with her, and he tried to get the beggar to give most of it back to her. Although Grandpa was a big man – a little taller than her father (and *he* was not short by any means) – and quite important-looking, that proved difficult, and in the end they just had to walk away.

"What would your mother have said to that?" he asked her. "I mean, at your age!" She could see he was angry.

"She'd have just given me a clout and then another one, and shouted a bit. I'm not bothered, Grandpa." He seemed very perplexed. Just being conventional, that was it. Was this what happened to people who looked after other people's money all day like he did, for the corporation? They were good people, as Mark said, but she wanted to do almost anything but stay there at Culver. The matter of her parents' not being properly together (she could not think how else to put it) worried her intensely.

When she went in the car with Grandpa on one Saturday morning in early April to see her parents, they found out that her father had left home. Her mother was there, in the kitchen in that low-cut blousy top and garish skirt.. She said he had left her with the bills to pay.

"Where is he?" Grandpa asked.

"How should I know?"

"Did you hit him, mother?" Marcelle asked, starting to clear some remains of a meal off the table.

"Course I didn't! Any road, you've no business asking things like that."

"Is she being well behaved, Henry," her mother asked, very obviously changing the subject.

"Oh very," he replied, nonchalantly. *Too* nonchalantly.

"Mum, do you mean it by saying you don't know where Daddy is?"

"Do you think I'm lying."

"We all lie, don't we? A bit, anyway. Even Grandpa. He did it just now," Marcelle burst out, feeling the tears come into her eyes and not knowing quite why she had said it.

Grandpa, surprisingly, smiled. "I think she means she may not always have been perfect."

"You shouldn't speak about your grandpa like that, Marcelle, or I'll be giving you one! He's being very good to you." (In fact it was some time, now, since the hand had come down and swiped her.)

. "I gave all my papers money to the man who sits begging with a dog by the railway station."

There was a long pause. It seemed for a moment her mother did not know what to say. Then she said, remarkably in a quieter voice than usual but all pent up, "Christ, Marcelle, You don't change do you?"

"Are you going to clout me, then. Give me one for Dad, too. I can stand it. `And please do you know where I can find him?"

At that, her mother clenched her fists and on the verge of tears shouted, "Why do you want to know? There's his address, on that bit of paper." She pointed to a scrap of paper on the dresser.

"Because I love him."

At that, Ida flopped down on one of the chairs at the table and buried her head in her hands. She was crying now.

"We must go and leave your mother in peace, dear," Grandpa said, but Marcelle went and put her arms round her hunched form.

At first, nothing happened. Then her mother seemed to come to. "Don't start that!" she said, and shrugged her off.

"Come on, dear," Grandpa said, and then, "We'll be off, Ida. I'm sorry it's come to this. Another day."

Marcelle picked up the piece of paper. As they left, Ida was still sitting bent over the table with tears in her eyes. Two people had eaten at the table. Obviously Larry, who was now serving a term, had a successor. When they were in the car she said,

"Grandpa, I'm sorry I said you lied. It was a kind of joke. Could we go and see my dad now?"

"I know it was," he said. "Yes, we'll go now."

They found him, in his usual worn jacket and brown cords, in a sparsely furnished room with a tiny kitchen over a pub further into town between the Leiston Road and the canal, the old Mondeo parked outside just off the road in a sort of unofficial pub car park.

"Tom, I had no idea you had left," Grandpa said. "We can get you a better place than this. How much are you paying?"

"Sixty pounds."

"Ida says you have left her with the bills."

"I am paying money into her account, but this job may fold. I have had to have a few days off, and they are not very pleased. But a thousand miles a week touting for the supply of food to every café and restaurant within a hundred miles..."

"What's wrong?"

"Just some virus."

Could that really be every week, that sixty pounds? Marcelle wondered in the silence that followed.. She would have to ask Mark. A lot of his friends were leaving home and looking for digs. Mark was staying a third year in the sixth.

A door slammed, followed by laughter downstairs, rousing Marcelle from her thoughts. She looked out of the window. The pub was almost the only original building in an area of mixed redevelopment. To the left you could see a couple of cranes of the old docks away over the new roofs. The old canal, brown and oily, passed close by and could be followed with the eye where it turned among some new warehouses opposite, flanked by derelict shrubbery and rubbish-strewn reed beds, and disappeared into a flat wilderness towards the city's outskirts.

"I could give you my papers money," she burst out, "instead of to that man with studs and rings everywhere, a woolly hat and a dog outside the supermarket," to which her father just said,

"He probably needs it more than I do."

Grandpa said something about it being "better if she keeps it herself". Marcelle was surprised, and a bit pleased, that her father had said what he had said, though he may not have realised she meant *all* the week's money. Grandpa didn't tell. She was pleased about that, too.

"But how *can* you pay that money into Mummy's account if you are paying all that money here?"

"Don't worry your dad about it, and don't worry yourself," Grandpa said. Certainly her dad looked worried enough, that same pointy face with small features as his father's now looking so anxious, so self-questioning, and his body so thin compared with Grandpa's robust form. Grandpa had once had the same very dark hair, but now it was silver and quite distinguished. Marcelle hated leaving her father there, in that miserable place. Back in the car she asked her grandpa why, if they didn't get on, it was her father who had left home and not her mother.

"You could put it like this," he said after a moment's consideration: "Because he is the one best able to look after himself on his own. And let me tell you something else, Marcelle." Grandpa put his big tweedy arm around her. "Your dad is very proud of you, actually, and how you are doing at school and everything."

It was strange, she thought, how someone who loved her could have let her mother knock her about so, but she loved her father nonetheless.

Until that day she had not felt she could talk to anyone except Mark about her parents and her concern for them. It was so hard to explain. And there was another thing, too, that she had never told anyone else about and had never forgotten, and that was the strange dream of years ago, the cry of the hunter as he fell into the river. It was as though she had another life and was cut off from it.

Back at the grandparents', she said she would go out for a walk. She wanted to think on her own. They told her to be careful and not to speak to strangers – the same old warnings. She walked by the canal, the same canal that came out of the city where her father was staying and – so she had learned at school – wound all the way to some factories in Leiston. It had been hoped to resuscitate it one day all the way to Leiston, but those hopes had long since faded. Something about economics.

She was not supposed to walk there, by the canal. They were not nice, safe places. Nevertheless, she walked slowly along the towpath till she came to one of the locks where there was a long seat by the upper gates facing the upper reach. She sat down in her jeans and sweater – it wasn't too cold – and found it remarkably comfortable for a battered, wrought-iron seat, and soon she was lost in thought. Away into the distance the canal appeared to widen, and the glistening light from the lowering sun expanded the water even further, blending it with the trees which themselves increased their extent so that they seemed to surround her. No person came, no breath of wind, nothing. She was still thinking of what Grandpa had said about her father: that he was "the one best able to look after himself" (did he mean her mother 'always has to have a man around her', like Lenie said?), when she became aware that the sound of the motorway where it debouched from the city a mile or so away seemed to have come much nearer. But the rushing sound in her ears was not the sound of cars, or of lorries rushing to Bathenhurst with everything from food to furniture as explained by Mr. Tattenhall years ago.

She was standing upon a slight eminence in noisy wind and rain.

The canal had become a wide, silver river bordered partly by forests reaching towards it from the horizon, partly by a more open landscape stretching flat as far as it was possible to see as successive squalls passed across it.

If the scene reminded her in its loneliness of somewhere often remembered, the man soon observed coming painfully towards her along the river's edge was more than familiar, with that funny walk and carrying all those furs and pouches and things. The sight of him brought everything into focus. It was *him! He had not drowned. He was alive!* She wanted to shout, to shout for joy. How often she had thought about him since the time her mother had hit her for listening through the floorboards. But could he really have survived all these years? Could it really be him? Now he was very close, but it seemed he did not notice her, so intent was he on making forward progress, fighting his way through the long, thick, sodden grass with the aid of a long stick and a spear. She opened her mouth to call out to him, but was hardly surprised when no sound came. How could she hope to communicate with him across the wide abyss of time?

The man appeared to be even more decrepit now, the deeply tanned skin of his face around that big nose scarred and wrinkled. The partially closed eye seemed to have healed but still looked a little odd, and he was moving with obvious difficulty, a sort of bow suspended from his waist adding to all his other stuff and his emaciated form swaying from side to side with that bad hip, or whatever it was, so much that she could not see how anything managed to stay on his shoulder. One thing was clear: there was a gap of years in *his* life, too, since his last appearance, a gap which he must have crossed with great courage. No animal appeared this time, no food for this hunter, yet despite his state she felt certain that if one did appear he would be quick as lightning and display that same agility as before. How she longed desperately for him to stop a moment, to be able to rest! Could she not carry some of the skins or furs, or whatever they were, for a while, or maybe just some stones? He passed, slowly, silent and unseeing. But it was him, and he was alive, and she feared for him more than ever.

There was a shout, but it was not from him. A man was standing on a boat entering the lower gates of the lock. "You could earn a bit working them gates, darling!"

"How much?" she shouted back. "But I might get a bit bored."

"I'd take you on in the galley any day!"

"I'll have to ask my dad!"

"You do that!" he said, laughing as he closed the lower gates. Then as the chamber started to fill he added, "There's more to the canal than meets the eye," and soon he was doffing his captain's cap as he tut-tutted his way into the upper reach.

Many a worse way to earn a penny, Marcelle thought, as she made her way back, and more fun than sitting studying for 'A' levels like Mark was trying to get her to do.

It occurred to her that she had not got wet. It was as if there had been no rain.

* * *

Her apparent concern for her parents did not cut much ice with Mark. He said she should be looking after herself. He had said the same thing after the trial, where they had let him into the gallery after some hesitation. And even he was stupid enough to ask her,

"Were you really too afraid to move a muscle when he attacked you?" to which she replied,

"I thought what's the use?"

"I'm glad you didn't put it like that."

"Anyway, he was very heavy."

"And how do you mean, it didn't hurt? Did it go in easily, then?"

"Of course not! What are you saying, Mark?" She hit him, and then started to cry and said she was sorry. "It wasn't like it would be with you, you know that."

"I'm glad," he said, distantly, and not very lovingly. Then, evidently relenting, he took her in his arms and held her there. That felt so good. "Marcelle, I'm afraid what you're doing, without realising it, is you're protecting your mother. Look what she's done to you. These men, I mean all these men she sees..."

"Two or three of them, not 'all these men'." She broke away from him.

"I'm not sure you're right there. They are a danger to you, and you said nothing about them in your statement or anything. I suppose you couldn't. I think she really let you in for that attack. Look, think about your future. Where does your father really stand in all this? Doesn't he ever do anything to stop these things? If I were there, I would!"

"Yes, but you are not, and you are not my dad. He's got this terrible job. He's out for days on end. Anyway, Mum can clout *him* when she feels like it."

When Marcelle had gone back to her grandparents Mark visited there often, and needless to say they fawned over him. It was a bit annoying how more and more now he agreed with them about everything, or at least with Grandpa. She admitted it *was* a bit daft wanting to do life-saving on beaches, though. For one thing they were a long bus ride away, and for a second thing she had only been learning to swim a few months, and then only because Mark had been taunting her about it and she told him she would jump in the river if he mentioned it again, which he did. He had to rescue her from a not-so-shallow pond in the Memorial Park, jumping in after her wearing his new black chinos and sweatshirt and his do-it-all watch that turned out not quite as waterproof as he had thought. She knew the incident rattled him, but he had tried not to show it, walking home as if nothing had happened. At least it made her really learn to swim. About Lenie his criticisms were probably justified, but to her Lenie was just Lenie: second-rate mum, poor housekeeper, occasionally untruthful, very lazy, extremely casual, but faithful to Jamie, though goodness knows why since he was brainless – which could not be said of her. Probably that was just it. Lenie could handle him like she could handle nothing else, helping him to hold down his job (currently delivering washing machines). And perhaps that was why she herself loved Lenie – because there was *something* in her that was absolutely watertight. Maybe their mother saw it, too. Even Mark had to admit that about Lenie.

Marcelle was even prepared to admit he might be right in agreeing with her grandparents about her staying on after GCSE's – except that with her dad having left home everything seemed so messed up and the future full of uncertainty.

"I think I need to go and help him," she said. That was the day after seeing her father and the episode by the canal, and they were at Mark's parents' house in Farston, which was quite a lot posher than the one where the Westons lived. It was a detached, four-bedroom villa at the top of a front garden filled with a rockery and spring flowers. In a hilly position, it overlooked a broad valley full of a patchwork of red roofs and the flowering of hundreds of cherry trees. Just out of sight round the spur of a hill was the security firm owned by Gerald Wharton,

Mark's dad, and on a good day there was a marvellous view to Marcelle's first school, miles away across the city with its memories of Miss Palmeson (and levers and sliders). It was a Sunday, and she had come over on two buses via the city centre after lunch. They were in the sitting room, or more precisely the drawing room as Winifred Wharton liked to call it, with its array of well-polished pseudo period furniture and dominantly pink floral curtains matching the cherry blossom of spring (she said) and the roses that would fill the foreground in the summer. "I want to take him a lot of things he left behind at home," Marcelle said. "We'll have to go there first."

"Can't we creep in when your mother's not there?"

"Why? What's wrong with Mum? Are you scared of her?"

"It's those grey eyes that look through me, the firm mouth and firm lips that may be beautiful but seem about to chastise you – you, not me. Don't repeat any of that!"

"As if I'd dare! It's because she's not herself, Mark. She's all strung up."

"Yeah, I know, I know. You were telling me that."

"I thought you were frightened she might seduce you or something."

"Much too old for me," Mark replied. "And I like blondes with big bottoms. And don't forget you aren't supposed to go there without telling your grandparents."

"I hate you," she said, aiming a sweep of her arm to just flick his ear. "I may not be blonde, but there's nothing wrong with *my* bottom."

"I was talking about your mother, Marcie."

"I'm not sure who you are talking about," she said, looking out of the window. She turned to face him – "Who will know if I go there? Tell me that!"

"Hold your horses, Marcie! Look. First, there's something I must tell you," he said.

"Oh my God! No more problems, please!"

"You know it was your grandparents who told the police that you'd been raped. Your mother wasn't going to, was she?"

"I know. I suppose she must have panicked and told my dad or something."

"It was me. Actually, it was my father who told your grandparents. You haven't forgotten that you phoned me just afterwards, have you? You were very upset."

"We thought it our duty to tell your grandparents who had been acting as your guardians, Marcelle." The voice was Winifred Wharton's. The fifty-or-so-year-old blonde, tall and with chandelier diamond earrings and in a short and shapely glittery blue dress had appeared between the open double doors to the next room as if from nowhere. Marcelle assumed 'nowhere' was probably two feet out of sight behind the door. Probably she had heard them talking about bottoms as well. "And forgive me for overhearing," she continued, "but I think that as Mark says you should not go to your mother's at the moment."

That showed she hadn't missed anything.

"She just wants to get stuff for her father," Mark said.

"Oh yes, Mark said he had walked out. Did he leave in a hurry?"

Marcelle did not like Mrs. Wharton's innuendo. "Will you excuse me, Mrs. Wharton," she asked without answering the question, "if I just go outside and make a call on my mobile?" Barely waiting for the grudging assent, she threaded her way to the patio at the side of the house and phoned her grandparents, asking if she could call at her mother's and take some things to her father's, for which permission was given provided Mark was with her – "We have some discretion, Marcelle," Grandma said, "but I'll have to ring your mother." Passing close to an open living-room window on her way back she happened to hear Mrs. Wharton say,

"That's a very belligerent girl, Mark, and I can see you would have your work cut out." Hidden from view she paused to hear the reply:

"She's very fond of her parents – remarkably so in the circumstances."

"I dare say. Maybe she is made of the same stuff! Personally, I don't know whether we can credit the half of what she says."

Marcelle beat a retreat and rejoined them.

"To answer your earlier question, Mrs. Wharton, my father doesn't hang about where he feels he can't be of any use. Believe it or not, it doesn't mean he doesn't care about us all." There were obvious tears in her eyes. She managed to say, "Grandpa says I can go with Mark."

"Well I hope you are able to help your father, dear," Mrs. Wharton said, Putting an arm round her – a move which, as Mark observed, was tantamount to aggression in Marcelle's book and rejected accordingly.

Mark was allowed to take his father's Audi. Marcelle was disappointed her mum was not at Hawthorn Road, though she sensed

Mark was relieved. She had been just going out when Grandma phoned, and had left a key. Marcelle got cases down from the loft and filled them with clothes from her father's little bedroom that she felt he would need, and some medicines he had meant to bring and had listed, especially some medications for a skin complaint. She collected up some bits of computer software from a chest of drawers, and also a couple of business files on one of the shelves above his bed which he said he had also omitted to pack into a trunk when he drove to his new address. As she did so, something fell out onto the floor. Picking it up she found it was an old envelope of photo prints from a chemist's in town. Glancing at the top one she saw it was a shot of them all sitting on the beach at Sandport long ago, minus herself of course, but plus her dad. How tall, dark and handsome he looked! And in the background was an ice-cream van with the name Piero Pirelli & Son written on the side. She was sure her father would have wanted to take the prints with him, and she stuffed the envelope into her shoulder bag just as Mark was coming up the stairs.

By the time Marcelle had packed everything she was going to pack, the tears were streaming down her face and ruining her make-up, what with collecting her dad's things, not to mention the photograph of happier days before she was even thought of, with everybody smiling and her mum with Lenie on her lap brandishing a spade.

Mark went and took her in his arms. "Don't you reckon your father could do something…something that would bring your mother round, pull her back from this abyss?"

"Of sexual depravity and general degradation? No. At least, I don't see how. When she gave up on Dad I suppose she gave up on herself. Dad has kind of retreated too, standing aloof like some men do and waiting till doomsday for everything to come right. But it's hard when you get into a spiral. At least I've got you to keep me on the rails, haven't I?", she said, quietly, clinging tightly to him. How strong his arms were! Did a slight smell of sweat, which was unusual, really betray an anxiety about her mother suddenly appearing? She was reluctant to let go of him, but eventually made herself. "Come on, let's buzz off up to Dad's," she said, and they loaded everything into the Audi. There was no sign of her mother as they left, or of any car outside in the road that she had come to recognize as belonging to a visitor. "It's going to get a lot worse yet," she said as Mark drove the four and a half miles into the city. On the way, she went into a supermarket and picked up all the food she could afford with the generous pocket money her grandparents allowed her plus the income from the newsagents, and also bought a Sunday Express, which she knew her father read.. She was fairly sure he wouldn't have bought one.

"How do you know you haven't wasted your money on that?" Mark asked as they drove away, tapping the paper.

"I don't know for sure, Mark, but it's like this. You are a scientist, aren't you? My dad's way is to reduce the metabolism of his life to a minimum. Spend and do as little as possible, curl up and wait. Wait for something better, except that it'll be something worse."

"So all this mess was inevitable," he said, resignedly.

"He could have done something, I suppose, before it was too late. I suppose the flip side of that is that we might never have seen him again. We're what we are, Dad's who he is and that's it. He's just kind of been there, with us, and we've all sunk together. How could I have loved him so much if, say, he'd divorced and married someone else and gone far away somewhere? He's quite good-looking, isn't he?"

"I guess that's what most people would have done. So all in all, as I said, it's inevitable and there's nothing to be done."

"You're too much of a bloody scientist, or mathematician if that's what you are. Answers to everything. I didn't say 'nothing to be done', but it takes two, right?" She collected herself. "*Lenie* was good at maths," she said, reminiscently.

"And?"

"She's pretty useless to everybody but Jamie."

"Perhaps I can be useful to *you*, at least," he said in a conciliatory tone.

"I don't want you to be *useful*. I just want you to try and understand me." Now the eyes were half hidden behind the frown, the pretty lips quivering. "It might be harder than you think, being 'useful' to me, as you put it." For a moment she was not sure whether she was going to tell him about what she had experienced by the canal, still less about a dream she had had, only that night. She hesitated. "You're going to say I'm stark staring bonkers, Mark," she said. "There's something I haven't told you yet."

"I hope you're not pregnant. If you are, it's not me, is it?"

"You prig!" she shouted. "You narrow, self-centred, blinkered, middle-class..." Her voice dropped a little."...Tory. Is that the most intelligent thing you can think of that I might want to tell you? You're going to need a lot more imagination, Mark."

He was silent as they approached her father's lodgings. He looked shocked. "What, then?" he asked at length.

"I'll tell you afterwards."

The room overlooking the canal looked even bleaker than it did the day before. Her father's few belongings had been tidied away. His computer stood on the table, and he was sitting at it trying to compose a CV.

"The other job folded, then," she said, gently.

"I am assuming it will. To tell the truth, I think I have exhausted my possibilities in the food industry. I am lowering my sights: traffic warden, furniture salesman, carpet cleaning demonstrator…carpet cleaner? The possibilities are legion."

"But Dad…!"

"No 'buts'. No money, no good job record, no permanent abode."

"Not now, no! But back to the present, I've brought your stuff, and some food. You will ring me, won't you, if I can do something else."

Her dad was very grateful, and kissed her. Mark said he would see if he could have the car another hour and take her back to her grandparents'.

Driving back to his house they said nothing for some time, and then Mark said,

"And what *was* this serious thing you were going to tell me?"

"I don't know whether I am going to. You'll only dismiss it."

"Now you're keeping me on tenterhooks."

"All right then. You remember that dream I had when I was little and my mother had knocked me about?"

"Yes. You've never forgotten it, have you? You've had another?" Mark's tone was almost serious.

"Yes, when I was sitting by the lock near Grandma's yesterday. It was the same man, only older and wearier, and there was a river, perhaps another river, and I could smell it, Mark, the wetness, the rankness."

"A dream, you mean?"

"I suppose so…" She hesitated. "But no! Mark, I was *there*, or half-there. He didn't seem to see me. But it was so real, Mark, the place and the man, and he was so alone I wanted to run to him and help him."

"How 'help him'? – even supposing you *could?*"

"I don't know...carry some of his stuff, sympathise..."

"And it was the same place, that river and forest and so on."

"Different, but the same. I mean the same kind of country, the same emptiness, the same sky, the same point in time. I mean in thousands of years, but a few years later – and raining. He looked that much older, Mark "

"Well he would, wouldn't he? After all, a few years have gone by here, too, haven't they. I mean, it's the same world, isn't it?"

"You're not being facetious, are you, Mark?" He was, of course. But there was more to tell him, more she *must* tell him, had been *wanting* to tell him.

"Why should I be? I mean, you are older, he is older."

"Yes, Mark, but now listen ...Ah! It will have to wait."

They were already in the Whartons' drive. Another car, a BMW, was parked there.

"That's Dad's yachting friend Logan Berry," Mark explained. "They used to play squash. Now they go to the same gym to work off the fat acquired sitting in the harbour at Filport waiting for the weather, or in the pub down the road afterwards talking about how challenging it had all been."

They went in. A girl in blue denims and T-shirt was in the hall, good-looking, tall, blonde, with eyes that were unexpectedly pleasing and reserving of judgement.

"Hi Avril!" Mark's voice was pleasant. "This is Marcelle."

"Hi Marcelle! Hi Mark! Dad's trying to get a crew together. Down the coast, beginning of May."

Gerald Wharton emerged in fairly discreet check jacket, cravat and white flannels. "Hello, Marcelle. Has your father settled down all right?"

"I wouldn't say 'settled down' exactly, Mr. Wharton. He's scanning the papers for a job."

"I thought he had a job."

Yes, but he's had to have time off and I don't think he can hold it. My dad's not very well, really. He's had a rough patch."

"I dare say he has."

Mrs. Wharton appeared and asked if she had seen her mother.

"No", Marcelle replied. "She wasn't there. I don't know where she is."

74

"I'm sorry. A pity there's no-one there when one *can* actually call in."

"Can we go, Mark?" Marcelle said after a polite two seconds' pause, trusting that the faintest of smiles would suffice as a reply to Winifred Wharton's remark.

"Okay if I take Marcelle back in the car, Dad?" he asked.

"Don't be too long. I want you to come down to the 'Lion' and discuss this trip with us."

"Okay, see you there."

Marcelle threw a little wave to Avril, who returned it.

"Carry on," Mark said as they turned out of the drive. "What happened next?"

"I'm glad that's over," Marcelle said. "Why is your mother so horrible to me? Avril yachts too, I take it."

"I thought you would have got used to it. My mum, I mean. And yeah, Avril sails. She wants to be a doctor. It's sort of like having a ship's doctor."

"Wow! I *bet* it is! Are you serious?"

"Of course I am."

Yes, he was, she thought. There was a quite down-to-earth, almost naïve side to Markie. She didn't know whether that made it easier or harder to explain her dreams or her experiences, or whatever they were. "Do you really want me to carry on?" she asked him.

"Of course I do! Just forgive me if occasionally I lose it because of the traffic." It was building up to the rush hour as they tried to get on to the Bathenhurst-Leiston motorway which cut round the outskirts and was the quickest way to get to Culver."

"That was all there was to that, but in the night I dreamed about walking up from the lock into that other time. It wasn't an ordinary dream, Mark, any more than the other one was, and I was so close it was unbelievable. It was a dark place in a forest. Maybe months had passed, or even longer. This time there was a woman lying on a bed of twigs and leaves and things and she was wrapped in animal skins. It's no good asking me how I know what it was she was saying, but it was something like,

'I didn't come looking for you, Big Nose. That's not why I left the camp.'

'And yet somehow you found me,' a man's voice replied.

'Years have gone by' she said. 'You could be anywhere by now.'

'Why did you come the way you did? You never told me that.' Then I saw him, Mark. His face had been hidden by a bough. But it was him all right, *large* nose, funny eye an'all.

'To find a new place, a friendly people.' Although evidently reduced, the woman's voice was clear, decisive.

'Like *me*, then.'

'But why should I tell you, actually. It's my own business. So don't imagine that by looking after me because I am ill gives you any power over me. I am who I am. I am beholden to no male!' And he retorted,

'Yes, I know. You never were!'

'What do you mean by that?' she asked, angrily.

He was stooping – though he was obviously finding it difficult – trying to get her to eat some morsel or other. A spear was leaning against a bough, and there seemed to be some protection from the rain that was falling – strips of wood covered with spotted skins and evergreen branches. 'I mean that you had many men and tossed them aside like old bones when you had had your fill. As I said before, I'm not blaming you, Red Hair, just telling you. Nor am I saying that I don't like you.' Big Nose seemed to have a voice to match, but he used it sparingly, gently.

She seemed to calm down at that – or was it that she was exhausted? 'Giant Man was terrible to me. I couldn't stand being owned by him. He was so jealous, so violent,' she said, very quietly.

'Yes, I know,' he said, 'I understand all that, but why should you think that I am looking after you for some other reason than to help you – help anyone in need'?

She did not answer." Marcelle felt Mark was trying hard to keep calm. He seemed to be taking corners a bit carelessly.

"Okay, you dreamed all this," he said. "Fine. Goodness knows where you dreamed up those names. You don't need to tell me. It's the same man. This 'Big Nose' is the same clapped-out old hunter. And she is just like him, tanned and dishevelled, and on the edge of starvation. She's obviously set her sights on him, whoever she is, even if she didn't set out to find him."

"You're very perceptive."

"And you have no idea how it is you know what they were saying?"

"No, I haven't," Marcelle agreed. Then she went on, "The food seemed to revive her. She said that as a matter of fact she had long admired Big Nose. She had brought him gifts; she had visited him on the night of spring revelries fearing that he might be going to leave, and when he was about to flee suddenly she begged him through another man to take her with him, but he would not. Big Nose asked how he could have known it was she who had come to him silently in the night. It was only the next day that the man called Strong had come to him and he realised, but he was already making his escape. It would have been dangerous, *then*, to change his plan. Then she said she had always loved him, but now she could kill him, and he said that would be pointless.

'I had a terrible beating from Giant Man when that sly Smooth Face let it be known that I had visited you', she said. 'I'll never know how he found out.'

'Pity you didn't bump *Smooth Face* off.' Big Nose said." Marcelle said she could imagine him smiling as he said it, though his face was hidden again. "'It was nearly the end of me, too,' he said. 'Don't imagine *I* had it easy after that, either.'

'I'm glad,' she retorted.

'Turned away everywhere – And my nose doesn't help'.

'I would have preferred *my* proper name, too,' she said, quietly.

'What was that?'

'Fairness – short for Fair Lioness.'"

Mark listened in silence, knowing it was useless to interrupt. He had to leave immediately they arrived at Culver, so Marcelle could not tell him any more, and they did not even fix their next date. He said he would phone. When he did so, a few days later, Marcelle said she hoped he would get over his disbelief. (How could she blame him for it, after all? The whole thing was something so personal, so close to her, so intense, so much a part of her.)

Days went by, school went by, an evening with him by bus into town to see 'The Return of the King', another to her school for a concert (though she admitted she did not much like him seeing or hearing her play the violin – she had only been learning for a year). He looked very smart in tie and new grey jacket, light chinos and polished shoes. But he didn't need to *point out* to her that he did not *always* have to wear jeans. Mark would always be just Mark. All she wanted was that he should properly understand what had happened to her, though 'understand', on second thoughts, would hardly be the right word, would it, for something she could hardly understand herself? Yet although nearly every night it was the same now – the dreams,

Mark did not seem to want to talk about them, even when he came over to Culver and they would walk by the canal and sit by the lock. He was by now preoccupied with his A levels.

Red Hair recovered from whatever had laid her low. The two could be seen moving for days on end through the forest, seemingly in no definite direction owing to frequent obstacles in their path. At times their way was barred by huge growths of brambles and wild rose, or fallen trees, and in places the forest floor was waterlogged and they would make but slow progress, bruising and soaking themselves as they stumbled against submerged rocks. Later, as the land rose slightly, time seemed to move more quickly, and Marcelle would get glimpses of them more distantly, small against the landscape. Now it was as if in spite of their debility the finding of each other had given them a new purpose, a new objective. Strangely, though, their determination when set against the formidable circumstances increased Marcelle's anxiety rather than the opposite, so that when things did not go so well between the two of them it would spill over...

"I don't know how they can possibly find food in these conditions, Mark," she said. They were driving back from her father's. Three weeks after their first visit her father had rung her mobile to say he had still got a chest infection and they had gone over with some more provisions and been to the doctor's for him for some medicine.

Mark gave her a funny look. "They'll be all right," he said. "They seem to be getting on all right now."

"What makes you think they are getting on all right? Did I say so? They fell out terribly a few days ago – our days, I mean.

'I thought you were a hunter, Big Nose,' Red Hair was saying, 'having survived all these years, but if a pigeon a day is supposed to satisfy the pangs of hunger, I reckon I might do better!' They had stopped somewhere, Mark, dropped all their things and spent ages trying to light a fire until it started raining. I could see her eyes. They were flashing angrily as they stood there barneying, flashing behind matted hair that she kept trying to stave off with her muddy arms, poor thing. But even in that state, you know, it was easy to understand her attractiveness.

'Take my spear, then,' he said finally, and for most of a day they went miles apart from each other. It was only a big tributary entering the river that forced them to come back together again. She was flaked out. He spent hours trying to catch a particular fish for her that seemed almost to be waiting to be caught, and he didn't look too good himself. Eventually he caught it, and they ate it raw."

"I'd have tossed her in the river," Mark said, as they approached Culver. "She really gets my goat."

"But I think you would have been wrong, actually," she retorted. "You know what Red Hair said to him? She said,

'I've missed you terribly. Whenever I came across animal tracks – especially a rhino's, I was terrified that it might be heading towards where I thought you'd be.'"

"I bet she did miss him!" Mark said, "And I expect she's frightened she might be on her own again. It's not so easy to get by on your own in those circumstances – as I expect she's beginning to find out."

"Big Nose didn't joke about it, Mark. Out of the blue he asked her why she had left the camp. 'You never told me why,' he said.

She said Giant Man got killed by a lion, leaving the women free to vent their pent-up anger on her not only for having been his favourite but also for hogging the other men. Then she said, 'But Big Nose, from the time you left I didn't want to have anything to do with other men, really – except GM. With him I had no options... I was always thinking of you.'

'Didn't want to'? There was a faint smile on Big Nose's face, Mark, not an unkind smile but a signal of...I don't know what. Love, understanding...?

'Don't be too hard on me!' she said. She was in tears. 'Sometimes it was as if I had to throw myself upon someone else, so dreadful was everything with Giant Man. But it could never be the same as with you.'"

The last time she saw them, Marcelle said, she thought the most they had been able to obtain in the way of meat in the last two or three days was an injured fox which they had roasted on a kind of natural rock table on a fine day and squatted down to share it. Marcelle said she had fallen asleep while poring over her 'World Citizenship' project work, and told him how Grandma's voice calling her down to her tea cut her off from a precious moment of domestic harmony. "I don't know how they have survived in those endless forests, or how they *will* survive, but if you'd seen how Big Nose moved when he nearly caught that deer the first time I saw him..."

"Judging from your descriptions, it'll be spring there – wherever 'there' is (he paused, significantly). They'll soon dry out, and then they'll sail along – to somewhere." It was a bold attempt at empathy on Mark's part, as his big hands manipulated the controls with almost exaggerated aplomb, and his fair head craned this way and that with super-vigilance. They were silent for a while.

For Marcelle it was almost as if the fate of those two in that wilderness in some way depended on her, though she didn't begin to try to explain that to Mark. Nevertheless there was no holding back her anxiety. "If it's coming up to one of those ice ages, winter might go right on to the beginning of summer," she said, barely audibly.

But he caught her drift. The heartfelt tone of her voice finally overtried his patience. "Heavens above, you can't be really worrying about these...people...or whatever they are, visions, self projections, whatever...For God's sake, if it is something real, it all happened aeons of time ago and finished."

But it was as if she wasn't registering.

Mark drew up at the Westons' house. They could see Grandpa working in the garden, and Grandma was just emerging with a cup of tea for him. Mark had that distant look indicating non-comprehension.

"You don't get it, do you darling?" Marcelle said.

"Jesus, I hardly know what you're talking about," he said. "Surely you can't be drawing a parallel with us." He was quite angry now.

"Not with *us*. Are you coming in?"

"So it *is* with your parents," Mark said, quietly. Neither spoke for a moment. "I must get back, Marcie. Dad says I am having the car too much, and I have to go down the pub again to fix the details of this trip. We'll be away a week from this weekend, back on the thirtieth." Then he faced her, the fine, regular facial features all screwed up. "Marcie, I *don't* get it. Why can't your grandpa help your dad more?"

"He's a proud man, my dad."

"And *that* in addition to all the other things...curling up and waiting, and so on, while your mother invites these men into the house?"

She didn't answer that . "By the way," she said, " I didn't tell you what happened after they'd caught a couple of fish and eaten them raw... Big Nose and Red Hair, I mean."

"What?"

"They made *love*, Mark, right there and then."

"And only you to see it." He smiled. "And was it nice? Was it nice to watch?" But she was crying. He drew her across and hugged her.

"I wish you could understand," she said. "I wish you *wanted* to understand. I think something terrible is going to happen to them, Mark, something terrible." After a couple of minutes she recovered, and he released her. "Are you sure you're not coming in?"

"Marcelle, I've got to get off."

"Yes, I know. See you soon." She kissed him, jumped out and ran indoors and to her room. Closing the door behind her she lay on the bed and burst into tears..

It was while Mark was still away sailing that her father phoned to say he had landed the job with the carpet cleaners'. A van came and collected him every morning at seven-thirty . He had had two days' training and he was going around assisting somebody. It was part of a big company. It was a job. The antibiotics had cleared his chest within a week, and he was fine. When she told her grandpa he went very quiet.

"Things are not so good, actually," he said. "They are re-possessing the house. The instalments were not being paid."

"Mightn't Dad be able to pay now?" Marcelle asked.

"They won't wait. The bank won't. In any case, he would not have enough."

"I thought you had always helped him, Grandpa."

"Of course I have, but it's like this, dear…" Grandpa flopped into a chair and he motioned her into the other one. They were in the sitting room and Grandma was in the village, shopping. "…There is so much I can do and so much I can't. I know you won't like this, Marcelle…" She knew what was coming. "…Your dad has left your mum. I just won't go on paying out money for your mum to live there. Your mum has practised no discretion in the spending of your father's hard-won income. Yes, I have helped them – quite a lot."

At least Grandpa could lay down the law, which her father never seemed able to do, at least to her mother, but she said, "Yes I know. But he loves her still. I know he does."

"Love is a two-way thing."

"Yes, I know that, too." She thought of that confluence of rivers in an epoch long ago. "But she will think no-one loves her. I love her, Grandpa!"

"Yes, yes, Marcelle." Grandpa looked very troubled. Obviously her father had been worrying him and Grandma a lot. But she knew he would not hesitate. "I know you do, in spite of everything," he said, "but there are realities." Yet there were other realities, she thought...realities that Grandpa – and Grandma – in the tramlines of their staid existence, would never know. And she could not tell them about the faithful hunter and the woman, either, about how much they mattered to her, never mind convince them of her fears for them.

Mark was quick to come round and see her when the sailing trip ended. He said they had had a fabulous trip, calling in at several places. They had been to some rally or other, taken part in a race out to sea and back and had a huge barbecue. Now he was just praying for an A or B in maths and physics to ensure entry into university.

"And Avril?" Marcelle asked, as cheerfully as she could.

"Oh, yes. Avril. A great sailor, a lot of fun. Do you know, she's an amazing organiser. There was this barbecue for about eighty crews. She ran the show."

"Really?"

"She's great, but not my type."

"No?"

"Oh no, not really."

She told him about the re-possession of her parents' house.

"I suppose it was inevitable," he said.

"Nothing is inevitable, Mark," she replied.

That night Marcelle had a dream. The hunter and his mate had been on the move slowly during several nights of her dreams. Several months of the Stone Age had passed. Things had been terribly hard during the winter, their way rocky and mountainous, progress painfully slow. They must have become terribly short of food. Sometimes he was carrying her, and in this particular dream, to Marcelle's amazement, she was even carrying *him*, across her shoulders. Only then did she realise the breadth of Red Hair's sinewy body and strength of her arms, the muscularity of her thighs when occasionally the smaller, lighter animal skin drawn round her (for it was getting warmer now) parted.

In the last bit of the dream she remembered, probably several more months had passed. They were both half walking, half crawling – apparently through sheer fatigue – towards an encampment situated around a clearing part-way up a steep, forested valley. It was raining hard. Men were running towards them. Two carried them into the trees on their backs, others their belongings. Then the nightmare began. They were separated. Red Hair was told she must stay with them.

Women were useful, especially older women who were less likely to cause dissension. Big Nose would share food and then he would have to go. Men were not needed – at least, not ones who couldn't run.

It was already getting dark so they let him remain, alone, till dawn, but he did not see Red Hair again before they told him to fend for himself and sent him away.

Marcelle was crying as she awoke from the nightmare and could not get back to sleep for a long time. Before morning, she had another dream…

CHAPTER FIVE

There had been too many accidents lately, Lexin was saying to himself as he descended to the living space. Only momentarily, however, did he think to cast blame on himself for not being more forthright in expressing his fears about the whole business of communication using the wormhole. How could he prove what he feared? Everybody knew all such work was hazardous. They knew that, and they went into it like lemmings. But what good would it do to try and tell them about his latest glimpse of troubles besetting other times and other places and try to explain his concern with such apparently remote things – a concern which he could hardly explain himself? It certainly would not sound rational.

It would not sound even mildly relevant, and it hardly fitted into the scientific world of his personal mentor Prof. Tang. And even if he could allow himself some disagreement with aspects of Tang's theories of human perceptions, human behaviour, which he suspected of excessive subjectivity (in his case a reflection of his sensual predilections), when he put his own convictions alongside *Malinovsky's* work on spacetime and on dimensions, his own concerns would surely appear unwarranted and quite beyond the pale. And this despite his sensing in Sergei Malinovsky a kindred spirit and despite the professor's admission of gaps in his own knowledge. As for

Lenica's suggestion about a tête-à-tête, it was ludicrous. Anyway, how could he, son of Olaf, say anything at all after that build-up about himself.

His father had spent the morning working at home. Expecting to find him bewailing the fact of another disaster, Lexin was amazed to hear him saying, in an unusually excited tone as he stepped in from the terrace, pocketing his multicom,

"It was a response from Lyra. There was just enough time to be sure of that before it all blew apart."

Meanwhile, Felicitas, propelled from her room in her dishabille by the gravity of the emerging news, was exclaiming, "What's that? A reply about the comet business?"

Olaf seemed lost in thought just for a moment. "A reply from HVC 0092 in Lyra," he said, "confirming receipt of our message transmitted a matter of minutes previously. It must have been. It will go down in history."

"When was it? When did you receive it?" Lexin asked, unsure whether he was more surprised by the news or by his father's upbeat tone in the tragic circumstances.

"Twenty minutes ago. It has been years of hard work here at the Station."

Funny how they still called it a Mission Station, Lexin thought. Nothing solid, at any rate, had been 'sent' from there since the twenty-second century, when the last massive fusion rockets went up on a twenty-year mission to the Saturnine satellite system. Since that time it had been reserved for the Society in its long and arduous pursuit of galactic enlightenment for the human race. He felt strangely unexcited. "But there was no time to retrieve the message before the explosion, you say?"

"No, unfortunately." That seemed to jar Olaf into a sombre mood. After a moment he said, "You must come down with me to the Mission Station, Lexin. It would not look good, after all this publicity about you, if your concern for this heroic loss of life were not to be made obvious."

"Is the damage well contained?" Felicitas asked, knowing full well that Olaf would hardly suggest exposing Lexin to a mass of unfriendly particles careering about at some phenomenal speed out of control – at least, that was how she probably imagined it.

"Just the three compartments were destroyed," Olaf said. "We have lost the teams of G.T Hu, V. Baker and J.P.Meunière: nine persons. That is all I know, and I am very sorry. They put everything into their work. The only compensation for us is that their thoughts will have been preserved up to the last moment. Naturally, the last few seconds will have to be analysed exhaustively."

"I hope the public continues to be patient with us," Felicitas said.

Lexin ran with Olaf the two kilometres down to the maglev terminal, Lexin still in his three-quarter lengths, Olaf in the tracksuit he had been wearing all morning. Olaf ran everywhere, and expected Lexin to do likewise. "It makes a good image," he would say. "Remember the rule – Be as 'normal' as possible, always." And: "The Normals love running, so we run. It was emphasised in the Bods' text, remember."

"I don't know where Felie and Lenica get this idea about public impatience," he said as the maglev whisked them with some engineers and other mobilised off-duty personnel through the bowery greenery of the suburbs and out into the desert on the fifteen minute journey to the Mission Station. "People are with us one hundred per cent. They can see we have one objective, namely an objective that will one day transform *all* our lives beyond our imagination. We are just doing the donkey work."

His father was not always so self-effacing. And Lexin was not so sure, now, about the public's patience. He also wondered whether his own questionings about progress towards the Galaxy could be eating away at his mother's confidence in ultimate success. If so, he regretted it, but she might have to wear it. "Those last three minutes, yes, certainly they must get the full treatment," he said after a while, "but I think we need to go back much further, analyse even more carefully where we might have made unwarranted assumptions in our procedures and their execution."

"Unwarranted assumptions?" Olaf said. The steely blue eyes demanded an explanation – of some sort. His father was putting the heat on.

Lexin was glad they had a compartment to themselves. He felt his response formulate. "It is easy to forget," he said out loud, " because in so many ways we have made astonishing progress, that it is a cardinal rule to analyse the thought processes of workers in all areas – engineers, even the laboratory technicians at critical experimental stages – against his or her simultaneous biological indices."

"Aren't we?" There was a certain vagueness in Olaf's question.

"Well are *you*?" – Now it was Lexin turning on the heat, looking his father in the eye, albeit with a genial smile, as the yellow desert beyond the padded upholstery and curved glass rushed past near-silently at five hundred miles an hour.

"Probably I make some assumptions that…"

"…Well what did I say? And I reckon Sergei Malinovsky may have reservations about our thoroughness, too. I hardly need tell you that I believe this whole thing may be much more difficult than we imagine."

"As I have said before, I may be getting a bit old for this job," Olaf muttered.

"There is another thing…" Lexin began again, but the amber light and gentle musical beat indicating 'station ahead' had come on and the maglev, which had been decelerating, was descending beneath the gleaming canopy of the semi-underground terminus and alongside the platform. As many as twenty or so journalists in their customary individualistic and often colourful attire, plus camera crews, were waiting in the adjacent, unusually busy transfer hall. This was probably unprecedented, such a number evidently being the compounded effect of the reaction to the first reply received (almost) from outer space and the tragic accident connected with it.

With Mackenzie, Head of the Mission Station, together with the Head of Wormhole Research and Operations standing beside him Olaf made a statement. He explained that the accident had occurred milliseconds after commencement of retrieval of the transmission, that is to say retrieval in the wormhole terminal of a message no doubt confirming receipt of our transmission of a minute or two earlier. They assumed they had corrected certain errors in the procedures during laboratory simulations, but these had evidently not dealt adequately with the problem. Every effort would naturally be made to find out once and for all what was bugging the retrieval process. The only compensation – though he hesitated to say it in view of the tragic circumstances – was that *something* had been received, if not actually *retrieved*. Given the procedures followed in transmission and attempted retrieval, and the timing, he said – just in case anyone should have any doubts –, the origin must have been HVC0092 in Lyra:

"The home of our saviours of 2073. This constitutes an enormous step for which those who have lost their lives – and those who have gone before them – will always be remembered."

Lexin for his part told them it saddened him greatly. The 'Guardian Interactive' reporter wished to express similar feelings but said that so far readers' reactions indicated acceptance of the situation as an essential part of progress.

"As an aspirant to membership of the Conference may I say something outrageous, Father?" Lexin asked Olaf, aside.

"If you must," he replied. "Better not tell me what. I might have to say 'no'."

"That is ridiculous," Lexin declared to the GI reporter. "In my view there must be a sea change in our approach to our work at the Mission Station. We should not accept the inevitability of accidents, even if it means a general slow-down. That is the view of young hothead Lexin. Report it!"

The woman, smart in a sand-smooth dress decorated with desert flowers, was simultaneously writing his words into her 'Galactic Progress' column, which had been located at page fourteen for as long as anyone could remember.

"Why did you say that?" his father said to Lexin as, free now of the reporters, they and an accumulating bunch of officials crossed the vast hall. The place always reminded Lexin in its 'feel' – its expanse of marble and resonant echoes – , if not actually in its style (which showed the beginnings of mondialism), of the pictures he had seen of splendid Russian railway stations of the steam age. In fact it was a relic of that effusion of Chinese power in the mid-twenty-first century which saw the beginnings of serious international interplanetary exploration on the back of those ancient rockets. The rest of the complex, with its administration headquarters and its laboratories, testing facilities, deciphering rooms and all the rest founded upon the rock beneath the sand, in fact bore little resemblance to the bunkers of the original one. Its strange, smooth, gleaming shapes were only ever visible above the surface to an extent that depended upon the winds and their effect upon the sand mass. Even less, Lexin mused as he tried to formulate a reply to Olaf's question, did the delicate architecture of Galaxy City bear any resemblance to the severely functional City of the Planets that the Chinese had built before it. As for the huge wormhole terminal twenty kilometres distant from the Mission Station, a kilometre and a half in height (with more below ground) and one kilometre in circumference – one of the largest free-standing structures on Earth –, it was of course something entirely different from the massive launchers of old.

Any reply to his father was postponed as they were taken to view whatever images there might be from the ubique video cameras. Most of the camera system had been destroyed in the explosion. That done, Lexin, a grim-faced Olaf and several equally grim-faced officials then boarded the desert rover and headed for the terminal. Even if virtually everything had been captured on video, Olaf explained, it would still have been necessary for him to inspect everything personally in a show of solidarity – if for no other reason.

No sign of external damage could be detected as the entrance to the main access tunnel came into view, the tower looming ever vaster and brighter above them. The massive, white gate – the first of several gates – opened automatically, allowing them to drive in and then down through the three hundred-metre outer shielding towards the core area and the mouth of the wormhole itself. At the last gate before the core-perimeter tunnel they stopped to park the vehicle and put on protective clothing. Once in the perimeter tunnel, they walked to the observation gallery, entering through the multiple doors giving access through the five-metre-thick duron wall that represented the inner casing surrounding the core. Looking through the heat- and blast-proof window across the circular core space illuminated by emergency arc lights, the extent of the damage became clear. While the gallery itself remained intact, the explosion had virtually ripped two of the working compartments out of the duron wall across to their left. Elsewhere, huge chunks of the wall surface had gone. The bodies of the workers in the compartments (six men and three women) had already been removed. Over towards the mouth of the wormhole could be seen a melted tangle of collapsed walkways and observation platforms, and initial reports indicated damage extending a short distance into the mouth. Not all the working compartments in the core wall had been destroyed, however, and the teams in the intact, or in one case damaged, compartments had been rescued via emergency exit tunnels and transferred to the Station for decontamination, and in two cases hospitalization. Olaf said that in layman's terms the failure had almost certainly occurred owing to stabilization problems in the capacitors designed to facilitate safe passage of the message-bearing waves.

"As you know," he said, "the energies involved can scarcely be imagined. We'd frizzle in there. It's still something like five hundred Celsius."

There was the usual air of powerlessness, and that strange smell everywhere, even here behind the window, somehow – the after-smells of an explosion. He had smelled them before – the smell of failure.

Since closer access was not possible either to the damaged compartments or to the wormhole mouth, there was nothing more to be done but return by the same route. Updated 'Guardian' coverage was already entering Lexin's brain as they returned in the buggy, arriving back to a scattering of cheers from press and staff: "Experts misread wormhole parameters in retrieval process. Lexin advocates sea change in work of Mission Station". An expensive mistake, Lexin said to himself. Nevertheless, all in all, given the potential for disaster, what had happened and what had not happened confirmed his long-standing impression that the Bods took the matter of safety, like everything else, extremely seriously, though it would not be appropriate to say so publicly at the moment. He could not get out of his head the conviction that those men and women need not, *should* not, have died.

An hour later, with official statements released, the counselling team activated, and the decommissioning team briefed, they were on the maglev again. Restoration after previous accidents indicated that despite the rapid building and engineering techniques by now acquired the process would take many months. Part of the inner core block would have to be rebuilt, and extensive repairs made to the wormhole mouth.

Olaf looked thoughtful. "I do think you should explain yourself, Lexin," he said. "Fancy coming out with that! What 'sea change'?"

"Half the Tarim Basin could have been blown sky high. The thing is, there have been too many accidents. By now I feel sure that with proper operation there should be no damage, no accidents."

"No need to advertise *that,* anyway – about the Tarim Basin!"

"What, Father? In this transparent age?"

"What evidence might you have to say it?"

"More to the point, Father, could you deny the possibility? Obviously we are still dangerously ignorant of some of the parameters of message retrieval. Fortunately it would appear that we might be slightly better at sending messages than at receiving them, although there have been accidents there, too."

But Olaf was engrossed in thought. "Unfortunately," he said after a minute or two, "we do not know the timing of any follow-up message."

"Or whether any replies to earlier transmissions might have been tacked on."

"We may know some day."

"I don't want to sound too pessimistic, "Lexin said, but I do confess I have often wondered whether, if they were not such nice beings as I think they are, they would not be able to stop laughing their heads off looking at the stuff we had cobbled together to send them. It will be interesting to read their replies – *some* day."

"Oh come, Lexin, we must not demean ourselves like that. That is too extreme!" By now his father's fresh and open face had become transformed into one almighty frown, but Lexin ploughed on...

"In my opinion it's all a bit too much like putting seven-year-olds in a sub-surface transit control centre. And I did not 'advertise' anything, as you put it. All I did was register a view, the possibility of a change of direction. Perhaps I should say a change of approach. Actually, I mean not just in wormhole procedures but in the day to day work of experimentation, testing *and,* yes, decipherment. We may be failing, or be slipshod or lack patience, in the way we decipher, not to mention the ways in which we apply the results worldwide. If we are not in the right frame of mind, we will not get the whole story, and that goes for our knowledge of time-crossing. The papers would not want to know, Father, even if I were to say it. It sounds..."

"...Boring?"

Lexin was conscious of the fact that he might be appearing intolerably big-headed in his father's eyes, but he did have a good knowledge of all these fields, and although he had not been allowed in the transmission and retrieval block he had been through the process in simulation many times as part of his advanced education. To many it would sound boring, he supposed, but he added in some attempt at palliation, "Don't worry! Old attitudes die hard, and it will take more than a few words from me to change anything. They have a great respect for you."

"What exactly do you want to change, Lexin? My brain is not receiving you." Olaf had regained some of his composure.

The maglev started to slow down. "Damn!" Olaf shouted. "Always just as one is about to explain something!"

"Our 'future guidance prompt', Father. I'll bring it up later."

The run up the Hill of Lyra dissolved some of the antagonism between them, but Lexin was continuing to turn over in his mind the fact that this was just the last and most serious of several accidents with the wormhole.

"Daddy! Thank goodness you are back. Mother was so worried," Lenica exclaimed from the terrace. "Mummy!" she shouted at the top of her voice, "they're both all right." Then, as the two men ran up the last few steps she added, quietly, "You know how hot and bothered she gets."

"You would have heard on your multicom if we had been vaporized," Lexin said, casually. Olaf, who, unusually, had flopped down at a table laid for coffee and was pouring himself one and another for Felicitas, gave him a funny look.

"If it's so dangerous, Father," Lenica said, mildly, "you shouldn't have gone."

"It isn't", Olaf said. "Ignore the boy – and his strange humour."

"Thank God you are back! I have too vivid an imagination." It was the Russian Princess advancing from the living space. "But since you are both back, now tell me, how do you like my coiffure de Sirius?" She had changed, and drawn her voluminous head of hair into something highly noticeable. Lexin assumed both its style and its name were her own invention. The very full dress was in a matching but paler blue. No doubt she considered that a star-studded stole completed 'l'apparence d'une princesse à la mode', since colours of the stars and planets were all the rage, with Sirius to the fore at the moment.

"Mother!" exclaimed Lenica, resting her back on the balustrade, sunny in a simple, one-shoulder yellow dress, mug of coffee in hand, "you really are pressing this 'blue for Sirius' thing. I know you like to make the running at the Societan Ladies Branch, but personally I am getting awfully tired of it. And today of all days!" Lexin knew that their mother enjoyed her sallies into the exactitudes of world mood assessment, using all the opinion synthesizers, in order to maintain what she considered her role in giving a lead in ladies' fashions. He wished Lenica would stop digging at her 'colour correctness', as his sister called it. "But then she asked, "Isn't the meeting at the Ladies' Branch being cancelled in any case, in the circumstances?"

"When I am trying to be calm and...normal – even in the present circumstances?" Felicitas interrupted, with a flick of the coiffure. "We must not panic, must we? But keep our eyes fixed on the road ahead."

"But *should* it not be cancelled?" Lenica persisted. "I think it should be."

Oh dear, she was bossy today, Lexin thought. Like mother, like daughter. How direct, how irritatingly direct Lenica could be. Sometimes it was hard to believe that that same expressive mouth and flashing eyes that could be so aggressive could also be soothing, pacifying.

"I refused to cancel it."

"According to Lexin we would do well to look *down* a little, turn our minds earthwards and ponder," Olaf said, "never mind Sirius. What was it you said, Lexin? Something about self-guidance?"

"Sounds like some rocket of warring times" Felicitas observed, coolly, and then, turning to Lenica, "and with reference to blue, today I am following the tastes of the Normals rather than the reverse."

"Nothing military at all, Mother", Lexin assured her. "Father knows I am talking about a little self examination, including using our personal activity synthesizers in fact. I trust we all use them diligently."

"Of course," Olaf said.

"So do I, when I can find it," Lenica said. "And I bet those chaps did, the ones who died. You would not get into retrieval engineering without it."

"Not necessarily true," Lexin retorted. "We should analyse every worker's biological indices – all of them – for a long period before using the wormhole, also data from the future guidance prompt, and including in training and simulations. Our FGP's can tell us a lot. We may find some pattern…"

"…I fear I am not into all this at all," Felicitas complained. "Yes, I read my print-outs sometimes, but the assessments are always the same. As for my FGP's, I hardly have any requests. I mean, housewives don't need them, do they?"

"Mother, could you possibly sit down and drink your coffee?" Lexin pleaded. "All that blue is putting me off too, now. But to answer your question, my instinct is to suggest we could all do with making requests for guidance, if only because we all have this facility. If we do not take advantage of these possibilities – though especially of course in the initial decipherment process – it may spell a lot of trouble."

"Don't you mean it already has," Lenica said. "And in the meantime, what happens to the drive for communication, the wormhole tests? I cannot think future guidance requests could make all that much difference."

"Possibly you could suspend it all for a bit." Felicitas suddenly sounded very subdued. "Stop and consider everything. Everything we are doing."

Lexin wondered whether his mother might actually be getting the message. If so, he hoped it was not only because she was afraid for Olaf.

Olaf was sitting very quiet, glancing occasionally at a newspaper but plainly not concentrating. He seemed upset now by the day's events, even if he was not admitting it. "I have a good idea of the Conference's response to that, Felie," he said at length. "I cannot for one moment see us stopping everything. Don't cancel the meeting. Have a moment's silence, perhaps." So saying, he downed the rest of his coffee put his mug down with a definitive clunk, got up and ambled into the house.

"Lexin," Lenica said, putting her empty mug down on a table, "I hope this is not just you procrastinating again. We surely must not lose what momentum we have. What do the big boys think: Malinovsky, Mackenzie? We can only listen to the experts in the field. For God's sake we must not allow those chaps to have died for nothing. I mean, has that occurred to you?" The aged but still very much active physicist Malinovsky had been one of Mackenzie's predecessors as Head of the Mission Station several decades earlier.

"Of course it has. How could you think not?" he added as she disappeared after her father into the house. But he knew she did not really think it. His sister was apt to speak carelessly. And big names tripped off the tongue easy enough, too! Anyway, he had an idea the two physicists might not each be of the same opinion.

"Tell me now, my boy," Felicitas said after the others had gone in, standing up and going and putting her arm around Lexin and drawing him closer, "Is it the girl again? What is she doing now? – If you are willing to tell me. I am sorry I was not very receptive this morning. Everything seems to have happened at once. You were telling me about sharing her thoughts and so on."

It had always been like that with his mother, that closeness. He was glad of it now, when day after day he lived in two or even three worlds and needed to talk about the apparent improbability – some would say impossibility – of it. Maybe in a past, feminist age it would not have been so easy to confide in her – or bear her criticisms. "It is strange," he said. "Sometimes I can follow her progress using my PAS. It is not just a matter of blips in computer programmes now. Sometimes, if my PAS is 'on', sequences appear on-screen automatically even if there is something else on the monitor. Occasionally, yes, I may actually feel I am sharing her thoughts. She is living with her grandparents in the country again – because of the abuse, which has now ceased. Often she visits her passive father, who lives in a dingy place in the city and is ill, and separated from his loose-living mother. I have been there. She takes him food, a paper. Her boyfriend goes with her."

"Where is all this, this city?" She had let go of him now, gone inside, and he had followed. She was casually rearranging some spring flowers in a vase.

"I don't know. There are all those car things and a filthy old canal, and what they eat looks really weird, all out of packets labelled 'low' in this, 'high' in that… You'd think they had a struggle to live very long."

"Well you cannot help that! She will just have to make the best of it. But the newspaper. What was it called? It was in English?"

"Yes, I suppose so. You know, we are wired up to so many languages I tend not to notice. I remember it now. It was 'The Newchurch Chronicle'. The boyfriend loves her but says she bothers too much about her parents."

"So you can hear what they are saying?"

"Sometimes if I have the sound on I can hear everything. Near where the grandparents live, the same canal runs through the fields, still and peaceful. She likes walking by it, but is not supposed to unless the boyfriend is over and they go together. There is a lock, where the canal goes up a level, and they often sit on a crumbling old seat there. I am not privy to all their conversations."

"I should hope not! Just enough to motivate you, it seems"

"That's all."

"And her mother used to beat her, and men abused her."

"Yes, but she bears them no malice."

"Some girl! Must say it beats me! No joke intended."

"She is completely unselfish."

"And the date – on the paper?"

"I did notice that. It was two thousand and four."

"My God. And they do not know you are there, if 'there' is the right word. I don't get it, Lexin. Are you a ghost from the future, then? Lexin, if it were anybody but you I wouldn't believe a word of all this. And what are you supposed to do about it? Obviously she can look after herself...and there's her boyfriend." Felicitas looked on the verge of throwing up her hands. As it was, she kept sitting down and getting up again, rearranging flowers here and poking about there, so that her bracelets jangled incessantly.

"I don't know, yet, but I will know."

"And is that all it is? This girl, and you in another time? No, it's not all, is it?"

"She matters here as well."

"But how, Lexin, how?"

He had gone to the open glass doors again, was looking at the view down to the city. Felicitas came and stood behind him, her hands resting on the shoulders of his tunic shirt – not difficult with his short stature.

"I don't know, but it is something out of time. All time is one when she is there."

"Sounds as if you love her. That would be a bit unfortunate, would it not?" Her fingers dug into the padded shoulder of his jacket, the middle, aquamarine gemstone of the three stones in her past, present and future wedding ring, seen from the corner of his eye, gleaming blue in a chance gleam of spring sunlight.

Lexin had a good laugh – he loved his mother's dry humour. "It is more simple than that," he said at last: "I think it is a question of being there to help her – and her boyfriend, and her family. It is as though something is missing from *my* life here."

"From *your* life!"

"From all our lives, something we have lost but she can help us regain."

"Isn't she in enough trouble herself? Do not imagine I am not sympathetic, Lexin, but you have work to do."

"I think it's all right. It will work out." He grinned as he said, "I have great faith in my future guidance software. Remember that it is interactive and uses – apparently – data received from an advanced civilization. Most important of all, it is a civilization which seems to care about us."

"I must say I would worry even more about you if you were not so confident about your future, *our* future. It seems it may depend on the past even more than we might have supposed. But I cannot help but be worried about you and your girlfriend. It all sounds so incredible, even dangerous. I mean time crossing *is,* isn't it?"

"I agree it is strange, but you must not worry about it, Mother." Felicitas, however, showed every sign of worrying as she released her maternal grip on her son's shoulders, picked up her stole and the new Lebinsky novel 'Phoenix America' and disappeared to her room without saying another word.

Picking up his father's 'Times' (the one 'daily' regularly read in the house in hard copy) his eye fell on the press release about candidates for election to the Conference. He was not too surprised to see that it led with his story on page four and then finished off on page nine. There was no sign there of the lost woman and her story.

* * *

Regardless of the fact that no-one knew whether or not there might have been valuable information in the communication from Lyra, or whether another message might have followed – and there would be a delay of many weeks in all our work at the wormhole now in any case because of the accident –, the very fact of having received an acknowledgement of receipt, from a distance of some hundred and forty light years, of a transmission sent minutes before was mind-boggling. It was mind boggling when considered in relation to every sphere of human life, even bearing in mind the amazing things already achieved.

That was the message put out to the ten thousand million inhabitants of Earth by the indefatigable workers of the Society, and such were the thoughts of Olaf Solberg as he stood with Lexin in his office a couple of weeks after the accident at the Station, gathering his papers together on the big, polished oak table before a policy meeting of the Conference of Societans in the Great Hall of the Palace of the Galaxy. Out of deference to his position as President of the Society he was in a tailored, tan longsuit that set off his slightly ruddy complexion and added great elegance to his stature. More often he might be seen in three-quarter trousers and white tunic shirt like Lexin now, or even in the toga favoured by many elderly men.

Lexin was conscious of his favoured position as son of the President. His popularity among Societans and Normals alike, like Olaf's, was undeniable. It was an advantage of which he was proud and by which he was untroubled, for competitive rancour of rivals was not characteristic of the Societans, accustomed as they were to the long, painstaking endeavour to achieve intragalactic progress in a peaceful world freed for so long of the blight of instant opinion, precipitate reaction and inevitable conflict. In general also, people – both Normals and Societans –, like the Solbergs, lived long. As an aspirant to membership of the Conference Lexin would be allowed in too, but would sit with other aspirants in the gallery.

"These events are surely inevitable, are they not, Lexin, despite what you say?" Olaf said. "It is not as if it were entirely unexpected, is it? I am sure that will be the view of delegates – and I should think aspirants, too. But we nearly managed it this time, didn't we?" His father had by now recovered his poise, and for him and most members of the Society and for the population at large the accident was just that, and would eventually pass into history as just another falter in the long march to enlightenment.

"I don't know whether we nearly made it or not," Lexin replied, "or whether accidents are inevitable."

His father was taken aback. "My brain seems to be functioning well, I am optimistic, any doubts are reasonable doubts, I review my position regularly to keep on track, and I have no reason to think those under me, including the deciphering teams, are any different."

"All this, and yet it seems failures are inevitable?" Lexin asked. "What you say may be so, but as I see it, despite the fact that our progress depends on the interpretation of a 'text' the process is something like being let into a secret so deep that we can be let into it only slowly, while at every stage we may expect to be surprised but not to be coming to grief."

"Lexin, there are limitations. As I say, I am optimistic. Sometimes we just have to go on. We cannot be forever looking around us for a 'green light'."

"And I am saying that there is a difference between optimism and the bright light of illumination, of enlightenment if you like." From that elevated position in the Palace, if he were to glance out of the window he would catch glimpses of the three great Avenues (often referred to collectively as the 'Avenidas') – of World Harmony,

Remembrance and Enlightenment – fanning out in six directions towards the city's boundaries, and in his own mind far beyond. But his father's eyes, as he stood at the table opposite him, were trained firmly upon the papers before him.

"I feel there might be another implied question there, Lexin," his father replied without looking up. "Are you really asking me whether I use my synthesizer to assess my position...*our* position? Of course I do. It gives good readings for brain functioning, stress levels; it says my understanding of our task is good."

"What is the meaning of 'understanding' in this context, father? Have you pressed your FG prompt button for future guidance on that point?"

"That is ridiculous, Lexin. Our task is our task..."

"I use my FGP for *general* guidance, too, and quite often it comes up with things I never thought of. We're not superhuman – and how the Bods know it! "

"If they know it, do they not make allowances?"

Lexin hesitated to persist. He hated to question Olaf's renewed confidence but felt obliged to. "It is not so simple, Father, is it? I mean the work we are doing. Subjective concerns, tiredness, impatience, instead of keenness to gnaw at a tricky point, may deprive one of an entirely new depth of understanding, so that one gets the one-word answers one expects. All that is explained in the text, the software as it were – as I am sure you know."

"I suppose it is, somewhere, but we're not perfect; we need to progress, indeed to forge ahead. Our situation is becoming more and more ridiculous."

Lexin detected a growing irritation, but still he persisted: "Why 'forge ahead'? If we do not test ourselves – I mean with all the means we have available – we may lose the plot. Indeed we may have already done so."

"Look, son, are you suggesting that even after umpteen years – how many is it now? Three, getting on for four hundred – we still do not understand even the part of the text we have deciphered, and that it is not simply a matter of failing to get the retrieval parameters quite right?" Olaf was looking hard at Lexin now, puzzled, perhaps, more than disapproving, irritated more than angry, as he gathered his notes together.

"Probably we do not. Probably we are collectively inadequately skilled in the use of our synthesizers, and we have missed stuff and are still missing stuff, and I don't quite know what happens next. Perhaps one should even have the humbleness to re-read ones study notes on the use of one's PAS."

"That is very discouraging, Lexin. We are only human – I mean at rock bottom – as you say. We make mistakes, we are not always as thorough as we might be, we are finite beings with a life span – albeit up to two hundred and odd. Yet here you seem to be saying we have got to get down on our hands and knees and look for clues like looking for needles in a haystack."

"We might get our retrieval parameters right. We could start by going more slowly."

"We have checked and rechecked our procedures and parameters – and in the laboratories, too. Sure, Tom Matovu has left no stone unturned there, either."

"Maybe the procedure is okay as far as it goes. It may not go far enough."

"What do you mean by that?"

"I don't know."

"Really?" Olaf's tone changed to one of a condescending irony. He paused significantly. "Clearly then, in deference to your suggestions, to be quite sure of the effectiveness of our text processing, presumably we should at least retrain all our decipherers." He was really annoyed now, frowning as he paused again, momentarily, leaning forward slightly with his large hands spread upon the table, the small file now containing his papers for the meeting the sole object lying between them. "As a matter of fact, I have already taken steps in that direction."

"It may not be enough, Father, with respect."

"I don't doubt our mission Lexin," Olaf said, hastily, as he turned to press the button for his private lift down to the Great Hall.

CHAPTER SIX

It was one of the times when his father always refrained from running. Lexin ran down the stairs to the Hall, entering with the delegates and other aspirants. It was a lofty place in the style of the previous, i.e. twenty-fourth, century, in which massive, soaring lines were designed still to give an impression of lightness, as if to symbolize our supposed fearless advance among the giants of the Galaxy (some, however, reckoned it had been built to replace the previous structure in an act of pure frustration following the reticence of the twenty-third). Lexin occupied his accustomed place in one of the gallery seats suspended unobtrusively among the intricate arches.

The Conference meeting was chaired by Leonard Mackenzie, a big man in physique as he was in the hierarchy as head of the Mission Station, an Australian with better understanding of negative energy density and pressure fields than most, and more than passing acquaintance with Einstein's many successors. These included most recently the late X.H. Wang, the person responsible for initiating, from the deciphered blueprints, the building of a terminal to a wormhole system engineered by the Galactic Community.

Mackenzie gave weighty support to Olaf's upbeat analysis of galactic progress. He was determined that the Society should step up its efforts to increase the rate of fundamental text decipherment and ask for more financial resources from the relevant departments of the World Government. In view of the near unanimity in Conference, it seemed that despite even this serious accident more resources would be forthcoming from the Treasury for all the work of the Mission Station, especially since in the view of the Conference it was painfully obvious that apart from the need for an intensification of decipherment, the failure of two-way communication with Lyra was a grave hindrance to progress. "Of course," Mackenzie said with the matter-of-factness that Lexin would have thought appropriate to some discussion of a rebuilding of the Australian cricket industry, "attention must also be given to re-examining and/or stiffening the procedures, and if necessary making design modifications. Appropriate steps are being taken." All this evoked audible support not only from the delegates but also from one of the three or four of Lexin's local rivals listening in the gallery with maybe fifty other aspirants from the Northern Eurasia and Northern Africa constituencies (these being the two constituencies currently presenting candidates). This was Angelo Vidano, a smart young Italian already publishing in both hard-science and psychology media. His family had influenced the Society's input into educational programmes over a long period, and had recently settled in Galaxy City.

"There is hope for us yet," he was muttering, but this drew an opposing view from X.F. Li, a young lecturer in pure and applied history from Beijing with razor-sharp mind and a pleasant turn of humour who was now splitting his time between the two cities and working in the Galaxy City University of Many Blessings:

"You need to re-study everything we have deciphered so far," he was saying. "Those two, Leonard and Olaf, they are hand in glove. It is not good for civilization. What say, Lexin?" Such discussion during meetings had become a long-accepted subculture over the long history of the Conference. By mutual consent it could be shared, at a different brain level and via their multicoms, by the delegates themselves, although in recent times this facility had tended to be largely ignored – such was the stultified transparency of Society politics.

"To respond to the point you were making, Li," Lexin had time to say in a quick flit to one of the bars, "our problem may be more fundamental than a need for re-study. It may be that something has just not clicked in the way we decipher." Li had become aware of Lexin's scepticism about progress on previous occasions when over from

Beijing. Later, back in the Hall when one of the North American delegates was suggesting more stringent education guidelines for the genetically modified part of the population, Li reckoned it would do no harm, but Lexin said it was like using big diggers to shift a molehill. Of course he knew it was possible to modify education programmes – on whatever scale and for Normals as well as the enhanced population – almost instantly, at least on a trial basis, but such powerful electronic psychosocial educational facilities had generally been used sparingly. "Anyway," he said, "if you're talking about our recent failings as a Society, you miss the point altogether: I don't think it is a case of more resources, more money, more effort, or even more education. It may be a question of trust."

"Trust in what? In whom?" A broad grin spread across Xiaofeng's chubby face.

"Presumably those guys our ancestors saw disappearing in a spaceship here three hundred and eighty years ago."

"Don't we trust them?"

"I don't think so."

"It was a long time ago." Now the grin had become a little laugh that sent his rounded frame into gentle ripples.

"No time at all for a historian, Xiaofeng! I think we should meditate awhile."

A figure was weaving its way towards them through the gallery seats.

"Oh dear, old Mauré's going to be getting on his hobbyhorse." The humour disappeared from Li's face.

Jean-Paul Mauré's line was that malign forces were disrupting attempts at intragalactic communication. Another immigrant, the tall, blond, well-dressed Frenchman from an eminent and respected family of the Society and with a string of qualifications and publications in the neurosciences as well as in ethics and comparative religions, was a somewhat older candidate whose writings included a recent paper entitled, 'The dilemma of the Society. A Problem Within or Without?' "I could not help overhearing you," he said, none too quietly. "I point out that where there is a vacuum, who knows what may step in."

"I think we all know, don't we?" someone joked. The others around smiled benignly.

"Sounds kind of religious," another commented.

"Less noise in the gallery, please!" It was headmaster Olaf's voice.

The education theme rattled on until eventually Lexin heard Leonard Mackenzie announcing in the flat, droning tones from down under, "So now, ladies and gentlemen we come to the final question on our Agenda: 'Especially in view of the importance to us of obtaining vital information on possible comet diversion, should we not continue our work towards message retrieval despite our unfortunate setback?'"

And we all know the answer to that question, too, Lexin thought, and in fact there followed no more than ten minutes of debate in which no amendments were put forward and delegate after delegate stood up and talked of 'consolidating and increasing our efforts', 'not being distracted', etc. etc.

"And so we will put this to the vote, while also – I suggest – taking note of, but not be too distracted by, the opinions of some in the gallery who would have us relax our single mindedness."

To this, Olaf added, with the permission of the Chairman,

"They are our leaders of the future. We must not belittle their views for they are the future torch-bearers, but I think they may come to modify their views." Delegates greeted Olaf's words with a well-known mixture of approbation and laughter.

The motion to continue was carried without opposition.

*   *   *

Jogging for home after the meeting, Lexin quickly covered the couple of hundred metres of the ceremonial way leading from the Palace of the Galaxy to the ever-open northern gateway of its precinct, but as he passed through the gateway he suddenly no longer recognized where he was. There was no sign of the great triangle of lawns and fountains in front of it. Instead, his feet were pounding across a wet, trackless landscape that stretched away as far as the eye could see. No sign either, as he ran on, of the public buildings and private and cooperative emporia lining the straight and splendid Avenida de Ferrer de Lorenzo (the Avenue of the Enlightenment) stretching ten kilometres from the Mount of Plenty in the west to the Arturo Mendez Sports Complex in the east, and so named after the great Spanish linguist of the twenty-first and twenty-second centuries whose skills had facilitated initial elucidation of the alien text in the early days. Now everything had simply vanished in a cold landscape in which this Avenue and the other two Avenues intersecting it had likewise dissolved in an all-embracing plenitude of swamp and forest. Yet still he ran, though how he knew where to put his feet he did not understand.

Now he came to a steep, rocky valley full of rushing wind and gushing water. Where there should surely have been the Hill of Lyra rising before him in its resplendent synthesis of private residences sunbaked in pastel shades, white-walled terraces bright with fruits of many colours, and the rich floral and arboreal tracery of its public gardens, was now an unkind place, icy, wild and wet. Climbing up and up he came, exhausted, to a place uncannily reminiscent of the encampment of hunter-gatherers that he had seen in that anthropology lesson in level-two basic solar system studies so many years ago. But it was not the same. Dark and uninviting, many of its shelters of skins and tangled twigs and branches among the trees were dug partly into the hillside, which was shedding streams of water, while the few men to be seen had their furs pulled close about them

As he climbed, Lexin's eye was drawn to a man ahead of him hardly able to walk, either because of a deformity or because of tiredness or the weight of his belongings, or all of these impediments, and being urged along by two tough-looking individuals. It was as much as the man could do to keep on his feet. It became obvious that he was being expelled from the camp. A woman rushed out from somewhere, screaming so loudly Lexin could hear her above the sound of the wind and rain. She tried to follow, only to be roughly driven back by other men who appeared out of nowhere. Lexin, impelled to follow too and pushing himself to the limit as he struggled against the mud and the steepness of the slope, stumbled after the men as they disappeared among trees above the encampment, catching as he did so a glimpse through the trees of a distant sea. Suddenly a voice hailed him,

"Lexin, you look whacked. Has it been a bad session?" The last few yards up the garden and the terrace steps were taxing. The woman's screams were still ringing in his ears, but it was his mother's voice. "Someone is insisting on seeing you. She's waiting in the hall. See if you can get rid of her quick sharp and come and have a drink. You look as if you need it. "My goodness, you *are* dead beat. I will get Robert to tell her you cannot see her. He said to warn you she is dangerously pretty."

"No, mother, I will go and see her straight away. I'll go in the back way. And would you please tell Robert to bring her up in a minute or two."

Lexin continued running round the terrace along the side of the house and in by the outside door where his own apartment joined the main house, then up the spiral staircase to his office, where he sat at his desk for a moment to collect himself. Normally he would have gone and showered, made himself 'respectable', especially since he was out of breath and could still feel the mud and wetness of that hillside clinging to him. But now all that seemed irrelevant.

Two minutes later Robert showed her in. He stood up. Yes, it *was* her of course, just the same as in the images, beautiful as ever. Just a little older, a little more grown-up in her slim-line bleached jeans that her body filled elegantly, yet not too tightly, topped by the whitest T-shirt with a 'Newchurch Angels' band logo with its flourish of flowers. On another day it might have been like a garden of flowers on summer hills, but today an unkind shower must have intervened, for it was wet with her tears.

"Hello, I'm Lexin, Marcelle," he launched out, nevertheless. "This is amazing. I have known about you so long and now I see you are as beautiful as ever." He said other things, welcoming, understanding, sympathising – though he could not remember afterwards what those words had been; it was as if they had not come from himself only.

She stood a long time appearing unable to speak. Then gradually, like the sun percolating through clouds, she began to smile. It occurred to him that he had not even invited her to sit down, but before he could do so she asked, quietly, "How have you known about me, or perhaps I should say 'why?'"

"It was because I needed you."

"Mmm...Needed me?" Was there a coquettish flicker of the moist eyelids?"

"It is a bit hard to explain. I don't mean in the way Mark needs you."

"Does he? That's nice to know. How do you know Mark?" The smile had faded.

"I know you all, in a way. Although I cannot explain it, I believe we need each other."

"Please tell me where we are, Lexin." There was a glimpse of sunlight again.

"We are in the Takla Makan Desert, in China. The year is 2452. We have a bit of a problem here, but I won't trouble you with that. I want to help you, Marcelle. I know what a rotten time you had, how you were beaten but how you still love your mother and father and how you are convinced that they can re-kindle their old love and be reunited." The words seemed to roll out, and many more of them.

Marcelle looked at him in astonishment. After a long silence she said, "How do you know all that? You seem to know my parents like I do: my mother's warmth that went cold, my father's bad luck, the way he is such a lovable stick-in-the-mud. How can you do that – help me, I mean?"

"I do not know exactly how, any more than I know exactly how you are going to help me, but I know these things will happen.."

"Are you real?" She asked. "Can I touch you?"

Lexin took the few paces to reach her, offered his hands. Hers were warm as she took them, grasped them. Close to tears again, she said, "Please help me, then, Lexin. I know you can, although...," and she stepped back slightly without letting go of him, "...although I can't explain why I think you can. At least, I think I can't explain it except there's just one other thing..." She was looking closely at him, searching his face. Surely half a minute went by in the silence.

"Something from the Stone Age?"

She looked at him open-mouthed. "So you do know about that. You know my hunter? You know Big Nose?"

'*My* hunter', she had said. *Her* hunter! She had stepped back from him now. "So that is his name: Big Nose. Did you think I might know him, Marcelle?"

"I thought you might..." She hesitated. "I didn't know...and I still don't understand." There was just a whiff of indignation in the tone. It was as though she both wanted and did not want him to share her secret. Eventually she collected herself, and the words poured out: "He's such a good man, Lexin. He had a long struggle after fleeing the camp. I am sure he really loves Red Hair. They've had terrible hardships since they found each other again. But I think you already know all that, and what has happened now."

"Red Hair has been taken prisoner, and Big Nose sent away. And that is why you were crying."

At this she broke down in tears. He led her gently to a chair.

"Yes, and there was a child," she said when she had sat down and recovered her composure; "*his* child he said, but the mother had died earlier. After he fled the camp, Red Hair had looked after the girl for many years – I heard them speak of it. She hopes the child – a girl – will succeed in finding her one day. Later she had a baby boy herself, but the chief had it raised by someone else." Her voice was shaking. "Somehow I have to help them. I expect you know that, too."

"As I said, I don't know everything, Marcelle: far from it. But I am not surprised, and I understand how much you really care about them. You do, don't you?"

"Yes, Lexin, and I wish Mark did. He doesn't believe me, really, when I tell him all this stuff. You do. Can I get to know you better? You're so understanding." He felt she was on the verge of tears again. He thought she was at least becoming reconciled now to the sharing of her secret.

"I am four hundred and fifty years away, Marcelle, but there is a way in which all time is one. I do not have words to explain all this. There will be more difficulties, more disappointments for us both, but what we are both really seeking will come about. I know that now."

"Are you telling me to go?" She managed a smile.

He was not, but perhaps it was best that way. "Remember what I have said –that things will work out – even if you remember nothing else of our meeting."

She stood up. "Don't forget me, Lexin," she said, smiling broadly for the first time to reveal a countenance in which vivacity and serenity vied for supremacy and those deep, dark eyes abolished rationality and created their own certainties, their own logic. "Please don't forget us."

"I never could," he replied, as Robert saw her out.

*   *   *

When Lexin returned to the terrace his mother had just emerged in the nude, carrying a folding chair and her favourite footstool. Normally she was equally at ease with or without her clothes, and it being already April in the Tarim Basin the sun was pleasantly warm even at five in the evening and she opened the chair and relaxed upon it.

"Glad there's a bit of rain tonight," she said. "We will leave the garden shield completely open to allow it to percolate nicely. Aren't we lucky that everything is so well organised? It is hard to imagine the trials that people once went through."

"Russian blizzards in your case, I suppose." Lexin felt he ought to laugh, or at least say something a bit light-hearted to his mother, but the last five minutes made it impossible. The commitment he had made to Marcelle was sinking in. "Not to forget those Arabian sandstorms, of course.

"So tell me, how did it go, then, the meeting?" she asked, putting down the last part of Lebinsky's best selling trilogy about the vicissitudes of an American Societan family and removing her sun glasses to see him better.

"The meeting? Oh, at the Palace. Predictable. They are going to try and continue with retrieval of course – as soon as possible." He paused, his mind still on other things. "Father spoke to the gallery mutterers in kindly but, I have to say, patronising terms," he added after a moment.

"You do sound less than enthusiastic." Felicitas had risen agilely from the sun bed to occupy a chair at one of the little tables and motioned him to the seat opposite.. It was a sign of more serious interchange. "What were the mutterers saying?"

"Only Vidano was really agreeing with the Conference', Lexin replied, sitting down. "Li Xiaofeng was of the opinion that Leonard Mackenzie and Father were hand in glove…"

"Unanimity of purpose has got us a long way, Lexin. At least there is peace. No terrorists to blow us up. Fifty million died in the United States on that day."

"Yes, but you are reading too much. Too much time reading Lebinsky. I find him rather depressing."

"I thought not so long ago you were telling me that time was not important." She grinned, but she was eyeing him closely. "Lexin, you do have a very abstracted look. Did you manage to get rid of your visitor without any trouble, by the way?"

"No. I'd…I'd kind of been expecting her. We had a useful meeting." He knew that would not satisfy his mother;

"Was she as pretty as Robert was suggesting?"

"Every bit."

"I see. And may one ask about the nature of your meeting. Forgive me if I seem to be over inquisitive. You know how anxious I am about you. At least we are not talking about supernatural things, are we? I mean your 'cyber siren'?".

So there was to be no getting out of an explanation! "She is no siren, mother. And as a matter of fact, this has very much to do with her."

"Is she in more trouble, then?" There was that look of patient resignation..

"She will be unless I can help her. We have a dream in common."

"A dream? A dream about what?"

"I don't know what you will think about this. Long before I knew about Marcelle I knew about a hunter from the Stone Age, a crippled man struggling to survive in some forest. I never told you about him. He appeared on my computer just like she did later. She *dreams* about him, is desperate to help him. We spoke, Marcelle and I, upstairs..."

"It was her up there? You spoke? She spoke? To each other, she in her time, you in yours, *here*? Has she gone now? Look at me, Lexin. No, on second thoughts, pass me my dress over there. I suddenly feel a bit cold, and very vulnerable...feel I am being observed from another time or something." The purple creation from Anastasia Mikhailovna in the Novy Nevsky Prospekt rippled easily like water down the shapely dunes of her breasts, over the smooth sands of her stomach and through the dappled woods of an Arcadian corner of old Mother Russia... Lexin went over to the balustrade. His mother seemed a shade disoriented by his change of position.

"Lexin, I do think..." she began. She was going to remonstrate with him, obviously.

"There is no 'time' when I am with her, Mother."

"Certainly you were not very long with her. A couple of minutes. You were dreaming, perhaps... But of course, Robert saw her."

" Yes, of course" he replied, and that seemed to calm her, actually. "She is an innocent, Mother. She is a most exceptional person, full of good thoughts, no malice. The hunter, too. He is innocent."

"Does he have a big enough brain to be anything special?"

"Oh, he does. And he is a good man..."

"For goodness' sake, Lexin. Innocent? What is this? Original innocence, something from Jean-Jacques Rousseau? I don't know...something supernatural? What?" She got up, went and joined him, stood staring out over the city. "We are in the here and now, Lexin. You will have very important work in the future. At least, I thought you would. You seem sometimes to be in denial of all our progress...the conquering of disease, social cohesion, justice, racial harmony...yes, happiness! What better? I hoped you might have..."

"...Grown out of this stuff?"

"I did not say that, Lexin. Let us be positive. What *is* your opinion on the future policy of the Society? At least the other guys – your rivals for the Constituency, I have to point out – take a line on things...Vidano, Mauré..."

"...Yes, I know, and Li Xiaofeng. I feel it would be presumptuous of me to offer an opinion, except to suggest that we might think we are too clever. Well we *ought* to be clever enough after having so much revealed to us, but are we?"

"And this Marcelle, and this guy from prehistory, are more important to you than the Society and its aims? For God's sake keep it to yourself – like I said before."

She was pretty worked up, Lexin saw out of the corner of his eye. She was fiddling with her jewellery. He turned to her, took hold of her hands. "You must trust me, Mother. Please trust me!"

"Hello there, you idlers!" Lenica's voice as she ran up the garden came as from another world. Quickly she was on the terrace in running shorts and vest top. "The papers are full of you again, brother. And in the pubs in town, too. Called in at the 'Jupiter' when I left the office. The Normals want to know why you think we don't trust the Bods. It seems a reasonable question, and they are seriously concerned."

"Very reasonable, Lenica, and I will make it clear in due course. How could I put it? It is a matter of humbling ourselves."

"Will that go down well? You know the Government is very upbeat about solar system mineral resources, major climate control, interplanetary travel promotion, and heaven knows what else at the moment."

"Yes, I know. All worthy ambitions."

"Mother!" Lenica said, pulling up the Russian footstool embroidered with Parisian scenes that Felicitas had been using, and sitting down on it, "you are looking a bit down. Has he been depressing you again?"

"No, Lenica dear, and I am fine."

"When I say 'trust', Lenica," Lexin said, "I mean it. Look what might have happened if we had not learned from them how to deal with the long-term after-effects of the bombs. Look how closely we followed the instructions they left for that. To the letter. And why not everything to the letter now? That is my point."

"So you know better than the Conference," Felicitas said, haughtily.

"Possibly I do," Lexin replied. "Oh, and by the way, sister, with friends like that to help us to greater things, why be in such a hurry to terraform Mars? There might be more important destinations if we listen carefully. Just a thought!" And amid warnings from Felicitas that he must not neglect his physical needs and must descend for dinner in half an hour, Lexin said he must return to his room, leaving the two of them talking excitedly about the forthcoming trip of the 'Ladies for Travel' branch round the Red Planet.

He activated his PAS, his abstracted gaze falling upon the view filling the south-facing window of his 'eyrie', out beyond the steeply pitched multi-faceted roof of his father's first-floor study and the adjoining clean, white domes of his sister's room and the guest apartment. It was a descending view past the profusion of shapes and colours of the Hill of Lyra first to the central part of the city below, reflecting in its exciting urban geometry the lingering light of the lowering sun. Behind that, and beyond the variegated suburbs and dense riches of the urban forest, his vision became arrested for a moment by one of those vast clouds that so often billowed out at the edge of the distant desert – swirling yellow masses spreading across the horizon and replacing the settled patterns of the sky with another of those magnificent sandstorms, so near, and yet so far removed from them.

In view of his recent public deviation from what he saw as the Society's current norms, and taking into account a few subsequent exchanges with the press, he was not exactly surprised, when he focussed his attention, to see that the positive deviations in his bioindices were greater than ever, and was relieved to note that his overall assessments were also encouraging. When he requested guidance, the first thing he read was, "Your interests and concerns in the timeless zone have been logged. Refer to new files". An interesting sign, he thought – some kind of new recognition of the way he was thinking? Pulling the feedpad towards him he found the new files without too much difficulty in a directory called 'Out of time'. In a 'People' file, for 'Mark' two submenus could be coaxed out: 'Career' and 'Decisions'; these seemed to have something to do with his movements from school to college – setting out possibilities, options which seemed to indicate a far from passive role for Mark in the 'timeless sphere'. For 'Big Nose' and 'Red Hair' there was just the submenu 'Properties', including dates, parents, physical characters, life expectancy, and *'galactic significance'* (Must look into that last one, he told himself). Interesting that Big Nose seemed to have inherited his father's hip dysplasia. As he closed each file he became amazed at the effort that seemed to have been put into helping him understand the significance of his 'visions' – for want of a better word to describe his experiences. Another file bore the name 'Shining Face'. Who was that? Nothing in the file – yet. The child Marcelle had mentioned, perhaps? Interesting!

For all the enduring idyll of the last three centuries and more (explosions apart), for him the road ahead seemed hard. It was not at all how he had envisaged life. He asked repeatedly for guidance, speaking into the apparatus: "Am I up to this task?" The reply came up on the monitor: "If you want to be. Do you?" The only answer to that could be, "Yes"; "Is it fair on my family?" Reply: "You will have to convince them of its importance." Mother, yes, but Father? Lenica? He would have to have it out with Olaf *sometime*. He tried a bolder question: "How can the Society's attitude be changed?" Reply: "Ball in your court. Note the following 'Help' file..."

He leaned back in his chair. The daylight had almost completely gone. He closed his eyes for a few seconds, opened them again, looked back at the screen at the topics emerging from the darkness, the near-impossibility of it all: 'lack of concentration by the Society', 'low recognition of universality beyond time and place', 'low spiritual input'...; and after the topics, suggestions as to solutions: 'promoting humility', 'recognizing local limits of rationalism', 'potential for self-sacrifice'... He was about to switch off when a warning appeared: "Do you really want to continue with this exceptional task of unknown length? See Future Guidance menu." (hints on self-testing? – Olaf please note!) But for himself the answer could only really be "yes", anyway, though in truth it was a lonely prospect. For the moment it seemed that if there were specific scientific and philosophical questions to be answered, it was not his worry.

In 'Comments' he wrote: "Will need much guidance and encouragement." Reply: "Good!" To a final question, "Is there a religious connection?" the answer was, "Not a direct one."

It frightened him to think of the task he had undertaken, for he had only the vaguest notion of how the events he was witnessing – even supposing they turned out well – could be translated into the sinews and certainties of galactic progress. He sat back again, letting the tension in his spine and shoulders relax, and said out loud, "I trust". The machine switched to audio-vocal. It had never spoken to him before. It said, "Good!" And then, louder, "You must come for dinner now," but that, he realised as he came out of a state of intense concentration, was the intercom voice of the Russian Princess.

*　　*　　*

Mark was finding it harder than usual to contain his disbelief on hearing Marcelle's account of her meeting with Lexin when they met the following Saturday morning in the city and she told him about her two dreams. They stopped for a cappuccino at the Barino, wandered around a cemetery talking about family trees and watched an archery competition in the Memorial Park. When torrential rain brought that to an untimely end they took shelter at a table of the pavilion café while rain beat on the canopy and rivers of water cut across the paths and transformed the acres of grass into lots of little islands.

"Sorry about your hunter friend," he said.

"He's my father, Mark, he's not just my friend."

"Yeah, I know that's how you view it."

Marcelle knew he was trying hard. He would make a good dad, give good fatherly advice. "*He's* not all right, either, my real dad," she said, calmly. "That job with the cleaning company was a dud. He's left. Do you know what they do? They go to these places and start cleaning carpets, and of course there are always difficulties. Then it's all 'hidden costs': charging for areas under 'unreasonably heavy' furniture, specialised spot cleaning, recent price increases, excessive distance from base, difficult access, etc., etc."

"Yes, I know, I know," Mark said. "You wonder how they get away with it."

"It's not how my dad does business," Marcelle said, "and he can't work like that. It hasn't done him much good, either. It *was* heavy work *sometimes*."

"What's he going to do now?"

"He's going to do supermarket phone-order deliveries. Mark, if Big Nose gives up on Red Hair, my dad will give up, too."

"Why that's crazy, Marcelle! You really have got caught up in this, haven't you?"

"It was raining again, just like this."

"Well that's one thing we all have in common, I suppose: rain. You mean your dad will give up on your mum? Is that what you mean"

"*Vice versa,* more likely. But Markie, the good news is that Lexin said we – I mean he and I – can help each other...that there are things we cannot do alone."

"What things?"

"You are dumb, Mark. I am really upset about Big Nose and Red Hair."

"So you said." Mark muttered. "You were crying when you woke up."

"I don't know exactly what things. I told you, Lexin knows all about me and how I feel. He knows about my father and mother and about my dreams and what I so much want to happen, and said things would work out for us both, for my family and for them, there, didn't he?"

"Who are 'them'?"

"I don't know."

"It gets crazier by the second." The waitress brought a pot of tea and some cakes Mark had ordered. He put his feet up on the chair next to him and poured out desultorily. "At least let's be *this* ordinary and enjoy our tea and cake. What's he like, this Lexin?"

"He's short, with curly dark hair like me, and deep dark eyes a bit like mine I suppose, but with a sort of built-in friendliness, though a bit sombre. He seems to know everything, Mark, though he says he doesn't. That's just it. There is some gap I have to fill for him."

"But he doesn't tell you everything he could."

"How could he, Mark? How could I know all about the future? I don't want to know that. Would you want to? He said the year was 2452. He was in this office, Mark, all glass, polished wood and concrete, but softer, gentler, seeming to be part of him, almost, and he was humming something that sounded a bit like Brindi Betson's 'The World is a Flower', but different, more satisfying."

"You seem to know enough, anyway!" Mark was tucking into his cake.

"Yes, enough, that's it. Oh Mark! He will help me."

"Well I don't see how I can," Mark said, and poured himself a second cup.

But Marcelle had no appetite, and her cake was still on the plate as they got up and headed towards the stop for her bus to Culver.

CHAPTER SEVEN

Shining Face half walked, half ran till she could go no more. She felt as if she had travelled half the night.

Summer had come late, after a late spring with big rains that completely surrounded the camp with water. It had not been a very happy time, with some of the menfolk drowned after several old people had already died of cold during the long winter. She told no-one she was going to run away, but for days she had been gathering a few things together secretly.

She carried over her shoulder a couple of deer hides in addition to the one she was wearing over her undergarments, some scraped hides that could be useful for holding water, and a woolly rhino fur. The fur had been given to her by the women earlier. She regarded it as some sort of offering to make up for often shunning her; she knew they were a bit afraid of her because of who her father was. For the same reason, despite her young age she did not think they would bother to pursue her, having made such a determined departure. Her feet were wrapped in layers of skins bound with thongs. The spear she carried she had made herself, secretly, and one day she would carve it nicely. It had a long stone-flake point, and she had already killed a hare with it when practising away from the camp. Fastened to a willow-fibre girdle round her waist was her bow for fire-making, and attached to the same girdle a deer-skin pouch containing what tools she felt she could carry and another pouch containing, in skin wrappings, a multitude of other items including a collection of meat morsels amassed over several days and dried, and various fruits dried in the previous autumn together with a quantity of nuts. Deep in the pouch, which she removed for a moment as she sank down to rest in a rocky hillside cleft illuminated by the moon, were special things, little objects, which her mother had given her at different times, like a long, pointed cutting blade quite exceptionally sharp and able to slice through the toughest hide, as well as a necklace of seashells strung on a thong of bear hide and a little bunch of fir cones decorated with ochre – "You never know when you might need help beyond yourself," she would often say.

She rested only long enough to get her breath back, and then she was on the move again, guided by the moon's path. The land was rising now. That was better. She was glad to be rid of the still waterlogged flatlands, felt herself drawn upwards, away from possible pursuit, away from uncertainty.

With her load thus feeling lighter, her spear firmly in her hand, and her feet treading ever more confidently on the hardening ground, something reminded her that her mother had once said: "Your father sometimes talked of powers guiding us – until one of them takes us." She had always thought that was a bit strange. She had never heard a good word said about her father. As a bringer of bad luck his name could barely be mentioned. But then her mother had added, "It's a pity he left without me, because now I don't care whether he is alive or dead." Only for brief moments had it occurred to her to question how he would have existed out here on his own, since she had heard that he was crippled, or indeed whether her mother really did not care. Anyway, she did not much like the sound of him. As for how she herself would fare as a mere woman on her own against bears and mammoths, well fortunately she had so far had to endure nothing more than the blood curdling calls of owls! The hills and forests were being kind to her.

At the top of a long slope where the forest had become all but impenetrable she decided it would be safe to pass the night there if she could find a suitable spot. She came to a place where the undergrowth was so thick that she judged nothing larger than a hare or maybe a fox would have a reason to go there. It was a bare patch amid a mass of briers. The moon shone clear above. Without a qualm she threw her things down, lay on one of the deerskins, pulled another close around her, and was soon in the land of dreams.

* * *

Lexin Solberg was becoming impatient with – not to say bored by – the Culture Committee of the Society, chaired on this occasion by an American mathematician and linguist called Callum, from Texas, a senior lecturer at the City's university and, in his writings, a renowned commentator on the alien text. He would have liked to turn to his PAS for something more 'enlightening', but he resisted. On the face of it, progress on the basis of the Society's deciphering work had been steady over a very long time. More recently, however, and particularly after the latest accident, the Committee had been debating whether the deciphering teams might be encountering consciously or unconsciously some ethno-psychological cultural or linguistic problem of sufficient gravity to hinder further progress. They might even (according to one of the newly emerging tabloids) be annoying the Bods in some way and causing them to have fits of temper to the extent of blowing up the wormhole terminal – a preposterous idea in Lexin's view.

Although aspirants could attend as observers, no discussion 'on the side' was possible in the way it was possible in the Great Hall, but afterwards in the Sirius Bar of the Palace with Li, Lexin exploded:

"How could we possibly think of them like that? That is completely contrary to everything they have shown us."

"Well yeah," Li said, "but that's just it, isn't it? We are not sure we are right about everything they have said. I mean, they might have been warning us without our realising it."

Lexin told himself to calm down. "We have had warnings all right," he said, "but I do not take the view that they were punishing us."

The two of them sat in silence for a minute or two, sinking their glasses of trad to the strains of Johnny Raithatha's thirty-two piece emotium band. Then Li said,

"I still reckon it's a good idea to look again at *everything*. You don't know what may be interfering in our brains. We may have got the wrong end of the stick about communicating with Lyra, not understood the rules of decipherment well enough."

"You make it sound too complicated," Lexin retorted, as the

rhythms and harmonies expanded and merged and the simultaneously jarring yet softly satisfying tones of the guest soloist on a Richardson cornet came in over the top. "There is nothing wrong with our genetically modified brains. Do you like Raithatha's stuff, Li? With the crowd milling about and the noise of the band, it was hard to keep his voice down, but he did not want to sound angry.

"I suppose I could not envisage life without being able to listen to it," Li replied"

"I can see that. Look how your body moves to it!" Lexin said as Johnny started up with his next number, 'A bit of that old time veneration' – a medley by Johnny himself, actually, which (according to Jason in 'Every Guy's Guide to Superpop) brilliantly recalled some of the pop cultures of history and, quote 'reflected so beautifully present understanding of the physiology and psychology of our reasoning and our emotions'. " So I say go for Johnny's way in your work , Li, and his emotiums.".

"What? dance to work!"

"It's good for the emotions *and* our powers of reasoning according to Jason. You know Jason?"

"Sure."

"He reckons Johnny gets through mind barriers. Don't shut him out of your mind when you start work and strain your brain with rubbishy new theories!"

Li laughed in that broad, innocent way that he had. "Okay," he said, dumping his glass on the table and standing up to head for his hotel, "Can't fault Raithatha, that's for sure." But Lexin kept talking:

"We need to let go, be more optimistic, go with the music, brother, have *faith*!"

The historian looked startled. He stopped. "Faith?"

Of course, his father, Professor of the Philosophy of Science at Beijing University of Science and Technology, was a celebrated atheist; (Xiaofeng was at Renmin, the People's University). Clearly the word 'faith' had switched on a red light. "The Bods did us a bloody good turn," Lexin said, backtracking a little. "Why don't we take them at face value? It is our galactic attitude we need to question!"

"I'll analyse your complaint to the sound of music, Lexin – Johnny's," Li said, grinning as broadly as ever, and headed off, but not before Lexin had added,

"And then test the result against your synthesizer!"

Olaf was just coming out of the Palace when Lexin started for home, and they ran together, past the Meeting of the Avenues and finally up the Hill of Lyra – that unremarkable little eminence (before its transformation within the city) from which some camel drivers were said to have been the sole witnesses of the arrival and the departure of the Bods' spaceship hundreds of years before.

"Was Callum okay, then?" Olaf asked as they ran.

"Just fine," Lexin lied.

"I knew you'd say that."

"It is just that he forgets a) that we're standard humans – some very clever, admittedly – adapted to do a special job: to decipher and apply the text; and b) that the Bods know that, and are surely anxious not to make it so hard we cannot do it. It is not our job to be rattling our brains inventing new theories of ethnic compatibility or whatever. As I seem to remember I mentioned to you earlier, I do find Callum's later writings on ethnology and linguistics to be too much about Callum to be truly enlightening."

"I wish I fully understood you, Lexin," Olaf said as they ran up the garden, adding as they came up on to the terrace, "He's coming up with Leonard for a quick drink and a chat in about a quarter of an hour. I hope you'll come and join us."

"I wish you did, Father," Lexin replied. "Yes, of course I'll drop in." Heading for his room still in his running gear, something made him pause for a moment in the central hall. It was a much passed-through but nonetheless hallowed space in the middle of the house kept permanently in a state applicable to about one hundred years earlier. Having such a space was a practice inculcated by the Bods, and implied a sense of humility, a reverence and respect for one's progenitors who had striven for galactic belonging long before.

The room, lined floor to ceiling with books, many of them indeed written by his father's forbears, and on historical as well as physical topics in a tradition continued by Olaf, had been the scene of many celebrations of family and world events by the Solberg Societans over the past two hundred and something years. But now, as often, Lexin found himself wondering just how far subsequent additions to the library would be considered worthy of their place there a hundred years hence, and he was in the middle of his ponderings when Felicitas appeared in slacks and no make-up and looking very dejected. He knew his mother was packing for the three-week fly-by of Mars with the Ladies, and in view of that he was surprised to see her anything but very excited.

"The papers are not being kind to you today," she said, taking his arm and drawing him close. "They cannot believe you have nothing to say except all that stuff about 'trust'. Thank God it is not like those days long ago when the papers destroyed people, like those politicians in the twentieth century."

"Not yet, at any rate. That is thanks to the Bods."

"Yes, and there is such an enormous fund of confidence invested in us, Lexin; it is a pity to let it go to waste."

"Ah yes! Even old Li has caught onto this theme that something has gone wrong with our brains."

"Lenica walked up with him the other day. Introduced him."

"Really?"

"You were upstairs. He did not like to disturb you. Knows what a busy bee you are, dear."

"Yes, yes, I know that," he replied with a sigh. "Well the point is that nothing has gone wrong with our brains."

"You could talk to the press."

"Yes, and I would tell them to listen to the beating of their hearts and thank the Bods for all they have done."

"That's a strange thing to tell them – if you could," Felicitas said quickly, letting go of him.

"It was a strange business, wasn't it, when they came here in that ship."

"*Yes, but...*"

Felicitas was clearly not going to let him go easily, but Lexin was in a hurry. "...I could inform them," he interrupted, that there are many more truths that the Bods could tell them if they would listen," he said, interrupting her, "but for the moment I have something I must do. You will have to let me go, Mother."

"I am almost afraid to go away while things are all uncertain like this. It is bound to come up on the trip, since it is Mars that started all this."

Certainly questions to do with the creation of a Martian atmosphere were central to the first time-crossing initiatives. "Maybe now it will be Marcelle who leads us to the answers," he suggested in as transparent a tone as he could.

"She gave him one of her half-despairing, half-pitying looks. I am going for a walk," she said, squeezing his arm. "Do be careful, I love you very much." She paused. "Have you seen *her* again?"

"No."

Activating his PAS back in his office, the special new files came up a treat. The cursor was already on the 'People' file, and suddenly he was in 'Shining Face' and a primeval landscape with no further actions on his part.

As a matter of interest he tested his own bioindices. 'Attentiveness' and its biochemical and biophysical characteristics were through the roof, as were those for 'Satisfaction'. As for 'Overall assessment', it had never been higher. Before he had had time to think about all that, a figure was materialising in the landscape, but he insisted on staying in control for a moment and went for 'Properties':

"... 'Group': "H6/442"; 'Sex': "Fem"; 'Age': "14"; 'Father': "Big Nose (real name 'Racing Torrent') b. BP 38 822, d. "N/A"; 'Mother:' "Curvy Lips b. BP 38 811, d. BP 38 789 (Guardian Red Hair)"; 'Height': "1.48 m"; 'weight': "44 kg"; 'Sexual status': "N/A"... and that was all. It was enough.

It settled it about who Shining Face was. As for old Big Nose, it seemed that in his circumstances even his real name would have afforded him little benefit.

Before abandoning all conscious control of her files, he selected another submenu for Shining Face: 'Frame of mind'. It assured him that her mind was clear and optimistic – as if he had not guessed already!

Now there she was again, at a distance at first, then close up, her streaming, untidy hair flowing back from that high forehead, one or two teeth broken, her scrawny, downy arms protruding from the cut and sewn animal skin, and thin but evidently strong legs powering her striding, heavily laden, down a slope away from a stretch of woodland. "Good old *Marcelle!*" he exclaimed loudly without quite knowing why, "you are a gem! I knew you'd do it!"

Shining Face looked too fresh to have been out more than a day or two. He could only hazard a guess as to what had prompted her to leave at that particular time. A young woman, little more than a girl, in that wild country full of hungry beasts, only her clear determination gave him cause for any optimism.

It was still with unease that he followed her progress as she headed down to where low scrub petered out in a lake in a valley bottom full of bloated and rotting carcases, whereupon the scene changed and he found himself suddenly in another age...

This had to be Newchurch: a warehouse-type building of polluted dark bricks...an old building, probably, even in Marcelle's day. And there *was* Marcelle! She was just passing through the grim façade into a modern reception area, where, there being no-one in 'Enquiries' or the showroom, she soon found herself in a stockroom stacked with boxes and packages floor to ceiling. It was no more than a momentary shock for Lexin, Marcelle being no faint hearted angel, to find himself amid surely enough sexual accessories to stock all the outlets there doubtless were in Newchurch: fetish and SM stuff, love dolls and lubricants, lingerie… Surprisingly, no-one came. Doors led off marked 'Studio 1', 'Studio 2', 'Design', 'Laboratory', 'Despatch', and at the far end one marked 'Workshop' from behind which came the sound of machinery. Audible behind the door marked 'Studio 1' were sounds of men and women's voices and considerable activity, and some laughter. Marcelle pulled out pencil and paper, rested the paper against a carton of adult videos and wrote on it in her large, confident hand simply: 'Dear Mum I love you and just want to hug you. See you soon! – Marcelle'. A woman came out of the despatch department and suggested she might at least have waited in the office for assistance. Had she come in response to the modelling advert? Marcelle, smart in a grey skirt with pleats at the bottom and a frilly white top replied, pleasantly,

"No. My mother works here. I called to see her, actually, but if she is busy…" (She sealed the envelope and gave it to the woman,) "…perhaps you would kindly give this to Mrs. Weston." The woman said she would give it to her when she finished in the studio. Then Marcelle left.

Lexin noted a link on the monitor to another file, or part of a file: 'Ida. Sexual history', highlighting information from which he deduced that Ferdie, who traded in second-hand vans and cars and had taken over from Larry in Ida's affections when the latter began his time inside, did not have quite Larry's 'resources', finally running out of both money and libido. To avoid double embarrassment he had introduced Ida to a mate of his, Phil, an entrepreneur with proven resources and owning a string of photographic studios as well as importing, designing, making and distributing sex goods. Before the file faded, Lexin briefly glimpsed a pointer to a separate link, 'Sexual health in the sex industry', but he was already intent on following Marcelle as she headed out of the showroom, only to find himself not in Newchurch any more but trying to keep up with her as she struggled up the side of a scrubby hill thick with gorse and wild rose. It was no surprise to realise that with a smoothness of transition belying their very different appearances, but paying tribute to the undoubted similarity of their missions, Marcelle had been replaced by Shining Face already leaving behind her the stinking bog strewn with carcases. The scene faded, and he was just sitting in his office again. Clearly, time and its events were leaping on apace in other places if not in Galaxy City. He switched off, changed and went to the living space.

George Callum and Leonard Mackenzie were already sitting on the terrace drinking with his father. For once, Olaf was not in *his* running gear, having made a quick change to casual cottons. Already at a distance Lexin could hear they were going on about cultural differences and misinterpretation in decipherment. Mackenzie, as usual in his nondescript and probably colour-variable slacks and shirt that were somehow in keeping with his yellow-tinged tanned complexion and ingrained features, was saying he had examined and re-examined the scientific bases of message retrieval as deduced from the deciphered text and could not understand why the calculations had proved wrong. "But we have sure upset those guys somewhere," he declared in that droning monotone that seemed baked in the hot heart of Australia. "And Lexin, what does Lexin think?" he asked, catching sight of him through the open doors. "You're very reticent these days, my boy!" by which Lexin assumed he meant he was generally not given to toeing Mackenzie's line. "Glad to see you're keeping up the exercise, by the way!"

"In such presence how could I not be reticent," Lexin responded, but Leonard Mackenzie wasn't having that.

"Ah, come now! That's no excuse! Pure flattery! Maybe if Sergei Malinovsky and I could suss out our hidden cultural contradictions, some of the remaining problems with our much respected X.H. Wang might become a little less problematic. Come on, Lexin, it's important." And he added, "Certainly the professor is more laid-back than I am – as if he even knew the answers already." Unusually, Mackenzie laughed. "Maybe he does!"

Lexin wondered whether by 'laid-back' he could actually have meant 'natural', or 'open'. "Maybe the answers we seek are indeed not far away if we are patient...and ...and receptive," he suggested. Lexin took his father's irritated glance as a recognition of the thinly veiled reference to the kind of things they had been arguing over earlier.

If Mackenzie was at all taken aback, he did not show it. "Well what is *your* opinion, George?" he asked, turning to Callum.

The rosy-cheeked American was wearing one of his with-it personal-climate suits, the coat currently draped decorously across his shoulders to reveal a florid shirt loosely encompassing his ample figure. He took a few moments to respond. "I do not know what really drives Malinovsky," he said, screwing up his nose as he did when facing awkward situations, "but I tell you that tribal instincts, historical prejudices, lie close to the surface. Who knows what they may be turning up and warping our minds with, possibly even explaining why…well...why we still have no decent theory of everything."

"Shock horror!" Mackenzie rolled his eyes.

"Look, gentlemen," Lexin said, "Do you not think the Bods knew all those things about us when they took us on? They are not asking us to do the impossible."

"You did say that, Lexin," Olaf agreed, his smooth, rosy complexion of tolerant fatherhood having replaced the irritation of a few moments before.

"I could have said more, Father, but we were running up the hill. I do not want you to die before your time by over-taxing your heart through talking while running. A hundred is much too early."

"Indeed," Mackenzie said, and the others nodded, solemnly.

"If you really want to know what I think," Lexin said, still standing by the folds of the terrace door since he hesitated to sit down in such elevated company, "I have to say you are barking up the wrong tree – in my view. We had a unified linguistic and cultural theory by the year 2150 – and thanks to whom? You want to step back in time; the Bods want us to move forward. I guess they gave us the necessary clues on those disks. Sometimes, with respect, gentlemen, I wonder why they bothered and whether we have forgotten what they did for us back then."

"Harsh words, Lexin," Olaf said as the others took on expressions of what might have been genuine shock.

"Even a decent theory of everything might be just a little closer than you imagine," Lexin said, quietly. Another thought occurred to him. There was something about George Callum from America's Wild West (as the western side of the reawakening continent had again become, in a modern sort of way), something forward-looking, something demanding radical explanations, although at eighty the spark seemed to have all but vanished. Was he not still into modern household and personal technology like nobody else – and not only climate suits!? Lexin thought he could put a point. "I could have asked whether we had ever thanked the Bods," he said, looking at Callum. But it was Mackenzie who responded first:

"How do we do that," he asked, "hold services of thanksgiving?" The physicist had appeared only half engaged, and was starting to play with his concept enhancement toy, tapping concepts out on a little gadget and watching the ideas roll out of his brain.

It was remarkable, Lexin thought, how 'laid back' *he* could be, never mind Malinovsky. "We should have respect for them," Lexin replied, mildly annoyed by Mackenzie's latest irritating habit and reckoning he must have gone to the extent of having the electrodes implanted somewhere, since they were normally external.

"Don't we have it, then?" Callum frowned deeply. "Don't we have respect?" His tone was unusually sharp.

"Not much, but for what it is worth I have found that my indices – all my indices that contribute to comprehension and motivation – improve when I have thankfulness in my mind... in my *heart*, if I may use such an emotive word as 'heart' in such sophisticated presence."

Lexin was aware of Olaf's eyes on him, glinting questioningly, despondently perhaps, on either side of his big hands clasped in front of his forehead in a characteristic praying attitude.

"Well my! There's a thought," Callum said with slightly lightened tone and stretching out a flower bedecked arm to take an extra long draught of his Boddingstone's. "Must pay more attention to my indices."

"Incidentally, you would not believe how your *synthesizer* makes you *more* independent, or perhaps I should say more far-seeing, more discerning. Another way of putting it, as I said to my father, is that our work becomes like being let into a secret – not some childish thing of no importance, but deep, deep, good things, but possibly quite simple. To be honest, I am not even sure they want us to be doing things like terraforming Mars and stuff like that." They were looking at him with varying degrees of tolerance, his father by now probably the least tolerant of the three. And *purely* incidentally," Lexin added, gratefully accepting a glass of lemon and apple from a momentarily present Robert and seeing that he had the attention of all of them, "what makes you think, Professor Mackenzie…"

"Leonard, please", the professor interjected.

"…What makes you, Leonard, what makes us *all* think," he continued, looking round the table with uncharacteristic urgency and a little extra flush to the rosy cheeks, "that these beings who saw the 'incident' in the US over three and a half centuries ago, whether from a circling spaceship or from some scarcely imaginable distance in Lyra, what makes you think they might not know or be bothered whether the world was really grateful to them*? Who knows – they might even be able to see us sitting here thanking them?* Forgive me, Dr. Callum, if I appear an excessively self-disparaging earthling faced as we are with the knowledge of such awesome entities."

"Let us thank them now, then, just in case you may be right, Lexin," Mackenzie suggested, idly tapping away again.

"They may take our thanks as read." Olaf suggested, leaning back now in a kind of despairing attitude. "They may not want any more contact…until we 'come of age', whenever that is."

"Father, everything I know of the Bods, from the text, from my PAS, my guidance prompt, and for other reasons that I cannot go into here, suggests to me that whether these entities have the same number of eyes, arms and legs as we do or whether they are beyond our imaginings, they do not appear to be anything less than understanding, considerate, friendly beings – I almost want to say loving beings…" Mackenzie was bursting to say something, but Lexin wanted to finish. He continued, "…friendly beings that care about us, not as some kind of deities but as kind-hearted Galactans."

"Heavens above! What are we talking about here?" Mackenzie exploded, pocketing his enhancement toy. "This is outside my sphere. I am a scientist."

"What do we have here?" came a familiar voice from the inner recesses. "Christ preaching to the elders in the Temple?" Felicitas entered with a slightly more subdued flourish than usual, merely casting the stole matching her deep purple halter dress artistically over the back of the wicker chair into which she subsided gracefully, drawing the one knee over the other, as Robert reappeared for an instant with her Manzanasco. The others had stood up on her entry. "No formalities, please," she said. "Carry on – unless it is something private, of course."

"What secrets could we have from Felicitas?" Callum asked. "I would say that if we are endeavouring to do anything it is to 'reveal' more than to 'conceal'."

"Good. I hope Lexin made some good points. He is nothing if not original."

"In that respect, Felie, he takes after you," Olaf said.

"If you call being basic 'original', well then possibly I am," Lexin said.

"The Conference could probably do with a shake-up." Callum was draining his last drop of beer. "Obviously your son takes his work very seriously," he added, turning to Felicitas. "I hope he gets in, and now if you will excuse me it is time I headed for home. Fiona likes to keep an eye on me. I suppose there are worse faults in a woman!"

"I too," Mackenzie said. "My dear Céleste will be already dressed for the variety show at the World Harmony Theatre. And thank you, Felicitas, and thank you Lexin. You know, my young man, I am not so sure your mother was far wrong when she spoke of Christ in the temple, but it is never too late to train for holy orders. It is open to the genetically modified, after all."

"That was a bit of a swipe from old Mackenzie," Olaf said when he and Felicitas returned after accompanying the guests into the house and having them shown out by Robert. The light was going, and the scent of wallflowers wafting up soothingly from below the terrace. "I am afraid, Lexin, that he probably hardly remembers what a personal activity synthesizer is."

"At least, not since his days in Decipherment. In any case, I guess he's more interested in the city life and more concerned with keeping Céleste happy than sweating over his PAS. It's not for nothing that they live in that palatial apartment overlooking the Galaxy Mall. It is a pity, Father, since what I was talking about was working for a better relationship with the Bods."

"Maybe they don't reckon to need PAS's in Oz," Felicitas said, picking up her glass with the remnants of her 'fix' and cradling it in her hands. "They are pretty full of themselves, are they not, since their climate revamp and tenfold population increase? I would say he was rude to Lexin."

Olaf's eyes appeared to be trained on the tower ascending from the exuberant structures of the Palace of the Galaxy, its trilltinium pinnacles reflecting the rays of the setting sun in every colour of the visible spectrum, but his thought was clearly focussed elsewhere. "You must understand, son," he said, without turning round, "that admirable though your ideas may be, they don't sound – how shall I put it – very scientific."

"Science? There is more to it than science, isn't there?" Felicitas said, gently, taking his arm. "Come, Olaf, you know that! Look at our social and ethical advances, absence of crime and social degradation, artistic endeavours..."

"Of course there is, Felie, but Lexin talks of thankfulness, love...why! Then it will be..."

"Joy and gladness and going to church next? Yes, and much more. Come, come Olaf, you are forgetting so much."

"Those things you both mentioned," he retorted stiffly, "those qualities of life, those benefits, have depended on scientific advance, let us be honest. No science, no long life; no science, no time to enjoy life. It is not only Mackenzie you lose here, Lexin, but me too." Olaf grabbed his jacket and put it on against the cooling, and made to go indoors. "Ah, here comes Lenica," he said as his daughter strode through the glass doors and, pausing only to thank Robert for the big jug of squash that appeared on the table in the fleeting instant of his presence, fill a glass with it, and top up her mother's Manzo, sprawled in one of the seats with her white running briefs so high up her gorgeous thighs, Lexin reckoned, that had one of her supine admirers been present – and she had plenty among the Normals as well as in the Society – he might assuredly have believed himself in a position to glimpse up at the top there the bosky valleys of Elysium. "Anyway, Lexin," Olaf said as he turned to go in, "think about it, son, or I at any rate will be disappointed. Meanwhile I strongly favour heading straight for the Galaxy.

"So what is all that about, then?" Lenica asked. "Father *is* preoccupied, isn't he? And if it is about the sort of thing I suspect, I have to tell you that Angelo Vidano is coming up well in the stakes for Central Asia."

"You are referring to press opinion, presumably," Felicitas said. She had sat down. Lexin was now standing leaning back on the balustrade..

"In the papers certainly, but…"

"Don't forget it is the Matriarchs who decide it, Lenica."

"That may have been so in the past, Mother, but things are on the change. The Normals do not understand what is going on. There's plenty of muttering in the Palace, too. You know the Conference is getting tired of negative attitudes in certain quarters." She was looking pointedly at her brother.

"Negative attitudes?" Felicitas appeared to be gazing not at Lexin but past him towards the softly illuminated urban expanse, and to an infinite distance beyond indistinguishable from the emerging starscape. The concern in her voice was evident.

"I mean blaming it all on ourselves. You know there are some really weird ideas around. I don't know whether they originate with you, brother." The full lips were accumulating some venom.

"Probably they do," he replied. "And I suppose you have been muttering, too."

"Things like looking at how we feel," she went on, "our frame of mind, our attitude to our work and to the Bods, even. To the Bods! That is the latest thing. I tell you, it does not go down too well with my boss. You know Harry Beckenthal made his name in big engineering projects – space stations, elevators. But we do not need any more of these. He assumes he will get that comet job. Now what? All that is happening, he says, is that his firm keeps having to rebuild bits of the Mission Station and wormhole."

"That's boloney. Father was saying they still do a lot of work for the Government."

"But now you ask, 'Why terraform Mars anyway?'"

"Leaving that aside, as a Societan he should not be getting involved in big business deals with anybody."

Lenica did not seem to be listening. "He is going to Canberra tomorrow to update the Government on the latest situation here. There has never been such interest in the Society in centuries, they say. I don't like to think what Harry will report – about the *dissident i*n the camp." She spat the word out. "You are well known, you know. There is money, big money at stake, brother, and not *just* money to power comets. Don't forget that although this is a world of sovereign states it is the World Government that sets the seal on all our big international endeavours, from…I don't know…everything from greening of the deserts to galactic exploration."

"Lenica, I fear you are forgetting what you are: that you are modified, and that the Normals expect special things of *us*, whatever Harry might report. We have to keep to our task, which is what we are endeavouring to do despite certain difficulties. He certainly is not keeping to his."

"You are saying we are superior?" she asked, springing up and facing her brother, eyes aflame. "How do you suppose the Normals would take that?"

Lexin could see that Lenica was probably too angry to be rational, but he said, "You know I don't mean that! Different, yes! We have a special task. We cannot rule, govern, hold powerful positions in industry or academia or the law, have big financial interests. We are experts in our fields, facilitators, advisers, encouragers..."

"Tell Harry all this!"

Lexin could imagine the big man's response – while scarcely even removing his electronic pipe from between his lips as he waggled his bushy eyebrows and dismissively gathered up his toga: 'What I do is perfectly legal, son. May I respectfully suggest it's time you grew up, Lexin. You know, I think I should speak to your father!'

"He of all people, as the Society's representative in the World Government and Assembly, ought to know better," Felicitas said, quietly.

"All right," Lexin said, "and to complete the picture nor can we fuck around freely and live the ordinary and yet now vastly enlightened lives of the Normals. At least, some of us might, but our task, our destiny, is special, and tragically we *all* seem to be forgetting what we should be doing, Harry not least."

"So all except *you*!" Lenica let out, scornfully.

"I think he would like to tell you to use your personal activity synthesizer as well, Lenica." Felicitas said, Twiddling the stem of her glass between her fingers. "I must say he could have expressed himself in more refined manner."

"The bloody thing doesn't tell me anything," Lenica retorted, "and you ask anyone in the Palace, or tonight in Canberra at Mackenzie's lecture on the latest on message retrieval. So good night, dear brother," she said, and with that his sister strode indoors just like their father would, and in ten seconds she would have leapt several at a time up the curving stairs to her dome retreat like she often did when they had fallen out as children.

Felicitas had appeared very thoughtful during Lexin's little clash with Lenica. There was nothing unusual about him having strong words with his sister, but the fact was that Lenica knew everybody and talked to everybody. To have her against him publicly – if that was indeed the case – especially now when things were getting more critical, was not good. With a boss who was both a Conference delegate and the Society's representative beyond the Society itself, she had wide contact with those working in the offices and committee rooms of the Palace, visitors staying in its accommodation, or Societans living in the city and attending lectures, forums, readings, social events...

"So Harry, from a long line of German Societans, is forgetting *his* destiny, too," she said, twirling the glass containing the remaining drop of her fortifier slowly between her fingers.

"He still wields great influence in the business he relinquished to his cousin when he joined the Society."

"I know it even worries Lenica, privately," Felicitas said,. "But tell me, Lexin, all this synthesizer business, is it really so vital? You know how un-technical I am."

"To recapitulate what I am sure you know really," Lexin said, going and sitting next to her, "it is part of our modification. When you joined the Society to marry Dad and underwent that long operation to implant new genetic material and a nanocomputer 'wired' (for want of a better word) to your brain, access was also provided to a kind of personal adviser – your data synthesizer. Incidentally, it took twenty years to develop the nanocomputers, and another thirty to achieve the personal synthesizer – at least we managed all that successfully (with the help of their blueprints in the text and our genetic enhancement, of course). So it took fifty years to get completely modified. Okay, so why are we not using our synthesizers much? Answer: because we seem to be able to do without them. Remember, great scientific and social advances were made with just genetic implants and the texts."

"*Just* those!" Felicitas had remained dutifully attentive and silent up to that point, elbows in the cosmic table top, chin resting in her hands. "But we could use them, we *should* use them you say?"

"For some reason our neglect of them is showing up. I do not fully understand why. It might be the stage we have reached in our progress – or lack of it, and/or because of the density or complexity of the data.. The point is that the neglect is now becoming evident."

"Hence the accidents?"

"That would be my guess. I guess too that the reason why many say their PAS does not work for them or does not work very well, even if they want it to, is that it has become rusty." His mother was looking at him curiously. "But that may be reversible. As I said to Father, there may appear to be nothing wrong with wormhole operation and procedure per se, but there has possibly been – how could I put it? an accumulation of ignorance in the use of our – I mean everybody's – synthesizers in general that shows up not least in wormhole procedure, although we do not know precisely where." I must admit that that is speculative.

"What did he say to that? 'They have already started retraining'?"

"How *did* you guess?"

"I would say that 'rusty' is the sort of word *I* would use more than a scientist. But anyway, the point is that yours works."

"Yes, though I don't know why I should have had the visions, and certainly not why it should just be me – if it *is* just me. It is very humbling. But our calling is a very humbling one."

"That's what worries me most, Lexin. Why you?" She gripped his hand. "And why you in particular to have to spread the humbling news?"

"God knows. And it works so well, too, my PAS!"

"So we have missed things in the text. So how do we find them now?"

"We may not be able to do that, and it may be too late to worry. Mother, I reckon our neglected PAS should be our *ultimate* advisers, and that just as surely they will point the way out of our difficulties."

"And how will they do that, Lexin?" Felicitas's patience was being tried – he knew that.

"For a start, the particular fact that my PAS mediates my visions must mean that the visions are something very important to me, probably to all of us. There was another instalment today."

"That hunter? You saw him today? Or was it the girl?"

"Not actually the hunter, but his daughter. You see, like Marcelle she cares deeply about her mother, or rather, the woman she believes is her mother. She is trying to find her. It is a hard trail to follow, and I have been close to her just like I am close to you here now."

"A good daughter, at any rate," Felicitas said, "and what about the father – what was his name?"

Lexin explained that first Big Nose, then Red Hair for different reasons had had to leave their community, but how (whether by chance or design) they had come together again, only to be separated a further time, leaving Big Nose wandering hopelessly and Red Hair effectively imprisoned in another camp, another community.

"Another family with family problems! My God, Lexin, it's uncanny. It frightens me a bit that this should be so important – important to you, at least, you of all people in a happy home (I hope), and supposedly to us!"

"It has never frightened me, mother. Mystified, amazed, but not frightened."

There was a silence. Then Felicitas said, "I *am* frightened, Lexin. Yes, I *am* frightened." She did not even stop to finish her drink, but sighed, and stood up to go indoors. "I am frightened for you, for Olaf, for us all."

It was completely dark but for the low glow from the City's illumination, and for the desert-bright stars, which were not obscured by it.

CHAPTER EIGHT

Looking back into the wide, flooded, valley, stinking of rotting animals, Shining Face could not remember exactly how she had been able to cross it. She was aware, though, that whereas the little bunch of decorated fir cones had been in a piece of animal skin, carefully wrapped up and buried deep in one of the pouches carried around her waist, now she was clutching it in her left hand which was holding down the hides balanced over her shoulder as she made her way slowly up the slope.

The rest of the day revealed vista after vista of rolling scrubby grassland with occasional views into the flatter landscape behind her. That was the lower country which had been her home for perhaps two years and to which she knew that the people among whom she had always lived had journeyed from their last camp by the sea. She thought it was just before that move from the sea that she last saw her mother. She was about ten. One night her mother had said goodnight to her on her bed of evergreen fragments and dried leaves, and the next morning she was gone. She had cried and cried, but understood that her mother had not gone by choice. Henceforth she would have to fend for herself, but ever since that time Shining Face had always had it in her mind that by keeping the fir cones safely she would one day find her again.

Thus it was with no lessening of her determination that she arrived late in the afternoon at a thicket with some bigger trees and was thankful to put down her belongings, eat some of the dried meat of the hare she had caught before she had left home, and find plenty of tasty green leaves close to the ground already gathering a refreshing dew. It was only then that it came to her fully, and with a sudden rush of apprehension, how she was really and finally on her own.

Thinking it best not to dwell on it, however, and being too tired to try and find a more secure place – if there was any – or even to try and find the fresh water she had now begun to crave, she put down her things, quickly made her bed on a carpet of oak leaves, drew the woolly rhino fur close around her and fell asleep. When once or twice in the night she awoke and stared up through the gently moving tops of the trees at the stars, she imagined animal shapes in their patterns as she had always done, and it gave her comfort because for all the strangeness of her new surroundings those remained familiar.

The next day, having sampled the nut supply and sucked dewy grass to ease the dryness of her mouth, she gathered up her belongings and moved on again, aiming for where the sun would be by early evening and hoping for a stream in which to refresh herself. Eventually, at the bottom of a slope she found it, almost buried beneath a tangle of unripe blackberry and rose, barely noticing the cuts and scratches it cost her to get to it. By the time she had washed herself, quenched her thirst and got moving again the sun already shone warmly. By the middle of the afternoon it was hot, and she surprised a slow pigeon, felling it with a boulder, and then likewise another, agitated one, probably its mate. She considered herself very lucky, and spent the rest of the afternoon in that spot, collecting wood with which to light a fire in a small hollow in the ground which she enlarged and lined with the few stones she could find. It did not escape her notice that the hollow, like others nearby, was almost certainly made by a mammoth's foot.

From a tiny girl she had often watched the women making fire and had achieved a good skill herself, under supervision. How long it took her now, though! But how relieved she was when, using tinder from one of the old bird's nests she had also crammed into one of her pouches for emergencies, she succeeded finally, after much work with her cutting tools and many spins of the drill, in getting a fire going and roasting the pigeons. She felt proud of her achievement and ate one of the birds, accompanied by a satisfying dip into her stock of various dried berries and what green stuff she could see around that she knew was safe to eat.

Although quite high up, it was a sheltered place among trees, so she decided it would be a good idea to stay there and keep the fire going all night for safety and for another cooking, so she enlarged the hole and created a reserve pile of wood, but was disappointed not to come across the pigeons' nest as she hoped she might. Shining Face finished by staying in the same place three days during which time the other pigeon's carcase dried in the sun. Little forays, keeping the 'camp' in sight, brought her in the evening of the second day to a grassy place where some little holes in a bank betokened the presence of little animals. They were the sort that the women generally despised, saying they were too much bother. But since she had time to 'bother' she waited with a stick and was rewarded with several little creatures no bigger than her thumb. Soon after, she was able to stun and kill a hare with a stone. The day's offerings cooked on the resuscitated fire went a little way towards alleviating her growing hunger.

It was her friend who had taught her to throw a stone properly.

"Do you want to throw like a boy?" he had asked once, and she had replied,

"I don't want to be a boy!"

"You may need to be a boy one day," he had said, and she had laughed. Then he said, "What if you go away like your mother and father."

"Why should I do that?"

"Mother says you could be bad for the camp, like your father, Big Nose, and your mother, Red Hair, were. She says you are headstrong."

"My *mother*?"

"They say she ran loose like a doe in the autumn." It was only later that she understood what that meant and thought probably he didn't understand it at the time, either.

"Do you fear I will bring bad luck?" she asked.

"No, I like you, Shino. There are only good things about you."

When she hurled stones it was as if his hand was over hers, guiding it and giving it force. He was stronger than his skinny body might have led one to assume.

They called him Toothy because when he grinned he seemed to be all teeth and ears. She had been glad to have a special friend in that lonely time after her mother had left, but she hoped he would not try to follow her as he had wanted to, so she had not told him when she was leaving and had therefore gone while he was out hunting with the men. It was not for her own sake she did that, for he would have been a great help to her, but because he would make a good hunter for the camp. As it was, he had done the next best thing for her. It was he who had once told her something that he said was in fact widely believed: that Red Hair had gone to find the great sea beyond the sun where it sets in spring, hoping to find Big Nose there.

And that was the direction she herself had taken.

On the third day in that place, returning from an unsuccessful foray which had taken her out of sight of the 'camp' she was just in time to see a large animal making off with the pigeon, even though it had been hidden under some pieces of wood. The fire was nearly out and obviously not big enough to scare it away. More concerned at the presence of what were probably hyenas in the vicinity than at the loss of the meat, she decided to strike camp immediately and with a little daylight left was soon descending into the next valley. With just a little food left from her original supply it was possible to stave off the pangs of hunger enough to seek out a place to sleep among some trees near the edge of a lake.

Again there was no difficulty in finding plenty of the oak leaves which she knew were good for the skins and helped to preserve them, and the sound of water birds as she laid her skins on a thick bed of them gave her hope of being able to kill one of the birds the next day and maybe make another camp. She fell asleep looking at the friendly stars.

In a half-waking state around dawn she dreamed of Toothy, seeing him running with the men trying to divert some threatening mammoths, though that puzzled her just a little since no mammoth had been seen in the two years spent in the camp. Toothy was only twelve years old and had no beard, and she was afraid for him, for she knew he wanted to prove himself, and although he was great with a spear, and had helped her to make hers and could run fast, he saw no dangers. The men were making a lot of noise, and after a while the animals wandered off.

Shining Face was woken at sunrise by trumpetings and heavy splashing and saw that she was at a narrow point in the lake, which stretched as far as the eye could see in both directions. The dark, massive forms of several mammoths were visible in the water. It was a relief – and somehow no surprise – to see that instead of following the route she had taken through clearings in the oaks along the lakeside they were leisurely wading across to the other side of the lake. The reddish-brown tops of their woolly heads as they raised them to bellow and the tips of their huge upturned tusks were catching the rays of the early morning sun until the massive beasts slowly ambled up out of the water and disappeared into the long grass beyond.

Prompted by a gnawing hunger now, she waded to a point where it was possible to cut off one of the water birds and send it onto the shore among trees, where she pursued and speared it. The chase exhausted her, and the making of a fire in a stone-lined hole in the earth beneath a big tree was a long job despite the dry twigs available. But the effort was well rewarded, and by the middle of the day she was enjoying all of the duck, which was nice and tender after cooking half the morning on the hot stones beneath sticks covered with a pile of moss. Another achievement! She decided to press straight on, since there was now no sign of the mammoths. With an immutable feeling that it was Toothy who had diverted them from their normal path, Shining Face struck up into what appeared to be some higher hills, buoyed up by a satisfied appetite and a conviction that her friend was very much with her.

Three moons passed – a period of considerable hardship. How she missed the men coming back from the hunt! If they had had a good day, two of them might be carrying a deer, or four of them a bison. Somebody would pull out half a dozen hares, or there might be a surprise, like a pair of geese and some little ones. The women would have the fire stoked up and be ready to manoeuvre the carcases above the flames. By dusk the stuff would be smelling good, and everything would go quiet as they ate until someone started recounting the events of the day and others would add to it as it turned into boasting. Life had been much better for most of them, and food plentiful, at the new camp under a new leader. It had been just before her mother left that Giant Man had been killed by the lion, and Shining Face had come to realise since then how those two events were connected but also how her mother had suffered at his hands. Not that that had evoked much pity for her by the other women.

Now, out here on her own, it was as much as she could do to find enough to eat once in the day, and certainly there was nothing to boast about as far as hunting was concerned. There wasn't much to boast about when you were scavenging from a deer carcase, even if you were trying to keep a hyena at bay at the same time. Actually, though, Toothy would have been quite proud of her there. For the rest it was a case of perhaps some baby hares (she had learned at home where to look for them), or a pigeon if she was lucky, or in one case a late brood of duck eggs. Some small fish that she managed to isolate in shallow water made a welcome change.

She would remember, as she struggled slowly on through rolling hills and deep valleys, through forest and marsh, how back at home she could easily get to the front when they crowded round to eat, because people were still a bit afraid of her on account of her father. It had not worried her too much, especially with Toothy around, and it could make her smile now, but only for a moment or two, as she felt a renewed determination to find that one person who would accept her for herself – and who might need *her*.

But meanwhile her feet had become very sore, and even the ointment from marigold flowers that both the women and the men used, and which she had brought with her, did little for them, or for her legs and arms, which were cut all over. She felt exhausted and had become very, very thin, to the extent that the usual bleeding now never happened. If this could be said to be one advantage, another was the appearance of berries with the approach of autumn.

Autumn also meant mushrooms. Her mother had long ago explained which of these could be eaten raw, which only when cooked well, and the one or two which would kill her. It was while gathering mushrooms in a boggy forest one wet morning after spending the night in a makeshift shelter close to the biggest river that she had ever seen, and which now seemed to bar her way, that she had an unfortunate setback. She lost the stone point on her spear – that point which had taken so long to prepare before she had set out, patiently working at it for half a day with a piece of deer antler. The spear had been leaning, point downwards, against a tree, but when she came to collect it the point was missing and no amount of grubbing around in the mud revealed it. The one thing she had so far omitted to do was to fashion one or two spare points. Since these had first to be splintered off a larger piece, then perfected with the antler and finally grooved in order to be able to attach it to the shaft, it might take more than half a day to make another one, assuming a suitable stone could be obtained. However, as it was also raining and blowing very hard she took a decision to stop everything else and try to improve her shelter. Hiding in the shelter it might even be possible to run and pounce on an unsuspecting duck, though she did not know how she would go about making fire in such rain. On consideration, she decided to move up to a slightly higher place, and as luck would have it there was a massive yew set into a bank only a little way away, where stretching a few more evergreen branches above her head should provide good shelter at least for a while, which could perhaps be improved later.

It was only after starting work on several large flakes that she managed to fashion a good point from one of them with her antler punch and hammer, spending ages leaning against a low branch perfecting and attaching it. By the time she had done this she was noticing that the silver line of the river could now be seen through the trees and seemed to be expanding even as she looked, indicating that after a night and half a day of rain the water level was now rising rapidly.

Although the heavy rain showed no sign of letting up, hunger overcame her weakness and tiredness and she went down across the boggy ground to where she could see some ducks swimming. At first it seemed they were having a fine time enjoying themselves, but as she got nearer it became evident how strong the current was, and how it was swirling around among the trees and sweeping away debris and even ducks and their ducklings. It might give her a chance. She waded as far as she dared, beginning to regret carrying her spear, and made a grab at one of the ducks with one hand, but as it struggled it was necessary to let go of the spear for a moment in order to release her other hand, and in that instant a passing uprooted shrub carried it away, and she watched in dismay as it vanished into deeper water, her morning's work *and* her precious spear all lost. In despair, her sole consolation was the knowledge that at least she still had the duck, but although it would have been easier to twist its neck there and then, and stop its flapping, something that she could not explain prevented her from harming it. Struggling back through the swirling water with the squawking bird under her arm, she was aware of her load becoming heavier and heavier, so that by the time she reached a point where water gave way to bog exhaustion overcame her and forced her to put it down. It sat and looked at her for a moment, then flapped its wings and took off into the trees. It was as much as she could do to struggle up to the shelter of the yew, fall on the bed of litter that she had prepared for herself, draw her rhino rug around her and give in to her weariness.

*   *   *

"So tell me how the meeting of the Culture Committee went." Felicitas caught Lexin as he was crossing the hall on the way from his room to the kitchen to get himself some breakfast. It was not long after his latest little spat with his sister.

"Could you hang on a minute, Mother? I need to get myself something. I feel stressed."

"I cannot imagine why. I thought you had got all that stuff sorted out."

Was she meaning his latest issues with Callum's ramblings on tribal instincts, and being disingenuous? "It is not that, Mother. It is the other stuff."

"Ah, the other stuff. Not of our time. Look, Lexin, come to my room and let us have a chat."

These kinds of cheerful opening moves in dialogues with his mother could so often lead to the most taxing interchanges. And today he feared he might lack some conviction in countering his mother's taunts, her fears, her questions... "First let mes get myself something," he said.

"Perhaps you want one of those energizer packs. I mean the ones with psycho-boost. I think you need this, Lexin. You are getting run down. You need a booster."

It was the last thing he wanted. "See you in a minute," he said, going through and doing himself tomatoes on toast. There was nothing like it to abolish the nervous void that his stomach was increasingly becoming. He made it himself on the prehistoric toaster. They really hadn't changed, toasters, since the turn of the millennium. Thank goodness some things were best if they stayed in their long-established ruts.

He was at one with his mother on that. But now he was going to have to report the extraordinary matter of Marcelle announcing to Ida that she would walk the streets if her own mother went on stripping in Phil's club (the club being another of his 'interests'). Felicitas would probably say, "for Heaven's sake, she is crazy, Lexin". Her suggestion about his needing a booster sounded a bit desperate. Surely she understood that his brain might benefit from a bit of slowing down rather than the opposite. He took his plate with him and found his mother sitting on her bed, staring into space and still in her cortilan morning gown brocaded with Martian motifs. It had been a present from Lexin on her last birthday – her eighty-fourth, and Lenica had given her the sumptuous slippers that went with it. Lebinsky's novel languished on her bedside table. He wasn't surprised that she had not finished all of its thousand and something pages. It was just so predictable. He had studied it by fast-read. That had been enough. Let the nanocomputer weed out the mountains of chaff!

"Come and sit by me," she said when he had wolfed down his breakfast in two minutes flat. God, how awful this was going to be, Lexin thought. It was when she was in this state – no make-up, hair all tied up, just the two of them, – that his mother was most challenging. "So where is Marcelle now?" she asked.

"She is trying to get her mother to agree to the two of them finding a place to live together. Time has moved on a couple of years there, mother – if not here – since the business with Larry. She has left school and got a job in a supermarket. Like I told you, Ida has for quite a while been modelling illustrations in a brochure of sexy underwear...you know, that kind of thing...for this friend of a friend of Larry's." He had referred only briefly to the converted old warehouse, just as earlier he had revealed only the sketchiest details of the Larry episode, and how Marcelle had eventually with some difficulty traced her to Phil's studios via Larry's friend Ferdie who had taken pity on her after the house in Hawthorn Road had been repossessed. She had actually seen very little of her mother when she was living with Ferdie – usually only in town in the company of her grandfather. "Now for many months Ida has been working in Phil's strip club, too, which is in another location in the city, but Marcelle wants her to..."

"...Reform?"

"Get back to her real self. She knows there is a real Mum inside her and is threatening to walk the streets herself in protest."

"Knows...?" The tone was gentle, caressing, doubting. Do you really think this hard, selfish – I was going to say cruel – woman is reformable

"Yes."

"Do you believe her? Marcelle, I mean"

"She has her mother's drive, but in Marcelle it hasn't gone rotten, and I doubt it ever will. She has her father's solid goodness, too.. It counts for a lot."

"So you believe her about walking the streets?" Felicitas's tone was suddenly ice-cold. Now it was the northern legacy. "And what *about* her father?"

"She's quite capable of it, walking the streets, but I hope she doesn't. Her father? He's delivering for a supermarket. Before that he was cleaning carpets. Hated the job. Don't know how he stuck it. But that's just like him."

"What about that girl, the hunter's daughter, trying to save *her* mother from herself..." Felicitas paused. "...No, of course that is not right. I mean trying to *seek* her *out*."

"You are not so far wrong, actually, Mother, in talking of 'saving her from herself'. As I think I may have hinted, Red Hair, while she was the chief's favourite, had something of a reputation among the other men of the camp."

"So it *is* another case of rescue, then?"

"Shining Face loves, *believes in* Red Hair like Marcelle loves and believes in her mum."

"So she figures still, then, th*at* girl, your *other* girl. I guess she is finding things tough." She was looking at Lexin, close by her side. Now she was half teasing, half serious.

"She is struggling. It is terribly lonely for a fourteen-year-old fending for herself in a flooded northern valley umpteen thousand years ago, losing her spear head, making a new one then having the whole spear carried away in the flood, catching a duck and then losing it, and finally – I saw this happen only today – dragging a drowned deer out of the water to save herself from starvation."

"You have seen these things on your monitor?"

"Yes."

"And Marcelle knows this, too – about her hardships, I mean."

"Well no, she doesn't. Remember, two years have passed for Marcelle. For two years Marcelle must surely have been beside herself wondering where she is."

"Haven't I always heard you say she trusts you?"

"It's a long time not to hear anything – and she hasn't."

"Oh come on, Lexin, didn't I hear you say even your great Malinovsky doesn't know the answer to those kinds of questions? And who talks more about 'trust' than you? No one!"

It was true, his mother was ahead of him here, and he sensed a real thawing of the ice of – dare he say it? – disbelief on his mother's part. He was not immune to disbelief himself. But Marcelle was patient. Look how many years (he said to himself) she had once waited to see her hunter again. Nevertheless, when it came to Shining Face, he felt an anxiety for her in her hazardous mission, and its outcome, to be entirely legitimate.

"I think I should tell you, he said, not only do I not know how Red Hair is faring, presumably in captivity, or have any idea where Big Nose is, but if and when Shining Face comes across him, the unfortunate thing is that she probably won't want to know *him.*"

"Why not?"

"Because nearly everybody in their community reckoned he was a bringer of bad luck." Lexin explained how Red Hair had come to foster is daughter Shining Face from babyhood, and the circumstances precipitating Big Nose's and later Red Hair's flight from their community. "I believe Big Nose is her true love, and I think – I just hope – that one day Shining Face will come to meet and love her father like she loves her foster mother.

"Anyway, so much for Shining Face. The last thing I saw on my PAS early this morning was Marcelle trying to stop her mum entering Phil's club, and having a row with her in front of a crowd of people. I suppose Marcelle will be back there tomorrow – *their* tomorrow."

"That was a plus, then." Felicitas was playing with her necklace of little stones that Grandpa Dubai had given her as a child. She stood up and went over to the tall window, then sat down at the little dressing table under it.

"Shining Face is tough inside, like Marcelle, Mother, and just as single minded. She still has her tools, of stone and antler, enough skins to keep her warm, and her precious cones to protect her. If she can just light a fire and roast that animal…" They were silent for a moment. "Marcelle desperately hopes they will all be re-united some day – the father, too. She *must* survive."

"Must?"

"Then Marcelle's own parents will surely come together again."

There was a long silence. Felicitas sat staring, unseeing, out of the tall window, where golden sunshine flooding the upper parts of the gently swaying trees indicated that the scene was being set for another perfect day. "You certainly know a lot about them all, don't you?" she said, quietly, "I don't know how they can be connected, these people, Lexin, but they are good people, and I hope they survive and everything works out for them. There now, you have got me caught up in it, but it's still frightening."

"*We* are connected too."

"Yes, I know. You have explained that." Felicitas's tone was one of near-belief, or was it tired resignation?

Suddenly she stood up. "Lexin, you are a good, kind boy. I admire you." she said, walking over to the bed, and as he stood up she threw her arms around him and hugged him. "You carry the weight of the world on your shoulders!" she declared.

There was the sound of movement in the house, and then of Lenica's voice. Felicitas did not let go of Lexin, and when Lenica entered in her running shorts she was still hugging him. Only after a final kiss did she let him go. "Don't you think he is a good, self-sacrificing, kind, loving, caring boy, Lenica?"

Lenica was used to seeing Felicitas's touching expressions of maternal affection – sometimes lavished even on herself. She smiled. "Yes Mother, he is, but you should tell him also that in politics…"

"…Oh, damn politics! It was not always like this."

Lenica firmed her lips a little and continued, "…that in politics it is a matter of finding concrete solutions, not of elaborating airy-fairy notions. That is all."

"You were not always quite so dismissive of such idealism, Lenica." There was something more than motherly concern in Felicitas's tone – a renewed questioning?

"It's the papers, Mother. They are reminding me of the old adage that politics is the art of the possible."

"Yes, very old. Positively twentieth century – or earlier."

"The 'Telegraph' is the latest to take up its position…"

"Its position? Latest? What can you be talking about, Lenica dear?"

Now she *was* being disingenuous, Lexin perceived, but Lenica took her words at face value: "Dear Mother, you really are a dreamer, aren't you?"

"Yes, I was and I am, and I am thankful for it," Felicitas agreed, "and before you get all serious, and before you worry poor Lexin any more – because between you and Olaf I think you are in danger of making him quite depressed – let us have lunch. I have got Robert to do everything today. You know I wanted to get into the garden. Quite neglected since our trip, the garden. Lexin, please give us five minutes to change! We can discuss the meeting of the Culture Committee later."

"I expect Father will be last," Lenica said. "The press will have nobbled him."

Lexin went across the central hall to the dining room on the west side of the house facing the arboretum. The room was peppered with family treasures and heirlooms. The latter might have been calculated to make a happier impression on him in his present mood had it not been for the haunting reality that the exquisite matushka dolls and other toys in their glass cases were his mother's (somehow) only as a (distant) consequence of the Russian princesses, to whom they had belonged, having been murdered by the Bolsheviks. As for the several original collaborative paintings of the new Group-Art School much admired by Olaf and expressing, with characteristic unsubtle boldness, new resolve in the face of disappointment with the pace of galactic advance, Lexin felt they missed the point. However, all this was more than counterbalanced by the grandstand view, through the long window, of the slight eminence from which the International Concert Hall soared above a sea of trees offering a bewildering array of species from temperate and subtropical regions of the globe.

For Lexin, now more than ever the scene symbolized the international co-operation in land reconstruction and climate control that had transformed this part of the Takla Makan – one of the most inhospitable places on Earth. Once no more than a remote and empty place such as was required in dangerous work for space exploration, now it was somewhere so important in its own right, and the sand-buried ruins of the City of the Planets had become the lush oasis and renowned centre of scientific and cultural excellence that was Galaxy City. He forced himself to try and imagine what would happen if stagnation were to occur, a period of no advance leading ultimately to a gradual abandonment of hope in what might yet be achieved. But he could not. The prospect was just unthinkable.

"Olaf will be here in a few minutes," Felicitas said, returning in purple splendour (clearly she had tired of blue, at last), followed by Lenica in jeans and shoulder drape. "He's just popped a message in my ear. I have telepathed Robert. I hope he won't go on about the Culture Committee meeting too much. Callum's been telling him about it. Apparently they have been talking about self deception, the subconscious and all that. Some people are even putting about a suggestion that our internal computer can lie and stop us deciphering properly."

"I tell you this," Lenica said, "the papers are getting a bit fed up with our Cultural Committee. I was just on the point of telling you, when you took pity on Lexin, that the 'Telegraph' thinks…"

"… The 'Telegraph' thinks we cannot go on for ever with our self-examination." Lexin sang, monotonously.

"'Self doubt' and 'time-wasting' were other terms used," Lenica said, tartly, "and as I expect Father will confirm, the Culture Committee itself may well be coming round to the same view, though George Callum is doing a lot of dithering, apparently."

"Perhaps that is a good thing in this instance – that he is dithering. His personal activity synthesizer might be able to confirm that – if he were to put a few questions to it."

"There is another thing, Lexin: the proposed historical review of the decipherment process, possibly some reworking of the text. Even the 'Guardian Interactive' is not pushing that idea quite so hard. Anyway, rest assured Father will go with The 'Telegraph'. You know what he's like." Reminded by the view beyond the window of so much progress achieved so patiently, it pained Lexin to hear the present problems being suddenly so much press fodder. It seemed at odds with the orderly progress over so many years, and he did not know what to say. But Lenica, settling down sideways on a dining chair, was bent on continuing. "To further inform you both about press positions," she went on after pausing for a moment to listen to some messages, "I am afraid the support for cessation pro-tem coupled with intensive self-analysis, which seems to be associated with you, dear brother, tends to be reserved for the tabloids – that is, press elements reflecting the views of those Normal citizens who claim never to have been in favour of developing our galactic relations at all."

"That is very perverse!" Felicitas exclaimed. "Many agree with what he is saying, only they are not the noisy ones,"

But Lenica seemed not to hear. "I have just picked up something from the 'City Independent': "More self-analysis might show us what fools we are". And there was something in the papers this morning, I remember." She sprang up and went into the living space, opening, as she returned, one of the dailies that Robert had been down to the city for. "Here we are, the leader in the 'Delhi Sketch'. It's about trust:

'Trust by all means, and we might get a big surprise, but not the one we want!'"

"That would be a complete travesty," Felicitas said angrily, stamping her foot and causing her bracelets to jangle.

"How do you know that?" Lenica was flicking through the pages. "It is not only the papers carrying all this, but 'World Blog Synthesizer'....all the opinion researchers, 'World Conversation Analyser', and the rest."

Were even *their* days numbered, Felicitas wondered – the days when these publications were patiently mulled over, thought about, used to generate constructive relationships, social harmony? Like the newspapers – once the unhurried biodigesters of all that was complex, controversial, or simply new in a world that had long since passed through the information explosion and emerged on the other side – were they not once again creating impasses where there were none and darkness where there were thin shafts of light? "Lexin wants the best for us all," she said. "He is the most public spirited of us all – and I mean all, enhanced and Normal."

"He doesn't appear like that."

Through the partially open window Lexin could hear the splash of water flowing among the trees where barrenness had existed before. It reminded him once again how the world was a better place since those shattering events of not so very long ago, and how all the things that had been revealed to him proved that out beyond time there were constant truths and a lasting goodness and rightness that the Bods knew about but we were choosing to ignore. At last words came to him: "Lenica, even with all our enhancements we are still children in galactic terms and need their help to succeed, but it has not occurred even to most of us Societans that the Bods are struggling – yes, *struggling* – to keep in touch with us."

Lenica had stopped flicking through the paper and was resting her head on her arms on the dining table, looking sideways at Lexin. "Struggling?"

"Yes, struggling."

"And the wormhole disaster? Is that the best they can do?," she asked when he had finished. "I don't know which of you is the bigger dreamer."

" And now let us say no more about it," Felicitas said. "I don't think your father will want to talk about all this, either."

"He won't," Lexin agreed as the sound of Olaf's voice announced his arrival and Robert came in and placed a silver soup tureen upon the table.

*   *   *

Ida went back to the Venus Club the next night. Marcelle left it for a night or two, then phoned her (at last she had her telephone number) to remind her about the idea of coming to live with her.

How could she possibly do that, she replied. She shouldn't be even seeing her.

"But I'll soon be eighteen," Marcelle protested.

"Phil will be paying me a hundred pounds for each of two nights a week, and I'm living in one of the apartments he rents out. Apart from that, I'm doing a little modelling for Phil's friend Brian – Brian Bluff, who photographs the lingerie for Phil – with me in it. Brian sells pictures to magazines."

Marcelle had to give it to her mum that she did not look forty-three. "Do you reckon Brian would take some pictures of *me*? I've got a good figure, haven't I?"

"Too good. Why don't you get together with that nice boyfriend of yours?"

"Old Markie? Haven't seen him since he went to Bathenhurst uni. We kind of fell out. He's written once or twice. He's doing computer science. Maybe the last time he wrote he was testing the water a bit, but I am afraid we've drifted too far apart."

"Pity. Seemed just your type."

"What type's that?"

"Sort of know where you're going."

"Where do you suppose I'm going?"

"I don't know, but I think *you* do. I think I know where *I'm* heading."

"What, to the pits, you mean?"

There was a silence. "Lenie put it more kindly", she said at length. "And Brian's really nice, Marcelle, very kind. It's not everything that you might assume. And he does pay me – a lot."

"What did you think I was thinking of? Fucking and all that? Well I didn't think it was all holiday magazines and shower advertisements."

"Marcelle! Do you have to use that word?"

"Well is there a better one?"

"Marcelle, this is not hardcore, okay? If this weren't on the phone I'd give you..." Her voice trailed away. "Marcelle, please don't come to the club on Thursday."

"Someone might employ me, you mean? Mother, if you can get me some work from this Brian bloke, I won't embarrass you again..."

The receiver had gone down.

A few days went by. Brian Bluff was not in the Yellow Pages, but she found him on the Internet and sent an E-mail by Hotmail at the library using Mark's account (she would delete everything afterwards), saying her name was Judy, she was eighteen, experienced, and needing cash to further her studies. Could she have an interview? A reply in the affirmative came back almost immediately: Could she go Friday evening? Telling the grandparents she was going to the cinema she stayed in town after work, having spent some minutes in the staff toilet making herself up and changing into her tightest jeans and a top both of which – according to Mark – revealed her ample qualities, though she did not care to dwell on what he might think of her now. Taking her normal clothes with her to change back into, with some difficulty she found 'B.D. Bluff Photographic' on the third floor of an old property in the newly emerging Bohemian quarter above the premises of 'Simone and Angélique. Holistic Full Body Renovation'.

Brian, fifty or so and with wavy hair down to his shoulders, and dressed not-very-smart-casual, was very nice to her indeed. Before she had been there more than ten minutes, in a room at the back of the building well blacked out and in a blaze of lights she had discarded most of her clothes behind a screen and a male assistant was taking streams of photos from different angles and in various poses "for a preliminary assessment". Another young woman hovered around. Then, passing her a glamorous silky gown to drape round herself and motioning her to a nearby rug-covered box seat he said,

"Excellent, Judy. I am sure we can be a considerable help to each other. You have the very relaxed attitude our work demands. I should warn you the work is quite... how could I put it?... demanding, even rigorous, but if you are agreed perhaps we could take this a little further..." Marcelle was just getting the feeling that things were warming up when there was a noise outside the door, which was flung open, and her mother was standing there, filling the doorway. It occurred to her how fetching she looked in a flamboyant tiered dress.

There was plenty of time to take it in because Ida was speechless for several long moments.

"Brian," she declared in that familiar voice which regularly preceded physical action, "you'd better ditch all those pictures. I don't suppose you realise this is my daughter and she's underage. Didn't you ask her age? Is this how you do business?" And then, turning to Marcelle, "I'll see you outside – when you've dressed." The photographer and the woman had disappeared into an adjoining room, where Ida pursued them. From behind the screen where she had gone to put her clothes on, Marcelle heard her mum come back in the room and say, "I know where your stuff appears, Brian, and if I see any pictures of Marcelle – and believe me her mother will *always* recognize her – I might consider some action. Goodbye!"

"I must say you are a person of conviction," she said when Marcelle joined her.

"So are you. How did you know I was here?"

"You must have sent your E-mail to me as well, by mistake."

"How could I? I don't know your E-mail address."

"For God's sake don't do it again, Marcelle, or we'll have lots of trouble. Anyway, it's wrong."

"I enjoyed it."

"Don't say that, Marcelle." Ida was all but in tears.

Marcelle put her arm around her. "Can I come back with you? Bugger the Social.."

"No, you can't. Phil's coming round. Ring me tomorrow."

She found her in a nice terrace house in a smart-ish street not so far from Phil's warehouse and showroom. She was padding around in slacks and slippers, with hair freshly washed and netted and no make-up. Marcelle could see more lines on her face than she remembered.

"I'll just go and make a cup of tea," Ida said. "I've got to go out in about twenty minutes. Don't look at the pictures too hard,"

It was all quite posh, actually. Just the odd item of the old furnishings from Hawthorn Road could be seen around the room, like some nineteen-thirties bookends with a trellis-and-roses theme and some figurines, but for the most part the décor was classy, with green and gold striped wallpaper, and period stuff that looked genuine and Indian rugs on wooden oak strips. It was definitely more worthy of the title 'drawing room', she thought, than the Wharton's. The pictures which covered the walls were definitely more interesting than theirs, too: explicit line drawings of sexual acts, the crystal-clear photographs of spotless naked ladies in interesting positions, and tucked away on illuminated built-in shelves in discreet corners the small photos, montages and drawings of the genitalia of both sexes in various stages of arousal – all immaculately framed or clipped on backings. Looking out of the big sash window she had a good view of a tennis club just opposite, while the new City Hospital gleamed through the trees.

"I like it, Mum," she said when Ida returned with a cup of tea for her and what she said was a gin and coke for herself. "What does it cost?"

"Nothing. It's all right, I suppose. Sit down. I'll stay standing. If I sit down I'll never get up. I'm so tired. I'll have to go in a few minutes."

"All *right*? Is that all?" Marcelle sat down in a huge, leather-bound armchair.

"I'm not getting too attached to it. It may not last long. The stripping's awful. It kills me, and he says I should smile more – not too much, just a bit more. Then there's the lingerie, and I've gone and upset his photographer." She paused, put her drink down, went over to the window. "I shouldn't even be talking to you about this, your mother, but he says there are these men who just go for my age…"

"…waiting with their tongues hanging out."

"You're very graphic, Marcelle. But I suppose you always did say what you thought. And with an imagination like yours…" She had turned and was looking at her. "Yes, I suppose they do. He says I could even make a good fist of lap dancing." Marcelle couldn't stop a little smile. "Yes, I know. Funny, isn't it? I won't do it, or the hardcore stuff." She drew in her breath, sighed. It was interesting how the lines on her cheeks and around her mouth seemed to take some of the severity of her away, as though in some deference due to age..

"There's some of that, too? What's he like? Does he love you?"

"Tall, dark and handsome, isn't he? Loves all the girls." Her voice had perked up a bit.

"But why you specially? I mean, all this…" Marcelle gestured about her.

"Must you ask? I must go in a minute, Marcie. I'm on tonight."

She could not remember when her mother had last called her 'Marcie'. "I'm going to see Dad," she said. "He's done six months delivering groceries since finishing with the carpet cleaning. He wants to drive trams. When I last saw him he wasn't very well again." Then she noticed her mother was not listening – or was it that she was trying not to hear?

"Why do you come to see me. Are you patronizing me?" she asked. She was staring vacantly out of the window.

"Do I seem to be?"

"No." Ida blew her nose, seemed to be shedding a tear. She picked up a handset and phoned for a taxi. Then she said, "You're not a naughty girl really, are you Marcie? Why do you bother?"

"Bother?"

"About me."

"I've said before, I love you. I always have."

"Go now, Marcelle. Go, please."

Marcelle picked up the shopping she had with her, gave her mother a little kiss on the cheek, and went out with a brief "See you!"

It was a couple of miles to where her father had been living, across the city centre, over the river, past the university and through the Memorial Park. There was a free bus, but she decided to walk. The day was warm for October, but rain was threatened. They said a cold front might mark the start of autumn, and she was glad she had a little umbrella tucked away in her bag. The trees around the hospital stretched tall above her like guardsmen. She crossed the boulevard into the Inner Ring and mixed with the crowds in the East Side. Passing Fenninghams and Mackenzies department stores, after popping into a chemist's, dropping some shoes off at a repairer's and picking another pair up, she turned into the newly enhanced and extended covered Mall. It was teeming with shoppers, students and schoolchildren coming out of the schools and colleges, and quite a few tourists, not to mention multifarious touts and vendors.

She came to the new part of the mall, and a much advertised promotion of outdoor equipment by 'Venturelife Expeditions', where a brawny youth tried unsuccessfully to interest her in inflatable camp beds and microlight rucksacks. There was an impressive mock-up of a stone-age encampment under the banner 'How it was'. It was crawling with mums and kids, and there was even a replica fire in a stone hearth with 'women' dressed in skins tending it and roasting an animal. Others were sitting around on mock stones and fashioning 'stone' tools. She stood watching for a moment, fascinated. There were artificial trees and primitive shelters draped in 'snow'. The odd flurry of feathery white flakes blew across, emitted from some concealed source to an appropriate wintry sound accompaniment.

Suddenly the men were coming back, shouting and singing and bearing booty, including four of them carrying a reindeer. Everybody was on their feet. A little jump in time, and the men were squatting and eating, and women were waiting on them, sometimes feeding them, touching them and being touched, laughing. Suddenly one woman's face came out at Marcelle like a beacon, and Marcelle caught her breath. Next to her was this guy who looked older and important and was clad in a splendid outfit of leopard skin held together by a thick cord that looked just like a lion's tail. They were sitting a little apart from the rest, and the man was keeping her to himself, fondling her when his hands were not too busy with his food. Despite his tender attentions he had an unattractive appearance and an aura of cruelty and domination. She was not resisting him, but looked indifferent to him.

Marcelle would have recognized Red Hair anywhere. She had followed her often enough. She no longer looked as wiry and agile as as when she had seen her carrying Big Nose just before they had taken her captive. She too was dressed differently from the others, with a long skirt of strips of skins in different colours and sewn together...

Then suddenly it was all mums and kids and the false stuff again, and Marcelle was walking out past the all-weather this's and that's, and on towards the other end of the Mall and the university grounds with a new spring in her step and a renewed hope.

So she was still there and they were still apart, then, she and Big Nose. Where was *he*? Still wandering? And the daughter – Shining Face? And how come she knew her name?

When Marcelle arrived at the end of the Mall there was no bridge over the river, and no university buildings were to be seen among the trees beyond it. To be sure, she was at the river, *a* river at any rate, but far from seeing the hordes of students that would normally be there, not a person was in sight. As for the rest, there was a familiarity about it, but the more she looked the more it was different. The white, multi-layered shapes slightly to the right, which from the direction in which the water was flowing appeared, curiously, to be *upstream*, might have been the halls of residence – but those should be downstream from where she was. Or were they just a cloud shape above the trees? And where were the distant warehouses marking the position of the old canal wharves? Were they being obscured by a trick of the light?

Puzzled and a little frightened, but keeping her cool, unable to cross the river Marcelle decided to try and follow it upstream until she could do so. Now she perceived that she was alone on a raised promontory full of thorny thickets. The river was wider than she had imagined. She began to follow its course as best she could, the skins wrapped around her sore feet miraculously protecting them from injury by stones and thorns. Was it Lexin's whispered encouragements that she heard? Was it Toothy's hands that she felt guiding her as she fought her way through bogs and brambles, under fallen trees, up and over tree-packed spurs running down to the water? Her bag of shopping was more like a pouch slung in front of her. It contained two or three large stones. She knew she could not afford *not* to have them at the ready, heavy though they were for her thin, weary body to bear. The pouch with all her *little* belongings, and another heavy with dried meat of the deer – were slung behind her. The new spear, meticulously pointed after another long struggle with the antler, made her feel good, for who could know what unsuspecting source of food might suddenly be encountered on rounding a spur. Just at first, for one fleeting moment she had been afraid she might have pinched it from that sideshow in the Mall – until she felt how solid it was.

By the time the light began to go, and she was realizing she would have to give up the idea of crossing that day and set about looking for somewhere safe to sleep, on getting to a slightly higher point she found herself overlooking a big curve in the river where it had broadened – so far as could be seen in the level landscape – into muddy shallows. Surely the moment had come to conquer her tiredness and put behind her this river which in its overflowing anger had almost deprived her of all hope and now stood in her way!

For a day and a night she had lain exhausted under the yew knowing nothing, and it was on the following morning that she had struggled in her weakness down to the receding water and seen the deer drowning and managed somehow to grab its body as it floated past. It had saved her life. Each succeeding day had provided her with more strength and more reassurance, and ever since the events of those two days – the saving of the duck and the gift of the deer – it had felt almost as though their lives, Toothy's and hers, were in each other's hands. She could not say she had been surprised to have found a deep spear mark in the deer's body when she had prepared it. He too it surely was who had given her the confidence to cook a big animal in the same way that she had dealt with the duck, this time collecting many stones from the shallows of the now placid river to line the much bigger and deeper hole. For sure, his hands must have been upon hers as she spun that drill and with great difficulty created the fire and later dragged the deer to the hot stones and covered it. She had decided to take the opportunity of staying put and building up her strength as long as the meat was good to eat, and only then to move on (and good it was, and well worth the labour of having dried some while it was fresh!).

Finally there had been the dream of last night that had filled her with renewed determination, a dream that had been at the same time both wonderful and terrible: wonderful because her mother lived, and that was the news she most wanted to hear. But ugh! How loathsome was that man being fed by her, putting his hands everywhere! How vividly the dream had brought her mother back to her. It had been years, but the same eyes, the same anxious, uncertain eyes, enticing eyes, determined, occasionally wilful, angry eyes, yes, but anxious! How terrible it was now to see her brought so low. But enough daydreaming! It was the dream that had finally made her decide that she was strong enough to go on, and for the whole of this day she had made her way upstream hoping to find a place to cross...

Baring her feet, she put the thonged hide that had covered them, and whatever belongings she could, into her stones pouch to keep them dry. Then, taking off her deer hide and her warm undergarments and carrying them, too, with everything else over her shoulder, she waded naked into the river, steadying herself with the blunt end of her spear. It was slow work crossing, and further in fact than she had thought. When the water reached nearly to her shoulders it was only with difficulty that for a considerable distance she managed to keep her balance and prevent everything from being soaked, and for many stumbling steps near the opposite bank she had to carry the spear between her teeth. When finally she struggled onto the bank, Shining Face lay upon it for some time before summoning the strength to dry herself with one of the hides and clothe herself. There was very little light left as she set off again with all her belongings through low-lying country in the direction of the sunset. Sleep would have to await the first sheltered spot.

For her part, once on the other side of the river Marcelle found not its boggy hinterland but the Arts Faculty of the University and its halls of residence – as if she had crossed by the bridge as usual –, and visible beyond it the towering trees of the Memorial Park arboretum. Taking stock for a moment it occurred to her that Shining Face had been travelling only since the spring and that it was almost as though the last two years in her own life had not existed and she had missed nothing. She was amazed – and glad.

Still clutching her bag and her umbrella as she walked along the familiar path towards her father's, trying to disentangle her thoughts from those occupying the mind of Shining Face, she fell to thinking about the boy Toothy. Impressed by what she had gathered about his remarkable skills in spearing and throwing, his prowess in running and his courage, she might have felt envious of Shining Face were it not for an overwhelming relief that Toothy seemed always to be hovering there like a guardian angel, ready to pluck his girlfriend from all dangers and keep her moving against all the odds, for surely in the end she herself and Shining Face shared a common goal.

The finding of Shining Face, and Shining Face's determination, now gave a fresh impetus to her mission. If she could not recall her having any thoughts of her father, Big Nose, but only about the woman she believed to be her mother, Marcelle knew this must be because neither Red Hair nor anyone else had had any kind things to say about him. But Lexin had said they had a task to do which was "beyond time", and what both he himself and she herself were seeking "would come about". Since it seemed that all their lives were intertwined, this surely meant that Shining Face would finally come to a realisation that her father was a good and courageous man and that she would hope to reunite the two of them just as she, Marcelle, was seeking to reconcile her own parents.

Marcelle had almost given up hope of gaining Mark's sympathy in *her* quest to reunite her parents, and although there had been a couple of other boyfriends she had never felt she wanted to let them into her 'other life' She believed Lexin, the beautiful boy far in the future. How she wished she could see him again! Yes, he was a bit short – barely taller than she was – and that wasn't so good in a man. But all that faded behind that agility of body and mind which brought him instantly to stand in front of her and take her hands, enlivened those lips from which issued such mellifluous tones, and animated those features so earnest and yet verging on humour that understood everything (almost), and promised so much.

There was no sign of her father when Marcelle arrived at the place near the canal. The pub was closed. After she had rung the bell repeatedly, a dyed redhead with jangly jewellery came to the door and said she had heard he had had a fall and been taken to the City Hospital. Something at work, she said, and she was owed two hundred pounds in rent.

"I'll pay it," Marcelle said. "Just give me a day or two."

"I've re-let it from Monday," the woman said.

"It's gone then."

"Yes, 'e said to. Are you his daughter?"

"Yes."

"Ran away from your mum, did he? Ought to be ashamed of 'imself."

"Ran away?" Marcelle was furious.

"I put two and two..."

"I'll be back in two hours for his stuff," Marcelle said. "Goodbye!"

She found her dad in a surgical ward with his leg in traction. He had fallen and broken it at the tram depot on the same day as he was commencing training as a driver. He was philosophical about the fact that he would very likely not now be able to be a driver – ever.

"Ironic," he said. "Fell getting out of the damn thing. Don't tell your mother, Marcie. I don't want her coming fussing. She is still working for Phil, is she?"

"Just, but she doesn't think it will last. And I think it's my fault." She told him what had happened at the photographer's.

"My God, Marcie dear, you don't change, do you? It's no wonder your mother used to do her nut."

"Aren't you going to do yours?"

"I s'pose I ought to, but not today. My leg's bad enough, never mind my nut."

"She didn't hit me, but I'm pretty sure she hit the photographer's assistant."

"Blimey!" Tom went very thoughtful, staring at the yet untouched plate of schnitzel and mashed potato perched on the tray in front of him. "All that hitting, Marcie...when we were at home..."

"Forget it, Dad. Home was home."

"Was it?"

"Yes. Now look, your room's gone,"

"Ah, you saw the lady."

"Yes, and I'll pay her and take all your bits and bobs to Culver and keep them in my room. I'll find you another place. Look! In not many weeks I'll be eighteen. I can get a place of my own then, and you could come and live there."

"No, no, that is just what I must not do. I must make my own bed and lie in it, and you must keep your own life for yourself." It seemed pathetic, saying that as he lay there unable even to arrange his long body comfortably. Her father's face was ashen. It must have been the shock.

"That's just what I'm not going to do, Dad. I haven't even given up on the two of you coming together."

Tom had turned his head away, towards the window and the big cranes hovering over the assertive concrete of the new university extensions and the East Side developments beyond. "Nor have I," he said at length, "but your mother would have to make the move."

"You might have to go to *her* one day. She may need you."

"As long as it's not today. Bless you, anyway!" he said, turning towards her with difficulty. Then as she collected up her things he added, "Keep reminding me!"

"I'll come tomorrow, Dad. Ta-ta for now! Don't worry about anything." As she walked out of the hospital to catch the bus to Culver she was glad she had talked about them getting together. There had been a noticeable lift in his voice. But then, he had always been like that: open, waiting for a signal, an encouragement...

Tom's leg failed to heal perfectly, necessitating repeated operations, and he spent many weeks in hospital. Grandpa and Grandma visited often, but he would not hear of living with them when he came out. Ida had phoned up a few days after the accident and apparently said she would not come and fuss over him. She was sorry about his lodgings. She was parting company with Phil, her only real regret (apart from the income, naturally) being the loss of those luxurious deep armchairs with several cushions each, which made her feel so good. However it was no surprise to Marcelle when she soon announced that she intended to sign on with an escort agency in the city centre and had found a nice flat by the river promenade.

In the November Marcelle became eighteen. Grandma and Grandpa – especially Grandma – didn't look pleased when Marcelle said she was going with her mother to dine at an expensive place in town and then back to see her new flat. She had told them about the escort agency. They would have found out anyway. Grandma was always asking her about her mother.

"You know you can live here as long as you like," Grandma said. She was having trouble getting a brooch central in her silk scarf before going into the village. "Oh darn it, it still isn't right!"

"Grandma does like to get things just right, doesn't she?" Grandpa observed, waiting patiently by the front door, the car in the drive bulging with a load of discarded items for the Conservative Association bring-and-buy. Marcelle was leaving to catch the bus. She could not resist a smile at Grandpa's tolerance.

"And if you want to go to college, to do teacher training or anything," Grandma was saying, "you know you need not worry about the tuition fees and all that. I think you could still go back and do 'A' levels."

"Yes, Grandma," she heard herself saying, "I'm very grateful." It was true that she had been talking about helping in the primary school in Culver. It seemed that the grandparents had decided she was their last chance to feel that their procreative efforts had not been wasted (her father had no brothers or sisters).

"I should take her advice," her mother said when they arrived at the new place after dining at a new Chinese restaurant in the East Side. "Start the long journey to successful womanhood – if Grandpa will pay what's necessary..." The flat on the embankment was large, and furnished contemporary style with chunky, well-padded chairs and sofas and plenty of white leather, glass, and lighting of intriguing design. It seemed her mum was sharing it with a young Brazilian woman, Nadia, a big-busted brunette who could charge six hundred a night and had her own suite. "This is her internet entry," Ida said, flourishing some printout. The colourful pages seemed full of big breasts and bottoms, and Gstrings threatening to cut her in two.

"She's gorgeous," Marcelle exclaimed. "She's got the boobs, but on consideration I reckon I've got the bottom."

"Marcelle! I'm not sure I should have asked you here! I just wanted you to be under no illusions about the sort of person I am." They were sitting back in one of those big sofas with coffees and 'After Eights'.

"You'll always be the same Mum to me."

Ida seemed short of words. "I shall only do 'out' calls," she said at length. "Can't have blokes coming in and out all the time, can I Marcelle?"

"Make a mess of the carpet with their shoes, too." A little smile passed between them. It was the smallest of signs, but somehow it neutralised so much anger of the past... ("Marcelle, you never even *think* of wiping your feet, do you?" etc.)

"Tony – he's the proprietor – he runs a very nice massage parlour, too," Ida added later, walking back with Marcelle along the riverside avenue towards the city centre and a cab rank. "Nadia works there as well." Marcelle realised she had passed many times its extremely discreet portal advertising: 'Holistic massage. Stress Relief. Shiatsu. Acupuncture'. "Marcie," her mother added, "you follow Grandpa's advice. He's a good man, and he can help you a lot."

"Don't remember you saying that sort of thing about Grandpa before."

"We've never talked about anything much before, have we – not till our little set-to a few weeks back. Marcie, yours is another world, a fresh new world."

"Are we that different, Mum? You know, I reckon I could outbid Nadia!"

"Marcelle! You are the end! No, Marcelle, don't ever do anything like this." There was a long silence. The wind was cold off the river. Marcelle wished she had been able to buy one of those rockhopper windproof high-necked coats she had seen in Venturelife the other day in the Mall, and worn it instead of her denim jacket. "Marcie," her mother said, "You say you love me, but God knows why."

"Does it matter why?"

"Well this is how I am. Heaven knows if I shall ever be any different."

They had come up to the parapet of the University Bridge. Marcelle's thoughts turned to her encounter – how could she put it? – her close walk there with Shining Face. She thought of Red Hair, and of Shining Face walking alone into one of those winters to find her, but a question had come to the surface which she was burning to ask: "Mother, do you love *me* just a little bit?"

"Marcie!" Ida seized her daughter, and they hugged each other for a long time, oblivious of the night-outers, the students, the old folk out for a stroll... Then she said, "I am anxious for both of us, Marcie," and as Marcelle climbed into a taxi (her mother gave her the money for it) grasped her hand, adding, "Marcie, tell Dad I am sorry." She was crying.

Tom left hospital after Christmas, and Marcelle quite quickly found him another couple of rooms, unfurnished, ground floor, near the Memorial Park about a mile from the city centre in the inner suburb of Kinley's Fields. It seemed clean and practical. She was just able to make a month's rent down payment out of some savings she had made from her supermarket earnings. Grandpa helped her take furniture from Culver – where most of the furniture from Hawthorn Road had been stored in the spare bedroom or distributed around the bungalow. He insisted on making a local authority bond investment for her as a 'counterbalance' to her generosity towards her father. Of course it was worth a whole lot more.. She gave him a big kiss – something she had never done before.

By the February Tom had got a job cleaning toilets in the parks. To Marcelle it was almost as if the job were a self-imposed penance, and it must have imposed considerable strain on his leg, but he said it was infinitely better than cleaning carpets and no worse than delivering groceries, and he was more or less his own boss. Marcelle looked in often and found him looking after himself well and keeping his couple of ground-floor rooms neat and spotless.

Except briefly at Christmas she had not seen her mother since going with her to the flat, but at Christmas she had said the massage (for which she had trained in evening classes for six weeks) was going well; she was quite popular among the male clientele. She had found a niche. About the escort side she was not so forthcoming, but on being pressed further she said everything was fine. When Marcelle phoned her and told her the latest about Tom she just said,

"Who would be a man?" – by which she assumed she was referring to a man's need to assert himself, to maintain his self-esteem. But then she added, "Come to that, who'd be a woman. I'm not very well. May have to go for some tests. Not been right for a good while, actually."

Marcelle left her grandparents home at Culver and found a little first-floor flat above a hairdresser's a stone's throw from where her father was now living (the Memorial Park was just across the road), furnishing it with second-hand stuff advertised in the paper plus some more Hawthorn Road items still in store in the bungalow ('Just check it out with your mum,' Tom said – which she did over the phone). It was good to be close to her dad, but she was more concerned now about her mother, and wondered if she was hiding something from her.

CHAPTER NINE

The strips of meat of the baby deer that she had been able to dry in sun and smoke after the flood lasted a long time, and her strength increased, but by the time the events at the flooded river were a whole moon away Shining Face was becoming short of food, and in rationing herself to a scarcely visible amount of the remaining meat in her bark dish each day she was becoming exhausted again. The absence of a big river and what it might (in the absence of mishaps) provide in the way of food was hardly compensated by the addition of mushrooms and berries and then hazel- and chestnuts readily available as an early winter approached. Its advance was clearly visible ahead, where snow was increasing on mountains that came a little nearer each day. She had never seen mountains before – only heard tell of them. The way now lay predominantly upwards and through forest. Once, close by, she saw smoke and heard sounds suggesting a community of the other people with the overhanging brow. The smell of cooking wafted towards her. These were the first humans she had come near since leaving home, but she hastened on, anxious to avoid all encounters.

Each morning she would take the fir cones out of her pouch and hold them tight in her left hand as she made the first few steps of the day. The power in them sustained her when all else seemed ever darker – the darkness of creeping anxiety as much as darkness of the shortening days, anxiety about her strength, her ability to find enough food. Of the certainty of finding her mother, provided she herself could hold out, she had no doubt.

With the weather becoming rainier, increasingly she was driven to stop in sheltered places longer, and try and get a fire to stay alight and keep her warm between short sallies to search for food, but it became harder and harder to find dry places and dry wood – and food. Finally she entered a deep valley through which a wide torrent flowed towards her from the mountains close ahead, their white-flecked precipices now looming high up behind the tall evergreens covering the lower slopes. At the sight of some small crevices in rocks just above the river she decided to investigate. The crevices offered limited shelter, and by blocking one of them about two men's height higher up with branches retrieved from the river bank it was possible to keep it dry enough to make a fire on the flat rock forming its base. Earlier, she had picked up the fresh carcase of a red fox being scavenged by crows, and she skinned it and roasted it by resting it upon stones taken from the river and raised up around the fire. It was not very appetising, but she made herself eat most of it, leaving the rest to dry out on the hot stones. The crevice was a little wider than had at first appeared, especially further back, and she was able to keep warm without getting burned. She had never slept so close to a fire, but it was becoming so cold that even the awesome closeness of the flames was endurable.

Then came the snow, snow at first mixed with the rain, then on its own, thickly and for two days. It was all Shining Face could do to keep the fire alight, and it was a case of a starvation diet. During this time there was nothing to be done but wait, moving and eating as little as possible, mostly roasted nuts,

When the sky cleared, the cold became intense and something Toothy once said now assumed overwhelming importance: "They say the only good thing about the mountains is the caves. The caves provide shelter from the cold." She could hear his squeaky voice now. Maybe the steeper and the rockier the slopes, the greater would be the probability of finding a really good cave.

The going higher up, when Shining Face set out again, was indeed hard and steep, but she was glad to be on the move, and the walking, and sometimes clambering, helped to keep her warm. In places where the snow had swept down the steep valley side it had drifted to depths that took it over her head and there was no obvious alternative but to seek a higher route that forced her across treacherous slides of snow and rocks. On two nights it was possible to make a snow shelter at what were no more than angles in the rocks. Surrounding herself with every fur and skin she had it was very snug in those, but she was more frightened there than she was of sleeping by the fire – frightened of being too comfortable and falling asleep only to freeze to death –, and had to make great efforts to pull herself together at first light and move on. Far up the valley a barrier appeared in the form of an impressive, ice-coated waterfall that reminded her of the long, ragged beard of an old man. To avoid this she was compelled to climb much higher, eventually arriving, exhausted, in another high valley possessing a river of its own.

Desperately hungry now, and struggling in the late afternoon in a dazed state, the realisation came to her that she was staring across the new river at what appeared to be a cave in the side of the mountain opposite, which grew as she got nearer into a yawning black gash in the vertical face, surrounded by scrub.

Having crossed the small, partially frozen river easily enough it took an age to get up near the cave, weighed down as she was with everything she possessed, and as she stumbled through the snow she became very afraid, remembering that other thing which Toothy had said about caves:

"Remember that what's good shelter for humans is good for hyenas and lions, bears, rhinos and anything else."

Even if it had not been necessary to approach the cave mouth step by slow step because of the steepness and the snow, she would have done so regardless, stopping, listening and sniffing the air repeatedly.

At the entrance, when she finally made it, there were bones everywhere, but at a cursory glance no hints of any human occupation past or present. 'Somebody' had had some good meals here, though, Shining Face said wryly to herself, but after a cautious snoop around to check for hibernating individuals she decided the next meal there would be hers – though she could not imagine where it would come from. Thankfully depositing her load just inside the entrance, she sank down and, against all her best instincts and despite her hunger, fell asleep there and then.

Fortunately, it was only the cold that woke her, and most of what was left of the light was spent getting a fire going just inside the cave using wood gathered close by that had remained dry owing to an overhang sprouting small bushes above the cave entrance. At dusk, alerted by the sighting of a hare just outside the cave, she discovered a hare hole, a crevice in the rock, tucked away just inside the entrance. A patient wait with a heavy stick rewarded her with two dead hares. A scattering of loose rocks on the cave floor enabled her to build a support around the fire, and although hardly able to stand with weariness, driven by hunger Shining Face very quickly skinned one of the hares by the light of the fire and cooked her best meal over it since Toothy's deer, devouring it eagerly. Although it was definitely less cold deep inside the cave, after stoking up the fire and adding wet stuff to make it last, for fear of being trapped she cautiously made a pile of her skins near the entrance and slept on them, wrapping herself once again in her rhino fur.

Awakening finally in the morning feeling much better, she discovered that by struggling up the mountainside she could emerge over the top of the cave, where there were many deer prints. However, much of the day was spent dragging dead wood up from the river through the snow and allowing it to dry by the fire which she had managed to resuscitate, and also carrying up skins full of water to fill a big skin water holder which she set up at the back of the cave. In the late afternoon she took her spear and a pouch of stones and again scrambled up over the cave to get a closer look at the lie of the steeply rising land behind. The snow was too deep to go far, but by incredible good luck on the way back she inadvertently drove a young deer over the sheer drop above the cave entrance, killing it. Incredibly, another met the same fate almost immediately.

With the precipice promising such a fruitful food source it seemed a good idea to stay the winter out in the cave rather than risk struggling on. It was a decision she did not come to regret when, for days on end, sometimes fog, sometimes swirling snow would hide the far side of the valley, isolating her in total whiteness. Much of the time was spent first of all dealing with the two animals chased over the precipice: gutting, skinning and dismembering them, cutting up the best meat, roasting some of it for immediate needs and starting to smoke the rest on hot rocks by the fire.. The skins she buried in snow to make them ready for scraping and preparation. Luckily, the hares in the cave entrance never went into long sleep or learned by their mistake of appearing at the same time each evening. Thus although it was some time before she chased another deer over the precipice, there was for the time being enough meat to keep her going, and being resigned to remaining at the cave there was plenty of opportunity to sharpen her tools and make new ones, build up a reserve of firewood from logs washed down the river and also make herself a permanent water bag to carry water up from there.

Eventually the sleet and snow relented, and for a whole moon a searing wind piled the snow into huge drifts in some places and swept it away entirely from others. When the cold abated slightly, despite what she had thought earlier it seemed this might after all be the moment to press on. It would be just too easy to stay there and finish up going nowhere. Another storm might cut her off for ages. One afternoon she went up to have another reconnoitre on the steepening slopes of rocks and (in the wind-scoured places) tufts of grass and moss leading up the mountainside at the back of the cave, taking only her spear and a few throwable rocks in her pouch for safety. Venturing higher than she had climbed before, it was possible to see the mountains stretching far away in the direction she wanted to go, and in the farthest distance long, grey clouds like strips of rhino fur lay right across the sky, shutting off the most distant view. She wondered whether it could be true that there really was another sea out there?

Returning towards the cave congratulating herself on the absence of competition for its shelter during her time there, on looking down from above the entrance she saw five or six lions standing sniffing the air. Hardened though she was to frightening situations, frozen to the spot, Shining Face shook with fear. Collecting herself, however, she could not fail to appreciate her luck at not meeting them at the cave entrance, and that not only was she high above them, but also, while her scent must be everywhere, they seemed not to have seen her. She shrank back out of sight. Should she go away for a bit and hope that they would too, hopefully before they found her or sniffed out the considerable amount of dried meat that she had stored – in several places as a precaution? What if they stayed here? How would she ever retrieve her skins, including the new ones she had spent so much time preparing, and the precious rhino fur, and her stores of fruits and nuts – as well as the meat? There had been plenty of time to get herself well supplied and organised. Then there was the beautiful knot from a dead tree that she had found, and which looked like Toothy's face, and most important of all there were her cones, her precious cones. All she had with her was the skins she had on her and her necklace of seashells, and her spear and a few pretty useless rocks. Disaster! One thing was clear: if she was not going to go away and wait she must at least try to make herself safe

Creeping forward, she saw one of the animals entering the cavern. It was not a good sign, but there was one thing in her favour. She knew there was a place where she might hope to hide and hopefully await their departure. Earlier she had discovered an entrance to the cave from above which she had been able to explore using burning embers. Close by her now, it was an obscure, small hole in the ground opening into a tunnel which led beneath where she was standing to the roof of the cave below. Down there it was inaccessible from the cave floor – inaccessible to her, at least, and, as far as she had been able to tell in the near-darkness at the back of the cave, to large animals as well. Managing to get to this upper entrance without being seen, she squeezed down – it was easier now than it would have been a year ago when she was not so thin. The tunnel was rough, but in places quite large, and at two or three points it admitted a little light through small crevices above. Roars echoing from below sounded much too close for comfort, and very quickly she recognized the smells that lions emit – there had been lion scares at the camp – and could now hear them grunting and growling ominously. With the air rising in the cavern there was a chance they would not catch her scent above them, and she waited in a small widening of the tunnel, hoping that the obvious animal remains that were down there would satisfy them and that then they might go away. Just a chance. She remained there till well after the middle of the day, listening, sweating with fear as she heard them padding about, in and out of the cave.

Shining Face was beginning to realise that they were not going to leave in a hurry when suddenly there was a commotion and she sensed one of the animals was very close – close enough to be able to hear it breathing. There was only one way it could have got there, and that was by clambering onto another animal and jumping. She remembered now that they were supposed to do that. How she wished she had the cones to hold! She was terrified. It was a forlorn hope, but if she could injure one it just might deter the others. What else was there to hope for?

"Toothy, help me now," she whispered, holding the spear pointing firmly in front of her and keeping quite still. Now the lion was directly before her in the darkness, growling. There was a rush, and the blunt end of the spear was driven back against the rock wall. Amazingly, it did not break, but she lost her hold on it. The animal seemed surprised, and that gave her time to find the shaft again. She decided to go for the lion rather than wait for it to attack her, and lunged forward. The flint point went into something soft, but the beast broke free. Nothing happened immediately, and she thought of Toothy again and let him take hold of her spear. There was a tremendous roar, and the lion came at her again, but she was ready for it and jabbed forward with renewed force in the darkness. She guessed the point of the spear must at least have gashed its neck, but again it broke away, growling ferociously. Suddenly there seemed to be more lions, snarling and jostling. Surely there was no hope now! It must have been another one of them that attacked her the next time, because it came from the side, the weight of it throwing her, dazed, against the rock wall. The next moment she was lying on the floor of the cave, a lion standing over her, sniffing her. A casual grope and a claw ripped into her side. Then something completely unexpected happened...

If the lions' roaring had been loud, then the huge trumpeting that suddenly filled the cavern seemed to shake its very walls. The lion grabbed her leg and started to drag her, now barely conscious. There was another great bellow from below, followed by many others, and to her amazement, at that the lion let go of her and headed away downwards. The other lions, too, must have retreated, for she could hear no more of the growling and snarling around her. It dawned on her in her dazed state that it could not be lions bellowing like that. Only one animal could have created such a din. And probably only a herd of them could distract a pride of lions. That Toothy must have heard her was her last thought as she lost consciousness.

*   *   *

With his synthesizer 'on', and following the course of events in his monitor, or sometimes nowadays directly in his head, Lexin viewed Marcelle's colourful but unsuccessful attempts to woo her mother away from her dubious lifestyle with some alarm as well as disappointment. He did not seriously consider, though, that she would be swallowed up in its ramifications herself. As for the father, sometimes Lexin wondered whether Marcelle had an unjustified faith in him and in his desire – and his ability – some day to win Ida back...

"It's no good trying to hurry things," he would say. "Your mother has her own life, her own decisions to make," as if the same did not apply to him and he could only react to situations and not create them.

And yet... Lexin had to admit that Marcelle moved towards the hoped-for fulfilment of her objectives seemingly with never a falter in her love for her father or any doubt about such an outcome. Her strange power, her dedication, amazed him. If he had been a Normal he could, as he admitted to his mother, have indeed fallen hopelessly in love with her. Felicitas teased him good naturedly about 'his' Marcelle, and her efforts – "not entirely without effect, apparently" (in his mother's words) – to help *her* mother "get back to her real self" (his words).

"So did you actually see her at that fellow Brian's photographic place...I mean, *in all her glory*?" she asked, naughtily, and with a little giggle that made her purple drop earrings rustle and glitter in the sunlight. They were in the garden below the terrace, she in a patterned floral top and cream trousers and carrying a basket which she put down occasionally to snip off lilac blooms, and he in old jeans and sweat shirt, walking beside her. A dense lilac shrubbery fell back towards the side of the garden, beyond which could be heard the sound of cascading water, and beyond that the challenging harmonies and instrumentation of what he recognized as Reissler's great 'Symphony for Nature and Man' issuing from the Concert Hall beyond.

"Mother, you are taunting me. You know that we have different feelings from Normals. And things have moved on, as I have said. Marcelle is eighteen. She has left her grandparents to be near her father. She is a sensible, fine young woman."

"Ah," she said, snipping off a bloom, "but I thought you might have switched off and taken a peek."

She meant switch off the part of the internal nanocomputer confining sexual interest to fellow-enhanced individuals. It could be deactivated. It was a concession allowing a form of escape to normality, and serious-minded men and women supposedly did not use it. Lexin knew his mother's, by contrast, was rarely *activated*. "Some of us take our duties seriously," he replied. "It is not difficult in Marcelle's case. It is not so much her body that is beautiful; it is her whole personality, her thoughts, her kindness, her incredible insight..."

"Her thoughts! Perhaps she has...interesting thoughts about you."

"She may have. But even if she does I don't suppose they would last for long – she has other things to think about. There is another thing: you must remember, Mother, that in effect I only see and know those things about her that…"

"…that you need to see and know. Yes, you have already told me that…"

"… that are my business to know. How else to put it? That I am privileged to know."

"I know." She was handing him blooms to hold.

"And you should use your *PAS* more, Mother," he said as quietly and gently as he could against the sounds of rising music and cascading water. "Remember if you've got your multicom you can flick it on wherever you are."

"Maybe I should," Felicitas admitted.

"You might see Marcelle yourself. But regarding the nanocomputer, even if I were to deactivate that part of it, I don't know that…"

"So you haven't switched off, even for a few seconds," she cut in, continuing to reach out and cut blooms, not looking at him.

"I dare not. And as I was trying to say, if I did, it would not be the same Marcelle, nor would I be the same Lexin, and we would be just nice friends, and the task…"

"Earth seemed so unimportant from out there, darling, so small, so weak…just a speck," she whispered, turning round and drawing him close to her. "'How great the universe is', the President was pointing out, 'and how much there is to be gained out here'."

"Yes, but we must learn to walk before we can run."

Felicitas seemed not to hear. "And from fifty miles up, Lexin, you cannot imagine it, the warmth of the colours: the browns, the oranges; the whiteness of the pole – like us and yet not like us…" His mother had hardly ever stopped going on about the Mars trip. "And then there *we* were down there, the humans emerging from the shadow of the night, the great domes that are 'us', the water, the greenness, the people you can visualize living, working beneath them, the vehicles moving between them…"

"Yes, I have seen the pictures," Lexin said, a little abstractedly. "Yes, it is promising." His mother resumed her work with the scissors, but never quite letting go of him, coaxing him gently along by her side if he seemed to linger in thought as she moved from shrub to shrub.

"It is only a foretaste of something, of course." Felicitas spoke more slowly now. "It will not be like that when the terraforming starts... but much grander, beyond our imagination."

"Yes, of course."

"All this would have been unthinkable before the 'visitation'. A pity it had to be precipitated by that terrible event..." Thinking of the catastrophe of 2073 evidently brought the recent explosion to mind, infinitesimal though it was by comparison, for his mother fell silent for a minute or two before adding, "There are bound to be accidents, Yin Zhang reckoned, in the face of such a challenging step forward," and sinking down for a moment on one of the stone seats.

"Mother, that is not right," he protested. "Such a thought, even of a great contemporary philosopher, is unworthy of the President of the Matriarchs."

Felicitas was staring ahead, deep in thought. The sounds from the Concert Hall were now ever more clearly audible above the noise of the cascade. "What lovely music!" she exclaimed. "What beautiful harmony!"

The Reissler symphony was indeed reaching a climax – a glorious variety of sounds of nature running, weaving, jumping amid an ever broadening, ever more complex, ever more colourful crescendo. Lexin felt his mind expanding with it, his understanding reaching new heights, new depths in which he found himself imagining planet Earth, viewed on returning to it from afar, in the form of a huge lilac tree sprouting blossoms in the garden of the Galaxy. "Yes, yes Mother, mysterious harmonies, perfect harmonies in space and time, the galactic oneness! And in some way we can scarcely conceive of, we can be part of that, too."

"*Perfect* harmonies, Galactic oneness! Now I *am* back from Mars," Felicitas said, putting her scissors and gloves back in the basket, "but they really do believe they are succeeding, you know, the experts, in their journey, their journey to the stars."

"And Father, too." Lexin's voice was distant.

"Yes, and Olaf." Felicitas's face darkened for some moments. Then she recovered: "but now I am back to my Lexin, my enigma."

"Marcelle actually walked with Shining Face, *became* her for a while. There was no time between them, in the same way as there is often none between me and either of them." He described, in as few words as he could, the walk by the river and then how Shining Face, set on one purpose, had struggled from the lowland into the snowy mountains, and finally after many hardships to the shelter of a cave. "And sometimes I have almost seemed to *be* her, like Marcelle was. Let me take the basket," he said, as she struggled with the huge blooms.

"I almost believe you, son," she said in a whisper as they walked up to the terrace, "though it terrifies me. And you too think you have all the answers? Something to do with pureness and goodness and, well...harmony?"

"To do with those things, yes, within human limits. But I would say also a 'certainty', an 'assurance'. Do I go shouting and ranting about these things?"

"No. But possibly you ought to. Plenty of others are shouting."

"And it is not 'all the answers', as you put it. Just a vision of something in those two, a fragment of the truth and what they mean for us, something... something to be grasped."

"Perhaps it is time to share it – share it with the world before it is too late."

"Yes, it may be," he replied, as they entered the living space.

*   *   *

There were certainly plenty of voices now zealously broadcasting their opinion in various sections of the media, and even in the Society's Conference, Lexin mused as he sat in one of the delegates' bars high up in the Palace during an interval in a Conference session. Several months had now passed since the last explosion. The tabloids were nicknaming him 'prophet of doom', and many were the cartoons of him, like those depicting him as dark clouds over the Mission Station, or even blasting off in an antediluvian rocket towards Lyra clutching a white flag. The broadsheets were more measured, but by and large the opinion was gaining ground that the Bods would hardly be punishing us for doing our best and that if we just kept our heads and plugged away enlightenment would come eventually. This was assuredly the view of George Callum, comfortably ensconced opposite him in one of the bar's plush alcoves. Lexin was pretty sure it was a view arrived at more or less by default.

"It is not a very flattering thought that we are but children in galactic terms," Callum remarked, doubtless recalling something

Lexin had said to him recently, as he took a last dive into the remnants of his half litre of Boddingstone's, "but it is a designation that we must surely endure. Growing up was never painless." Callum had sought him out in the bar on several occasions since the evening recently when Lexin had joined him and his father and Mackenzie on the terrace at home. Lexin did not know whether maybe his father, or possibly even Mackenzie, had suggested keeping an eye on the renegade or whether Callum was just being chummy. He didn't mind which. Callum was someone he could talk to, and Lexin had learnt quite a bit about linguistics and the new 'Wild West', and Callum likewise about sport – on which topic he confessed ignorance. Just occasionally they touched on problems of decipherment. It occurred to him that by contrast it would have been exceedingly difficult talking about anything to a *Mackenzie* constantly distracted by his enhancement toy.

There was another reason contributing to this general feeling of resignation: attempts to get going on a historical review of the decipherment process had soon proved extremely difficult. Going back hundreds of years, and comparing what had actually resulted from the decipherment process – both initially and after the usual calculations, discussions and trials at the Mission Station and in the world at large – with the carefully preserved original text was never expected to be easy. It could surely never be easy despite the vast information retrieval resources now available, but now something else seemed to block the way. It was something that had been suspected for quite a while: the actual original text, when a way was found of returning to it, never made any sense, nor had it ever been possible to copy it.

"How do you account for it?" Callum asked, screwing up his nose. "Why should it be impossible to rewind the decipherment process and go over it again?"

"I am sure you appreciate that the learning process in decipherment is different from that which we experience in general."

"Yes, of course, there are many theories about that. But Lexin, I am not a biologist. Another vodka and orange?" Callum had already managed to extract himself and take two steps towards the bar.

"This is enough for me," Lexin replied. Then as Callum returned, balancing his beer in front of him to avoid spilling it on his suit, he added, "but I don't think even the biologists have all the answers."

"I suppose we have always just accepted the text as it is," Callum said, vaguely, "a sort of 'given' – like many other things since...well, since the visitation…"

"…and have not seriously questioned our *ability to understand it*," Lexin said, leaning forward and tapping the table top emphatically with his forefinger. "That's more important to my mind. But something else has occurred to me. I know that occasionally in the past few years some of the decipherers have mentioned that when they are doing their deciphering it is almost like facing a living thing. You know, don't you, that they get advice and encouragement in the text, as well as the 'meaty' stuff..?" Callum was studiously wiping away some spilt beer on the table with a tissue before squeezing his voluminous form back into his seat. "One or two have said to me that it is as if, as the team decipherment proceeds, each bit deciphered comes alive. To me that would suggest that the whole 'organism' – meaning the whole deciphered text from beginning to end – is thus revitalized and can continue to grow. I might add, tentatively: and in some mysterious way everything 'sprouting' from it, all our advances in whatever sphere, will continue to prosper."

"So if you look back it's different because the whole organism has changed?"

"Not bad for a mathematician, George," Lexin said.

"Not bad for a non-biologist, your explanation, Lexin," Callum replied, "but it's a shade spooky."

"I would not say 'spooky', but 'worrying', yes. Look, what really concerns me is that because it is an organism it needs to keep on growing, otherwise it will wither. It needs to be revitalised from its source, as I said. That is one thing."

Callum was fumbling in his pocket. "Worrying, sure," he agreed, absently.

"Or bits of it might wither, so that progress already achieved might become stunted, even lost, or – which seems obvious – things just may not get corrected or modified or compensated that should be. In other words, regardless of the form of animation, with cessation of decipherment anything might happen." Lexin was struggling, and Callum was struggling no less to pay attention. "I have tried to interest Leonard in all that. Of course, poor decipherment, or poor application of its results in practice, could have similar effects."

"I expect he might find it as puzzling as I do. Important to get the deciphering right: one try, and that's it. Seems tough, no second chance." Callum was well into his second beer and had finally got his diary out of his pocket. "Just checking on the date of the next Culture Committee", he explained, apologetically. "Well what does *that* tell us – no second chance, I mean? What does that really tell us about the source of this animation, Lexin?"

"That ours is a serious task that has a beginning and an end – and is something that is expected of us..."

Callum looked unimpressed. "...And we have come to a tricky bit and we are just not getting it." Callum was looking beyond Lexin, presumably at the crowds around the bar. "I think we may get a visitor," he said. "Some journalist I half recognize."

Callum had obviously failed really to take in the significance of what he had said. "We cannot 'just not get it'", Lexin insisted with a degree of urgency. "We *must* not! Be encouraged by where we have got to: no-one murders, no-one even thinks of it, no starvation, life-span open-ended, optimism, religious fulfilment, sense of purpose, no blame culture – at least until recently."

"Not perfect, Lexin: still accidents, unfairness..."

"We're not through the text yet. But I am saying the bottom line is that not only can we not go back, but also we have to continue to go forward, otherwise our growth may be impeded, and Heaven knows what might happen then."

"Okay, so we mustn't just 'not get it'. Decipherment must continue."

"You've got it," Lexin said without great conviction, and then with unaccustomed passion, "but resumption of our attempts to communicate with Lyra before we are totally sure we can do it is ill advised. We could blow ourselves to pieces. At the very least, another explosion could scare the Government into forcing us to cease all activities – with unknown consequences, as I said." There was a silence during which he allowed himself to cool down a bit, after which he added quietly, as an afterthought. "It is obvious, isn't it, that there must be a connection between what is behind the decipherment process and our modified genetics..." – "and our PAS " he might have added – , but he sensed George Callum's relief when their conversation was interrupted by a long-striding, curly-headed young guy in trendy flashy shirt, floppy Mediterranean-blue summer suit and polished winkle-pickers who announced himself as Peter Hoffen of the 'Neue Frankfurter Allgemeine':

"Would you care your Ansichte to give on the proposal to report more regularly to World Government and the public on your activities." It was an appropriate enough question, Lexin thought, on a day when Conference hoped to ratify a new policy of the Society on publicity and public relations, although his autotranslator certainly needed an overhaul. 'Ansichte'? Rogue word, and inappropriate word order! German for 'views'. He must have borrowed somebody else's device, or he was trying to talk too fast. A new guy, no doubt. They had multiplied like flies. It was also only a few days before Olaf was to recommission the wormhole complex at the Mission Station, when a renewed attempt would be made to send and receive messages.

"More regular reports are a good idea. Why not?" Callum replied.

"Would you like to elaborate on that, Mr. Callum?" the man ploughed on. He was going to be a nuisance. Lexin had things he badly wanted to say to Callum, and in a few minutes they would be going into the Great Hall...

"If it increases your confidence in the Society."

Lexin would like to have added, "and if it kept you guys off our backs a bit," but patience prevailed as Callum admitted his own disappointment with progress but hoped the public would realise that the progress yet to come – with patience – would very likely put previous successes in the shade.

But the pressman was not so easily dismissed and had drawn up a stool and sat on it: "Can you foresee what form that progress might take, Mr. Callum?" At every word the wide mouth, now all the closer, had the appearance in Lexin's eyes of opening from ear to ear to reveal a slightly distasteful pulsating pink and toothy hinterland.

"No, I cannot at this stage. Our job is to get this work done step by step. Later, as I say, we will try and be more specific."

Lexin admired Callum for his tact, at least. He had seen how, in these last weeks, when Callum chaired meetings of the Conference he was no longer speaking to the delegates alone but with many an upward glance towards the galleries. It was obvious that he had one ear permanently tuned to the media. It was so different from the past, when days, even months would go by with the Society and its doings barely featured there. Journalists rarely appeared in those days, and until recent times transcripts had generally appeared in the back pages of the papers.

"Do *you* think the public should be better informed, Mr. Solberg?"

the man blabbered on. Now the vampire was trying to get his fangs into *him*, drive a wedge between them. He was still the favourite target, after all.

"I would not want to raise false expectations," Lexin replied. "I would say we are in a stage of absorbing data. We do not know precisely why things are moving very slowly at the moment. I hope you will trust us to overcome the obstacles."

The reporter obviously detected some discrepancy in the views of the two men. "Is it reasonable," he asked, "to tax the public's patience any further?"

Increasingly now the Society and its doings, or its non-doings, would find itself beamed out from the front pages, on the newsstands. As work got underway again at the Station, increasingly derogatory references appeared in many organs of the press from the 'Shanghai Evening News' to the 'Chicago World News' and the 'New Daily Mail'. The 'Mail' referred to "Doubts, Disagreements, Ditherings and Dismay" among the delegates. The leader column in the 'Guardian Interactive' in London spoke in slightly more sensitive tones of increasing hostility towards the Society "as the faith which the world has placed in it for hundreds of years continues to be questioned".

"As I say," Lexin replied, "my view is that it is a matter of trust. Trust us in the same way as we can only trust the powers that have brought us to where we are. I think my views on resumption of message retrieval are well enough known."

"Is it not hard to trust those who will not communicate directly with us?"

"I think you are making some unwarranted assumptions there, Mr. Hoffen." Lexin was glad for Callum's intervention – his friend had been screwing up his nose as his patience dwindled. "Look!" Callum said, "I think it is time to terminate this interview. Thank you for your interest."

"I have to agree that was an inane question, George, Lexin said as the reporter ambled off, but I suppose we should not be surprised, should we?"

"I would prefer to say it was just off the point," Callum replied, cheerily raising his mug to his lips. "But any of us can lose our way a bit, can't we?" he added with a naughty twinkle in his eye.

"We lost it. I do not dispute it."

"We will all get over it," Callum said, "once things really get going again...in a little while, well, perhaps a bit longer...a few months, say." He appeared thoughtful for a moment. "Why *did* we lose it? Just refresh my memory."

"Too much reliance on our modified brains, and not enough effort. It is not just the decipherers, either. All the stuff they churn out, it cannot just be swallowed whole and regurgitated by our advisers in every part of the world from the families and farmers of India to the planners and pensioners of America."

"Ah yes, wrong attitudes all round." Callum probably suspected personal activity synthesizers would be on Lexin's next breath, and he changed the subject slightly. "Couldn't we just ban the press from here?" he suggested, glancing round. "We do need a bit of peace. We hardly ever used to see a media person."

"But they were never disallowed. It would only be acknowledging the return of that twenty-first century problem of press hassle." A headline in somebody's 'New Daily Mail' caught Lexin's eye: "Lexin Out on a Limb on Recommissioning", and on another front page: "Mackenzie Openly Backs Vidano", with side-by-side portraits of a deeply lined Leonard in leather jacket and lumberjack shirt, and smart and suited young Angelo with black hair immaculately flattened. Lexin was noting the woman reading it, the intent look on her face.

"It wouldn't be a problem with young Vidano that was causing your dismay, would it?" A grinning Callum was following Lexin's gaze, but Lexin barely registered the remark. "No, that's unworthy of me," Callum retracted. "This is the big decisive moment for Mother Earth, then, is it? The break point?" The tone was not entirely flippant, was even emollient, but the starkness of the question roused Lexin finally as his eye took in the accelerated pace of life around them, the ultra-light taxi bubbles – ubiquitous feature of their exclusive city-centre domain – bunching down below, the journalists down there and up in the bar where they were sitting, waylaying delegates or speaking urgently into their multicoms.

"It could be disastrous for us, George; it could be disastrous for the Normals," he declared. Yes, let us keep the media informed, but tell them attempts at message retrieval will cease for the time being just to give us a chance to reorientate ourselves."

"That is much too stark, Lexin," Callum said, his puffy cheeks with their veined rosiness suddenly broadening into a wide, compassionate grin tinged with anxiety as he looked up from his deep brown ale at

Lexin swirling round the last drop of his vodka and orange. "Let me buy you another one, young man; you will feel loads better. Look, Lexin, we've had so much success, made so much progress."

Lexin seemed not to hear. "For well over three hundred years we had a purpose," he said, slowly, "a guide, an amazing vision. I don't mean the Normals, I mean *us*…"

"And the explosions wrecked it, and we've lost our way, is that it?"

Lexin saw a kind of barrier of distorting glass between himself and his friend. "Other way round. The explosions probably occurred *because* we lost our way. Look, George," he said with a touch of desperation as the lady folded up her paper and stood up and he saw Hoffen's Mediterranean blue disappearing with the media regatta towards the Great Hall, "we have transmitted the fruits of our vision to the world at large, and Earth, everybody, has reaped untold benefits – not of our making, I might add, but the Bods'. If we 'lose it', before long we could be having wars again or worse, and the only winners along the road, incidentally, will be…"

"…the press, the media? But you can't expect the press to be into all these abstracts: 'purity', 'peace', 'thankfulness', 'humility', even 'forgiveness'…those things which trip quite easily off your tongue."

"Not *so* easily". They were silent for a moment. Then Lexin said, "They will hardly take them seriously when we don't ourselves."

The humorous twinkle in Callum's eye faded before the seriousness in Lexin's. "When *we* don't?"

"You should remember, George. I wasn't even here, but I know it happened. Fifty years ago we believed in those kinds of miracles as well as the scientific ones."

"Maybe we did," Callum said, slowly. He was looking at Lexin curiously. "And no more about diverting comets and galactic communication."

"Hopefully not for long, George. I'm just saying here that because we spoke openly about those things, used those words, they were accepted among the Normals. Hence progress in social policy, moral theory and practice."

"And now that we have lost faith in the Bods…"

"…the Normals are getting infected, too, and what shall we have? The old time-wasting, soul-destroying politicking. And I don't blame them, not at all. I blame ourselves, and nothing will escape, George. Art, culture, religion, science…" The bell rang. They made their way with the others to the Hall, but Lexin was still talking. "We Societans will forget our heritage, and because *we* will no longer believe in, yes, the *miraculous*, therefore nobody will."

But the American was plainly fired more by the return to the final stages of the debate and what would probably be Leonard Mackenzie's 'drawing together of the threads', than by Lexin's admonitions. "In my view you are making too much of *ourselves* and our *problems*," he said, adding matter-of-factly, "At worst we might be on our own – I mean, without the Bods, picking up the residue of their legacy. Surely those loving beings would not be so unkind as not to leave us with something...some comfort."

Lexin recognized the echo of his own words and the irony attached to it. "I find it hard to swallow, George, that you are even *thinking* like that. It is a dangerous assumption." He gave himself a few moments to calm down. "We cannot be on our own. Remember we – I mean we modified ones – are inextricably linked to the Bods, unless an individual decides to opt out and join the Normals. Surely you still accept that." Lexin wanted to believe that Callum was testing him.

Mackenzie was upbeat in summing up the decisions of the Conference ratifying the new publicity policy and praising everyone for their patient and fruitful discussion of the issues. It was a time to be open among themselves, open with the Normals, he said, and to press on. He thanked those who had worked tirelessly to rebuild the Centre in readiness for the recommissioning. Delegates listened attentively and showed their approval. It must be said that clapping was not a common occurrence in that tranquil, august assembly.

"But we should be more open also in expressing our thanks to, and our faith in, our benefactors," President Olaf Solberg said in a closing speech – "I mean of course our saviours from Lyra. That much I commend heartily to you of what you have heard from the more cautious among us here. And do not," he said, raising himself to his full height and focussing with unaccustomed firmness upon an unusually numerous media contingent stuck up there in the press gallery across from where Lexin was sitting among the aspirants, "do not be diverted or discouraged by negative attitudes in those sections of the media which talk only of failure and would have us forget the origin of the great advances we have made." Then looking again round the delegates packing the Hall he said, "Most of all we Societans must look to ourselves and have confidence. I am convinced that we have the means, with all our enhancements, to one day override all our problems."

"It was a bit of a whitewash," Lexin told his mother afterwards. She was preparing something in the kitchen.

"Guess what!" Felicitas said.

"You have been giving your synthesizer an airing."

"How did you know?"

"I read you like a book. Was it informative?"

"Yes and no. It's worrying that you read me so well!"

Lexin laughed. At least someone was reading their PAS, and indeed some discrete information gathering using the 'Snowballer' opinion researcher suggested she was not the only one and that as many as five per cent of Societans might be doing so. But it was a trickle against a tide..

Five days later, drawn repeatedly to open his PAS by Shining Face's fortitude and daring, Lexin in his office had been witnessing with dismay, first on-screen, and then half-experiencing them himself, the events unfolding at the cave, from the moment she returned from her reconnoitre only to find the lions there, and the continuation of her journey thus in jeopardy, to finally the great bellowing of the mammoth that caused the lions to abandon her badly injured. Then he became aware that the vibration was not so much from the electronic speakers as from the foundations of the house beneath him, and instinctively he leapt up and looked out of the window.

Up above where the Mission Station was situated across the desert, a column of black smoke was already ascending very high in the sky. The terrible explosion at 10.36 a.m. on March 11th 2453 was loud and clear in Galaxy City a hundred and fifty kilometres away.

CHAPTER TEN

Going down to the terrace, from where the rising plume was equally visible, Lexin found his mother already standing there in a day gown, her face transfixed with fear and foreboding. Lexin was already receiving messages in his brain. He did not need to transmit them to his mother. They both knew few if any could have survived in the transmission and retrieval block in an explosion clearly so much bigger than the previous one, even though the Station as a whole, and especially, of course, the wormhole terminal, was built to withstand enormous shocks.

Lexin put a comforting arm around his mother and led her back into the house.

Robert materialised, unsummoned. "Can I help in any way, Mrs. Solberg?"

The fact that the robot was actually expressing sympathy, albeit by inference, tempered a sudden sickening fear that that was that, and so much for galactic aspirations! Robert did, after all, represent a tangible, known connection with the Bods. Might not that fact embody also a tenuous hope? But Callum had certainly given him a nasty shock talking about going it alone.

"Just my usual in my room, Robert, thank you," Felicitas said in an unaccustomedly shaky voice. "And please, I do not wish to have any visitors for the time being." Robert disappeared, and Lexin held his mother close.

" Let me go with you to your room. We cannot go to the Mission Station yet. I will be told when it is safe to go."

"Thank you, Lexin. You are such a comfort to me. You know how I feared this." She was being very stoical.. Then she said, looking at him through tearful eyes, and making no attempt to break away, "We won't be the only ones having trouble, will we? Your friends, the girls…?"

"They'll be our saving yet," he replied.

"I know you won't give up hope, darling," she said. He knew he would not do that, if only because she had said it, had encouraged him, was surely beginning to believe him, if only with a very fragile belief now strengthened perhaps by bitter experience. She knew it, too. "Actually," she added, "I know you will do what you think is right. It's Lenica I am worried about, Lexin. She was so close to your father. She must already have heard. Someone seemed to suggest she was not very well." Lenica was with her boss in Canberra at a session of the World Assembly. They were debating the motion 'It is time for a thorough investigation of the Society'.

They went to Felicitas's room. Robert appeared with her 'fix' and was gone.

"Sit down quietly, Mother," Lexin said, gently.

"Lexin, dear, haven't you got things to do? You go, I shall be all right."

"It's only reporters," he said. He had a feeling she might want to say something else. "They are all trying to talk to me at once. They can wait. Oh, and I am just getting word that the Assembly debate has been suspended."

"You did warn everybody about this…about what has happened, didn't you?"

"Yes, but there is a long backlog of misconceptions."

"So you have explained to me." He had. He had warned Societans of the dangers. He had spoken to the media whenever he could about the things he was convinced Societans and Normals alike were losing sight of. But calm opportunities arose less and less as the controversy about the reasons for the Society's difficulties intensified. Perhaps Marcelle and Shining Face *would* lead the way, though he had a feeling more might depend on himself now. "That's my Lexin," she said, squeezing his arm. "Now you go and do what you have to do."

Back in his office, Lexin did not at first reply to the messages pouring in. For just a moment his gaze wandered out of the window, down the Hill of Lyra to the city spread out below. He thought of those camel drivers long ago...the departing spaceship...the rescue from disaster...

Turning to his personal activity synthesizer, in the face of such an enormous setback, he hardly dared seek some kind of encouragement...

"Can I still have confidence in the ultimate success of decipherment?"

"Yes, Lexin."

"Should I project my personality more? Seems risky in the face of the media, and in the light of my father's probable death perhaps inappropriate ."

"Yes, you must project your view at all costs, otherwise the media will have every reason to complain. Do you understand that? Please confirm your absolute willingness to pursue the course you are on."

Such was the scale of the debate on the Society's work that it had all but obliterated the little wave of euphoria following the astonishingly received, but of course untranscribed, communication from Lyra of some months previously. It was a debate orchestrated by certain media elements awaking hungry from long years of quiescence against a background of uncertainty within the Society and a bemused public. Lexin was only too aware of the way in which, as he saw it, the newspapers in particular were degenerating. He must avoid being caught up in their negativity or just fatuousness, look after his mother, and stick to his guns.

True, all was not doom and gloom. Even as he was pondering the reply from his PAS his brain had been registering a low level message quoting the Chancellor of a university in Beijing interrupting an inaugural speech at the opening of a new department and praising the work of the Society. The Chancellor recognized that despite the accident – of which pretty well the entire globe would by now have become aware – Societans were not superhuman and *the Lyrians also recognized that fact.*

Accepting that for the moment at least the battleground was going to be the media, he was relieved and pleased at the firmness of the reply from his PAS, and answered accordingly. A check on biochemical and other personal indices (for example wellbeing, rationality, trust or confidence) then confirmed the continuation of the recent positive trends in his response to the hiatus in 'galactic progress'. The trends were especially positive when taken in conjunction with data which he keyed in from the recent Conference decisions and the media coverage, and technical information already arriving on the lead-up to the explosion of twenty minutes previously. In other words, viewed against the background of what he saw as recent negative movements in the Society, and probably in the Normal community (if the press was anything to go by – always questionable!), his own indices remained greatly enhanced. By their very positiveness, though, they presented him with a challenging, if not daunting, prospect.

Lexin wanted to tap into the special files that would lead him to Marcelle (indeed they would still often appear unannounced in his monitor if his PAS was 'on'). He would see her, personifier of certain timeless truths, and serene as ever.... But he judged that he had assurance enough that all was being done that could be done, both for those in time 'now' and for those in times 'then', that it was within his power to influence. It would be sheer self-gratification to seek her out, understandable though such a desire was, feeling as he did so drained by both the events at the cave and now the catastrophe at home. The logic did not make it any easier for him to turn away from his PAS to the unavoidable tasks placed upon him by its advice. He would have to turn away from Shining Face, too, for the moment.

He prioritised automatically the dozens of new messages that had arrived via his multicom or the house telecom.

"Mahendra Singh of the Indian News Service, Kolkata. While you must be greatly saddened by your father's death, as are we all, would you say this vindicates your opinions on the failings of the Society for the Advancement of Intragalactic Relations?"

What callous stuff! Lexin thought: Are we not all saddened! He was angry. He was angry too because he asked himself what Mr. Singh knew either of his father's untiring efforts or of the almost imperceptible chain of events over the years that had led to the breakdown. But of course, he was being unreasonable. The man could know nothing of what those young women in other ages had revealed to *him*...their singleness of purpose, their high aspirations...many things, and most of all the very fact that they could appear to him at all. Probably no-one knew but he himself and Felicitas. He could not tell anyone about his visions yet or explain how they had changed his understanding. It would have to wait.

"Mahendra Singh's office...You want him?... He's not available... Who did you say you are? Lexin Solberg?...Could we have vision, Sir?" A pause. "Okay, it's fine. Now I have confirmation. You're so like your look-alikes, Mr. Solberg."

"Hello, Mahendra Singh, INS Kolkata!"

"So glad I look like myself, Mahendra. Mahendra, as a matter of fact I am still awaiting firm news on the casualties and when I can go there."

"You mean you have not heard officially yourself? They very much regret the toll might be over a hundred." The journalist's expression was hard to read – he was being jostled, and there was much distracting noise and movement in the background – , but it appeared impassive. Yet Lexin could almost feel the sense of catastrophe in the Palace, which was where Mahendra appeared to be. There could be no-one now who did not know of the explosion. No earthquake had been expected, and in any case the shock and dismay must be evident on everybody's face like it had been on his mother's. At least the journalist had *not* added, "It is feared the shapes of those in the observation gallery will be imprinted on what's left of those walls like a memorial for ever."

From the gallery, sunk like the compartments of the transmission and retrieval control block in the duron wall, and with a window onto the core space of blast-resistant duron-glass possessing great thickness and a high level of transparency, Lexin knew that the observers could have expected to see everything there was to be seen. However, data currently being received by him and digested from various sources at a low brain level suggested that if fears were borne out much of the lower part of the core space and to an unknown extent the lower part of the wormhole mouth itself, despite their extreme toughness, were likely to have been badly damaged. The central unit and spacetime boundary were of course virtually indestructible according to the Bods. There was no report of any sign of life in the wall compartments or the area enclosed by the wall. "I shall be hearing," Lexin said, as calmly as he could. "In the meantime, Mahendra, there is something I want you to understand..."

"Mr. Solberg, before we get to that I have a further question. Do you think all these deaths might have been avoidable?"

"Mahendra, if you want me to discuss this tragic accident I suggest you choose another occasion." The man was being as abrasive as that Hoffen fellow the other day. "Step away from this accident for a moment, indeed, step outside the box, as they say."

"Seems a strange time to be doing it!"

"Make no mistake, my father was – if indeed it is 'was' – very dear to me, and to my mother I might add, and please don't imagine that I do not grieve for the others, too, but I have to ask you to take a leap and grasp this idea: the idea that there is still unimaginable knowledge out there, far more than we already have received, Mahendra, a realm of truth and goodness which the Bods intend us to be part of." He stared at the reporter. It was not easy to tell whether he was listening. He was having to move about a lot, get out of people's way. How far, anyway, could such a man be expected to comprehend things that even those with all the advantages of enhancement had forgotten – or tried to ignore if they had ever known them? "I have to tell you, Mahendra, although I am not a decipherer, that I know the work sometimes becomes very difficult – and very surprising – to the point where we are scarcely able to *believe* what we are interpreting, so that our own ideas might cloud the interpretation."

"Are you saying we, or rather you, have got to be more spiritual, more religious, Mr. Solberg? " At this point the journalist seemed to be swallowed up by the crowd and contact was lost. Half a minute or so later Lexin heard him just say faintly, "I think I follow you. Thank you for your time, Mr. Solberg "

Now the prioritiser was saying: "Contact 'News England', London."

"Rod Donington, 'News England'. Two questions, Mr. Solberg: Can we trust you, and can you trust the aliens?"

Lexin replied, "If it's the Lyrians you are referring to, I have no qualms about trusting them in view of all they have done for us. I hope that answers both questions," and he turned off and went down to his mother, having postponed reading the rest of the messages with apologies.

Felicitas was standing staring straight ahead, unmoving. In front of her, on the wall of her room was a photo of herself with Olaf on their wedding day. "Well have you made statements?" she asked, turning round.

"No, I have not heard anything, Mother, so how could I?"

"I suppose there is nothing much left to say anything about."

"I spoke to an Indian on the INS in Kolkata," Lexin said, taking his mother in his arms. "I did not get through to him much. Thought I was suggesting we should be more religious because I talked about timeless truths and said I thought we were not believing the Bods enough. Perhaps I should not have said that, but it is the truth. In fact I wanted to say more. It seemed important... confess our neglect, explain that I was not talking about gods or theology, but we couldn't hear each other. We *aren't* believing them, are we? At least, not fully. And it is something more earthy: friendship, help, and good and lasting things. But of course they are far beyond us in understanding. Far, far beyond..." He saw that Felicitas was crying, and he added, "...and I would say walking very close to the Creator."

"No, you were not offending my religious sentiments, Lexin. It's just that it is so hard to equate such...such beings with what has happened...so hard to understand."

"I know it is, Mother." He held her closely, and they remained thus entwined for a little while. "I can't think you want to talk about this at all," he said, releasing her.

"It's all right, my love," she said, and then, quietly, almost to herself, "I wonder whether Olaf would ever have understood it all in the way you do." Lexin wanted to say "He would, in the end", but did not, and he felt his mother probably needed to be alone. "But don't you want to go and see how 'the others' are getting on?" she asked, cheerfully, and he nodded. "I'm all right. I must go now and get dressed properly. You go. And come and tell me. I want to know."

Lexin reckoned the press could wait a bit if all the interviews were going to be like Mahendra Singh's, but no sooner was he back in his office than the prioritiser insisted he take another message. It was Rod Donington again, with a text:

"The crowds are going crazy here in Trafalgar Square, Lexin. People are very emotional, many shouting, others crying. They are not very sympathetic towards you. One guy came up to me. 'Lexin,' he complained, 'thinks he has the answer to the Society's problems, but how come so few even in the Society believe him?'"

Away from the chaos eventually, and back at his desk, Lexin soon found himself in Shining Face's situation without need for recourse to his monitor. At first, all was dark, with vague outlines, then suddenly he was *there*, in the picture.

The sensations were real enough: a dark, hard place...a cave, the dimmest light entering from somewhere, an intermittent roaring of beasts somewhere down below, a pervasive, bad smell... Time passed – or seemed to – until bit by bit the roaring died down and finally ceased altogether as full consciousness slowly returned and Shining Face began to remember where she was. Only gradually did she begin to remember the lion and how it had dragged her – and in the remembering became more and more frightened. Her first thought was that she must leave that place even if the lions appeared to have gone, but first her things – or those that were still there – must be retrieved from the main cave. Eventually she forced herself to crawl slowly towards the little entrance, taking with her no more than a few stones and her still intact spear – more in the nature of a comfort than offering any real protection. The pain in her leg was bad, and only a combination of utter necessity and absolute determination enabled her to drag herself out of the hole. She saw that it would very soon be dark. The mammoths certainly could not be counted on to come to her defence again! Indeed they seemed to have passed the cavern. Perhaps they were not settling down for the winter at all, or were simply migrating from one valley to another, taking advantage of the break in the weather. Of course, the lions might have just put them off temporarily. Of *their* whereabouts she had no idea.

Shining Face slithered cautiously down the rocky slope leading to the cavern entrance wondering whether the lions might have taken the carcase of the last deer (a young one) chased off the top of the cavern (making altogether four that she had taken in that way). That had been only on the previous day. And the rest of the meat, her other stuff...? Again she thought of the precious cones. Were they safe? She was shivering – that was unusual. Only when part-way down the slope did she become aware of blood leaking onto the snow from a gash in her side. She had not even noticed the wound. Strangely, it did not hurt as much as her leg, but she saw that the gash was long and the wound probably deep, yet for some reason could not remember now exactly how it had happened, only that if you were clawed by lions you sometimes died. She tried to stop the bleeding by packing snow on the wound like she had seen the men do. The wound did hurt then, but in this way at least she might not leave such an obvious trail.

Now she was near to the cave entrance, and with difficulty because of the pain in her leg she stood up straight. Everywhere she could see the snow was trampled. The entrance, once welcoming, now threatened, and she was definitely too close already to be able to retreat to her hiding place if things became desperate. Distant mammoth trumpetings occasionally broke the silence. There were certainly no mammoths in the cave, but might not the lions have been only momentarily distracted and one or more of them be lurking, finishing off the food remains in there? She advanced, terrified, towards the entrance. She admitted to herself that if she really thought one of the animals might still be in there she would not dare to move – not even to rescue her precious 'Toothy' knot, or – woe betide her if she should lose them – the dyed cones. But there was complete silence.

Shining Face advanced through the entrance, and relaxed. Amazingly, the half-hidden deer carcase was intact. The lions must have retreated quickly before getting to it. The ground inside was well trampled by the mammoths, as was one of the newly prepared skins, but the dyed cones were safe in their little piece of skin tied with a strand of creeper. And her rhino fur had survived! Alas! The really bad news was that the dried meat reserves had been discovered. Relieved at least about the cones she went to the back of the cave, put her head in the big water holder and took several gulps. Since she could not carry water as well as everything else she would have to come back with her water bag. Then she gathered everything else together that she could carry, and went to the cave entrance, furs and skins and the baby deer over her shoulder. But remembering suddenly a baby hare that she had killed at sunset of the day before the lions came, and buried temporarily in the snow a little aside from the cave entrance, she put the deer down for a moment and went and dug it up, untouched, and stuffed it into her pouch, having no idea how she might cook it. Resting then, and watching, she heard no sound but the wind, saw no movement in the valley but the slightly moving branches of nearby trees and the clouds of snow blowing off them every so often... Making her way back to the cave entrance, she gathered up the deer and started back up the slope with the intention of leaving at dawn and in the meantime trying to block the way up from the lower to the upper cave. But her load was heavy, and in agony from her wounds she moved only slowly, stopping continually, dizzy and exhausted.

Suddenly, almost at the top above the cave entrance, there came the sound she had been dreading: the unmistakeable grunts and snarls of lions close by. Only one option: get down the hole! Moments later she sensed the animals very close, sniffing and growling. Sacrificing the deer, she hurled it in their direction, made it to the hole, threw her things down it and herself after them and lay still, dimly aware of the beasts snarling and squabbling behind her. Almost immediately, however, she roused herself sufficiently to crawl past the little widening in the cave, and then with great difficulty block the way up through the tunnel as best she could by dislodging and heaping boulders at a low, narrow place still illuminated by a thin shaft of daylight.

When the dawn came, Shining Face realised she would have to remain in the upper cave for another day, feeling too weak and ill and too afraid to move even for the purpose of fetching water, of which there was now almost none left in her water bag, never mind continue her journey. In any case, lions had still been about during the night, heard from time to time in the cave below. They must have been coming back to the cave with their kills. Although the pain in her leg caused by being dragged was still bad, the shallow wounds there looked less angry, but the open rip in her side, just below the ribs, and going right down to her groin, continued to bleed at times under the piece of deer hide with which she had tried without much success to cover it using some lengths of animal gut from among the collection of useful items accumulated in her deer-skin pouch. She had been too weak to do the job properly. Now the pain was all but unbearable. She lay down all day taking an occasional sip of water and becoming less and less aware of the passage of time or anything else..

* * *

Lenica had returned on the day of mourning. She looked awful, frazzled, in a less than pristine travelling suit, and definitely funereal – though *definitely* not by design. She was not one to invite pity. Lexin knew that. It had been impossible to get away from Canberra earlier, she explained. The mood of the World Assembly was already less than sympathetic to the problems of the Society for the Advancement of Intragalactic Relations, and the disaster had sharpened things up no end. After long debate in the Assembly the Cabinet had ordered a wide-ranging enquiry to evaluate the crisis and make recommendations on the Society's future.

"Harry," Lenica explained to Lexin and her mother when they had returned from the memorial service for the victims in the Home of Many Faiths on the Avenue of Remembrance – at which both she and Felicitas managed to display a stoical tranquillity – , "Harry has been trying to explain the difficulties of the Society. In my view he has not been doing very well by us, talking about the Society being in danger of 'losing the will to succeed' and 'our great project' being 'derailed by mysterious unknown factors'." The three of them had retired to Felicitas's bedroom.

"And doubtless it's all rebounded on you," her mother said, her grief over her beloved Olaf momentarily displaced by her anxiety about her daughter, "as though you as his personal assistant were co-responsible. I must say, though I did not like to when you first arrived, that you don't look all that well. It must have been very stressful."

"It is true I have not been too well," Lenica said, a blotchy, tear-stained face and a now noticeable leanness having done nothing to improve initial impressions.

"Poor darling! I can imagine the sort of looks you were getting from members if that was Harry's message. What pompous rubbish!"

"Especially when the Conference's latest reports, which were what he was supposed to be transmitting, spoke of, what was it? – 'avenues of investigation... psychological, ethnological, philosophical, and, not least, physical'. Oh, and 'a determination to succeed!'"

Whatever all that amounted to, Lexin said to himself. The only thing that could be said about it was that it was better than Harry's angle. Lexin had been able to do little but stand there and make what he hoped were occasional helpful noises while the two women sat on the bed trying to comfort each other. Felicitas wore no jewellery. It made her look very subdued – so sad in one used to making waves. Robert's attire, he had noticed, was also subtly different – a little darker, but also a little softer, and in some indefinable way even kinder than usual. Lexin reflected that Robert was a much more efficient comforter than he was himself. In relation to those many friends, members of the Government (including Joanna Van Rensburg, the First Minister since 2445) who had travelled from Canberra, Societans from the Conference, and others working in the field who had come in the intervening days to express their condolences, his actions were exemplary. The Bods had surely revealed something of themselves when they had divulged some totally unexpected and unguessable principles of robotry. The solidity-mimicking dynamic pseudo-holograms incorporated a virtual presence of unfathomable empathy, and were yet another example, as Lexin had pointed out more than once, of the combined supremacy and virtue of the Bods.

* * *

Nearly one hundred persons had died among the personnel and visitors at the commissioning, the high level of attendance at it despite the recognized dangers having been testimony to the increased political prominence of the Society coupled with a worldwide wave of anxiety about the future and a concomitant desire to push things forward. In addition to all the engineers involved in the attempted retrieval and several top Conference delegates the dead included Vidano, one of two aspirants who had requested and been recommended attendance. Sure, he was brave. Lexin reckoned there was no shortage of contenders just as brave and just as blind to the truth. The Head of Wormhole Research and Operations, and many other scientists, World Assembly and local politicians, broadcasters, journalists and other writers also died. The process had failed at the same critical point as before, the explosion this time vaporising not only everything within the core space but also destroying most of the duron containing wall and tearing into the main tower structure to a depth of up to twenty metres. The extent of damage to the mouth of the wormhole was considerable, but no more extensive than in the previous accident. The funeral ceremonies would have to be postponed to allow the human remains to be identified collectively by wide-area DNA testing. Even the main buildings of the Mission Station, at a distance of twenty kilometres and partially buried, had been shaken and would require substantial repairs.

The cloud that had descended over Leonard Mackenzie, together with the majority of the Society Conference who had voted to resume recommissioning, had in fact the effect of reviving just a little the flagging media interest in the former blue-eyed boy of the Society and his hitherto increasingly rejected 'minimalist policy' as Lexin's views were widely, if inaccurately, interpreted by his kinder critics. Not that he could hope for any particularly sympathetic treatment by the various organs of the media flailing around for someone or something to get their teeth into. In fact, a week after the day of mourning, that is two weeks after the disaster, Lexin was being allowed no respite and

Mackenzie's fall from grace was not so far showing signs of being counterbalanced by any significant support for Lexin's repeated advocacy of a new kind of self-examination.

If Lexin knew that Olaf had not been entirely deaf to his suggestions about studying biological indices during wormhole operations, now he could almost hear his father saying, "But we all still died this time, didn't we, in spite of doing some at least of what you suggested?" Perhaps it really was time to see if he could have a heart to heart with one-time Head of the Mission Station Professor Malinovsky and see if he could shed new light on research in his sphere, since he was known to be still very actively engaged..

Some sections of the media were very unkind. In a one-to-one interview with Marcus Kastner on 'Europe Vision', Lexin in his tunic and baggy trousers (it was a sharp spring day) facing one of the networks' most aggressive and most feared interviewers had been forced to defend himself when Kastner asked him in his grating, expressionless tones whether he stayed away from the commissioning because he knew an accident would occur.

"Are you wishing me dead?" Lexin asked him. "My mother would not thank you. I had expressed my views, and I took my decisions." He did not say that Olaf had forbidden him to attend the ceremony. Next day, 'Die Welt' ran the headline "Lexin saved own skin" and reported that when interviewed he did not deny his ability to predict the explosion or that that was the reason for his staying away.

What did not get so much repeated was Kastner's next question, namely whether he thought the Society was "losing its will to succeed."

Lexin did not comment on the origin of those words quoted to him so recently by his sister. "What do you mean by 'losing the will to succeed'?" he wanted to know.

"I mean its courage. Your father was a very courageous man, and that must be a great loss to the Society. Maybe there are not so many left like him."

Lexin disliked the obsequiousness, and the innuendo that accompanied it. "Courage?" he had replied. "It was the aliens who needed courage when they entrusted us with everything. It is not so much courage we need. A leap of faith, perhaps, but I would describe it more as co-operation."

"Co-operation? A joint venture? – With whom?"

"Not quite. I would say 'following instructions'. Yes, I would say 'following instructions'. And we can save our courage for the football field, or save it for when we try and get a comet to Mars – if it ever comes to that".

"But haven't you Societans done that? Haven't you been following instructions?"

"No, not the small print, not always. Not even the large print sometimes."

The interviewer affected shocked surprise: "Excuse my saying so, but could that not be said to be a little ungenerous to....*them* – our friends out there – to talk of the 'small print'."

"No," Lexin replied promptly. "I am sure they will always tell us, as they have in the past, the route to follow in our work, often in great detail...I mean in terms of what to do and when to do it. It is what our modification enables us to do, taking it from there. We have really nothing to gain by questioning it, everything to gain by understanding it, but the work involved is often prolonged and very demanding."

"It sounds – if I may say so – a somewhat slavish procedure. Is no initiative required – or allowed?" The interviewer was sounding just a shade irritated by Lexin's forthright replies. His forehead glistened red below coarse hair that threatened like a porcupine's bristles.

"The initiative is with *them*, Mr. Kastner. It is almost impossible to explain to a Normal citizen how the following of instructions is still a skilful and fulfilling task, or to describe the satisfaction, the sense of triumph, that comes with such complete understanding of things that are often very difficult to understand. And that is the road to success."

But it was probably his response about being instructed 'what to do', and 'when to do it' that inspired the slightly mocking leader, "Who are you waiting for, Lexin?" in 'Die Welt', and the headline, "What now, Lexin?" in the 'Chicago World News'. It was as if, in the words of the London 'Telegraph', he might be waiting for the "eclosion of some cosmic secret", some revelation to him alone, something, they added with relish, "that could enable them maybe to bypass some small print which seemed to have bogged things down?"

Lenica had watched the Kastner interview. "I still don't really understand your views on the crisis, Lexin" she said to him over a late breakfast on the terrace the following morning. Nor does Xiaofeng, incidentally"

"Surprise, surprise!"

"The Assembly's terribly hung up on this question of subjugation to the authority of the Bods – or however you want to put it."

"Oh I was mentioned, was I?"

"More than once. S'pose it's not surprising they don't get it if most of the Conference doesn't either. That is what they don't like, either: the disagreement here, the lack of direction, lack of progress."

"It is not new, is it?" he replied. "I mean, I do talk about it. We are not their equals, but nor are we subjugated. It is not something Earthbound we are working towards, Lenica, it is something galactic and not attainable on our own; nor for that matter do words like 'success' and 'progress' possess quite the same aura against that background."

"You'd better get round and explain it all a lot more, and pretty damn quick or they'll close the whole thing down for good!"

There was an uneasy silence interrupted only by the crunch of cereals and scraping of yoghurt tubs. Then Felicitas said, quietly, "That would be terrible. All Olaf's work…"

"Get round where, Lenica?" Lexin asked. "I cannot go to the Assembly."

"The world. Press conferences. Then everybody will hear, ourselves and Normals. There is nothing like real presence. If all this is as important as you say it is, you must talk about it until you are blue in the face. It should be possible to televise what goes on, and of course it will fill the papers. Come on, I'll fix it. I know everybody. I was with them all at a party the night before this damn thing happened. It seems awful that we were all having such a good time. My poor father, it's such a bloody shame…" Lenica relapsed into tears again, causing Felicitas to do the same. "There is nothing to stop you," she said after a minute or two, pushing aside her plate, standing up and draining her coffee mug. "You would not be representing the Society. I will fix it if there is any trouble. I don't know why I am saying this, Lexin," she added, "but trust your sister." So saying, she picked up her still not quite empty wine glass and went and stood at the balustrade, surveying the familiar view – with a fresh eye, possibly?

Lexin offered his mother the fruit dish, which today was the large and ancient Russian silver one that would often appear, probably by some arrangement with Robert, when she admitted needing a boost to her confidence in historical continuity and purpose. He recalled that according to his historical studies the calm and fruitful period that had followed the visitation and burgeoned in the twenty-second century was marked by an unprecedented and lasting respect for the spoken, and especially the written, word, and it angered him that once again swathes of the media were seeking to dominate the hearts and minds of the population, Normals and Societans alike, and him in particular! With Lenica on his side it might be possible to make them relent and see for themselves the light which for him now blazed out more strongly by the day.

It was true that there was nothing to stop him, and every reason to take on, en masse, those in the media who were opposing, belittling him. By inviting them, it would be he who was on the front foot. He had not told Felicitas that when he had made that inquiry about use of their PAS by Societans on the Snowballer opinion gatherer he had also posed a cryptic subsidiary question: "Respond if you know Big Nose!", because a negative response would almost certainly accentuate her worries about his singularity. Fortunately, he did not think she had seen the question. No-one *had* responded. As far as he himself was concerned, the knowledge that the visions might be his alone, and the challenge they posed were thus his alone to explain, strengthened his resolve.

When after a minute or two Lenica turned to come back to her seat, despite her smart, even hard appearance in neat jeans and dazzling white top, knee-length and clinched by a Southern Cross brooch in red stone, did he not detect at that moment an indefinable softening in her manner? He had always known there was that other happier, gentler Lenica, obscured over the years, especially the last few years in a perceptibly more unsettled world and in the last few months in the uncharacteristically inharmonious environs of the Assembly. Could it be that now in the certainty of Olaf's death the hard veneer was disappearing to reveal the beginnings of a new determination to strive for some kind of solution to the Society's impasse, even if it meant going along for a while with her brother's peculiar ideas?

Suddenly, for a few moments, Lexin was back in the cave, feeling for himself Shining Face's partial awareness, as she lay enveloped in the new skins that she had recently prepared and with the safely retrieved rhino fur under her, of her weakness and the need to eat. It was an awareness that was increasing as the dim daylight in the cave faded. Yet she knew there was no more to eat within reach than the last remnants of an old store of nuts, mainly of beech, that she had been able to accumulate in the autumn, and the beech nuts still remaining needed cooking. In truth, Lexin could not imagine how salvation would come to this brave young woman.

Lenica was sitting now with her elbows upon the table, chin resting in her cupped hands, a slim, silver bracelet on each wrist, fixing Lexin with a studied gaze and unusual concentration.

All right," he said, "go ahead! But it is so hard when you have nothing concrete to offer like a politician has, but only warnings, hints, insights provided by a personal activity synthesizer...visions – however real..."

"Visions, brother?"

"Yes, visions. I don't talk about them too much."

"Do you know about these, Mother?"

Felicitas had risen from the table and come round to where Lexin was still sitting. "Yes, I do," she replied, running a hand through his hair. "You must be patient with him, Lenica; it may be our only hope." Felicitas said it with just a flicker of a smile.

"My God, it's a mother-and-son conspiracy!" Despite the touch of humour there was genuine astonishment.

"It took a long while for me to be persuaded."

"They are about people in trouble in other times – messed up families, actually –," Lexin explained. "It seems our destinies are intertwined." He admitted it all sounded horribly pompous.

"Really? Well tell me more, dear brother – later. But apart from all that, if you *are* right – God knows how – in your press pronouncements and all that, and I with my wayward lifestyle am leading the world to ruin, and if it is true that we have all been grossly neglectful of our vocation..."

Lexin did not wait to hear what his sister was about to say – whatever it was. An apology, possibly? Apologies did come occasionally. The important thing was to build on Lenica's initiative before she started getting miserable again. "*I* did not say anything about your lifestyle," he insisted. "Did *anybody*?" Then, releasing himself from his mother and going over to where Lenica was standing, he took her arms in his hands, and engaging those firm and confident eyes now clouded by sadness he said, "Lenica, trust *me* now, even if I hardly trust myself. We have to act now, immediately, like you said."

"I will do my best," she declared, kissing him, adding that only a trust that approached the outer limits of reason enabled her to say it. "I will get going this very day," she said, giving Felicitas a long hug, "I have to get back to Australia as soon as possible, in any case – much to Xiaofeng's displeasure. Actually, we could start there. Lexin. But you must explain to me about your visions."

"His displeasure?" Lexin said, after Lenica had gone out. "I did not know..."

"You are not omniscient, Lexin," Felicitas replied. "They are pretty close. He's been round often lately. You are always up there in your eyrie. Our Xiaofeng could be quite a calming, steadying influence on Lenica, you know. But tell me about those other women in your life."

Women in his life! Only now did he feel it was right to worry his sympathetic but still grieving mother with an account of Shining Face's hardships in the cave – how his body had come to be her body, invested with her thoughts, her sensations – not in some bisexual transformation but completely and unquestioningly. He had known her fear, even her pain...felt in his hands – her hands – the little bag of cones, the charm, and in those hands he had felt what remained of her hopes of finding Red Hair, and the power, the faith that sustained it. "I don't know about Marcelle," he said. "Perhaps she is there too."

"Lexin, I think *she* is having a lot of trouble. She may need your help before long. I gather her mother is poorly."

"You have not been using *your* PAS, have you?"

"This morning. You prescribed more use of our PAS. Isn't it better if we share out the visions – and the worries?"

There was certainly plenty to think about when you were living in three different worlds. Lexin managed a smile, thankful that his mother was alongside him, but wanting to protect her from the threefold pressures of the timeless sphere.

"Yes, of course it is," he said, coming over to her and kissing her on the cheek.

"There is plenty to worry about."

"Courage, boy, courage!"

"Touché!" Yes, he did need it. She must have heard all about the Kastner interview. He did not think she would have watched it. So Ida was poorly. He hoped there was nothing to really worry about. But... "a lot of trouble"...? *His* PAS had nothing to report on events at Newchurch. Clearly the visions *were* being shared – with his mother at least! That was good, very good, and he was turning it all over in his mind as Lenica travelled back to Canberra with him.

She had made a collection of media-coverage reports which she added to from time to time as they went along, and which he managed to plough through on the eight-hour journey by SST while she would go off and chat to friends on her much travelled route or do some exercising in the gym. He also found time, as they arrowed along their suspended tunnel a hundred metres below the surface of the Pacific off eastern Australia, to fast-read Reilly's latest novel, 'Retreat from Lyra', about a family that emigrated to Lyra. All but one member of the family returned because they could not stand the 'bright light'. The bright light was never quite explained. It was something they always had to turn away from. Indeed it was not quite certain it was Lyra that they had reached at all, and in the end they were given a free passage back to Earth – after sad partings, of course. The work, written by a Normal, seemed to be infected with all the current powerlessness and frustration of members of the Society, and he hovered between thinking it should be banned for Societans or made obligatory background reading as a kind of warning. Then it was back to thinking about the difficult days ahead on Planet Earth and those press reports.

"Lexin Denies the Bods are Gods" proclaimed 'Le Monde', but "Mr. Solberg proclaims that our alien friends are to be obeyed absolutely. How do you equate this with democracy, Lexin?" Certainly there were things to be put right, notions to be corrected: "It's Open War in the Society!" ('New Daily Mail'): "Lexin says the Society is on a road to nowhere". Did he really say that? Well that one was a bit more illuminating, but not very helpful, either. It was clear that appearing full-frontal in the world's media was going to be hazardous, but nevertheless he was looking forward to the chance of face-to-face exchanges with his detractors.

He thought of that amazing girl trapped in a cave, then of Marcelle and *her* single-minded devotion to her deviant mother, and made some notes: "Think of making two and two equal four," he might say to the assembled media, "that is what I mean by being obedient. It is because we modified humans have tried to pervert simple logic, because we have failed to listen, to allow ourselves to be enlightened, that we are in trouble. In the light of the galactic understanding of the Bods, ours must be a speck in an ocean of knowledge just as we are a speck in an ocean of spacetime. And yet it seems we matter nevertheless. We mattered in the year 2073, and there is no doubt in my mind that we still matter in 2453."

But how could such assertions be digested? The Bods weren't all that popular at the moment. What would the media want to know of decipherment, the use or misuse of PAS's, still less of visions giving insight into greater truths? Speculating on all this and trying with Lenica to arrange a timetable of press conferences, perhaps other meetings, he wondered whether any words would convey what had become evident to him only through personal revelation. Perhaps he *should* tell everyone of his experiences out of time. Perhaps he would have to. But even supposing he could convince Societans of the present reality of those subjects of one man's visions, and that in some mysterious way the future of the Society depended on their future, how could the rest, the Normals, be expected to swallow it? If Lenica was right, a change of heart by both Societans and Normals would have to come quickly. As to what might then follow if and when this happened, well he just hoped Marcus Kastner might have to eat his words.

Having finalized their itinerary in the calm of Lenica's old fashioned suite in the New Australia Hotel in Canberra, Lexin returned to his suite for a shower and a change before dinner. When they met again in the bar and found a quiet corner, she laid her little black handbag on the table, visibly gritted her teeth and said,

"Lexin, I am afraid there is really going to be a problem with Harry Beckenthal. He is not at all happy with me. He tells me cancel the tour or resign. Worse even than that, the Government has intimated that the Society may have only until the end of the year to 'put its house in order'."

"Or?"

"I don't know."

"Not closure, surely."

"Meantime, they say, it could concentrate on its advisory and applicational work, with no retrieval, experimental or even decipherment work allowed at the Mission Station, where at most only theoretical work would continue."

"So little appreciation!"

"It would be up to the Society to decide whether it wishes to proceed with the rebuilding of the Station, and up to the Government and the World Assembly to decide whether at the end of the year the criteria are likely to be fulfilled for fully recommissioning the Station and resuming decipherment and other work."

Lexin supposed the Government would hardly be willing to pour more money into a failing project, however important, and Harry Beckenthal's interpretation of the Society's struggles were hardly designed to inspire confidence in the institution. "Criteria! What do they know about criteria?" Lexin exclaimed, gyrating the ice round his apple martini in frustration.

CHAPTER ELEVEN

"A student in computer science and information technology is invited to participate in an online service supporting solutions to a specific anthropological and human problem. 'See' (highlighted) for further information." Mark had turned aside for a moment from his project notes on his 'Applications of information technology in world development aid' to examine on the net – purely for study purposes – the range of jobs actually being offered. The invitation was in a page of advertisements for IT posts in areas of academic research. It sounded like a holiday job.

Mark stared at the monitor again. A little unusual, certainly. Definitely something different. He had researched IT in community initiatives, conflict situations, but this? Suddenly the screen changed. Up came the heading, 'Problem focus: Big Nose', and he just sat staring at the words in disbelief.

It was not the first time, though, that something a bit like this had happened since that wet day when he had been with Marcie in the park and they had seemed at loggerheads about the business of those people in other ages. When later he had met blonde Jane studying on his course at the university and found that she lived in Newchurch too, and that her father managed a large company providing internet services to the entertainment industry, he had shown an interest, and her father took an interest in him. He remembered writing to Marcelle and telling her he had gone over to the business and economics side of IT and was excited about having a good contact. Soon after that she sent him a card on his birthday, and he sensed she might have felt a bit put out, since he had not been able to avoid mentioning Jane in his letter. He hoped he had not hurt his old girlfriend.

Then out of the blue he had happened, in the course of his studies, to turn up a website entitled, 'Ancient man and the long road to economic chaos'. But something he could not quite pinpoint about the way it talked of the harsh life of the hunter gatherers and the hazards of weather and accidents and disability had put his old girlfriend, and her enduring interest in that hunter-gatherer of long ago, firmly in his mind again. For reasons he could not entirely explain, his interest in business economics dwindled and there seemed to be not so much to talk about with Jane. He realised later it was the same website that had prompted a subsequent interest in more humanitarian applications of his science. The strange thing was that despite strenuous efforts he had never been able to find the website again; nor could he remember anything else about it.

The fact was, though, that seeing the name, 'Big Nose', in print, a name so personal to her and probably known only to the two of them (not counting Lexin), was a shock for which he was still scarcely prepared by that earlier experience and the subsequent change of heart about the direction of his studies. Surely there was no way Marcelle could be responsible for this!

He had wanted to write to her again at that time, but hesitated. For the life of him he could not fathom her rock-hard attachment to her mother, still less believe what she believed about her dreams – or whatever they were, and felt there was still so much he did not know about her. He admitted that the truth was he was afraid to commit himself and certainly he did not want to hurt her. Admire her he certainly did, loved her probably, if it is possible to love an enigma. In a way, he felt just a little afraid of her, too, because of her directness, her boldness, her other-worldliness. There could be more truth in describing her as 'otherworldly' than he wanted to admit. Some might call her daemonic. The word scared him, and even more so now, after this…

He told himself as he sat there in his room overlooking the modern buildings of the well-tended, leafy campus that he must not get carried away by this new revelation. If this file, this message or whatever it was, was about what he imagined, had he not heard it all before from Marcelle and been completely flummoxed by it? Would it be any more comprehensible now than then? But how the dickens... Even as he said this to himself, staring at the monitor, the 'Problem Focus' became subtitled momentarily something like 'Progress of the father as an active link in family reunification', but not quite that... something gentler, more personal, yet something more powerful..., before the screen changed to thumbnails. There were dozens of these, numbered and apparently making up a pictorial chronology: images of Big Nose walking in a forest, sometimes in the snow, weighed down with all his stuff or scooping water from a stream with an animal skull or collecting it in a skin bag. No sign of Red Hair. Certainly it was all just like Marcelle had described, right down to that peculiar, half-closed eye. Then came another change – a series of textual options, like 'objective', and then 'progress' (or was it 'characteristics'? – he could not remember later. 'Progress' certainly came into it), with detailed physiological and biochemical indices of fatigue, malnutrition, mental state...

In the end, but only after some months, he *had* contacted Marcelle again, with a Best Wishes card and brief letter on her birthday in November, mentioning that he was now more interested in humanitarian applications of his science as he embarked on his third year. By this time Jane had disappeared over the horizon. Marcelle had replied telling him she still worked in the supermarket, her father was in hospital having numerous leg operations, and her mother was working for an escort agency. She wished him well in his studies. No mention of Big Nose.

Mark played around with the miles of data for a minute or two...'Objective': survival...; 'Progress': travelling a year and a half alone... The medical indices, though he did not understand them well, looked kind of real, and there was no reason to doubt that they represented a man continuously close to the limits of human endurance. The thumbnails, unlike some of the text, could be re-accessed, and between them it added up to a story of great fortitude. The date, April BP 38 776, was stunning.

It couldn't be a computer *game*, could it? Sure, he was trying to fool himself with such a suggestion. Of course he was. It wasn't just that the name 'Big Nose' would not have just happened to come up; it was the fact that the whole file appeared 'tailored' for him, to convince him, yes, to involve him. There was no need to dwell on anything. What he needed to know was there, already digested. The one thing that struck him was the complete credibility of everything. There was nothing to disbelieve, everything to believe. No, it was Marcie's dream all right. She had latched on to some paranormal phenomenon or other, and now he had as well. Best forget it! See her, tell her. Maybe she needed help.

The screensaver took over. He sat looking out of the window, at the students biking in early to meet friends for a natter before the evening meal in hall, the gently random movement of the spring flowers setting off the solid geometry of the halls of residence and the landscaped lawns across which angular shadows progressed with imperceptible, complex yet predictable motion. He tried to think of other explanations. He asked himself who else could have known about those people... about Marcelle's dreams? Her dad, her mum? Had she told them about her dreams? But they would not, could not have done this. Nobody could have, could they? Some new friend, an acquaintance more like, deep into computers and eager to use his skills assembling plausible data to help convince him, Mark, that her dreams were true? Impossible! She would never have allowed such a thing. She was head-first into the story and would never have played around with her precious 'ancients' like that, even if it had been possible.

He returned to the monitor. There was the man again, full-screen now – a bag of bones – and now he was moving about. He was busy. It was rolling country, up towards the mountains somewhere, and he was breaking branches off the trunk of a dead tree lying in the snow across a torrent. The sunlight was bright, and a branch of a tree with white blossom came across a corner of the screen. It must be late winter or early spring there, too. It was very still. The man cast a lively shadow in the bubbling water. Suddenly Mark realised that he had forgotten to switch on the audio. Now he could hear the stream, the sound of cracking wood, even the sound of breathing. Big Nose was making a shelter in bushes above the river. The colours, the shapes, were vivid, tantalizing, beckoning, seeming to draw Mark in, enlist him in the building of it too, the building of a refuge with stripped branches and evergreen fronds, roofing it over with more fronds and a few skins. Was it his imagination, or did the shelter actually grow in its reality, its tangibility, its comfort even as he looked, with its carpet of moss and leaves from the dense forest and fragments from the forest litter, topped by a deerskin rug. Soon, hopefully, the air would be full of promise with the smoke from a fire, and later – given successful hunting – replete with the smell of roast venison. The scene was so real, so 'present', that it was downright mean and cynical to have thought in terms of tricks and games, or of anything other than the strong probability that the advertisement was for his personal benefit. He was driven unwillingly to the conclusion that, however inexplicable, what he was seeing was like an authentication – and, like the advertisement had said, an invitation.

Was it not obvious from the beginning? Probably. He just didn't want to believe it, or didn't dare – he wasn't sure which. The picture vanished, and the screen went blank.

"All right, Marcie", he said out loud, "You've got me here. I don't understand this at all. What happens next? What do I do? If I am supposed to do something, how could I possibly affect what happens to Big Nose?"

Mark dare not turn the machine off or come out of the file. He sat for several minutes looking out of the window again, gazing absently at the occasional stirring of the daffodils, the imperceptibly progressing shadows. Six o'clock. An hour to go before he need go over to the hall. It seemed wrong, he thought, supposing this was all real – and it was still near-impossible to get his head around it –, to be a voyeur into the man's hardship. Yet he knew that for Marcelle it was all very real and that he must ring her if only to set the record straight. She probably knew all about Big Nose and the others and what they were doing, anyway. At least he knew now what she was talking about, and if anybody did somehow have access to some plane of existence where there was no time but only a constant reality, he thought, smiling to himself, it was surely dear Marcie, and he realised that she was still someone special to him.

*   *   *

This was Marcelle's third visit to see her mother. It was three days previously that the City Hospital had got in touch with her about Ida's serious illness – Marcelle had known nothing more than that she had been unwell. She was propped right up now to help her cough up phlegm, towering so that it looked as if she would almost topple over as she shook with the effort. She still looked hot and feverish, but a little more comfortable now than on Marcelle's first visit. It was pneumonia, a special kind of pneumonia, the nurse was now able to tell her (having ascertained that, the husband being absent, Marcelle was effectively next of kin) associated with the human acquired immune deficiency syndrome.

"AIDS?" Marcelle had uttered the word involuntarily, like vomiting forth something unspeakably awful.

"I'm afraid so. But we'll get this infection under pretty quickly, hopefully. We can do a lot with AIDS these days. I gather your mother shares a flat with somebody."

"Yes, but it's not somebody who could be expected to look after her."

"She will be very weak for a while. And it being AIDS one doesn't quite know what's round the corner."

"I can call in and make things easier for her – if she'll let me."

"Independent, is she?"

"I wouldn't say that." Stubborn, maybe, Marcelle thought now as she sat beside the bed. Ida was averting her gaze, which was sad – more sad than Marcelle ever remembered her being, a self accusatory sadness. "Try not to worry, Mum, just take the medicines and I'll see you're all right."

Ida burst into tears. "Haven't I been enough trouble to you?" she managed to say between sobs.

"It's all right. You never hurt me that much, and I got used to it."

"I should have tried a bit harder, then," Ida said, managing a wicked smile which turned into another bout of sobbing.

It was now nearly May. The nurse could not tell her how long ago infection might have taken place.

Marcelle had never seen Lexin again since that vivid encounter in which he had appeared to care about her so much. But often, especially when things were difficult for her, she would remember his words, and how he had responded when she told him about her family and what she longed for. How could Lexin help her now? How could he help her mother escape from this cul-de-sac illness in which time was only too real and the prospects so bleak? How could he help Shining Face? Soon she would die in that dark place, that cave where she had got stuck, and then there would surely be no hope left at all. But Lexin had said things would work out. How could she not trust in the word of such a good man so far above her in knowledge, and not least knowledge about her own family?

About a week later, when the doctors seemed pretty pleased with Ida's progress in the circumstances, Marcelle took a call from Mark on her mobile. It was months since she had heard from him. He was saying something to the effect that she wouldn't believe it but he thought he had seen Big Nose walking in a forest. She was busy, busy tidying up her living room littered with pamphlets about teaching assistants, books about AIDS. She really hadn't got time to chat...

"Where was that, then?" she asked with a laugh. Mark was apt to make daft remarks, and postponing the moment when she would have to explain why she was not feeling very jokey she played along.

"How should I know? Just a forest, and it was snowy."

"Mark," she said sharply, "It is ages since you got in touch with me, and here you are talking about a man in a forest like Big Nose. So what? I am amazed you even remember his name. You were not all that interested before. I shouldn't think he's alive now, anyway, so the joke has fallen a bit flat."

There was a few moments' silence, then he said, "All I can say is that I know what you were talking about, now."

"That's *something*. Now what can it be that has caused this change of heart? Have you fallen out with Jane? Is that what you are trying to tell me?" Marcelle was conscious of being unkind, but the truth was that she did not really want to hear from anybody but Lexin. How could Mark help her? She was in any amount of trouble. There was a time when she would have been glad just of his sympathy, but she did not even want to tell him now about her mum and thus elicit unwanted pity from him. Still less had she any desire that he should return with her to that other world of lions and mammoths that he had despised.

"A lot has changed," he said. "No, I am not with Jane now, and I've changed course a bit. I told you. I am not concentrating on the business side any more, and I am getting interested in aid organisations."

"Really?" At least he was talking in some sensible way at last.

"It's still computers – you know how I practically live in them. And it's to do with my computer that I'm ringing". Well that was a confession, she thought, confessing that he practically lived in computers. His bedroom at home had been full of all that stuff, with leads and plugs everywhere. Could it be that he was beginning to know his limitations – or what? Marcelle wanted to say she had things to do: a sick mother to go and visit, not to mention a sometimes struggling father to go and be cheerful with before she tidied up *his* house as well, – and she needed a bath before she did all that because sitting on that stool in the supermarket made her so sweaty – but something about his tone, a kind of unaccustomed urgency, held her back. And what did he mean about his computer? "I've been seeing strange things on my monitor," he went on, "and just now, as I said…"

"Monitor?"

"Computer screen."

"Oh yes, of course. Everything on that would be pretty strange to me." There was a momentary pause. She felt he might be getting just a bit frustrated by her apparent indifference.

"Marcie, dear, I'm trying to tell you that my computer seems to have become a bit like your dreams, and I am seeing Big Nose moving out there, walking in that forest. The *real* Big Nose.. Either that or someone is playing an elaborate trick." He began to try and explain.

Suddenly Marcelle felt herself come into focus. "I'm sorry Mark, I had some things on my mind. Mark, I understand now. You say you really saw Big Nose? That would be wonderful, wonderful news! Just Big Nose? Not Red Hair, or a girl called Shining Face who is Big Nose's daughter? She left the camp later, desperate to seek out Red Hair who she thinks is her mother, but who in fact fostered her."

"No."

"Probably you couldn't. Shining Face is dying, injured and starving in a cave. I keep dreaming about her lying there. I don't know where Red Hair is, but I think she will be in a camp being a slave of one sort or another. I didn't even know if Big Nose was still alive. He has been wandering for so long."

"The dreams go on, then?"

"Yes, they go on. Just like before." She could almost see those bushy blonde eyebrows knit together. Was he still doubting? Couldn't he trust her even now, even when he had seen something himself? "Yes, Mark, it's like I told you. They are almost a part of me."

"And… Lexin? Have you seen him again?"

"I haven't seen him. I am sure he knows, though." She did not say she would badly *like* to see him again. That would be rubbing salt in, if Mark really did care at last. "Perhaps there is a way through now, then," she said. "Everything's in such a mess."

"Everything? Your father's not too bad, is he?"

"Still cleaning out the parks toilets."

"And your mother?" The tone was gentle, conciliatory – he could be both those things.

She would have to tell him now, pity or no pity, "Mark, Mum has AIDS and she is ill with pneumonia."

"Christ! I'm so sorry, Marcie. When did she find out?"

"Not long since. *I* only did ten days ago."

There was a long silence. "And you. Will you...will you be all right?" He was waiting for her to pick up a thread. Sympathy had become anxiety. She helped him.

"She doesn't think it was from Larry, Mark. He was tested when he went inside – on account of me. Grandpa told me. But in any case I had to have two lots of tests and I came out negative both times. She must have caught it long ago, anyway."

"What about your Dad. Will he be okay? I mean..."

She helped him again. "Mum said my dad could never have got it from her, and I was to draw my own conclusion from that."

"So what do you mean by 'a way through?'" Mark asked after a lengthy pause. "A way through for who?"

"For everybody." Marcelle could imagine Mark thinking, worrying, wondering whatever outlandish things she was going to say, the connections she was going to make across the barrier of time. But she was clear in her own mind, and she must say it: "Everything depends on Shining Face, Mark, and she can't move from the cave. Maybe Big Nose will find her and save her and then both of them could search for Red Hair. Mark, I know why you were shown everything."

The whole seemingly preposterous setup was there again, Mark said to himself, those parallel connections that he had been so cynical about, and which now again he knew neither how to believe nor how he could disbelieve. And here he was, involved once again with this dysfunctional family. His parents would be making their opinion clear, talking about him getting too involved with *that* girl, although to be fair to himself he did not feel bound by their opinions. The uncertainties, the decisions to be made, were his own. But how do I start if I really have to do this? he asked himself. What did it say? 'Participate'. So just do it. Just go with him, I suppose.

"I can't tell you how upset my father is," Marcelle went on, "though I know you find it hard to understand that he still loves my mother." She was crying now. "Mark," she said when she had recovered, "once I travelled with Shining Face, and for a while we were one person. I don't think I ever actually told you that. It is just a shame that she was taught to despise her father for the way he walked, but I am sure that one day she will come to recognize him for the good man that he is."

"You are incredible, Marcie," he said. Neither spoke for a moment. Then he said, "I could get over this weekend."

"Then you could tell me personally how Big Nose is progressing."

"I hope so," he replied, truthfully, "Yes, I hope I will be able to."

"I couldn't thank you enough, dearest Mark," she said finally. "I'm sorry I was so horrid."

*   *   *

Mark returned to his computer. It could have been several days later now as he observed Big Nose walking away from his shelter by the river now stripped of its comforts and abandoned.. Whatever the truth about all this business, Mark thought, it undoubtedly put the seal on all that Marcelle had said about the hunter, right down to the determination in his painful walk and even a suggestion of generosity in his expression, visible even beneath the shadow of his straggling, matted hair. Although reason told him otherwise, he knew Marcelle would recognize him.

It was a quarter to seven, and only a quarter of an hour to when he would need to go over to eat, but he could not tear himself away. He was heading upstream. There were signs that the snow was beginning to melt, for from time to time his shoes of thonged hide sank into mud. Mark caught the sound. It was a country sound. Marcelle often teased him for being such a townie – that was since she had been living with her grandparents in deep country at Culver with its fields, foxes and pheasants, and the canal winding through the flat landscape. Strange, then, that now he felt nothing odd about squelching up this muddy mountain valley, prodding continually with his spear to test for swampy ground or occasionally to test the depth of the mushy snow. Sometimes his spear helped him balance when his hip jipped and gave way momentarily and would otherwise have sent him sprawling into briars. It was as tough as its maker. Always keeping two spears, none had lasted him as long as Strong's.

As though at the flick of a switch, Mark had an impression of fast-forwarding in time, for now he realised it was already the middle of the day. Yet in spite of this the cold had become more intense, and he judged that he must have come up some hundreds of metres in altitude. Steep slopes stretched higher and higher on either side, their increasingly sparse vegetation struggling to stay in place amid the grey, tumbling screes and precarious snowfields. The sun, which had been shining when he first set out that morning, was now fading gradually behind a fog that was slowly descending the slopes towards the river, eventually enveloping him and freezing upon his eyebrows and upon his mammoth fur.

The way was ever upwards, but now at least there was frozen, level snow to walk through, provided he avoided the dense entanglements of vegetation swarming over the rocky sides of the river. But he was feeling increasingly tired, and there remained only scraps of meat to eat, scavenged and dried in the sun moons ago, plus the remainder of his store of chestnuts and acorns cooked the previous autumn and a few handfuls of dried berries. Certainly he would have to stop soon and rest. Of course, if some unsuspecting meal came running towards him upon its four legs…but he was dreaming!

It was with only a slight feeling of regret that in his daydreams Mark saw from his window in the hall of residence no movement yet towards the refectory and dinner. Daydreaming in these circumstances might be pretty normal, but now he forbade himself even to daydream. It was imperative to keep going. Only in this way had he survived so long since those distant times in Giant Man's domain. But by the middle of the afternoon, as so often by this time, the pain in his back and hips was intense, and with the way now becoming increasingly rocky and obstructed and everything shrouded in fog, he decided to call it a day, stop, and make what camp he could.

Keeping a sharp lookout for signs of the lions and other beasts that he knew from experience inhabited these high valleys, he began to search around for a place to build a shelter. Having found a spot close by the river where one or two overhanging hawthorns had kept the snow at bay, he had got no further than gathering a few main supporting props from material washed down by the current when his hands became so cold as to be without feeling and he decided to first try and make a fire and thaw out. It might also make his position safer. But alas! His best efforts working hard with his fire bow produced no embers in the damp air with which to ignite the less than bone-dry kindling which he had managed to collect from tree fragments scattered along the river's edge.

For some moments Big Nose fell to reflecting on what might have impelled him to come up into these mountains, so cold and inhospitable, and the truth was that he was still trying to work it out. Much of the winter had been spent by the sea away to the south, living pretty well off baby seals and seabirds' eggs and all the stuff the falling tide left on the rocks. So why head up here when it was still winter? He concluded that it had been many things: first the direction taken by a flight of geese before rain, then a diversion due to a flood, then a decision to follow a herd of reindeer...and so it went on, and every day he would run his hand round the precious necklace of acorns.

It was while he was trying to find drier sticks by the river, and at the same time the best place to scoop water into his boar's-stomach water bag, that his eye lighted on very large animal prints, clearly those of mammoths, along the river bank and in the ice and snow lodged among the boulders in the water. He had seen no prints the way he had come. Glancing round before returning with more sticks and the filled water bag to where he had left his things, he became aware of the jumbled prints of other animals. At almost the same time the fog thinned momentarily, and on looking up he caught sight of the shadowy shape of a towering but hitherto invisible rock face high above him. In the lowest part of the rock there appeared to be a gaping black hole – almost certainly the mouth of a cave. The sight of it injected new life into his weary body, and hope of a refuge much to be preferred to a roofed-over hole in the thorn bushes. The question was whether it might be already in occupation. And if so, by man or by beast? Neither seemed a very good prospect. Certainly, though, it must be investigated.

He waited some time, after collecting his things together, looking and listening. He felt that at least if mammoths were present (and if there were any there would be several), unless they were completely in the land of nod he would hear or see something. He detected nothing. For what use they might be, he put a couple of large stones into his pouch, and, since it was already dusk and time was thus short, taking a calculated risk he began slowly to climb the steep slope.

What with the weight of the stones, the water bag, the cumbersome skins on his back, and everything else it was desperately hard scrambling up, spear as near ready as it could be, among the rocks and the stunted birches. He had calculated that it was better to keep as much of his stuff with him as he could since he did not want to have to return for it immediately or get cut off from it. Even so, he had had to leave some skins and some heavier tools behind, intending to return for them later.

Now he could see everything more clearly. There was indeed a cave, its opening the height of perhaps three men. By the time he was just below the entrance, he hoped that any human or large animal present, unless in deep sleep, would have made their presence known.

Big Nose emerged cautiously on the flat rocks before the cave entrance. By now it was almost dark, but he could see the cavern was quite deep. He could sniff nothing suggesting living animals, only the lingering smell of the remains of some carcases that looked like the aftermath of considerable feasting, their smell reaching him on a current of slightly less cold air that he would have expected from a large cavern with another entrance somewhere. As for what animals had been feasting there, he preferred not to think about it! If his time had come, so be it! What he really did not expect to find were the remains of a very recent fire, and he hesitated. Any contact with his fellows had usually resulted in bad outcomes.

The event of a year ago when Red Hair had been taken from him was only too fresh in his mind. He had been back twice to try and get her back. The first time he had been allowed to see the headman, and he had summoned her. She had wanted to come with him, but the headman had said, "How do you suppose she will survive out there, a woman?" He persuaded her to stay and sent Big Nose away. The second time they did not even let him see her. "She does not want to come," they told him, "and she is too good a grandmother," and some youths had chased him off. He thought it might be true that she did not want him any more, and in any case it was the beginning of winter and it was probably better for her to stay there. Now he had walked so far in search of food and rest that he was not sure if he could even remember where that place was, or if he could ever find it again.

A cursory examination of the cave, however, revealed no sign of man or beast, and it being so late he decided he would have to risk an encounter – of whatever kind. There were scraps of dry kindling around where the fire had been, and under these sheltered conditions just inside the cave it was not too difficult to get a fire lit with the bow and pile it up with some bigger pieces of wood lying about. Exhausted, he laid his belongings aside, wrapped his heavy mammoth hide around himself, lay down and fell asleep by the entrance.

Mark daydreamed about Marcelle and about trying to get her to explain what she wanted him to do now that it was clear all Big Nose was interested in was to survive. He had tried to get Red Hair back and had failed. There seemed no hope of finding her again. But Marcelle was reminding him that Shining Face had not given up hope in her quest, and now was no time for him to give up, either.

"So if you care about me, if you love me, Mark, you must not give up," she was saying ever more loudly. Her voice had an urgency that he had never heard before. It was almost like a cry for help...

Big Nose awoke, imagined he had heard something and lay listening. Very soon he heard it again, but very faintly – a voice. It seemed to be coming from high *inside* the cave. It must be a spirit, he thought. A dead persons spirit? He had never heard of spirits of the dead ending up in caves. Nobody knew where they went. He lay still. Again, in the middle of a little gust of wind as it touched the dry ivy leaves clinging to the cave entrance, he again imagined he heard something, but was not sure, and he turned over and fell asleep.

The voice woke him from a jumble of dreams as it was just beginning to get light. How could he be hearing a *woman's* voice, here? He lay still. It *must* be a spirit. When it came yet again, faint but urgent, now there was no mistaking a cry for help, and *in his own language*. He decided that, spirit or no, he must answer it, and raising himself on one hand he shouted, "Where are you?" He was surprised by the shake in his own voice.

"Come over the top of the cave!" It was definitely human, a woman's voice, only just audible now.

"Who are you?"

No answer to that. "Watch for lions!" the voice came a last time, and again in his own language. It was strange and unnerving.

There was nothing for it. He couldn't pretend there was nothing there. He must investigate, whatever the risk. Picking up his hide and throwing it round himself, and taking just a spear, Big Nose went out of the cavern and made his way round to where a rocky, overgrown slope seemed to lead upwards in the right direction. There he saw what he had not seen before: human footprints in the snow. There were animal prints too, but he encountered no living thing while stumbling up among the loose stones hiding beneath the plants and shrubs. Where the slope levelled out the footprints ceased, and there he was startled to hear the voice coming out of the ground.

"I am here!"

Looking around, he could see nothing in the half light that might have been an entrance to anything until the voice repeated the words and his eye made out a small hole among the rocks. He stopped dead in his tracks. Had not Giant Man described these holes in the ground where bad spirits lived? Not in caves, but in holes in the ground. Spirits of bad men – and maybe women? A jumble of recollections rushed into his head. But the footprints? He waited, hesitated, looked around him at the rocky, snowy slopes stretching away, the fog having cleared and the sky now dark blue but still faintly starry above him and brightening every moment in the direction of the coming sunrise. Right by him, in the growing light, he could see many human footprints – quite small ones – leading to and from the hole. Again came the voice. Big Nose decided that even if it was a spirit there was no point in disobeying. If it was a bad spirit, what had he to lose, a marked man already? He went up to the hole and called. The answering words were hard to pick out:

"I was attacked by a lion. I have a terrible thirst."

He cursed for not having brought the water bag up from the cave. "I shall have to go back for water," he explained"

"Please tell me who you are." The voice was weak and hesitant.

"Later", he replied and scrambled down to the cave entrance, returning with the water, and all the food he possessed stuffed in a pouch together with a healing ointment made from many plants and which he always carried with him in a double sea shell. He called down the hole again, but again the demand came.

"Now tell me who you are"

"Do you want food and water or not?" he parried, always wary of revealing his blackened identity, and receiving no answer he edged his way with difficulty down into the hole and the semi-darkness and crawled perhaps three men's lengths along what seemed to be a low, narrow passageway in the rock.

"Wait! How is it you speak my language?"

Now he was very near to the voice." Here's some water," he said, without answering her question, and edging closer.

"Don't come any nearer. Put it in this bag!" She was speaking in little more than a whisper now. It was hard to see anything at all in the cave, but he could just see the little skin bag that she held out for him, probably a hare's skin. He filled it. She took several gulps. As his eyes became adjusted he could just make out that she was sitting leaning against the side of a passage which at this point had widened slightly and was almost high enough for him to stand up in. He sensed some heat coming off her, as if she was ill. The water revived her a bit. "Why won't you tell me who you are?" she whispered sternly, but it was a whisper tinged with fear. "You won't tell me anything. I am Shining Face, daughter of Red Hair." So it was all a dream, and he was still dreaming? It was all too much: spirits, and now a dream, and those names! "Please will you now tell me who *you* are? And whether you have any food." What *was* this? Certainly she spoke his language. But just supposing it *was* Shining Face here, a miracle and no dream, she surely wouldn't want to know him, however much he would like to have known her.

"I have no fresh food," he said. "I saw some bits of carcases in the cavern."

"The lions must have left them there. They came up from the cavern. Along there" (she pointed into the blackness beyond). "They may come up any time, but I have blocked the passage."

"I must get you away from here," he said. "Here is a little dried stuff. It's all I have. Hold out your hand" He reached into the pouch. After some hesitation she reached out, took the pieces of dried meat and chewed and swallowed them, drank some more water. "And you will have to let me see the wound."

"No!" she shrieked, and then whispered, "If my cones can't heal me..."

Big Nose knew the moment had come. That settled it, the cones! Red Hair had mentioned the cones. So the girl was real, and he was not dreaming. "Shining Face," he said, gently, "we come from the same place, I think."

"I doubt it. Name some of our people!"

"Strong, Smooth Face, Slanty Face..."

There was a long silence, then she said, "You say you knew Strong. He died years ago. He was trying to save somebody from drowning but drowned himself."

There was nothing for it now. "I am Big Nose, your father," he said, quietly. "Red Hair gave you the precious cones, didn't she?"

She gasped. "So you…you are my father? I don't want to believe you. But if you are," she cried, "stay away from me. Go away! Just go!" She was screaming now. He was amazed she had the strength to do it. "You bring bad things. Everybody said so."

Not everybody, perhaps. Not Strong, he thought as he backed away – so far as he could in that place. Poor old Strong! How the news saddened him. That good man! For long moments he was lost in sad thoughts. "Look," he said, "I can help you. You will die here otherwise."

"I will probably die anyhow, now." She was still trying to shrink away from him. There was a long silence. She seemed exhausted by her outburst. "You must go away. Please go away," she said eventually, in a faint voice and close to tears. A long time passed in which neither spoke. Then he said, quietly,

"I can't leave you here, Shining Face. Look, why did *you* leave the camp?"

She did not answer at first. Then, revived, perhaps reconciled a little, she said , "Does it matter?"

"Yes."

"If you must know, lots of reasons. There was a terrible flood. Anyway, I wanted to find my mother. I don't know why I am telling you this."

"Why do you think she left, your mother?"

"Because the women didn't want her there."

"Didn't they try and stop you leaving?"

"No."

"Why?" Big Nose felt he knew the answer already.

"They all reckoned I was bad luck, too," she said, adding almost inaudibly, "Only Toothy said that I am not, but I fear very much that he may have been killed when he saved me from the lions."

He thought she was perhaps rambling a bit. "Shining Face," he said, "it seems that we are in this together." He could hear her sobbing. "I'll go and try to cook something. It might be more appetizing. In the meantime, rub some of this ointment on your wound." Big Nose handed her the sea shell with the ointment. She took it, saying nothing He judged she was probably past caring. Then she held out something towards him,

"Take this," she said, "It smells terrible. I can't stand it here. You can roast it for yourself. I know you've made a fire. And there are some beech nuts. You can roast them as well." She fumbled around for a new moments, and he took what felt like a baby hare from her, and a meagre fistful of nuts.

"I suppose the smoke came up through the cave," he said.

"Yes, and if I'd known..."

"What? If you had known it was me? It could have been worse, couldn't it?"

"You are on your own, then?"

"Yes, just me I'm afraid."

She said nothing to that.

Down below in the main cave a slight breeze was encouraging the fire as it raced through the wood. Suddenly it was something fearsome, engulfing, like a burning away of the last years of his life. The thought of what might lie ahead scared him a bit, but it troubled him even more that if what they all said was true and he did bring bad luck, he might bring it to her (if he hadn't already). The matter of his bringing bad luck was something he had over the years come to half believe himself – but only half. Something told him that it was just that he looked different and could not walk or run properly that made it turn out that way. Neither Curvy Lips nor Red Hair ever spoke of such things, and whatever the truth of it all, how could he abandon anyone in such a situation, and least of all this daughter so marvellously returned to him. He must do what he could and then go on his way until the Power took him.

He skinned the hare in record time. The warmth of the fire, and the greatly improving smell of the hare as it cooked over the piled up stones of her hearth, encouraged him. He would like to have thrown most of the other smelly remains discarded by the lions down the hillside – they would make him sick if he ate them –, but they could attract more intruders. Anyway, the hides might come in useful. There were a few good bits of meat, however, mostly the remains of a deer, and these, too, he skinned and either roasted or laid close to the embers with the beech nuts, thinking he would try and dry them, and that the roasted nuts might tickle his sick daughter's appetite.

Now in the glowing embers he saw her courage. It might not be blazing now, but he recognized a fiery spirit behind her words, spat out like the fat in the cooking. She must be incredibly strong to have survived on her own. She could not be more than fourteen years old. He had counted the winters that had passed since Strong had seen him off in that wood by the camp near the sea. How long had she been travelling – she would hardly have left in the winter?

When the hare was ready, Big Nose piled more logs onto the fire before going up the mountainside again with roasted hare and nuts and two sticks coated with hare fat, ignited to give some illumination and stuck in the ends of two bits of one of the deer's leg bones. It was a struggle to prevent the flames blowing out, but fortunately there was very little breeze now. "Here is something better for you to eat," he said.

"I smelt it," she said. "It makes me feel sick."

"Its better than it was. Eat to live," he replied, "and now let me have a look at you!" He held up the sticks. He could see now that she was half-sitting, half-lying in a slight hollow in the cave wall, her deerskin drawn up round her shoulders, above which a necklace of seashells caught his eye. He recognized the necklace at once. There could be no doubt at all now that she was who she said she was, of course, but if even more proof were needed it hit him like a thunderclap – her face, the whole shape of it, but more particularly her lips, her mother's beautiful curved lips that dipped in the middle. He said nothing about that. "You see my nose?" he said. "You're lucky not to have my nose!"

She had been bearing his gaze stoically. "That's enough of joking." she said. It was the stern side of Curvy Lips now, ironically the side that had stood up for him when others got at him. She picked at the hare a bit, and it seemed to revive her a little more. "I suppose I have to thank you for coming to my rescue," she said, "but I don't hide my thoughts, and although you say you are my father I would have preferred to have seen almost anyone else. You deserted my mother and did no good for the camp, either." Her face had darkened: a cloud had passed across the sun. It seemed strange seeing a face so like that of Curvy Lips yet a body so thin, and none of those other curves – so far as could be seen in the low light.

"I will not remain here any longer than I have to," he said.

"You don't have to stay."

"Well I *am* staying." They were silent as she made herself go on gnawing at a leg of the hare. Then he said, "And have you put some stuff on that wound? I'd better see it."

"No, it's all right." She shrank away.

The lighted sticks had gone out, and he had put them down. "I'll have to go and have my breakfast," he said. "Then I will try and re-light the sticks."

"Why do we need them?"

"The wound. It may kill you. It must be treated." He crawled out and went down to the cave entrance. He thought he might have been wrong, but as he approached he had the impression of something leaving the cave. There were so many paw prints everywhere that he could not be sure, but it would hardly have been surprising with roasting smells drifting over the landscape. He ate some of the bits and pieces of deer that were well enough done and then quickly fashioned some more fire sticks to add to the others. As a precaution, over one shoulder and into his largest pouch slung behind him he gathered up as much of the rest of his belongings as he could, and holding all the lighted sticks together in the one hand he now had free, struggled back up the slope. One day he feared his body would give way completely – and there would be no-one to look after *him*.

She looked at him suspiciously when he humped the whole lot down near her.

"Don't worry, I'll find another spot," he said, "but now, that wound! Hold these sticks!" She hesitated. "Go on, I'm your father, aren't I, not Giant Man, so called, or one of those brainless women-chasers?"

"So you say." Her voice, as she took the lighted sticks in their holders, was full of mistrust, but a bit stronger now. The food seemed to have revived her again, just a little.

She let him take off the piece of deer hide that had been covering the wound, turning her head away while he did it. He saw that her side, and right across and down to the womanly parts, was red and swollen, and oozing liquid. She had not opened the shell containing the ointment. He opened it and handed it to her, taking the sticks off her, and watched while she slapped all of it on, making sure she covered the whole area. The raw bits made her squirm in agony.

"No, I'll do it. I'll get a fresh piece," he said as she tried to get the piece of deer hide to cover the wound again and was reaching for the gut to tie it with.

She took the sticks again. "But don't go on looking at me," she said, bitterly.

Seeing what was evidently the original hide lying close by, Big Nose seized one of the cutters lying about and carved out a fresh piece against the cave wall. Resigned now, she said nothing as he deftly fastened the hide over the wound. Afterwards, she said,

"You won't know Giant Man got killed by a lion."

Now was the moment to tell her. "I did know," he said. "Shining Face, I must tell you that I walked many moons with Red Hair."

There was a moment of stunned silence. "Am I to believe that? How could that just happen?"

"Somehow we met up, long after she had left our people." Big Nose paused, then he said, "Red Hair is with another people far away. I could not stay there. They wouldn't have me if I went back.

"Which way is it, that camp?"

"Back the way I have come. A long way. And when you are better, I shall go the opposite way."

She said nothing to that. If he could detect any expression on her face, as he took the still burning sticks from her, he interpreted it as one of relief. "You mentioned Smooth Face," she said. "He got killed, too, just after Giant Man. They say he was killed by another man angry because he had told Giant Man lies about him."

Big Nose made no comment. Before the sticks burned out he managed to find another nook in the upper cave just aside from hers, and planted his belongings there. It was a little closer to the entrance. When he came back to her she seemed to be asleep, though in the near-darkness he could not be sure. He spent the rest of the day reconnoitring. On returning once or twice he managed to get out of her that she had chased several animals off the cliff edge above the cave and that she had been in the cave since the middle of winter, but she would not say much else. That night he dreamed of leaving this place finally, and of her going off in the opposite direction.

But a voice was calling, pleading with him not to leave Shining Face now that he had found her, pleading with him to go with her to find Red Hair. But even assuming she became well enough, with her refusal to recognize her limitations and the unlikelihood of a successful outcome it seemed an unreasonable responsibility to place upon him, and it reawakened in Mark all the old uncertainties, all the old scepticism. In the end Marcelle, as though reading his thoughts, was screaming at him. He had never heard her scream like it.

Big Nose was wakened by it, wakened by Shining Face screaming. Grabbing a spear and a stone he ran, crab-wise and crouching, the few paces to reach her.

"It's there! You see its eyes!" she was shouting. "I kicked it off and it bit me, bit my side. Kill it!" The animal, whatever it was, lunged towards *him* now. It leapt up, its teeth just flicking his arm as he nudged it away. He smelt its breath. It was a wolf, he was sure of that. He realised it must have come straight up from inside the main cave and, finding an injured person, attacked. But it hadn't bargained for him, Big Nose, and it would regret it. When it jumped the next time he was ready for it, staving it off with his spear held in his two hands. Then as the animal fell back he kicked it hard, and as it fell over he lunged at it – or rather, at where he believed it to be – with his spear. Fortunately, he felt the point go into soft flesh and put all his weight behind it. Suddenly Shining Face was by his side, and taking a mighty swing with something heavy she struck the wolf with it as it struggled on the ground. It lay still. She must have had the huge club hidden by her somewhere Then she fainted, toppling into him, and he half pulled, half carried her back to where she had been lying.

He felt a wetness on his arms and realised that the wolf must have opened up the wound in her side. Things looked real bad, unless – and it was a strange thought to have at such a moment when she was so ill – unless she was *meant* to find her mother, meant by some power, meant to survive. He did not rule it out. There was something about her that he sensed he would never be able to explain...

Mark kicked himself. Surely he was daydreaming again. Or was it real after all? How could he be knowing all this if it *wasn't* : the cave, the warm breath of animals beyond his knowledge, his experience? It must be nearly seven o'clock, he thought, but his mind continued its journey, wanted a sequel, a good outcome for Marcie's sake.

Big Nose was listening, expecting an onslaught at every second. Shining Face was coming round. Her voice came in gasps as her body struggled with pain and exhaustion. "'Go further down, see if you can block the tunnel better. There's a chink of moonlight; I can see it from here. That's how I knew about that place. Take the club."

Further down, at a steep, low place, the cave tunnel became very narrow, too narrow now for him, let alone a lion, to pass (though not, evidently, a wolf). He saw that this was because she had cleverly let down a huge rock that must have been precariously balanced higher up. Even as he realised all this there were scuffling sounds beyond the blockage, and the amber eyes of another wolf became visible in the darkness. With his spear in one hand and her club in the other he was ready for it, and with a single blow of the club he smashed its skull as it struggled to get through. A second had no sooner tried to come over the top of its companion than a spear in its throat stopped it in its tracks for ever, the bodies now almost completely blocking the passage. Big Nose reckoned it was knowledge of the fate of their companions as much as this that stopped the onslaught, for there was no further sound.

He crept back, half expecting to hear sounds at the upper entrance, but there was none.

"Did my club come in useful, then?" Shining Face asked, quietly. She seemed *remarkably* quiet in the circumstances – but perhaps she was just beyond caring.

"Yes, it did. Thank you. I hope nothing comes in at the top."

"So do I." Then she added, "I am grateful to you."

But the wolves must have moved on, and in the morning an uneasy peace lay over the camp. Big Nose left the dead wolves blocking the passage in position for the moment, but the one Shining Face killed he carried down to the main cave where he skinned and dismembered it and, managing to renew the embers of the previous day's fire, put some of the meat on the ready-made hearth to roast, but keeping most of it to one side to start drying. Risking a longer absence he carried up as much water as he could from the stream, at the same time collecting the remaining skins and the tools that he had left in the first, barely started shelter by the river. Then he brought the water and the skins`, and later the roasted animal pieces when they were ready, and the re-lit fire sticks, to the upper cave. When he had eaten, and she had toyed a little with the wolf meat and allowed him to see to her wound, he descended again and spent the rest of the day sharpening his axes, cutters and scrapers and trying to keep a small fire going at the entrance in order to continue drying the meat and to be able to ignite more greased sticks when necessary..

The next day Big Nose recovered the dead wolves, found he did not like the smell of them, and took them and all the other bits of carcases a distance from the cave and dumped them. The rest of the day, after seeing to his daughter's needs, he spent collecting what stones and timber he could find to re-block the connecting passage and made it as secure as he could. He also found a way of blocking the upper entrance at night.

For a whole moon the two of them remained in their camp

undisturbed. *He* welcomed the tranquillity, for it was not only she who needed to recuperate. He made himself some new shoes out of a hyena hide that Shining Face produced from somewhere, and with a gradual relaxation of the cold he was able to do some limited hunting. Thus released, it was at such times that he would take Strong's spear and feel both thankfulness and sadness when he thought about his old friend.

Shining Face bore his nursing with resignation, listening attentively when he answered her questions about Red Hair, like how she looked, and whether she spoke of *her* (which she did, often), but otherwise saying little about herself. Unbelievably, almost, the wound had fortunately stopped bleeding, oozing for many days from the time the wolf opened it up, then beginning to heal. Her strength began to return, though at first she could not stand without considerable pain and remained in the cave, except when with great difficulty she crawled out to relieve herself.

A sudden improvement in the weather, too, having dispersed a lot of the snow in a day and a night, Big Nose went foraging in green places appearing for the first time and came back with wild garlic and other leaves and roots. For the first time he helped Shining Face down to the main cavern, and he dug a hole where she made a vegetable and hare soup in a deer skin using hot stones from the fire.

With the weather continuing kind, Big Nose decided to set out at daybreak the following day and hunt down the neighbouring valley the way Shining Face said she had come. Thus he might be lucky and surprise some animal drawn out of its winter quarters by the sudden warmth and bring it back. All morning, as he walked, the sun shone, and then all afternoon as he returned clouds gathered and it became very dark and started to blow a gale. He suspected the cold was about to make a return even though it was now full spring, and sure enough heavy rain turned to snow as the wind swung into the north. Several times he came across animal tracks and once even saw a retreating deer, but he obtained nothing, though a good haul of green leaves was some compensation...

Turning over in his mind how he was going to keep his end up while admitting his failure, he crept through the narrow entrance of the upper cave to find his skins and everything still there but no sign of Shining Face or her belongings anywhere in the cave or, when he came to look, in the cavern below. Half of the remaining dried wolf meat had also disappeared. Absence of her belongings as well surely meant that she had not fallen prey to a wild beast, but how could she possibly survive in the state she was in? There were no footprints in the snow. It seemed that she had decided to go in the thaw, thrown together her things and left soon after him.

* * *

Mark was annoyed to find it was seven o'clock. Although an awful lot had been packed into the last few minutes, he had a feeling of 'mission not yet accomplished'. However, another part of him was telling him now not to agonise over dreams, and when he came on the train to see Marcelle that next weekend in the middle of term and she met him at the station, he could at least say that Big Nose had tracked down Shining Face. But since that was not quite the end of the story, when they finally stood alone together in her sitting room above the tidy road in Kinley's Fields where she lived, with its pollarded limes, neat shops with flats above like hers, and the wide park opposite with its mums and buggies and its paths criss-crossing the greensward, and she threw herself into his arms and thanked him, he felt a little guilty.

With a little pirouette, she stood back in her cream skirt, colourful, eye-catching floral top and chocolate-brown neckerchief with silver brooch, and he realised that she had dressed to please him. She had judged well. But he felt ill-dressed in his jeans, however smartly sober his new grey shirt with button-down collar might be and despite the new gold ring through his ear lobe – of which new departure he was quite proud. And he did not know quite how to tell her that Shining Face had finally given him the slip.

She said she was preparing chicken with tagliatelli and tomatoes, and being excluded from the kitchen his eye roved over the family photos and the collection of artefacts, photographs, and drawings of the stone ages, as well as the many sketches of Lexin, and some, too, of Shining Face and the others, that she had made from memory. He had offered the opinion, when she had first shown him one of those sketches of Lexin, that with his short curly hair it made him look more like some laboratory-bound physicist than a herald of an advanced and seemingly enlightened humanity. He would refrain from saying those kinds of things any more. What most caught his eye, though, was a photo he had not seen before of her parents, Lenie and the maternal grandparents (whom he had met a couple of times) on a beach, presumably at Sandbay. Obviously it was before Marcelle was born. Lenie was preparing to head off to an ice-cream van and they were all sitting there on the sand, laughing. There was Ida with her arms clasped round those long legs drawn up to her chin. Mark had never seen Ida laugh. He could hardly believe it was she.

When he pointed the photo out, Marcelle she said that although he was very attached to it, her dad had not minded parting with it because there were plenty more photos of those early years. She joked that it seemed it was only when *she* came on the scene that things changed for the worse, and suddenly it seemed harder still to tell her that he had lost Shining Face again in the end.

"I'm afraid she is not in a very good state!" he said, adding, "and it was Big Nose who found her, not I. It's even worse than I've said, actually. I hardly dare tell you she went off again, left the cave, went her own way – while we, I mean I – was out hunting. I'm really sorry. But of course, she is resourceful."

Marcelle looked disappointed, but she could see how wholeheartedly he had thrown himself into his mission.. "I know she is," she said, "and so is Big Nose, and I am trusting Lexin, Mark. It's no good worrying about it." She came and hugged him again. "He knows what's going on. You must bear with me when I talk about him. It is *you* who are my special, dearest, darling friend."

"I don't mind you talking about him," Mark said, holding her tightly. "He must be very special, too, but when this is all over, Marcie," he added, encouraged by her unexpectedly calm response to his confession, "I hope you *will* think about yourself and what you want to do with your life…" He was half expecting her then to stand away from him and have a go at him, but she did not, and so he continued: "…I know how you see beyond what people usually see and recognize the good in people and can help them…" He hesitated, feeling there was something else to be said. She gave his hand a squeeze, and went to the kitchen, saying she must deal with the pasta.

"You still reckon I should get qualified and all that, widen my outlook, etc..." she said on returning to lay the table. "...Isn't that what you used to say?" He nodded. "When it is over, maybe," she said, thoughtfully. "I do like your earring, by the way." Then she said, after putting some things on the table, "Mark, if you hadn't stuck with Big Nose I'd be even more depressed about my parents than I am now."

"Things are very bad, then?" He was standing by the window now, looking out towards the familiar rectangular shapes of the city centre beyond the park.

Part of his mind was already elsewhere, she thought, probably, in some other place as yet unknown to him, a new world where he would make his own way, trusting in his own logic and ability. "Yes, they are bad," she said. "They have found she has a shingles infection as well. It's bad enough finding it hard to breathe without having this terrible pain down her side, and feeling even worse as well. I just don't know how it's going to work out."

"How is your father taking it?"

"He's hoping she will come and live with him when she gets over this crisis."

"Wouldn't that be risky for him? What does Ida say about it?"

"At the moment she is too self-critical to contemplate it, I should think." Marcelle had been expecting Mark's *next* question for some time, and she could not answer it.

"Marcelle, when was Ida first diagnosed? I was thinking of the clients.'"

"Yes, I know. And Phil. It was a self diagnosis. But she is very cagey about it."

"There has been no word from the escort agency?"

"No. Incidentally, Mother once told me Phil always used a sheath". Neither spoke for a minute or two. Then, going over and taking Mark's hands in hers she said, "we are not through this yet, Mark, are we?"

"I know. It's obvious, isn't it?"

"I do often question what it might be, happening in the twenty-fifth century…," she said, after retreating to the kitchen again and returning with a large saucepan of conchiglie and another of bolognese sauce and lowering them onto the table, "…what it might be that is so important to Lexin."

"Whatever it is, if it is so important to him that is all the more reason to keep on doing what we are doing. Other things may happen. You believe *him*; *he* knows your – our – circumstances here."

"I hardly dared to hope you would ever say that."

"I suppose," he said after a moment's hesitation, "I suppose that where time is of no account everything can get sorted, somehow. Let's trust your friend!"

She laughed. "And now let's sit down and you can tell me what exactly you are going to do with *your* life, Mark – *afterwards*. I haven't asked you lately."

"As long as it's with you, that's all I'm concerned about just now," he replied, heaping a mountain of pasta on his plate as Marcelle added the sauce, relieved that at least she would have him beside her on what seemed inevitably to be a rocky road ahead.

CHAPTER TWELVE

"Crabtree, 'Vancouver Daily'. Lexin! So you have visions using the special modifications enjoyed by all Societans?"

"And available to us in our work. Yes, that is correct." The matter of his visions had got about somehow. He had not tried to prevent that, though he had not expected it to come up so quickly. Possibly that was naïve, but then, really it did not matter where or when he started to try and explain them. It would all be difficult.

"And how long have you been having these...visions?" There was a contrived hesitancy.

"Since my late teens. They appear superficially to be a bit like a form of historical viewing. Of course, you are all familiar with that."

"Will you tell us what they are about?" The wiry, sun-tanned pressman, dressed in the resurrected twenty-first century battledress style somewhat à la mode among pressmen, and looking as though he might be no taller than Lexin himself, was sitting very near the front of one of the spacious auditoria of the New Humanity Conference Centre by the lake in Canberra. "And – supplementary question – do your colleagues have similar 'sight'?" There was a ripple of laughter around the representatives of the media, many of them in the individualistic dress styles long characteristic of the journalist fraternity. Lenica, chairing the meeting following some unexpected 'about turns' by

Harry Beckenthal, was hoping they were going to take her brother seriously.

"I do not think any of my colleagues have quite the same sort of visions – not yet, at least," Lexin replied, "and I cannot really explain them in scientific terms. As to the form these visions take, to put it briefly, they are about ordinary people in two different earlier epochs."

"And *our* fates are somehow intertwined?"

"To put it simply, yes, I believe so."

Lenica surveyed the uncomprehending faces down below. Several seconds' silence followed the expression of this novel concept – a concept almost as novel to her as it was to them. There had been little opportunity for him to tell her anything much about his dreams, or daydreams, or whatever they were. After she had refused to cancel the tour, Beckenthal had relented and asked her to stay on as his personal assistant provided she did not chair the press conferences; he said it could have damaging consequences for him as the Society's representative in the World Government and Assembly. The reason seemed a bit specious. She called his bluff and assumed it had been on a 'better the devil you know' basis that he had without so much as a twitch of those eyebrows withdrawn his proviso. It would mean she would both continue to have a finger on the pulse in Canberra (beneficial for Lexin) – and also satisfy her curiosity about his 'visions' and how they might fare when exposed to the cool scrutiny of the world press.

Rob Daley of the 'Sydney World News', whom she knew as an ascending star of the popular press and owner of a growing slice of a television industry showing signs of a sudden renaissance, was raising his hand to speak. The very causticity of this modern-day press baron might draw Lexin out. She hoped so, and gave him the chairperson's nod.

"Mr. Solberg," boomed the richly bewigged Daley, imposing and resplendent in his velvet-edged, pale blue suit, frilly shirt and well-known outrageous tie full of symbols of global influence, "so these people are living and loving in their own times."

"Yes, in their own times. I know those people are revealed to us for our benefit, but not simply as models or examples. It is like looking through a window into the past. There they are with the history of their lives as yet unfinished." That was as far as Lexin got. Bill Walmsley of 'Guardian Interactive' wanted some immediate clarification:

"Could we just get this straight, Lexin? You say you see them in their own *real* times."

Lexin had met the slightly corpulent, affable but mercilessly probing Walmsley through Callum. He knew the two of them had been firm friends since journalist had met linguist-cum-mathematician at a symposium on international relations many years ago. Callum had later joined the Societans with great enthusiasm, and indeed would probably soon find himself chairman if Mackenzie resigned as seemed likely, but nowadays his difficulties with "Lexin Solberg's highly original views" had become the subject of some light-hearted raillery on Walmsley's part. Even now, Callum, who was down there among the pressmen and others, was probably giving his climate suit some work to do as he sweated out his old doubts.

"Yes, I do see them in their own real time on my computer monitor," Lexin replied in answer to Walmsley's question. "Sometimes even independently of it. I mean, just in my head."

"Lexin, before you describe them – as I am sure you are going to do – do you have any idea why you should have been chosen to have these revelations?" Another ripple of laughter. "I think you will appreciate, because I know you, that I intend no disrespect when I ask why we should believe you any more than anyone else, normal or enhanced, who believes they have had some sort of paranormal experience?"

"That is a fair question, Bill," he replied, "but I am not asking you to. I do not see how I can expect you to; not at this stage at any rate. It is for my colleagues – my colleagues in the Society – to judge on these revelations in the first instance."

A murmured "O-o-o-o-h!" was audible around the room. "Then why have you called us here?" Walmsley continued as the television cameras closed in.

"In order to tell you just that, as well. Yes I know, I know" he said, trying to quell the rising murmur of surprise, "but it is important to tell you, as I will try to explain."

But Daley thundered again, precluding any immediate explanation and causing the speakers to crackle: "Mr. Solberg, is it true to say the Society has gone off the rails, lost its way?"

"Yes, it has a bit, and it is something only we can put right. There is a part of our modification that we are not using correctly. All we can ask you to do is to be patient."

"Maybe in due course you will tell us what your visions are about," Daley snapped impatiently, "who the people are, and where and when events are taking place. In the meantime we could be forgiven for thinking it could all be just something *in your own head.*"

Lenica stepped in as Daley was rewarded by more than a ripple of laughter. "I hope you will give Lexin some credit, Mr. Daley and other representatives of the media," she said, tossing back her blond curls more vigorously than usual. "I remind you that although only an aspirant to membership of the Conference, my brother's understanding of the work of the Earth Society for the Advancement of Intragalactic Relations is widely acknowledged there."

"I dare say, Madam Chairman!" a voice interrupted from somewhere in the sea of faces below in its disarming diversity. "We just want to know what the situation is – I mean about our future, if any – , and skip the fairy tales."

Lenica recognized the abrasive Werner Künstler of the popular German Daily 'Vox Humana'. She would have liked to say, but did not, something about having respect for their very surroundings, the building they were in. Even she, who was not specially artistic, could understand the historians when they talked of its 'pure and beautiful overarching lines', and a 'period of architecture supervening after the true dimensions of what had happened to humanity had sunk in.'

"When the Society gets its act together," Lexin said, "you will see that it is not my privilege alone to have been shown these things for which I am sure our protectors, yes our protectors, in Lyra are somehow responsible."

A kindlier, gentler voice intervened: "Freda Sonego, 'Brazilian News Media'. There's so much obscurity here, Lexin, I'm afraid…" The journalist had risen to her feet, smiling under copious, dark curls just beginning to acquire the silvering of age and wisdom. "…You say we Normals matter, but not yet. Again, you say the Society must take things seriously – that they must agree, presumably, which they don't do now, do they? Then there is the matter of the link with these other people. What is the link?"

So even little Freda Sonego, so poised, so gentle, and long a sympathetic if not uncritical commentator on the Society, was finding it very difficult! That did not augur well. But any answer to those questions was inevitably postponed as Daley stood up again and boomed away without waiting for the Chairperson's go-ahead:

"As I said before, perhaps Lexin could start by telling us what his experiences are actually *about*," adding, before adjusting his frilly cuffs and resuming his seat, "especially if they are supposed to be the key to preventing us accidentally blowing ourselves up in our galactic quest."

"Yes, I can," he said. Surely this was the moment of truth, and he was grateful to his sister for preventing things from getting out of hand thus far, and for giving him fair winds when she barely understood the choppy seas through which he was steering, the rocks and reefs lying in wait that might sink both of them in his efforts to explain the almost unexplainable. Even now the morning could so easily end in farce or boredom, not to say disaster. There was nothing apparently newsworthy in these days of historical data-extrapolation about an injured stone-age girl in animal skins facing cold, wild animals and starvation in a search for her mother, or for that matter on the face of it anything encouraging or comforting to be derived from a sympathetic daughter sitting with her boyfriend at the bedside of her mother in great pain and recounting a strange story of suffering in prehistoric times. People suffered, and people died. "Yes, I can tell you, Mr. Daley," Lexin repeated, "that these visions are about young women, girls really, who become involved in rebuilding their broken families. They are about healing, reconciliation."

Lexin paused, as members of the press stirred slightly – although some were shaking their heads in boredom or incomprehension. "One is an early modern in archaeological terms," he said. "The other is living at the beginning of this millennium." He saw Callum stiffen, look hard at him questioningly, anxiously, his features for a second or two screwing up into that characteristic self-torturing attitude. The TV crews adjusted themselves, seemed to sense an important moment. Of course, as he was only too aware, all this was as new to Callum as to everyone but his mother.

Suddenly he was telling them about the hunter, Big Nose, with the gammy hip, which was where it all started, and about Marcelle, an abused child who has dreams about him. Then in a few sentences – or that is how it seemed – he told them about their disintegrated families and what has happened right up to the ascent of that ice-cold valley by Shining Face in her search for her mother, her encounter with the lions, her desperate plight in the cave, and Marcelle's conviction that the girl's survival and finding of her mother are crucial to her own mother's recovery from illness and the restoration of both their families. Lexin was astonished by his own ability to be so succinct, and he hoped the translators were up to such an onslaught of, *yes, 'galactic significance'*!

Lenica was astonished, too. Here now at least was something that she could grasp hold of, something more than bland assertions, admonishments, rejection of present efforts, words repeated so often that she was tired of hearing them: failure, losing the way, loss of values, of trust. She had been watching Callum. He had looked really down in the dumps. She questioned now whether anything would ever spark off George these days if he could not analyse and compartmentalise it within the boundaries of his admittedly fertile mind.

Miraculously, even the most seasoned pressmen did remain attentive until, when Lexin paused having brought his audience to Shining Face's latest staging post on her journey, the very popular correspondent Émil Daugin, of 'France Soir', popped a 'very simple' question. It was the inevitable question that Lexin knew must come: what was the significance of the two stories in themselves, for *us*?

"On one level I suppose you could say it is the innocence, or even the 'other-worldliness' of the two girls," he replied.

"But this here," Daugin said, indicating with an artistic sweep of his hand the great hemisphere of the auditorium above them upon whose lofty boundary the celebrated twenty-third century painter Rostrand – a Societan – had with consummate restraint sought to represent man's place in the eternal scheme of things – "this is our world!"

"Is this going to be just preaching, Lexin? Is this what you are doing?" another voice interrupted in an impatient tone. Lexin thought it was Richard Strauss, well-known atheist broadcasting widely over European channels.

"Preaching what? Dedication to one's task? Well maybe," Lexin replied, but before he could continue Freda Sonego's voice re-emerged.

"Lexin, please tell us what we are to take from the visions in *practical* terms?" The voice had an unexpected ring of urgency. So she had got her question in at last! Lenica reckoned she would have asked the same herself, but Lexin's answer surprised her.

"That's the other level, Senhora Sonego" he replied, as the noise subsided a little. "I believe they offer a *remedy,* a way back for the

Society. To bring it back on track. We had become lazy, and as I said – and have been suggesting to my fellow Societans for some time – we may have lost our way."

Daley sprang up in a flash of frills and blue "A remedy to be taken, understood, pondered?" he asked in a tone of withering disdain "The truth is that you're not up to the task."

Lexin ignored the accusation. "I mean we must identify with those individuals," he said, calmly, "we must encourage them, go with them, become them almost. We shall need every skill, all the gadgetry of our modification to do it. Remember! Their goals will be our goals."

So there was a reason for the visions – of sorts. There were things to be done, that's what he was saying, though God knows how. The rest for Lenica was mystery, and as Lexin did his best to provide answers to questions about that old word, 'remedy', with a new meaning: , and she struggled to maintain order as some had hands raised while others were just chipping in regardless, it all seemed too much, too much to swallow in one go – and all across the barrier of time! Her eye caught Callum again, sitting stony-faced. Someone brought up questions of time difference, asked Lexin to explain. He said he could not, but pointed out that everyone knew we were making big advances in spacetime theory.

She had the impression Daley was not much into theories of any kind. "It's a test, you mean, the Lyrians are testing you?" The tone was mocking. "A kind of test by total submission!" This provoked laughter.

"Order, please!" Lenica had hoped never to resort to bringing down the mallet.

"I see it more as enlightenment," Lexin said, "but yes, I suppose you might view it as a test of our trust in the Bods."

"Isn't that the business of Societans?" It was Crabtree of the 'Vancouver Daily' again. "I mean, do you need to bother us with that?"

"I am telling you because – as I was trying to say earlier – it concerns everybody's future. The point is that finally, as you probably know, it will be for the Government and the Assembly to decide whether we have proved ourselves up to the task and whether we can continue with our work."

Sonego had her hand up again. "But how, but how?" she complained to sympathetic noises around her. "I find that all very strange. How could I put it? It's not quite the kind of way either we Normals or you Societans think, is it, unless we're talking about religion…believing, repenting, changing? That's another thing."

"That's it. It's religion again." The words could be heard around the auditorium as some of the audience began to disperse, and Lenica felt things slipping from her grasp. Battledressed Crabtree seemed to have decided the skirmishing was over, and was packing his bags.

"Possibly you could say it was a parallel of sinning and reconciliation". The observation came from Joseph Richards of 'United African Christian Churches News'. Those around him waited for Lexin's response, but Robert Daley had already gathered his things together and stood up:

"I reckon I'm about as direct as you are, Lexin," he declared. "Wouldn't you agree that all this stuff about remedies is too much for us Normals? For me, straightforward errors – whatever they are, and only veiled references have been made to the nature of your shortcomings – for me such errors require straightforward solutions. I say each to his own remedies. I like things on my own level, and by my lights you're all up a gum tree," and with a flashing flourish of frilly cuffs he promptly disappeared through a side-door to a buzz of approval.

Lexin followed that television moment as best he could, talking about trusting in him, progress towards the Galactic Community, "our magnificent friends the Lyrians…", but the auditorium was steadily emptying, and Lexin finished by talking to a faithful few, including Callum and some of the other Societans who had attended. Maybe when it came to the likes of slick and smart Daugin in his cloak and breeches it didn't make much odds, but the gentle, good-natured Sra. Sonego who wrote regularly for 'Brazil News Media' in the 'Times of Brasilia', a paper that had retained old values as well as any, she mattered. Perhaps he had sown seeds that would germinate later. He hoped so.

Callum must have found the meeting very trying, too, Lexin thought as he gathered up his things and Lenica disappeared to the Ladies' Room probably to have a good cry. Synthesizers (albeit referred to in veiled terms as 'gadgetry'), questions of religion, the very word 'vision', never mind 'remedies', must all have presented difficulties for him. Likewise maybe even the idea of such paternalistic Bods at all, (especially kind and loving ones). Lexin had been pondering why he had wanted to come to the press conference in any case. He concluded that George was not giving up on him easily. Viewed optimistically, the reality of it all was seeping through to him, and if he did not sweat so much over these things, but relaxed, he could surely save on his expensive suits!

"The religious bit is sure to come up. It's already on CBS," Callum was saying as they stood in the Speakers' Suite, downing much needed refreshments. Words were entering his brain thick and fast, he said. "'Times of Brasilia': "Lexin Finally Departs from Reason"; 'Corriere della Sera': "...Today's press conference in Canberra revealed a striking similarity between Lexin Solberg's 'visions' and those of many early Christians.""

Lexin laughed. "The media up to their ancient tricks!" he declared. But despite that, he was feeling a renewed optimism. It was connected with images of Marcelle and Mark floating continually on the edge of his consciousness...something very much to do with Marcelle's determination to see things through. So in that smart way that his PAS had of relating the passage of events in no time at all, even while the conference had been drawing to a close and Rob Daley had been making his melodramatic exit it had been revealing directly to his brain the events he had been anxiously waiting and hoping for. What a great inspiration it was to see how sceptical Mark had indeed taken Big Nose's journey upon himself also (just as for a while Marcelle had travelled with Shining Face), the two of them reaching the cave and pulling Shining Face back from the brink!

Moreover, when after many weeks in the cave Shining Face slipped away on her own, Big Nose had decided it was not safe for her to be alone and had hurriedly gathered up what food scraps he could lay his hands on, and his cumbersome belongings, and set out to follow her. He was sure she would have started off from the cave by the way he himself had come to it. If he could move fast enough he would start picking up her trail in the snow that was still falling but may not have started at the time she set out. She could not possibly move quickly with the terrible gash down her side...

There was no point yet, Lexin thought, in trying to relate these latest episodes to Lenica, and certainly not to George who had certainly heard enough for one day. No point either in trying to explain to them the way in which for a moment he had seen into Big Nose's mind and felt the comfort and protection of the forest despite the continuing cold, felt the moving power of the river as it accompanied him, and the will within him at least to see his daughter to the end of her journey.

One day he believed their de-rusting synthesizers would reassure them about the reality of those other lives in other times. They might even be drawn into the timeless sphere themselves. For the moment, though, Callum was definitely unhappy, going on about "the innocence thing", and "redemption and all that".

"I do not believe this misreporting goes deep like it once did, George," Lexin said, "pandering to some, dividing others, addling brains, and, in short, doing no good." At least, he was hoping it didn't.

"That may be so, but it's all a bit depressing." Callum had sat down, eyes closed. Lexin guessed he was being inundated by messages.

"That was Harry's line when I asked him just now what he thought," Lenica said, having come in and overheard Callum's complaint. Lexin thought she looked weary even in a very expensive two-piece in unlikely but gorgeous shades of pink and blue. She collapsed tiredly into one of the interactive chairs, hoping (*he* hoped) for some resolution of negative or conflicting thoughts, the flowering of some nascent understanding of what he had been talking about. "Says he can't imagine how we Societans will get out of the hole we're in, but can't imagine it's your way, Lexin. 'Since when', Harry asked, 'did innocence and progress go together?'"

"Not much progress in blowing ourselves up, though," Callum sighed wistfully, "if that is the alternative."

"I still don't see why they couldn't have warned us before." It was a frequent complaint of Lenica's.

"I am sure they did whenever they could – bearing in mind our lazy habits –" Lexin said, wearily, pulling up a chair to the table and starting to sort out his papers. They knew what he was talking about, but he could only guess how far away from his visions Lenica might feel, – Lenica with her years of work helping to interpret the work of the Society to the Assembly under Beckenthal. It must have become increasingly difficult for her, especially with her boss's idiosyncratic approach to the Society's task (to put it mildly). Very likely all this had been palliated by frantic good-timing, probably with deactivated libido discriminator, in Beijing, Rome, Madrid, Chennai, Buenos Aires, Miami and the rest. Lexin knew she had even pondered relinquishing her membership of the Society. Only the fact of the grief it would cause Olaf had stopped her. "But make no mistake," he said, "the Bods know all about our trouble."

"That is my complaint, isn't it?"

"Yes, I know it is," he said.

"Let's go and get something to eat," Lenica suggested when her brother had returned all his papers to his briefcase. "At least, that's *my* best *remedy* at the moment." She seemed by then to have recovered some of her self-possession. "I know the best place. Secluded in summer, cosy in winter. We all deserve it. I'll contact Mother afterwards. The press conference won't have improved her spirits. She is bound to have followed it."

It was Radichi's, an Italian place off Furneaux Street in Manuka, nice and intimate. They took a taxi. It was not hard to guess why his sister knew it well. Callum looked less than enthusiastic until they had taken seats in a very private 'Tuscan Arbour' with red-gum rustic chairs and tables and he had noted that the menu was far from only Italian, being unexpectedly elaborate and including, of course, gum-leaf soaked venison. Only then, Lexin reckoned, would George's heavily (some would say outrageously) dissembling suit be returning to neutral.

Lenica looked better already. "That's what I like about Canberra," she said: "nothing much is supposed to have changed here in five hundred years. It's fabulous here in summer, outside under the trees."

"Need more stimuli myself," Callum said..."Give me Madrid, Casablanca... And from your descriptions I do find your Marcelle a little..."

"...Boring, George?" Lexin suggested.

"A little too good to be true. God knows how you survived five minutes telling them about her."

"Nor do I. But I did. Not that I find her *boring*. Rather the opposite: too much to get your head round, never mind explain to people. As I think I said, I could not have hoped to *convince* them about Marcelle. Not yet, anyway. At least I told the story 'in black and white' so to speak, and hopefully they will get some idea. It will be hard enough trying to convince the Society."

"You reckon the Normals will accept it in the end? It doesn't look much like it to me. I mean, how can you expect them to?"

"I may not expect. Nevertheless, I have a shrewd idea..." But the hors d'oeuvres were about to arrive, and Callum's attention was being diverted.

"Look at that Brazilian woman, the older woman with the red jumper," he groaned after downing the first spoonful of his soup. "Never mind young Daley. You can understand...I mean, the woman was being utterly reasonable."

"Sonego, ah yes! Yes, she was, like you, George. And very well regarded. Writes for the 'Brazilian Times'. You will bring her round," Lexin declared. "That is what I was going to say."

"*I* will!" Callum's laden spoon hovered half way to his mouth.

"About Daley I'm not so sure. I think we are an obstacle in his path."

"You are suggesting *I* will persuade people about your visions? I'm still wondering when I'll get some clear idea about it all myself.

"I know. It's not something rational, George. I'll tell you why they'll get it in the end," Lexin declared: "It's because it is you who will be convinced. And when *you* believe that I am talking about real individuals and that they matter to us more than you can now imagine, the rest will follow: Societans and Normals. And I tell you something: the Normals might even be ahead of us. We shall see "

Callum shot him a quizzical look, manifestly still troubled, as he continued with his vegetable, bacon and risoni soup, by an absence of mathematical or any other logic in Lexin's prognosis, even if he was by now getting gradually more accustomed to his strange and unexpected assertions.

The nut and vegetable salads, and likewise, according to one's choice, the cannelloni, moussaka and cottage pie came and went before Lexin opened his mouth again for any purpose other than eating.

"I appreciate all this must be hard for both of you to take, having had no preview of my visions, if I may put it so grandly, but I was hooked on Marcelle from the beginning. I cannot explain it. As you know, I do not deactivate so as to take an interest in her in other ways. Nevertheless, the light – I could say the truth, the energy – that shines out of her..." He paused. "... for me is just as illuminating, just as powerful as any dawn in the Appalachians, George, or for that matter (he said it in deference to Callum's modern tastes) even the latest Reissler symphony." There was indeed no shortage of possibilities for comparison given Callum's wide interests in the contemporary arts.

"And when Shining Face emerged to carry the baton for *her* family there was the same energy, if not quite the same charisma."

George was nodding automatically.

"Does sound quite religious, doesn't it?" Lenica said, thoughtfully, "Not that we have to believe *all* that you are saying, I mean believe it unconditionally." She had remained pretty quiet during the meal. "Not that I don't *want* to believe it, either," she added, smiling. It was about the first smile Lexin had seen from her since her return.

"Redeemed women, saintly women, weakness of mankind, chosen individuals …yes, you name it, it's there: religion…" Callum was muttering as he wiped his face free of the remains of his venison and reached for the menu again. "…To tell the truth, I feel my brain is working on too many levels at the moment." Lexin noted a few moments later that the man who was one of the world's most accomplished linguists was staring blankly at the words on his menu and not taking anything in at all.

"Won't hurt to exclude all messages from outside for a bit, George," Lexin advised. "Let the internal computer take the strain. Anyway, any further comment on the conference?"

"Best not ask! " Callum replied, "But Malinovsky says you did very well, Lenica. He was watching."

"Really? " Lenica was thoughtful for a moment. "Whatever it is exactly that you want us to believe, or know, or *do,* Lexin – and I am a *doing* sort of person, as you know," she said, picking up a menu and studying it, "it's going to be tough going as far as I'm concerned."

Lexin knew that about the closest his sister came to spectating at anything was at 'total immersion' films, which at least gave her plenty of opportunity to interact if she felt like it and come out hardly knowing who she was and having to take a reorientation pill. "The fact is, both of you," he said, "that your PAS will not fully activate, things will not become really real, until you want to sing along with the Bods."

"So maybe we will have to sing songs without words," Callum said eventually, rousing himself, "if not hymns ditto."

"I don't know whether the Bods sing songs or hymns, but they want us to sing something!" He had stood up. "Look," he said, "Let's finish up this bottle! Let's drink to the Bods!" and he splashed the rest of a fine house red from the Capital Territory into their glasses declaring that the Bods wanted them to take a chance on it, except that he knew it was not a matter of chance, the Bods being "made of solid stuff – whatever the 'stuff' is."

"Sounds like fighting talk, Lexin," Lenica said.

"Better than your scary films, anyway."

"They are just for relaxation. You were never very good at that, Lexin."

"Now for a dessert, Lenica? Lexin enquired as the pervasive scent of the eucalypts coming in through the open window mingled with the aroma of some pungent dish as the kitchen door swung open yet again and the waiter approached.

"Just get me a wattle-seed ice cream, Lexin," she replied. "There's a dear. You probably hardly need to ask, actually. It's my regular bit of self-indulgence"

"Well if wattle-seed ice cream is as bad as it gets, sister," he said "there is surely still time to rescue you from the sins of high living."

CHAPTER THIRTEEN

"Was it the usual, Mrs. Solberg?" A simple command from her brain had summoned Robert to her room as she sat at her dressing table. It was one o'clock. Felicitas felt sure Lexin would be coming straight back home after an important meeting of the Conference (i.e. no post-meeting polemicising, no 'one-liners' to the press). He was ready for a rest after Canberra. As for herself, she wanted to look her best because Lenica had said she might bring Xiaofeng back for lunch.

"Yes, thank you, Robert...Robert!" She caught him before he had time to disappear – or was it that he sensed there was something else she wanted to say? "Robert, do you like my dress?" she asked, standing up and turning around. The only concessions to the state of mourning now were the dark purple rings around the full arms and encircling the lower part of the long dress with its high, unrevealing neck. For the rest, the quickly produced creation from Anastasia was of a (for her) unusually subdued, lightweight fabric in the most gentle mauve, with gold flecks to match her bracelets. Felicitas had been determined not to succumb to the trend of recent decades towards a return to the sombre attire that had gradually disappeared after the time of the visitation.

"Yes, I do," he replied immediately, "I am so pleased it is not too solemn. It must be difficult to know how to appear in such circumstances. If we robots have doubts or worries they are usually soon resolved."

"I have no doubts about that particular matter, Robert," she said, but worries about the 'circumstances' themselves, yes."

"About Lexin?"

"How *did* you guess?" She smiled.

He smiled too. "We are allowed to guess! I cannot help but know that you have special concerns about his vision for galactic communication!"

"Should I encourage him more, or less, do you think?" His treatment by some of those journalists in Canberra a couple of weeks previously had been quite shocking. She had watched the beginning and listened to the rest. It had become too awful.

"I'm afraid that is where my knowledge terminates, Mrs. Solberg, but may I suggest that your PAS may come in handy."

"That's funny, you have never said that before."

"I have not liked to, but somehow today it seemed appropriate."

"My PAS. Ah, yes. I have been persevering with it."

"I am sure you may trust it if you trust me." He was smiling at her. What a touching smile he had, she thought. "We have the same origin," he added. There was the sound of young voices. "I will bring your drink to the living space and take any further orders there." Felicitas thanked him as he disappeared. She stood up and went through.

"Mother, I've brought Xiaofeng back for lunch. He says it's pretty boring talking to Conference people at his hotel. All they want to talk about is miserable Mauré and his theories about galactic evil." Lenica, in a dark-green sari, had arrived at the open terrace doors, closely followed by the young historian.

"I am glad you adopt a sceptical attitude to all that, Xiaofeng dear, anyway," Felicitas said, offering her cheek. She approved of his silky, light grey suit with the enormously flared trouser bottoms, so informal and yet so smart. There was also the pleasant touch of humour in the stout little fellow, in which characteristic he differed a little from Lexin, bless his heart, who could on occasion be a bit too serious (shades of Olaf). Lenica had had many men friends, probably more than her mother would ever know about – or want to, for that matter –, but Felicitas liked Xiaofeng more than others she had met, he being a sensible fellow with reasonably comprehensible ideas regarding the

Galaxy and more illuminating conversation about other things than many, especially many of the scientists. Most important, he was modified, too. He belonged to the Society. She had thought Lenica might marry out of the Society and undergo optional gene-reversal, and used not to feel strongly about that, but more recently, knowing Lenica's problems with Harry and shocked by his attitude, especially since Olaf's death she had hoped that would not happen. "Is Lexin coming up?" she asked. "How did the meeting go? I haven't heard anything. Been sleeping."

"I am not surprised that you need some rest," Li said. "It's the nervous reaction. It's been tough for us all, never mind what it must be like for you, Mrs. Solberg. Lexin got nobbled by the press, by the way, so I think he may be a bit delayed."

"Sure I am tired," she said. "We will stay indoors. It's more comfortable than out there. It is a bit cool without the canopy today. Olaf was a little more Spartan than I when it came to the chairs on the terrace. So how *did* it go, then?" she asked, settling herself in the woven banana leaf armchair that offered her both comfort and physical 'presence' and motioning Xiaofeng to sit down also.

"It has to be said that the Conference is not at its best at the moment," Xiaofeng said, his short body sinking almost out of sight in an armchair. He was barely taller than Lexin, and definitely a little stouter. Interesting to speculate on the shape of any offspring, Felicitas thought – if it were to come to that. "So many different views, Mrs. Solberg: no direction, only arguments, and it always seems to end up with Jean-Paul Mauré."

"Nevertheless he must be taken seriously. And do not imagine that because Vidano is no more, the competition is less."

"Ah yes! Polyanova." There was a moment's silence to recall the deceased Vidano and ponder a new rival, the Russian lady from Siberia. "Then there's the big uncertainty."

"Big uncertainty?"

Robert appeared with her Manzo, took more orders and disappeared. Felicitas viewed the robot with a new admiration. She questioned whether even Lexin might realise his full depths. She certainly could not pretend to.

"About the Society's future."

Felicitas's features tautened. "Ah, yes. So you fear it may come to that."

"Xiaofeng says Mackenzie stepped down, and George Callum was approved as the new Vice-President," Lenica said, changing the subject slightly. She had remained standing by the terrace doors, seemed uneasy, uncomfortable. "He was the obvious choice, wasn't he?"

"I think you will approve of that, Xiaofeng?"

The Matriarch was expecting the answer yes, but not demanding it. He knew she would know if he lied, but he had no need to, even if he had been tempted. "I would say he is the best choice, Mrs. Solberg," Li said. "I would not envy anyone with that job."

There was a silence, then Lenica said, casually, "Callum's certainly pretty sceptical about Lexin's girlfriend in the twenty-first century."

"Aren't *you*?" Her mother asked, smiling. The question, beamed across from those slightly slanting, dark eyes astride that powerful nose, eyes that were as demanding as they were kind, was a little more open-ended than it might have sounded to Li Xiaofeng.

"I'm open-minded," Lenica replied. "I'm almost ashamed to consult my PAS after years of neglect."

"So you are consulting it? That's a bit of a change, isn't it, dear? What happened in Australia? Or was it earlier?"

"Oh, I don't know. It might have been Harry's pig-headedness...or the threat of explosions... No, I know what it was: it was Lexin saying the other day when we were in Canberra that he thought the Bods wanted us to sing something...'sing along with them'. *Sounds* a bit daft, doesn't it?"

"It does, a bit," Felicitas agreed as Robert soundlessly put drinks down on a side table. She thanked him.

"You know. Rejoice in them! Take them to our hearts! I mean, why not? I reckon he is probably right, my little brother."

"To our hearts via our synthesizers. What do you think of that, Xiaofeng?"

"It's difficult to imagine ways of taking to our hearts people with whom we might perhaps find it hard to, er, identify." He was grinning in that jolly way of his.

"Might we? So hard, Xiaofeng? And how are the rest of them taking to Marcelle *via their synthesizers*?" Felicitas asked, rather pointedly, causing the grin to disappear, but she suddenly appeared thoughtful and continued without waiting for an answer, "She's probably why I think I am a 'believer' – almost. If it were someone else and not Marcelle I would find the whole thing too overwhelming, and sometimes so raw... so explicit... that I might suspect there was some other... some... undesirable source of his...his fervour, even though Lexin's been confiding in his mum for a long time and I believe what he says, and no-one knows the truth about her offspring like a mother. But Marcelle, yes, there is just something..."

No-one said anything for a moment, then Xiaofeng said, sounding surprised, "You see the things Lexin describes on *your* PAS?"

"Where else? *Some* things I see."

"How? How do you see them?"

"I ask questions – about the people he talks about."

"And Marcelle. You saw her?"

"Just once or twice, but it has been enough! I have the picture. Does that answer your questions, Xiaofeng dear?"

He hesitated before replying, "I suppose it would have been possible to know everything through Lexin, and because he is your son you might have been influenced by the way he thinks – if I may say so."

"Do you think so?" The tone was Romanov. "I wonder..." She seemed to be dreaming for a moment, then added, "Actually, it is not exactly something one *sees* that convinces me; it's just...I don't know..."

There was a discreet pause before Xiaofeng said, "I'm afraid they did not seem prepared to put their official backing behind his press conferences, Mrs. Solberg. There's another one coming up at Casablanca, I gather. As a matter of fact," he added, "I must say I am finding it difficult to swallow – is that what one says? – to swallow this business of following those people, step by step almost, from what I could gather from the broadcast."

"And he is following them still," Lenica said. "It's a pity most of the media in Canberra did not really want to listen, but maybe in time they will, when they get used to the idea, like I may, and you too, Xiaofeng love," she added, taking his fruit drink from the side table and handing it to him, stooping at the same time to give him a chaste kiss on the cheek and returning for her coffee cocktail.

"Marcelle came here once, you know..." Felicitas began to say in a matter of fact sort of way. She had stood up and was feigning staring interestedly out of one of the side windows.

"What?" Xiaofeng exclaimed, jumping up too, from the depths of his armchair, probably out of astonishment as much as out of politeness.

"In flesh and blood, according to Lexin."

"That is almost too much for me," he admitted.

"Almost?"

"One should never close one's mind, but... did you know this, Lenica?"

"No," she replied, "I did not, but my brother is full of surprises. I'm not sure I want to meet her, actually. Sounds a bit serious, a bit too good..." She stopped herself.

"I suppose it is, isn't it?" Xiaofeng said, slowly. "Serious, I mean, if everything is as Lexin says it is. Possibly if we had known about her and all the rest of it much earlier..."

"Well we did not, did we?" Felicitas said, "and now we do," and Lenica was glad her mum could bring herself to say it, and in the releasing of that tension her mother had released a tension in her daughter, and its pang of sadness.

"Just wish I didn't feel so bloody tired at the moment," she murmured.

"You have been overdoing it, Lenica," Felicitas said, making towards the terrace "It's not like you to be feeling tired. And now you'll have to excuse me. I feel like a breath of fresh air after all."

For a brief moment Lenica thought Mauré might be right and an interest in the visions dangerous, even prejudicial to health, but then she told herself she didn't believe a word of all that! Above all, she regretted making her mother worry about something else, as if she did not have enough worries already. The news about Marcelle, though – that *was* a surprise!

*   *   *

Lexin ran out of the rear entrance of the Palace complex and into the Park of New Enlightenment with its array of evergreens and its intersecting paths, skirting the Home of the Municipality and the Lake of Refreshment and True Contentment before turning in the direction of the gates leading into the Avenue of Remembrance and the way to home and lunch. Visible to him from that part of the park, in the far distance upon the wooded slopes of the transformed dunes beyond the public buildings that formed the central part of the city, and impinging occasionally on the corner of his eye like a sore place, a wound, was the hospital. Accidents in general were few, but this was where the rising number of people were taken who had survived but been injured in accidents at the Mission Station in recent decades. At least, most *Normals* probably still assumed they were accidents, Jean-Paul Mauré's alternative explanation involving evil powers having not yet quite caught the attention of the wider world – even if among fellow Societans it was gaining some currency...

There were other runners , men and women, and high up around the park's perimeter could be seen the aerial urban transit modules appearing and disappearing among the tree tops, sometimes singly, sometimes in caterpillar trains. Because it was the holidays there were children everywhere, quite a few of them sitting with their real-time simulators playing virtual flight with the birds above them (the latest craze). Yes, there were boys being boys, or rather space marshals, hurling themselves about as they fired their electric booster backpacks to protect the Galaxy, while others were away among the trees, evidently playing cowboys and Indians, or was it terrorists and peace lovers? Other young people walked about in wired up worlds of their own in a way Lexin would like to have done ten years before. Occasionally recognized, he would pass men or women in twos or threes in unobtrusive uniform clothing, chatting or in deep conversation – staff of the Society or municipal departments, very likely, or of shops, financial institutions, museums and libraries in their elastic lunch breaks, workers restoring the Mission Station (ten minutes by maglev). Others walked alone, displaying when taken together a carefree confusion of colour and design that abolished every boundary of race and nation, age and gender... writers, musicians, artists, scientists, journalists, philosophers...? Just people! One musician, a flautist, had attracted an audience. Often, here, Lexin had passed people singing to themselves, and no-one would blink an eye, while people who were evidently complete strangers would stop and talk, prompted perhaps telepathically or by interactive clothing. And always, as today, people were sitting on the plethora of seats, talking or reading newspapers. Newspapers were everywhere, rustling as they were unfolded or brushed by the gentle breeze. It was not a noiseless place, but it was a comfortable place with its own tranquillity. Even the day happened to be exceptionally peaceful and temperate, obviating the need to activate the city's climate canopy. For brief moments (between transit modules!) you might have imagined yourself in some pre-industrial colourful, carefree age of peace and plenty, but if such times were past (insofar as they had ever existed), so also were the intervening years of worldwide pollution, mass starvation, conflict and universal self-questioning. Compared with those years, Lexin thought, now was a good time to be here, an epoch in which the innate optimism of the human spirit had found an amazing degree of fulfilment inconceivable prior to the visitation. Only the dark windows of the hospital stared out at him like distant eyes, like some warning of vulnerability, as he approached the Avenue of Remembrance commemorating the terrible tragedy of three hundred and eighty years before.

Too many good things had happened in the wake of that catastrophe in Lexin's view, too many things that made humans stronger and more resilient, kinder and less selfish, to be ready to allow ourselves – Societans and Normals – transformed as we were by countless social and scientific advances, to shrug off the present trouble, pretend it wasn't there, or simply fail to get to grips with it. Still less, for those same reasons, should it be attributed to some dark power that had newly arrived to afflict the world and come between mankind and the Bods. Since under special circumstances aspirants were allowed to join in proceedings of the Conference and speak from the gallery, sparked by the attitude of several delegates Lexin had tried to point all this out at a session in the Great Hall that afternoon. This had been called first to elect a new president or vice president, and secondly to discuss the impasse in the Society. Mackenzie's resignation as Vice-President since Olaf's death, and George Callum's election to a similar position pending solution of the present crisis, were agreed without dissent, and Callum was chairing the meeting.

Other aspirants also spoke from the gallery, including some at least *sympathetic* to Lexin's views as expressed at Canberra not many days before and widely circulated, and including Anna Polyanova. Although a rival for representation of the local region, Lexin sensed support from an unexpected direction in the form of this large and cheerful lady, an educational expert from Siberia and mother of six with a gentle, coaxing touch.

"So you see I understand Lexin's concern about our attitude to our saviours from Lyra", she had said, "and I am sympathetic to the possibility of an escape route from our difficulties. I mean the visions." But her message was gentle, perhaps too gentle. Her advocacy of continued investigation of "all possible causes" of the Society's impasse was well received by quite a number of delegates and aspirants, including, Lexin noticed, Li Xiaofeng. By contrast, Jean-Paul Mauré's uncompromising message welled up from the gallery through the speaker system as though from the very depths of a troubled soul. At every opportunity in meetings of the Conference the increasingly popular aspirant would seek to propound his theory of malign intervention, and on that afternoon it seemed to Lexin that he scaled new heights of dark fantasy. "It has occurred to me," the tall and imposing Frenchman had solemnly declared, "that Lexin may have become unwittingly involved in all this in his visions." Gesturing with characteristically smooth assurance he spoke of the release of malign powers rife in past ages, old devils, old sins – possibly in conjunction with "new devils for a new age, alien devils even." Several delegates spoke, gave Jean-Paul encouragement.

Callum was trying to call time on the loquacious Frenchman when a delegate stood up to speak. Lexin recognized Andrew McLintock, a figure of forthright manner and commanding considerable respect especially in burgeoning North Africa. A pioneering spirit, an agriculturist émigré from Canada, for many years he had been a familiar figure striding about his Moroccan vineyards and olive groves, an unruly mop of blond hair scarcely contained beneath his fubar hat. Nowadays, wearing another hat, as it were, the Canadian was also to be seen among the new cotton and cereal crops growing in a long swathe to the east of the Atlas Mountains. There he was acting as adviser to the Northern Sahara Development Commission.

"I do not see how Lexin could possibly object, in the interests of progress," he said amid a rising murmur of approval, "to the visions being subjected to physical and psychological scrutiny."

"May I remind delegate McLintock," Callum said, "that Lexin has been at pains to explain how his visions originate in the use of his synthesizer – which form part of the Lyrians' legacy – and not in his own mind."

"And *physical* scrutiny? " McLintock queried.

"Our PAS's are fairly simple in their structure, Mr. McLintock," Callum went on, grinning good-naturedly, "and yet we do not completely understand how they work. However, being sure of the authenticity of their source, it would be a mistake, in my view, to allow dark interpretations to cloud our appreciation of all that has been achieved through the decipherment process in which – as Lexin has been reminding us, actually,– our synthesizers need to play an ever more important part."

It was all quite remarkable coming from George, Lexin reckoned, suggesting a trust in him*self* that he could hardly dare to have hoped for considering his rough ride in Canberra. As for McLintock, he was an adaptable person, but perhaps buried in his expanding North African 'empire' he had been isolated too long from the current debate. Time might tell. Perhaps he had not followed Canberra very closely, or had merely read about it in the press.

For respected broadcaster The Rev. Adrian Dawes it was all a bit too sudden:

"Yes, Mr. Chairman," he countered when given the nod from Callum, "but images can be so evocative, so persuasive. We know too much about the brain's workings these days not to be worried by the possibility of manipulative forces..."

Needless to say, J.P. Mauré lost no time in interrupting the charismatic, gentle clergyman to press the point. The Rev. Dawes obligingly half-resumed his seat. "Evocative indeed," Mauré declared. "Those details gleaned by Lexin from such devoted use of his resources...I do not see a connection between our work and such vulgar intrusions into privacy."

Was Jean-Paul referring to his brief accounts of Marcelle's abuse by her mother, Ida's wayward lifestyle, and Marcelle's counteraction...the intimacies of Shining Face's journey? "I feel privileged to have to have been allowed to share, even enter their lives as I travel with them" Lexin said with some animation.

"To enter! This becomes more unwholesome by the minute," Mauré sneered. "It is fraught with unimaginable danger." There was an audible gasp from the delegates below.

"I must say I am not sure where this leaves us," the Reverend Dawes opined a touch wistfully, raising himself up again before finally gathering up his robes and sitting down. The clergyman had long been a dedicated adviser in decipherment of spiritual aspects of the Bods' legacy as well as being chairman of Interfaith Action.

But Lexin wanted to shout about the reality, the unavoidability for him, of those people – his 'own' people whom he knew so well – those living human beings in other times whose names were now, since

Canberra, being reiterated and talked about with enthusiasm on the social networks, as well as being chewed over endlessly (and with far less charity) in the press. Given permission to speak further, he asked Conference to visualize walking with Shining Face down a long and lonely valley full of wild creatures where every step in her search for her mother was one more step into dangers unpredictable.

There was a kind of embarrassed silence.

"And *we* lost our way." It was McLintock.

That was an admission, at least, Lexin thought "There is no going back, Andrew," he said, "any more than we can rewind the disks, for that matter, or reinterpret them."

Xiaofeng, among others, had been trying to get a word in for some time. "I don't feel I have lost my way in matters of historical synthesis," he complained, "so why should it be assumed physicists, agriculturists, educationalists or any others had lost theirs?"

"The path may just be rockier than they – or you – imagine," Lexin suggested, facing his friend and rival just a few seats away. "Gradually, imperceptibly, we may *all* have wandered – decipherers, field workers like yourselves (with a sweep of his arm he gestured to include all the delegates below) – made assumptions, *imagined* we had answers. It is no easy journey that our forefathers undertook. If you were to go and seek out Shining Face, Li Xiaofeng," he continued against a rising background murmur that he liked to think was more questioning than querulous, "torn in her mind between wanting Big Nose on the one hand to emerge out of the sleet and wind, and on the other hand fearing that things might end badly for her if he did, yet determined to carry on, come what may, I think you will come to understand what I am talking about. I want you to go that way, that apparently impossible way, Xiaofeng. "I was going to add,' to help her'. It is to help both of you – and all of us." Xiaofeng looked crestfallen. Possibly it was the thought of what would happen to that immaculate suit of his in such a wild country, Lexin thought, with a little inward smile.

"I have asked my PAS to explain the visions – without much success. Maybe my problem is psychological."

"I think you are trying to rely too much on yourself, on your own powers of reasoning ," Lexin declared. "The fact remains that these brave young women, Shining Face and, yes, Marcelle, too, in her determination to restore her family, both of them trying to do the near impossible…" He hesitated. "If you," he said, now clearly addressing all the assembled delegates down below, who fell silent – compatriots of Xiaofeng from distant parts of China, a very attentive Russian delegation, Africans, Americans North and South, Indians, Europeans, Mauré's supporters, and all the rest… Malinovsky, Mackenzie somewhere in the shadows –, but casting a glance also towards the many aspirants with himself in the gallery, "if all of you can bring yourselves to put your full trust in your synthesizer, you will see that these women are touched by some power…some power outside themselves. We have to go with them and be drawn by that power too." Mauré was anxious to speak, but several voices were raised, and one stood out:

"We ought to know exactly who or what we are dealing with in those people!" it declared. It was an unknown voice, but some others echoed it with shouts of "Hear, hear!", and Jean-Paul was nodding vigorously. Lexin sat down as Callum stepped in to quell a growing hubbub:

"So you cannot define that 'power' further, Lexin? " he asked, calmly, looking up to the gallery.

"No more than I can define it in Marcelle who believes she has it in her to prevail against all the odds posed by incurable illness and every kind of human weakness and ignorance, including her own. As for us" – he was clearly addressing everybody –, "we, all of us, have the resources to go with them now to their destinations whatever those might be. For sure, in them lies our path to the Galactic Community."

He had thought they might be critical of him for not telling them about his visions before they had fallen like a damp squib on the ears of the world media in Canberra. But no! Give them their due, they seemed to understand that it was only during these last days that he realised he would have to 'reveal his sources' and describe his mysterious 'other lives'. Whether or not it was at least partly as a result of Xiaofeng's questioning or Callum's interventions, despite the best efforts of a few delegates Lexin escaped any expression of official disapproval of his interpretation of his visions. Apart from confirmation of an earlier decision to continue rebuilding the badly damaged wormhole terminal, no new decisions on action were taken by the Society. While continuing rigorously to explore all the evidence as to possible causes of its problems, special attention should be given to the question of malign forces.

It was only after being waylaid several times by fellow Societans, some approbatory, others more disputative, in the Palace precincts that he was able finally to change into his running gear and head off for home. But it was not their arguments, the ominous rumblings of the clergyman and others, or even the maunderings of J.P. Mauré that were on Lexin's mind as he ran along the Avenue of Remembrance past the vast, honeycomb domes of the University. It was not even Xiaofeng's problems, either, as he flew past the Museum of Knowledge from Space – that wonderful interactive creation, changing in colour and transparency all the time, celebrating all that had happened since that fateful day in the year 2073, and visited, encouraged and recreated hourly by visitors from every part of the world. The more he ran, the more he thought of Shining Face and how *she* was unable to advance at anything more than a snail's pace down that rocky valley, and yet still she advanced, almost hidden from sight beneath the load of everything she possessed.

A few, at any rate, supported *him,* Lexin, for they were telling him now, even as he ran across the Avenida de Ferrer de Lorenzo and up the Hill of Lyra, that their personal activity synthesizers were affirming their confidence in him, and Lexin noticed that Sergei Malinovsky was among them.

*   *   *

Lunch was already over and coffee was being taken on the terrace when Felicitas, who had gone to the balustrade to look out for him, burst out with something less than her usual decorum, "Hello! hello! Here he comes, just like a little version of his dad, pounding up in his Paris Olympics shorts," whereupon her own little reminiscence caused her to shed a few tears as he came up the steps.

"Mother! You are upsetting yourself again," Lenica said, going and putting an arm around one shoulder and her head on the other.

"Now let me tell you some good stuff, both of you," Lexin said. "George Callum saved the day – with the help of X.F. Mauré did not have it all his own way."

"You didn't tell us that, Xiaofeng love," Lenica said. "Whatever is my dear brother talking about?"

"I suppose I just helped, indirectly, to get some points clarified," he replied. Xiaofeng had stood up, probably because the others were all standing now. To remain seated when Felicitas was on her feet never seemed quite right anyway.

"I must say I cannot help but be relieved if this means Lexin will have some respite from this constant questioning," Felicitas said, recovering and sitting down.

"I would not say that, Mrs. Solberg. The debate about Lexin's experiences is only just hotting up, you know. Lexin was very impressive. Talked about a power. I almost thought you had cracked it, Lexin!"

"Cracked your psychological block, is that what you mean?" Lexin joked, giving Li a friendly shove.

"Don't know about that," he replied.

"Of course there is a power behind all this," Felicitas said. "Look at the power in the text from Lyra, look what happens when things go wrong. Don't be surprised when power seems to be leaking out of every joint in Lexin's visions...To be honest, it is that which frightens me."

"It frightens me too, pretty much," Lenica said.

"Anyway, Lexin," Felicitas said, "I hope you are grateful to your friend and rival. And you yourself, Xiaofeng," she went on, "What *do* you think about all this power floating around?"

"I don't know." The young man looked uncharacteristically nonplussed. "I just think we must exhaust all avenues to understand what is happening, including Lexin's interpretation of it."

"Look, Xiaofeng," Lexin said, cheerfully, "I do not know what you will find on your PAS, but I think you will get at least a glimpse of the visions I have been describing. I am certain they are for everybody."

"What worries me," he replied, solemnly serious, "is that there seems to be no latitude, no freedom there. These visions, it sounds a bit like, I don't know...a runaway train."

At least the fellow was thinking about it. With even Felicitas still a bit dithery on the subject it seemed it rested upon him, Lexin, to face the young man's scepticism head-on – not easy with the guy's prospective wife and mother-in-law there like helpless onlookers at an impending accident.. "The fact is, X.F, that as long as you are content to play around with your PAS..."

"...I have asked it questions on the mechanics of historical vision, dynamics of historic perception..."

"Were they answered for you?"

"I sometimes think I could have got the information from anywhere."

"I wonder whether you have really plumbed its depths, whether you have let the machine really work for you? Have you felt its power?"

"Nobody ever described anything like this to me, except Lenica a little bit. If I try it, it usually ends up pointing to the visions."

"And you don't go there!" Felicitas looked thoughtful. "It's not a runaway train, you know," she added.

"Maybe not yet." Xiaofeng was looking at Lenica, who had gone to look out of a window.

"I hardly know anything myself," Lenica said. "As I said, it's pretty scary."

"We learned nothing of this in our education, except perhaps at the very beginning, briefly, and then things became more ordinary: historical methods, techniques of synthesis, and so on. But Mrs. Solberg," Xiaofeng continued after a few moments, emerging evidently from a brief and unusual bout of introspection, "with respect, your PAS doesn't seem always to inspire you with confidence."

"You are a much more dedicated person than I am, young man," Felicitas said, standing up and putting everyone on tenterhooks. She went over to Lexin and Xiaofeng and put an arm around the shoulders of each. "Look, boys, listen to this: Something very interesting happened this morning. I happened to mention to Robert our robot that I had a few worries, and he told me he knew I had concerns about Lexin's visions to do with galactic communication. And what did he do then? He advised me that my PAS would come in useful and said – listen to this – 'I am sure you may trust it if you trust me. We have the same origin'. But you are right, Xiaofeng," she said releasing them and going and sitting down. "I am a bit hot and cold. You could put it down to age and motherly concern – and – dare I say it?– a certain unwillingness *sometimes* to take life too seriously. But I have seen enough. Frankly, it is what comes up...how could I put it?...by default, unsolicited, that has been most convincing, so I can no more ignore it than I can ignore Robert. Unthinkable!"

"I might come to trust it," Lenica said, "but God knows what it will tell me about myself."

"It might help you a lot," Lexin said, "and Lenica, I wish you *would* use it. It might even help Harry, actually, if he used it. I tell you, if we cannot exploit this power...no, I do mean *use* it..."

"…What's the difference, Lexin?"

"It is a gift. You can use a gift, but 'exploit' does not sound right to me. Be that as it may, the fact is that if we do not use it, if the Government does not see something happening, i.e. that my visions – our visions – are being shared, if they see only a divided Society, they will send us all packing. As it is, I am going to have a hell of a time on this tour – next stop Casablanca in a week."

Lenica and Xiaofeng soon departed to meet some friends. When they had gone, Felicitas got up and came and gave Lexin a generous hug:

"How's it really going, my boy?"

"Couldn't be much worse," he replied.

"Oh yes it could! I'm very proud of you, Lexin, and I think Lenica's got the message. If she turns Xiaofeng round…"

"*If*, Mother. But how hard it is for him. He has a long way to go. They *all* have, in the Conference. How easy it is to say 'examine all avenues!' or blame somebody else: the Devil, or aliens, or gods of prehistory, but refuse to grasp the nettle. Yes, if he does see the light, maybe others will be encouraged, but I don't see much sign of it." Releasing himself from Felicitas's firm embrace, Lexin walked away a few paces and stood wrapped in thought. The name of Malinovsky was never far from his thoughts. When he turned round he had an impression of his mother staring at him forlornly, as though at some receding comet, and he went and gave her another hug.

"Now you'd better come and have some lunch," she said.

CHAPTER FOURTEEN

"Welcome to Algiers, Mr. Solberg!"

"Thank you. Sorry there is no time to take a walk ashore. Looking forward to a good sleep before Casablanca. Hopefully, I will get it on the boat."

Lexin was picking up his hand luggage to join the passengers transferring from the failed SST from Galaxy City to a travelator heading towards a distant vista of masts and wingsails crowding the clear Mediterranean sky.

"Another press conference, I understand," the friendly official went on. Lexin nodded. "I hope they treat you better there. I saw you at Canberra. Those girls!" He was grateful for the sympathy. "The girl in the lions' cave especially." The official had put down his check list and was helping a Moroccan woman with a horde of children.

"You saw it all on TV, then."

"Yes, we were all watching." There had been much heralded worldwide coverage, of course. "It was almost as if we were with her there in the cave. It was the way you described it. These press boys don't want to believe anything, do they? It's not the sort of thing you'd make up, is it?" The man looked as if it had been on his mind all day. So something 'galactic' had travelled through the ether! Lexin could have wished for no better news.

He paused a moment before sitting in the travelator. "Thank you. Thank you for your encouragement. Look out for me in Casa!"

"There's not one of us who isn't bothered about them," the man said finally, "and good luck, Sir!" he added, touching his cap as he explained to the next traveller, "Yes, we apologise for the disruption today, Madam. Some overheating."

Lexin heard the woman say "Sounds like something out of the twentieth century." Her words stuck with him as he transferred to the relief boat laid on to complete the journey. It would put on fifty knots across the rest of the Med and down to Casa. They would be there in time for the conference to start mid-morning as scheduled, but he was puzzled by the overheating of the motors – if that was what it was – suddenly becoming a problem on SST's. There had been one or two such occurrences lately. The trains ran on maglev principles, and the long and highly automated maintenance cycles were normally utterly reliable. Then he remembered his own words. "Growth – our growth – may be impeded". Was this it, then? Was it a case of coincidences, or was it some kind of retrogressive effect resulting from non-decipherment – the first sign of something? If so, that was the worst kind of thing he feared. Perhaps he was being too pessimistic!

There was a lot of satisfaction in being propelled by an emissionless and independently produced mix of wind, wave, sun and hydrogen, he mused, lulled by the gentle hum of the wind in the wingsails high above the deck and comfortable throbbing of the complex propulsion systems down below. But when he retired to his bunk, the gentle, encouraging sounds of the ship's progress were obliterated by the imagined voices of press men and women clamouring to unravel the carefully knitted fabric of his thoughts.

"Lexin, how do you quantify the girl's chances against the hazards of a primeval epoch?" And he would like to answer,

"Better than yours!" But there was no point in clever answers when so much was at stake, and when people as close and potentially valuable to the 'cause' as Xiaofeng remained unconvinced about any power beyond the end of his nose, it was no time to talk in riddles. One day they might have to plead for the Society's survival. When the steward brought him his breakfast of fruit and cereals, the sea racing by was flecked with pink by the early morning sun, and between the flecks were a million dark sides to the wavelets giving an impression of endless uncertainties...

"Sixty minutes to Casablanca, Sir. Do you need help disembarking?"

Lexin decided not to take advantage of Rapid Disembark, which would have transferred him to one of the taxi modules on the urban transit net, the taxi then delivering him to the door of his hotel. He needed to pause, acclimatise. "No, I will walk off," he replied. "Thank you all the same. Please deliver my things to the Nouvel Hotel Canada."

Out on deck, he found a seat away from the passengers heading for the disembarkation points, fished out his multicom and activated the PAS. It was a struggle to select and focus. Menus, images, appeared unexpectedly that were too extensive for the hand monitor and probably too much altogether...crowded perspectives of events in Newchurch passing semi-subliminally, condensed texts that spoke logically only to inner brain processes and could hardly be unravelled. He was forced to ask for selection advice. Eventually it was Big Nose, and not Marcelle, who materialised out of the confusion. But if the fact of his appearance at least had a reassuring, timeless effect, the rest was less reassuring. Big Nose had caught up with Shining Face, but they were having words...

"Couldn't you have taken a hint?" she was saying. She was pale, moving with difficulty. It was impossible to say whether it had taken hours or days for Big Nose to catch up, but whenever it had happened she would probably have seen him coming up behind her, and he must have approached with a good idea of the kind of reception he would get.

Lexin had to admit that she certainly did not have great charisma, but he supposed it wasn't a place or a time where charisma counted for much. "How do you suppose you'll manage. Look, at least I can hunt – in a fashion." In fact he could barely stand after stumbling for hours alongside that treacherous rocky river. He had never felt more hindered in any sort of movement, never mind hunting. It would be understandable if she thought he was not as capable of doing things as he said he was.

"I managed before, didn't I ?" she protested, stopping. "I managed even though I am only a girl. Any girl can get trapped by lions – just like any male can – if she's not content to just sit around all day. I have a job to do. Okay, okay, you got me out of a fix. And thank you!" The snow had turned back to rain here, further down the valley, but despite the fact that the days were long and it was nearly summer the wind out of the north was stronger than ever, beating on their faces, soaking them. It didn't improve her looks, and it was almost as if she took advantage of that fact, screwing up her face into a scowl that matched beautifully the grey sky and the darkness of the river and the forest around them.

"It's because I am who I am, isn't it?" he said. "But I may turn out to be the lesser of two evils."

She looked down and said nothing, then began to move on.

In other circumstances he might in the end have lost his temper with the way she treated him, but when he thought of her fortitude in her endeavours he could forgive her a lot. Then her defiant independence became tolerable, even touching. When he kept up with her she offered no resistance, and they walked on in silence.

Time shifted. It was evening as they approached a defile which appeared safely passable only on the opposite side of the river. "We'll have to cross," he shouted. "It's getting dark. I'll build a shelter here on this side, and we'll try and cross tomorrow." He stopped and put down his load.

"You can stop, but I'm going on," she spat. Ignoring his warnings she carried on walking on the same side until he saw her disappearing next to a shrubby overhanging rock where the water appeared poised against the rock in a slowly turning pool before plunging out of sight down a rapid. Suddenly, at the limit of his vision she must have slipped, for he was horrified to see her being swept away, and he lost sight of her.

Lexin pocketed his multicom and walked off the boat with just a shoulder bag and onto the travelator. But now that other part of his brain had taken over, and he had thrown down everything he was carrying and, imbued with scarcely explicable agility, was racing along the rocks of the defile perilously close to the plunging icy water. Below the rapid, the river entered another deep pool, its surface ominously unbroken, but by the time he had reached the end of the travelator at the Boulevard Aberrahman he had discarded his mammoth fur, waded in and swum with the current to where something was moving in the water...

Diverting from the Boulevard Mohammed el Mansour and plunging into the crowded alleys and hotchpotch of stalls of the Old Medina with its traders now from almost every part of the world, he was recognized on more than one occasion with a smile and a wave or a "Peace be with you", but people did not crowd him. He was glad there were no journalists about. While he was bargaining with an American stallholder for some fruit, another stallholder standing nearby was poring over the top newspaper in a pile for wrapping. The headline said something about growing discontent of the World Government with the Society and questions about its future. There was a picture of Van Rensburg the First Minister.

As he emerged from the narrow passages, having meantime grabbed hold of Shining Face and struggled out of the whirlpool, pulling her behind him, another news headline was flashing on a billboard – "Unprecedented World Food Shortages Inevitable. Failure of 'Successful' South American Agroprogramme". It was almost unbelievably bad news when viewed, as he walked towards his hotel, against the emerging confident background of modern Casa: the French colonial city of the end of the second millennium interwoven now by that of the increasingly multicultural and prosperous third, and finishing with the intricate aerial creations of the present day – and the hotel, semi-transparent and harmonious against the settled blue of the sky.

By the time he was no more than half way there he had managed to empty the water out of the half-drowned body of the girl and was doing his best to comfort her. Realising by now that he had been dawdling as he drifted in and out of two worlds, he hailed a taxi bubble, calling out "Nouvel Hotel Canada!" in as calm a voice as he could.

*   *   *

"Lexin!" The tanned, blond figure of Andrew McLintock in timeless military-style khaki shirt and trousers and deck shoes advanced nimbly to meet him across the glittering high foyer with its view across to the Mosque Hassan II and the ocean beyond, and inland across the arborified suburbs to the World University where once the airport had reigned supreme. "Bienvenue au Maroc!" he said, warmly, as they embraced. "You've made it!"

The conference would be held in the banqueting hall, renowned for its refinement and detail, chaired by the very man who had suggested a special scrutiny of his visions. He had in actual fact *offered* to chair it.

George Callum thought it was a good idea. "Somebody with a critical mind who is coming round to Lexin's way of thinking. Very good," he said, "Very good!"

There was no question of its being Lenica, since Harry Beckenthal definitely put his foot down this time. Things were too hot in Canberra, her boss said, and she had had to return there. It was surely no coincidence that, following on the enquiry into the Society's problems and its conclusions, discussions were starting there, in committee, on a re-framing of the law on the status of the Society. Not since the earliest days of decipherment had it been found necessary or desirable to dwell on such things. The world had suddenly come to feel a much less secure place.

McLintock had not made clear when he had called Lexin what exactly had prompted his "new way of seeing things" (as he put it), but a growing optimism on Lexin's part soon proved justified.

"We *are* in trouble; I begin to see it now," McLintock said when they arrived in Lexin's room. "And believe it or not, I have been having glimpses of your visions, just glimpses, but nothing that I can hang anything on yet."

The other part of Lexin's brain had just seen Big Nose pick up the girl in his arms and start picking his way back along the river's edge, so that for an instant it was the agriculturist's voice and the view between the elevated structures surrounding the hotel towards the famous Hassan II mosque that were of another time than the here and now. "And you were questioning its authenticity!" he said, automatically.

"What I have seen has been enough. Ever since the last press conference I have had the feeling that the crisis was somehow to do with us, the Society, including me – some short-cutting in our work; 'imagining we had answers' is what you said. Yes, a little 'furring up of the arteries', I reckon, rather than the intervention of some malign power. I must say, though, that we are beset here by unprecedented climate control problems right across to the headquarters at Ghardaia. I thought we were through our problems long ago...My PAS seems to attach significance to our situation here, but it has been short on explanations. Now it is saying – and this is what has really set me thinking –'proper solutions may have to await a continuation of decipherment'. I must say I don't give much for Mauré's diagnosis."

Indeed it was hard to visualize satanic powers in the presence of those two, Lexin mused. One perceived there only fortitude, even if now he was hearing Big Nose say, "When you have completely recovered I will leave you to go your own way, and I won't be chasing after you when you fall in." Surely just a few cross words! Next, in a seamless transition it appeared already to be the day following the rescue. He was aware that Big Nose had struggled back up the defile with the girl, retrieving what he could of her belongings, and made a shelter against the rocks, where they had spent the night. She even had her pouch still, with its precious contents, including the irreplaceable cones in their skin, but they were all soaking, as had been the hyena skin and deer hide that she had been wearing and her body beneath it – and this frozen, too, to the extent that Big Nose had worried that in her state she would fall ill. She had been mortified at having to strip and be helped to get dry because she was so exhausted, and those beautiful lips were quivering with a mixture of cold, anger and despair, not least because once again she had lost her spear, her very own spear, to a river's power...

"If you ever did suffer from metaphorical furred arteries, Andrew," Lexin commented, laughing as the real present took over again without perceptible break in their conversation and the wiry Canadian, glancing at his watch, let himself agilely into one of the armchairs, "from what you are saying I don't think you are suffering from them now!"

"I am relieved to hear you say it, Lexin," he said, sipping at the mint tea that a porter had had sent up on their arrival.

Andrew was getting there fast. He must try not to overload him with too many dire prognostications. There would be no *concrete* basis for them, anyway. Nor was there any point in referring to what was likely to be an increasing problem: the question of how far increasing worldwide dysfunction might be due to inadequate decipherment and how far to its complete cessation.

"Things don't sound good at the Crisis Committee," the Canadian went on. "They keep calling in more Conference delegates – including me, incidentally –, and they all disagree. It doesn't help much, does it?"

Lexin, too, had heard the same from Callum about the Crisis Committee. Mauré and supporters were getting the best hearing. "It is easy to dismiss the idea of visions," he admitted, subsiding likewise into a chair, and McLintock nodded thoughtfully. But even as he said it, Lexin recalled the official's words of encouragement at Algiers. Evidently there were those, and perhaps many, who had taken Marcelle and Shining Face to their hearts. "The trouble is," he said, "that time is almost impossibly short for us."

* * *

"How will we know when it's all over – Will there be a family party in the local cave when they find the woman, and will they in fact make it up, do you reckon, she and the guy with the nose? And will you be telling us about it, and in half a dozen words why it matters to us.? And the other girl's family.....the one who was knocked about by her mother..."

"Marcelle."

"Yes. Can the mother possibly survive...?"

"...And will *we* all live happily ever after?" someone else called out.

Émil Daugin was going to be a pain. The olive-skinned Mediterranean native sat down with the satisfied air of one who believed he had given someone something to think about.

It was perhaps not surprising that in such a beautiful setting as the banqueting hall Lexin's sombre and often self-deprecatory message, and the novel antidote offered, looked like getting a cool, not to say flippant, reception. The vulgarity and irreverence of 'France Soir''s roving correspondent stuck out there like a sore thumb. Before Lexin had time to answer, somebody else shouted,

"Will you Societans ever agree among yourselves?"

"Eventually,"

"Eventually!".

Lexin refused to be diverted. He tried to shut everything out of his mind but the ongoing events that shouted out to be pointed to.. He pressed on: "Allow me first to update you. Marcelle's mother is suffering from the incurable human acquired immune deficiency syndrome, or AIDS, almost certainly as a consequence of her sexually permissive lifestyle. Marcelle is telling her mother that she will look after her at her own (Marcelle's) place..." Somewhere in a compartment of Lexin's brain Ida was sitting up in her hospital bed, with Marcelle holding a basin in front of her as she rinsed out her mouth with Listerine. "Her mum is too weak while recovering from

AIDS-related pneumonia to look after herself," he told them, "and as well as suffering from a painful herpes infection called shingles – again resulting from lowered immunity – , she also has a mouth infection which makes eating difficult."

Already they were finding it hard to concentrate. "Promiscuity's no great issue now," Daugin was saying, "and there's not much prostitution or live sex entertainment... and where there is, there are ways of countering any ill effects."

"This is not a lesson in moral behaviour, M. Daugin, It is not even a history lesson. It is just the living lives of these people, just like it's the living lives of Big Nose and his family that I've told you about. And in answer to your questions, the outcomes cannot be known."

Lexin was conscious of facing an audience just as colourful in terms of the visible light spectrum as that at Canberra, and even more restless and inattentive. He could hardly be surprised, could he, if while in the back of his mind Marcelle became busy discussing the details of her mother's discharge from the hospital with the ward sister, and Ida was full of remorse as usual and not understanding how Marcelle could love her, he found himself being driven to the conclusion that only a second visitation, a *'second coming'*, might be capable of restoring sight to those glazed eyes in the hall below?. He wondered whether Daugin might even seek to denigrate him for having a morbid interest in these people if there was nothing else to write about for his wretched paper.

"And your job is to get alongside these people. That is so, right?" It was Russell Johnson, now, BBC. The voice had an authoritative ring.

Here at least was a glimmer of understanding! "That's right," Lexin replied just as Marcelle was telling her mother not to worry and they could get help at home if necessary. They could get through this, he said, upon which Ida's face lit up.

"And to do this you use what you refer to as your gadgetry. But hasn't there been trouble with....what is it...your synthesizers?"

"Trouble with ourselves. Not with our equipment." Lexin's admissions seemed to give a moment's pause for thought.

"Well yours works, at any rate? You have been speaking as if you have just viewed these events, now, today."

"Yes, I have, though actually at this moment everything is being transmitted directly to my brain *via* the synthesizer."

If only that was all he need say! He wanted to apologise, apologise on behalf of the Society for the lack of dedication, the missed opportunities, the mistakes, loss of life…, tell them point-blank of the probable consequences of his visions being ignored by his fellow Societans. But it might switch them off for ever, banish all hope. Fingers might soon be poised over multicoms to warn the world of the disasters at hand. Daugin could have read his mind…

"I can't imagine," he said, "why so many Societans should have been misusing their synthesizers for so long, causing explosions, never mind correcting their mistakes by reference to a lot of folk in other ages with more earthy problems. And if it comes to that," he announced smugly, "I am increasingly concerned at how little Societans appear to understand about their own modification. It is a pity there is not somewhere where you can take yourselves for psychorepairs – those of you who need to."

Lexin felt more sorry for McLintock, as he tried to restore order in the ensuing laughter, than for himself. Oddly enough, he did not feel angry with the oh-so-witty Frenchman, but just despair, a despair in a way exacerbated by the fact that in his own mind he sensed an unusual clarity in the latest news from Newchurch: a harmony of many levels: a serene Marcelle, a family fractured, yet increasingly drawn together again in that same tender tissue of bonds which surely embraced him, too. He remembered how Marcelle had once or twice begun to tell her mother about himself and about Big Nose and the rest, and how she had shown an understanding that her daughter had scarcely dared to expect.

"M. Daugin," he said, quietly when the laughter had died down, "It is the Bods, the Lyrians. They are offering us help now, even without our asking: Marcelle, Shining Face. I have been trying to tell you. They are our 'psychorepairers'. I prefer to say our 'remedy'."

"And on their own terms, on the Bods' own terms."

"Yes, on their terms – terms I could not possibly have imagined. Who could have imagined knowledge of those people from other ages?" Again he wanted to warn them. He wanted to warn all of them, ranged in their ranks high up there in the banqueting hall of the Nouvel Hotel Canada, with all the richness and prosperity of the city spread out below them, the boulevards, the crowds, the sounds, the colour…, that their very existence was now so fragile, so vulnerable… But another journalist burst through the ranks and said it for him:

"Lexin, are you really wanting to say to us: 'Accept my story or the consequences may be...' What? *What* might they be? I have heard whispers of dire effects resulting from cessation of decipherment. Is 'catastrophic' too strong a word?"

The implied accusation raised a growing murmur of agreement. It was also the more worrying for its origin. 'Guardian Interactive' commentator Bill Walmsley, today in white salwar kameez, had a reputation as a peacemaker and multiculturalist. In common with his newspaper, he was generally a strong supporter of the Society, although it was true that the paper had recently become noticeably less sympathetic. At any rate, the interest of the TV crews had certainly redoubled when he got up to speak – as it had at .Canberra.

It would help, Lexin thought, if he himself could really explain 'retrogression' to them – or even be sure it existed. But theory might be overtaken by events anyway. " Trust me, Andrew" he said under his breath, resuming his seat as McLintock, standing and leaning forward over the table in front of him and brushing aside the lank, blond hair that for some might erroneously evoke a certain casualness, even carelessness, stepped in, but not before another voice had rung out:

"No-one has answered my question: Will we all live happily ever after? "

"To be sure, we understand your concern," McLintock replied, "and yours, Mr. Walmsley, but I must point out that at rock bottom Lexin's analysis is one of optimism, and certainly not one dwelling on any consequences that might result from a failure of the Society to accept the remedy offered by the Lyrians. These people in other times that we have been talking about are meeting their difficulties, overcoming them, swept along by hands seen and unseen, as I am sure Lexin can confirm..."

"Willingly!" Lexin said, and stood up to describe how Big Nose had caught up with little Shining Face and managed to pull her out of a whirlpool that would probably have drowned her, and how Ida had now already moved to Marcelle's flat to be looked after there: "Marcelle has made the front room her mother's room," he told them, "and given her her own bed, borrowing for herself a put-you-up from the Sandbay grandparents. Devastated by Ida's downward spiral, they are full of admiration for the way Marcelle is caring for her – as I am," he added emphatically. "Time has actually moved on several weeks, probably," he explained. "Bactrim treatment has overcome another bout of pneumonia, but even as I speak Marcelle has come home from her work at the supermarket to find her mother in the bathroom desperately searching in a low-down cupboard for something to ease the candidiasis which has now invaded her throat. Now she asks her whether she has swallowed the yoghurt she left for her:

'If the lozenges and the mouthwash don't work, what's the use?' Ida replies, dispiritedly.

Now Marcelle is kneeling down and putting her arms around her. 'Do it, Mum,' she says, 'just to see. It's step by step, this is.'

'I suppose I had better do as I'm told,' she says. '*You* did, didn't you?'

'Did I?' Marcelle replies. 'I wonder why you used to hit me then.'

'I shouldn't have,' her mother admits, and Marcelle says,

'So let's forget it.'

'Thanks, my love,' Ida says, 'It was all wrong.' And they exchange an awkward but tender kiss kneeling on the floor."

An unexpected moment of tenderness and accompanying silence, in the auditorium, followed by a brief appreciative word from Bill Walmsley for 'an interesting insight' but pointing out that his question about *possible* consequences had not really been answered, gave way to the well known voice of the 'Vancouver Daily's Crabtree. Neat and tidy in his battledress, he suggested while meaning no disrespect that he feared "all this" might be just part of Lexin's fertile imagination or attributable to wish fulfilment. "And this J.P.Mauré has a strong following, hasn't he? They say he either cannot or does not want to see these things, insists they are dark manifestations, a culmination of the otherwise unaccountably bad things that have overtaken us."

"I have to say," McLintock retorted, lifting his voice against a rising murmur of agreement, "that I regret the short shrift you are giving to Lexin. I believe others may well have had these experiences – which Jean-Paul Mauré has not had, on his own admission..."

"But you?" Crabtree cut in, "May I ask whether you have had them, Mr. Chairman, whether on your monitor or in your head?"

The hair had flopped again. McLintock flicked it back vigorously. "Just the beginnings, Mr. Crabtree, but enough, yes: visions as real, as undoubted as the revelations in understanding which have driven us forward in our work in Africa. And I can tell you that we would not have got as far as we have got there by following mirages."

Lexin nodded. He was watching Marcelle set down on her mother's bedside table a tray with a dish of yoghurt and a small vase containing a little cluster of roses. A few minutes must have passed. Her mother was sitting in bed now, near the window with its view across the Memorial Park.

"You shouldn't have done that, but I forgive you," Ida said, and they both smiled.

She dipped into the yoghurt, and Marcelle slipped out. Between reading magazines and listening to the radio (television, as she put it, seemed to give her no time to herself) her mother would sit staring out of the window. Through a gap between a petrol station and St. Luke's church it was just possible – as Lexin had observed – if she looked that way to see where Tom was living in a house adjoining the end of a row of shops in a similar terrace to hers, with its red bricks and white sills and lintels.

Meanwhile, several press people were trying to make themselves heard, questioning how many Societans had actually seen things that Lexin said he had seen. When McLintock had managed to restore a semblance of order, a request by Crabtree to speak again was granted:

"Mr. Chairman. I hear what you say about the revelations which you have received and your work in Africa, but the fact is – is it not – that most of you have *not* shared the visions?" Lexin knew the complaint was justified and understood the irritation. In the face of the restless crowd in front of him he feared more and more that one way or the other time could just run out for Ida – and for all of them. For her, the possibilities for opportunistic infections were legion, and it was clear that there was no cure for AIDS at that time – his own researches for historical information confirmed it.

But McLintock had already sprung to his feet again. "A week ago," he declared, "I had no glimpse of Lexin's visions. Now I have, and in the coming weeks," he declared to the hard-nosed ranks before him, "I hope to see much more of them and that many more of us Societans will see them, and I fervently hope their purpose may be fulfilled, if for Africa's sake alone, and its future"

"No doubt it *is* your *fervent* hope," Victor Rodriguez of 'El Pais', a man of short stature and sharp nose, declared tartly as Andrew sat down again. "You are doing well out of the new Africa." Of course, he was referring to the continuing transformation of the Sahara, resulting in the creation of new cities and thousands of farms and villages, and the Canadian's not inconsiderable part in all this over the past thirty years. "You have a lot to lose if it all seizes up, not so?" he added.

"Yes, that is true," McLintock agreed. And yes, that included money if that was what was on Rodriguez's mind. Societans, in their role overseeing the implementation of new advances, new projects in every sphere, benefited greatly from successful developments like everyone else, and he told them so, adding that it was not only a case of Africa. "Look at the transformation of Australia, look at South America, its standard of living, its vast cultural contribution."

"They are in trouble, too," someone called out as more hands were raised, and everybody was starting to talk at once. The conference seemed to Lexin in danger of getting out of hand. Could it be that things were moving so fast that McLintock had not heard the latest bad news about the South American agroprogramme? That was a bit unfortunate.

"Don't you think...," Rodriguez came back with some vehemence, "don't you think Conference delegates should always have declared their interests like World Assembly members have had to. Under the new laws they may have to. What do *you* think, Lexin?" Judging by the general murmur of agreement, the old-fashioned left-wing journalist and broadcaster, in his dark jeans and sweater, had struck a chord, and suddenly Lexin felt the disbelief and cynicism festering among many in the audience now beginning to weigh upon himself.

"Surely you must know, Mr. Rodriguez," Lexin replied in a sudden silence, rising to his feet and managing (he hoped) to conceal his anger, "that Societans are not allowed to amass great wealth or power. But it is more than that. The special abilities conferred by our genetic and other alterations are intended and designed to be able to further *everyone's* interests." Yet even as he said it a doubt assailed him. Yes, in McLintock's case he was sure that was as true as for anybody, but for all those other Societans out there charged with bringing to worldwide fruition the hard-won results of decipherment? And Beckenthal? And now with everything blurred by the possible effects of retrogression? He could only hope so.

But the man had a bone to pick. "Isn't all that difficult to prove," he asked, "– that it is being done in everyone's interest? Shouldn't all of this – I refer to questions both of wealth and power and also of personal advantage versus public good – shouldn't all this have been looked at thoroughly long ago? I think so."

Lexin wanted to say, "Proof, proof, proof, that's all you think about!" "It's because it was not considered necessary, not called for," he replied. "In any case, it's a bit late now." Societans were not perfect, as had become patently obvious. He wanted just to reiterate their special mission, the principles of dedication and fidelity to the human cause, but he spoke carelessly: "We have special insights," he went on, "we can make special connections between principles and situations, we can make far-reaching decisions, safe choices," adding "usually" when he realised what he had said, upon which ironic laughter drowned the rest so that he had to give up. As for any idea of reminding them that any action on resumption of decipherment would have to have the agreement of Government and Assembly, and in a still democratic world, thus the approval of the population, and not least journalists themselves, any such reminder would be pointless or worse

After somebody had finally suggested that, in view of how little was apparently understood about the processes and consequences of human modification, it might be best to throw in the towel now in the hope that the Bods would forgive us our stupidity and look elsewhere for a more intelligent life form to encourage, Andrew, no longer troubling to control his unruly head of hair, finally closed the conference on as cheerful a note as he could. Later, he and Lexin retired to lick their wounds and then, with a few other Society members who had attended, they headed for a nearby restaurant to sample the local fare.

CHAPTER FIFTEEN

A tired Lexin, glad to be on his way home, toyed for a minute or two with the destination menu of his compartment and decided he would not allow himself to bask in the well-known eulogies and subtle cycloramas of Galaxy City. Having turned it all off he tried to give his mind to the business of getting his convictions across as the SST transported him at 1500 kilometres an hour at first underground and then – suspended – beneath the surface of the Mediterranean (the SST problems now being attributed to *tunnel* overheat, and hopefully resolved). At first he feared calmness would never catch up with him, and only gradually was he able to substitute the negative attitudes expressed by many at the press conference with calming thoughts of Marcelle.

"I suppose I had had *my* doubts," Asad Malik, a young hydrologist from a remote part of Pakistan, had admitted as they sat enjoying their B'Stilla pastries at the little place in the Rue Chaoui. But his PAS had no doubt about her uniqueness. "For me, now, Marcelle abolishes all the clever complaints of those journalists," he declared. "She could not do that if you were not convinced she was real, could she?" Lexin had had to agree – nothing in his own life had prepared him for Marcelle. "I could share her thoughts, you know," Asad said, his dark moustache pressing forward, earnestly as he rested his arms on the table, "share her conviction that time will not run out for her mother, and that there will be a cure, a real cure." He added that with the help of an ethnic culture transfer mode which he had come across (probably not by chance, he thought) he had been able to understand and follow Tom's struggles to get on the care workers' course that Marcelle said he was aiming for.

The almost imperceptible vibrations of the SST as it raced though its vacuum tunnel were the very gentlest but ongoing reminder, in the midst of such optimistic thoughts, of the passage of time in the here and now and the threatening finiteness of its events. But Lexin had suspected it could not be long before other Societans, too, began to share his visions. And how else could his words carry conviction? First it had been Andrew, now Asad Malik and also another worker out on the front line, a seasoned Australian climate control engineer presently based at Ghardaia who had also spoken up at the restaurant. Rupert McDonnel, like Mr. Malik, had witnessed Marcelle's untiring care of her mother. He felt he had had a remarkable insight into changes going on in Ida's and Tom's state of mind.

"It's not as if I had always known them," he said. "It's just that I suddenly knew where they were coming from and where they wanted to get to, if you see what I mean. Felt the same motivation. Can't explain it."

Lexin couldn't, either. "But I wouldn't worry," he said, "Better just accept it – and expect more of the same!"

It was no more than a momentary surprise for him when, after activating the personal mind-clearing and relaxation option of his resting facility and enjoying for a while being surrounded by its dynamic pseudo-hologram, in the near-silence of the tunnel and with PAS activated he was startled by Ida confessing to him that she was a stubborn old cow and he realised part of him was Marcelle.

"Marcie," she was saying, "It must be rotten being my daughter."

"You had better explain yourself, Mum," Marcelle replied – she was in her dressing gown, having just come out of the bath – "Is that any different from how you were before?" She did not know how she could have dared to say that. It just came out.

"How dare you say that to your poor mother who is not in a position to clout you?" Ida was grinning. Gone completely now was the old fixed expression, the distant staring at nothing. Then she said, "But the point is, Marcie, I *have* decided I am not going to carry around my old burdens any more. Marcie, I want you to settle up with Nadia for me, but first I have a confession to make to you; two confessions, actually. My symptoms drove me to test myself, and *then* get tested so as to be sure. So you see I was never an escort. Could never have been. Nadia let me stay on. I had nowhere else to go. I continued at the massage place until I became really ill, then resigned. Nadia knew everything." There was a silence.

"I had just wondered. In fact I hoped that might be the case." Another silence.

"And now the second confession: we have, or rather had, I suppose, a relationship."

Marcelle had not seen that coming. "You had a relationship with Nadia? What sort of a relationship, or shouldn't I ask?"

"Best not to ask too much. She does everything, including s and m."

"Sado-masochism."

"Sometimes. I was 's'; she was 'm'." She stopped. "Marcie, I'll have to get back into bed. I feel terrible. You could bring back some little things from my bedroom, and the kitchen stuff that's mine. Nadia is the kindest person, but I shall never go back there, or *back* anywhere. She will understand. And there are my clothes and things. She will help you. We shall always be friends. I'm sorry to put this onto you. The s and m stuff is hers, of course. I'll ring her."

"It's all right. Where *will* you go?" Marcie went and sat on the bed and put her arms gently around her mother, around that form which had so many times borne down heavily upon her..

"Where but here for the moment? But not too long, for your sake. Then, who knows? – If I am still in the land of the living."

"You *will* be."

"I mean, the past is finished. I mean I am not even going to go on blaming myself any more, or even feeling guilty. What's the use?"

"None."

"Can you accept that, then? It was just all wrong, and I am sorry"

"Yes, Mum." Marcelle held her tighter and kissed her, and her own tears welled up to join her mother's. Her mum had said similar things before, but this time it seemed different. It was not a denial of the past so much as trying to set her mind on the future – or so it seemed. There was just one worrying thing. "You don't mean you are giving up, do you? I'm sure you don't."

"No, Marcie, but I have to rely on you, and on that young man."

"You mean Lexin!"

The 'young man' was finding it hard to sustain the account visually in his brain (and it *was* a bit embarrassing when he himself was part of it). Slipping out of the resting facility, he switched on the compartment's monitor and activated his PAS code.

Quickly then he was in Marcelle's shoes again and recalling that many weeks had passed since she had talked to her mother about Big Nose and eventually Lexin. She tried not to show her excitement now at her mother's evident willingness to trust him, and judged it was the moment to bring up another subject. "Dad wants to help you, Mum," she said. There was a long silence. Ida's eyes, still questioning, demanding, were fixed on her daughter, searching her. Marcelle wondered whether she had blown it.

"Does he?" she whispered. "I'm a wreck, darling. Useless." Pale and drawn, her gaze had moved out of the window. Pneumonia, drug side effects, candidiasis, shingles, the totality of the disease and universally accepted inevitability of its consequences, all had taken their toll....

"He wants you to go there."

The scene blurred, and Lexin switched off the monitor, slipped out of the resting facility and consulted his multicom. A quick glance showed that the quantity of messages had built up considerably, especially since the press conference. Even so, he allowed himself to drift off to sleep confident that he would wake up with the change of motion as the train touched rails and pulled up at Cairo. Returning to his messages somewhat reluctantly as it plunged to working depth again beneath the Middle East, and prioritizing them on the desk monitor, he noted without surprise that Lenica's name was high on the list.

"Main news is decision of the World Assembly to give the Society thirty weeks to resolve its crisis. Lucky to get that. Other bad news: Callum was no help in preventing that decision. For breakdown of reactions to press conference and status of Society in terms of galactic attitude: see attachments."

The deadline had a final ring about it. 'Galactic attitude'! He liked that. Good old Lenica! But it could all wait. It was George Callum that worried Lexin the most. It was funny how it was only he who ever came near to making him really angry. Callum the ditherer, and the thought of his friend totally failing to 'take the medicine'! Not a magic cure for the world's problem, more a treatment. If there were those who wanted to laugh at the idea of a 'remedy', let them! Before contacting George he questioned his PAS on the monitor.

"Is it first necessary for Ida to be cured?" he asked. "Sorry. Stupid question!"

"Stupidity is understandable....," came the answer, firm as a rock, on the monitor. "...What do *you* think?" More difficult, he said to himself, was the question of how soon a cure could be expected, but he did not fancy asking the question only to receive another jokey answer.

Contact with Callum did not raise his spirits…

"Privately, I am getting the feeling that Mauré may be right, and that other mechanisms must be harnessing the thoughts of those who are seeing the visions."

His friend's tone shocked him. Lexin tried to hide his exasperation and was glad not to be televiewing. "You mean to say that the visions are not from the Bods?" How could he explain it all yet again? Why should George assume the worst? There were no PAS warnings about false sources – but of course, that wouldn't cut ice with George. "Look," he said, "several friends here… we have been sharing visions of Marcelle… They felt the same as I did, that they were real, that they were important."

"Could be a kind of hypnosis. You know, like Bernadette," Callum suggested.

He really was scraping the barrel. "That's very much *your* interpretation of Bernadette, George."

"And people don't like being threatened, you know, Lexin. It came out at the conference, didn't it?"

Lexin did not know what exactly they had been saying at the Crisis Committee, but he could hazard a few guesses. "I have heard of telepathic images being called on to account for my visions," he retorted. "Now it is hypnosis. Next it will be self-inducement or something. Don't say you're believing everything in the papers. Not these days. The intelligent are very vulnerable, George."

But it was the matter of retrogression that was just as much on the man's mind. It was not a word he himself had used at the Conference to describe a possible consequence of breaking some sort of organic link with the Lyrians. Indeed he thought he had not mentioned it to anyone but Callum and a rather uninterested Mackenzie – and Malinovsky. It was just a concept floating around in his head, expressed in one word and unauthenticated. George Callum had clearly not forgotten it, and clearly it was more than just a word to him.

"I'm not saying there's no such thing as retrogression," he was saying. "Because agricultural projects are in trouble all over the place, I s'pose you *might* say there's something retrogressive there. My PAS – when I have felt obliged to consult it for my linguistic philosophy lectures (so he was using it, at least!) – has been trying to tell me something of the sort...I mean in warnings I have been getting about 'curtailment of decipherment'."

Lexin reckoned he could not let that one pass. "Surely, then, it should be telling you something else as well," he said. "I'm serious, George."

"Yes, I know, I know what you are saying. Your warnings, the visions, the whole conundrum... It's just that people don't like being bullied. *I* don't like being bullied!"

"I know they don't. But no action on the visions, no decipherment! But to return to retrogression, you are talking about the failures in Irish potato cultivation in Louisiana, aren't you? Mmm ..." This was the latest crisis. Lexin thought a moment, hearing the sound of Callum's heavy breathing and not wanting to discourage a thought in the right direction. "Just poor decipherment, *maybe*. And of course, one could not rule out poor local application of the results of what was highly detailed work in the decipherment unit. But yes, perhaps it is indeed that the techniques and parameters the unit came out with are simply no longer sustainable now, after curtailment, and that they reveal unexpected faults, unforeseeable snags that are no fault of the unit itself – or anybody. I see you took on board what I said when we were talking several months ago, just before the explosion – took it on board theoretically at least."

"Up to a point. Yet still I waver on this. But I did try and explain to them your metaphor, Lexin, the metaphor (or perhaps not just a metaphor) about the growth of an organism, the living text, and all that. You must appreciate that I do understand what you are trying to say. I explained it as best I could, your insight into the unknown depth of the text, its power..."

Wasn't that all stuff from his own mouth? He supposed it was. Callum certainly hadn't given up the struggle to understand his point of view, but it *was* a struggle. Nevertheless, in view of his precarious state of mind he thought it would hardly be helpful to bring up the serious worries about rainfall patterns across transformed parts of the Sahara that were preoccupying Andrew McLintock – areas with supposedly established new climate. But Callum brought the matter up himself.

"True," Lexin responded. "It seems there are things we have not fully understood about the new pressure patterns created by our afforestation and greening of the land with maize, wheat and such like."

"Low-pressure cell trajectories, that sort of thing?"

"Everything about pressure patterns. Formation, characteristics... Sometimes it is as if we had learned nothing, Andrew says, as if we had grasped something but now it had no substance, like an empty shell. You could say it was a case of never having got to the bottom of the text. Yes, possibly it is that, or that we are missing new or correctional data through poor use of PAS, but our misunderstanding seems so total."

"Or maybe there too it's a case of the whole tender plant wilting a little?" Callum's tone was more despondent than mocking.

"Possibly it will come to that: unsustainability of the whole project."

"Lexin, I felt I should reiterate your warnings to the Committee about cessation of decipherment, its unknown consequences –'like rejecting the advice of wise friends', you said."

Had he really said that? He supposed he had. "And scared the life out of them!" he exclaimed. "I see now!"

"Committee members sensed something powerful going on that they didn't understand."

"Something pretty powerful has been going on for hundreds of years – and now may not be."

"Yes, yes, I know. I think they half believe you, half want to take your warnings seriously. The trouble is they reckoned that despite your warnings it would probably be advisable to bite the bullet and cease all decipherment for good as being the lesser of two evils."

Break off diplomatic relations! It was the very worst Lexin had feared. Of course, it was obvious, now, what had happened. They were just running scared. "There certainly is a power, George," he said, "but acknowledging that fact, *that* is the bullet that has to be bitten."

He must have dozed through Teheran, for quickly, it seemed, he was at Peshawar in the train's disembarkation bay saying goodbye to Asad Malik and wishing him all the best – "in both present time and time past" – before going back to his seat to strap in for kick-off on the final leg under the Karakorams. With only an hour to go, Lexin took a deep breath and opened Lenica's press quotes and reports:

"Lexin's Warnings Turn to Threats", "Society Conference Delegates Challenged on Personal Gain", but probably the worst quote was from 'El Mundo', with "Lexin Reckons Society Takes Sound Decisions. Lexin Solberg's assertion that Societans have special insights and the capacity to make far-reaching decisions and safe choices met with mockery at yesterday's conference for the world press at Casablanca."

As for 'galactic attitude', seventy per cent of Conference delegates were now estimated to be for Mauré according to a poll, notwithstanding a noticeable upsurge in an interest in Lexin's timeless sphere (particularly, now, among aspirants themselves also). Even Polyanova was ahead of Lexin in the election stakes. Of course, it would be up to the Matriarchs finally to select the new delegates, but they did not often deviate wildly from the perceived wishes of the Conference in issuing their verdict. It might be no more than academic, anyway, in view of talk of closure of the Mission Station, and termination of the Society at least in its present form, in little more than six months failing a real breakthrough.

Lexin felt the train slow down and judder a little. It had been running a bit erratically for some time. The seat belt sign illuminated. As he tried to steady the jolting cursor, by chance the name of Li Xiaofeng leapt centre-screen – as usual in connection with his advocacy of multiple approaches to the crisis that would lead nowhere! How he hoped Xiaofeng would leap 'centre-picture' and follow Lenica's promptings! One day, when this terrible business was over and done with, would not new blood born of the Solbergs be needed to revitalise the task of leadership? – a task which for the time being, nevertheless, he unashamedly ascribed to himself. Surely he could allow himself to dream a little about his family's future – and his mother's, and her hopes in the same direction! Had she not said it was no fault of Xiaofeng's that his Societan parents had long been among those who believed the cosmos to be an entirely physical force of its own creation that would one day grow its own god in all dimensions and yet none. Anyway, when long before that Earth's people became full participants in the Galactic Community and thus maybe attained to a fuller vision of the Creation, they would realise their mistake. As it was, she reckoned Li Snr. was as well up in galactic philosophy as anybody and surely 'only a short leap away from true Belief'.

He called his mother. Robert answered, saying Felicitas was resting but that he would put a low-level message through to her so that if she was asleep or even dozing she would not wake. "She is exhausted, Mr. Solberg. I think it is worry."

"What about?" A silly question, maybe, but the answer was unexpected.

"It's about your train. It's reported to be breaking down. It's the third or fourth this week. Something about overheating, warp in the tunnels."

Overheating my foot, Lexin said to himself as the vehicle ground to a halt deep under the Karakorams. But what, then? Those giant machines had melted, bored and vitrified at a rate of five miles a day. One might have thought it was almost too much to expect that the remote inspection and automaintenance systems ensuring tunnel fastness, track alignment and safe traffic control would adequately look after such a magnificent operation for ever. Yet the fact was that everything had continued without major problem for two or three hundred years. The sophisticated above-ground control centres, the magnificent stations which had become great meeting places, magnets for inspiration and international effort, and the totally individualised travel facilities ending in the sleek silver trains shooting around under the world's surface like friendly bullets, stood in bold and lasting rejection of the polluting effects of air travel and were potent success symbols of the post-visitation era.

Now Felicitas was on the televiewer, wearing (unusually) a baggy pair of trousers in changing colours and a diaphanous top in subdued tones of the same colours. It was as Robert had said: she looked pale and upset, and her bracelets chinked and glittered as she manoeuvred a handkerchief.

"Lexin, are you all right?"

"Rather self-satisfied, actually."

"On what grounds? You must have heard the reports of the press conference."

"I mean that we're stuck. Did I not forecast trouble?"

"It's nothing to joke about, you silly boy!"

"It's all right. It will be some unmodified, or new and inadequately tested, maintenance procedure, probably." It was no good worrying her by theorizing on the full spectrum of possibilities posed by retrogressive effects – if they existed. She might erroneously imagine the molten core of the Earth pouring through the tubes even though they were only a mile or two down at the most! However, she seemed to be satisfied by his calm response.

"*They* are not moving very fast either – Big Nose and the girl, I mean. He's carrying her, and she does not like it."

"She will have to put up with it. She won't be able to shake him off."

"Do you reckon she could still have the idea that he may be an impostor – that he might know of the cones and the necklace of shells from somebody else?"

"I shouldn't think so! But old fears do die hard. Her one goal is to find her mother – and to avoid anything that might conceivably put its attainment in jeopardy." He resisted praising his mother's 'sleuthing' successes now that it seemed spontaneous, and Red Hair being increasingly at the forefront of his mind, he asked his mother to try and find *her*.. "And when you do find her, don't let her out of your sight!" he said.

Stuck two hours while they cooled down the tunnel – or it just cooled on its own or something else put itself right+ –, they arrived unprecedentedly late. One of the ever solicitous robotic assistants quickly took his luggage and escorted him through the vacuum lock to the transfer hall. The change from the always surprising spaciousness and unhurried atmosphere of the train, even in its disembarkation bay with its body- and morale-boosting upholstery, hit him hard. The transfer hall looked smaller, dark, and travellers were few, seats unoccupied, cafes near-deserted.

"What do you think was the cause of the delay, Lexin?"…"Is there a jinx on the SST's?"…"Could J.P. Mauré be right about supernatural influences or negative extraterrestrial intelligences?"…"What is likely to happen if we don't start deciphering again?" and "Can we still trust you?" "Can we trust the Society any longer?" The press were there, of course!

He had a word or two for each, likewise for bystanders who recognized him...

"Will Marcelle save us from catastrophe?" an obviously tired and distraught woman being clung to by children with tearful faces asked as he passed.

"Marcelle is doing her best, but there's a long way to go. Try and be patient"

An old woman was desperate to ask what would happen if Shining Face got drowned or Big Nose got eaten.

"They face dangers like we do, but are all working together and I think we will overcome them."

But no-one is immortal, in our time or any other, as he kept telling himself, and when a press woman asked whether he had a doomsday scenario (somebody from 'Le Monde', was it?) he decided it was time to feign deafness, and he ended by sprinting off in the running gear he had changed into in the train, leaving his luggage for Robert to pick up. If he could have been sure no-one would take him seriously he might have answered, "The world may spin out of control." But it might have been a joke too far. There had indeed been pretty ticklish geomechanical operations under the Bods' guidance after the great catastrophe (which had caused a perceptible Earth-rotational perturbation), and continuing decipherment had led to repeated adjustments. If all advances resulting from decipherment were initiated in accordance with a living galactic system, whatever its form of transmission or animation, when it came to all those plans, programmes, algorithms, processes, and procedures, and their modifications and adjustments, it would be best to keep one's guesses to oneself as to the outcome following its cessation.

* * *

The camp was just like Lexin had described it, in a level clearing in an otherwise steeply rising wooded valley, its shelters made among the trees or built into the rocks of the hillside. It was a summer evening. Red Hair was directing women tending the embers of two fires in a single large hearth placed in a wide, open area among the dwellings and surmounted by an ingenious system of trestles to bear the carcasses. Many of the women wore only a brief skin round the waist, but Red Hair also a very thin skin draped around the shoulders, tucked in and covering her breasts. She was not like Felicitas had imagined her. Nor, she suspected, was she like Lexin would have imagined her, either, from his description of her when he saw her in that first camp during his studies. The colour had mostly vanished out of her hair, and it was as though having put on more weight had had the effect of binding her to the primitive earth. She did not look quite the stunning woman that he had enthused about, and yet Felicitas felt herself drawn to the firmness in her gaze and an authority about her as she moved about among the other women.

It was clear after a while that the others were in awe of her. After a while, a modulation in the low tones of her voice caused several of them to redouble their efforts in fetching wood from piles of branches among the trees, while more women and some older men began to appear from the dwellings. The reason was soon made clear by a prolonged, bloodcurdling yell from the forest. The men were coming, and in triumph by the sound of it. Pouty Face, a worn-out forty-year-old with a terribly scarred face helping to tend the fires, and moving about only with difficulty, gave Felicitas a good scowl and went and dug some fat out of a bone container and dropped it in the flames of one of the fires, causing them to leap very high.

"Well get some logs on it, then, Pouty," she yelled as the woman stood looking at the flames. "Nothing cooks on fat!" Pouty was slow and surly, but she could forgive her a lot with her disabilities. And she had never had a man – another sad point that struck a chord with her. The woman ambled slowly across to a wood pile. The way she walked always evoked thoughts of Big Nose and a feeling of sadness, because he still occupied the biggest place in her heart, and so much so that, as it turned out, it might have been better not to have seen him at all when he returned to try and get her back. As it happened, though, it was after that that Big Bear started to make a fuss of her and things did improve.

Several carcasses had been deposited on the trodden ground a few paces from the fire – a young hyena which they said had fallen over a cliff, and part of a large one which they had managed to take off a bear, some hares, two geese, two deer. The fire tenders were doing a good job, but now it was a case of all free hands to the carcasses.

She suspected too many able bodies were lurking in their shelters, and she wasn't the headman's woman for doing nothing…"Hey you, Smiley, and you, Oak," she shouted to two boys still among the trees arguing over a game of five stones; and then to some idling women: "You, Sunset, and the rest of you who never stop talking, you know what to do. Boys! Go and join the skinners!" (they won't like that). The girls seemed reluctant. "Go and get on now," she ordered them, "or your food will be dried for the common good. I did warn you." She *had* warned them, many times. The boys obediently went off to join those who had already started the messy job of skinning and disembowelling the booty. The gossips grumbled as they headed off to their tasks. But they knew Red Hair meant what she said.

Last home, a little while after the others, she could just make out in the failing light the outline of a large beast being carried in on the shoulders of two men. It was surely a reindeer. It *had* been a good day, and it should do more than anything to put the boss in a good mood!

When the preparation of the other carcases was nearly finished, the skins were tidied away, the large bones broken and the marrow removed, and the meat and offal were brought to the side of the hearth. She knew which women would do the best job cooking the meat to Big Bear's satisfaction, and these were soon engaged skewering, turning and manipulating the carcases on the trestles, while others fried the offal on the hearth stones. Meanwhile, with the fire going well, she ordered some of the fire tenders to go and help the skinners who, having finished skinning the reindeer, were preparing to dismember it and cut it up. Most of it would be left by the fire overnight to start smoke-drying..

It was nearly dark now, and the smell of the cooking began to draw the men from the pool in the dammed-up stream among the trees where they had been cleaning themselves up, drinking their brews and chatting, and were now leisurely throwing something round their middles before returning. She knew that some of the younger women had been consorting with them, and she went over and gave them a round telling off for avoiding work.

"You can go and help finish off the reindeer," she told them. "The men have done their work; you haven't done yours. They can't be doing with you. Anyway, this is their place."

"You're saying they can do without us? They can't, can they?" one of the women said, with a dirty laugh. It was the young and desirable Golden Hair, flaunting her magnificent breasts as usual.

"There's a time and a place for that," she retorted.

"Really?" Goldie smirked.

"Yes, now go and get cracking on the reindeer, all of you."

"Keeping your hand in then, Red Hair? Showing him who's boss around here?" The other women were tittering as they turned to go. Goldie was the only one of the women in the camp who dared answer her back, and the woman unnerved her. By sending them all to finish off the reindeer she would be keeping Goldie from joining the serving girls later, when they served Big Bear.

"You're just jealous," Goldie said as they went unhurriedly to their task.

But it was more than jealousy, and Goldie knew it.

It was now time for two or three of the older women to cut up the meat, which they did very quickly, apportioning it among the men of the camp as they crowded round, including several who were no more than youths. But only when the headman came out did eating commence, and soon after, at a sign from her the young women (the 'serving girls'), overseen at first by herself, brought round skins loaded with green leaves, bags of fruits, nuts and berries, and a water skin into which the men could dip their drinking shells or barks. She knew that one of the youths was eyeing her and brushing against her, but she ignored him.

At a signal, she went and sat next to Big Bear on his log seat, and meat and fruits were brought to them as the rest fed squatting. The other women, the very old, the infirm, and the children would have to wait their turn to eat.

Big Bear was as big as his name suggested, and Red Hair never felt quite so safe as when she sat by him even though she and everyone else knew he was a hard and cruel man. Once, on the spot, he had used a boulder to smash in the head of a man who argued with him about the apportionment of food – Big Bear had had a bad day. She had not wanted to go to his shelter at first when she had been taken in, but she had been weary of wandering, and here there was security, so if she was resigned to staying here, the rest could be put up with. He was always gentle with *her*.

*   *   *

Felicitas had asked Robert to wake her in half an hour so that she could greet Lexin when he arrived, but he must have escaped serious confrontation with the press, for Robert said she had been asleep for only half that time when she awoke and rushed into the living space in a day gown on hearing his voice, relieved to be released from her responsibilities in Big Bear's camp, temporarily at any rate.

"Darling, darling Lexin, are you all right?" She hugged him. "I wish you could avoid them altogether, those press people. I wish you could just not see them!"

"What, and let Jean-Paul Mauré convince them all finally?" Just the smallest suggestion of a drop of perspiration was visible on the boy's brow after running the two kilometres from the station. The power pack looked inexhaustible, and from the rest of the thinly clad body did she not detect the lightest fragrance of some Moroccan balm unsullied by the long journey through earth and water?

Robert put fresh water on the side table, and a large Manzanasco for Felicitas. Breaking away from Lexin, Felicitas took up her glass and tipped it more steeply than usual in an effort to clear the still clinging vestiges of the camp from her mind. Thank you, Robert," she said. "Robert, Lexin doesn't look any the worse, does he?"

"As fresh as a daisy, Mrs. Solberg. He's unstoppable," Robert said, and retired.

Was that a prophecy? "I suppose Mauré doesn't need to hold press conferences," she said, taking Lexin in her arms again. Now he's talking about extraterrestrial intelligences, whatever they might be."

"I *had* heard," Lexin said. "The press might be putting words in his mouth."

"They feed on each other. Lexin, you'd better talk to George Callum. We need a shepherd, and he's like a sheep. He was trying to explain the visions away again apparently…some other force, Fiona said, some other factor.. Did he talk about self-fulfilling prophecies? I think so. Talked about everything and nothing, actually, according to her. And George hates using his synthesizer," she added.

Lexin told her about Mr. Malik and the others in Casa, and about the change in Andrew McLintock. "I am still hopeful George will come round to using it," Lexin said. "He is just too rational, that is all. If he does come round – quickly, I hope – he could be such a powerful *force*."

"What is Malik doing?" Felicitas asked casually.

"Finding out why some Himalayan snowfields have suddenly started melting, pushing unprecedented quantities of water down the Indus."

"Why had they?" Felicitas had not sat down, and was standing looking unrelaxed, taking frequent generous sips at her glass, which was nearly empty.

"To cut a very long story short, it is to do with unexplained loss of control of artificial temperature reduction in the North Indian Plain. It's very complicated.

"'Quickly', you say. 'If George comes round quickly'. It really is serious now, isn't it, the situation ?"

"Sure it is." He told her about the climatic problem that had begun to appear in the Sahara, talked about the growing food shortages in South America, but he did not mention his conversation with Callum on the train, not wishing to burden his mother with even more bad news.

Despite the grim sound of things, Felicitas could not help being surprised at a certain optimism, the upbeat tone. It was his father again, the same unstoppable energy in mind and limb – those pure olive limbs so different from Olaf's, so much less athletic-looking, yet remarkably agile and just as beautiful, that freshness in the dark, boyish eyes...

"The weather's not too good here, either," she said. "It's dark. Some say it's the climate, some the canopy. Talking of climate, they are talking of a reclamation problem in Australia, a danger of forests dying back, something that might even return it to being the dry continent." Suddenly the revitalizing effect of the drink seemed to leave her. She sank back into *her* armchair. "Lexin, I cannot say I am anything but terrified, though I would only tell *you* that. For Big Nose and Shining Face the summer will be short, won't it? Can I be forgiven for wishing all this was a dream – those two and Newchurch and *its* problems, and ours. Lexin, it is not good with Red Hair. She is in the thrall of the headman, and is resigned to staying in the camp. She practically controls it. But she is afraid, and the women taunt her, one in particular."

"You walked with her? "

"I *was* her". He smiled briefly. "Things could go wrong, Lexin. The chief is very volatile." The probing nose, the searching eyes seemed momentarily to have lost their electrical charge.

"Yes, I thought it might be like that," Lexin said. Only then did he look really anxious.

*　　　*　　　*

Two weeks later Lenica returned from Canberra. She arrived home in the afternoon in a cheerful suit in a purplish floral pattern from what had become the world's fashion capital. It did something to cheer Felicitas up – or would have done if despite her outfit she had not been looking so upset. Felicitas was feeling down, too, what with Red Hair being glued to the headman. She also suspected that there was something now between her and that other guy who had been eyeing her. It seemed a dangerous situation.

It came as no surprise when Lenica announced that she had finally resigned as Harry Beckenthal's secretary.

Obviously, despite her criticisms she had formed a special, if strained, relationship with him and would have to give herself time to get re-orientated. "I performed all my duties to the letter and in spirit where I could – researching, taking soundings, everything," she explained. She had got up from where she had been sitting with Felicitas on her mother's bed and was standing disconsolately staring at one of the many interactive family moviegraphs. "I liaised with absolutely everybody, smoothing things over. He's such an abrasive man; I can't understand how the Society appointed him. His supposed interest in galactic progress is now entirely at odds with his interest in expanding the family business despite the restrictions."

"Smoothing things over?"

"The idea that the Society was close to giving up, close to collapse."

Felicitas thought for a moment. "If he feels the Society is hampering him, why doesn't *he* resign Why doesn't he just leave the Society?"

"I think he would just like it to fade away."

Felicitas raised herself off the bed and went and put her arm around her and drew her close. In the old days, before Olaf's death, Lenica might have resisted this from her mother, but this time not. "It was just all too difficult," she went on, "but especially his connivance with the press-driven opposition of the World Assembly to Lexin." They were silent a moment, then she said, "As a matter of fact I hate to have let the family down by leaving him – our involvement with the Society and all that."

"Don't worry about that. I have ceased to worry about us, I mean us as a family. Everything is in the melting pot. It's not just us, Lenica. But I must admit I am afraid for Lexin!"

"You always were!"

"Yes, but I mean whatever the outcome of this crisis, what will happen to him? These visions that I do not understand but cannot deny. They don't seem to be working out, though you wouldn't think so from his attitude."

"You're seeing the visions a lot, then."

Felicitas told her about the camp. "I can hardly deny all that, can I?"

Lenica was amazed. "Hardly, no."

"And my PAS replies leave no room for disbelief."

"So Lexin said find her and don't let her out of your sight? Is that what he said?"

"Yes, he is so sure of something – like my PAS is."

"Oh yes." Lenica sighed. It was a sigh of frustration. She broke away from her mother. "I am following what I can of his visions. I never thought I could follow any of it. Now I have changed my mind and wish I *could* meet Marcelle like Lexin did…"

"I don't think we can," Felicitas said, quietly, "and yet somehow we matter to them, don't we…*really* matter?" Her voice drifted off.

"…I wish I could just see her, hear her even." The transparency of her daughter's clear eyes seemed suddenly less penetrating, the firmness of mouth softened slightly. "I'm finding it very upsetting, actually – I mean about poor Ida, and Tom trying hard to understand it all, wondering whether if he had tried harder to reach a working understanding with Ida long ago she might not be where she is now. On top of everything else, Mother, Ida has gone down with another bad bout of pneumonia."

"This is from your PAS, I take it, not the 'Lexin's People' website which he has just set up. This is certainly a change for you, dear, to feel so strongly about these things."

"Only glimpses. But it is nearly always those two, whatever I do. It's just so much nearer to our time than that camp. It all feels very close, actually. I have seen the website too." She explained that when Lexin had told her about his latest idea a few days earlier he said his chief inspiration had been Mr. Malik, the hydrologist. She found his story very impressive. "Sometimes," she said, "I have the distinct impression that Lexin is relying on others, in some mysterious way, to fill in gaps in his account on the website."

Felicitas had sat down on the bed again. She said nothing for a moment, but then, recollectively, "As a matter of fact, when I first saw the site I did feel that it must have somehow been I myself who had found everything out about Red Hair, I suppose you might say *pioneering* the images for him. I *was* Red Hair, after all."

"It's not just a matter of Lexin having visions, is it, and that's all there is to it? Yes, they do depend on us, those people," Lenica said in uncharacteristically sombre tones, and repeated it: "They do depend on us, like you said."

"And the world must be told," Felicitas added, "and told again and again", at the same time catching sight of Lenica examining herself in the long mirror set in the wall-length wardrobe. Yes, her daughter's anxieties were certainly telling on her. She did not look her old self for any amount of beautiful floral tracery in delicate purple.

Neither spoke for some time. Then Lenica, turning away abruptly from the mirror, said, "But how can it possibly work out when George Callum doesn't know where he is and has no influence on Harry, takes all his decisions autonomously, and is doing anything but trying to wean the Government away from towing the press line and adhering so slavishly to Mauré's miserable prognoses. In fact, often you would think he was actively promoting Mauré's theories himself. It's certainly nothing to do with George that Lexin's views have actually gained slightly better currency at Conference these last two weeks."

"They have, have they?"

"According to Xiaofeng. And George is disgruntled because I'm going with Lexin to meetings in Paris next week."

"I didn't know he was going to Paris. And why is George upset?"

"Because I have told him I want to chair the meetings."

"And he has agreed? He is the boss, isn't he?"

"Yes. I don't think he wanted to go, anyway. I think he's had enough. *I'm* going to chair it, and the next one if I can." (She owed it to her mother to do what she could, anyway. She hated seeing her so un-princess-like).

* * *

Xiaofeng did not think much of the latest utterances of Mauré (well covered by the media) postulating planet takeover by a malevolent alien power in order to explain an increasingly dysfunctional world – a notion on which the Government Crisis Committee was said to be keeping an open mind. Instead, despite Lexin's persuasions at the last session of the Conference pointing to his own experiences he was endeavouring to elaborate his new theory of guilt – guilt on the part of the Society sparked by an excess of success and causing some kind of hidden mental breakdown with all sorts of consequences. Lexin was finding it hard to digest along with the very fine vegetarian casserole prepared and served by Veronica and Robert. It was the day before he and Lenica would be leaving for Paris.

"*I* see our situation in terms of a breakdown in nurture," Lexin countered.

"Whatever can that mean?" Xiaofeng exclaimed. "Nurture." There was that incredulous look.

"Nurturing the technology – the opposite is what I like to call retrogression, which I am convinced is what happens when decipherment stops. It may explain the breakdown in desert transformation technology, and I am sure it lies behind the latest problem to do with a breakdown in some advanced types of telecommunications cabling here in your country, Xiaofeng. Apparently it is as though some component or mode of manufacture of the materials that had previously worked now did not. Stop nurturing the technology and problems will arise, as though the knowledge handed down to us in decipherment can be explained by our part in some wider biological or pseudobiological system."

Lexin had tried to explain 'retrogression' to Felicitas. One day, he said, it might be possible to prove his hypothesis of 'world provolution', or an accelerated development of the human race towards full participation in the galactic community. The mechanism remained unknown. It was obviously beneficent, but required commitment on a grand scale – and continuation of decipherment – to power it. Xiaofeng was sceptical about all this. He considered it far fetched, but against Lexin's, his own hypothesis with its roots (in Lexin's view) actually in a primitive fear of vengeance (by defeated rivals?) seemed very negative. The remedy, Xiaofeng suggested, lay in group psychotherapy. By the end of the evening Felicitas was not surprised when Lenica burst out,

"Xiaofeng, love, is that how you explain Marcelle, wonderful Marcelle, and Big Nose and his endurance, his steadfastness? How do *they* fit in?"

Lord, how Lenica had changed! Felicitas thought.

"I don't know. Look, Lenica, it's just a theory. I don't doubt the reality of Marcelle. But it may be that the visions are...I don't know... a sort of timeless extension into universal problems and human dysfunction."

Lenica was incredulous. "That's not how I see them," she declared. "You sound more and more like Mauré!"

"No, no. I mean, reflections of our own self-punishment, reflections that we have to disown."

"Those are real people who are going somewhere *for a purpose*," Lenica declared. "Just trust them. Trust Lexin. Forget your Tangian psychology for a moment; it's simpler: trust the Bods. For God's sake trust *me*."

The poor man seemed to have no appetite for his compote du jardin, looking more crestfallen than Felicitas had ever seen him. She saw the fellow's friendship with Lenica hanging by a thread. Inevitably she found herself questioning her own relationship with him. Had she been too 'matriarchal', for example in pulling him up for sometimes continuing to address her stiffly as "Mrs. Solberg" instead of "Felicitas" (as she now requested), or for very occasional dissembling in order to pacify or please her? She would hate to lose him, and she was thankful that the smart young man from Beijing could generally take criticisms in his stride. However, it was some days before his usual smile reappeared.

Lenica had found it hard to gain the interest of the television networks for the press conference in Paris held in one of the meeting halls of the Hotel Mendes-France, and the network coverage was probably less than at Casablanca. She did all she could, as chairperson, to get her brother a fair hearing, to draw out signs of empathy with Lexin's People, of optimism among his listeners, or appreciation of the Society's dilemma. It was proving hard to dispel bad impressions lingering after Casa. Worst of all, Lexin was forced onto the back foot not least by the fact that his visit coincided with rumours emanating from elements of the press that preparations were being made to counter an alien threat.

Felicitas felt drained of hope. Did not the hopelessness of Red Hair's situation give some credence to Mauré's gloomy theories? It was hard to see how she could ever make it out of the camp, never mind get together with Big Nose. Big Bear was old, and it was a long time since he had called her to his bed (though his judgements on usurpers were well known), but she knew that in the camp they feared her, too, both men and women, and almost as much as they feared him.

Things had never run so smoothly there! Every night she slept in Big Bear's shelter, safe from the boys who might otherwise have been more than just a nuisance to her, for despite the effects of ageing there remained more than vestiges of her old attractiveness. And yet at the same time for any number of reasons her position was obviously precarious.

As for the salvation of Humanity (if that was what was at stake), was it not possible to imagine, she admitted inwardly, that (never mind Mauré) if there were good guys out there (Lyrians) there might indeed also be good old-fashioned baddies, though she would not burden Lexin with her shifting thoughts? With some such scenario at the back of her mind she had to admit there were moments when she thought George Callum's unwillingness as Vice-President of the Society to point a convincing way forward made even the Government's extreme measures look better than no response at all. It was action in preference to inaction. The aliens might not even be so bad, anyway. After all, probably no-one – if you discounted the explosions, which might or might not be connected – had actually died yet. Or there might not *be* any aliens, and it would be back to square one, wherever that was. Nevertheless, the impact of news of preparations was quite shocking, and the absence of any statement from the Government disturbing.

In contrast were the encouraging answers to questions Felicitas put to her PAS for her own future guidance – in her own life, and in Red Hair's by proxy. In terms of 'galactic significance' – a concept she had taken completely on board since the time when she had first heard it (with alarm) from Lexin, and which she understood to refer to probable outcomes in galactic terms – an apparent lack of progress was, it seemed, not necessarily a cause for concern!

Viewed on television, many in the crowds gathering to see him as he emerged from meetings could be seen holding multicoms and leafing through the 'Lexin's People' website. Felicitas might have been gratified were it not for the fact that those people who could be seen asking him if there was any more news on 'the red-haired woman' seemed to be viewed with a faint, even patronising disdain by commentators. Visits to the website were already soaring, so it was ironic that the interest he aroused among the population at large only served to turn the spotlight on his beleaguered position vis-à-vis those in authority, the press and – disappointingly – even some of the small number of Societans who had been at Casa and seen him struggling there.

She was bitterly disappointed when Lexin informed her that he and Lenica would be going straight on from Paris to Brasilia, where the next press conference would be held in a couple of weeks. They would take a short break at a quiet place Lenica had found in the French countryside. The fact was that despite the support of good friends, as a gregarious person Felicitas was feeling increasingly isolated and would miss his constant encouragement. She realised, nevertheless, that he would be laying great store by hopefully making a good showing in what had become the largest city in the world. In fact he would be hoping to reverse a Maurian tide now given added force by the report of a survey by the World Council for Social Affairs showing a significant and sudden decline in "feelings of wellbeing" among young adults worldwide, and a concomitant increase in disputes and disorder especially in educational establishments, both among students and among teachers. Mauré referred darkly to the recruitment or activation of 'hostile forces within'. As concerning Lexin's People, he had been quoted as saying he saw them now as part of a 'softening up process', pre-invasion implants designed to demonstrate the futility, in the end, of all human endeavour.

Xiaofeng came to see Felicitas often during Lenica's absence abroad but did not seem anxious to discuss the reasons for the disorder or the world situation in general, leaving the two of them free to roam over other subjects, bringing Felicitas considerable solace but also giving her some insight into life in Beijing, and that of the Li family in particular.

Unfortunately, by the time it came to Brasilia events in Big Bear's camp had gone from bad to worse. Red Hair was well aware of the dangers of consorting with other men, but as Felicitas sensed, this had been a temptation ever since Big Bear had lost his first enthusiasm for her. Her comeuppance came when (as she learned later) Pouty Face, who had been spying on her, told him about Mountain Ash, the slender youth of fourteen years who had been hanging about her much too obviously for the good of either of them. Only the boy's potential as a hunter saved him, and only the fact that she was pregnant saved Red Hair – at least temporarily, although she found herself replaced in Big Bear's favours and in her position of authority over the other women, who at best now ignored her.

Even the better media outlets mostly seemed ready to put the lid on Lexin: "Hopes for Lexin's People Crumble as Alien Threat Grows?" ('Japanese Times'), "Lexin's Threat Cedes to a Greater`?" ('BBC'), "A world at the mercy of 'believers' whose naiveté may leave us at the mercy of malign forces." ('Sydney World News'). However, it seemed to Felicitas that much of the *popular* press, probably sensing that its readers might be in danger of deserting, was content to devote less space to the alien threat in favour of a detailed treatment of Red Hair's downfall and speculation about her future, and spicy items or even any slightly more encouraging news concerning Lexin's other 'protagonists'. Meanwhile, Felicitas could see many interviewed in the crowds, and in the audiences in public meetings at which Lexin spoke, obviously upset by the news about Red Hair. It was a matter now close to her heart and never far from her mind, and enough for her to keep her PAS on permanently.

Felicitas cut out all the accounts of her son from the papers (several of which she had taken to ordering in hard copy in Lexin's absence and regularly sat on the terrace reading), and kept them – even the negative ones – in a scrap-book. It was a way of coping with things.

She put Lexin's popularity among the general public down to a continuing fund of good sense among a population not quite believing the dire predictions, a population immunised, as it were, against cynicism and ready to accept Lexin's accounts at face value. It was as though too many years of peace and reason and progress had elapsed to jump easily to other conclusions. All this was despite food shortages unknown for centuries, and despite being caught up in the increasing violence around them, or having to join the growing numbers becoming unemployed because of failing technology and collapsed projects.

"The hand of the Bods is still felt in every human project from increasing our longevity to boosting world fishery reserves," Lexin declared when they had a good chat by televiewer, "...and from space research projects to a deepening of religious understanding. It's in all our writings, enshrined in our libraries. That trust, that confidence, does not just disappear. It's surely part of our provolution. Unfortunately that is not to say it is indestructible."

CHAPTER SIXTEEN

George Callum and his bright little wife, Fiona, and Leonard Mackenzie and Céleste came up to the Solberg residence for dinner several times while Lexin was away in Brasilia. On one such evening late in September no-one seemed inclined to get into the subject of Earth's possible unravelling and conflict with external forces until Céleste piped up,

"But what about Jean-Paul? Such a horrible man. I mean, can he be right?"

"No," Felicitas said, "he can't."

There was a silence of some moments as the sounds of cutlery and the mastication of braised chavass fish and beetatoes and giant lamb's lettuce salad continued.

"Leonard," Céleste asked, "what is your opinion?" Getting no answer, she raised her piercing little voice and repeated the question:

"I hope not, Céleste. That's all I can say. Must say I have never much taken to the smart fellow from the Parisian Seminary of Enlightened Souls or his theories, but something's wrong, isn't it? Unfortunately, Lexin offers no *concrete* explanations for the breakdowns in our various systems. Nor can I offer any, with research stymied, and nor, more to the point, can J.P. Mauré. No-one has anything but theory - *unless the Government really knows something.*"

Callum said nothing, even when prompted by Fiona, and seemed disinclined to express any opinion on Earth's predicament or its remedy.

The next day Fiona came round full of apologies for George's 'negativeness'. She was in a short silver and black dress sporting warrior motifs in gold. Felicitas had never seen anything like it before. Was it a sign of something? "I am sorry, he is very odd at the moment," she said as the two of them sat on the terrace straw-sucking fruit juices. "He is saying very little. Of course, you know with him everything has to have an explanation and a proof, and there is no room for anything else at all, but he is very, very quiet these days."

"No room even for his PAS?"

"Not unless he can rationalize what it says to him."

"Sometimes difficult."

"Of course. But some people are using them, aren't they? And *I* am."

"You are?"

"It doesn't have much to say, even if I coax it, though I did glimpse Marcelle."

Felicitas laughed. "I thought you would, Fiona." She paused. "They may be the only way we have, those people," she said, looking out over a deceptive late-summer kind of calm and a silence over the city that belied the tangle of questions churning around in her mind and demanding answers. She told her about her chat with Lexin, and his 'galactic thoughts'.

Fiona nodded. "I must say I am beginning to understand him better than I did, but it's a big step to take on this 'provolution' idea – a kind of fast-track evolution, I suppose."

"I suppose so, in some way. How else to understand the confidence they still seem to have in us, the friendly bits of advice that were said to emerge amid the hard data poured out by the decipherers – and which we now find in our PAS's? It sounds kind of personal, one-to-one. Even the jokes..."

There was a long silence, then Fiona said, with an unaccustomed display of resoluteness, "I am even considering putting up for the Conference the next time round."

"Somebody with a bit more oomph, anyway."

Fiona laughed. "I reckon George would be happy to stand down, actually. He has been finding things very difficult. Personally, *I* cannot stand that arrogant man, either, with his smart alcron three-piece from De Vigny's and his silly, curly blond mop." The reference was to Mauré again, of course.

"Well," Felicitas said, "I confess my aspirations are more pleasure seeking."

"A close moon fly-by, you mean?"

"Isn't that a bit ambitious, in the circumstances? What about the Great Wall by airship?"

Felicitas got a welcome boost from her chat with Fiona.

*   *   *

Lexin came home for a break before making a planned tour to Los Angeles later in October, and was invited (somewhat to his surprise, and probably as a result of lobbying by aspirants) to speak at the Society Conference. Amid persistent reports in the media concerning the installation of Earth- or space-based defence systems, the Government had just announced that subsequent to the conclusions of the Crisis Committee (which, Lexin knew had been far from conclusive) preparations were indeed well in hand to counter a presumptive threat of alien aggression. The Emergencies Minister Erich Blunck had appeared on TV to reassure the public that there was no immediate threat, no cause for alarm, and the public would be kept informed of any further measures – as if the word 'presumptive' in the cool delivery of such frightening information exculpated the government in the event that no threat ever emerged!

Speaking in the Great Hall with Marcus Kastner's gritty voice still ringing in his ears following a programme relayed from 'Europe Vision' to half the world and sardonically asking Lexin (in his absence) whether he thought the Society "might yet find the will to succeed" and "pull a rabbit out of the hat", Lexin warned delegates to think independently of the Earth-bound media. He suggested they should treat the Government position with respectful scepticism.

He expressed his concern regarding the SST breakdowns and the increasing number of long and hazardous rescue missions. Delegates waited, eager no doubt to hold on to any suggestion of a breakthrough in understanding. Many had been involved themselves in such incidents like he had. But when without any mention of breakthroughs he went on to try and explain the repeated malfunctions in the network of *urban transit modules*, especially in Galaxy City, which were leaving countless people having to walk to work as winter approached, and said,

"I reckon it may be due mostly to failures of the integration of driverless, off-track module pathways," he sensed their patience was going to be limited.

"They work in bigger cities than this! " someone interrupted, to be gently reprimanded by Callum.

"Ours is the most recent, the most sophisticated. That may be the reason," Lexin replied.

"You mean the most modern things may be the most vulnerable?" Another interruption, and then another:

"So retrogression, then!" The speaker's tone suggested he had been hearing the word too often and was tired of it.

Although obviously displeased, Chairman Callum said simply,"Friends, these things are of grave concern to us all. We must give Lexin his space, let him speak without interruption. But Lexin," he added, "before you do that, may I as Chairman put a question to you here since I know it is on many people's minds? Most of us know that you were on one of the first SST's that failed. And if I remember correctly, that failure was put down to retrogressive effects. Are we in fact any further advanced in our knowledge of this 'retrogression'?" So George was at least still involved – enough to interrupt on his own behalf, anyway!

"The recently introduced type of electrodynamic suspension is thought to be behind the SST problem," he replied. "Yes, I look on all these as cases of retrogression, but as I think you will all appreciate, we do not yet completely understand the phenomenon, which seems to be connected with the nature of the 'text' – I mean the form of transmission or animation of the link with the Lyrians. This may have been *broken or weakened.* Perhaps it is beyond us to understand it at this stage," he added, aware of many expressionless and, he feared, sceptical faces filling the front of the auditorium. "The point is, Mr. Chairman that, as you imply, we Societans cannot simply forget about it. My Uncle Sverre may have done so. He did not take my father's advice and move south, but stayed in splendid isolation in Bergen, well away from SST's and their problems! He does take occasional canal holidays in southern England, where his wife comes from. Goes by boat." That produced a few smiles. "But of course, he is a Normal and a businessman. He can do as he likes. We have to find solutions. And you know my – *our* – solution!" he said, to some vigorous clapping from the gallery – a rare occurrence. It was not echoed – at least not noticeably – in the main auditorium.

"I suppose our teachers have retrogressed, too" a voice suggested, wearily, "and that that explains the trouble in our colleges." The topic had become a red hot one in recent weeks, not least in the colleges themselves, and its mention produced a questioning buzz in the audience.

"Yes, teaching too" he said, "but teachers are rising to the challenge, and not least in the College of Aspirants. The teaching of such subjects as galactic sociology presents many difficulties because of the intricacies of multiple time integration and accelerated thought maturation. How could it not require patience, trust, dedication? We know something about the *structure* of the Galaxy, but anything more? Not all that much, I fear. The same may go for galactic philosophy. I suggest shortcomings in these areas may have done more than anything else to weaken the galactic link. But mastery of the problem of retrogression – whatever it is precisely – can be achieved with our existing resources, and I am sure you know I am referring to your synthesizers. As always, we have to take advice, and in the end we have to act together and resume decipherment, otherwise we may lose everything."

Some wished to take issue, but Callum did not allow any discussion.

When he had been thanked by Callum and dutifully applauded (and more enthusiastically by the aspirants), and the meeting came to the matter of alien aggression, some doubted that the conclusions of the Crisis Committee about such a threat were based on the kind of rigorous scrutiny known to have been urged on its members by Andrew McLintock when he was called before it. How Lexin wished Andrew could have been present, rather than dealing right now with his climatic problems in the Sahara! What solid evidence had the Government come up with? Many pointed out that there was far more evidence of the reality of Lexin's People, and several delegates were prompted to rise and praise Lexin's untiring reporting of them. Then, to his delight – and relief – more rose to describe their own experiences.

One was Rupert McDonnel, the Australian engineer from Ghardaia, who had managed actually to take time off from mounting problems to come and talk about Tom and Ida's gradual but unmistakeable rapprochement. Encouraged by such dedication, several delegates expressed great concern for Ida and would try and stay close to her. Others felt drawn to Marcelle and Mark and had themselves sensed the depth of Mark's experience as Big Nose and the great uplift this had given to Marcelle in encouraging her very sick mother as well as giving hope to Tom.

One or two others followed, and just a few aspirants were allowed to give their experiences, like a lady in colourful kaftan suit who said she was a midwife and was determined to stay by Red Hair when her baby was born. But when more of the possibly seventy or eighty aspirants present wanted to make themselves heard, both men and women, Callum seemed more inclined to let the 'doubters', led by Leonard Mackenzie, show their colours. These were, after all, the mass of the elected delegates (with just a few aspirants), as Lexin had to admit. One by one they called for calmness and reason to prevail and were applauded. Many, while in some cases insisting that their respect for Lexin remained, said that their PAS was telling them nothing about his People, despite seeing them on the website. Meanwhile, the state of Lexin's protagonists as a whole did not give too much cause for optimism, and many still hoped 'straightforward' reasons might yet be found both for Mission Station explosions and for the current chaos.

The name of Jean-Paul Mauré and his invocations of sundry evil influences was on the lips of many, and he was on his feet to speak when Anna Polyanova asked permission. She had not spoken hitherto. If Callum had now wanted to move on, he seemed to relent. Lexin was wondering whether this could yet be a turning point.

"I commend to all of you," she said, "Lexin's advocacy of humility and trust vis-à-vis the Lyrians, who have brought us so far along the arduous path to the Galactic Community, and the example he has set..." Lexin held his breath. But then: "...As things stand with me, to my despair at present I appear blind, but soon, pray God, I may see the visions, like many of you have. Perhaps I am too proud," she added, before sitting down. Callum thanked her for saying it.

Asked by Callum to be brief, Jean-Paul's ever more dire warnings, uttered in an aura of grim stoicism that Lexin would have found laughable under any other circumstances, was heard in gloomy silence. Anna, the open-hearted, generous Anna Polyanova, was in tears.

Despite the significant breakthrough by some delegates (a breakthrough that might already extend beyond the Conference), Lexin's inability to stir the mass of delegates, and get more of them involved in the plight of those in other times whose lives seemed almost to have been entrusted to him, seemed to him to be almost a criminal failure. But he realised that if he had gone on to tell them it was their own lives that could be at stake, too, he would have been wasting his breath.

Callum declared that the Conference having arrived at some sort of agreement, although it was not unanimous, he was not inclined to allow further discussion on the situation, or for the moment to announce any change in the Society's position (whatever that was, precisely, Lexin wondered).

"I think we are going to have a situation to contend with," he said, adding, with a sublime devolution of responsibility, "I have to say that at this time I am not sure what that is or how we might contend with it."

Lenica was not well enough to go with Lexin to the conferences and meetings in Los Angeles. Instead, she was in and out of bed with fever and diarrhoea, causing her mother a lot of worry and Robert competently to take on nursing duties that they had had no idea he had been qualified to perform. McLintock chaired everything. The events were packed out, and (as far as Lenica could see on television), by an enthusiastic public as much as by the media – the media perhaps marginally more receptive and less hostile now in the face of the seemingly unstoppable interest in Lexin's People and the absence of any other signs of a resolution of the crisis (or any real sign yet of an alien invasion). But Lexin's journey home took two days because of temporary breakdowns in eastern China on the last leg from Los Angeles that nobody seemed able to explain satisfactorily. At the same time it was clear that, sadly, little had happened meanwhile to raise hopes about his People.

After a brief summer of painfully slow progress, winter was already closing in on Big Nose and Shining Face, he said, and the two of them had been forced to take refuge beneath a rocky overhang above an ever widening river. Meanwhile, Red Hair in Big Bear's camp was becoming more and more fearful as the time of her delivery approached.

Lenica had hitherto caught only frustratingly fragmented glimpses of Lexin's People in her PAS, but now when she opened her synthesizer she found she could follow Tom and Ida clearly. Both appeared weighed down by a broken past and a present fraught with intractable problems. In a second bout of pneumocystosis back in August Ida had apparently suffered severe gastrointestinal side effects when taking the Bactrim tablets that had dealt successfully with the first attack. Although the antibiotic was successful in driving off the pneumonia, she was left weak and feeling very low. This was no doubt part of the reason why, when Tom had been to see her at Marcelle's, taking CD's of some 'Queen' albums which they both used to listen to at her parents' house twenty-five years before, Lenica saw that she was upset by his visit, saying she felt unworthy, that she must 'put together the shattered vessel', make a new life, etc. etc...This was the first time Lenica had walked so closely with Lexin's People. It had been while she was standing in one day for Veronica in the kitchen (which she enjoyed doing when she was at home). The transition to Tom and Ida's timespace in Marcelle's room overlooking the park, was almost imperceptible. The intimacy, the closeness to her despair and his earnestness, felt strangely more real – and more sad – than she could ever have imagined, and so much so that she could hardly bear to be there. How could Ida make a new life with Tom with such an illness hanging over her?

Just as real, and just as daunting, was the discovery, following some tests taken actually just before Lexin's return from Los Angeles, that she too was afflicted with something resembling AIDS, which had not been known in the human population for nearly four hundred years. Felicitas hoped that this 'unlikely' diagnosis would prove insubstantial, but the very real decline in Lenica's health suggested that it might be a forlorn hope.

Any hopes of a more favourable turn of events in present time seemed finally shattered when disaster struck the very next SST from Los Angeles after Lexin's, which came to an almost instantaneous halt from a thousand kilometres an hour deep under Tsinghai Province in northern China. When Lexin returned to the station as the bodies and the few passengers who miraculously survived were being brought out he was met by a press reinvigorated in its hostility towards him, later being forced to endure such headlines as "Lexin Gets Away with it Again" ('Delhi Mail') and, so unjustly, Felicitas thought, "Stop Talking and Stop *This*, Lexin - If You Can!" ('World Messenger').

All but emergency SST travel was suspended.

In the face of all this, Lexin maintained a stoical attitude of which Felicitas could be proud. After a week of intensive investigation of the disaster, engineers claimed to have diagnosed the problem in terms of a slight track deformation. This meant that, in the absence of any discovery of a systemic fault in a new track-laying procedure introduced in this recently replaced section, or any other possible reason for the deformation, running would probably be able to recommence, at reduced speed, after two or three months following complete tunnel replacement over about ten kilometres. In a move that implied a degree of deference to Lexin's concerns regarding newly introduced modifications, running over several similarly replaced sections was suspended for two weeks to allow full inspections. But Lexin could not help but focus on what he saw as the increasing fragility of that bond – whatever it was exactly – by which the Lyrians had bound us to themselves. So much for 'provolution'!

*　　*　　*

As with most of the population, both modified and normal, outside extreme old age illness was relatively uncommon. It was only when the episodes of illness became more frequent that something had prompted Lenica to try a routine self-diagnosis, and she could scarcely believe the result. She found it hard to believe that her own life style was to blame, yet a visit to a consultant and a further test suggested she was already close to full blown AIDS. In the quietness of her little work den in the dome one misty morning, she consulted her PAS. The result was less than enigmatic:

"This is where absolute trust is needed, Lenica. Whatever the reasons, it can be no surprise to you to know how much Ida needs your help."

So that *was* it! In a way it was a relief, but 'help'? AIDS was AIDS. It occupied a prominent enough place in the history books, at any rate. "I suppose in your timeless world there is timeless death as well," she said to her PAS. "That is to say, shall I survive?" She was thinking of the consultant's report, her CD4 cell count of less than five hundred, the symptoms she had dragged up from recent memory: discharges, intermittent fever, nasty mouth infections… which, when you looked back and saw them as a whole, spelled out something so terrible.

"Can't *promise* anything," the machine wrote in response to her question..

How laconic can you get? And yet still in a way the light touch was peculiarly encouraging. Then – a rare occurrence – the machine acquired a voice, a voice so friendly that she felt she would still have trusted it under far worse circumstances:

"Lenica, your adviser is not timeless."

Bur she still did not know whether the news was good or not. On consideration she thought the former. At least someone was there, not just something disembodied.

For some reason Harry came into her mind – Harry Beckenthal, looming large on the world scene (though notably absent at Conference), and probably about to loom even larger if the rumours about defence preparations were to be credited. Perhaps it was a sense of humour that Harry lacked most. For sure, he would never appreciate the lightness of touch, the humour even, sometimes, that her PAS offered her, and which for some doubtlessly good reason allowed her that optimism despite everything. As for her other fellow Societans, how she wished now that more could appreciate it. They should use their PAS! Sometimes you asked yourself why the Bods were interested enough – or determined enough – to help us. They were so…well…, so *cool!*

Possibly, Lenica thought, this newfound measure of confidence she felt in herself could be attributed to transient fervour of the newly converted, for many questions, especially important ones about time-crossing – already such a sharp thorn in the side of the Society –, still lurked just below the surface, defying all rational explanation. The apparent impossibility, the inexplicability of those encounters with Lexin's People – failing some watertight (and probably incomprehensible) explanation by Sergei Malinovsky – always hovered there, seemed to immobilize the 'anti-Maurians' in the face of more persuasive arguments on the other side. Jean-Paul Mauré's latest one trumpeted Lexin's "infatuation with alien implants" and the dissemination by him of their "ruinously demoralising effects" on mankind, and the consequent "ruination of the Race". Only a Mauré, she thought, could propagate such stuff, and yet, if those girls' missions were to fail spectacularly who could deny that that might seem to give some substance to his diagnosis any more than that the ongoing SST and other problems might, say, suggest the exertion of a negative effect on world events by an outside force of unknown origin. There was little serious challenging of Jean-Paul's pronouncements, and all the indications were that the Government now took his pronouncements very seriously.

Despite the tumble Lexin had taken in many people's esteem, various individuals, sometimes even ones openly disagreeing with his views, could nevertheless be found increasingly at the Solberg residence on the Hill of Lyra, meeting there for discussion and, hopefully, illumination. He was, when all said and done, the only person openly optimistic about the possibility of a happy resolution of the crisis. Thus it was that on a mild morning early in November Lenica, in a brief period of respite from her illness, came down quite early (by her standards) to find people already sitting out on the terrace in their coats (necessitated by an only partially working climate canopy), and someone saying,

"If George with his enhancement gadgetry is still riven with doubt, how do you expect me, a Normal person who can see no visions, to believe that this Marcelle might be capable of pointing the way to our salvation like some latter-day Saint Shevaughan ..." Lenica quickly recognized the stout form and eloquent tongue of 'Guardian Interactive' veteran Bill Walmsley. The reference was to a saint often referred to by her mother in respectful tones: that saviour of men and women on their way to Titan by her mysterious correction of the trajectory of their spaceship, which had veered off course during an unprecedented gender dispute among the crew. "I've never too much liked the religious feel to all this, you know," Walmsley said. Nor – as Lenica knew – had he ever ceased to question the authenticity of Lexin's claims for his visions. George Callum's difficulties in that direction were of course as well known as his even-handedness – usually – in debate. One arm leaning on the table, and staring anxiously at the multicom clasped in his other hand, Callum remained silent.

"Is it any easier to prove the existence of malign forces, Bill?" Lexin asked, but after a few seconds' silence it was Prof. Malinovsky, now Lexin's most faithful advocate and certainly, at one hundred and thirty-odd, the oldest in years, who spoke. For Lenica, his gentle tones were like a shaft of sunlight penetrating the gloom. The professor spoke quickly, like he usually did:

"I have to say, as a physicist as close as anyone to the frontier of our theoretical knowledge of spacetime – though the Bods are many notches above our present state of knowledge – I have to say," he spluttered on, supporting his slightly bowed frame with a stick and his words, as always, tripping over each other, "that I do not have too much of a problem in a general sense, personally, with these 'real histories' as I call them." There was not a hint of pomposity in the old man – in his shabby, tweedy overcoat resurrected, as he often explained, from physicogeographical investigations in a Latvian winter a century before. "Some things are clarifying in my sphere. This has resulted from fresh clues – both scientific ones on the basis of a prolonged re-examination of some of X.H. Wang's conclusions, and also philosophical ones. These – as you probably know – are both areas in which I have been able to suggest answers to several outstanding questions relating to communication through space and both forwards and backwards in time, and including the problems of retrieval at our wormhole terminal. However, as for the way Lexin's People are actually connected with each other and with us – I mean how exactly, how far, and by what agency we are able to impact upon each other in a physical sense – that strikes me as much more difficult. And some things, I do suspect, are beyond the knowledge even of the Bods. So what? I might say, 'Thank God for that!'" And he added, leaning towards Bill Walmsley, "Sorry Bill, but I do go for the religion."

"Anyway", Walmsley responded, rearranging his kameez rather ostentatiously, "what cannot be doubted is that whether we are talking now about alien implants, or saviours from our own stupidities, our transportation and manifold other very terrestrial problems, have brought us to a parlous situation here,. Either way we have a highly dangerous situation, have we not?" The journalist could not quite hide a self-satisfied expression behind the fleshy folds.

"Hopefully things will improve a lot when we start deciphering again."

"You reckon we will, then, Sergei?" Callum said, still staring into his viewer. "I see they are calling up fifty thousand reservists. I didn't know there *were* that many."

"I do. I don't deny the existence of malign forces per se, but I don't see them here. What we do have here is some powerful intervention through spacetime. I am talking about Lexin's People now, of course. Benign. What we see on our screens...these individuals... they are telling us something, and it is something we need to know and appreciate."

"So what are they telling us, Sergei?" Callum asked.

"I have suspected all along that Lexin was right and that it is a question of our complete – or rather our incomplete – trust in the Bods. In my opinion it is just as important to trust them now as it was back in 2073."

"What do *you* think, Lenica?" Walmsley put the question.

Lenica was glad of Malinovsky's diversion of attention away from Lexin. Her brother's smile had become rarer, especially after the latest SST tragedy. He was suffering. As for herself, she had listened with fascination – and relief – to what the physicist had just said. It was a relief, too, from the endless media talk about Maurian theory. A return to the sterile flounderings of those, like Leonard, who still could not accept the reality of her brother's visions, was surely unthinkable now. Malinovsky in his old age, and his colleagues, treading a divergent path in spacetime and wormhole theory from that of Leonard Mackenzie, had long been a thorn in the latter's side, and now in the chaos of a deteriorating world situation it seemed that a tide might be turning in their favour. Everything seemed to have become more ordered in her mind in the space of five minutes. 'Authenticated' might be a better word, since he had not said anything she did not already believe possible – the quantum leap to a resolution!

"You won't be surprised, Bill, when I say I am at one with my brother's views – especially after listening to you, Professor."

"Afraid *I* don't really follow you, Prof.," Walmsley said, shaking his head. "And these parallel histories: too speculative! I regard it as all highly questionable! Of course, I am not a philosopher, I have no PAS. I just see the situation."

Lenica badly wanted to divert this doyen of the intellectual press from a dead end. She wanted now to tell him about the dissolution of time, her optimism despite the beginning dissolution of her own body, but somehow she could not find the moment to say it, and when Veronica appeared with refreshments (Robert was having the day off for servicing) conversation moved to speculation about the possible causes of the disruptions according to Lexinian hypotheses. If there were some niggling questions in her mind consequent on her medical diagnosis, Sergei could not have given her better reassurance. The upshot of it all surely was that in another Earth time there was indeed an emergency into which by some inexplicable means she had been thrust to her very fallible human core. Two other things occurred to her about Lexin's 'timeless sphere' – into which both she and her mother had now been well and truly plunged: one was Callum. Without him, nothing could progress. It occurred to her that if he could be plunged into Big Nose's world it might trigger the rationale he so much needed. Perhaps it would happen. The second was Xiaofeng. How she needed *him* to change, too! Poor man, poor sweetheart! He was in such a state of uncertainty. And how upset he had been when she told him about her illness. He had enough troubles of his own, with an over-filled work timetable, and now Renmin were wanting him to spend more time over there.

In the weeks following, Lenica experienced a marked change in a now very poorly Ida. It seemed that she could no longer reject the peace overtures of this steadfast husband whom she had brought down, on her own admission, in her own *degeneration* – there was no other word for it. Tom was no longer just the passive father and husband, waiting for things to mend. Add to that, much to *his* father's relief he had graduated in the parks department first to toilet facilities manager, then recently to assistant manager in the Memorial Park Restaurant – incidentally an interesting return to something like his original calling. He would appear at Marcie's with a smile and a bag of fruit, or the touching, tangled tale of the latest park bench dosser, to enliven her. He would kiss her gently and for a few moments at least they would recall their first intimacies at Sandbay when she was a single mum living with Lenie in her parents' house and her parents were at the pictures or one of the new nightclubs in Newchurch. Always for Lenica everything came back to Ida.

Soon the season of fogs was engulfing the city. Trees in the park, houses, people receded as everything changed in status, the outside world dimming to the point where only fading silhouettes were there to remind Ida of it. The relative lightness of the room gave its contents a new reality, a new importance: the tray with the empty dishes from her yoghurt and fruit-juice lunch; her bedside table with the miconazole tablets for the fungus that had now spread to her oesophagus; a pile of whodunits that Tom had picked up at a church fete; her normal clothes draped over a chair – just a little tantalizing now as, despite her illness, for reasons she only dimly understood she found herself beginning to be able to refocus her life; and the new dresses Marcelle had got for her against fierce competition in a bring-and-buy scrimmage – fresh clothes for a new life. She had never read whodunits. She looked forward to it. It might take her mind off things when – as still happened, sometimes – she felt she could slip back into despair. Even the daily visit of a nurse who now came in when Tom was at work, and had seemed a kind of confirmation of the seriousness of her illness, was now an unexpectedly welcomed event.

Perhaps it was because it was a small room, and there seemed little beyond it, that she felt, as she sat there looking out at almost nothing, in a strange way in control of her own life at last. Moreover, she had nothing to hide. Earlier, she had stopped taking her antiretrovirals – she had been so depressed. Now there was every reason to persevere, things to talk about with Tom, not least Marcelle's and Mark's revelations.

It had been difficult for Marcelle to explain to her father about Lexin and all that. It was really only when Mark had come round and told him about Big Nose and Shining Face in the cave that Tom had to admit that if Mark – no-nonsense Mark Wharton – was actually involved, there must be some reason, some reasoned explanation, behind the whole business. Later she had been able to describe to both her father and her mother her dreams about Big Nose following Shining Face after she had left the cave and eventually catching up with her, and how she, Marcelle, thus felt renewed in her hope that soon, despite the flare-ups between them, they would find Red Hair one way or the other. Tom saw nothing was to be gained by dismissing Marcelle's dreams, and everything to be gained for both himself and Ida by holding fast to the reality of them and, as Ida said, trusting Lexin, however hard it was to explain the how and why of everything.

So it was that even though the beastly pain refused to go away, the spreading candidiasis infection continued to be unresponsive to her antifungal lozenges and made eating almost impossible, and the pentamidine antibiotic that she had been taking prophylactically since her last bout of pneumonia was producing its own skin rashes and causing a lot of nausea, under Marcelle's healing hand and Tom's love and practical attentions (already he was into a care worker's course), Ida dared to believe in the future – her future and Tom's.

Felicitas, meanwhile, fought hard to preserve a tranquil exterior when Lenica came down with an intractable pneumonia – such things had long been a rarity as a result of the excellent level of health worldwide. As usual, however, her mother's automatic responses of calming tenderness and love prevailed:

"My poor Lenica. Why you? Don't tell me. I know why. It's Ida," she had exclaimed. Now she was trying to keep her voice steady while pouring some fruit juice and swinging the bedside tray across the bed, which nestled in one of the curvaceous alcoves geometrically dividing her dome domain like the petals of a flower. "You are too kind, too empathetic. I thought it was almost extinct, pneumonia. Workers in the SST tunnels got it for a while, apparently. Occasionally there was a hospital case."

"This... is the sort that always... always went with AIDS, Mum," Lenica said, stopping for breath repeatedly. She was propped up, coughing a dry cough, just like she knew Ida had been doing a few weeks earlier.

"So they say."

She knew, too, that they were making up some stuff for her like the medication they used back then. "It'll take a few days, you said, the new medicine."

"Yes."

" It's caused a stir among the medicos, apparently. Worried them quite a bit."

"Yes." Felicitas was staring fixedly out of the window with eyes glazed. "A few days. Let's hope it's not more...that's all..." Her voice trailed away.

It was not unusual to see her mother anxious, though it was strange to see her lost for words. But how superb she still looked, even at eighty-four, profiled against the clean, flowing lines of her room, a room normally flooded with light – the 'daffodil' room her father called it –, but on that day just a little dimmer in the sunless weather that according to Lexin was now affecting the whole Takla Makan. It had to be admitted, though, that her mother's worried expression did have the effect of softening those regal features just a little. "I might die, I suppose," Lenica said, "but it's difficult to die these days. We're too good at prolonging life, at life support."

"Life support! Lenica, darling! I should not have said anything," but Lenica had gone into another bout of coughing. "No, I shouldn't. I must let you rest, build up resistance, fortify your immune system. There is something different for you for that, too – something different from the old antiretrovirals of Ida's day."

"So I understand. They've developed something just for me, haven't they."

" Robert has just fetched the capsules. The doctor texted to say they had got them."

The warm, burnt-orange dress her mother was wearing kept catching Lenica's eye, and she smiled. Mars was in vogue, of course. Such steadfastness in leadership and example, even now! She hoped she could be as steadfast herself. Now was the time! Her mind drifted...

The doctor was talking to Marcie outside the door. Ida wondered whether she was still dreaming. She had been dreaming about being someone else...somewhere quite different...

"It's the very latest approach," he was saying, "and on the basis of her tests it should give very good results. And none too soon. There is absolutely no point in not taking them, with the pneumonia threatening again."

Marcie was muttering something to him.

"Is that the doctor?" Ida called out, suddenly fully awake. "He isn't taking them away, is he?"

A new doctor came in, a big man with sturdy features. "As I was saying to your daughter, Mrs. Weston," he said, flourishing a small parcel, "these are the very latest. There would be absolutely no point in not taking these."

Marcelle took the parcel from him, opened it and put the packets of capsules and some other stuff on the bedside table.

"Of course there wouldn't," Ida said. Did he think she didn't understand the seriousness of it? But the man's high forehead and square jaw had collapsed into a grin, and she realised Marcelle must have split on her back then, when she was refusing the antiretrovirals, and her own doctor must have put it in her notes: 'patient non-compliant'.

"We'll have to have you in for more tests in a couple of weeks to check on progress. I am making arrangements for an appointment for you."

"What exactly made you change your mind and start taking them again, Mum," Marcelle asked after showing the doctor out. "I told him you were."

"I don't know... Tom...you...Mark...Lexin...?" Now *she* was grinning.

"Are you taking the first lot now, then?" Felicitas's voice came from afar

"Yes, Mum." Lenica was hardly aware of taking the first capsules and the glass of water to wash them down, just that she was filled with a euphoria that was so much more than a relief about her own situation. She indeed hoped that, as she had been told, AIDS was now understood in a way not dreamed of in an earlier age, and as consciousness faded into dream she knew that for Ida *that* was what mattered.

Lenica became very ill indeed for several days before the archive laboratories came up with the Bactrim substitute that would deal with the pneumonia. In the meantime she was conscious of being Ida in Newchurch and going to the City Hospital with Marcelle in a taxi, and being told that her CD-4 cell count was already a little higher and her viral titre lower.

Then Marcelle had mystified her mother by taking her back to another house in a different part of Kinley's Fields that Tom and his father had succeeded in secretly renting for the two of them. She had collapsed in the doorway, though whether with sheer fatigue, or amazement at finding Tom and Henry and also Mark there and seeing what they had been up to, was not clear. Marcelle thought probably both. The men had hired a van for a couple of days (Mark was on vacation) and brought the rest of the family furniture over from Culver, including the king-size bed and its suite and the lounge suite, as well as the chairs and tables already at Tom's and an attic-full of soft furnishings, books, pictures, light fittings and the rest. Marcelle had incorporated it all into a scheme which she was at pains to say was 'a suggestion only – for her mother's consideration'. At least it did not cost anything as far as it went. When they finally got her inside, Ida was flabbergasted and broke down in tears.

"At last I'm back home," she declared, hugging Marcelle, followed by the others in turn, and then adding, "but if I may make a suggestion about the curtains...", which caused some hilarity.

When the others had gone with the van to pick up the rest of Tom's belongings and they were alone, Tom took her wholly in his arms and kissed her. It had not happened quite like this for years. Then he helped her undress and get into bed.

"Damn it, Tom, this is ridiculous," she said when he brought her a cup of tea. "It's time I looked after *you*. I never have yet."

"Never mind all that, Ida. We have both had to sweep up our back yards a bit," Tom said, kneeling down by the bed and taking her in his arms again. They were silent for a while, then he said, "We both let Marcie down, to be honest."

"She bears us no malice. That is what I find hard to understand."

"So do I – and I am grateful for it – what's important is that she says she believes you will be cured, too."

"They say that would be impossible to prove..." Ida drew Tom tightly to herself. "...that saying it raises false expectations."

"Let them say it!" he exclaimed. The words came out almost involuntarily. "Yes, let them say it!"

"I'm afraid I raised some for you...some false expectations...in the past."

"And I for you, darling. But that is exactly where it all is: in the past. Isn't it?"

She was looking right into his eyes, *her* sad, grey eyes, now with just a touch of brightness, the whitish cheeks just catching the last of the afternoon light, for a mild breeze and a glimpse of the sun had replaced the fogs of the previous week. "I love you, Tom," she said, kissing him, and then after a minute or two, "I don't think these are false expectations of Marcie's, not after all that's happened." After a while, breaking away gently she said, "Give Lenie a buzz. She's quite upset about me."

"I think Marcie's been."

"She's an angel."

"Probably," Tom said.

Ida gave him a queer look. "It's a good thing we got together all those years ago, then, isn't it?"

"It is," he said, getting up to go, but Ida held him back.

She said nothing for a moment, then whispered, "To think that I..." But he interrupted her,

"It's in the past, Ida. Don't think too much."

"I have to say it, Tom, just to you, so that I can try and forget it for ever. To think, yes, to think that I did not want her..." She broke down completely.

"And to think that I even dared to suggest you would regret it," Tom said after a while with just a touch of irony, clasping her tightly to himself.

"...that I just couldn't stand her being there," she went on, appearing not to hear what he had said, after which she said repeatedly, "How wrong I was, how terribly wrong," as they stayed locked together until she started coughing and he had to let go.

"And now we have to close the chapter," Tom said, gently. "You could not go on blaming yourself for ever. It's been a miracle, and we must just accept it. I'll go and see if there is anything more to bring over."

Pondering the subject of angels as he started back up the length of Acacia Road with its solid stone bays and dry-cleaned curtains drawn back behind gleaming windows, and headed for his old place to help the others, he found he could not stop thinking about that other young woman, Shining Face, and her father not knowing whether they were any nearer yet to finding the woman she believed was *her* mother. How he hoped now, hoped beyond hope, for a good outcome for all those people back in time and the young man in the future who seemed to know everything and yet needed them, it seemed, as much as they needed him! For there surely could be no doubt now that the lives of all of them – those in the past, those in the present and those in the future – were linked, and dependent on each other even, it seemed, for their survival.

*   *   *

Lenica had been only momentarily surprised to find herself in the hospital away out in the slopes of the old dunes above the Avenida de Ferrer de Lorenzo. Mostly it was for accident and maternity cases. Felicitas was there by the bed in a soft light tinged with blue. Lenica could hear the music being filtered softly through her head via the autoheal system, cradling her thoughts. There might have been no gap in time since they had been speaking before, though Felicitas said she had been barely conscious for several days. Now the Bactrim was working. Xiaofeng had been to see her several times but had not woken her. Lexin had called, too, more than once.

"You look much brighter," her mother was saying, "and you're breathing much better."

"Things are good at Newchurch, Mum. That must be why I feel brighter!"

"I'm glad," Felicitas said. There was a comfortable silence for several minutes, then Lenica asked,

"What news of the others?"

"I did not want to tell you about the others just now, darling," Felicitas replied kindly, but because you ask I have to tell you." She perched on the bed close to Lenica, gently straightening the bed clothes. "Red Hair ran away when the baby was born. It was a couple of days ago. Life had already become unbearable in the camp."

"The baby?"

"A girl. She has it with her."

"You have seen them, then."

"Yes, sheltering in the forest in a blizzard. The babe had hardly had time to be born. It will certainly die. How can she possibly hunt for her food carrying the baby? She should have left it behind."

"She might not have wanted to do that a second time."

"Like Shining Face you mean. I suppose not. Not in that camp."

Lenica assumed they would not have bothered to pursue her, reckoning that nature would take its course only too quickly. She would be a liability to them now, and as for the baby, well it was only a girl. "And Big Nose, Shining Face?"

"They seem to be moving again after abandoning the shelter beneath that rock. It looked a horrible place, wet and freezing cold – just an overhang, really. A flood forced them out. I think she was almost giving up, but he made her eat. In fact, they had recuperated fairly well after the long stay in the shelter, and Lexin reckons the problem was more in her mind – even she can crack! I don't think Red Hair is too far from the sea, but I don't know how close they are to her. Lexin does not know, either. It could be some way to the sea yet. Big Nose is making the running, but he is relying on Shining Face to navigate."

Even for a girl like that, Lenica thought, there must be limits. "Where is he? Where is Lexin?" she asked.

"At a Conference meeting. They have postponed the elections, by the way, for what difference it makes in the present situation." Felicitas looked tense and sombre. It was hardly surprising, Lenica thought, in the face of such confusion and unpredictability. "The aspirants are an asset," her mother went on, a bit more cheerfully. "They talk more sense than the rest, Lexin said. Don't repeat that! And, you know, George Callum gives them a very fair hearing, which is interesting. Actually, the news on the world front is not so good – to put it mildly. Even inexplicable confusion in the world stock exchanges. – and, less surprisingly, lots more problems in urban transit. There was another sub-surface transit accident."

"Another case of tunnel deformation?"

"No, though I must say Lexin was no more surprised this time than last, but don't repeat that, either."

"What happened?"

"It was between Lagos and Rio. Train nearly got drowned when the sea started coming into the tunnel. Some new sort of seal between sections. No trains running."

"Casualties?"

"Two drowned in the rescue. The section had been replaced only a year ago."

"It will be good for Mauré's ego – evil forces trained on the SST's...!"

"But there is nothing you can do about it, my love. You must rest, continue the improvement. So rest!" Felicitas leaned forward and kissed her. The Princess's favourite perfume hovered close...

"For a while, at any rate," she whispered, adding almost involuntarily, "until the next thing comes along." She caught her mother's frown at that as she closed her eyes, and felt guilty to be causing her pain, and when the familiar fragrance moved away and went quietly to the door and out of it, her spirits fell a little. How hard on her to have both her children involved in such dangerous events whose galactic significance she sometimes thought her mother had difficulty in fully accepting even now, despite her experience in Red Hair's woven shoes...Lenica fell to thinking about Xiaofeng. He had withdrawn his 'guilt' theory, said he had changed his mind. Moreover, she knew he had half-believed her when she had first tried to talk about her close walk with Ida, however difficult an idea it might be for him to fully accept. But it would be some time before she saw him again, since he had finally had to return to Renmin for two, possibly three months to fulfil some teaching obligations. She would miss him. She needed him now to help her, give her confidence. She was going to need him more and more. Only after a long time did Lenica finally fall asleep.

In a few days she was able to walk about the recovery areas of the hospital under the watchful eye of the robotic nurses, much encouraged by being told that it seemed unlikely she would have passed on the virus to anybody else, although the doctors were not very forthcoming when she enquired further, and some were openly sceptical about her interpretation of the circumstances surrounding her acquisition of a virus eliminated from the human population centuries ago. The nursing staff were much more receptive in this respect, and Lenica put this down to the large robotic representation on the staff. She was aware that most robots were created according to the same decipherment parameters as Robert.

Armed with warm garments for her, Lexin came to fetch her in a taxi module (obtained with some difficulty) on a very cold day in January. An unusual expression on his face as he approached her in the healing ambience of the recovery block suggested a strange mixture of anxiety and excitement. She waited for the explanation, but he said nothing as they left the intricately engineered, many-faceted structures of the hospital and the bimodal taxi headed for the urban transit net – this section fortunately still working –, eventually lifting up onto the slender, snaking track and accelerating above the wooded slopes down towards the central area of the city.

Even while she had been so ill there had been times when she felt part of herself had been floating, gossamer-like, in Newchurch, and during these last few days in the hospital, as she gained strength and confidence, that part of her had spent a long time close to Ida and Tom. Henry and Florrie Weston had been over to their new home at Christmas, Florrie submerging her dislike of Ida in her pride in their son's faithfulness to his marriage vows. Ida continued to improve slowly, and it seemed the pentamidine, while continuing to exert unpleasant side effects, was sufficient to ward off another threatening attack of the pneumonia bacterium. Marcelle came to see her mother every day, sometimes with Mark if he was home from uni.

Lenica's thoughts came to rest on Big Nose and the girl.

"They are making slow headway," Lexin said, reading her mind. "Many people are seeing it using their PAS. The two of them are barely speaking, though. When she does speak, she is very sharp with him. It seems that her old fear of him and his influence – all that stuff – has come back a bit." Her brother spoke with his usual matter-of-factness.

"So full of rejection for so long, Lexin!" Lenica suddenly felt irritated by her, but Lexin was gazing away into space. Then he faced her:

"I was going to say she is nervous. But I think she is more like terrified. I am sure it is because now he is really in the lead, even if she is navigating, and not just protecting her. There is a new determination in the man, a determination to see things through. That is good news for us."

So it was *that* that he was excited about! But then another thought came to her: "You don't think it might be that she is worried her mother might after all have no time for her, but only for Big Nose?"

"I don't think so."

"Shouldn't she be pleased, then?"

"You are forgetting her prejudices," Lexin went on as the Avenida opened up thirty or so metres below them, now almost bereft of people, bicycles, multifarious bubble vehicles – just a few pedestrians to be seen, probably on urgent or essential missions, occasional runners undeterred, exercising under the leaden sky. The module slipped off the net at the International Theatre exit, and the driver headed north on the central ring road guideway through the colourfully integrated constructions of the business zone towards the Concert Hall and the Hill of Lyra. "It is the thought that if her still-lurking fears about him, and about the effect he might have on her, are in any way justified, with him now in the lead her mission might fail spectacularly. It is a risk for her. If she does find Red Hair alive and well – which Heaven knows I hope she will –, when she knows the full story you can guess how she will admire him. At the same time, like you suggest, I suppose you cannot rule out a bit of jealousy either, can you?"

'See things through'…'the full story'…? She looked hard at her brother. The clear features, the calm voice, were signalling that assurance which once she had often regarded as over-confidence, but which now was a lifeline. Could he be that sure?

"Put it like this," he said: "I think he sees a purpose in his wanderings now, if not an end to them – some resolution, yes, but I suppose that is all he knows for sure. As for the possibility of taking up with Red Hair again, even if she were no longer a prisoner he might understandably remain fairly phlegmatic about that."

"It's very public, isn't it? Their life, I mean, or what's left of it."

"Everyone is willing them on, Lenica – all those who have bothered to find out about them from their awakening PAS (not to mention the good wishes of my web fans). Remember, you did not know what to think at one time, did you?"

There was that hint of excitement again, but suddenly for some reason she was thinking of Harry and noticing that the excitement, stemming no doubt from thoughts of a resolution of Earth's problems, had vanished and his features tightened into a frown. She thought *he* must have transferred his thoughts to *her* this time. "What is it about Harry?" she asked, impacted suddenly by a cocktail of emotions...

"It is something I have to talk to you about. The Government is thinking about aliens, Lenica, but the world has enough problems of its own."

"Mother mentioned the SST accident, the sea coming in, so no trains at all."

"Ah yes, that! They reckon they have bypassed the problem."

"The seal between tunnel sections."

"Yes. Patching up, autochecking the seals over three hundred kilometres, with a return from now on to the traditional process, and the trains should be going in a week or two. But where to in the?long term? – I mean figuratively speaking. I don't like to think about that. Lenica, the sub-surface transit system is our life blood. And it is not only the transit system, it is all our technological advances that are threatened. Our computers are going haywire. Almost nothing is happening in Galaxy City. The world is slowing down. In Europe there is far more civil disturbance than can be explained by problems in the colleges, as well as widespread transportation problems and God knows what. Now as I said," he went on, "the Government seems to believe there may be some... some aliens, but, you know, I think something else may be going on, something both more subtle and more ordinary, more *earthy*."

"I don't suppose the Government would see it if there were. They seem deaf to everyone except Mauré..."

"...And the media."

"Deaf especially to you, my dear brother, and to any suggestions of 'provolution'!" She took his arm and drew him to herself for a moment.

"It's not a word I use in public, since I do not know exactly what it might be. The idea of retrogressive effects means nothing even to many of us Societans. But Lenica, I am not even talking about retrogressive effects now. I have had a warning from my PAS, and it is that which I need to talk to you about. It was a spoken warning...," he added as the taxi detached from the net and came up through the trees in the Park of the Nations, stopping a few metres from the upper part of the house, "...a warning in a friendly voice that somehow you felt you would trust anywhere. I am telling you about it with a mountain of misgivings because if I am right it is unprecedented and indicates how far we have sunk." They walked out of the craft, Lexin stopping for a moment – was it with a touch of wistfulness, or lost in morbid thought about the future? – to watch the ultralight and its driver disappear before walking slowly with her to the house and into his office. As the door slid to behind them Lenica said,

"I'm sure you don't think I'd be surprised to hear Harry's been misbehaving."

He smiled. "I don't think you will be, then" he said, going to his desk. The dark waves were still emanating strongly from his brain. "This...this must not come out, Lenica, nor is it something I wish to burden our mother with. I know this sounds extreme, and you know Harry better than I do, but he seems so opposed to me, and in fact to the Society, that I question whether he is abandoning us altogether, gunning for post of first minister or something. I have been trying to contact him in Canberra. Always he is away somewhere. Lenica, he hasn't been at the Conference for several sittings."

"I am sure you are not saying you have information that he hopes to seek alien co-operation to achieve that!"

"You never know," Lexin said without a flicker of a smile. He had gone to his desk and was checking his messages on screen. "Damn, it's not working properly."

He *was* joking of course – they were a family of jokers, except Olaf. Even so, the mere *thought* of Harry the *traitor* coincided with a passing faintness that was perhaps not due entirely to an empty stomach – a lingering candidiasis did not encourage eating.

"You look a bit pale," Lexin said. "Sit down. No, I am not saying *that*." He indicated the huge easy chair by the book-lined wall and visual/audio resource across from his swivel seat, a comfortable chair that had served for centuries of relaxation in the knowledge of the Bods' leadership. It was where Olaf would occasionally sit to read or meditate in the days when this was his office before he vacated it in favour of a son expected to continue the family's pre-eminence in the Society (setting up his own in a part of the house once occupied by *his* parents). No relaxation for himself today! But as Lenica sank into the chair he could imagine no-one more deserving of it than his sister.

"So what *are* you saying?" she asked.

"*You* know how well in he is with Blunck at the Ministry of Emergencies. But if something is going on in some space factories – or anywhere else – that is not bona fide, we need to know. Something detrimental to us in the Society, perhaps, or to the world at large. I have no knowledge of what it might be. I don't suppose it concerns aliens for one moment, but..." He was still fiddling with the computer.

So this was what was working him up. A conspiracy! "...And this just when things are already getting really desperate, aliens or no aliens."

"None we *hope!*"

There he went again! "And just when *you* are at a low ebb in media esteem."

"There could be a connection."

"You must tell me more about that! By the way, aren't there checks and balances on what they all do?"

"Possibly the roving inspection teams are spread too thinly, or maybe the inspections don't happen. And a lot of Beckenthal's work may be classified these days. Whatever there is," Lexin said, emphatically, "little or a lot (and I cannot imagine anything little in Beckenthal's book, to be honest), we must find out about it."

"Do you assume his interest would be purely monetary?"

"That would be my guess."

"So others may have other interests. Blunck?"

"I suppose so." Deep furrows had appeared on her brother's forehead that were clearly not due only to the recalcitrance of a computer, annoying though that doubtless was. "My PAS is insistent. It is a pity, Lenica, because while it is not a majority of the Conference, I am beginning to see signs of a real turnaround among the delegates."

"I don't know how it took me so long to see the light."

"And if it has taken *you* so long, Lenica, I am sure you cannot be surprised about everyone else? Long tradition can stultify. But now I sense a firmer desire not to allow ourselves to be defeated – by the media, or by vague assertions about aliens, or by errant politicians or governments. More and more are studying their PAS. The aspirants' testimonies are having a huge effect, you know."

"Maybe."

"And *you* have had an effect," he added, turning briefly towards her, "Your illness." He got up and went to the window behind his desk.

"Sympathy, you mean?"

"Yes, but more than that."

"Yes, more than I would prefer."

He seemed not to hear. "Your gradual change of mind had got around, too, and then there was your resignation. Now with X.F. himself getting the hang of it..."

"I could do with him here now," Lenica sighed.

"Yes, of course you could," he said sympathetically. He thought how fragile she looked now, despite her recuperation, as he turned and went over to her and gave her a big hug as she sat there, which she returned in full. "Not as effective as X.F., I'm afraid," he said as he gradually released her.

She was glad he had believed her when she told him she was sure Xiaofeng was 'beginning to see the light'. "It's just that you have been talking about the visions so much that your evidence is at last convincing people," she said, smiling. "No-one has produced any evidence of aliens, have they? Least of all Mauré! Polyanova for all her eloquence hasn't exactly advanced the situation one way or the other. The emptiness may be beginning to show."

"I don't know. It's still an uphill struggle." He was standing in the middle of the room now. She noticed that with his curly mop protruding slightly forward over his forehead he could appear almost belligerent, in his three-quarter trousers and his tunic with a military flavour, profiled against the other main window, the west-facing one. Behind it, the International Concert Hall dominated the winter skyline through the trees. But travel and communication problems, and a general and growing tendency of the public just to stay at home, had resulted in ever fewer events and a sad silence in the Park of the Nations. One could become very despondent looking *that* way, but Lexin's gaze was directed firmly through the other window, down towards the Palace of the Galaxy and the Society's heart. "We shall see whether my PAS is telling the truth," he said, turning towards his sister. "I cannot imagine it is not. Say nothing to anybody. I had to tell *you* about its warning, and I am sorry to have done so while you are still not well. There's one other person I have to tell, absolutely have to, because somehow in him may still lie the way through all this."

"Callum." He had not conveyed it telepathically. It was an

automatic response. McLintock might have made more sense in some ways...

"How did you guess?"

"I don't really know, but I hope we are right," she replied. "And I hope he will play ball."

It was a welcome relief to see a grin on his face. "I think we are," he said.

CHAPTER SEVENTEEN

George Callum had entered the office of Mr. Nawale, Deputy Minister for Emergencies, in World Government House (situated like the offices of the executive and the judiciary on State Circle in Canberra and erected in the year 2222 for Australia's first hosting of the World Government), with little confidence that he would discover anything that would confirm Lexin's suspicions. He was simply "doing the boy's bidding," as he had told Felicitas with an unusual touch of humour, and glad at least to be in the warmth of an Australian summer.

His late-afternoon appointment with the deputy, whom he had not previously met, was quite legitimately to get a briefing on the alien threat, preparations underway, etc. In his position as acting head of the Society for the Advancement of Intragalactic Relations he had access to the highest levels of government at short notice if the circumstances demanded it. Obviously these did, since one way or the other Earth's intragalactic relations were in danger of suffering their most serious setback ever.

"Mr. Callum, all the indications are of an approach of hostile forces," Mr. Nawale was explaining. The Deputy Minister, a short, very dark southern Indian, had stood up from his desk to stand uneasily by his chair when Callum was shown into the book-lined office with its restrained, not to say minimalist, lines and a dash of polished marble and red native timbers, all in keeping with the rest of the complex. He was chewing something, which Callum found a little surprising in so high an official.

"But I thought there was no immediate threat," Callum said. "I assumed the measures were...how can I put it?...precautionary."

"We would hardly issue the warnings which we have issued without good cause."

"Yes, Minister, but surely there is a difference..."

"Mr. Callum," Nawale interrupted, clearing his throat, "I am sure you understand that caution is advised when presenting the general population with information of this kind."

"What *is* the evidence?" Callum asked.

Nawale definitely looked ill at ease, remaining standing and fidgeting constantly after motioning Callum to a rather fine, very shapely and beautifully polished chair the colour of chestnut that looked as if it deserved a longer occupancy than it was likely to get on this occasion. Perhaps what he was chewing was one of the mildly psychostimulatory edible gums, and indicative of an acute attack of nerves, or simply of the level of apprehension in the population as a whole, or both. He might well be feeling uneasy in the shadow of the autocratic Emergencies Minister. His formidable chief, the low in stature but high in self-importance German, Erich Blunck, was reported to be stuck in an SST somewhere (to do with a power reduction affecting computer networks, apparently). Callum had his doubts about that explanation for his absence, but at all events it seemed there was little prospect of a meeting.

"Weird radio sounds or signals and visual images, jamming, mysterious civil unrest, effects on Earth power systems of all kinds," the Minister replied in answer to Callum's question, "inexplicable technological failures in projects worldwide." He was chewing busily.

"Serious, but I question whether it is very conclusive," Callum said.

"On the contrary. There is the evidence of analysis. Patterns in the disruptions, patterns in the signals and images that suggest thought processes. We are confident that we have detected layers of malevolence and its effects."

"You mean they – whoever they are – think like we do."

"Only more so. Perhaps I should say 'worse so'. I need hardly remind you that these days we have advanced considerably in

332

knowledge on a galactic level. These allow us to extrapolate hypothetical processes, even moral systems – or amoral systems –, that may differ from ours."

Shades of Mauré! He wouldn't mention him. It might fog the issue. "Presumably they could be much more advanced," Callum began to say, "much more..."

Mr. Nawale interrupted. "...much more dangerous," he said, quickly, "yes, but that is no excuse for inaction. We have to do what we can, even in the face of modes of alien interference, possibly even in the face of modes of outright attack that might be very strange or beyond our imagining. It seems one does not experiment with spacetime with impunity, as you will appreciate I'm sure, Mr. Callum."

"And what might one do by way of counter-offensive?" Callum asked, detecting the innuendo but not at all anxious to get into pointless discussion about the Mission Station disasters. But Nawale was pursuing his own line.

"We have planned our response, based on the evidence, including that based on the types of analyses I have just indicated, but also on the conclusions of the committee investigating the Society's message retrieval and decipherment problems, Lexin Solberg's experiences, etc., etc. Obviously I am not able to give you details." The Deputy had taken to standing at his desk and leafing through some papers on it – probably, Callum suspected, to suggest he was busy and hoping the interview might soon be brought to an end.

Callum tried another tack: "Supposing 'they' are, or were to be, already here. Are we prepared for that?"

"For that, too." Nawale replied.

Ten more minutes and more shuffling of papers, and it was clear that if he was going to get closer to obtaining concrete data it would not happen here. Callum walked out of the campus feeling quite depressed. It wasn't just the gloom about the Government's view of the Earth's predicament – he wasn't sure if he should swallow a fraction of what Nawale had been reciting –, it was the Society, and how vulnerable it suddenly appeared to be. He had to confess it was a long time since he had really wanted to stick up for it all that much, rather than just making an attempt to do justice to Lexin's strongly held views.

Walking back to his hotel an odd thing happened as he was crossing the lengthening shadows of Telopea Park. Suddenly there was nobody about, and just as suddenly the view was not towards an array of trees aleaf in summer warmth, nor towards the sprawling city, but of a forested, snowy valley in some cold, cold place under a leaden sky, and two figures nearby briefly glimpsed struggling along beside a river in the falling dusk. Then equally suddenly everything was as it had been –.the park, the willows, the poplars, and, topping all, the sequoias, still and lazy in the evening. It was all over in a moment. He thought he must have been daydreaming.

Reaching his hotel in a leafy little backwater he set to thinking about precisely what line he would take at a meeting arranged with First Minister Joanna Van Rensburg the following afternoon. But as he stared out of his window at the gardens out there dissolving into the sweet-smelling night he found he could not put out of his mind his little experience in the park, and he suddenly felt very isolated. It had thrown him a bit, he had to confess. He no longer really thought it was a daydream, and what with that and the somewhat strained interview with Nawale he felt uncertain of his direction and an urgent desire to share his concerns. The whole matter, Callum reasoned, might be more complicated than he had imagined. Bill Walmsley came first to mind. Surely Bill could be safely confided in. There was a man with whom he felt a special affinity as a fellow rationalist and relentless investigator – even if in the sphere of journalism as distinct from languages and mathematics. What's more, weren't things coming to a head now here in Canberra on those government decisions to settle the future status of the Society. He would surely be here for the 'Guardian Interactive'. Callum just hoped he wouldn't plead Society fatigue, what with press conferences as well. The one thing he was absolutely sure about was Bill's ability to keep his mouth shut when necessary.

It was a welcome surprise when just before turning in he received a message from the man himself. Callum knew a bit about telepathy – its connection with linguistics and so on – and thought he might have contacted Callum inadvertently. He knew journalists were regularly receptive.

"Lexin says you are in the den of diplomats. I am in Sydney. Can we meet?".

"By the swimming pool in Telopea Park at ten tomorrow?"

"Okay if the maglev is operating and bush fires are under control."

"Are those the latest things under threat, then, the maglevs?"
"Seems so. See you later."

*　　　*　　　*

They walked across the grass in their summery slacks and short sleeves.

"So the maglev worked," Callum said.

"Yes, but it was touch and go. Have you seen the papers this morning? Maglev workers the world over are going to cease working tomorrow."

"Why?"

"To get ready for the invasion."

"What are they expecting? Star Wars stuff, or giant spiders rolling in in cotton wool balls, or what?"

"I'm joking. It's about lawlessness on the trains, lack of policing. Joke over."

"Look, Bill," Callum said as soon as he was confident they could not be overheard, "Could you do a little undercover job for me on Beckenthal? He has disappeared, and Lexin suspects something is going on to do with the invasion, or with the non-invasion if there isn't one. Lexin reckons there isn't."

"Ah, Lexin! Yes, he did say something." There was a pause. "Well, George," Bill Walmsley said in that wise and searching tone for which he was famous, "whether Beckenthal is a prospective fifth columnist or not, whatever he's doing let us hope there isn't an invasion, eh?"

So much for telepathy! Callum mused. This sounded more like Lexin playing his synthesizer. He felt Walmsley was going to find it hard to take him seriously. "Wait! How can I put this?" he said, hesitating, "Yesterday when I was walking here..."

"...You had a vision."

"Ten seconds and it was gone."

"I thought there was something," Walmsley said, and to Callum's surprise nothing more was said for a while. "Have you seen anybody?" he asked eventually.

"Only the Emergencies Deputy Minister, Nawale. I wanted to see Blunck to check up on the invasion and proposed countermeasures, all innocent-like. As you probably know, he and Beckenthal..."

"...are close. Yes, I have noticed. I suppose it's not entirely surprising in view of their mutual interests, is it? Did you get anything?"

"Not really. Blunck is supposed to be away, but I don't believe it." Callum told him about Nawale's somewhat reluctant recitation concerning the possible nature of the threat. "I suppose Blunck could be making the whole thing up," he said finally.

"He's not known for being too straightforward." Walmsley said, then after a pause, "but it would not have got past van Rensburg, would it? There must be some substance in it"

"Sounded pretty tenuous, I would say."

"Obviously he couldn't tell you everything."

"Enough, I reckon. It sounded like a regurgitation of all that stuff the Frenchman spouts constantly."

Walmsley laughed so that his jowls rolled about. "And countermeasures?"

"Nothing divulged. I have to tell you, Bill, that I cannot ignore Lexin any more."

Walmsley affected no surprise. He must have seen that coming. "Only the fact that it is my rational friend who now tells me that the scarcely possible seems quite probable makes me able to do your bidding. Regarding Beckenthal, leave it to me," he said.. "I'll have a good nose around."

Over lunch in an Italian brasserie in Manuka they chewed over the latest disruptions and a couple of Murrumbidgee pizzas.

"You want to know about my vision, then?" Callum said, as they were about to leave.

"I wish there would be one final vision to settle it," Walmsley said, "what with Lexin's People, and now your vision. It's of Lexin's People, too, is it?"

Callum nodded. "Probably."

"No need to tell me. Don't know what to make of it all, to be honest, but anything to get out of this bloody situation."

The paper stands when they emerged were full of the bother on the trains, the 'intolerable inconvenience' to the travelling public.

"Canberra catching up with the rest, then," Walmsley commented, "Must be the international students. Well leave it to me while you go and pump old Van Rensburg."

Having arranged to meet at an insignificant location in Dixon, time to be agreed later, they went in opposite directions. Callum walked casually at first in the warm sun. He would like to have enjoyed it for longer – the Australian Fathers certainly had a good idea when they invented this paradise, he thought –, but he had the feeling of being followed. Or was it just that his nerves were on edge? He took a taxi bubble passing opposite.

Arriving at the offices of the First Minister in World Government House in the middle of the afternoon he was able to get only as far as the receptionist. Told to wait, and looking casually out of a window expecting to see the gardens and possibly a view across Lake Burley Griffin to Civic, he saw only what appeared to be the same snowy forest that he had seen the day before, and then suddenly, surely not many yards from him and quite clearly now, that primeval man, that Big Nose, now recognized on so many monitors all round the world from Lexin's website. It was quite incongruous. There he was, George Callum, having just come in from twenty-five degrees Celsius, and yet now looking out on a cold, snowy place how many thousand years ago was it…?

Big Nose in his mammoth fur was actually carrying the girl over his shoulder, moving with that distinctive, slightly crab-like gait. He was towing something. Then to Callum's surprise he put the girl down and she walked a bit. Evidently it was just that she could not keep up with him. Now he could see he was pulling a kind of sledge made by binding branches together. On the sledge were skins and a carcase. The girl, arms protruding from a thick fur, was walking a little distance behind the sledge. Now she hastened forward, put her hands on it and pushed it. Perhaps it gave her some support, for she seemed to move with difficulty. Callum remembered hearing about the girl's bloody encounter with a lion. Was it really possible that he was actually in on the story himself now, and not merely second-hand, via Lexin and his website? A minute or two later and the girl – what *was* her name? – got on the sledge. Big Nose did not complain, but simply struggled forward until he had apparently had enough and shouted something and she got off and walked again. They seemed to have reached some accommodation.

Callum found himself thinking about the older woman, Red Hair, who the girl thought was her mother. Presumably Big Nose did not know she was in grave danger. It suddenly seemed important, making the receptionist's voice an unwelcome interruption.

"The Minister's been called away. Her Secretary will contact you."

"I shall be at my hotel another two days," Callum said, "leaving Thursday."

"I will tell her."

That was strange, Callum said to himself, and for some reason, instead of heading back to his hotel he headed for the 'gents' without feeling the necessity.. Once in the quiet of a cubicle he remembered that Lexin had fortunately warned him to keep his PAS connection 'on'. It occurred to him that that might explain his experiences of a few minutes before and on the previous day. Taking out his multicom he struggled frustratedly for some time before remembering how to request the guidance from his PAS which now, for the first time ever, he realised he really needed.

"You are on the right lines," he was advised – to his astonishment. "You must keep close to Big Nose. They need protection." There was nothing more.

Callum stepped boldly out of the building into a layer of snow (not an action he would normally have relished), and a wall of cold air that momentarily took his breath away. He found himself alone on a high hill, or more exactly a promontory. He was looking at a wide plain stretching away into the distance. Automatically he cast his eyes round, looking for the man and the girl. To the left, off the end of the promontory all was forest. He saw no person until on turning another ninety degrees his eyes came to rest on the two dots far down in the valley behind him. They were moving very slowly along the side of a swollen river. Soon they would pass beneath the promontory to where the river entered the forest.

Only now, prompted by the advice he had received, did Callum take stock of his own situation, dressed (as he now perceived himself to be) not in a sophisticated personal climate outfit suitable for an Australian summer, but in layers of skins topped by a bison fur, and carrying a spear bound at the end to a beautifully sharpened pointed stone. The warmth and dryness of his feet was accountable to their being surrounded by well-made skin and hide shoes through which he felt nothing of the hardness of the stony ground. But he was not *old* Callum – if indeed he really could be Callum at all –, and he was slim, and felt more agile than he had ever felt before – or at least he felt that he *would* feel so were it not for the burden of all his life's belongings upon him.

Scanning round the frozen landscape with ever more accustomed eye he made out in the distance, advancing slowly across the open plain, other dots, prowling dots. Almost at the same moment he became aware of activity closer at hand, down the slope where it merged into the flatness. Now he did shed his clobber, and armed only with his spear and a pouch of good stones for hurling he slithered part way down the hill. Undoubtedly those were lions out there, and now he saw that they were coming on steadily. He waited a little among the bushes. Quickly he caught sight, much nearer, of the front runners of what was probably a whole herd of mammoths appearing from the right and about to advance through the bushes at the bottom of the slope.

It quickly became clear that both mammoths and lions were heading in a direction that would inevitably bring them to the river where it flowed beneath the promontory, the mammoths probably first, very likely arriving at the same time as the two travellers. It might be a long shot, but Callum reckoned that if the mammoths could be headed off and caused to stampede in the direction of the lions it might give father and daughter time to get clear. There was no time to think of an alternative, and anyway, he could hardly fail to see, could he, that by some inconceivable means he had been placed there to do that very thing?

Crouching spear in hand, he raced through the low vegetation right down the hill and was almost at the bottom before the mammoths detected his presence, probably through a sudden strengthening of the wind. Now he brandished his spear and charged, summoning a volume of sound that he had not been aware of ever possessing and yelling at the top of his voice, hurling the stones with unbelievable force, flushing the mammoths out of the bushes, cutting off their advance and causing them to head out into the plain. Two or three animals broke away and continued towards the river, but he continued to pursue the others before returning and climbing back up the hill, where he had the satisfaction of seeing them in the distance still moving towards the now retreating lions. He was asking himself where the other three mammoths were now when a voice hailed him. He had not been aware of anyone near him, and it startled him. Moreover, it was a woman's voice...

* * *

"George! It is not like you to ignore me!" It was the small, rather plain figure of Van Rensburg herself, in a nice short gown over floppy trousers, her hair now in a slightly greying bun and with a cardigan over her arm.

"I was far away," he said, realising after a moment's confusion that he was still at World Government House, just outside among the trees and still in his suit (somehow).

"Something made me look in my security monitor. I never used to look in it at all, but now occasionally. I could not see why you did not come in." The voice was clear and undistinguished as ever.

"I am very pleased to see you," Callum said. "I did come in. They said you could not interview me, or rather, that you had been called away."

"Couldn't interview you? That's rubbish." Her sharp features puckered into a frown. "What a pity that we have to become all security conscious. I am afraid they are still a bit nervous about the whole thing – security, I mean."

"Joanna, could we get out of range of security?" Callum sensed a slight, uncharacteristic shake in his own voice.

She hesitated, looking at him questioningly. "Why, yes, of course. We can go to my flat. I was hoping to catch you before you disappeared." She extracted her multicom and told her secretary she would be out for half an hour plus. "...And no thank you. I prefer to be alone."

The official residence of the First Minister, also dating from Australia's arrival on the World Government stage, was situated nearby in a little enclave off Queen Victoria Terrace. They walked there. A friendly robot admitted them to a substantial building in the bungalow style, and through an interior redolent with the sense of a changed Earth and the gratefulness of Earth's people – murals portraying peace and reconciliation... a room embodying in subtly interwoven vistas the transformed rural economies of Africa... another depicting the first century of progress in science and humanitarian living 'post-visitation', the prospect of earthly harmony and hope of entry into the Galactic Community. In the wake of his experiences of that day, all this evoked in Callum a severe attack of self-questioning. It was a consoling thought that he was not the first to see Lexin's People; if it had been otherwise he might have thought he was losing his marbles. But did he really want to be involved? Doing the boy's bidding was one thing, but now, and a future with so much at stake, and he himself alone only a moment ago on that snowy mountain! What would be next? He would bide his time. It was all he could do!

Another robot, a female, materialised as they came to The First Minister's private apartment, to be quietly thanked and dismissed. There were no public statements here, rather the expression of Joanna's own preferences, a person conscious of public service and a person knowing her own mind but of modest aspirations – but not too modest or hidebound, he hoped, in the face of present challenges. Or was there more to her than might appear? It was the general consensus, actually. And anyway, couldn't it be he who was being too modest, too timid?

"I will come straight to the point," he said once they were inside and he was barely yet seated in one of the spacious old armchairs. "I fear we have a potentially dangerous situation, but possibly not one you might be thinking of."

"Isn't the present one alarming enough?"

"Joanna..." Callum was finding it difficult to step back in time from those retreating lions thirty something thousand years away. "...Joanna, you will appreciate that there is controversy concerning the causes of the current troubles here on Planet Earth, but quite apart from all that, this danger I am speaking of originates, we feel sure, not from alien influences but from within." He was aware, as he spoke, of being surrounded somewhat incongruously by family portraits, and paintings of the glories of her peaceful and productive homeland of United South Africa. He knew her husband was an eminent physician in Durban and that she commuted there frequently, while her own family could be traced through a long line of politicians and lawyers back to the Voortrekkers. The First Minister was attentive, the small, dark eyes fixed firmly upon him. "The first thing I want to say," he went on, "is that I am having Beckenthal investigated. He has been grossly misrepresenting the position of the Society, indeed belittling the Society, thus creating fertile ground for the prevalence of stupid and/or dangerous ideas. Secondly – which may not be entirely unconnected – may I strongly recommend that you ask your Emergencies Minister for a full breakdown of all supposed evidence on alien interference? And don't take any second-hand stuff from Nawale, whom I saw this morning, upright man though he no doubt is." Callum paused.

So far she had let him speak on. She had remained standing and now appeared to be looking at him as though in some kind of trance. "Carry on, George," she said, seemingly automatically.

"I fear somebody could be pulling the wool over his eyes..."

"Really?" Again the featureless, hoarse tone.

"The wool, in short, of theory and hypothesis and a marked absence of fact. May I suggest that you could send the evidence for alien interference – I don't know...accounts of technological breakdowns, population behavioural analyses, other things that you may know but not I – perhaps to a university outside Australia for a composite interdisciplinary assessment. Meanwhile may I suggest alerting all security? For the rest I would advise silence."

Secured by no more than a robotic caretaker and graced as it was with a charming gyndroid, the residence of the First Minister seemed a world away from dangers of planetary upheaval. Canberra, although now by rotation the seat of world government, was as yet little affected by the chaotic developments of recent months, so all in all it was perhaps understandable that Joanna Van Rensburg should have been taken by surprise.

He had the impression that if she had been an inveterate smoker or even a modest drinker, she would have reached instantly for the relevant articles. As it was, her small but firmly drawn features tightened, and the corners of her mouth turned down, a bit like a child about to cry. It was a figment of the imagination of course.

"With respect, Joanna," Callum added, "I have a feeling you should look at your own department, too."

The First Minister's initial shock suddenly turned to annoyance bordering on anger: "My God," she exclaimed, "are not things just bad enough as it is, with the chaos? First it's Nawale. Are you speaking now of my deputy, Faust? I'm not quite sure I understand exactly what you imagine may be happening in the Government here..." She paused, seemed to cool down a little. Then she said, more calmly, "I have the greatest confidence in my deputy."

"In summary," Callum said after a polite pause, "some people may be cashing in on the chaos, as you call it, in a manner endangering world security. Faust may know something. As I said, I have a trusted friend making some discrete independent enquiries on Beckenthal. I hope you don't mind."

"I don't suppose I have any option, George, if your view is that everything – whatever 'everything' is – should be kept at a very low level."

"I think that's best. Then if there *is* something – I mean some 'irregularity' (I hesitate to say 'plot') – it might be sorted with a single shot, as it were."

"But tell me, what real evidence can you possibly have other than the vague suspicions you have communicated to me?"

Callum hesitated, but only momentarily. She must know about the synthesizers, and certainly about Lexin's visions. "As you may know, Lexin is way ahead of all of us Societans in the level of his enhancement – I mean the way in which he is able to use it. The warning stems from him. I am conveying it to you as the Society's Vice-President." He found himself starting to try and explain about under-use of the synthesizers, its disastrous effect, and then about Lexin's extraordinary insights, but he had the feeling she had heard too much of it already and left it at that.. After all, the business of the Society and the tensions within it were not a secret.

Joanna van Rensburg stood quite still, without speaking, for as much as a minute, hands clasped under her chin. "I thought we left such stuff – I mean, plotting, all that sort of thing – left it behind long ago." She began to speak of her determination to preserve "our wonderful civilization", but evidently stopped herself. She would not be drawn on her understanding of the nature of the alien threat or on any details of countermeasures. "Tell me, George, tell me, what do you suggest is behind all this? A 'coup de monde'?" She wasn't smiling.

"The answer to your question is that I don't know. With the greatest respect, however, I have to say that I have come to the opinion that nothing, not even that, could be more serious than a future without the Society if that were to happen from whatever cause, terrestrial or other."

"Are you...how can I put it....on Lexin's wavelength, then?"

"I think I am moving towards conversion."

She looked hard at Callum for several seconds. The firm, tight features relaxed momentarily into a faint smile. "I think I should know who your sleuth is."

He told her. She had no comment. He was sure she would have said if she had any qualms about Walmsley, and he was relieved.

"I am shocked," she said. "If anything transpires, you will know."

Nevertheless, Callum had the impression she was more shocked than believing. "From my end also," he assured her. She did look a bit shaken. In view of that, he accepted her invitation to join her in a quick fix consisting of a dubious orange liqueur from her own country to which she said she resorted 'only in times of stress'. There's a back entrance," Joanna said when they had finished those and resisted a second round. "I don't think anybody knows about it yet. It may be a different story soon at the rate things are deteriorating. I'll let you out."

As he returned to his hotel, brief sequences appearing – much to his surprise – on his multicom indicated that the lions had dispersed in the far distance, while most of the mammoths that he had chased in their direction appeared to have stopped to browse on the scattered shrubs in the open ground. He could not be sure of their number. There was no telling where the three were that had broken away. His hope was that they would be dawdling now, waiting for the rest to catch up, thus giving Big Nose and the girl a chance to get ahead.

Callum met Walmsley in Dixon that evening, and then again briefly in Manuka three days later, having allowed himself a few days' break before the next meeting of the Conference, when Lexin would also return from a tour of Chinese cities. He had hired a bike for two days and explored the bush around Canberra, and felt a great deal better for it after the tensions of recent weeks. Bill Walmsley said he had had sightings of Beckenthal, who seemed to be in Sydney as much as Canberra. However, he pointed out that if anything was going on that should not be it *could* be happening anywhere at all, even thousands of miles from the Ministry of Emergencies. Meanwhile the World Government had refused to interfere in the maglev strike, relinquishing all responsibility for negotiations in favour of national governments in a move typical of a developing policy of leaving acute problems to be sorted at that level and concentrating itself on 'the main task in hand'.

Homeward bound, as news viewed via the desk monitor in his compartment began to indicate that the defensive cover – whatever that was – would soon be ready for commissioning and ready to counter any alien offensive, Callum was equally aware of, and certainly more worried about, the potential for some kind of domination by Earth-bound powers if Lexin's fears were justified. It presented an unimaginably terrifying prospect in a rapidly degrading society given the state of modern technology: population elimination or alteration? Forcing of the Society into new paths…?

His PAS yielded nothing more on Big Nose and Shining Face and their progress via the desk monitor (when he had managed to dig out his PAS code to use it). Yet the fact was that whatever was happening, and whatever might happen in the future, gradually and painfully Callum was already beginning to reject the 'one-dimensional' views of his old self (his words). 'The word 'trust' came to mind. It was Lexin's favourite. So was it now to be all a matter of trust?

Not many days earlier Callum would not have seriously believed in the reality of these people at all, any more than most of the press did, despite all the press conferences – or the Government, apparently, or even at that time the majority of Societans –, seeing them, if not as of alien origin, then as psychic experiences of Lexin himself. He would not have believed that they could be connected with what was happening here, nor that they could matter to him, and least of all that their (probable) escape from those lions and mammoths might actually have *depended* upon him.

He doubted there would be anything on the 'Lexin's People' website for some time, but on checking later, another, sadder story was being portrayed there and picked up on maybe a billion multicoms worldwide – that of a wandering Red Hair trying to feed her dying baby.

*   *   *

Towards the end of January, Tom and Ida went to stay with Henry and Florrie for a few days. Just afterwards, Ida had to attend outpatients for a biopsy and CT scan to determine the cause of some unaccountable bleeding that had started before she went away. This was despite the fact that on the whole she had been feeling very much better, the shingles having at last subsided and the candidiasis of the oesophagus at last responded to treatment. It was a worrying development, but by now both she and Tom had learned to live day by day and face each difficulty as it came. Thus it has to be said that when the diagnosis of cervical cancer came and a proposal was made for a radical hysterectomy, Marcelle thought the pair appeared less fazed about it all than she was herself, though she was determined not to show her disappointment.

The surgeon, a short, thickset man with tanned complexion, black, bushy eyebrows and a cheeky grin, was as nice as he could be when she and her mother went to interview him after all the tests. It was at stage 'One B', he said, and was still confined to the cervix, i.e. the lower part of the uterus. It was about one and a half inches across. Quick as lightning he produced a diagram of the pelvic organs, pinpointed the location of the tumour and in detail what the operation would entail.

"This is a very common cancer with AIDS," he explained.

"And radiotherapy or chemotherapy would not be suitable?" Marcelle asked.

"Not on their own, but we would probably combine it with a post-operative course of both radio- and chemotherapy."

It seemed an awful lot of her mum's inside to be taking away for something not all that large, which Marcelle pointed out, and which led to more explanations...

"I think we must leave it to Mr. Chappel, dear," Ida said finally when Marcelle had run out of questions. "He has his reasons."

The surgeon's grin blossomed into a smile. A man seemingly in no hurry, and displaying an expressive agility of the hands, Marcelle thought that at least he looked as if he could do the job, which did sound horribly complicated, removing this and that and hopefully leaving behind everything essential.

Florrie took a dismal view of the situation, and kept on airing it when Ida had gone back after the New Year: "Didn't Ida have smear tests?" etc. etc. Marcelle could have hit her. No, she didn't. Her mother was never that good at looking after herself. But it got Marcelle down whenever she and Mark called at her grandparents.

Mark was a great prop. "Come on, Marcie," he said, "We've come so far and we're not going to give it neck. You've trusted your blue-eyed boy up to now. Do you think he will let you down?" They were by the canal. It was foggy and cold as they walked along the towpath.

"I know, Mark, I know, but we've come so far and yet there seems to be darkness at the end of the tunnel. Before, it was you who wouldn't believe *me*. Now you are so confident."

"I didn't follow Big Nose all that way up to the cave to no purpose, did I? It was pretty dark in *there*, incidentally."

"No, Mark, you didn't, love." She was staring into the distance. A boat was just discernible, coming gliding across the fields.

"Did I save Shining Face for nothing?"

She turned to him, closed up to him, resting her head on the fur lapel of his expensive 'polar extremes' coat. "No, of course not. At least, I hope you didn't." She was silent for a moment, then she said, pouting, "Mark, I confess I am just a little jealous...about you and Shining Face."

"Marcie, you know my position," Mark said, studiously avoiding her eye, "I don't know by what means we have had these dreams, or these experiences, but they happen, and now it's *my* turn to have my say, that's all."

"You have not seen Lexin," she said in a mock peevish tone.

"Your word is good enough," he said, laughing. "You must know me by now, Marcie, that once I get hold of something I don't let go. I haven't let go of you, have I?" He kissed her, first on one cheek, then on the other, then on the lips.

"Mark, it is so hard seeing Mum struggling."

"I know. Men can be so objective in some ways. I s'pose if it were my mum..."

Marcelle did not hear the rest. She was recalling her various encounters with Mrs. Wharton, and at the same time trying to forget them while blaming herself for her nasty thoughts.

"I know what's going through your head," he said.

He surely did. And in other ways too. How relieved and thankful she was that he had drawn closer to her, tried hard indeed to come close to her way of thinking, her vision! She hardly dared to believe how far he had come, and it was interesting that his vision of himself in the future now seemed to encompass the poor and the needy and the dispossessed.. Had he not just recently sent off for info on IT involvement in Action Aid programmes in Africa? It was the old Mark 'plus'. Mark's parents, evidently seeing the relationship between the young ones prospering, had even had Tom and Ida over for a meal.

They were approaching the lock now, and the boat was alongside, edging through the lower gates into the chamber... A man was guiding it with a pole.

"Nice day for a picnic!" he shouted as the lock filled and the boat slowly rose up..

"What have you got for us, then," Mark shouted.

"Winter coats, rainwear, snow-wear, boots, capes, anoraks...," came the scarcely expected answer, "...long-sleeved warm shirts, long underwear, polar fleece sweat shirts, snow pants, warm jackets, fur caps, foam sleeping bags..."

They laughed, and sat down on the seat as the vessel moved past the opened top gates, watching it until with all the gates secured and a wave from the man it was heading out into the upper reach.

"Let's walk on a bit," Marcelle said, and they got up and started along the slowly rising path. The boat was already out of sight in the haze, and soon no upper reach could be seen but only a greyish whiteness, and soon they were advancing through another country, hemmed in by forest, slowed down by deep snow. Marcelle was thinking how lucky they were to have some really warm things, when suddenly Mark stopped.

"Wait!" he shouted. "There's something ahead there, in the bushes. Get behind me!"

Shining Face stopped pushing the sledge, grabbed her pouch off it, and a stone out of the pouch, a stone that might have been thought too big for her to hold until her spidery fingers closed firmly and unerringly round it. Big Nose had dropped everything and was already brandishing his spear and preparing to rush forward, eyes fixed ahead and his gaunt features tautening beneath the thick beard glistening with ice drops.

"Stop! Stop!" she shouted suddenly. There were long moments during which nothing at all happened. From all that could be seen of whatever it was, crawling out of the snowy undergrowth into the clearing, which was chiefly its spotted coat, it might easily have been a hyena. It was very strange, though, she had reckoned, that such a beast was approaching them fearlessly like that. That was why she had shouted 'Stop!' When it was perhaps six men's lengths away Big Nose might still have rushed at it nevertheless, had she not grabbed his arm and shouted to him again:

"Look ! The face!"

They both rushed forward, then stopped in amazement. The woman, emaciated, extremities blue with cold, had stopped crawling. She was clutching a thick stick, but her eyes, though upwards cast, looked right through them. She appeared unable to speak. Shining Face knelt down and cradled Red Hair's head in her arms. The eyes blinked occasionally, and the lips moved just a little, but there was no sound and no recognition.

"She must have a shelter. She must have come out when she saw us approaching," Big Nose said. Though sapped of strength himself, he picked her up and placed her gently over his shoulder. They followed her trail back into the trees. There indeed was a shelter of evergreen fronds with a carpet of the forest litter, deepened in one place to make a bed. There were some skins and other articles, and the remains of a meal. Two pigeon carcases were suspended over a long dead fire, evidently intended for smoking and drying, but not smelling too good. Snow was sparse here, as was the light.

CHAPTER EIGHTEEN

"You are on the right track, George, but there was never a time when it was more necessary to await a go-ahead, to wait while things happen, and to be reticent." The stern warning from Callum's personal activity synthesizer was sparing and to the point, as in his limited use of it hitherto he had found always to be the case.

Back in his very modern and palatial residence on the edge of Galaxy City, with its variable layout, personal activity prompting and traditional robotic staff of three (chiefly for Fiona, and for show), his art treasures, his books and the rest, and his views across green suburbia, he was aware that '*some*thing' had indeed happened. As he awaited Lexin's return he was aware of the latest turn of events now filling the millions of screens still able to display Lexin's website (despite the increasing incidence of computer crashes worldwide, suspected of being due to some newly introduced software): new images showing Red Hair being carried to her den, evidently having been rescued by Big Nose and Shining Face.

Now at least, Callum reasoned, in the shelter of the den the three of them might have a chance of enduring the worst of the winter together. With the (hopefully extendable) deadline for the Society now imminent he realised how much the event must mean to Lexin if the repair of broken families was indeed at the heart of his gospel. He had talked on the phone of a 'seismic moment', and Callum had to admit – if he set aside his wretched mundanity – that he could see Big Nose justifiably dreaming of a brighter future from that moment on. He even had some sense now that it mattered to him, Callum. And if there might be a brighter future for Big Nose and those with him, then maybe also for those struggling in Newchurch and, by some incomprehensible process of redemption or reparation – or whatever it was –, also for the green and pleasant oasis that was Galaxy City and all it stood for, despite ominous indications to the contrary. His PAS was markedly reserved when he asked it about all that, and for that matter so was Lexin when they had spoken..

Obviously, there were good reasons for its warning about reticence. If even rumours of a dire plot reached the ears of the public, a population already disrupted and frightened by the possibility of an alien strike and having received little enlightenment from the authorities would soon be impossible to control. A sense of deep unrest had already become a repeating feature of the city's life, with strange and unusual confrontations between individuals, a general air of pessimism, suicides, demonstrations...

Callum looked out of his study window at the distant pinnacles and domes visible beyond the greenery clothing the residential limbs of the suburbs: the University, the Museum of Knowledge from Space, the Palace with its trilltinium pinnacles where the Conference would meet in a couple of hours. He was struggling to translate so many uncertainties into something meaningful to put to the meeting: uncertainties about the precise meaning of the deadline, the solidarity or otherwise of the delegates behind Lexin, Malinovsky and his work, Lexin's People (unfinished saga), Beckenthal, the world situation...not to mention aliens, if any. He found that if he imagined himself charging down that hillside driving those mammoths out of the bushes, or even let himself somehow float in galactic space, the task became marginally simpler. Certainly it would clarify things if they knew exactly what Beckenthal was up to.

Naturally, he had kept Lexin informed of events in Canberra, but was it just possible that when Lexin came round in a few minutes, incidentally after a more enthusiastic reception in China than anywhere hitherto, apparently, he might have caught some inside news: that, say, the Government was going to come out openly and admit the discovery of an internal plot to take advantage of a nonexistent alien threat, or to grossly exaggerate the threat? Either of these eventualities might at least provide a breathing space for the Society, and greatly strengthen Lexin's hand. Very likely Beckenthal would have been found to be involved. Of course, if there *was* a real and imminent alien threat... But it did not bear thinking about!

"It's just got to be a holding operation, this meeting," Lexin said when he did finally arrive, looking smaller than ever, his multimodal suit creased and tacky from constant wear and crowd contact and his round eyes betraying a tiredness that even his most inspired utterances could not hide. It seemed he had no further information, no inside news (and nor had he himself, via Van Rensburg). His warning seemed merely to corroborate that of his own PAS about keeping things to themselves – for the time being.

"Yes, I know," Callum said. "You know, I'll never understand these Bods," he exclaimed, almost involuntarily and in sudden exasperation as they entered the living space. "Is there a threat, or isn't there? I mean, are they with us or not?" He regretted his words almost before they were out. Lexin's response was utterly predictable...

"I hoped you had swallowed all the medicine," he said, looking for somewhere to put his winter coat until a robot appeared and politely took it away. It was true, Callum admitted to himself, there *were* things he could not quite bring himself to accept. "Did you take the proper dose? Possibly not, eh?" Lexin was going on, good humouredly, declining to occupy one of the reclining chairs that Callum press-buttoned out of nowhere, saying he needed somewhere to rest things. "But how about a drink before we start, George?" (Did the boy never rest?). Callum tapped other buttons and the space around them reconfigured, holographically at first, into a space for discussion and note-taking and personal light refreshment. "The Bods may be active, they may be stemming some evil tide, George, though I doubt it," Lexin continued when the transformation was complete and he had perched with his brief case on the edge of a seat and snapped open a pack of refreshing juice, "or juggling our options, or planning a pathway for us, for our future. Or they may take things step by step like we are having to do, or be waiting for us to act, or again, they may be doing nothing. I don't know what they do or what they don't do, but what they are telling us is to hold our horses and not to mention Beckenthal if possible."

Yes, that was it, 'waiting for us' – Callum saw it, but still in a mist.

He had even been searching his PAS for the names of those whom he suspected of taking advantage of the chaos, but no names had appeared. He supposed it wasn't his job, then. At least, not at present. Yet it offended his rationality to have to wait, to have to wait as it were outside the timeless sphere. "I did get involved at least," he said at length, anxious to restore Lexin's faith in him. But he might have known that Lexin knew it already.

"Yes, and thank God, and I am sorry if I sometimes seem impatient and over-critical. It is because time is short. I had a warning, a warning I was half expecting and could not ignore. I asked you to investigate, and you did. Thank you! We don't know the results yet, and we must keep our mouths shut."

"And at the meeting."

"The same. Remember! More of us have got the message now and are using our synthesizers. Many are seeing images, their own as well as mine, and following events. They will not need explanations, just encouragement in the face of chaos and uncertainty. And they trust you."

He looked so young, so immature, Callum thought. So there was to be no speech as such, just play it by ear. "And so all manner of things shall be well?" He grabbed hold of the words, half serious, half not.

Lexin picked up the quote. " I know you don't believe it," he said, "but my mother feels religion could blossom now more than ever before. She is very angry with old Mauré, actually, banging on about evil, but I was trying to tell her about the great encouragement I got from Christians in China. I tell her thousands of faithful Christians who are Societans, from Haerhpin to K'unming, are optimistic, convinced that Mauré's time is passing, and not only Christians but Buddhists, Taoists... But we all have to work at it, work for our futures and for the futures of those others we know in other ages, like you are doing now." Lexin was fishing a newspaper out of his bag while Callum imagined himself back on that snowy hilltop with its view of potential disaster, wondering whether he had *really* helped Big Nose and Shining Face, and helped them enough, and whether he was missing something even now, some fervour, some inner assurance that all could indeed be made well with the world. "But I don't much like this," Lexin exclaimed, pointing at the front page of the 'Shanghai Times': "'Lexin Finds Religious Consolation in China', etc. etc. 'Finds *inspiration* in China', that would be okay, but 'consolation'! When

Felicitas gets depressed, gets worried about everything, including me, she prays a lot but forgets to use her PAS. Of course, I tell her she needs to do both, like religious people are doing in China now in a big way."

"I did get involved with Big Nose and the girl," Callum said, not sure if Lexin had taken it on board when he had mentioned his 'involvement' a few minutes before.

"I knew someone must have, and I thought of you straight away. The lions, wasn't it? It must have been not long after that that they found Red Hair." It was all so matter of fact with Lexin, as if all the time it was some far bigger thing that was concerning him. He would never get completely used to it. "And my mother," Lexin added, "for brief moments sharing Red Hair's wanderings after she fled the camp with her baby, finished up experiencing the same event. She said those glimpses of her were terrible and unforgettable. The baby had died many days before."

Lexin had wandered into the living space and was looking out of a south-facing window in the direction of the distant yellow band. Callum went over, followed his gaze. Despite all his assurances, how close they might be, he thought, to everything unwinding, how close to the fruitless aridity of the Takla Makan filling the horizon like a threatening tsunami!

Half an hour later they had run through the form of the meeting and headed off through the grounds of Callum's residence and along the frosty walkways to try and find one of the rare taxi bubbles to whisk them along the Avenue of World Harmony to the city centre – this line of the urban transit net at least, with its modules, being currently suspended. It was a longer walk than Callum liked, but again if he thought of himself charging across that plain in pursuit, spear poised, single-minded, powerful, the adrenalin would run and before he could stop himself he would be quickening his gait. A taxi came eventually.

They helped themselves to good strong coffees in the only one of the Palace's four eating facilities operating – the public self-service restaurant on the ground floor next to the main entrance with its view across the near-deserted Gardens to the Meeting of the Avenues. The others were suffering from staff illness or lack of supplies, or both. In the now unmanned information area, usually thronging with visitors, an air of neglect prevailed, and it was cold, the solar-electric heating system (normally used only minimally) being unable to cope in winter with the heat deficit caused by the non-functioning of the canopy – now a persistent and most unwelcome phenomenon here as in many other cities.

"A retrogressive effect on canopy structure," Lexin declared, in passing.

Callum did not question Lexin's diagnosis, reckoning he was only too likely to be correct. They went up to his office – the same room where Lexin had often gone before meetings with his father – to collect his papers, and from there through a security check to the Great Hall. The sign 'No visitors. Public gallery closed!' was unprecedented. Orders from the top, apparently.

They were handed new passes before heading for their seats – Callum to the president's rostrum, Lexin up to an aspirant's seat below the slender, light-controlling windows. Callum thought it was the first time he had seen Lexin betray such unmistakeable anxiety.

The Hall filled right up almost to the last seat, many delegates in warm capes, overcoats, even ski-wear. Callum had put on a toga over his suit. Lexin had brought a couple of rugs. He did not take off his winter coat. Full attendance – barring pressing business back home – had become a leading feature in recent months, and especially in recent weeks. Maybe it was imagination – and would be paradoxical in a way, in view of the present crisis – but never before in Callum's experience had the great space of that Hall with its sublime curves and unimpeded lines of vision given him such a sense of having at last come into its own! Could it be that only now were so many beginning to be aware of the full extent of their responsibilities to the Society and therefore their responsibility for the successful realization of a galactic future for Mother Earth?

"First and only item on the agenda," he announced: " 'Status of the Society, and what happens next'." He hoped nobody detected *his* nervousness. "We have a matter of days, now, to convince the Government that we can continue our work safely and effectively. In the circumstances this may seem a daunting task, but you will know...," he continued, buoyed up suddenly by an unmistakable feeling that his listeners were ahead of him, and strengthened by an unaccustomed conviction, "...you will know that Big Nose and Red Hair are together again after many tribulations, no doubt much to Marcelle's relief as well as mine. I hope you will agree that despite their precarious situation this gives great cause for optimism amid a grave situation worldwide. Therefore, friends, I ask you to live as intimately close to your PAS as to your most beloved." The laughter at the suggestion, coming as it did after so much sombreness at meetings of the Conference, was encouraging. Quickly, though, several delegates requested permission to speak. "Professor Malinovsky!"

"Yes, yes," the sprightly old man declared, springing up most impressively in his everlasting carbon-nanotube and super-wool Latvian overcoat, "I too feel that we have reached a turning point, that we..." He hesitated, stumbled a little in his speech, "...have...how could I put it?... wandered off our path, but are finding it again. In addition, I must point out in particular that Lexin's experiences have provided fresh impetus for re-considering our time-crossing theories."

Callum saw that Leonard Mackenzie was pressing his advisory speak-button repeatedly. In the end the professor, barely recognizable in long, shabby overcoat and balaclava helmet, stood up and interrupted with characteristic abruptness, causing Malinovsky to resume his seat:

"Mr. Chairman, my good friend is surely being irresponsible. In my opinion we do not know the true cause, or causes, of the disruption to our civilised way of life, never mind theories of time-crossing."

"Professor Mackenzie, please allow Professor Malinovsky to continue!"

"I fully understand the doubts of my good friend," Malinovsky said, on his feet again, "but... if I may continue, I want to say to my fellow Societans that with my colleagues I have now finally been able to project a new scientific and philosophical hypothesis. We have been able to set out with much greater confidence and clarity than previously certain principles governing interaction and communication with other people – or intelligences – through space and time." Here he paused, seemed to lose himself for a moment before resuming, "I would not have publicised this quite so soon but for the recent very serious accident and its aftermath. As I have said before, I have no difficulty in accommodating Lexin's People in this framework. But now, if I may continue, regarding the impact of our work as affecting the safe resumption of wormhole activity…"

"May I respond?" Mackenzie had risen to his feet again.

"Please let the Professor continue, Professor Mackenzie," Callum insisted, at the same time hoping the venerable Malinovsky would curb his tendency to wordiness. Callum had noticed signs of restlessness in the auditorium. Mackenzies sank wearily into his seat.

"Thank you Mr. Chairman, and thank you, Professor. Very briefly, then, I am thinking here chiefly of the details of wormhole *operational procedure*," Malinovsky continued, "since I do not consider that there is any problem with the *design* of the wormhole mouth, in particular the central unit and spacetime boundary. I think if we – I should say X.H. Wang and to a less extent we ourselves – had not ironed out any such faults a long while ago, I don't suppose we would be here to talk about it, would we? No, it is all a question of operational parameters." There was already more fidgeting as the old man's words slurred into occasional inaudibility, and two or three hands had gone up and buttons been pressed for permission to speak (the speak-button system had been in place for only a matter of weeks, and being also only advisory was receiving scant regard in that place where informal and unhurried debate had long been the custom). "Frankly," he said, "at risk of disappointing some, in my opinion the procedural modifications already worked out theoretically since the latest accidents occurring during attempted retrieval are also unlikely to bring any improvement, at least from the safety angle…," and that was a bombshell!

An audible complaint swept through the delegates.

It was too much for Mackenzie: "Are you *really* saying that Wormhole Research and Operations have been wasting their time over the last…how many months since the first major accident?"

"Perhaps much longer than that."

"They will close us down tomorrow!" someone from Wormhole Research complained, and one or two others followed suit.

"Delegates," Callum said, "it is important we hear Professor Malinovsky out, so that he may be able to explain himself."

Malinovsky had only half relinquished his seat. "Never forget, fellow Societans," he went on, with unusual emotion and without any stumbling over his words, "that stars may have been sacrificed to construct this scarcely imaginable galactic channel of communication with many portals, and power it. A myriad factors occurring in different parts of spacetime and involving different intelligences will all have to be taken into account in both retrieval and transmission procedure, and I think this is where we have slipped up – badly. Here on Earth we cannot possibly identify, still less quantify, all these factors. My contention is as follows: there are some parameters we can calculate precisely (and I will simply call those 'calculable'), others that we cannot, and still others maybe that we can do no more than speculate on. Indeed, *new* factors might come right out of the blue at any time." Everyone was listening carefully now.

"I am glad you are at least not saying, Professor, that there are *no* calculable parameters." The speaker was Edmonde Lamonte, Mackenzie's number two at the Mission Station, and the man in charge of Wormhole Research and Operations since the big accident, in which his predecessor died. Youngish, unprepossessing in appearance and manner, with scraggy hair and of short stature and dressed in a somewhat bizarre top-to-bottom padded zip-up suit, Lamonte shone chiefly and remarkably by virtue of his cerebral capacity – and sense of humour. A little laughter at his good natured remark reduced the tension.

"To be more precise, I suppose you could say some parameters are calculable *according to theory which is sound as far as it goes*," Malinovsky said. "Now, when it comes to the non-calculable parameters, or to any unknown ones, what can we do? Is it not reasonable at this stage to suggest getting together with the Bods?"

"Get chummy? How the dickens…?" The Frenchman had popped up from his seat like a jack-in-a-box.

"M. Lamonte, they know things we don't know, can't know. When you are all on board, I know they will be glad…yes, I think I can say *anxious*, to talk. They have not had much chance so far."

"That's your opinion Sergei," Mackenzie chipped in from his seat. "We are going to get a lecture from them, then… from the Bods?"

Callum thought it might be best to allow the Professor's sniping. It might help Malinovsky to keep to the point as well as being a safety valve for Mackenzie's own considerable following, who so far were actually being quieter than might have been expected. He said nothing.

"Is that so unreasonable, Leonard?" Lamonte asked. He had remained standing.

"If it's as easy as that, why bother with the wormhole?"

Malinovsky must have picked up the 'Hear, hears' coming from some quarters in response to that question. "Maybe…" he spluttered, "…maybe to successfully use the wormhole is…how shall I put it…the easiest way to convince the world that we are capable of continuing with our work, and decipherment in particular? So when you are ready, Dr. Lamonte, I strongly suggest you request a get-together with the Bods, all of you: team chiefs, team members. It's important.

'Research', too, perhaps. Yes, the Research team as well."

"Everybody?" Mackenzie interrupted with evident irritation. "What about the waverers. renegades, doubters? " He had removed the overcoat to reveal a more familiar toga. He sat down again. Clearly he was getting hot under the collar.

"I was not talking about coercion, Leonard. Just about common courtesy, especially in view of how long we have kept them waiting. These are Galactans!"

There was a silence now in the Great Hall, not to say an atmosphere of strained attentiveness. Lamonte looked troubled. "It's a bit daunting, Professor. Some kind of a PAS conference, then?"

"Yes. I don't know how you do it. You will have to find that out."

"You don't know? "

"No."

"And do you think they will advise, give us clues, warnings, I don't suppose they will let us into any galactic secrets..? They don't usually say very much, do they?"

It was true. The Bods were as sparing with words (if not as reticent) as Lamonte himself.

"Give you facts, point in new directions more likely," Malinovsky said. "I don't know, but maybe they will correct mistakes in your calculations as well."

"I *have* been noticing some unexplained discrepancies in one or two supposedly calculable figures," Lamonte admitted.

" Led by the hand, then." Mackenzie again. "Little children."

"Yes, if you like to put it that way, Professor," Malinovsky said

"It's a new concept, isn't it?" Lamonte said to nobody in particular.

"Professor Mackenzie is long accustomed to working everything out for himself rather than having things handed to him on a plate."

Lamonte agreed. "Aren't we all the same?"

"Certainly it will be a collaborative process, and none of us knows how it will go, Dr. Lamonte," Malinovsky replied, "but I reckon that if becoming Galactans means anything, surely it means new dimensions of respect on all sides and, thankfully, an assumption of tolerance in relation to ourselves that in no way diminishes us."

"I'm thinking it's not as if we've got all the time in the world."

"And they have all the time in the Galaxy," Mackenzie added, resignedly.

"We may have almost no time," Malinovsky said, "but I feel sure

that this being so, the Bods will cooperate with us more quickly than we can imagine. They won't let us down. That is the one thing I am sure of."

Lamonte sat down. He looked thoughtful, but those last words of the Professor's produced a round of applause, including, Callum noted, among many of Lamonte's men and women. It would have been understandable if some of those who had worked so hard – to little avail according to Malinovsky – should have wished to challenge him. Callum put this, and the solidarity of perhaps the majority of the meeting, down not least to Lamonte's willingness to listen.

Nevertheless, many delegates of all colours found it hard to understand how there could still be so much to learn when we had apparently come so near to successful retrieval more than once, albeit with disastrous consequences.

"Apparently so near, *apparently,*", Malinovsky responded. "I take it to be a measure of the Bods' generosity of spirit, They will go as far as they can to accommodate, but there comes a point…" He paused…

"…where they lose patience?" someone suggested.

"I don't think so. I was going to say a point where we lack the extraterrestrial data to handle *their* transmission, whereas…whereas… they apparently sometimes may have the means to accommodate *our* transmissions, however imperfectly they may have been put together. But I admit this is supposition."

Callum felt fortified, by the proceedings, against the tsunami of doubt verging on disbelief that still so often threatened him. But now Mackenzie was on his feet again.

"Yes, Professor Mackenzie!" Callum said, noting at the same time that other buttons were still being pressed, including Jean-Paul Mauré's.

" Personally," Mackenzie said, gathering up the toga to reveal the accustomed slacks and shirt sleeves beneath, and adopting an uncharacteristically gentler tone now, attributable evidently to genuine reverence towards his elderly rival. "I do not wish to cast any sort of shadow over my good friend's philosophical considerations, but in truth I am asking myself just how far – as I understand them – they take us in matters of spacetime, or indeed whether they take us anywhere new at all in relation to our present predicament, although of course I have noted what he has been saying and will be pondering it carefully…" Callum picked up the short but sharp burst of applause at

Mackenzie's 'although'. "At present, though," the Professor continued, "I don't go for any of the analyses of the present mess we are in – neither the Government's, nor M. Mauré's, nor even, I'm afraid," he said, casting a glance across at the aspirants filling the gallery, "anybody else's, tempting though they may be to some."

Some from Research and Operations did echo his sentiments, but Callum noted that still others showed no reaction who he knew would have expressed their disagreement openly if they had seen no substance in what Malinovsky was trying to tell them.

Only one hand was raised now, and one button being pressed.. He sensed an atmosphere of patient expectancy, a calm attentiveness despite the fact that many must have been feeling the cold badly. He wondered whether he should say anything…a word of encouragement fair to both the professors, perhaps? He decided against it.

"Jean-Paul Mauré!" Callum, looking up at the inscrutable Frenchman, was more than a little interested to hear his latest position, aspirants again being permitted to speak. It had never in fact been quite possible to see beyond his hypotheses concerning evil powers and be clear exactly what he was saying in concrete terms about the threat posed to Mother Earth, other than vague references to planet takeover and interruption of intragalactic communication, 'hostile forces within', and some very unpleasant remarks about Lexin and his People. Perhaps that mysteriousness, that vagueness, were what had continued to make him so captivating to many.

"So the hunter and his family have made it," Mauré said, standing up in a spectacularly smart, padded and polo-necked outfit, no doubt bespoke from de Vigny's, "assuming they do not freeze to death. What about the other family? I mean the young girl it all apparently started with. They are not out of the woods, are they? In fact, we may have a tragedy on our hands, not so?"

"It is true we have to be cautious, M. Mauré," Callum replied, thinking of 'coups de monde', but no sooner had he said it than he was conscious of being in another place than the Great Hall. He was in a hospital operating theatre. Once over the initial shock of undergoing another translocation, he was just a little less surprised than he would have been a couple of weeks earlier to discover that he was not only in the theatre but in green scrubs and himself entering the final stages of performing a radical hysterectomy. He was in fact not now George Callum, thank God, but Mr. Edmund Chappel, F.R.C.S., of Newchurch

City Hospital, and a man as confident in his team as he knew they were confident in him. How many times had he performed one of these operations? An hour and a half ago he had been making the initial cuts in the tissues around the patient's uterus and top of the vagina and tying off the blood vessels. Thereafter time had galloped fast as with great dexterity under the steady, intense light, surrounded by his team, he had gone through the complex processes required to remove the entire uterus and upper vagina with the attached ligaments, confident that he had left ureter, rectum and bladder intact. Blood loss had been minimal. He was a meticulous man.

When he had met patient and spouse together a few days before the operation (a practice he insisted on wherever possible), he had found him intelligent and cooperative, tidy, very presentable in neutral jacket, pressed trousers and shoes well polished. But the daughter who had appeared with her mother at the initial consultation, with her thick, dark hair, those large eyes and full, firm lips, in some way inscrutable in an immaculate two-piece that was just 'her', and yet possessing what one might normally have imagined to be a barely compatible softness and gentleness – she was very striking. He sensed there a confidence, a far-sightedness, that probably more than matched his own, and a degree of trust that boosted his own confidence and his optimism. He sensed, too, that these qualities would be likely to react favourably on the patient.

Now finally he was dissecting the patient's pelvic lymph nodes, since these were potentially sources of metastases. Then, when the counting out procedures were completed and the clamps removed and he began the six inch horizontal suture, his assistants would be judging (he had heard it said) from the cool look in the eyes above the mask that he had hopefully given it his best shot – 'hopefully' because he was not so self-confident as to be blind to the levels of recurrence of malignancies in AIDS patients.

Callum returned to the present with his mind poised between exhilaration at his experience and disappointment at such a severe setback for Lexin's People. As Edmund Chappel he had not known the patient or her husband before their first interview; as Callum, he had, by their names and from Lexin's descriptions and his website. But there was no crossover in his mind. It was very extraordinary how he felt easy with both his roles. The upshot of it all was that he had begun to have doubts, up until the events of the last few days, about whether he could continue with the vice-presidency of the Society. But now, after this experience, how could he possibly abandon Lexin at such a critical time?

Feeling none too warm in that cold Hall after his session under the theatre arc lamp, he was still conscious of having just heard Mauré saying "a tragedy on our hands, not so?" against a rising noise of background discussion. "You are right about the precarious state of Marcelle's family," he replied, having called the meeting to order, "but I point out that for it to be effective you have to work it hard, your synthesizer, Jean-Paul. You have to be ruthless in self-questioning. Are you? Sometimes one's PAS speaks to one uninvited, forces reconsideration, progression step by step..." Could he, doubting Callum, really be saying this? "What does your PAS tell you about the young girl and her mother? Read what it writes, listen to what it says. Remember it holds the power, not you. Let it work for you. You will see these young women are real people, wonderful people imbued with something of the same power.

Callum reckoned he had never really questioned Mauré, asked him in detail about *his* visions. Now he might be about to hear.

Mauré hesitated. Then he seemed to collect himself: "All right I will tell you," he declared. "My synthesizer has been invaluable to me. It was a powerful agent in my sociological studies, in helping to forge new theories of the dynamics of our civilization." There was excited fidgeting among his supporters, sounds of "Hear, hear! Hear, hear!" began to be heard, even something close to applause. "You know my work," he went on," my work on ethnic parallels, universal sources of guilt, the evolution of evil, theories of retribution, patterns of conflict, harmonized living. I have a good understanding of psychology, yes, parapsychology, psychological deviation, manipulation – in fact, of the nature and sources of evil."

"I do not doubt it," Callum said, "but these people...our situation today. Did you ever query the relevance of your research for us?"

"Yes. And I know our chaos possesses a most powerful source."

"An evil source, presumably. But did your synthesizer ever write or speak to you about it specifically?"

"It is a power of tremendous force, Chairman. It could not be spoken about."

"More powerful than the Bods, I suppose." The laconic interruption was by Mackenzie. "How can you possibly substantiate that?"

"Leonard, let Jean-Paul finish." Callum said sternly, then put on his most solicitous voice: "This may be very important for us. We must respect the opinion of our long-standing colleague." Callum asked himself why he was being so deferential to Mauré, calling him by his Christian names. Surely his stuff couldn't be credited. Was it pity for him, therefore? He didn't quite know, but he felt surer now, since stepping yet again miraculously into the dynamics of Lexin's People, that Jean-Paul would simply talk himself out, that whatever the truth or otherwise of his theories of good and evil on the cosmic level, they would be of no account here. "Please continue, Jean-Paul," he said. But Lexin in the gallery pressed his button to interrupt. Callum, deciding Lexin's contribution was likely to be more fruitful than either of the others, requested Mauré to wait even though it was against his better democratic judgement, and let him go ahead.

"And my visions," Lexin said, "are just a softening-up process. Is that what you were reported to have said; some evil processes implanted in my brain by external forces which I am now, by my belief in them, driving forward to their conclusion and disseminating in the population?"

There was just a moment's hesitation, then the Frenchman said, "Perhaps... perhaps it is sufficient for me to point out that your People, Lexin, just supposing they are real, have suffered a great deal. I do not find their histories – if we can call them that – inspiring in the way that some of you do, so much as indicative of cruel forces beyond our control. Surely it is not too great a step from there to infer that whatever the real nature of the events you have described, Lexin, you have been drawn back unwittingly into the deep and timeless miasma of all suffering, and by your belief in those implanted processes you are continuing to deepen their destructive effects and, yes, propagate them." This line of thought was continued for some time to the accompaniment of encouraging noises from Mauré's supporters until Callum began to detect rising discontent in Lexin's camp. They were ahead of him, now, ahead of the chairman. They were tired of hearing Mauré. He was about to bring delegates to order again, when another, familiar voice intervened:

"What *is* your vision of things, of the present threat, then, Monsieur Mauré?" It was the resonant Canadian accent of Andrew McLintock. Probably he was oblivious of the button system anyway. Callum had hoped to see him before the meeting, but he had apparently been delayed on his journey from Ghardaia. The fresh voice and the open ended question seemed to invigorate the Frenchman.

Raising himself to his full height he announced in sonorous, alarming tones, "I fear that if I could tell you my whole vision, if I could describe it, it would be too terrible for you to bear. I cannot. I do not know its shape or its reason, or anything concrete about it. It is...just... *there*, and I fear it."

McLintock, uncowed by the scenario suggested (albeit dimly) by Mauré, continued, "The explosions, do you consider they were part of it, part of your... 'vision'?" to which he replied,

"That would be a reasonable assumption. Yes, I would say so. And much that has followed, as I have been indicating."

"And the force or power you have referred to, do you consider that it is distant, or already here, or not anywhere to our perceptions – I mean, not in our dimension?"

"I do not know, but we have to prepare for it as best we can," Jean-Paul Mauré replied.

When others tried to penetrate this nightmare, little of substance emerged, although the effect the questioning had on Mauré himself – his tremulous voice, his grotesque expression and graphic gesticulations – was frightening enough in itself.

Callum, cold and hungry, decided to call a break in the discussion until after lunch. Delayed for a moment talking to the Proceedings Secretary and then leaving the hubbub in the Hall and making for the usual delegates' bar and Andrew, he became aware with mixed feelings that he was already in Mr. Chappel's shoes again, heading for his office between the Outpatients Wing and Surgical, and looking forward to dipping into a flask of strong coffee.

Pouring out a mug of it and placing it beside him, he leaned back in his chair by the window overlooking the car park and turned up the patient records files in his computer where he kept, somewhat individualistically, highly detailed records of the histories and backgrounds of all his patients. He turned up Ida Weston and entered essential details of the operation. Before he closed the file, his eye drifted over her recent data... the progressive rise in CD cell count at the last three checks, albeit from a very low level but (he believed) with good self-medication discipline. For a case of such rapid progression to AIDS a remarkable reversal! Just some concern about the viral titre, though, he said to himself, moving up and down the file and studying it. Due to latent reservoirs? Virus particles in the bone marrow, genital tract? But if ever such a seriously ill patient could be helped, it was her. Cured? In the case of the cancer, he had hopes.

Picking up his mug he happened to glance out of the window and thought for a moment he must be dreaming, for his eyes were met not by the view of the usual car park but, to his surprise, indeed amazement, by a leafy prospect and beyond it a cityscape of towers and green avenues, strangely shaped buildings, pinnacles and domes. He looked away, and then back again: the same view. His eye wandered to the record file again. Now the pages in the monitor appeared strangely semi-transparent. Beneath them he was able to discern other pages. Yet when he examined them, trying every trick he could think of to adjust the monitor or clarify the text, it proved impossible. It was as if there was another file in another place and – he did not know why the idea should have come to him unless it was that view from the window – another time. His experience at first alarmed and then excited him. He told himself to relax, and sat there with eyes closed for a minute or more before closing the file. When he looked up there were no domes, no towers, just the car park out there again and the green trees of the hospital grounds and along the city's Inner Ring where it curved round to join the river.

Callum surfaced in the bar, his spirits this time definitely raised by his further excursion into the work of Mr. Edmund Chappel. Although also puzzled by what had happened there, he was determined not to be distracted by it and was already intent on fishing for the multicom in his briefcase to prioritize his messages as McLintock thrust a half litre in front of him. The meaning would become clear enough in all probability.

"Still the same old Mauré," McLintock said.

"Were you expecting something different, then?" Callum asked, casually, still reaching for his multicom but failing to find it.

"I'm thinking it sounds far fetched – 'too terrible to bear', etc."

"I s'pose it might be...too terrible to bear, but to be honest I doubt if Mauré has ever had a proper conversation with his synthesizer." Neither spoke for a moment, then McLintock said,

"He might have to change his tune a bit. I don't know. Anyway, I need to talk to you." The indefatigable Canadian leaned a little closer, the usually forthright manner now a little more tentative. "Could we retire to your quarters for a few minutes? Something's come up."

McLintock grabbed his fur coat and Callum his beer, and they walked in silence along the corridors to the lift down to the president's office. Callum was glad to get into a quieter environment.

"So do I gather you might have some other explanation for Mauré's 'tremendous force?'" he asked when the door had closed behind them.

"You remember I have been talking about problems of climate control – in the Sahara, I mean."

"Yes, Lexin told me," Callum replied, wondering whether he could politely fish for his multicom again but deciding to postpone it and picking up his beer instead.

"You know I have regular access to climate control headquarters where they are studying the data..." Callum nodded. "...We have been noticing a new pattern of disturbances, not in fully re-climatised areas on this occasion but in ones where the climate is undergoing establishment. The same kind of operational fault or breakdown in automated control would be reported across a number of stations – too little emergency irrigation, say, or unnecessary requests for cloud-treatment balloons."

"Not another of Lexin's retrogressive effects?"

"Could be, but too neat and tidy somehow. What I am talking about is something necessitating the same *type* of manual correction across many stations, e.g. faults of minimization, exaggeration, uncertainty, even self-contradiction."

"Some overall system fault?"

"I think that is what they were working on at HQ. I am not so sure."

"Sounds feasible, doesn't it? Any reports from anywhere else, similar schemes, etc.?"

"Just one. I have only learned of it in the past couple of weeks. In Arabia. Another Government-sponsored scheme. Similar situation."

"Excuse me, I'm getting a reminder," Callum said, tapping his head. "Must deal with this." He picked up his case and delved into it, sitting down at his desk.

"George, my theory is that someone is controlling things."

"Someone in the system?" Callum was prioritizing his messages.

"Or outside it."

" How would that happen?" Callum asked, absently.

"Don't know. *Could* have locked into the system somehow. The system is no great secret. It is certainly accessible." McLintock was standing at the window that looked out over the quadrangle down below, usually so colourful even at this season of the year. He was looking at the frosty grass, the dead bougainvillea flowers, the frozen fountain....

"Sounds unlikely," Callum said, staring at his multicom.

But McLintock was following his own thread. "Especially," he was saying, "since the latest info from Rupert McDonnel at Ghardaia is that station engineers may not actually have been acting on the data they were receiving. May have even been causing the faults in the first place."

Callum, however, was reading a message from Walmsley, something about 'electromagnetic radiation'. He realised he must have spoken the words out loud, because McLintock turned round,

"EMR? Could be," he said, then, realising Callum was talking to himself, "What's that, George, about electromagnetic radiation?"

"Oh, it's a message from Bill Walmsley," Callum said, dismissively. "Says he has been accumulating evidence of illegal crowd control, possibly control or manipulation even over a wider area. Sources are implicating non-ionizing radiation..."

"... or the influence of extraterrestrials? – if you believe in that sort of thing." McLintock was grinning.

"Bill reckons that would be the favoured and official view – alien interference."

"Seriously? I suppose one could believe either to be the cause of civil disturbance anywhere."

"I suppose we could. I suppose we might have to, God forbid!"

Neither said anything for a while. McLintock was the first to speak. "George, it could be that the effect is being exerted on minds, and not on machines."

"Difficult to prove," Callum said, but his brain was doing overtime.

"I am not sure you heard me when I mentioned the station engineers – how they might have been making unnecessary decisions, or failing to make necessary ones. Actually, they were sometimes correcting corrections."

"Yes, yes, I heard you," Callum said, quickly.

"Rogue satellites, George!" McLintock said with a degree of urgency. "There are plenty of satellites up there. Too many for comfort, actually."

"But isn't this beginning to sound like the big-time mind control of science fiction?" Callum protested. "Reminds me of the sort of thing folk probably had nasty dreams about back in the bad old days!" he said as he belatedly and apologetically press-buttoned a chair out and motioned McLintock to it, which the Canadian declined, saying he could keep warmer standing up.

"I only said Mauré *might* have to change his tune a bit."

Callum felt cold, too. He pulled his toga more closely around him. "It never happened, did it?" he said. "Mind control never took off. Discredited. Come on now, Andrew!"

McLintock reckoned Callum might be playing Devil's advocate. "Not so much discredited as disused – fortunately", he said. "As a matter of fact I looked into the theoretical possibility of this kind of explanation – I mean telling the guys 'on' is 'off' or wet is dry or hot is cold, whatever the agency employed to do it, including satellites. I need to know what's happening in my patch. If it's not retrogression or aliens, then what is it? I had to explore all avenues, especially when I heard the same sort of thing had been reported in Arabia. My PAS was encouraging."

"Ah!"

"And now we get suggestions of illegal use of EMR. And I know a bit about satellites, George; we use them routinely in monitoring and control, obviously – geostationary and orbital ones, though that's not to say I know anything about mind control from personal experience!"

"So what are we talking about here? Microwaves, sounds in the skull, very low frequencies, subliminal messages…?"

McLintock laughed. "Maybe, but I fear things have moved on a lot in the electromagnetic spectrum. But I *am* thinking in terms of polar-orbital satellites."

"But those pass at God knows how many miles a second, and how many hundred miles up?"

"New power sources, amazing microengines? No one is inaccessible anywhere. A millisecond may be enough. Obviously, one doesn't want to believe all this – such a backward step. But things come together: my information, your new information, and things begin to take shape. Now I can tell you something, George: whatever the explanation, when I compared the data from different stations with all available data from the Tibesti Space Complex relating to satellite orbits – you will appreciate that I am thorough – I got a tolerably good correlation with one particular polar-orbiting satellite. Not the one we have access to in our work, by the way."

"Correlation? Meaning what, exactly?"

"I mean their precise location every twenty-four hours over an EMR-affected area."

"And activation just over this area?"

"In this case, as far as I can ascertain, yes, in a traceable trail."

"And in Arabia?"

"The same satellite, I think. I suppose climate projects could be considered a good area in which to carry out tests. Not exactly headline-grabbing. Of course, satellites *could* remain activated all the time."

"What a ghastly thought." Callum's head was momentarily filled with fleets of circling satellites beaming poisonous messages unceasingly round the globe. He looked at his watch, and was considering whether he might have to make a change to the way he conducted the afternoon session. "But getting blokes to doubt what they are seeing," he said, "it's pretty crude science, I suppose, and as I suggested, pretty discredited."

"I don't think you realise, George, the level of sophistication your American compatriots reached with mind control. And world wars may have ceased, but brain research hasn't. I can imagine that several changes might occur in the mind in the split second it takes one of those things to pass over."

"You have talked to the climate guys, presumably?" Callum imagined Andrew striding about in a wilting landscape in his green denims, baking in fifty degrees where cloud and rain should be changing everything.

"Not yet. They just know I have been snooping around. They are used to it."

"PAS's? Are they immune to these effects? Are *we* immune?" Callum asked, suddenly feeling vulnerable.

"I detected no effect on my PAS. And I feel our other modifications may give us some protection." Both men were silent a moment. "But who would be doing this? And is there just one satellite involved? For that matter, how could the Government not know about it? And to what ultimate purpose the disruption? Plenty of questions!"

"I have a feeling Harry Beckenthal would be the one to put them to!" Callum said.

CHAPTER NINETEEN

"Beckenthal?"

"And Blunck, and others – probably a very few others – in the Ministry of Emergencies. Lexin suspects they are up to something. In view of your observations, Andrew, this might be where we get some clarification. Let's go and get a bite – if we can. I told Lexin I would meet him for lunch – insofar as the word still has meaning."

McLintock came over from the window and gathered up his things. "It's extraordinary about Beckenthal. How long have you known? Of course, he's into all kinds of space technology. I gathered he was not being too helpful to the Society, but *this!* You *have* been stringing me along!"

Callum laughed. "How could you possibly think that, Andrew? I've only just heard about the radiation, and I have no confirmation that there *is* anything definite on Harry, actually. But as I said, we suspected *something*, or Lexin did, and when I went to Canberra a few days ago and saw Blunck's deputy, Nawale, I smelt a rat and confided in Bill Walmsley of the 'Guardian Interactive' – an old friend. Set him sleuthing. I assume he deploys persons less conspicuous than himself, of course, and that he has been reporting to Van Rensburg. I saw her too. She *appeared* to know nothing at that time. Still pretty fixated on the aliens idea – probably failing anything more convincing. Now if you and Lexin were to go there in a day or two and try to get an extension for the Society, things might become clearer. I'll try and raise Lexin," he said, tapping his intercom and waiting a few seconds. "Must be talking to all and sundry. Come on, let us hope it's a bit warmer in the restaurant."

"*I* go with Lexin!"

"Why not? You have some concrete information that something's going on that shouldn't be. Joanna ought to know about it – if she doesn't already. And if in the meantime you or we find any further info on dodgy satellite activity, that would give added weight to your visit. I am sure Conference will agree to asking for postponement of closure."

"If she doesn't know already...?"

"Only joking. Let's go! And by the way, there was another bit to Walmsley's message. Mauré's been visiting the Emergencies Ministry for months. I'll mention it to Lexin now."

"Do you think *he's* involved. I mean directly."

"Depends what's going on exactly."

Callum admittedly had not been entirely joking when he had questioned what Van Rensburg might or might not know. After all, there were implications in what McLintock had told him. Was not the Government very keen on its 'clean sky' policy? Would it not be keeping track of all new satellite launches from space stations? A couple of questions put to his PAS as they went down the stairs and along to the lobby and the restaurant yielded no more than a measure of reassurance about the direction of their investigations.

The Chatterjee Self-Service Restaurant (the name belonged to a Conference president in the heady times of long ago) was a bare, cold place (despite the soft, comforton veneer) with now much depleted clientele and the most basic menu and, needless to say, no sign of its auto-diet selection menus – or for that matter its quick-meal tablet dispensers. It was mostly a case of stuff from the fast-emptying freezers and vegetarian dishes of ingenious concoction.

Lexin was filled with renewed optimism, he said, following Malinovsky's remarkable address to the Conference and its favourable reception by many. But he was not pleased when, after they had sat down and started into their dishes, hungry enough to praise the desperate efforts of the severely handicapped cooks, he heard about Walmsley's messages. However, he perked up again on learning about

Andrew McLintock's findings in the Sahara and from Arabia. After some discussion, to Callum's relief he agreed that he himself would go with Andrew to Canberra, where, if Conference agreed, they would try and get a 'stay' for the Society at least pro tem. Presenting Joanna van Rensburg with the new – admittedly somewhat slim – covert evidence on mind control would provide some backing for such a request. Whatever else happened as a result, they all agreed it might just take the pressure off the Society.

"I suppose the radiation could be aimed at an occupying entity," Lexin said, and agreed with Callum that it was a pity there was hardly time to look for more evidence, but then Andrew pointed out that he had online access to Tibesti. Perhaps he could try and correlate areas of actual disruption in badly affected parts of Eurasia precisely with the passage of one or more satellites.

"Supposing we could see Van Rensburg in two or three days time," Lexin said, "would that give you time to get hard data, if any, bearing in mind that it should be possible – assuming you can go online – to get an idea of the current geographical distribution of disruptive effects from the Planetary Data Base?"

"It might be difficult, but it's worth a try."

"George'll help you with the maths," Lexin said with a grin.

"I will do what I can," McLintock said.

"And I will try and fix things in Canberra, but first, George, you will have to make sure the delegates are behind us this afternoon about seeing van Rensburg. As for Jean-Paul, if you will bear with me this afternoon I will find a moment to tackle him during the session."

Callum frowned. "Can you do it without giving the game away about our suspicions?"

"I shall be very discreet, and I am sure Jean-Paul will let nothing out."

Callum recounted his recent experiences in the operating theatre, and (for McLintock's benefit) when he was in Canberra. Hearing about the hospital experience Lexin merely nodded as if he was not all that surprised. Evidently he had not known about Ida's cancer diagnosis.

"A pretty clear indication that we are nowhere near out of the woods yet," he said. "I have some more news about Chappel," he added. "Tom was 'over the moon' about an introduction he had promised to give him to a surgeon with special skills in his type of leg fracture. It came quite out of the blue. Said he 'wanted to set them both up for the future'. I find that very encouraging. You know what? I think Chappel is fighting with us." The latest threads in the lives of his People would be drawn together, he told them, when he came to update his website that evening. In spite of the communication difficulties the site was still receiving millions of hits. If Callum wondered at times how or under what form of guidance everything was being coordinated (if that was the right word) in the timeless sphere, he contented himself with the thought that even Malinovsky himself had indicated that the 'mechanics' of it all were far beyond his understanding.

"We may have to mention Beckenthal's absence at Conference," Callum said.

Lexin thought for a moment. "I think we should mention straight away that we're trying to find him, and..."– he paused – "how could I put it? We could add, lightly and with a touch of humour: 'We suspect his business interests are preoccupying him'. It would not be for the first time, would it? At any rate, I am pleased that at last we have a bit of circumstantial evidence for certain suspicions," he said finally, scooping up the last scraps of his chow mien without much relish, "but we must keep it to ourselves – everything. I am confident that Conference trusts us – well, you at least – and will be glad we are intending to make contact with the Government to plead for an extension. Even Anna Polyanova knows we are already getting, quote, 'in better touch with the Lyrians', unquote. I think she just means Societans in general. And I agree with her. She said it to me this morning in those very words, and she was most impressed with Sergei Malinovsky. I think she is very fed up with Mauré, and I know she is reading her PAS. 'Mauré is too proud to consider that his PAS might solve more than his technical problems,' she said." Lexin got up, pushing aside his empty dish. "Whatever our prospects for the future, today a man must eat," he declared. "I will go and see what I can find for us in the way of puddings."

Callum and McLintock, tiring a little of their unidentifiable stew, stared out at a scene that had become only too common: an atmosphere of despondency, occasionally even panic, with many places closed and few people about. As Callum realised, most citizens preferred, if they could, simply to stay in the tranquillity and safety of their own homes. A leaden sky lowered over all. In the distance, no urban transit modules could be seen gliding above the Avenues. Close by, outside, he saw a man begging – or was he asking for some other kind of help? He did look desperate – as the occasional taxi bubble that somebody had been able to grab drew up at the entrance and discharged its load.

And this the unique city, centre of the Society, of hope for intragalactic relations! Yet according to the pictures filling those papers that were still circulating and obtainable, and the television screens on channels still broadcasting, such scenes were not to be compared with those of fighting in Nigerian village markets, rioting in South American shopping plazas, or the widespread turmoil in daily life even round the smart Mediterranean. Callum knew that even where a semblance of order prevailed at national level, this was the result of the most desperate efforts of national governments to keep hold of the situation.

Eventually Lexin returned with portions of the latest edition of Galaxy Tart at least two days old, and they sat eating them, while Callum questioned in his mind how even the improving self-confidence of Societans and their trust in the Bods could possibly prevail against the explosion of so much disorder and – if it proved so to be – so much malevolence.

"As for whether 'terrestrial malevolence' is involved in any of this," Lexin said when Callum – unwisely, perhaps – voiced his thoughts, "we would have to await the evidence. Whether it is or it isn't," he burst out with unaccustomed anger, "I am just sorry that there are those who cannot get to see my website, or cannot read it. Not because it is my story. It is not. It is everybody's story"

Lexin's way of not talking about the coming Dark Ages, a Callum in negative mode said to himself as they joined delegates returning to the Hall. Then he could have kicked himself for his pessimism and faithlessness. McLintock was offering much more encouragement to Lexin in his despondency. It was interesting, he said, that some latest newspaper headlines featured a vast but relatively orderly protest march along the Avenida Principal of Brasilia triggered merely by absence of information in the public sphere. "Amazingly, your good name was on many lips, Lexin," he had told him, "and was displayed on banners."

In the afternoon the mood was at first edgy, conducted as it was against a background of breaking news of severe unrest in cities across Eurasia that seemed to mark a significant escalation in events. The

Vienna city administration and executive had collapsed after weeks of dissension, while east as far as Baku whole populations were out on the streets of towns and villages. Lexin had to admit that it was very hard now to ignore a feeling of malign influences of *some* kind. And on such a scale! It should be noted, however, that in some other areas, notably in parts of India and China, orderly anti-government demo's were being reported -- and even tolerated.

A few delegates were even in favour of requesting immediate resumption of all the Society's activities on the basis of Malinovsky's positive stance on Lexin's experiences and fresh proposals on wormhole operation. Others wanted 'partial' resumption. None of this found any widespread support, however (and certainly not from the Professor himself), although his positive position itself did. Lexin felt they were waiting for a lead, but Callum seemed to be biding his time. Things were brought to a head by Leonard Mackenzie calling for a resolution to demand a definitive and detailed statement from the Government on the world situation and the probable threat faced.

"At least," he maintained, "we shall know what they know. Otherwise, what basis is there for us to act upon?"

Lexin was relieved that nothing much came of Professor Mackenzie's proposal. Such a move would at best have led nowhere and at worst provoked unpredictable events. It was so vital above all to maintain the momentum of trust in Sergei Malinovsky and put his theories to the test. A few, including two or three Mauré supporters, agreed with Mackenzie, but there was no rush either to support or to oppose the resolution, which was dropped. Clearly, Callum had been right to bide his time. Lexin was sure the reticence of the majority, when given plenty of opportunity to have their say on Mackenzie's proposal, did not represent indifference. They were obviously giving their synthesizers a good work over, and it was gratifying that George was not immune to the growing confidence Professor Malinovsky was inspiring among the delegates.

Mauré, normally punctilious about the use of the 'speak' button, had been pressing it for some time, and now rose in some frustration to a resurgence of vocal support. Lexin, however, deciding it was now or never, stepped in hoping the chairman would again give him precedence, which Callum did.. It was not a popular decision among Mauré's supporters.

"Mr. Vice-President," Lexin began amid the barracking, "I do hope we can soon decide on our 'status' and future action as a Society. However," he went on, noting more relief than annoyance on the Vice-President's face at his interruption, "perhaps at pain of repetition I could ask Jean-Paul again whether he could enlighten us any further on what he believes it is that we are facing. I am aware, Jean-Paul," he said, turning to face him, "that you have been in touch with the Ministry of Emergencies recently."

If Jean-Paul was as surprised as many others by Lexin's question he did not show it, and the noise of barracking gave way to absolute silence as he replied with customary suavity, "I have been in discussions about hypothetical types of threat. They were also interested in my theories on evil influences. This was some time ago."

"Types of threat such as what, if I may ask?" Callum asked.

"In the first instance, disruption in various ways."

"Disruption?"

"Reversal of the progress achieved in the world by our efforts. I should add that in the worst scenario there might be no limit on what superior powers might do to us in the way of total subjugation, or even worse things against which we could have no defence – as I was intimating earlier."

"Such as?"

"Malign interventions defying the limits of our imagination."

There were no smiles at that, but nor were there any gasps of horror from the packed meeting, only a bemused silence.

"And you were able to assist them, the Government?"

"Of course, from my knowledge of sociology, psychology, and yes, the sources and nature of evil, I was able to advise them on some forms of attack that we might hope to counter." Mauré paused in that pompous way of his, most perfectly parading his well-padded elegance. "Mr. Vice-President, it is in the present chaotic and demoralizing situation that I see the clearest signs yet of the external threat which I fear – signs foreshadowed in your visions, Lexin, which as I explained, embody the beginnings of a process of destruction of the human spirit."

With an effort, Lexin remained calm: "And can you tell us how the Emergencies Ministry hopes to counter these assaults, in whatever form they may come, and when, because...?"

"...I'm afraid I am forbidden to speak of that."

Lexin had the impression of a Maurian camp stunned as well as silent, shocked by the realisation of the closeness of their hero's involvement with the Government, and that it was more than a case of his theories simply giving credence to the Government's actions.

"Fine, Jean-Paul," a supporter exclaimed, "but surely you might voice the Society's desire for greater urgency on the part of the Government, more information?" One or two others followed.

"Well what do you say to that, Jean-Paul?" Callum asked. Was there a suggestion of anxiety in the Vice-President's voice? Lexin thought not. He was sure Callum realised that if Mauré was involved in setting up a satellite-based EMR programme he would only be likely to say any more if it was totally above board and open to scrutiny.

"I have supplied the Government with all the information I can," Mauré replied. "Whatever it is possible to do, I am sure it will have been done, or will be done. And whatever can be made public will have been, or will be, made public whenever possible."

Apparently no-one wished to query or applaud all this any more than they wished to press him on defence preparations, but his supporters roused themselves to applaud him as he sat down. Lexin could not help asking himself whether he had gone to the Government uninvited, or whether it had been at their invitation.

Meanwhile the Vice-President, with more than a suggestion of a smile in rosy cheeks glowing (Lexin guessed) with animation rather than with overheating beneath his voluminous and no doubt very adaptable toga, was saying, confidently, "Nothing that I have heard today leads me to conclude otherwise than that we should ask for an extension of our deadline? Is it the view of delegates? We'll take a good break, then decide."

The remnants of the world's telecommunication systems were enough to convey a strongly affirmative answer which thus came not just from those present but from the tens of thousands of Societans – possibly more – with whom their delegates were in direct contact. It seemed quite possible that even Mauré's Societan supporters out there in a world harsher than they had ever known were more prepared now to give some credence to Lexin's visions (and to the importance of their PAS), and maybe even more so than to Mauré (or the vague reassurances of the World Government). Few 'noes' were registered when Callum proposed that Lexin should go and put their case to Van Rensburg, or when Lexin suggested Andrew McLintock should go with him. Jean-Paul Mauré's expression betrayed no clue as to his feelings.

* * *

Lexin and Andrew McLintock were in Canberra by nine a.m. local time, the SST journey having been remarkably uneventful in the circumstances. Lexin had had great difficulty arranging a meeting with Van Rensburg for a discussion on postponement of closure, but in the end she agreed via a secretary to meet them in her office. McLintock had booked a room in the cosmopolitan waterfront area of Kingston, and from there they took a municipal taxi to World Government House, McLintock no doubt glad to be back in his time-honoured khaki shirt and shorts in the summer warmth of the southern hemisphere.

"My fellow Societan, Lexin explained, introducing him to a slightly testy, trouser-suited First Minister, has shared important information with me that *may* be relevant in connection with what you were discussing with George Callum at your meeting with him a few days ago. He will explain in a moment. And by the way, we have still not caught up with Harry Beckenthal."

"I have not seen him, either. But be that as it may, I have to tell you straight away," Van Rensburg said, "that neither the Assembly nor the Government is keen on your continuing. We may be facing the worst threat in Earth's history since the giant asteroid. The trouble is that we have to face the possibility that the Society has provided the vehicle for interference, even an invasion, by aliens."

The First Minister's offices – situated in a modern wing of the originally twenty-third century complex – reflected the contemporary 'mysterioso' style: calm, reflective, with studied patterns and inviting recesses. Lexin was momentarily distracted by a framed painting, illuminated in one of the recesses, of a pretty little South African mole threatened, apparently, with extinction. Collecting himself, he said, "You are referring to some connection with the explosions...?"

"I am not referring to any one thing specifically." The First Minister's expression was uneasy, irritated.

"...or to my experiences out of time, my 'People' (forgive the expression) trying to restore their broken lives. You are somehow connecting that..."

"...To be honest, Lexin, I am neither connecting it nor not connecting it. The point is, there may be an alien presence, or imminent presence."

"What evidence is there, if I may ask? I hardly need to tell you how important it is for us to know this."

Clearly she would have preferred them to just go away. They were still standing. Facing them, and raising herself to her full, small stature like an interviewing headmistress, Van Rensburg reacted with barely disguised anger:

"Indeed it is important for all of us, but I cannot discuss this. We continually review all the evidence."

"Andrew has some evidence, obtained in the course of his agricultural work, suggesting the possibility of experimental mind control." Joanna was regarding them closely now, her eyes moving from one to the other. The female secretary, who had been recording everything, looked up for a brief moment. Was this a delicate area? "But I am referring to control of human origin that may be the source of at least some of the present disruption."

"Mind control? That is impossible!" Van Rensburg exclaimed.

"Control quite possibly through subtle manipulation by electromagnetic radiation. I understand Bill Walmsley..."

"Mr. Walmsley did inform me of something, and I did look into that and assured myself – and him, I hope, that there were perfectly good explanations."

"I have summarised my evidence in these documents rather hastily put together," McLintock said, stepping forward and handing her an envelope.

"You had better sit down, both of you," she said after a moment's hesitation, motioning them to two interactive, deep-upholstered chairs as with a deep sigh she took the papers out of their packet and went over to her spacious desk and laid them out on it. She sat down and thumbed through them, then read the page of conclusions.

After perhaps five minutes of intense concentration she stood up, went over to a window and stood staring out of it for perhaps two more minutes without saying anything. In spite of her known grittiness, she looked slight and vulnerable now. Turning round, she said, "You must understand that it would not be out of the question for a defence system to employ satellite-based methods. But this!"

"First Minister, a colleague in the Arabian Desert has come up with some similar information probably involving the same satellite. Added to that, my researches of the last few days have suggested more widespread illegal use of satellites," McLintock continued, a slight urgency now in the Canadian drawl. "Foci of serious social disruption developing in several cities in southern Russia, and through Iraq, *may* be correlated with the EMR activation of another polar-orbiting satellite."

"Am I not right in thinking a polar orbit covers the entire Earth – eventually. Is it so easy to implicate particular satellites?"

"First Minister, I believe the effects, or particularly a trail of effects, should be able to be accurately correlated with the passage of a particular polar-orbiting satellite."

"Look, I do not doubt there is great anxiety about the situation, but many governments in various parts of the world have nevertheless been able to calm the fears of their populations..."

"I'm not so sure of that, First Minister," McLintock protested.

"Well sure, all's not well, but as for all this about mind control, I feel you are being quite irrational."

"EMR is widely used in psychotherapy, and with high levels of selectivity and precision, and long ago it was capable of being used militarily at very long range.."

"What about normal human failure, or what about the retrogressive effects that have been so much spoken about? What about general anxiety, tensions thus arising...?" She paused, seemed for a moment to be waiting for an answer, then she continued, "Are they not bad enough? As for the real threat," she added, assertively, "my Emergencies Minister informs me that we are prepared."

"Since, therefore, our defences are prepared to confront what is surely still a highly theoretical threat of alien interference or attack," Lexin said, after a moment's silence, "and we the Society are not undertaking wormhole testing or even decipherment work, might we not therefore be granted a stay of execution?"

"Highly theoretical? I hope you are not making light of this, Lexin!"

"With respect, the Deputy Emergencies Minister did not greatly impress George Callum. I hope the Minister is not pulling the wool over *your* eyes."

Van Rensburg was fixing him with her steely glare. "So do I," she said, angrily. "You will not deny," she added, bitterly, "that something went drastically wrong with your work, I mean not just yours but all the Society's work?"

"I would not deny it," Lexin said.

"Not just some errors, but something...something of a different order? Something that changed everything...that *has* changed everything?"

"I do not deny it."

She went to the window and surveyed the view once again. "Nor does Jean-Paul Mauré, I am told", she said, turning towards them, "possibly the foremost expert in his field."

"Ah, yes, Jean-Paul. Very likely he is. He mentioned some advice to you."

"*Did* he?" She was livid. "And yet you..."

"...Most of us do not agree with his belief in *alien* intervention, Joanna."

A few more questions followed, mainly about the recent deliberations of the Conference, punctuated by reflective silences during which they had plenty of opportunity to study the threatened fauna of the southern hemisphere (of which, judging from the illustrations adorning the walls, the First Minister was obviously a champion), and she in dwelling on the arboreal calm beyond the window had time to cool down considerably.

"Very well" she said. "They won't like this, and I don't either, really, despite your evident sincerity, but since the Society is not actively engaged in decipherment or testing I will try and set aside my deep misgivings and get them to agree to a postponement, say one month, initially – always supposing we have that much time. The position could then be reviewed."

They had the impression it was the only way she could think of to get rid of them.

* * *

Bill Walmsley did not seem surprised at their cool reception by Joanna when, disguised in journalists' garb like himself, Lexin arrived with McLintock late in the evening at a rendezvous in the under-illuminated garden of a bar in Kingston and detailed the latest findings. Still in his shorts, and just a light zip-up jacket slung over the corner of the chair back beside him in case the day's heat should fade more quickly than he hoped, McLintock had the look of a horse restless at the starting gate. Lexin hoped he was not going to be too frustrated by the rate of progress in their enquiries.

Walmsley mentioned that he had passed on to the First Minister the evidence on illegal use of low-energy EMR. She had explained it away in a brief communication. "But I reckon there *is* something going on," he said, "and your information appears to confirm that. I feel Blunck may be playing a dangerous game – if it's him. Experimenting maybe, but only a game. As for terrorising the planet, though, I'm not sure that fits. I am short on new leads," he admitted, "but I am asking myself these questions: What sort of a guy is Blunck? Emergencies Ministry top-brass disposing of idle forces (until the recent emergencies at least), with no battles to fight and badly bored. And Beckenthal? Well, an engineer entrepreneur with plenty of interest in making and launching satellites and possibly not caring much how or where he does it."

Beckenthal's inaccessibility was still central to Lexin's suspicions. He had not been seen at the palatial offices of Antipodean Planetary Systems in North Ryde – officially his cousin's business – for over a month, though this was not unusual; Lexin knew his interests were widely spread.

"And what about Faust?..." Walmsley was about to go on, but he broke off suddenly to change the subject to some triviality as the aboriginal waiter approached to deposit a second round of drinks and paused to point out how visible the Southern Cross was that night.

Walmsley craned his neck round quickly. "I guess you're right," he replied before any of the others could, adding when the waiter had disappeared, "Just testing to get an idea of who we were... see if we were Aussies. Seems they...somebody's got some spies out."

"Testing *us*?" Lexin could not say he was surprised, actually, in all that fancy gear.

"Journalists in general. I expect our reactions would have told him something."

"My fear is that it is all going to take too long" McLintock said. "I probably understated my findings to Van Rensburg, if anything. Someone's playing a very dirty game. So many reports now." As Lexin appreciated, Andrew found it difficult to sit still and do nothing. He did himself, too, at the moment. So many obstacles, *so little power to do anything*. Sometimes he even found himself thinking like those others who wanted to run straight for the wormhole terminal. Wasn't Malinovsky nearly ready? But then, what about his People and their aims and ambitions? Ida? Red Hair? Hardly. He supposed one sometimes had to think the unthinkable in order to turn round and come back on plan.

"I take your point, Andrew," Walmsley said. "But to return to Deputy First Minister Faust: American Right. Virtually unknown, rarely seen. Faust might be going for a 'world cleansing'."

"Scary! Even in my anti-American moments," Lexin said, "I don't really go with that. Always thought he was pretty sound."

"He could be trying to cool things down – from behind the scenes," McLintock suggested, and then after a pause he said, "It's not Mauré, is it?" clearly expecting the answer 'no'.

"No way. I doubt he has ever had any such ambitions," Lexin said, trying not to fiddle with the false buttons on the upturned cuffs of his braided and embroidered jacket and the sides of his breeches, "or that there is any malevolence in him, though he may talk frightening stuff. I must say I sometimes ponder if while we rake around here a plot is being controlled from some station in the Gobi desert or some clandestine hub in Paris or London."

Walmsley seemed to be in more of a hurry with his beer than usual. "I don't think so," he said, quietly. " I think it's here. I *have* got one or two others in my sights," he continued. "The Filipino Alviola – in the executive. They are supposed to have sent him here to get rid of him. His country was going downhill. He's one of these scientists with radical views on genetic regulation of populations, for instance, not to mention moulding of the solar system. He's quite 'anti' the Society. Or there's Ramzan – a Pakistani industrialist working for Emergencies. He's one of the resurgent Islamist radicals, again a bit anti-Society..." He lowered his empty glass gently. "But I think we should go from this place, and not in too much of a rush," he said, already lifting his sturdy frame agilely but unhurriedly out of his seat and pulling his fleshy jowls into a grin just detectable in the low light. As he hailed the third taxi bubble that came along outside he said, "Fear not, things are winding up."

"They had better do it quickly" Lexin said with unusual gravity.".

"Steady, though," Walmsley warned, "or we could blow the whole thing. And look after Lexin, Andrew. Some avid supporter of Mauré may bear him a grudge!"

Later, Lexin and Andrew McLintock took a private box at the Murranbea Theatre in town, and saw 'A day in the Chaotic Life of Loboste Henriques'. It was a humorous tale of misunderstanding and reconciliation in a circus. It was a pleasant antidote to the troubles of the day for them, as it certainly was for the audience in general until the performance was cut short by a lighting failure just before the end, with resulting panic. They were lucky enough to find a taxi, paying it off in a busy night spot and walking through unlit streets from there to where they were staying.

The return to Galaxy took two days. Fortunately there was a day in hand before the next meeting of the Conference, so that Lexin was back in time for it and, invited now to join Callum on the rostrum, was able to report to a packed Conference that the closure date had indeed been extended by four weeks. Naturally, no mention could be made of the details of his interview with the First Minister. Lexin felt moved to ask delegates to share with each other privately, in the meeting, their experiences involving his People. From this it was clear that much sympathy and indeed respect centred on Ida – who having shown such resilience in dealing with AIDS was now suffering from cancer too. It was a terrible blow for Tom – and so disappointing for Lenica.

However, there was light in the darkness. A couple of weeks later, a delegate involved in transport engineering reported some clues to an understanding of the current SST problems, and others subsequently began to bridge gaps left after decades of what was now seen to be poor decipherment in various areas. Indeed, until the present critical situation intervened it had already been possible to shed light on a swathe of half-solved problems ranging from the reconciliation of clashing religious, ethical and philosophical viewpoints to that of opposing views in urban planning and the appreciation of pictorial art!

Nevertheless, Lexin made it clear that in his opinion the various welcome improvements achieved by greater recourse to PAS's would never halt the overall downward trend resulting from cessation of decipherment. He agreed with Malinovsky that the key to the all important resumption of decipherment, and the rest of the Society's work that stemmed from it, was to prove that time-crossing difficulties had been overcome – if only because this was the way the world, and especially the Government, saw it.

When somebody suggested replacing Beckenthal as their representative in the World Government and Assembly, Callum agreed this might be necessary but asked delegates to be patient. He said afterwards that the trust in him implied by their acceptance of this delaying tactic was most gratifying and a great relief. It was only then, he told Lexin later, that he realised no-one had hitherto even mentioned Beckenthal, so that no explanations for his absence had been necessary. Meanwhile the ever-present Mauré remained silent, and despite some hints from Bill Walmsley of a possible breakthrough no tangible evidence of a plot had emerged, to the frustration not least of Andrew McLintock, so far removed from his beloved North Africa.

The truth was that now, with such chinks of light appearing in the darkness and in their own minds, many said they felt overwhelmed by a desire to head for their own countries in order to offer their encouragement, insights, and in some cases special skills, not least for alleviation of the social and economic chaos. Lexin, however, made no bones about telling them at a meeting in the middle of February of 2454 that even if they could get home in what would soon be a virtually transport-less world, here in the Conference was where they were most needed. Here resided the beleaguered heart of a Society in whose hands the future of Mother Earth truly rested and where their presence and their solidarity were still critical.

"I suppose we shall think twice about letting our synthesizers get rusty in the future at any rate," Callum said as they were leaving the Hall after the meeting, which was not prolonged in view of the persistent cold.

Lexin thought he looked pretty tired. It was not surprising, he thought, since in the end, despite his earlier persistent 'disbelief', probably no-one had done more to keep the Society on the rails. "Well I'm glad you see it now, George, anyway," he replied. It was a salutary thought, though, thinking of his own words about the Society's responsibility for the safety of Mother Earth, that with no more than a dispensation to allow some crucial laboratory tests at the Mission Station, a renewed attempt to send and receive signals, being an all-or-nothing event, would be the sternest possible test of Societans' genuine trust in the Bods.

It was thus gratifying to hear from Callum quite soon that under a now less reticent Edmonde Lamonte the Wormhole Research and Operations people had really got their act together despite Mackenzie's doubts, and made promising contact with Lyra. Many personnel, already using their PAS to good effect, had formed a good relationship with the Bods so that when the time came to resume use of the wormhole the procedure would be carried out with input from both ends – ourselves and the Bods – via a highly complex PAS conferencing system. Altogether it seemed a vindication of Malinovsky's understanding of the Lyrians' intentions.

"I guess we have to play it their way, Lexin," Callum said.

"I guess so, George," he replied,

By March, tension was mounting everywhere, made worse by the fact that the Government seemed chronically unable to say or do anything to alleviate it. It was at this time that in a survey by McLintock identifying further separate areas of population disruption across Asia apparently due to satellite-based EMR, and sadly resulting in many more fatalities than previously, news emerged of the horrifying story of the boys of Szechuan.

Acting on an unaccountable impulse to cause harm to their own friends and families, it was said, boys in a remote town had poisoned the food in the local supermarket with chemicals from a local agrochemical store. It seemed to Lexin to mark the beginning of something of a different order. One might have been inclined to liken the story to one of those unthinkably awful one-off events in a comparatively remote and primitive place until other equally bizarre and deadly events began to be recorded. McLintock said their complex nature suggested extremely sophisticated timing and control. At about the same time, reports emerged of a sudden increase in a strange but debilitating sickness among young babies in a swathe across Africa and Eurasia. In this case he thought one satellite was involved.

Although it might have appeared incongruous, even obscene when viewed from outside, in the face of these shocking events a mood of calm solidarity nevertheless prevailed in the Conference, with many delegates even reporting a scarcely accountable optimism among Societans in their regions regarding ultimate outcomes. However, if many were having new insights it was not the time to be blazoning them to the world at large, and if it was possible to speak of a new enlightenment it amounted as much as anything else to an only too clear understanding of past deficiencies.

"As for the present," Callum said during a short break over a drink in his office during a Conference meeting later in the month, "despite the optimism in some quarters I am not at all pleased with the way things are going. These show the pattern of disruptions developing this past week as plotted by the Planetary Database..." He was picking up some papers and spreading them on his desk. His expression was grim, the cheeks less rosy. "I am beginning to see elements of a pattern, a complex spatiotemporal rhythm of events, probably also of different types of effect, as though everything is indeed being controlled automatically according to a programme and using many satellites." A bewildered Lexin was staring at a map of the world decorated with variously coloured and *apparently* randomly distributed symbols. "The personal info networks suggest I am not the only one to be noticing it, either," Callum said. The news was very bad; Lexin knew it. It confirmed all his fears "A truly malevolent programme," Callum was saying. But Lexin was beginning to receive an urgent message directly in his brain, and George Callum's words were becoming a background irritation. The message was an automated one. Lexin's mouth went dry.

"Better stick to your guns, George," he croaked when he had finished listening. "Message from somebody at 'Guardian Interactive'". He played back the message: 'Regret Bill Walmsley dead. Daley of 'New Australian' arrested at the newspaper's offices in Sussex Street together with Blunck and others 'on charges of involvement in illegal EMR activities and suspicion of being accessories to murder.'

CHAPTER TWENTY

"So are you coming to join us?" Felicitas asked.

"Don't know whether I can stand Mackenzie, Mother."

It was three days after the arrests. Lenica had been gloomily examining her blotchy face in her mirror when Felicitas, determinedly dressed for dinner in a vadolin and velvet sage-green cocktail dress against (as she said) the 'shocks and despond of a world riven with anxiety', came and sat herself on her bed just as voices were heard in the living space.

"Lexin says he has changed remarkably, Lenica. Leonard was very impressed with his spotting of Beckenthal. He was actually enquiring after Lexin's People today, apparently, believe it or not. I have a feeling that his wormhole chief, the very unassuming little Frenchman… Lamonte, isn't it? has taken Malinovsky very seriously, and the rest are following suit."

"Yes, I'm very glad Lamonte has taken the bit between his teeth. Malinovsky's found a valuable ally!"

"…and Mackenzie, feeling upstaged, is pulling himself together."

"Well good for him. And you can't ignore Lexin's People these days, can you? They're even getting on the back pages of the papers, like a cartoon serial. No cartoon, and sales plummet."

"So I am told. I suppose that has got to be good."

"Yes, Mother, though I don't think the editors appreciate they are real people now to most of the population – like they are to you and me."

"No. By the way," Felicitas said, "Leonard was so impressed when Lexin told him I had seen Red Hair on her feet."

"*You* have?"

" Those were Lexin's words when I told *him*. He doesn't know everything does he? Anyway," Felicitas added with a wry smile, "didn't he ask me to follow her, come what may? And didn't I, in the camp? He went to check it with his PAS."

"I suppose it's so important."

"His PAS said, 'Trust your mother!'" They both laughed. "Yes, Red Hair is looking loads better. It's good news, dear. It's already in 'Lexin's People'. But now to the present," Felicitas said, springing up. "Céleste is here, too. She will be a bit lost without you. You know what she is like. George and Fiona will be late. Yet another emergency meeting of the Crisis Committee." Then she saw that Lenica, still examining herself in the mirror, was crying. She went over, and they silently embraced.

"Sorry, I'm feeling very low," Lenica said. "I suppose they are all talking ten to the dozen about the crisis. Tell me, why do you always assume I can humour Céleste?"

"Don't imagine I don't understand about Céleste," Felicitas said, gently. "It is that you are basically a sympathetic person."

"Really? Sympathy! It's poor old Xiaofeng I'm sorry for, never mind silly Céleste. Mother, it's good news about Red Hair, of course it is, but no matter how quickly they reckon they can sort things out in Sydney – if they can –, and whatever else remains for Societans with their best efforts to do, there is unfinished business with Tom and Ida. I know that now."

"And your future depends on their future, yes?" Felicitas said after a few moments' silence.

"If only it were only mine that depended on it!"

"Lenica!" Felicitas hugged her tighter. "It doesn't seem right that you personally should have to bear all that, you and Xiaofeng, and you in the state you are in."

There was still something very Earth-bound about her mum. It was always an effort for her, that projection into the 'timeless sphere'. There was good reason, of course, for her worries, knowing how deeply both her offspring had become involved. Lenica understood that. It was only a couple of days before that she had been able to get through to her beloved to tell him about her latest 'trial', her latest 'burden'– she did not know how else to describe her cervical cancer diagnosed but a few days previously and for which she was receiving out-patient treatment. Like Ida's, no doubt her own, too, was AIDS-linked – even present knowledge, it seemed, did not allow the viral reservoir to be banished all at once. But there *was* no way she could think of it as anything but part of her burden, something 'contrived'. She hoped that was not an impolite word to use of those possessing unfathomable depths of galactic compassion. Whatever else, it had all been another big blow for Xiaofeng. "It may not seem right, Mother, but to me my new illness is the surest possible indication that they matter, Tom and Ida – if that doesn't sound too self-centred on my part!"

Felicitas sighed. "I know, I know what you are saying," she said, "but I *am* your mother. Don't think I am criticising you – how could I on this matter?" Lenica had moved away now and was standing by the window. "…But Xiaofeng is very fond of you. Supposing you *can* get married."

Lenica knew her mother was thinking 'assuming she is cured of AIDS but loses important bits of her insides because of the cancer'. "He can think for himself," she said. "It's hard for him, but he *is* reorientating, you know, after his theories let him down. It was a brave try, his 'guilt' theory, to explain the Society's failings and the mess the world is in, but it's behind us now. Anyway, nobody's into theories any more, and with the Crisis Committee doing nothing and Jean-Paul in the wilderness the Society will take Lexin's lead. Hopefully dear Xiaofeng may come to see the light fully – and understand why, if it so turns out, I have no procreative capacity. There is no way I can opt out of my twenty-first century obligations now."

"I know that really, I know that," Felicitas said. "Lenica, everything seems so dark – out there as well!"

It was true that darkness had fallen very early that evening. Lenica had noticed it.

"You saved up some stuff before I was born didn't you?" she said. "They might be able to do some reconstruction." She saw her mother wince, and didn't pursue the subject of storage of her placental cells. "But as I say, it's not all over yet, though I'm damned if I see which way things are going to go. I can't seem to find Ida any more – for myself, I mean. Maybe I'm losing my brain capacity like a lot of others are."

Lenica went and straightened her bed. Even that was an effort. The only sound was that of an unusually boisterous wind outside.

"I've really got to have a rest," she said.

"I don't know about Jean-Paul 'in the wilderness', as you put it," Felicitas said. "In prison, more like."

"Oh, Mauré! I don't think Lexin takes that view."

"I suppose the point is who clears up the mess?"

"The Bods may need to."

"The Bods! What, after all that's happened? What a charge to place upon one's friends!"

"At least they might if it's not too late!"

"My God, my children! You terrify me," Felicitas said, flinging a good thick lamb's wool stole round her shoulders in preparation for making her entry, the day having been dark and the warm embrace of the urban canopy – that 'epitome of modern civilization now so rudely taken from us', as she put it – being absent.

Leonard Mackenzie and Lexin were standing by the closed glass doors to the terrace. Lexin was defending himself against the incoming draught and the general heating deficit with a toga, while Leonard had donned a tweedy outfit that was no doubt as cosy as it was dated. Felicitas heard Leonard say that he thought even if things started to improve now that Blunck and his fellow conspirators in Emergencies, together with newspaper impresario Daley and the infamous Beckenthal, were being held by the police, it would take at least a week to get everybody off the SST's.

Robert, who had seen to everybody's drinks, was conversing with Céleste pending his mistress's arrival. Plump Céleste was draped in a home-made shawl as bulky as a small blanket from beneath which there emerged baggy, tartan trousers that made no concessions to style. How marvellous it was to have Robert, Felicitas mused. He could converse – as far as his position allowed him – as well as any human. In fact better than most! She signalled to Robert that she would get her own drink. At the same time, she heard Céleste saying how brave she thought Lenica was.

"I'm sure I couldn't be like that," she was saying, "so unselfish. Do you think she will recover?"

"I don't know, Mrs. Mackenzie. I indeed hope so, but for various reasons it's very difficult to predict," Robert replied, vanishing as Felicitas approached with her Manzo. Felicitas noticed Céleste's puzzled look at the robot's response.

"I couldn't help overhearing you, Céleste dear," she said. "Sometimes it seems you are even more naïve than I am. The whole world's in a mess, never mind Lenica."

"Yes, but with the healing of time?" Céleste whined.

"Time is just what there isn't enough of, Céleste." How could she explain to this simple woman her growing but unwelcome acceptance of the painful fact that in a certain way – and certainly a way hard to explain to Céleste – her *own* future, everybody's future, might somehow be wrapped up with Lenica's, and the future might be very short? Her thoughts were interrupted, and she was relieved of further comment, by another announcement from Leonard that the Sussex Street offices had not suffered any kind of damage prior to or during the police swoop, and those arrested had very little warning.

"Hopefully there should be something to work on now," he was saying, when, about to lift his glass again, he seemed suddenly to be conscious of his omission in not noticing her, for in five strides he had reached her, planting a discreet kiss on each cheek. "Dear Felie, how could I ignore you even for two seconds. It must be the stresses of the day...and Lexin being so gloomy."

"Not gloomy," Lexin countered, overhearing and coming closer. "Just thoughtful."

"Now Lexin" Mackenzie said, "you were starting to express doubts to me about whether it will be possible to reconstruct...I mean work out... the programme of terrorization, world domination or whatever it is, which you fear these criminals may have perpetrated. So there may be no solid evidence with which to bring them to justice." Felicitas knew Leonard was paraphrasing for Céleste's sake, probably taking care to avoid saying anything more specific, like mentioning the words 'satellites' or 'mind control', which would not have been a good thing for Céleste to go blabbing about.

"I think I follow you, Leonard dear," Céleste said, "even if the details escape me."

"It may be possible to bring them to justice, if solely on a charge of murder," Lexin said. "Regarding the programme, I should point out that despite not having had much time they might have been able to destroy much of the evidence of any illegal EMR activities – according to my 'Guardian' contact."

"Anyway," Celeste whispered, "let's hope they have at least switched everything off...I mean, the computer programme, or whatever it is."

It was only when Lexin had heard about Walmsley and the arrests that he remembered something his mother had said to him after the events at Brasilia. Lenica, she said, had noticed the Australian newspaper tycoon Robert Daley there. She had gone on about how "the ambitious young man not that much older than her brother had not so long ago inherited a fortune from a newspaper proprietor uncle and gone into journalism himself after turning down a professorship in cybernetics and linguistics at Adelaide". He had just bought up the 'New Australian' which was moving into new premises in central Sydney (together with the 'Sydney World News' and other media organs in which he had a commanding interest). These, as she now realised, were the sixty-something storey state-of-the-art premises newly opened with much fanfare in Sussex Street. Now, at any rate, things began to fit together, although any thoughts of a journalist terrorising the planet had never crossed more than a corner of Lexin's mind, there to be instantly and thankfully dismissed.

It seemed that minutes after the 'Guardian Interactive' offices (fortunately still well staffed) were alerted to Walmsley's shooting, and the dumping of his body on waste ground, by a disseminated tracer tag, a colleague obviously previously delegated by the journalist to act in such an eventuality was in touch with Van Rensburg implicating Daley (whom Walmsley had presumably come to suspect). The same person probably communicated the news to Lexin. The police swooped immediately. It was not at once clear why the plot required the 'execution' of Bill Walmsley, but his death must have brought forward the arrest of all the men. It was followed by a complete news blackout for twenty-four hours, during which time Lexin was able to confirm a mounting suspicion that Beckenthal was the main contractor in the provision of communications technology for the new offices in Sussex Street.

"Well if it *isn't* 'switched off' – or worse – at least we'll have something to go on" Mackenzie was declaring as he strode over to the bar where Robert materialised to produce a half-litre of his favourite ale. This caused Felicitas to catch her breath momentarily on remembering that owing to the cancellation of cargo airship flights beer transport from Europe was almost at zero and her stocks likewise (Robert *had* warned her). "If it *is* 'switched off', or has been deleted without trace," Mackenzie continued, oblivious of how close he was becoming to being denied his Budweiser as well, "we'll just have to take it from there. The detainees might talk, for a start, or we might be able to re-access the programme. But just give us time, and – assuming *something* is left – I think we would surely crack it...the codes, the system, the programme, whatever it is. Not so, Lexin?"

"Yes, surely, isn't that right?" Céleste chirruped, drawing her stole closer round her. "Aren't we always able to crack codes these days?"

Felicitas hated herself for thinking so low of Céleste, hanging onto Leonard's words and reducing them from the mundane to the ridiculous. Not so low as she thought of the miscreants, though. It was a big enough shock for an innocent population to come to realise that those responsible for protecting them had been abusing them. But mind control! That was one of the horrors of ancient times and no mention was made of it in the information as yet released, in which, while notions of an alien attack were firmly put aside, vague references were made to 'brain washing experiments'. The media – those still publishing – were rife with much more speculative rumours, and with very real stories, not least from Galaxy City itself, of schools in difficulties through teacher incompetence, industrial plants closing for safety reasons... There could be little doubt, now, that some kind of mind control was going on.

"Well come on, Lexin," Mackenzie said, pursuing his point with some annoyance, "We're not talking about alien intelligences, are we? We'll surely crack it, won't we?"

Lexin had started to say something when two shadows that were definitely not aliens appeared on the darkening terrace outside the glass doors. "I see George and Fiona are here," he said.

Looking out at the passing figures, Felicitas noticed again how black it was out there, with no sign of the city lights. That was peculiar. At the same time she was becoming aware of an unaccustomed wind discovering hitherto unimportant chinks in the windows. Instead of waiting to be let in, the Callums passed round the side of the house. That was a bit strange, but she knew Robert would have become aware of them and would let them in at the rear. A couple of minutes later he appeared:

"There is a sandstorm, Mr. Solberg. Dr. Callum and Mrs. Callum are absolutely covered in sand. Perhaps Mrs. Solberg could help me find some alternative clothing for Mrs. Callum. Dr. Callum is already taking a shower, and I have put out some clothes."

Felicitas went to meet Fiona, who was cheerful but exhausted. She could hardly believe it, she said. They had never seen anything like it. It had got in their eyes and everywhere. Veronica had gone home earlier, so Felicitas looked out what she could for Fiona. When she returned they were still talking about the sand. She told them that Fiona had had to go and lie down in her room. George had told Robert that the sand had drifted to knee height in places and walking was difficult everywhere. Practically nothing but sand was moving in the city.

"Why are all these things carrying on when I thought they had caught the people?" It was Céleste again. "Does that mean they can't have switched off?"

"Maybe it does," Felicitas said, hoping it would keep the poor woman quiet.

"Do I detect from what you are *not* saying, Lexin," Mackenzie bulldozed on, "that even supposing they have not destroyed everything they might have concocted an electronic control regime too difficult for us to fathom?..." adding, after stepping over to the glass doors and staring out at the blackness, "...whether or not this is part of it. Good Lord! You can hardly see anything down there."

"Nothing like it has ever happened before that I know of," Felicitas said, going and looking too. The others followed.

"It's more likely an effect of climate canopy breakdown," Mackenzie muttered. "Remember that sand exclusion is part of the system. This might have happened even sooner. Ah, here comes our sandy-haired friend."

Callum had entered in a remarkably sober (for him) long-coated dark suit with baggy breeches a-la-mode, which lent him a certain unexpected look of venerability, although he did look a little agitated. Felicitas reckoned Robert had done a most ingenious outfitting job. She could not imagine where he had got the suit.

"I overheard what you said about the sand, Leonard, " Callum said. "Believe me, it must be more than just the climate canopy. One of your retrogressive effects, Lexin, yes, but I would guess some kind of knock-on from climate modifications in other parts of the country.

There it is, it's terrible, but there are more urgent problems to be dealt with, .I'm afraid. An EMR programme operated from satellites is still running – 'fully activated', as they put it. We have been sent what appear to be copies of software, printouts and other supporting data from Sydney," he continued amid complete silence. "The prisoners may not have had time to destroy them, or may have had other reasons not to. The stuff is hard to understand. There are parts, or 'steps', they just can't understand in Sydney. And there's a lot of it." Callum refused a seat when offered to him by Lexin. "We still don't know much," he said, "about exactly what's involved."

"So it was there, the evidence," Mackenzie said, cautiously. "That's something."

"Well there's *something* there."

"Where are the prisoners?" Céleste piped up.

"Helping the police with their enquiries, so I hear from Joanna van Rensburg's new deputy, and consulting their lawyers. Faust was suspended from office."

"Is that all? Only suspended?"

Callum was screwing up his nose. "I'm afraid the detentions are about all there is to be thankful for, Céleste. As a matter of fact, at the moment some of the detainees, Robert Daley among them I believe, are being taken individually back to Sussex Street. Engineers, programmers, cyberneticians, psychiatrists, all sorts of experts and officials are there, and Van Rensburg herself by now, probably. They are trying to get them to shut the thing down, slow it down, reverse it, do something with it. Experts say it's too hazardous to try and do it themselves. As if things are not confused enough already. At least they don't have Melbourne's trouble," Callum went on. "The latest thing there, I hear, is that nobody can count any more. Shops are chaotic, timetables of all kinds have gone by the board, teaching in the schools is impossible."

"Oh yes!" Céleste exclaimed, "like the violence in African village markets because people can't bargain properly.":

That some kind of mind control was going on was now plain for all to see, and Callum looked too worried to be irritated by Céleste's remarks, or to even notice them. "The trouble is," he said, "that they may not be cooperating genuinely, could be stalling, or could be even trying to manipulate the system to threaten something sudden and overwhelming – as a bargaining position, a sort of 'Plan B'. It's all very tedious – and very dangerous. You have to consider things like suicide, erasure of everything with unknown consequences."

Van Rensburg, Callum said, had been visibly shocked on arriving in Sydney. Agreeing to make a full statement in due course she had nothing to offer as regards resolution of the immediate problem. In the meantime, she had felt obliged to suspend both Faust and Nawale from office pending clarification of the situation.

For Felicitas, irritation had already become replaced by anger – anger at an already beleaguered world being faced with such dire prospects because of Blunck and his accomplices. It was anger born of fear for Lexin, for both her children, and, God Almighty! fear for everyone's children. It occurred to her that Daley himself might have had something to do with the actual programme. It was his office. It didn't seem impossible from his qualifications. She wondered whether Céleste knew what an EMR programme was. She would, very soon.

Evidently Lexin was still pondering electronic control regimes. "Can't help thinking about what you were saying the other day," he was saying to George Callum. "Something about mathematical patterns in the events, something about automaticity?"

"Now what are you saying exactly," Mackenzie asked.

"The thing might be running itself entirely," Callum said, "in a progressive programme."

"These mathematicians have a mathematical explanation for everything," Mackenzie said, resignedly, in a slightly bad tempered tone that did nothing to lighten Callum's solemnity. "Strikes me they have one pretty impenetrable system entirely under their control."

"I don't know how far it is under their *control*," Lexin said.

"And how would they manage to *do* that – something that we can't handle, and even they can't themselves, damn it?" Mackenzie said, loud enough for everyone to hear.

There was a silence, then Lexin said: "Perhaps Jean-Paul Mauré is the one to put that to," upon which the wind seemed to make a determined effort and odd grains of sand could be seen landing on the carved Arabian coffee table by the terrace doors. Felicitas even felt some on her face.

* * *

As Xiaofeng waited for rescue from his SST with its powerful electromagnetic motors broken down and silent somewhere deep under northern China, and reflected, when he was not thinking about poor Lenica, on his recent lectures on 'Convergence of Truth and Historical synthesis in Prehistory', he wondered whether there would be anybody at all to look back in the future and try and see what had happened to Earth in 2454, never mind whether or not he would have Lenica to look back with.

If he had been imagining that the almost total inability of Beijing Metropolitan Authority to function, and the fact that few of its twenty-two thousand employees were actually at their posts, constituted an exceptional, if catastrophic, local problem, it soon became clear that this was not so. From what could be gleaned from confused press reports before the train broke down, the steady increase in disruptive phenomena worldwide was matched only by its variety: here a hyperactive Kazanian politician going on a murderous rampage, there French children taking over a school and administering summary justice, and, most bizarrely, in the last few days reports of not one or two, but three catastrophes in mid ocean, with two cruise ships colliding and sinking in the North Atlantic, a fishing fleet vanishing in the Arctic ice and a macrocargo vessel likewise in a not very major storm in the Pacific. Earlier, of course, there had been the much publicised incident of village poisoning in his own country.

He had known, naturally, of Lexin's visit to Canberra with Andrew McLintock, their successful request to extend the life of the Society, and the unmistakeable sense of hopefulness in the Conference despite everything. It was a confidence that in his most optimistic moments, like when Lenica was actually with him, cajoling, encouraging, infusing him with the steadfast confidence she showed in her own mission, he shared. Then, just before his departure from Beijing there had been garbled news of the discovery of some plot at the Emergencies Ministry. Now, however, trapped far beneath the Earth's surface where such communications as were possible were directed to the rescue, he had only his PAS to rely on. Yes, he gathered, there was a plot, and while the messages never abandoned a fine thread of optimism, it was clear that the potential consequences were grave. This puzzled him. A terrible situation, yes, but...with no solution?

It seemed solutions were not readily forthcoming to their situation here below the endless deserts of Eurasia, either. An attendant had been by, announcing complete failure of the SST with loss of subsidiary power systems and a consequent delay while emergency vehicles came from Galaxy. Meanwhile conditions were becoming very uncomfortable. Everything was 'emergency': air conditioning, sanitation, drinking water... It was also hot. He picked up a two-day-old paper, re-read the speculation surrounding the plot – if such it was, the involvement of electromagnetic methods of mind control (official), of satellites (unofficial), 'world-wide effects'. But if the plotters had been caught, then why...?

So it was locomotive failure this time, not tunnel warp. It seemed so random and unpredictable, all this trouble. Were not Lenica's illnesses like that – random? It was the opinion of his parents. They were not too sympathetic towards Lenica's different interpretations, nor to Lexin's theories, nor to his 'People'. They had had quite a philosophical *discussion* (to put it politely) amid the sleek lines and vitreous translucence of the sitting room of their house in a smart Beijing suburb. Again and again Xiaofeng's thoughts came round to his beloved Lenica and how desperately he wanted news of her. He had tried calling, then texting, from Beijing to say the university was virtually out of action and he was returning, but could get no reply. Thank God he was nearly there, now. Or was he?

Half an hour later they came round with an announcement of a six-hour expected delay arriving at their destination, suggesting passengers might make use of their resting facilities. It would also conserve oxygen. For some reason it was not possible to aerify the tunnel – the normal procedure in similar circumstances. Anyone with breathing problems should report to the office. He chewed over the plot question again, but couldn't seem to get his head around the idea. Wasn't all that the stuff of history – and hopefully not of today ? He had read enough about it! Perhaps his mind was slowing up, like everybody else's. Or was it the lack of oxygen? Questions to his synthesizer produced no answers, which was supposed to mean that he was being trusted to 'play it by ear'. But was it a safe assumption – the assumption that he could be trusted in that way? A synthesizer could be irritatingly uninformative! Or was he just being impatient with it? Was he asking it the wrong questions? It would not be the first time!

Later, emergency food packs were brought round, and passengers were again advised to stay lying down to conserve oxygen. It would take the rescue vehicles three hours to get to them for continuation to Galaxy. He ate the date and apricot bars but was having a job to keep awake. Soon he was dreaming about trying to solve all kinds of impossible puzzles.

*   *   *

Xiaofeng returned to full consciousness only with the aid of a handheld oxygen cylinder being brought round by an attendant. After a few minutes he was fit enough to walk through with most of the other passengers to the rescue vehicles waiting to transport them the three hundred or so miles to Galaxy City.

There, normal disembarkation procedures being suspended, and being obliged to manhandle his luggage as best he could to the arrivals hall, he was surprised and a bit perturbed to find himself passing medical emergency teams hastening past him in the direction of his train. Then passing through the lock (now simply excluding air from the outside) into the main concourse he was met by curtains of flying sand.

Passengers had been warned before arrival about "the worst sandstorm ever experienced anywhere in the Takla Makan", and an announcement now gave that as the reason for breakdown both of vacuum running and of subsequent aerification. But it was far worse than he had imagined. Even there, under cover in the concourse, the spinning eddies made it very hard to open one's eyes even with one's back to the wind. Almost immediately, however, he was amazed to hear Robert's voice and feel his arm firmly taken hold of.

"There is no transport," he explained. "We shall have to walk up to the house. Here, wear this coat and these goggles and allow me to guide you." In a flash he had helped him on with a preheated sileron cape and hood held magnetically close to his smart zhong shan jacket and trousers and exchanged his shoes for tall boots, popping the shoes into a bag. The goggles were skiwear type with wipers. "If you can do without your luggage I can fetch it later," he said, then disappeared for a few moments to deposit it.."

'Lenica got my message then? Xiaofeng asked when he returned.

"Yes, but we couldn't get back to you," he replied.

Outside the station, and along the boulevard to the Meeting of the Avenues and then the Avenida de Ferrer de Lorenzo, sand up to a metre or so deep was swirling about, and above it, with only a vague line of demarcation, was the totally airborne sand being carried along with other objects in the storm. The dark shapes struggling to move about comprised only groups of people. No vehicles of any kind were to be seen. It felt even colder on his face than in Beijing. Robert was in the outdoor coat and beret he often wore above his shirt and jeans in winter for appearances. As Xiaofeng knew – and robotic science never ceased to amaze him –, he did not need it because although you could 'feel' him and he possessed dynamic properties he was not solid, being in reality a figment of the senses, a notion.

If being met by him was a surprise, the walk – if it could be so called – the walk to the Solbergs' was something else again. While Xiaofeng could feel his legs moving in the normal way, the speed of progress was far greater than the depth of moving sand could have allowed. It was as though for him the sand was not there. Was it that Robert was sharing some of his power of almost instant translocation?

Soon he was hearing him speak, or more precisely receiving telepathic messages from him that sounded like him speaking.

"Lenica will be delighted to see you," he was saying. "By the way, she says she thinks you will not mind if I call you Xiaofeng."

"Of course I don't, Robert," he found himself thinking, while at the same time wondering whether there was some reason for the suggested change in practice – for Robert had always been punctilious in his politeness in addressing him always as Mr. Li. "How *is she*?" he asked, again without opening his mouth.

"She is poorly, Xiaofeng. The cancer gives great cause for concern."

Xiaofeng's heart fell. He was puzzled. "But I hoped Ida was making good progress...the operation..." He was coming, reluctantly, to accept the way in which Lenica was in some way 'linked' with Ida, the mysterious intertwining of their lives. They were climbing the Hill of Lyra, taking giant steps in the moving floods of sand with their load of dead vegetation and living and dead animals… gerbils, rabbits, mice scoured out of the desert, little birds powerless against the storm. "The cancer, will that be banished? Can it be? Do you know that? I hope so, Robert, I do hope so!" The unspoken thoughts poured out of his brain. The city was spreading out below them now, the dark, blurred outlines of spires, domes, and other familiar but slowly fading shapes. As he strained to hear an answer, with the whole world seemingly dissolving before him, he remembered those words of Lexin's that had hurt him quite a lot: "Have you let the machine really work for you.. have you felt its power?" Then the robot answered the question for him in his thoughts:

"You must continue to place your trust in it. You must let it work for you, feel its power." The words were in the flying debris as they half strode, half levitated upwards. He felt Robert was smiling, though how he could be smiling in that storm he could not imagine.

They arrived at the house.

"We will go in the side door," Robert said, somehow covering the entrance in such a way that a minimum of sand entered. Lexin in body warmer and baggy trousers, and Lenica and Felicitas in warm, fleecy gowns) were sitting in the living space discussing the day (it was already late afternoon) when Xiaofeng entered, apologising for his sudden intrusion looking like a spaceman.

Lenica ran to him, and he took her in his arms. "I didn't hear you arrive for the storm," she said. "Is it really as bad as they say?"

"Could hardly be worse," he replied. "Couldn't have made it without Robert. You have an incredible ally, there, Mrs. Solberg," he added, offering a kiss on both cheeks, to be reprimanded for not addressing her, in his slight confusion, as "Felicitas" and told to go and get tidied up.

"No doubt you recognized my bossy mum's kindly reminder of your membership of our family, X.F.," Lexin said later, meeting him on the way back from his shower room, summoned by the mistress of the house to describe the rigours of his journey.

He smiled. "Yes, I did," he said, "and I am realising that family membership also brings great responsibilities. But Lexin, what's your take on all this? I suppose the sand is some kind of a retrogressive effect."

"Yes, we think it is."

"But the disruption in general, the plot – if there is one?"

"The Callums and the Mackenzies were here yesterday," Lexin replied. "George reckons things are very bad indeed. The detainees appear confused and unable or unwilling to open up on the programme, either because they are affected by the radiation just like many others, especially Normals, or because they do not understand it fully themselves, or..." Lexin hesitated.

"...or because they are being obstructive?"

"Possibly. The police commissioner just hopes the guys will get the system under some sort of control eventually, if it isn't already."

"The detainees?"

"Yes, or anybody else... if they can," he added as they entered the living space again. "Then we can go from there."

Xiaofeng noted the scepticism, and it confirmed some growing fears, but at first he could only think to ask how the guests would have got home.

"Robert took them," Felicitas replied.

"Does he ever tire?"

"Not so long as we keep him serviced properly."

It occurred to him what strange words those seemed now, applied to an entity so knowledgeable, so superior. "Robert told me you had not been so well, Lenica," he said, softly, going and taking her in his arms.

"No, I've been feeling rotten."

"I think he has put the ball in my court," he said.

"How do you mean, he put it in your court?" Felicitas asked, a little haughtily.

"About Ida!" Lenica burst out. "It must be that. Isn't that so, darling? Don't say you don't understand, Mother!"

"I want you to be better, Lenica," he said, releasing her. "That's all I know!"

"And he discussed all that with you on the way up, Xiaofeng?" Felicitas exclaimed. "You discussed all that, about Ida and Lenica, on the way up, in the sandstorm?"

"I don't know about 'all that'. We didn't *discuss* anything much. It was kind of telepathic." There was a silence, then Xiaofeng added – "I have to let my PAS work for me. Robert is very persuasive."

"Why should they not have discussed everything, Mother, even if they didn't?" Lexin observed, adding with a wry smile. "Just possibly it is not only to you that he talks seriously, but to other members of the family as well." He gave Xiaofeng a wink.

"Mother, you have to believe him," Lenica said, manoeuvring herself very close to the bemused young man and taking his hand so that they were both facing Felicitas. "What was it you said about Robert, Mother? 'If you trust me...'?"

"Yes, yes, Lenica, I know. I s'pose I fear for all of you. I do not know which is the more dangerous place for you: Galaxy City or Newchurch, wherever it is – or was. Lexin, I am tired and I am going to retire – after I have bathed this sand out of my person. Bring me a nice 'special' to my bath (i.e. the usual plus a dash of gin), there's a dear. And my dear Xiaofeng," she said as she went out and Lexin followed her, "The Lord be praised for your safe return!"

The absence of others in the room allowed the sounds from outside to dominate – the now violent wind and the hissing sound of sand upon the glass doors like sleet, and no doubt just as cold. Repeatedly Xiaofeng caught the gritty sound of sand grains under his shoes, felt a soreness in the eyes. He folded Lenica close to himself – the reduced, tired body of the beautiful Nordic woman that once strode fine and agile among so many admirers...

...A nurse came, said the consultant would see them now, and took them along...

"We have a little problem here, Mr. and Mrs. Weston," Mr. Chappel said as another nurse entered the consulting room and placed what were presumably some CT prints on his desk, "but one I can deal with". A couple of nimble movements of his fingers had spread these out in front of him. "Because of Mrs. Weston's medical history I decided to check progress unusually after only three months. Our latest CT scan shows two recurrences of the tumour in the pelvic region. That is the *bad* news." He paused, and then, probably relieved to see stoical faces before him, continued, "The good news is that because I am confident of the location of these recurrences and that they are not situated in the pelvic wall, there is a good chance I can eliminate them, and have a good chance of preventing further recurrence. The operation is called posterior exenteration."

Tom noted the glazed look in Ida's eyes. He doubted she had heard a word. *He* certainly hadn't taken it all in – but enough. "I take it that it is pretty drastic," he said.

"That I cannot deny. Yes, it is. But in view of your wife's medical history I consider it offers the best option."

Mr. Chappel had come from behind his desk and was already unfolding a very large diagram. Tom began to have a fair idea of what was coming. Now the surgeon flipped the diagram of the abdominal organs over a whiteboard. "By means of the operation we clear the whole pelvic region affected..." he was saying. The diagram clung to the board remorselessly, and his hands moved about it likewise, and in uncanny harmony with his voice as he began to explain...

"I take it radiation is not a possibility," Tom said after the first few sentences, chiefly because he could think of nothing else to counter a feeling of doom and despondency.

"Because she also had adjuvant therapy, that is to say radiation and chemotherapy, it is not possible to have it again." He paused. "As I indicated, this *will* involve removal of the lower bowel and rectum."

Tom realised fully what the surgeon was talking about – the word everybody whispered about with gravely nodding heads: "colostomy"... Was he even saying it right?

"Yes indeed you are," Mr. Chappel replied, flipping up another chart over which his hairy hands fluttered with all the ease of a weather forecaster's as he explained about bags and stomas, and how millions had benefited from it all.

Tom was visualizing all too easily what a stark, two-dimensional chart meant for a multi-dimensional process in a fragile body already subjected to unspeakable pressures. "She has been through so much," he said, and the surgeon nodded slowly. Then Ida said, suddenly,

"It seems a lot of trouble to be taking for a fallen woman. I feel I'd be taking up your time unjustifiably."

"Ida, Ida," Tom exclaimed, "that is all behind you now!"

"Your history in the way you describe it does not enter into it for me, Mrs. Weston," the surgeon said, gently, before sitting down again. "And no-one should undervalue him- or herself. As for the operation and its aftermath, as I said, it's very common, and you get used to the idea, I can assure you."

Tom was looking hard at Ida, a bit of the old Ida. Surely, she had not given up! He did not think she lacked courage, but he feared she might slip back into her old self. Her resigned look belied the new trousers and smart top she had put on that morning with the very purpose of making her feel better about herself. He felt he might slip too if he were in her position, and he was feeling very despondent until just something in the surgeon's manner, something about the way he looked – as if he was waiting for something to happen – caused him to pull himself up. At all events, there was no point in beating about the bush. He felt impelled to probe further.

"What if you find more recurrences, as you call them, when you are operating?"

"In that case it might be necessary to change the plan slightly, maybe to remove another organ, like the bladder. When it came to the operation, Mrs. Weston would have to sign up to that possibility. But I don't think it's likely."

Tom was determined to hit rock bottom. "Would it be possible to put a figure on the success rate for this kind of operation, Mr. Chappel?"

"Forty to sixty per cent."

"What does that mean, exactly?"

"Survival rate after five years." Survival. The word rattled round in Tom's head. It seemed a far cry from their optimism of recent weeks. Ida looked blank. "Your HIV indices remain good, Mrs. Weston," Mr.Chappel said. "They are much better, in fact. Remember we were starting from a very low base. Yes, this is serious, what we have here, but that at least is a good sign."

The words of reassurance were genuine enough, but they seemed lost on Ida. And yet her seemingly negative response did not appear to faze the surgeon. In fact it was almost as if he was inviting more questions. Tom took the opportunity, and when he *had* asked more questions and Ida said she thought they should have a good look at any alternative approaches before taking any decision, and could he advise them, he was in no way disapproving. Indeed he appeared glad and smiled broadly, as though he had arrived at some opportunity, even some kind of a green light. But what kind of green light? Wasn't he the boss? It was strange.

"I can give you the name of a cancer centre," he said, "which aims to counteract cancerous cell processes without making wild claims about cures. It combines various approaches such as cancer-combating vitamins and the immune system protein interferon, plus the use of various substances slowing tumour growth, together with relaxation and psychotherapy. Let me give you that address and a letter of introduction. Go and have a look, and if you don't feel it's for you, you *must* come back and see me."

He appeared to have the details in his head, and he wrote for a couple of minutes. It was as Tom's gaze wandered idly through the window behind him that something very odd happened. To his astonishment, instead of an expected view, probably across the car park to the university, he had a hazy view of spires and domes and other, even stranger shapes. It was an unknown cityscape, somewhere far, far away. Only the friendly smile of Mr. Chappel as he folded the letter and placed it in an unsealed envelope addressed 'Professor Lansdowne, Lansdowne-Clarkson Holistic Healing Centre' and shook hands with both of them, urging them not to delay too long in making a decision, reassured Tom that he was not dreaming. He could only put the changed windowscape phenomenon down to the latest innovation in smart décor.

"You must stay here tonight", Lenica said, breaking away and going over to the window. "It's getting really dark now. I expect Veronica will have already prepared a bed for you. I'll ask her to get something for you to eat, if she hasn't already." She came away from the window. "George Callum and Lexin are going to try and get to Sydney with a team of experts tomorrow night – at Van Rensburg's instigation. She admits Jean-Paul Mauré was involved in developing the satellite-based EMR programme, which was to be used in the event of an actual invasion by hostile aliens. There is now believed to be no invasion threat. The First Minister hopes our experts might be able to break into it, which the plotters either won't or can't do, as Lexin may have told you. Mauré has vanished. Mackenzie will lead a Societan group to work on it from this end if necessary. Mother's pretty cross, as you know. She certainly won't be pleased if they want you to go to Sydney as well," Lenica added.

"I cannot imagine any particular use for an expert in historical synthesis."

"It's just that Lexin often feels very much on his own. You would be a great support." She went up to him, looked into his eyes for a moment, then kissed him on the lips. "Not that *I* want you to go. And *she's* very fond of you too, my mother is – however hard you may find that to believe sometimes," she added, teasingly. "And it's so dangerous, Xiaofeng, everything at the moment. Look how black it is out there. That's how it gets with the sand."

"She is very fearful for *you*, Lenica," he said, "and so am I. Sometimes I feel that the responsibility for you is almost too great for me." Xiaofeng said nothing for a few moments. Then he said, "I will not be going to Sydney. I will be staying here with you. It may all come down to us in the end, us here."

"Us?" Lenica released him, looked at him curiously for a moment, at the wide smile overflowing from the delicate folds around those captivating eyes. "Were you there, too?"

"Yes, of course. We both were, weren't we? But how, I don't know. My PAS was not even switched on."

"I couldn't wait for the surgeon to start writing," Lenica said.

"I don't remember what all the therapies were."

"I'm not sure it matters. It could just as well not have been about alternative therapies at all. You unburdened yourself, Xiaofeng, plumbed the depths, emptied yourself for Tom. Isn't that what you did? I didn't do the same for Ida."

"But you trusted the surgeon, Lenica, put yourself in his hands for Ida's sake. I felt it. He was not just fobbing them off."

"I know. On the contrary he was waiting for them, Xiaofeng. He knew something...everything."

"Waiting for their trust?"

"Maybe just acceptance This is not over yet, Xiaofeng, is it? And did you see the funny window?"

"Onto our city. Yes."

" We cannot desert them now, can we?"

"No, we can't," he said.

She kissed him. "By the way," she added, "it can switch itself on – when necessary, your PAS..."

* * *

The next morning, he heard five people had died of suffocation or cardiac arrest on the delayed SST. The world network was in fact close to complete suspension, with all resources concentrated on keeping a few trains running for officials, repair gangs and disaster relief.

It took Lexin and the others thirty-six hours on two or three of these to reach a baking Sydney, with a breakdown at Kuala Lumpur due to power failure, with some non-vacuum running. It seemed the Melbourne 'numeracy' malaise was showing signs of spreading to Sydney, too. And even the seasoned cabbie seemed confused about the exact location of the Murrumburra Hotel situated in one of the old streets in the central area and refused to trust his autonav. Having left their luggage there, the bubble took them on quickly to the Planetary Police Headquarters overlooking a deserted Hyde Park; the cabbie knew where *that* was. It occupied a modern building which, however, owed little to the contemporary 'gossamer' or 'mysterioso' styles of architecture, much more to the current parallel trend defiantly harking back to certain ponderous, even fortified styles of the pre-visitation epoch.

Appropriately, perhaps, the Metropolitan Police chief was no-nonsense Alistair Ackroyd, a redhead whose robust form amply filled his colourful tunic and breeches decorated with cummerbund and shoulder sash, and just as amply reinforced his known attitudes. Explaining that he had handed over interrogation of the prisoners to an ad hoc panel of experts for a while, he conducted the party to his own office, reached via a bewildering operations room that had obviously undergone rapidly improvised expansion. The office offered a degree of comfort in its cumbersome armchairs, surrounded by Australian motifs.

"I don't know whether you know about the bush fires, Lexin," the Commissioner said before they sat down. "Never had anything like this, or till so late in the season, not for centuries. They just haven't stopped since December."

"Where?"

"In the Blue Mountains." Lexin had the feeling it was where they always seemed to start, historically. Since the reversal of climatic warming, and the 'greening', they had not been a serious problem. "Blazing all summer," the Commissioner said, "and now heading this way. Something really unpredictable has happened. Looks real bad.".

The word 'retrogression' was firmly planted in Lexin's mind.

His own men, Ackroyd said when they were seated, were already hard pressed in their attempts to on the one hand maintain order in the city, and on the other hand, this being the chief one of the four world police control centres, maintain full contact and co-operation with the others in Paris, Brazilia and Beijing. Several secretaries in a side room could be seen struggling the whole time to prioritize the Commissioner's own incoming communications. Lexin had the impression that at any moment he might be called away, leaving them in the hands of his deputy, a hawk-eyed little man clutching his hat and fixing each of them in turn with a disdainful eye, especially later when they were all made to swear to secrecy about the results of the interviews with the felons. Lexin felt the deputy was enjoying his newfound responsibilities and that he did not like these Societans any more than he liked the felons.

"There are times when I can hardly talk to my own men and women because of befuddled brains, never mind bad telecommunications," Ackroyd said to Callum, "And then there's this excessive desire to go to sleep. It's hard enough as it is getting enough reliable information to advise everyone from the First Minister to local medical teams everywhere concerning the situation in addition to our normal duties. And we Normals don't have quite your language abilities at the best of times. Not that I really put the blame on you Societans for all this – at least, not much," he added.

Callum was stung by the chief's scarcely diluted taunt, and the faces of the other Societans took on wryful expressions. Apart from Lexin they were Andrew McLintock, the biologist and Lexin's former tutor Prof. Tang, computer scientist J.X. Wang, criminologist M. Patel, one of the two women psychologists, and two text analysers from the Mission Station. The other members of the team, chiefly computer experts, were Normals.

"Never mind," Callum said, trying like the others to ignore the comment. "Perhaps we can get some sense out of these naughty boys." The feeble attempt at humour did nothing to improve the atmosphere.

"All I can tell you is that they're as bloody scared as we are," Ackroyd said.

"We'll have to see why, then," Lexin said in as pacifying a tone as he could.

"I'll say we will," the chief said. "If you boys and girls – with your special insights (he paused, significantly) – can't bloody well get it out of them, who can? Now what about this guy Mauré they all used to be so enthusiastic about?"

Was it Lexin's imagination or was the air conditioning struggling against the heat emanating from the overwrought commissioner? "We don't know where he is," he replied.

"Do *you* know what could have made such a programme unstoppable?"

"Not yet."

"We have to find him," the Commissioner snorted.

"Thank God there is no invasion, anyway," an overhearing Prof. Tang put in. "At least we are dealing with humans. It could be even worse, couldn't it?" The remark of the diminutive professor had a faintly quaint ring, and Ackroyd looked unamused and distinctly unappeased. Lexin supposed the complete absence of humour in the Commissioner, and his sharp tone, might result from a combination of stress plus strenuous efforts to overcome the 'sleep' effects.

As for himself, he spent a restless night, not helped by a faint but pervasive smell of smoke and the disturbing knowledge that the eastern edge of a massive bush fire was no more than fifty kilometres from the centre of Sydney and heading towards him.

During a day of individual and group interviewing at the Police

Headquarters, this time by the Galaxy City team, the prisoners, detained indefinitely under unprecedented emergency powers, asked to be taken to the newspaper offices a mile away in the south of the central area, and again they were accompanied there individually. What transpired confirmed Lexin's worst fears. The men, at their request, were allowed to confer with each other. Afterwards, in the presence of their legal representatives they issued a statement confessing their inability to stop or in any way modify the programme, which they admitted to being targeted on humans, pleading somewhat lamely that they had been convinced – until it proved otherwise – that it would remain fully under their control. Even in the uncompromising Commissioner's view, if they had been obstructive at first he did not think they were now. The prisoners' bland admission quite took Lexin's breath away, but the admission of unstoppability of the programme was only too comprehensible if Mauré had had a crucial input into it. He did not say so, since he did not want to raise hopes of Jean-Paul being able to stop it himself.

Blunck claimed to have believed in the reality of an alien threat two years earlier, when explosions at the Mission Station became a more frequent occurrence. It was apparently not long after that that it was decided to prepare a second line of defence in addition to a defensive shield developed long ago, and gathering cosmic dust, in case it proved impossible to stem an actual invasion. He had asked Mauré, with his particular combination of expertise in aspects of neurology and supposedly special potential as a Societan, to advise a team in drawing up a secret programme of satellite-based psychological defence using electromagnetic radiation and able to counter any occupying biological entity. Further questioning by Prof. Tang and Andrew McLintock pointed to automatic adaptation to the target organism and honing of the programmed effects once full activation had taken place.

"Can't we just destroy the programme?" Ackroyd suggested afterwards.

"What? The control centre?" Tang asked. "Then you lose everything, lose any possibility of a reversal. Or you may leave people's minds in a mess for ever."

"Or just switch it off?"

"Unknown effects, surely," Lexin suggested. "It is possible a whole fleet is already whizzing around up there anyway, scattered in goodness knows how many independent pre-programmed satellites. That is George Callum's view. Unfortunately he could not be here today."

"Surely, Jean-Paul Mauré *could* help us – if we can find him," one of the psychologists suggested. The others looked at Lexin expectantly.

"My feeling is that he would have reappeared if he knew he could help you," Lexin said. "Even being the individualist that he is, he would hardly withhold such information – if only to save himself."

"I've got a good part of my Force looking for him, anyway," Ackroyd said, "but we can no longer put off telling the public what we know."

"It's hard to see how a Societan could go off the rails like that!" It was Patel the criminologist, a bright young fellow from Mumbai University obviously shocked by the turn of events since his rapid rise from the ranks in India, the cradle of modern technology and, significantly, a country blessed with a world-renowned tranquillity.

"As I say, we'll hunt him down," the Commissioner declared, coldly.

"As I pointed out," Lexin said, "I don't think he will be able to help either. As a matter of fact, despite what *you* may think, my feeling is that he may have been acting in good faith in his advice to the Ministry." George Callum had told him he came to much the same conclusion. Patel still looked puzzled when Lexin reiterated that he did not believe for one moment Mauré ever imagined humans as the final target. The Commissioner maintained a steely indifference.

Upon further, urgent interrogation by the Galaxy City team from early on the following day – day eight of the activated programme –, Beckenthal said experiments in electromagnetic mind control had been carried out in view of the assumed threat of an alien invasion. Several experiments were in fact authorised, leading up to an EMR programme jointly concocted by Mauré and Emergencies Ministry scientists, and ultimately to be delivered via a state of the art system of polar-orbiting satellites designed by Beckenthal. These took place first on terra firma in some limited tests on crowd manipulation, but later, crucially, *from September* some "harmless, brain-confusing experiments" were conducted using one satellite each time, including the one in the Sahara.

When questioned by McLintock about the ultimate objective of the radiation, Beckenthal said simply that the intention was gradually to mentally degrade every invader organism of whatever type targeted once it had been identified. He explained that a progressive spawning of daughter satellites would take place, which seemed to remove a remote possibility that had been suggested of identifying the satellites and destroying them one by one.

Intensive questioning by police and experts, including Lexin and Callum, indicated that around late November it became clear to Blunck from close analysis of past and present events worldwide that in spite of plausible interpretations in terms of Maurian theory there was actually no hard evidence of alien influences. One of his co-conspirators, Alviola the Filipino biologist on secondment to the Emergencies Ministry (and one of Bill Walmsley's suspects), even acknowledged the plausibility of Lexin's theories on 'retrogressive effects' and had (as he confessed) pointed out to Blunck the measure of cover this could give them if they were to continue experimenting. They assumed, apparently, or perhaps hoped, that those retrogressive effects would eventually stabilise in a post-Lyrian, post-Societan era.

"And you couldn't bear to stop playing around. That's it, isn't it?" Ackroyd put it to Beckenthal finally. "You couldn't quite resign yourself to your system never being fully implemented and activated," to which the German replied,

"We agreed to continue some testing at that time, but later..."

"But you did *agree*, didn't you?" the Commissioner asked rhetorically, addressing all the prisoners in a briefing room in the presence of the Galaxy team and others, "and if my memory does not lie, you certainly achieved considerable successes in mind bending, from swathes of rural Africa to fishery settlements in the northern tundra. These successes probably acted like a drug so that by the middle of January of this year your drunken electromagnetic revellers were causing disruption in all sorts of places across central and eastern Europe and southern Russia and probably disrupting the Japanese stock exchange. And then came Szechuan in March and more mass mortalities. Another satellite? And the sick babies – yet another of these devils launched from your space stations! Yet still you carried on." The Commissioner was getting redder in the face again, constantly wiping it with his handkerchief. He seemed to be having difficulty in holding himself together. At the mention of Szechuan all the men interviewed remained silent. To Lexin the whole thing seemed so much the very antithesis of all the progress achieved since the visitation – the mental cohesion, proper use of scientific discovery, mutual respect. "And you were building up the network all the time," Ackroyd put it to Beckenthal, who nodded. "Obviously the system was not fully activated." Now he was looking at Blunck.

"Correct," Blunck replied, "but the hardware was in place by two weeks ago." No good dwelling on the undeniable part played by Societans in triggering all this, Lexin thought, as the men were led away, but the Commissioner did so anyway:

"It's a fine mess you people have got us into, Mr. Solberg!" he declared as with obvious relief he dismissed most of the experts, saying he would continue with a normal police interrogation in the afternoon after an early lunch. "Meantime if I don't get a rest I shall be asleep. It's only the taramils are keeping me awake as it is."

"Wasn't that a *little* unfair, Commissioner?" Lexin asked. At least, he thought, Van Rensburg might have taken a warning about Beckenthal from her interview with George Callum. Ackroyd knew about those interviews, and his attitude had been to describe them now as 'water under the bridge'.

"Well haven't you been saying it yourself?" he replied, " – that you Societans blame yourselves? And what *about* Beckenthal, Mauré himself?"

He was certainly rubbing it in. "And we will get you out of the mess, too." Lexin's confident tone surprised even himself.

The Galaxy team tried to relax over wine and pizzas at Circular Quay, having arranged to meet in the evening when the Commissioner would address everybody and give an assessment. Callum had been sending regular reports to the Society Conference in Galaxy City, and vice versa. In a step of faith, Callum had asked Mackenzie to take over the chairmanship in his absence. Whether it was owing to inner conviction that Leonard had suddenly become interested in the fate of Lexin's People, or whether it was, like Felicitas reckoned, through discomfiture at being outpaced by Lamonte, his 'number two', Lexin did not know. It could have even been attributable to rank fear in the knowledge of an unassailable orbiting programme of annihilation. On the whole he thought the Professor was anything but a 'follower on' and that he knew what he was doing and had taken his own decision. But Lexin had made sure Xiaofeng, whose PAS had now sprung fully to life and who would attend regularly in the gallery, would also keep the acting chairman informed about Ida, Tom and the others at Newchurch if Leonard Mackenzie's own awakening resources should fail him.

The team was by now aware of the return of Ida's cancer, and of the consultation with Edmund Chappel. Lexin confessed, over their meal, that Lenica's acquisition of the disease and the return of Ida's had been a great disappointment and very worrying. He had not needed any further confirmation of his sister's closest possible connection with Lexin's People and said that in recording it in his website the heaviness of his heart had been lightened only by her own and Xiaofeng's total acceptance of their 'burden' and their optimism about how it would all end. All this did do a little to relieve the general gloom, but Patel found it hard to stomach.

"We have come a long way in our country," he said aside to Lexin as they got up from their tables. "But it all seems so different now, so far from our expectation."

"So when this is all over and done with, be vigilant! Enhancement is not for sleeping on!" Lexin responded.

"When this is all over..." the Indian said, thoughtfully. "...You think it *will* be over?"

His words trailed off as it became evident that a fight was in progress at the till over an argument about a bill.

Outside, despite the perfect late-summer weather the quays were near-deserted where normally the buskers would be playing against the contrary rhythms of the scenic railway above, now silent. A man approached them for money to buy petrol. He knew a place in the Blue Mountains where life was still possible. He would willingly take them along with him. He wandered off. Perhaps he had not heard about the growing conflagration there. Everybody else was talking about it, and could smell it, even imagine they could hear it in the strong wind. When the group split up, Lexin decided to return to the hotel and rest.

CHAPTER TWENTY-ONE

A signal from his multicom wrenched him from his dozing at about three-thirty, followed by the discontented voice of the Commissioner:
"We've got Mauré, trying to board an emergency SST for Galaxy."
"Oh, really? Has he said anything?"
"Yes, but perhaps you could come round and see me."
"Now?"
"Yes please. I need your help."
The Commissioner was at his desk, looking severely overworked. He dived straight in, barely giving Lexin time to take a seat on the other side of the desk. "Mauré told me he had no idea the threat of an invasion was anything but very real."
"As I said, I believe him."
Ackroyd ignored that. "And by the way," he said, "Beckenthal considered Daley and the others might be wrong if they reckoned it would be possible to halt the fully activated programme, and he was trying to warn them."
"I'm not surprised."
"Why didn't you bloody say so?"
"I only had an idea that he was trying to put the brakes on. He is a Societan too, after all. Doubtless he knew how thoroughgoing Mauré would be."

"They are probably wishing they had listened. I have a feeling they are pinning their hopes on Mauré, with his enhanced insights, to put things right. Some hopes! Mauré said that in Blunck's terms the array of electromagnetic *options* in the *deployment* of the satellite *fleet* permitted almost infinitely varied ways of automatically *homing in* on *the enemy*" – Ackroyd spat out the offending words. "All cut and dried. Sounds like some World War II admiral talking up his campaign! Mauré reckoned he was appalled at the games they had been playing with his programme."

Lexin saw a certain irony in the fact that the solution offered by Jean-Paul, with his 'enhanced insights', to deal with an invasion had turned out to be so much more watertight than his diagnosis of evil powers. "What are you going to do with him?" he asked. "If stupidity is culpable, then I suppose he is culpable, but all I am saying is that whatever you are going to do with him I am sure he did not foresee the terrible consequences when he was at the Ministry working it all out with them. I do not like to be a pessimist, but..."

"...I didn't know you people could be so stupid," Ackroyd fumed on. "Bloody Hell!" There he went again. Surely the Commissioner's reliance on certain stereotyped expressions was another sign of brain suppression. "I didn't imagine it could get any worse. Let me tell you, it gets worse by the minute."

"What do you think I might say to that? 'I knew it would'?"

"*Yes.* As you might guess, then, when things got out of hand the felons needed somewhere secret to operate from. They had been at one of the Ministry's places out in the bush, directing everything from there: satellite launching, everything. I am not sure precisely when Daley actually got involved... " The police chief paused. "By the way, I hear Daley gave you some trouble at your Canberra Press Conference. Did you *know* about his move into press ownership big time, in Sussex Street?"

"At that time, no. My sister told my mother. Said he was at the Brasilia press conference and that he was super-ambitious. He did not bother me there."

"He was at all your recent conferences. I checked. But now, when did he get involved, or perhaps I should say 'openly involved'? Was it only after it became clear there was no real threat? I am not even sure Blunck ever believed in a threat in any case and whether he might not have been planning something with Daley for quite a while. Anyway, as you will know, Beckenthal equipped the building at Sussex Street for Daley's media activities – and more, filling it with every means of collection and dissemination of information, surveillance and indoctrination known to man, plus the means to link up with and control a fleet of satellites. Look, Lexin..." The Commissioner emptied two more taramils out of a phial on his desk and swallowed them, then leaned closer, "...What amazes me is that this guy Robert Daley follows your every move, denigrates your People, Beckenthal abandons the Society, and then provides him with the equipment to take over the world, all of it without you even noticing!" All the important words were emphasised.

Lexin kept his cool. "So they transferred everything there."

"Yes. Now I discovered that Blunck's son had been at an Emergencies Ministry training academy with Daley. Young Daley seems to have decided that such a life would not satisfy his ambitions, and he went off and studied cybernetics, but, as I understand it, a friendship that had formed between him and Blunck senior on visits to the family home persisted. Presumably it was a friendship founded on mutual respect and interests. They *could* have been collaborating closely for quite a while – some plan for total media domination , – *or worse*? Anyway, operations control was transferred to the top of the newspaper building, maybe under some pretext or other, probably as early as in December...."

"...to form a top secret command centre – with or without the full knowledge of Van Rensburg. I see. Where is the launch site?"

"Without her knowledge, I hope. An old Emergencies Ministry tower in the middle of a five thousand square mile no-go area somewhere in the Gibson Desert, updated and semi-automated."

"I hope so, too. I suppose when it came to the transfer there was nothing much Beckenthal could do about it anyway."

"Probably not. If my understanding is correct Beckenthal never bothered too much about the possible long-term consequences of his contracts."

"And that was surely the point where he began to get really worried."

"As well he might have done, because the point about Robert Daley – which nobody had properly realised, is, to put it bluntly, that he's a megalomaniac if ever there was one, and this was surely the point at which the megalomania really kicked in."

"Or perhaps Beckenthal did realise it. But look, Commissioner, are you sure you have got time to be telling me all this?"

"You might as well know, having such an intimate connection with it. I am just surprised – because I know that you think you receive guidance from those you refer to as our 'Saviours' in your work – that they did not warn you about Daley and, yes, about Mauré. Or were you just not listening? Was not your neglect of our safety so great as to be almost criminal?"

"I didn't need to be told by anybody that Jean-Paul Mauré was talking rubbish, however clever he may be."

"His defence system wasn't rubbish."

"I believe we are on the verge of offering an alternative way out of our predicament."

"Isn't it a bit late?" Ackroyd sighed, sank back in his chair, closed his eyes. Lexin thought he might fall asleep. After a full two minutes he said, quietly, "I still harbour a small hope that with your special powers you, you yourself, may see a clear way through our trouble." There was a pause before he seemed to pull himself together and continued: "Now I do not think Blunck ever really believed, actually, that adjustment of the basic EMR programme prior to full activation was limited to identification of the target organism. But very quickly, it seems, Daley persuaded him that the programme was not only capable of radical modification but could, following its modification, indeed be controlled *after* activation."

"Beckenthal must have been very worried too, by now" Lexin said.

"Daley clearly had no qualms about proposing full activation at the new premises, with a radical modification embedded in a Mauré programme now targeted on the human species. Its intention was to clear men's minds, temporarily or permanently, and substitute a malleable mindset receptive to a new political philosophy in the pursuit of which he was happy to enrol the others'. He was quite open about it this afternoon. Reckoned he already had the software. Within two weeks he could have it ready for substitution – which indeed was what transpired."

"Could not Blunck have done something to stop it at that stage if he had wanted to?"

"...or the dedicated crew around them, two of them with Blunck, the others Daley's cronies? I don't know. Possibly Blunck and his two colleagues even agreed with his philosophy, whatever that is, or was."

"Or hoped to scale down Robert Daley's ambitions," Lexin suggested.

"Or maybe Blunck reckoned he had sussed Daley out, believed his software was rubbish and would simply make full activation impossible. As for Daley's pals on the 'New Australian', they have said very little all along. They seem to have been entirely taken in by him. Anyway, in the event," Ackroyd went on, "the substituted software failed to kick in. But unfortunately Mauré's intricate, mind-destroying system went into full activation from scratch, already targeted on the human species, as I said, and borne along by a large number of satellites and possibly others subsequently launched from them."

"At least we have got all the perpetrators. I am sure of that. All seven of them. Our investigations have been very thorough given the short time-span since all this blew up. Lexin, I just thought you would like to know that my respect for your enhanced status is exceeded only by my despair in that you refuse to cooperate with me by making use of it for the world's benefit – salvation even. Some unwinding of the programme …something beyond us mere… *mortals*…"

"I don't have those powers."

"I don't know whether to believe you."

"I'm sorry. By the way, how far away is the fire now?" Lexin asked, changing the subject.

Ackroyd fished out his multicom. "Forty kilometres."

"And how are you coping?"

"My head is spinning. Every available fire fighter, every available reservist, Emergencies personnel, everybody is fighting it. There is a terrible shortage of water, and firefighter numbers are reduced by seventy-five per cent through sickness or death. Thousands of houses are threatened."

"Was Daley penitent?" (another change of subject).

"Not particularly. As I said, he's in a world of make-believe. He is a bit puzzled about why his software failed. Lexin, I do have the power to arrest you, you know. Think about that!"

Lexin's head was spinning, too, and more with the Commissioner's update on the satellites than with his personal threats. Then there was the fire situation. "What good reason could I have for not wanting to help you? "

"That is what puzzles me."

"Commissioner," Lexin said, assuming you are not arresting me I intend to go and have a good rest. And may I politely suggest you do the same and let your deputy do the work." But on the way back to the Murrumburra Hotel he decided to change his mind and take the ferry for the Taronga Park zoo – if it was still working (One of the vessels at least had still been working at lunch time). He had some notion that in that place, with its famous 'solid' dynamic pseudo-holograms representing Earth's zoospheres of the past and in the present and, (work in progress) speculatively in a galactic future, he might be enabled to get a calm perspective on things. It might be the best way to pass the time before the evening's meeting.

But as the craft glided across the harbour, its high wingsails glinting in the hot, rising wind, and Lexin, leaning over the top deck rail, watched the great Harbour Bridge first soar away on the port side, then sink imperceptibly into a smoky fog from the advancing fires, unmistakably in another part of his mind another scene was playing out, another reality. Tom in an anorak and holding Ida's case, and Ida, just as tall and a little unsteady, in plastic mac with a hood that kept blowing off in the cold wind, were heading out into the car park of the Lansdowne-Clarkson Holistic Healing Centre. With them were Mark and Marcelle.

"It's not that I do not accept vitamin C can help to restore my immune system," Ida was saying. "People are wrong if they make such assumptions. That's not the reason why I have decided not to stay here."

"I know," Tom said.

"Nor do I deny that I may be deficient in melatonin and thyroid hormones..."

"I know."

"...and that detoxification therapies, nutrition and all that may help."

"I know it too, Mum," Marcelle said, gripping her mother's arm. "Even what you may think is a sensible course of action may not always be the best. People tell me to go back and take A-levels and study for a degree in social psychology or something, and all I want to do is be a teaching assistant and show kids how to make levers and sliders."

"Make what?" Tom asked as he bundled stuff into the boot of the old VW Golf that Mark had recently acquired.

"Do what Miss Palmeson showed me years ago."

"Ah, yes. But what *about* some qualifications, like Mark says?"

"Yes, yes, a*nd* Grandpa and Grandma say, too, and I still love them!"

"Sometimes you have to take your own decisions, don't you, Marcie love?" Ida said as Marcelle helped her in to the back of the car. "If you'd done all the 'right' things, love, where would Daddy and I be now? I'd be dead, probably. Tom, where would you be?" she asked as Tom got in at the other side. "Divorced and remarried, probably." Tom had barely had time to think about that when Ida leaned forward as Mark started the engine and Marcelle climbed in beside him. "And Mark, now" she went on, "*you* didn't always do the 'right' thing, either, did you?" She waited while he edged the VW warily out of the grounds of the Centre into the driving drizzle of the main road and headed for Kinley's Fields. "I mean not by your parents' lights."

"True enough," he replied. "I became seriously involved trying to sort out a prehistoric family that seemed to have found itself in a lot of trouble, though now we seem to have lost them again. And if I had not found those weird websites that started it all," he added, making a good stab at sounding indignant, "I might have been looking forward to a lucrative career in business IT instead of information resources for development aid in Africa on a shoestring budget."

There was a long silence. Then Ida said, quietly, "It's all true, isn't it, about those people, about your friend, Marcie? I mean, this isn't all happening *on its own*, is it? I mean...just...*happening.*"

"Of course it's true."

"You know they found Red Hair," Tom said.

"Yes, we know that," Ida said, "but supposing she doesn't make it. You said she was barely conscious, didn't recognize you. She didn't recognize her daughter."

"Don't give up now, Mother – for both their sakes, and Big Nose's!" There was an urgency in Marcelle's tone that took Ida by surprise. "Lexin won't let *us* down."

"Do as she says, Ida," Mark said as he headed on to the motorway and put his foot down. "Marcie knows what she's talking about." And she did. Had not Marcie been telling him how for days now she had been sharing Shining Face's thoughts and how with Red Hair having suddenly taken a turn for the better they and Big Nose were heading slowly seawards. Marcie had told no-one else – she wanted her mum to take *her* own decisions. But now she just needed a *bit* of extra help, a bit of encouragement.

It was the first time Mark had called her Ida. It lent urgency to his words – as well as tenderness. And it was not jokey Mark now, but serious Mark. Had he not taken twenty-four hours off from uni to be with them? And for Mark that *was* serious. To Ida it was still a mystery she could only half see through, but there could be no doubt she believed now that there was only one way for her to go, and that was fast-forward, wherever that might lead, and as if putting the seal upon that she leaned over and hugged Tom. "I'd have given up without *you*, Tom," she said, "and I won't stop now!"

"And I won't let you," he replied.

'Lexin could not see into Ida's mind in the way he often could with Marcelle and Shining Face. His mind was definitely working a bit more slowly, too. He did not know whether Ida would go back to Chappel. Maybe she did not know herself. And what good outcome could be expected if she did? Perhaps he should say, 'If she *had gone*? For a moment his optimism deserted him. The vision faded and was only slowly replaced by the Mossman skyline gradually appearing through the invading smoke.

The ferry moored up quietly. Lexin joined the visitors wandering in sight of cave bears and mammoths to encampments of ancient humans who would greet and welcome them, sometimes observing in the distance, or close by, groups of men hunting, and eventually ascending to the second level representing present time.

There they soon encountered mammals large and small, glimpsed reptiles, saw many beautiful birds and from time to time came across people – some real, some no doubt holographic – from many races and many parts of the world, and walked and talked with them, hesitating and sweating a moment with them on seeing a pride of lions moving nearby, thrilled as they caught sight of a tiger's stripes illuminated by a stray ray of sunlight in the shadowy greenery... But already smoke was beginning to spoil the vision of ourselves in our bit of spacetime. The way up to the third, the galactic level, and towards a hoped-for vision of our proper place in the wider scheme of things, was barely visible now in the ever thickening blanket. It was a project barely yet begun.

Lexin fought to put dark fears and sadness out of his mind. Just once he felt bombarded by indelible thoughts of Tom and Ida,

* * *

As the ferry returned across the Harbour, Lexin's multicom was tapping into his brain again.

"Ackroyd here. Lexin, I'd be glad if you would come half an hour before the meeting tonight. Seven-thirty."

There was no saying 'no' to Ackroyd. Not as things stood at present, anyway!

He found a spot high up, aft, with an all-round view of the bay, or as much of it as could be seen in the smoke. The fires seemed a lot nearer already, and along the whole western horizon, and extending far above it, was a perceptibly fluctuating orange glow. The lowering sun – or was it the glow of the fires? – was just catching the high pinnacles above the dizzy trafficways threading the multilevel commercial and residential structures of the city, as if bestowing a final kiss upon the dying achievements of a world that had overreached itself.

* * *

"So you visited Ida..."

"Yes, I was there," Lenica replied. "I was going for another observation, but I was suddenly shown into a room and she was there sitting up in bed. I suppose I shouldn't have been amazed. You know what happened when we were very close to Ida and Tom at their consultation with the surgeon. I told you, how he seemed to be moved, guided by some authority, some power beyond himself...

"Yes you told me. As if he knew Ida would find her cure in some other place and not his hospital. And there was the strange window."

"Yes. Anyway, now she was about to be discharged *from our hospital*, completely free, she had been told, of both virus and cancer." Lexin, sitting now on a seat on Circular Quay, relaxed. So it had happened! "She looked as if she believed it" Lenica went on, "and I reassured her, too. She knew who I was and thanked me."

"Xiaofeng was pleased when I had had my tests and got back home and told him all this, even though I knew my results would be awful, and said so. Everything does seem to have fast-forwarded in the end, Lexin, doesn't it?"

"I am glad it has!" It was the great leap forward, and a more than welcome leap in view of the rigorous demands being made by the 'present' in terms of our available time. It gave substance to those fleeting yet indelible thoughts experienced at Taronga Park. "So *your* cancer is not good, Lenica."

"It's pretty bad. But, you know, I am sure it will get better now." The line sizzled, and nothing could be heard for a few moments. Then he asked,

"How is the situation with the sand?"

"The sand. Well, we could not move without Robert, and Conference delegates are mostly holed up in the Palace complex. Supplies are getting round. I have seen one or two Emergency bubbles just above the surface of the sand in the occasional lull. Funnily enough, Robert says he would call the mood in the city not so much tense as expectant, actually."

Lenica sounded resilient, but her voice was coming and going. Lexin guessed it was the effect of the sand, if nothing else. "I find that encouraging, too," he said "– about the mood of the people."

Felicitas came on from her room. "Lexin, Lexin! Lenica is so ill. Encouraging maybe, but when *are* we going to come out of this?"

Lexin sprang up and started pacing along the quayside, feeling obliged to walk off his unreasonable impatience with his mother. "Think out of time," he said, "like you have been doing, and Lenica, and all of us. Ida is cured, and not only that: she and Tom are together. As for us here, we have done all we can and it is all Marcelle asked for. Now it is in the hands of the Bods. Everything is: Lenica's recovery, everything. I reckon even George Callum will accept that, and certainly Xiaofeng... and even the formidable Polyanova." Even the jokes perpetrated by my PAS suggest it, he said to himself.

"I take your word for it. But Lenica! If you could see her," Felicitas said, breaking down in tears.

"*I* see it as a privilege," Lenica interrupted. "I certainly felt that when I spoke to Ida Weston."

"Look, go right now to Lenica's room and give her a big hug from me, Mother," Lexin said. "Father would be so proud of you, Lenica – and of Xiaofeng."

Lenica came on again: "Is it true they've caught Mauré?"

"Yes. He doesn't give much hope of reversing the EMR programme, but I'm afraid Ackroyd still has the idea that either Jean-Paul or yours truly can wave a magic wand and work a miracle. I think it does all depend on us, but not in the way he is thinking."

There was no comment from Lenica, and Lexin realised after a moment that it was because contact had been lost. He found a bench and sat down. It was too hot to move about much. The ferry boat he had come in on was just being moored up.

"Not many more trips, probably!" a ferry hand said.

"I hope it's not like that."

"We've been lucky. The zoo's kept us going. People still want to go there. I think I know why. I look in there myself. It's what keeps me sane. But if it's not this fire, or problems with the boat's new photovoltaic cells, it'll be something else. The country's really in trouble, brother. There's not one state that's not in real trouble: epidemics, no food...and now the fires! They've even started killing themselves over in the west. What with the depressing press reports and that Commissioner..."

"You reckon it is the boat's photovoltaic cells themselves that are the problem, and not the smoke?"

"Definitely the photovoltaics. We reckon it's one of these new problems. But hi! Isn't it Lexin? This is amazing! What do you reckon the score is, then, Lexin?"

"You mean are we going to get out of this? The answer's 'yes!'"

"That's bloody good news!" the ferryman said. "Good luck on us!" He shook Lexin's hand and went off to see to a couple of intending passengers. There was still no reception from Galaxy City, so Lexin took the opportunity to contact Callum at the hotel and update him about Robert Daley and Ida. George seemed a little less surprised about Daley than about Lenica seeing Ida in the hospital. By that he was flabbergasted. "I suppose it's just too big to ignore," he admitted eventually.

"Sure it is!" Lexin agreed.

There was a silence before Callum said, "And by the way, something *you* may not know which I heard today. Did you know Daley has had a controlling interest in Europe Vision for some time now? I recall your set-to with that Kastner fellow."

Lexin whistled. "No, I did not. A nasty pair, then!"

"Anyway, so Lenica spoke to Ida and Ida is completely cured. That really takes the biscuit!" Callum declared. It also brought to mind what he had experienced in Chappel's consulting room. How was it that he did not recognize the city beyond the window? Of course he didn't. He was Mr. Chappel. He had never seen Galaxy City! "So are we through the woods?" he was able to ask with a renewed though as yet not unclouded optimism, adding "I speak privately. The world is suffering, including our dear Lenica."

"I think we have to trust the Bods for all that, George," Lexin said. "So do we now seek authorization from Conference – from a distance – to propose to the Government and the Assembly that we recommence all activities, including operation of the wormhole? "

"I don't see why not – subject to *PAS confirmation*."

Lexin visualised the grin on George Callum's face. "Of course! I was just testing you. Mackenzie and Lamonte are happy with the new operational regime?"

"Going by the latest reports, yes, they are, though Lamonte told me there is genuine puzzlement, if not amazement, at the new types of calculation..."

"...and some mind boggling factors to be taken into consideration Yes, I had heard. Puzzlement but acceptance, I hope.".

"Acceptance, yes, full acceptance."

"Leonard, too? "

"Yes, he accepts. I think he grasps it now. It has been difficult for him like it has for me just coming to terms with Lexin's People, never mind the wormhole procedure and the astrophysics."

"He has come to terms with that? "

"So I understand. I do not know how the Government is going to take this, though," Callum said. "As for the Assembly...! By all accounts, members have little stomach for a Society that had got them into so much trouble, still less for any discussion of the way the Society imagines it might redeem itself and in so doing save the world! Joanna is in quite a state, as became clear in a televisual call I had from her half an hour ago. She wanted my opinion on how things were going."

"*Did* she? "

"Just checking up on you, I guess. Still has her doubts about you, dear boy."

"I guess so. Must have been talking to Ackroyd. He has this idea that Jean-Paul and I have the answer to his problems. Even that I am keeping something from him. Wants me to see him again before the meeting tonight."

"Both of them are looking for any other way out of this but your way, aren't they? So are you going to see Joanna? One thing is sure: if you are able to work your magic on her, she has great pulling power, has she not?"

Lexin agreed, although he knew there could be no recommencement without the Assembly's approval. If there had been a Society constitution, that would have been part of Article No.1. "Yes, I agree it's time for a little chat with the First Minister, though I do not know how it will go."

"Felicitas? How will *she* take it?"

"I hate her to be tormented by thoughts of what could happen to me if it all goes belly-up, but what alternative have I?"

"I just hope you can get there, Lexin."

"Get where?"

"To the re-commissioning! Anyway, leave it to me. I will get in touch with Mackenzie."

Thank God Callum was still on board. "I hope we can *all* get there," Lexin said. "Just make sure Mackenzie gets the message, and Xiaofeng. An awful lot depends on us now, otherwise Ackroyd and van Rensburg between them...?"

"I will do my best. You know things are no better in Galaxy than they are here. We have fire, they have sand. And it's not just the sand, according to Mackenzie. People are dying."

"What are they dying of?"

"Apart from suicides, which include two of my colleagues, it's hard to say. People ignore the personal survival recommendations, basically, or can't find a doctor, or just plain disappear."

Lexin wasn't feeling too good, either. The smoke seemed to be drying him up, depriving him of any appetite, draining him. "I shall be trying to get the First Minister to see it the way we do," he said to Callum finally. "I don't believe there is any other way, in any case."

Lexin tried Joanna van Rensburg's private number. Her secretary put her through immediately. She said she was expecting to hear from him and he had better come over. She could see him in her office next day in the evening.

Looking up as he walked back to the hotel through near-deserted, unlit streets in the dusk it seemed as though the entire sky was a huge, blazing blanket and the dark land around him, already hot and expectant, longing for its engulfing embrace. As soon as he got back he put a belated update on his website, as detailed as he could.

* * *

Lexin was in the Commissioner's room overlooking Hyde Park at 7.30 prompt. No point in irritating him unnecessarily.

"I trust you have had a good rest," he said.

"I decided to relax a bit at the zoo."

"Try and forget everything, eh?"

"On the contrary, I have been trying to point the way *through everything* for a long time. Blunck & Co. are just a diversion. Visit my website."

"Oh yes! And just how are Lexin's People going to help us now?"

"With respect, Commissioner, if you had been following you would understand."

"I hope you're bloody right, anyhow," he said, barely controlling his anger. "Your Mauré's really spilled them now! Says Daley activated in effect a global programme of increasingly severe effects. The elements of it are now scattered beyond recall in numerous virtually invisible daughter satellites set to cover every square kilometre of the globe. He was angry, damn him, and yes, so am I. Incidentally, according to Mauré there was never any chance of Daley's inserted software taking hold. And now," the Commissioner continued after a pause, in a tone of something between resignation and disbelief, "with a five thousand square kilometre fire sixty metres high already carving its way into the suburbs I don't know where it will end, I bloody don't! Talk about playing with fire, Lexin!" (Was that a dart aimed at himself? He thought it probably was. So what?)

"I am glad you are not panicking, Commissioner," he said.

"I never do that! Emergency measures are in progress for Sydney, as elsewhere. The bottom line for me, Lexin, is that – fires apart – I am not convinced about the inevitability factor here. I mean the inevitability of total population destruction. That spark of hope is something to do with you, and I have tried very hard to make quite sure that spark is not extinguished."

Lexin found it difficult to share the Commissioner's spark of optimism, having more respect (if that was the right word) for Mauré's brain power and preferring to rest his confidence in Tom and Ida and the fact of their re-emergence from their tribulations, in like manner to that other family in the ice and snow of an earlier age. Now was the time to tell him. "I have to inform you, Commissioner, that Lexin's

People (I hesitate to say 'my' People – it sounds presumptuous) have now just about achieved what they hoped to achieve, and Conference is likely to agree within the next twenty-four hours that the Society has also overcome its problems at the Mission Station to the extent of being ready to resume all its work. Therefore I do ask you most earnestly to please leave the solution of your problems to us."

"Leave it to you! Can *you* put out the *fire*, never mind stop the programme?"

"You know I cannot, Commissioner. Meanwhile I have a simpler question which *you* may be able to answer: Tell me," he said, "Can you clarify one thing: why they murdered Bill Walmsley?"

"Walmsley! Yes, sorry about your Bill Walmsley, but if you'd come to us sooner..."

"...It might have been difficult to prove anything We might be even worse off now. But you didn't answer my question."

"What was that? Ah yes. I don't know why he was murdered. They deny any connection with his murder. My guess, however, is that he blew their plot early. I speculate it was Daley who organised his murder for having been identified by him. He may have suspected for some while that Walmsley had him in his sights. No opposition can be tolerated by such a person as Robert Daley."

"Can I come and see Jean-Paul?"

"I shall think about it, under supervision. I want a solution to this, Lexin. I am still not entirely convinced that you – or the two of you – cannot reverse the present catastrophic situation. I'm sorry to have to keep repeating this. Now we must go. I have to get to the meeting"

He had calmed down a lot. The meeting was held in a committee room. The Commissioner left no-one in doubt about the gravity of the situation, of which the public had already received details in two TV appearances of the First Minister. The grim details had, he said, been received by the public with remarkable calmness and fortitude. The media had been very cooperative.

He explained that all parts of the globe were liable to exposure to the radiation. Moreover, the characteristics of the development of foci of harmful effects appeared to be changing and we must be prepared for very bad experiences. Lexin realised this was entirely in confirmation of both Mauré's and Callum's predictions. From what he was hearing, the effects ranged from light mental incapacity to increasingly violent and often unpredictable or strange behaviour.

Earth's people were long *un*accustomed to severe mental and physical trauma, and in most cases had no-one to turn to and nowhere to go for medical treatment. In urban populations in certain longitudinal belts the pace of loss of control at all levels of government was alarming.

"Roaming, self-accreting gangs are an increasing phenomenon in a growing disorder worldwide," the Commissioner said, "and we must be on our guard. On the positive side, everything is being done that can be done both nationally and locally in the face of a totally unprecedented set of problems." He was hopeful that a multidisciplinary team that he had with some difficulty called together, consisting of both Societans and Normals and collaborating televisually, would be successful in complementing the efforts of Societans in Galaxy City to unravel Mauré's devilish design. He hoped also that the team might be able to establish a model to counteract or neutralise, even reverse, the effects of radiation.

So saying, he picked up his hat and marched out in a flourish of service medals, no questions having been invited. Lexin managed to catch him in a hallway afterwards.

"There's something else I feel I must reiterate…," he said.

Perhaps it was an unusual note of desperation in Lexin's normally calm tone, some change in attitude, possibly, that pulled Ackroyd up. "I've every faith in your boys back in Galaxy," the Commissioner said, "and if there's anything relevant in the material they're continuously analysing I'm sure they'll spot it if my team – or Monsieur Jean-Paul Mauré – doesn't come up with something before they do!"

But Lexin persisted. "Even if by some good fortune we were able to nullify the EMR programme, and in time to avoid total catastrophe, it is possible, you know, that all our efforts to do that might turn out to have been a waste of time involving enormous and unnecessary loss of life."

Ackroyd sighed, shaking his head in desperation. He was fatigued, said he had a blinding headache and was finding it hard to think straight. "I think you had better come back to my office for a moment," he said, wearily.

"Well?" he said, when he had flopped down in his chair, offering Lexin another.

"We might do better to leave resolution of the problem to superior powers."

"Now I fancy you are talking in riddles again, Lexin, if (as I suspect) you think I am barking up the wrong tree and it's your 'People' you are wanting to talk about."

"It is not they who are the 'powers', Commissioner."

"So who, then?"

Was he feigning puzzlement, or was it the radiation effect? "The friends from constellation Lyra," Lexin replied.

"Jesus, Lexin, that was hundreds of years ago!" Ackroyd yawned.

"No less important for that! Anyway as I explained to you, the long and the short of it is that I am suggesting to Conference that they should finally decide whether they think it is now time to seek permission for the Society to resume all its operations, and I am pretty sure delegates are going to say 'yes'."

"I hear what you are saying. It scares me like I should have thought it would scare you. I ought to have you locked up." There was not a flicker of a smile.

"Assuming you are not going to do that, I hope to see Van Rensburg tomorrow to inform her that Wormhole Research and Operations are now very confident that past errors of procedure have been corrected and that two-way communication can be safely attempted."

"And the satellites, the unstoppable programme, the fires?"

"Our friends are very powerful. Commissioner, I would not want you to remain uninformed about the situation."

"My view is that you should wait for the multidisciplinary team to come to an interim conclusion, and I have told the First Minister that, and my views on the Society's role in all this – and yours especially! By the way, you may not get back from Canberra even if you get there," the Commissioner added as Lexin got up to go.

"Oh?"

"The fires are bad, real bad."

Returning to the Murrumburra Hotel Lexin could hardly credit the fact, on turning up his website, that in a week it had received five million hits despite an estimate that perhaps only one in ten thousand computers worldwide was able to work online. Obviously not everyone out there was as sceptical as Commissioner Alistair Ackroyd about Lexin's People.

A brief meeting early next day, under supervision, with a somewhat defiant Mauré produced no surprises. He had been dismayed to discover that his advice was being used against Earth's people, not to protect them. Lexin even had the feeling he might still believe in the reality of an alien threat. He said the programme was actually intended, by its multifaceted, steadily more severe approach, to be a fail-safe way of reaching all the invaders and encouraging them to leave the planet or take the consequences. He spoke darkly of universal lethal effects.

In the afternoon a message came from Galaxy City that in an emergency session the Conference had unanimously agreed to ask permission to restart full operation of the Mission Station. Lexin had already arrived in Canberra when Callum forwarded the message.

Callum said that according to Xiaofeng Mackenzie had taken the line that present attempts to break the impasse would probably fail, or at least be too late. At the same time, no destructive consequence of an unsuccessful resumption would be likely to be any worse than the consequence of no resumption. "As for the rest," Xiaofeng said, "I am convinced that most of them contacted their constituency organisations and plumbed the depths of their synthesizers, and came up with an unequivocal 'yes' to resumption on *that* basis." To his credit, and for all his lingering doubts, Leonard had stated his wish to be among those in the observation gallery at the inauguration of the reconstructed wormhole.

*   *   *

Some sense of optimism felt by Lexin during the thirty minutes to Canberra in the maglev, which became reinforced by the news from Callum, proved to be not unjustified. Lexin's reception at World Government House was very civil.

"I have not had the chance to say to you personally how sorry I was about Bill Walmsley," Joanna said when the secretary ushered him into her office. "Without his help things might by now be even worse than they are, might they not?"

Lexin nodded. He felt a bit sorry for *her* in the present situation. She certainly looked paler than usual, but the determined look on her face plus a smart costume in which red and blue predominated, topped by a voluminous silk neckerchief on which elements of the threatened fauna of her country could readily be distinguished, suggested that his response to her inevitably severe questioning would require maximum skills of persuasion. Stepping aside to reveal a sallow- and sombre-faced fellow standing behind her she said,

"This is my new deputy, Andrew Borland. He is English. Andrew, I know you will recognize Lexin Solberg, de facto Society representative in the World Government and Assembly post-Beckenthal, and not only from his website – which to my own discredit I had not visited until recently." Lexin would like to have confirmed with her what exactly the American, Faust, had been up to. Rumour had it that her deputy had learned what was going on and had tried to contain and conceal the antics of Blunck and company from her in order to preserve political stability at least until the unauthorised experimenting stopped and its effects became lost in the general chaos of retrogression.

"Indeed I have visited it," Borland replied, stepping forward and shaking hands, rousing Lexin from his thoughts and unexpectedly smiling beneath a mop of lank, blond hair. He looked surprisingly 'cool' in an uninhibited, long, flowery shirt and linen trousers and sandals. A young-looking forty-year-old, Lexin reckoned, he looked interested, but tired. "Of course," he said, "they are in the papers now, are they not, Lexin's People? It seems there is no putting them down!"

When they were seated in the First Minister's intimate and now familiar surroundings, the atmosphere so restrained, so controlled in contrast to events elsewhere, Joanna said,

"Just clarify for me, Lexin, these terrible events; they are not solely the result of criminal activity, are they? You are saying that something went basically wrong with our relationship with...with the Lyrians, I suppose?"

Lexin was glad she was willing to go back to basics. "Yes. As I have tried to explain – and it was hard to explain even to fellow Societans at first – , for many decades we had not been thorough enough, trusting enough in the use of our personal link with the Lyrians, i.e. our synthesizers, especially in our decipherment of the text on the disks left behind by the Lyrians. After a number of explosions when trying to contact them via the still experimental wormhole in order to fill in some gaps in our knowledge, it became a case of our – and particularly my – progressive vilification by certain unsympathetic or even malign elements in the media – not so difficult to imagine against a background of scepticism about me and my funny ideas."

"Malign elements? Really?" Borland sounded doubtful, or a little confused. It was difficult to tell. He appeared to be struggling against the creeping lethargy, too.

"Yes. The big explosion forced cessation of decipherment. It was like losing a living link – or put another way, it was like a teacher leaving the class on its own and things going a bit pear-shaped (Lexin thought Borland would appreciate the English understatement). And *there* was Beckenthal, already tired of his work at the Mission Station repeatedly going up in smoke and only too pleased to follow the media, rubbishing the Society and latching onto something more 'productive', and Daley relishing being master of the press hounds."

"Daley!" Borland seemed to catch up. "So to get this quite straight in my mind, you mean the media were rubbishing your attempts to explain how the Society could redeem itself, as it were, if Societans put themselves in the position of your People?"

"Yes. But at the same time, under cover of the chaotic developments following cessation of decipherment, this gang, the real criminals, were unfortunately able to hijack the valuable skills of human enhancement..."

"I don't follow," Joanna said.

"...which you had engaged for purposes of second-line defence – albeit unnecessarily."

"Ah yes! Mauré."

"And very quickly things spiralled out of control."

She looked pretty uptight at that. Lexin again found himself questioning how Borland's predecessor Faust might have kept her in the dark for so long, allaying any suspicion that might have been aroused by her meetings with Callum and with himself and McLintock. He thought all this – if it was what happened – was most likely to be interpreted as an example of the kind of trust in public office that had been instilled over centuries. Possibly, however, it did not happen quite like that, and, as Ackroyd had seemed to infer, the smallness and tightness of a group protected by a self-imposed curtain of 'security' could have been enough to shield the perpetrators from any close investigation, or even suspicion, in spite of everything. Time would tell – if there was enough of it!

"Concerning Lexin's People of the two different epochs," the First Minister said, recovering her poise, "these really are – or should I say were – real people?"

"Yes. The tense is irrelevant in the sense that although they are real, now, in their own epochs our PAS's enable us to identify with them, even sometimes almost become them. Lives become intertwined."

"And they represent salvation for us is what you have been saying, isn't it?" Borland asked. His expression was entirely neutral, his attention fully focussed now.

"And for them of course, but for us I would describe it more as 'a way back'. But it is the *Lyrians* who represent our future, our future in the Galactic Community, as I was trying to explain to Commissioner Ackroyd. I know he would like to put me behind bars. He thinks I believe in fairy tales, but the fact is that the Lyrians must have revealed them to us." Both ministers were regarding him closely, Joanna with the sharp attentiveness of that little African mole, and both evidently with Herculean efforts of concentration. Lexin had to admit to himself that the kinds of things he was saying were not the most digestible food for politicians at any time, never mind in times of cerebral meltdown. Outside it seemed to have become darker.

Joanna had got up and was pacing around. "He is a practical man. He is afraid you are following dreams, and I find it hard to disagree with him. Why these people, Lexin? What exactly is happening here? What is their significance...no, I mean how do you define their *status*, actually? I am a bit late into all this, as I said, and not as clear in my mind today as I would like, though – I shouldn't say this – I think his accusation that you are actually putting your dream before any real attempt to stop the EMR programme may be a little unfair. Nevertheless, I know he would like to have you in for interrogation."

"Would like to?"

"Yes. Would like to. You can see how critical this is, Lexin. Actually, Commissioner Ackroyd's view now is – to put it bluntly – that the Society should be closed down."

"To answer your question about the 'status' of the People, I cannot read the minds of the Lyrians, but obviously it is being made clear to us that the People need us and we need them. I think it is not irrelevant to mention that the two chief 'people' are very remarkable young women in different epochs who become instrumental in uniting their fragmented families. Could it not not be imagined that the Lyrians might have wished, by facing them with this real-life task in their own times, to awaken in *us* the desire for our relationship with *them, the Lyrians*, to be fully restored – a reconciliation, a restoration of trust?"

The initiative was theirs, the Lyrians', and the offer thus made to us humans was surely made in the same good faith that we on our side have to a large extent lost."

There was a long silence, then Joanna said, "I don't see how the Assembly will ever swallow this in its present depressed state. I am afraid it is the radiation and what it is doing to us. Everything is black for them. They will say the darkness now is the same as the darkness at the beginning of the troubles, the explosions, only worse. They will say that what went wrong before will go wrong again, and even worse this time. The rest will just sound kind of religious. Arresting you, that's...well..." She did not pursue that. "… But to allow you to go on, it's a step too far."

Borland seemed lost in thought. "Restoration of trust. Mmm... interesting," he was saying, half out loud, but Joanna had that near-tearful look.

"This is impossible!" she declared. "Now that the criminals have been caught, may there not be shades of grey in the blackness, if I could put it like that, where the investigating team might yet break through, order be restored? Commissioner Ackroyd takes this view, doesn't he? And even your Mackenzie is less than convinced. Moreover, Mauré cannot be the only clever guy in his field; others may be cleverer. It is very difficult, Lexin, to disagree with the logic exercised by the Police Commissioner."

"It is impossible to say whether there may be shades of grey. The point is, Joanna (though it is hard to have to say it), that it does not matter. The medicine is for the Society, but it is the cure for the Earth and its restoration."

"You must admit that when you speak of our world like that, I mean as though one were abandoning it – as an act of faith, as it were –, it puts me in a difficult position in terms of my perceived responsibilities" The First Minister was standing by the window overlooking the gardens. "I cannot get away from the fact that for whatever reason you are actually saying, if I understand you correctly, that there is no point in waiting for the report of the multidisciplinary team – with all that that may imply for the future of the Planet."

Before Lexin could saying anything in reply to that, Borland, who had stood up and was taking a couple of paces here and a couple there, with head bowed, said,

"You say most Societans have accepted the 'medicine', in effect?"

"Yes, almost unanimously."

"The justification for recommencement being...?"

""...That families once divided and entrusted to our care are restored.""

"And that is enough justification for resumption of testing?"

Lexin scarcely dared to hope that the Deputy had 'got it'. "It means that we are using our gadgetry correctly," he replied, "and also by inference that the wormhole teams' confidence in their procedures is justified. Our PAS's confirm it unequivocally. That is vital."

"It implies complete trust, then."

"Trust on both sides. The wormhole procedures involve much closer co-operation with the Lyrians, actually."

Joanna swung round. "*Co-operation* with the Lyrians?"

"There's been co-operation all along, Joanna – 'trust', if you like –; just not enough of it."

"Ah! Your PAS." She relaxed visibly.

He nodded. "I cannot overstate the part played by Professor Malinovsky in this connection,. He has been a truly guiding light in restoring our relationship with the Lyrians.."

"I gather Mackenzie always disagreed with him."

"Leonard Mackenzie did not use his PAS, never followed Lexin's People himself, personally – until recently, anyway."

"Ah yes. Of course." The First Minister emitted a sigh. Was it a sign of some understanding and/or of resignation? Borland, who had been scrutinizing Lexin's face during this exchange, was nodding almost imperceptibly. He turned towards Joanna, who was staring out of the window again, staring at the faintly pink sky. What remained of the light was reflected in her face in a pink- and orange-tinted flush. Even up here in the Capital Territory the sky seemed to be shedding blood. After all, the Blue Mountains were not that far away. "They will never allow recommencement," she declared before he could say anything, and without turning round. "Everything that has happened, they will place it all at the Society's door. Lexin, Commissioner Ackroyd believes you had many opportunities to halt Robert Daley in his tracks."

"Hindsight is not always helpful. At least, now we have a lasting solution in prospect. That is not in any way to diminish the terrible damage caused. I wish we could have reached this point earlier."

"I think we have to trust those who trust the Lyrians," Borland said.

"It is they the Lyrians have always communicated with – with our consent and to our benefit."

"I wish I had your faith in those People of yours, Lexin," Joanna said. There was a long silence. Then she said, "I suppose I am more of a plodder than my Voortrekker forbears."

There was a short silence, then Borland said, "I should just like to ask Lexin, if you go ahead, what the outcome might be?"

"I hope the mind-destroying programme will be stopped," Lexin replied "It is a hope – hope and trust that the Lyrians will help us once communication is restored. But that would be only the beginning of Earth's restoration and – hopefully – the continuation of decipherment and our progress towards Galactic participation."

"And what do you suppose will happen if the Assembly does not 'get it', Andrew?" Joanna asked, turning to face him.

"I shall be surprised," he replied.

No-one spoke for some time. Then the First Minister turned and said, with a suggestion of a sigh, "I see I am upstaged by my Deputy. In view of the urgency of the situation, I think my colleagues will agree *subject to the agreement of the Police Commissioner* to my summoning an extraordinary session of the Assembly for tomorrow at which I shall put the proposal of the Society to them. I guarantee nothing. Who can guarantee anything at the moment, anyway? Even that we shall still be here tomorrow? Meantime, I have every confidence in the Police Commissioner and will continue to support him in everything he is doing."

Smoke was thick in the air as Lexin left and made his way towards the same hotel in Kingston that he had stayed in with McLintock previously. He was picking up news that the fires were now indeed threatening the maglev route to Sydney, as Ackroyd had warned. He would have to stay the night.

CHAPTER TWENTY-TWO

"Your father would never have stood still and done nothing to try and help you in that situation, Lenica," Felicitas said, still distressed by her daughter's self-sacrificial utterances. "I feel *I* should be helping you – somehow." Robert had cleared away the breakfast things from the table, but they were still sitting at it. Xiaofeng, the only one properly dressed, and sitting next to Felicitas, was fiddling with his multicom, trying to contact Beijing and find out about his family. It would not do to be appearing there in his dressing gown.

"Mother, what could you possibly do?" Lenica said. "Even supposing the worst comes to the worst, then like I said they might be able to fit me up with new bits." It was now a week after the last scan. The cancer had spread. No reason could be found for its unresponsiveness to the latest tailored procedures. She had resisted major surgical intervention. "The cancer hasn't spread to vital organs," she said.

"Yet."

"No, and I am optimistic. And I have got those cells stored up. It might pay to have been old-fashioned yet." It had all been at Felicitas's instigation, of course, a bit hypochondriacal and introspective as she was, and like her Russian forebears were supposed to have been. In these days of even more perfect health it was no longer so fashionable to make such provision at the birth of one's offspring.

"The thought appals me, darling." Felicitas leaned forward on the table, burying the disordered remains of her latest coiffure in her arms and showing the grey hairs on her nape. Such neglect of her appearance in semi-public was most unusual.

"Mother, in any case it may well be that very soon now we will find ourselves closer to the Bods than we ever were before."

Closer to the Bods! It was twenty-four hours earlier that Lexin had let them know members of the Assembly would be deciding next day whether message transmission and retrieval, and decipherment, could be resumed. As Lenica contemplated that house where she and her brother had lived all their lives, the house with its centuries of patiently accumulated memories, set above the city and so proudly poised for the future, she hoped beyond hope that those hearts and minds so misled, and so disillusioned about the Society, might rise above paralysing despair and hostility boldly to take what was surely the only possible route to a resumption of progress towards galactic participation.

Felicitas might have read her thoughts. "I hope they believe that in the Assembly – about the Bods! Or do I? It's a nightmare!" she burst out, clutching Xiaofeng's arm, causing him to lay aside his multicom.

"Felicitas," he said, putting his arm around her shoulders, "Too much has happened this last week not to have confidence that we'll get through everything."

"And my children? And that includes you, Xiaofeng."

"They will be all right! Look, the Society is single minded now, strong. Even Leonard Mackenzie's put his head on the line. Anyway, there can be only one way to go, and that is forward. It is the least we owe to the world – and to Lexin! I just hope Lexin can get here, and that they can get them to the Mission Station."

Meanwhile the media – a fragmented remnant struggling to find some cause to espouse in the present confusion, and in particular one that might give some cause for hope – were now at least sniffing drama and conclusion ahead in the form of a final showdown between two opposing but increasingly unequal forces. Ranged against the dwindling forces of what looked increasingly like persistent stubbornness were many, like the Brazilian, Freda Sonego, and (much to Callum's surprise) even pompous old Crabtree of the 'Vancouver

Daily' and a growing number of others (including most of the tabloid press), adding to the voices (where they could be heard) of those now expressing increased confidence in Lexin and his People. It embodied a real hope – if not exactly a solid expectation – that in them resided the salvation of the Race.

"The words 'Mission Station' fill me with foreboding," Felicitas murmured as she rose finally from the breakfast table and went to her banana-leaf chair, sinking into it most un-imperiously, head lowered slightly and eyes staring blankly forward, her hands fingering the arms nervously. Lenica went and comforted her before gently breaking away and going to the window overlooking the Park. The sky was dark yellow with the thickly blowing sand. Nothing was visible out there. "I keep on thinking of that attempted mass suicide in Australia, in Perth," her mother said (Thousands were preparing to lie down on a maglev track, but fortunately the electricity had happened to go off minutes before).

At another time, Lenica thought, it might have been the stuff of tragicomedy. "Yes, yes," she said, "but *they* survived and we're going to. You know, Lexin told me how many hits the website was getting. He says it is what gives him the most hope now."

"And if we don't get permission, billions around the world looking to Lexin's People will scarcely credit it," Xiaofeng said. He seemed to have given up trying to get through to Beijing.

"Permission!" Felicitas exclaimed sourly, rousing herself and forsaking her chair to go to the glass doors of the terrace and stare out at the sand drifting in the garden, the obscurity beyond.

"Mother! You know it has always been a cardinal principle. Let's not try to ignore the Government even if we've failed to listen to the Bods."

Felicitas did not answer. Instead the house telecom rang and Lenica answered. "It's Lexin!" she said in as steady a voice as she could.

"Well let us all see him and hear him, then, and vice versa!" Felicitas demanded, suddenly regaining her old composure, and Lenica activated the room screen.

To Lenica he looked strained, miserable. "Bad news, I'm afraid. By a big majority the Assembly has decided that my visions, whatever they really are, provide no basis for any resumption of the Society's activities, and that we should await the Commissioner's report in order to determine what action to take – this despite the fact that the multidisciplinary team is getting nowhere. Failing such action, we must all just 'weather the storm' – whatever that can possibly mean."

"I don't believe this," Lenica exclaimed. "They must have just given up. It's the radiation. It's killing them! The Assembly must have been targeted."

"Quite probably," Xiaofeng said. He had stood up. "Like I am sure they targeted Beijing. It has completely disintegrated, with gangs roaming the streets."

"What more can I do?" Lexin crackled over the poor connection. "Van Rensburg's deputy got the message, and Joanna went along with him. I don't think it is her fault. But this is democracy, isn't it?"

"I've never thought much of that word," Felicitas said, angrily.

"I reckon it's the Police," Lenica said. "You know Ackroyd never believed in us." She felt ill and wanted to sit, but did not want to worry Lexin by showing it.

"Don't they know your sister is dying for their cause?" Felicitas complained.

"Mother, don't talk in those terms!" Lenica protested. "It would be no help."

"My God, it's all terrible." Felicitas had sat down again. "I agree with Lenica," she said. "They *must* have been targeted."

"They are in a strange state," Lexin was saying, "suicidal, even. It is as if any explanation for the visions will do except the one we know to be true. Lenica..." He paused, and Lenica suddenly knew what was coming. "...You must talk to them. Who knows what it might do? A new face, voice of experience."

Lenica was steadying herself against the back of Felicitas's chair, scarcely daring to believe she had heard her brother aright. She was hardly able to see him on the screen for the sand interference. She heard herself say, "*Could* I come?" and immediately wondered what Xiaofeng would say. Then seeing him apparently making no discouraging signs she said, "I'm sure I have the power to convince them." Still he remained silent, but had come and put his arm round her. At any moment she expected to hear a maternal voice of stern disapproval.

"How could you get here?" Lexin's voice was clear, and that and the fact that the beloved had not tried to go against her gave her confidence beyond her expectations, so that when the maternal voice resounded,

"She's ill and in pain, Lexin, she couldn't," Lenica knew there was only one possible response:

"I must, Mother," she said, and then to Lexin, "Could I be broadcast onto a big screen for the Assembly to see?"

"The picture would be so bad it would be counterproductive."

"It could be broadcast from the Palace, Felicitas," Xiaofeng suggested. "via the three hundred-metre antenna. At least the sand shouldn't be too much of a bar. The great bulk of it is below that height. It is the best chance, Lenica. This is an emergency, isn't it?..."

Later that day, Lexin phoned saying that having spoken to Joanna he had received a message from her saying she and her Government were sorry about the negative response of the Assembly. The Government had now agreed that Lenica by her very presence could be a catalyst for a breakthrough, and the Assembly would be recalled. She had admitted that possibly she should have been more proactive.

Was she moving in his direction? At least, he said, he had not been taken in for police interrogation. She said he had come very close to arrest, and the Society to closure. He had politely suggested she might have to be even more proactive yet.,

*   *   *

Lenica appeared on a large, wide screen set up in the awesome minimalist surroundings of the Chamber of the Assembly in World Government House in Canberra whence the proceedings were being relayed to wherever they could still be viewed throughout the world. In a long purple dress that buttoned up to the neck at the top of a long white vertical overlay bearing her Southern Cross brooch in red stone, she had tried hard to look her best and inspire respect rather than sympathy, still less pity. Any fleeting (and on her own admission, ridiculous) feelings of envy on the part of Felicitas, seated in her room with Fiona Callum, on seeing her daughter elevated in large dimension queen-like on the world stage were quickly abolished by her haggard appearance. It was something which no immaculate presentation would have been able to hide completely.

Lenica tried to explain to the thousand members of the Assembly ranged across another large screen in front of *her* that her brother's only thought was for the world at large and its future. When she spoke of the great gifts decipherment had brought, Felicitas could only exclaim 'Yes! Yes!'– this despite the fear in her heart of the possible consequences for him of any recommencement that turned out to be premature. For the present, she knew she must bury her own fears now and hope, no doubt together with the Conference delegates also watching the proceedings from the Great Hall, that the Assembly members in Canberra might come to believe her daughter. Few, at any rate, could fail to have heard of Lenica's great suffering in the cause of her brother's visions.

A voice called out ,"Give us back ourselves, when we had to fight to live. Give us wars, heroes!"

"It's not an option," Lenica replied. "Your ancestors chose another way."

"So why did you ruin it?"

Felicitas winced at the harshness of the question. The television crew in the Chamber had not been able to pick out the questioner.

"Because we were fools and did not obey the Lyrians. It has been a hard and testing process, and we have not lived up to it."

Now a big man stood up to speak, growing bigger and increasingly formidable as the cameras closed in: a man with full black beard and pronged moustache, an Armenian or perhaps an Azerbaijani – Felicitas's language selector faltered for a moment. "Perhaps we do not wish to follow them any more," he said, and declared passionately, "but go our own way to freedom, even if it means our destruction." To this there was a murmur of agreement, which became louder when he was asked to repeat it in one of the preferred languages of the Assembly.

Felicitas gasped. Lenica's image, when it reappeared, was becoming hazy, owing perhaps to the blowing sand or to disruptions due to some retrogressive or other effect on transmission, for it was with only intermittent clarity that Joanna van Rensburg next appeared, sitting tight-lipped among her ministers. Involuntarily, Felicitas stood up, wanted to shout something across the world in response to the last speaker, though she did not know what. But Lenica spoke instead. She stood up:

"Should any survive the coming catastrophe," she declared, "they would not forgive you! Look, I want you to listen to me because I will show you there is no need for us all to be destroyed." How daunted the poor girl must have been by the grim, stony faces before her! "I want to explain to you that things began to go wrong long before the explosions, but it was only then that we began to realise that our dear friends, our patient friends, the Lyrians ..."

"Some friends, Lenica!" a voice shouted, but the person was called to order by the Leader of the Assembly in the sturdy, authoritative figure of the Moroccan Rita Ouchelh in her red kaftan.

"Thank goodness *she* seems in her right mind, anyway," Felicitas said quickly.

"Only then, after the explosions", Lenica continued against a background of continuing interruptions, "did we realise our friends had not abandoned us but offered a vision of hope, a wake-up call to make us realise our shortcomings – yes, our serious shortcomings..."

"...Vision? There *is* no hope!" voices were calling out, and others: "Why should we trust you now? Is not Mauré one of you? How do we know there are not more fools plotting?" until the Leader finally restored a degree of order, but not before someone was heard to ask,

"How is it that you a Societan are so clever, so intelligent – supposedly –, but never foresaw what happened in the Ministry of Emergencies?"

"We did see it, we did see what was happening – in the end," Lenica almost shouted, but her voice faltered. ..

"But it was too late!" a lone voice pointed out. Felicitas recognized Werner Bergmann, a German industrialist big in body and in biosynthetic fibres.

"Yes, it was too late to halt the programme of irradiation," Lenica managed to say, before a torrent of complaint almost drowned her assurance, faintly uttered, that it was "still not too late to act."

Felicitas, still standing, registered with dismay the pain on Lenica's face as she waited to continue, prevented just as much now by her discomfort, probably, as by the noise confronting her – a noise, an unruliness, an intolerance such as Felicitas had never seen or heard of in the Assembly. Joanna, too, was looking forlornly in her direction, but others were trying to speak, and finally one person in particular, to whom – to Felicitas's surprise – Mdm Ouchelh gave the floor and said she would allow no interruption:

"If you had understood our galactic 'friends' as you call them – and I don't particularly dispute that word –, if you had trusted them, all this business and the events which apparently led to it might have been avoided. You would not argue with that, would you?" Close up, Felicitas recognized Yoshida, as Lenica would have done as well. She had often mentioned him, a Japanese lawyer, slim and fresh faced, a clever but moderate man. Unlike the mass of those present, he appeared still quite lucid and rational.

The question stung, and Felicitas sensed a wave of concordant anger among members. Had not Lexin talked so often and so passionately of 'trust'? She was forced to acknowledge that it was a perfectly reasonable complaint expressing fears on behalf of a world facing a terrible threat that had resulted from the Society's self confessed failings in that very matter of trust. Who could blame them? The anger crescendoed.

Van Rensburg was captured by the cameras looking pleadingly at Rita Ouchelh, sitting opposite, for some palliative words, but eventually the noise subsided into a heavy murmur of complaint of its own accord. Lenica appeared to be about to reply when the German stood up again as Yoshida sat down:

"What assurance can you give us that it is not too late to act? Tell us the truth!"

"Yes, for goodness sake, tell us," Fiona said under her breath, and then, "Felie, why don't you sit down. It's hard enough for you as it is."

"I cannot," Felicitas replied. "I cannot sit while this awful thing is going on."

Lenica seemed to recover herself. "I don't dispute the other member's accusation, I mean about our lack of trust," she said, "but there has been a reconciliation. At last we are reconciled with those who have brought us unbelievable benefits. We have a good understanding – of hearts and minds, if they have hearts and minds like ours. Now I can tell you that the disastrous effects *can* be reversed, but they cannot be reversed by us." Her words became barely audible as a growing sound expanded to fill the great circle of the Chamber, a wave of sound that was maybe part complaining, part questioning, but the German had evidently caught the words, and as this wave began to dissipate into a babble of conversation he asked,

"Reversed? By who reversed? Did you say the Lyrians?"

Was Lenica actually nodding? The intermittent fading in sound now, as well as vision, was becoming more persistent, and Felicitas could not hear what she was saying as the industrialist sat down again, staring up at her in apparent disbelief as she took full screen again. How many others among the confused and unhappy members filling the Chamber had picked up the fragile message of salvation?

"Mauré! You have not answered about Mauré!" a persistent member was calling out repeatedly above the babble.

"He was foolish. Don't be too harsh on him," Lenica responded, sitting down.

"What if he was right after all?" It was Yoshida. "What if there *are* evil forces waiting out there. Has it been disproved?"

On the Leader's nod, Van Rensburg stood up and intervened. Felicitas could imagine Lenica's relief at being able to sit down even for a moment. "I have to tell you that there *is* none," the First Minister said, an unaccustomedly slow, even agonised but nevertheless determined delivery matched by a defiantly immaculate appearance in a warm gown with lapels, white scarf and deep, white belt. "There are no evil forces out there, ... and we know…we know now that there never were any. Furthermore it is irrelevant at this stage to judge whether M. Mauré is guilty of anything…of anything, I should say, more than extreme foolishness." The slowness had the effect of reducing the buzz of disparate voices to a brain-stopping silence, and the Minister sat down.

"Commissioner Ackroyd still reckons *we* can reverse Mauré's programme even if Mauré himself cannot." The cameras picked out Yoshida again, out of the silence. "Ought he not to know? How do you answer that, Ms. Solberg?"

Lenica, coming to her feet again, paused for a moment as the voices resumed, seemed for a moment not to know what she should say. The Leader stood up and asked members to allow her to rest a moment, but Lenica replied despite the noise,

"Commissioner Ackroyd has to deal with the situation he sees on the ground and make his own judgements..." Felicitas could not hear the few words that followed.

"What about the Multidisciplinary Report, then?" Yoshida continued.

Van Rensburg took the question. "There may be no time left to consider it," she said. "The investigatory team has not – at least so far – been able to come up with a model…a model that might… that could in any way counteract, or indeed neutralise, the programme." Still the slowness, the coming and going of the Minister's image, and of her voice, but her speech was a little more fluent now.

A sullen silence resumed while the cameras panned round the Assembly, as though Mauré having been dismissed, Commissioner

Ackroyd let off the hook and aliens likewise, and Lenica already having made her vicarious confession, there was no-one now to latch onto, no-one to blame, no-one else to have any hope in.

"Members of the Assembly, I hope you will trust us Societans as you have always done," Lenica said, standing finally, and then, as the transmission lurched towards a breakdown before partially recovering, "for all our aims, yours and ours, are the same." Then she sat down.

If there was more to be said after that, Felicitas feared Lenica might not have the strength to say it. So much seemed to rest on her – the way out of this bondage. How shamefully slow her mother had been to grasp what was at stake, namely the very imminence, now, of a galactic belonging!

As if to give substance to a terrible fear that that prospect might slip this very day beyond human reach forever, Felicitas had no sooner sat down than she was horrified to see a certain American spring to his feet, causing her instinctively to grip Fiona's sleeve. Lennox Bright, the member for South-West USA, a disputative person with deeply etched facial features and bearing an expression of hardened disdain, had become a persistent thorn in the Society's side.

"He's never forgiven the rest of the world for America's eclipse," Felicitas said.

"I guess this is where we come back to the matter of your re-education," Bright launched out. "So you think your reconciliation, your re-education is complete? It's important to be sure, isn't it, in the circumstances?"

Now a fresh wave of sound began to well up in sympathy with the American. How impossible for her, Felicitas thought as Lenica stood up once again, to retrace and reiterate things that were well-nigh impossible to explain to fellow humans with brains and emotions in such disorder!

"We know it," Lenica began as the noise continued, her figure disappearing from time to time, "we know it because of Lexin's People, whose courage my brother has been broadcasting round the world...", but Bright interrupted,

"I have never thought these people were other than fictitious, created by you or the Lyrians to put us to shame. By blaming yourselves you are blaming *all* of us."

What might have grown into a tsunami of despair died away to a background of indecipherable sounds in the wake of this accusation.

Perhaps they had heard it too often, heard this man too often. But the cameras held on to him as somebody declared, almost chanted:

"Nobody can get us out of the mess we're in...," upon which the American lifted his voice into a kind of response, a chanting that at times seemed on the verge of being taken up around the Chamber:

"The only certain thing is that you blew it somehow and everything since has been a disaster," he began. "The tragedy's the same; only the actors are different...whether it's that scoundrel Daley, or Emergencies, or some alien force, or the idiot Mauré, or you yourselves bringing disaster after disaster upon us... "

That was only the beginning. Mdm Ouchelh was trying to put an end to his maudlin ramblings, but in the end she allowed him to continue his chanting until he ran out of words and there was silence.

Lenica, who had sat down during the tirade, rose again and obviously struggling said, "My friends, distinguished members, despite what you hear, we *have* done what we had to do. We have walked far with Lexin's People. It was a small thing and a good and necessary thing to do to compensate for our foolishness." Whereupon she sank down, burying her head in her hands upon the table in front of her as somebody came to stand by her and comfort her. Nobody else said a word. The Assembly appeared to Felicitas to have simply been brought to a standstill, thoughts suspended.

Felicitas expected Mdm Ouchelh to stand up and take charge. She seemed about to do so when suddenly the picture cleared completely for a moment, and Felicitas saw that it was Xiaofeng standing by Lenica. She had had no idea he was there.

"Lenica is exhausted and can say no more," he announced. "She wishes me to say this storm cannot be weathered by Earth's people alone."

Unusually, Felicitas barely noticed when Robert appeared with some refreshment. Her gaze was fixed on Joanna van Rensburg, who was staring at Xiaofeng as though mesmerized. She was sure Joanna would have recognized the reference to the *Assembly*'s earlier verdict about the need to 'weather the storm'. And how after all this, she said to herself, could members fail to have been moved by Lenica's modesty and gentleness? They seemed almost to have neutralised the accusatory tones that had threatened to fill the auditorium – or was that wishful thinking? Whatever the answer to that, how amazed, how sad Olaf would have been at the turn of events, but how proud of her!

Mdm Ouchelh had gone over to speak to Joanna, who after what seemed like an age, but was probably half a minute, rose to her feet:

"Members," she began, "many, perhaps most of you, have followed Lexin's People, have followed Ida Weston's progress to enlightenment. Lenica bears the marks... I should say the wounds... of her journey with Ida most modestly, having taken it upon herself to share Ida's severe illnesses." There was a silence during which she seemed to be bracing herself, summoning up all her courage and powers of expression amidst the sullenness around her and very likely a still unresolved confusion in her own head. "Now Ida has recovered ," she continued, "and I have become convinced that Lenica, too, will recover. On the one hand you can vote for the dark and disdain of disbelief," she continued in a stronger, if occasionally faltering voice. "On the other hand, you can vote in the certainty that the Societans, by their renewed dedication, yes their *renewed* dedication, have been shown the way through these difficult times by guiding lights. Trust them! Today Lenica, sorely tested herself, is *your* beacon. She has suffered on our behalf. Lexin's website was visited by millions last week, including me. I have watched those people in distant ages, and I know now that we, like them, will pull through, and that through them and the resumption of our work at the Mission Station our damaged Earth will be restored and we will be enabled safely to resume our galactic journey."

"I never thought Van Rensburg would do it," Fiona said.

"She had to do it!" Felicitas said, quietly. "Let's hope their eyes are open to the light," and the two women clung to each other as the First Minister sat down, pale, and obviously exhausted. No-one else spoke in the Assembly, and no-one clapped. Members remained for some time in an apparently dazed state in their seats, their eyes drawn to bland and hazy shots of the Palace viewed from the Gardens through a cloud of sand. There was little incentive to leave their seats, for they knew only too well that once outside the Chamber their eyes would be smarting with the smoke from distant fires now drifting over the capital.

*   *   *

Major parts of the wormhole terminal had been completely rebuilt in a matter of *little more than a year* after the big explosion, notwithstanding chronic shortages of materials and difficulties in their transportation (in particular the freighting of ultra-high-density material from the production plant in central Russia for repair of the tower), and also the highly complex structure of the lower part of the wormhole mouth. Meanwhile, the big changes in sand distribution in the desert, presumably related somehow to retrogressive effects, were necessitating round-the-clock work by robotic sand-shifters to keep the maglev line to the Mission Station open. Televised pictures showed ten-metre depths of sand across the line in places, making it easy to understand how so much sand had infiltrated the city.

Now everything had become overshadowed by the events of the last few weeks. But in the moments after those closing words of Van Rensburg's, Lenica's proud mother had put aside her fears and prayed that Joanna might have persuaded the Assembly to reverse its decision on resumption of the Society's work. Whether it was chiefly Lenica's persistence and her heroism, or Joanna's words, or indeed a mother's prayer, or a weariness and finally a blankness in the minds of already befuddled members induced by that tirade by Lennox Bright, when half an hour later a motion was proposed to resume all activities at the Mission Station, including inauguration of the restored wormhole, it encountered little opposition. It might, Lexin thought, even have been a result of some awakening receptiveness to the very visions the American was rubbishing.

Lenica's pain, discomfort and apprehension due to the still intractable cancer had been compensated by knowledge of the hugely increasing confidence of Societans in their work. But now, as she stood with the largely silent crowds (that is to say those in the population still well enough to turn out) watching the giant television screens in the reception hall of the Palace and awaiting, with the crowds outside, the inauguration of the rebuilt Station and wormhole, the harsh reality lay in this question: despite everything, would that confidence among Societans prove to have been justified?

She knew that the direction of projects conducted in centres worldwide had changed. It had already begun to move away from what had been little more than a barren raking over of the ashes of failure in a vain attempt to find reasons for the explosions. Even the investigation of suspected retrogressive effects had been sidelined. Now the direction was inspired, throwing up suggestions for the solution of the most widely varying and thorniest questions that had evaded understanding as a result of so many decades of poor decipherment. High in Lenica's thoughts now, and in her expectations of a coming mental, physical and spiritual restoration for Earth's people, was a hope that the criminal and the foolish could be dealt with using fresh knowledge that would far outpass present understanding of justice and the recompense of victims. It was something that stretched her faith in the Bods to the limit – and could, she supposed, like many other things come to true fruition only with the resumption of decipherment.

Full statements made to the police showed that "very limited field experiments" with EMR from satellites had indeed been authorised, but everything that had occurred after it was appreciated by the accused men (on their own admission) that there was actually no alien threat, occurred completely without authorization. As for the rumour about Faust, this appeared to be untrue. Nawale believed everything Blunck told him, which was next to nothing, and if he did have any suspicions he was probably too scared of his boss do anything about it. Whether he was under any kind of threat was yet to be established. The plot was thus limited to the few.

Much of the underlying optimism was due to Sergei Malinovsky's patient endeavours to demonstrate more clearly than ever before the possibility of participation in an interactively functioning Galactic Community. The validity of his conclusions about the present impasse in communication with the Lyrians, and how to overcome it, had near-universal backing. Now it was ready to be put to the test in a renewed attempt to make two-way contact through the physical time barrier. It was an attempt that would certainly enshrine a request for help with an overriding problem: the rogue satellite programme and alleviation of its effects. Lenica had only the haziest understanding of the difficulties that had hopefully been overcome in wormhole operation – mountainous algorithms, questions of stellar personalities, opt-ins and opt-out..., yet her recollection of the impressive effect Malinovsky had had on *her*, and how he had made sense of her illness, even if only in confirmation of her own conclusions, was crystal clear. Fine words? Perhaps it had been all too easy to be carried away. Today would be the acid test. Out there, somewhere in the driving sand, was the meticulously repaired terminal, waiting within its fortified tower…

A large part of the western environs of Sydney was by now all but deserted and destroyed, its aged and infirm mostly transported to safety in a massive rescue operation. The accused men and their 'control centre', with its incriminating evidence and the fast-diminishing prospect of Earth's rescue residing in it, had been evacuated back to the fire-protected Emergencies Ministry facility in the bush where it had been before. Both in order to keep the men under close surveillance while in detention and also as part of the general evacuation of public employees, Ackroyd and his entire staff were also transferred to the same complex.

Emergencies Ministry vehicles had got Lexin, with Van Rensburg and senior members of the Government, from Canberra to Sydney Air Station, from where their progress on the journey to Galaxy City with Callum and the others (though Andrew McLintock was on his way back to the Sahara) had been driven by the sheer urgency of the situation. First there had been the flight by airship round the east coast of Australia, avoiding the fire-ravaged continent. This was followed by an SST journey via Indonesia and Malaysia temporarily interrupted in Djakarta as a result of the outbreak of a civil war, and finally a series of hops by airship, maglev and even private vehicle. They were lucky to have completed the journey in ten days.

It could not have been accomplished without the co-operation of fragmented local populations already suffering under the effects of nearly three weeks of radiation, and Lexin had been enormously encouraged to see the way in which they had taken Marcelle and her reunited family, and Shining Face and hers, to their hearts. At the same time he had vividly sensed the remorseless thickening of the web of electromagnetic influence, an impression reinforced globally by the reports of increasingly serious medical effects and a realisation of the terrifying fragility of human life under these conditions. The World Health Bureau was announcing that it was extremely difficult to get any sort of precision about total death tolls but losses due directly or indirectly to the radiation might run to millions. Meanwhile, even hostile media elements seemed to have ceased their invectives against Lexin in a belated hope that the Society might actually bring about a final resolution of the world's crisis, and not least because of him.

In the briefest of televised ceremonies in the reception hall attended by Government and Society bigwigs and led by George Callum, Joanna van Rensburg had also said a few brave words before she, Callum, Mackenzie, Lamonte, Lexin, other observers and a few officials departed for the Mission Station. Without doubt it was a real demonstration, Lenica reckoned, of the spectacular way in which the First Minister had succeeded in surmounting the steepest of learning curves.

As Lexin knew, Leonard Mackenzie, now boarding the desert rover along with himself and just a handful of other observers, for the twenty-kilometre ride, preceded by sand blowers, from the Mission Station to the terminal, would have been the first to acknowledge the risks implied by the whole process of opening a 'gateway to the Galaxy'. Most of the others would remain in the operations room at the Station, but partly by her sheer powers of persuasion, partly in recognition of the solidarity of Societans which it implied, the well liked and once doubting Anna Polyanova was also allowed in the party.

The worst of the winter cold was probably over, but the dirty-yellow, ever drifting and shifting sea of sand was tempestuous as ever, and as the approaching tower stood out ever more clearly, it seemed to Lexin to be almost presumptuous to assume that everything would work as planned. Arriving at the tower, the desert rover entered via the same three-hundred metre access tunnel that he had travelled along with his father after the first big accident. It was a salutary thought, as they slowly decoded themselves through the security doors leading to the observation gallery, that only a very few months after that event there had been nothing where they now stood but empty space and debris, the duron inner casing at this point having been completely destroyed in the second big explosion and blown into the core space. In fact, the space would have started twenty or thirty metres back up the access tunnel, dramatically marking the extent of the destruction caused on that day just over a year ago. When they came to stand in the rebuilt observation gallery with its battery of monitors, it was impossible not to recall those ninety-eight men and women – one of them his father – who, filling the gallery to the limit on that day, were gazing as they were gazing now at the wide and spectacular view down to the control block compartments and across to the mouth of the wormhole itself, looking to the dawn of an unimaginable future. No such proud numbers hoping to witness such a dawn this time! Was that due to a lowering of expectations, natural caution, a kind of latent fear of failure? The question kept running through Lexin's head…

Meanwhile in the buildings of the Palace there was silence save for the incessant sizzling and spattering of the sand upon the windows.

Beyond the people huddling out there in the cold and the driving sand, Lenica could see crowds waiting in the Gardens and in the distant Avenidas. Television screens revealed glimpses of crowds gathered expectantly, anxiously, in public places in cities round the world wherever life staggered on. Many European cities teetered on the brink of catastrophe. Hundreds of thousands had fled from London to a makeshift existence in the countryside. It reminded her that Lexin had told her how Uncle Sverre and his family had decided not to try and get back to Bergen after a canal holiday and were living on a canal boat in the English Midlands.

As she stood looking out at the figureheads of the early Societan Fathers adorning the terraces, as crowded now as the reception hall itself, something began to change for her as gradually another part of herself found itself in a different place. Such experiences were, of course, not new to her, but this was different. It was not like stepping yet again into Ida's shoes, Ida's thoughts, her slow and painful restoration. Now she was an onlooker. Marcelle was there, with Mark beside her. It was the first time she had seen them really clearly; always when she had been Ida they had been just a shadowy presence in the background.

They were standing hand in hand by what she recognized after a moment to be a canal lock in the countryside. It was one of those old features she had seen pictures of – historic symbols, with their spreading arms, of that first industrial expansion in a yet earlier age. They were watching a boat glide away from it into a higher water level in the gathering dusk. It was surely the same place that Lexin had described to her once when he had seen them walking together. And *there* was the rickety iron seat, even! The man on the boat appeared to shout some farewell from the vessel as it receded in the fading light. Then after responding the two of them hugged each other for several moments, and as they turned to walk on Lenica caught just one thing that Mark said:

"The point is that Ida needn't be anxious about Lenica any more now," before they disappeared into a strange brightness like that reflected from snow.

Lenica was trying to imagine what exactly had prompted those words of Mark's? Perhaps it did not matter. It was a spontaneous remark from Marcelle's boyfriend, a down-to-earth guy in Lexin's judgement. The fact was that it was her own life, now in 2454, that was in question, a life that had seemed, and still seemed, to hang by a thread! Was this really the assurance she hoped for? Minutes passed... half an hour... Still there was silence from the terminal. Just....silence... Yet how, after everything that had happened, could she possibly not believe what the words surely meant, despite what she felt in her body? And as if to punctuate that, a murmur spread round the crowd as an announcement appeared on the CCTV: "Outbound message transmitted".

Confirmation of the transmission was received in the observation gallery monitors following prolonged visible and audible procedures in the control block. The request had gone out successfully! The tension on the faces of those around Lexin was apparent – not least in the case of Ryman, Deputy Head of Wormhole Research and Operations, and laboratory chief Matovu, the sweat glistening on his shiny black forehead. Lexin was surprised to see these two men there, having assumed that they had been the whole day at the terminal with the engineers. Several more minutes of waiting ensued in agonising silence. Then, suddenly, activity commenced in the control block accompanied by noise in the wormhole mouth, continuing in fits and starts. It was as if the team personnel were being given time to accommodate. After perhaps ten minutes, stability data began to be registered in the monitors, continuing for some time and eventually reaching high levels before gradually dropping back. Lexin's understanding of the display suggested full control had been maintained at the critical point of message retrieval – an assumption confirmed when he caught sight of Mackenzie looking at him and daring to grin. A good sign, especially from him!

All eyes remained focussed on the monitors:

"Incoming transmission retrieved".

Still nobody spoke. Then after no more than another two minutes the announcement came:

"Transcription in progress in Mission Station."

Down there in the control block, personnel continued to move about. All Lexin wanted to do was sit down and recover, but the others were cheering and shaking hands, especially with him, until finally Anna Polyanova seized him in a bear-hug of truly Russian proportions, from which he was released only by the appearance, in almost no time at all, of the transcript on a monitor.

It began:

"Earth people, welcome to the Galactic Community! First, we must reassure you that deactivation of the rogue electromagnetic programme has already commenced. It will take some time to complete. We are very sorry indeed about the death and destruction caused and will do our best to alleviate all suffering. We must point out, however, that our experience indicates entry into the galactic siblinghood is rarely a painless process.

"Your earlier attempts to communication with us via the wormhole," the message continued, "were as you now know somewhat premature, your decipherment capabilities not being up to scratch. This resulted in considerable loss of life, which we again very much regret, although the above remark about entry into the siblinghood again applies. We realise, however, that it became necessary for you, for various reasons, to more fully understand and be able to use the basic principles of wormhole technology. We are glad that through your dedication you have now achieved this. We thank you for your sympathy and active assistance in the timeless sphere of Earth. Incidentally, it is not unusual for Galactans to be asked to help in the timeless sphere of their worlds.

"The replies to the questions which you successfully transmitted to us being necessarily complex, they will be merged into your ongoing decipherment programme (He had guessed correctly here). Guidance on world rehabilitation following your upheavals will also be merged. From now on, although decipherment will be more thorough, because of your dedication it should also be much quicker. Although you have some distance to go to full participation in the Galactic Community, you are well on the way!..." The transcript went on to express renewed confidence in the Society and in its ability to lead the way.

So it was as he had suspected – and hoped: the living 'text' was able to regenerate, change and adapt.

Returning in the desert rover, Lexin imagined Malinovsky, in the Great Hall with the delegates, quietly and justifiably smiling. The arrival back at the Mission Station was a little emotional. Even Van Rensburg, who had remained there all day, by all accounts calm as a rock in an impressive display of renewed confidence in the Society, shed a few tears. She and Callum, Lamonte and the others there had been able to follow progress simultaneously. "Perhaps we may call ourselves *second-generation* children of the Galaxy, " Lexin said to Callum, grinning.

"I regard that as very presumptuous, Lexin," Callum replied with manufactured pomposity. "All right, then, let's hope our 'teens' won't be too rocky!"

When, having sped with the others through the angry desert back to Galaxy City, Lexin was besieged by the press at the maglev terminal, all he would say was, "Our work goes on", before standing beside the First Minister while she made a short televised broadcast.

After congratulating those who had braved the dangers of the wormhole, she admitted the slowness of the World Government to realise the threat upon the world's future posed by criminal elements. For this she took full responsibility, but she said she wished finally to make an historic announcement:

"I am pleased to report," she said, the usually matter-of-fact expression transformed by a scarcely contained excitement, "that our good friends, our saviours in Lyra have, in their words, welcomed us into the Galactic Community. The full text of their reply to our transmission will of course be published immediately. Suffice to say now that they express their sorrow at our sufferings and loss of life and say that deactivation of the EMR programme has already begun. They also say that we can now be confident that certain failings of the Society in the fulfilment of its complex task have been rectified. They assure us of its ability to lead the way to world rehabilitation and ultimate full participation in the Community."

Half an hour later, having fought his way with Callum and Van Rensburg through the crowds in the reception hall of the Palace and been persuaded to say a few televised words there, and also been thanked by the First Minister for his crucial role in preventing what was still mankind's only home from "plunging into the abyss", an elated Lexin was in the Great Hall of the Palace being formally welcomed by George Callum. Asked to speak to delegates, Lexin was quick to point out to the assembled Societans, all of whom now held in their hands a copy of the transcribed message, that his role had been essentially that of a messenger. He advised them never to forget the massive potential for galactic advance that now resided in them and told them that they had the power to bring it to fruition. Now a very sad and difficult time would have to be endured by everyone, and he encouraged all Societans never again to make the mistake of neglecting their PAS.

Lenica had never felt so happy to see him – or so proud of him – as when they met in a quiet corner of the Palace a few minutes later. She could not wait to tell her brother about the event by the canal and what Marcelle had said, but already it was as though an enormous weight had been lifted off her shoulders..

"Thank God for that," he said. "Everything *is* going to be all right, then," and he gave her a hug. "I thought there was something queer about that canal ever since I used to see them sitting there," he said, releasing her. "I expect they are going to give their friends a hand."

Lenica looked at him. Sometimes his deadpan expression could be annoying, but not on this occasion. She grinned. "I'm sure they are," she said. "I hope everything works out for all of *them*."

"I expect it did, like it will for you," he said, giving her another big hug, his face bursting into a broad smile.

Outside in the city, every television seemed to be switched on, and every source of music playing. Machines were stepping up their efforts to clear the sand while trying to avoid a few crazy individuals celebrating by floundering in it. A few taxi bubbles were battling in the wind and sand, one of which Lexin hailed, but the driver would not risk the Hill of Lyra in the blizzard, and it took them all of twenty minutes to struggle up to the house on foot.

Xiaofeng had volunteered to go and join Felicitas (who had stayed at home in the company of Fiona and Céleste) – much to Felicitas's approval (and very likely at her suggestion!).

He and Robert were attending to an emotional Felicitas, who had apparently already fainted twice. Fiona was trying to calm down Céleste, who could not stop talking. Felicitas, seeing Lenica and Xiaofeng fall into each other's arms and Lexin coming stumbling in behind, flung her arms around them all exclaiming repeatedly, "My children, my clever children." Robert beat a discreet retreat.

CHAPTER TWENTY-THREE

"So what are you going to do now, Mum?"

"See Mr. Chappel, Marcelle. He'll understand." Tom nodded. "He said I could phone him direct...well, via his secretary, I suppose."

Tom had obviously been disappointed at first when Ida had decided not to stay at the healing centre. His questioning of the surgeon Chappel seemed to have paid off and led to the possibility of a less invasive approach. But her determination, and the fact that she had made an appointment to see Mr. Chappel again – as the surgeon had insisted she should – had been enough to reassure him. Her confidence was definitely infectious. That was the only word for it. A new fire burned in her, fuelled by some inner and incontrovertible certainty, and *he* felt the heat of it too. She knew that he had been hugely encouraged by Mark, as well – sober Mark, yet a man who had undergone a transformation, walked in another time, and endured that cave. She knew that it was not only for the sake of Big Nose and Shining Face that Mark had done it, but in a roundabout way for herself and Tom as well.

Just a couple of days after returning she went to see Nadia, who had said she was having a couple of days in hospital for a check-up. But a strange thing happened. She had not seen Nadia at all. They told her that her check-up had been postponed two weeks at the last minute.

Drinking a cuppa' in the canteen before taking the tram home, she was more than surprised when Tom appeared and said he would walk back to the ward with her. Only then did she come to 'remember' she was in her dressing gown and a patient herself, but it was not the hospital she thought it was, being strangely shaped and full of unknown experiences. There had been tests – tests she could not possibly have merely dreamed about, but not too uncomfortable, and treatments likewise. Those must have lasted many days, for she had lost count of the number of daily data sheets completed and affixed by the bed in her little room so spotless and tidy. She did not know much about the other patients, only that however bad their circumstances they were cheerful and encouraging. Normally, the nurses had explained, there was a lovely view of the park and the domes and spires of the city beyond, but now there was only the yellow haze. It was a sandstorm, and it had been going on for days. Most unusual. There had been delicious foods unknown to her. There had been times of which she had no memory, but if there had been any surgery, there was no sign of it on her body.

When she had finished her treatment, and after the doctor had finally discharged her, reassuring her amazingly that she was completely free of both cancer and HIV, and had left the room, the nurse had come and said there was someone to see her. There had not even been time to get out of bed. She thought it could not have been merely because Marcelle *might* have mentioned once that Lexin had a sister that she knew straight away who the tall, blonde lady was who came into he room. Somehow she recognized her immediately and knew her name even before she announced herself.. It was Lenica. She was clearly not well, yet so natural, so assured in her manner, but somehow so indefinably different that it was like looking through to another world. Now she felt she knew how Marcelle had felt in the presence of Lexin in his office.

"We have had terrible trouble here," she said, "and still have, but now, just like I know you are completely better in your time, so I know now that everything will be restored here in ours. I couldn't possibly explain all this to you, though. We can hardly put it into words ourselves." There was that same sense of mystery that Marcelle had described, the same sense of a world facing some awesome danger and yet overcoming it. "Please tell Marcelle that I came, and that we love you and cannot thank you enough, all of you." Ida felt her arms surround her, and her kiss on her cheek. There was a faint aroma of perfume, and that same total reassurance that she knew Marcie had had in Lexin's presence, and had continued to have ever since *her* encounter. Ida had thanked her, for she knew there was much thanking to do and she felt the gratefulness in her heart. Then the nurse came in and Lenica had disappeared.

The next thing Ida knew was that she was finishing her cup of tea in the canteen and picking up her bag to go and catch the tram to Kinley's Fields.

Marcelle drove her parents to the City Hospital in her grandpa's car to see Mr. Chappel a few days later, having just passed her driving test. Henry had been giving her extra lessons. The surgeon was happy to see her as well.

He spent a minute or so looking out of the window, apparently engrossed in thought. Her mother had told her about the window with the strange 'cityscape', and now she could see it for herself. Eventually Mr. Chappel said,

"What do *you* think we should do, Mrs. Weston, Mr. Weston?"

Under normal circumstances it would have seemed a strange question, but now... "I don't know," Ida replied. "I feel a whole lot better." Tom nodded.

"Can't always go by that," the surgeon said. "Better check, I suppose. I'll try and arrange another scan and some tests this week"

Marcelle took her mother for the scan and tests two days later and both her parents for another consultation on the following Monday. The results showed no sign of the secondaries, no primary recurrence, and negative results for AIDS.

"You've done me out of a job," the surgeon said.

"You get your consultation fee, don't you?" Marcelle was smiling cheekily. Ida didn't know how she dared, but he took the joke.

"Nothing like what I would have got for an operation," he replied, grinning back.

"I'd better come back for check-ups, I suppose," Ida said, to which Chappel replied,

"It won't be necessary." Marcelle nodded. The surgeon gave her a big smile. "Sometimes these problems just disappear," he said.

" And you are confident they won't recur?"

"Yes. I should go to the canteen and celebrate if I were you."

"Always thought there was something odd about him," Marcelle said when the VW drew up back at the house in Acacia Road. He really did know, didn't he? – about that other place. I mean the place you had that experience of, Mum, when you went to see Nadia in hospital, and you said you remembered the nurse describing the view from the window and it sounded just like that window illusion in Mr. Chappel's consulting room."

"You know, I can recall so little of what happened that day now, only that it was something very important."

"Except that his window is not an illusion," Tom said as they got out of the car. "I could see that plainly from where I was sitting when we went the last time. I was having a good look, I can tell you. Mind you, this morning it was back to the normal view". The others agreed, and they went into the house. "You go in the sitting room, Mum," Marcelle said, "and I'll bring you your cuppa and then sort something out for you and Dad for supper."

Marcelle went through to put a kettle on while Tom went upstairs to change for his work at the restaurant – he had managed to take just a half day.

"Marcie!" – Ida had to raise her voice for it to reach the kitchen. But it was not the hard voice of old.

"Yes?"

"He didn't seem at all surprised that I was cured, did he?"

"I know. But I wasn't surprised that *he* wasn't surprised."

"I could never have imagined all these things happening when I was being so unkind, yes so cruel to you. I could have been sent to prison."

"Well thank God you weren't. Let's not even mention it any more, Mum."

There was a long silence while the kettle boiled.

"It all started with that hunter, didn't it" Ida said as Marcelle came in with the tea.

"And then there was Lexin," Marcelle said, and added, "But you never imagined getting ill, did you? It's been so hard for you – and Dad."

"Or getting better," Ida said

"No, but you are."

"Looks like it, Marcie, and with a bit of luck Tom will be a lot better too." Then after a few moments she said, "Do you think we shall ever know what happened to the hunter and his family?" at the same time sinking back into one end of the vast four-seater pillow-back sofa with the sponge-roll whirly patterns as her daughter wheeled up the little tea trolley beside her, poured out a cup of tea and placed it in her mother's hands. The tall china cabinet graced the wall behind her, and on another wall Grandpa had been busy assembling units upon which family photographs figured large. A wood-burning stove emanated a heat that helped to project into the view of the yet leafless garden outside the window, with its scattering of spring flowers, a pleasing suggestion of warmth and impending summer.

"Oh yes, we shall know something – enough, I reckon."

But there was something else on Ida's mind. "And Lenica?" she asked after a minute or two's silence. "Will *she* get better?"

"Lenica?"

"Lexin's sister. She looked so ill when she came and saw me in that hospital. You know, the one in that city through the funny window. I told you that I could remember almost nothing about what happened that day – until just now. Suddenly it's all coming back, Marcie!"

"You saw Lexin's sister? She came to see you?"

"Yes, I remember now. It was after the doctor had been and told me I was cured. She came and thanked me, I know now it's to do with the way our lives have been mixed up with each other's. In fact she was overflowing with thanks to all of us and wanted me to tell you that, while I felt it was I who should be doing the thanking, and I did. I remember. She sends all of us her love. And says things will get better there now, wherever 'there' is and whatever the 'things' are".

Marcelle was bubbling with excitement as she got a stool and put it and a cushion under Ida's feet.

"Now just rest, and rest,. She ordered."

When Ida's eyes blinked with sleepiness Marcelle eased the cup and saucer out of her hands and placed them back on the trolley. Ida had been through a lot, but if she felt at peace now, as Marcelle hoped she did, she herself felt at peace, too, as never before.

"I hope Lenica gets better, Mum, I really do. Its absolutely wonderful that you met her."

Marcelle couldn't wait to tell Mark what Ida had told her on regaining memory of her experience. Communication was difficult because he was very busy at uni, but she had already told him about her mother's strange experience on going to see Nadia and her return to the surgeon. Unfortunately, when she phoned with the latest news his mobile played a pretty tune in the middle of a difficult tutorial and it was only when he got back to his digs that he phoned her and she was able to tell him everything. About Ida's meeting with Lenica all he could say was surely there couldn't be any more surprises, to which she replied,

"Can't promise anything," and, referring evidently to herself, "You've got a right one here!"

"I know," he said.

Mr. Chappel had been busy on another front. A few days later, Tom went for a consultation with the orthopaedic surgeon as promised. The place was way out in the country. Mark took more time off (Marcelle knew only something really important would make him skip lectures and risk being late for a tutorial), and he and Marcelle took her mum and dad in Henry's car. Then, after the consultation, which went well, they all drove over to Culver for a little celebration of Grandpa's birthday. They would stop for a meal afterwards.

Marcelle had got the day off and had decided to afford a nice dress from M&S – tasteful, tubiform and strapless. Mark was most impressed and bought a new pair of chinos and some really shiny black loafers in an act of solidarity

."Lenie will be coming with the kids," Marcelle explained, "but won't stop. Grandma will give them a nice tea, I know."

"I am so glad about the consultation, Tom," Grandpa said when they arrived. "And glad you could help them get there, Mark. I really enjoy driving less and less these days."

Ever since Ida's illness, Marcelle noticed, Grandpa had gone out of his way to be helpful to both her dad and her mum. On a number of occasions he had been over on the bus to help them with matters which she guessed were to do with claims and benefits, or even to do jobs in the garden – for in spite of being seventy-five the modest bungalow and garden at Culver were scarcely enough to occupy him. He would always drop in on Marcelle at the same time, if she was in, or even if she was not, when he would find that taps needed washers or some incipient rot in a window frame needed getting out and replacing with plastic wood. Today he was looking very spry in a new suit and the cherry-red waistcoat. But Grandma never seemed to be able to forget Ida's past.

"And how is the recovery, Ida?" she asked when they had managed to find somewhere to sit down and rest a moment before the expected arrival of Lenie's tribe. Grandma spoke in that harsh tone which she could adopt when something was narking her. "I consider you are very lucky. Things could be so much worse, couldn't they?"

Marcelle winked at her mother, but Ida did find Florrie difficult, especially now that she knew in her heart that the seal had been set on her recovery. Naturally, Florrie could hardly believe that she had given up the holistic centre as well, even though she had had to admit she had been pretty sceptical about it herself. "The recovery is over now, Mother," Ida said.

"Over?"

"I mean I am better, full stop."

"I am glad you are so sure."

"I am sure she would agree that Marcie has been a great inspiration, Mrs. Weston," Mark said. "Marcie has never doubted that her mother would get well."

"I dare say she hasn't! Well if it means Tom gets his due care and attention..."

"Mother, how can you say that after the hell that Ida's been through," Tom said, trying to adjust himself in one of the big armchairs so as to get his leg comfortable. "And Mark's right. Marcie has been a tower of strength."

"I am glad to hear it," Florrie said, and then, seeing Lenie parking the old estate car and coming up the path with the children, who now numbered four, she added: "Marcelle, be a tower of strength to me and help me lay the table in the dining room, there's a dear." Jamie couldn't come. He was doing overtime on the vans, and Lenie was thankful that as long as people had children – especially when they kept on having them – they would never be able to do without washing machines and Jamie would be bringing the money in.

Marcelle ran into the kitchen, gasped at the spread that Florrie had prepared and threw her arms around her. "Grandma, you are a darling," she exclaimed as she put a cloth on the dining room table and set about carrying in the plates of mini-sandwiches and cakes, and dishes of trifle and stewed fruit, pizza fingers, mini sausages, fairy cakes and a large tub of ice cream.

Pandemonium now reigned in the sitting room as the children chased their roboraptors around the floor and sprayed each other with their foam guns, abolishing serious talk for twenty minutes after which the juniors disappeared into the dining room for their tea.

A minute or two later, Marcelle was amazed to hear Mark's parents being ushered in at the front door by her grandpa. She was amazed because she was pretty sure the Whartons had never been to her grandparents' house before (and they had only met her parents a couple of times). It must have been Grandpa's idea, she thought. Then something else struck her: *she* had not breathed a word about the fact that Mark had proposed to her on that day when they had returned from the Healing Centre with Tom and Ida...

She grabbed hold of Mark as he came out of the dining room, where he had been separating Tracy, aged seven, and Derek, six, who had been in dispute about who was sitting where. "Is something afoot, Mark? Something of your doing?"

"What do you mean? Is *what* my doing?" The voice, the expression, were deadpan.

She let him go.

"Pleased to meet you. Take us as you find us," Grandpa was saying to the new arrivals. "Florrie's somewhere. Ah, there she is, feeding the starving." Grandma was hovering with a plate of tarts between kitchen and dining room.

"Of course, of course," Gerald said with an affability perfectly in tune with a jolly green cravat awash with white spots. "I must say I quite envy you out here in the country. Marcelle was partly country raised, wasn't she?" he said as they entered a sitting room miraculously tidied up by Marcelle in the space of ten seconds.

"*I* would say her upbringing was a bit hard to categorise," Mark said, grinning, before Henry had a chance to answer.

"Now what can you mean by that, Mark?" Marcelle asked.

"I think he means you are an independent spirit," Tom said just as Ida came out of the kitchen where she had been helping Florrie.

"Surely that cannot be denied, Ida" Winifred Wharton said in that same cold tone she had spoken in when passing those remarks about her behind her back at their house, but there was just a hint of a twinkle in her eye.

"Something's made a fine young woman of you, at any rate," Gerald declared.

Marcelle had had a moderate dislike of Gerald Wharton – for his innuendos about her father and his work – or lack of it. His remark came as quite a surprise and, it had to be admitted, warmed her to him not a little.

"I couldn't have done without her," her mother said.

A question to Gerald Wharton from Tom enquiring after his business took the pressure off everything again for a while, during which time Marcelle took Mark aside and gave him a good old thumping for (as he admitted) revealing their secret (though she had to admit that it had not been all that secret).

"They're just dropping in for sherries and birthday cake", he whispered..

"Oh really?" she said, as Grandpa called for silence and said how pleased he was that Mark and Marcelle intended to get married – sometime.

"How long will it be before you can afford to keep me, darling?" she asked.

"Not for a long time yet," Mark replied with studied unconcern.

"Now if you had taken my advice and taken the business side…," his father said, but Winifred interrupted him:

"It's the boy's choice," she said. "They'll have to rely on Marcelle's wages. You are going to be earning something, aren't you, Marcelle?"

"I hope to get a teaching assistant job," she replied, upon which Winifred Wharton gave her a steady look that was neither critical nor approbatory. "Anyway, Markie, I love you whatever," she said, hugging him. Everybody clapped, and Ida was reduced to tears.

Grandpa's birthday celebration passed with a minimum of fuss – which was how he liked it. Florrie dispensed slices of birthday cake from a trolley, and Mark filled glasses and proposed a toast while Lenie tried to keep one eye on the children in the dining room, who were getting very noisy. Tom made a little speech. He said Pop and Nan had hoped to come over from Sandbay, but Nan's sister was very poorly and they had had to drive over to Bathenhurst. They were thrilled about Ida's recovery, sent Mark and Marcelle congratulations on their engagement, and wished Henry a happy seventy-fifth. Gerald Wharton echoed all these sentiments and was about to offload a sailing jingle which he said was about the upside of old age, but it was disallowed by Winifred.

Grandpa said there had been times recently when he would have despaired of ever seeing them all gathered here "like this". The poignant moment of silence which followed was broken by Marcelle going and putting her arms round him and kissing him, and then doing the same for Grandma.

Meanwhile Lenie was already getting the 'overtired' children ready to go home, but not before they had insisted on coming in and singing 'Happy Birthday Great Grandpa Henry' to general applause. Grandma filled an old biscuit tin for them containing extra slices of birthday cake wrapped in paper napkins and other tasty leftovers.

Soon the Whartons made their excuses, and after the Audi had thundered away and Lenie had bundled the children into the estate car and driven off too, Grandma took Marcelle aside:

"Tell me, love," she said, " is it true that you have visions – about the future?"

"And about the past."

"And that you have some healing powers."

"Just some insights, perhaps."

"I'm so glad you could help your mother," Grandma said, earnestly. "Tom is so different now."

There was time to take a walk with Mark before Florrie had the evening meal ready. Neither said to the other where they intended to go, but in five minutes, oblivious evidently of their scarcely suitable party wear, they were crossing the fields to the canal.

"I heard Grandma asking you about your visions," Mark said.

"Yes, I couldn't possibly explain it all to her, after everything that's happened. And when all is said and done we only know part of the story, don't we?"

"Do you know, Marcie, even after all that's happened there is still something that keeps telling me it must all be in our minds."

"How *can* it be? Men are so self-centred, Mark."

"It *can't* be, I know. It just shows how stubborn the mind is."

They came to the lock. The light was beginning to go. They sat on the rickety iron seat. A boat – surely the last one of the day – was gliding across the landscape. The chamber was empty, and the boat slipped into it. The young man at the helm signalled a greeting. He clambered up the ladder set in the opposite wall of the lock, wound a line loosely round a bollard and strode around closing first the bottom gates and paddles, then with the windlass gradually opening the paddles of the top gates. The chamber started filling, and the boat began to rise. When it was nearly full, Marcelle saw that Mark was staring at the vessel intently and asked him what was interesting him particularly.

"The name!" he said. She looked. It was just distinguishable:

'Lenica'. Both were bereft of words. The noise of rushing water ceased as the lock finished filling. "Interesting name, 'Lenica'," Mark shouted to the man, who was leaning on the arm of the further of the two top gates and opening it. "Was the boat always yours?"

"It was my father's," he replied. "Renamed it after my uncle died. Doing dangerous work. A big engineering job. Catastrophic accident. It was a terrible time."

"And Lenica?"

"My cousin."

"What happened to her?" Marcelle hardly dared wait for the answer.

"My cousin was very ill too, after her father died...but she recovered – against all the odds. Married a Chinese boy."

Mark wanted to ask the uncle's name, but something stopped him. The man dropped the paddles and performed like clockwork the rest of the sequence of operations required before the boat could proceed into the upper pound, darting hither and thither and finally stepping into the cockpit from their side of the lock and starting the engine. But there was something else Mark wanted to know: "I hope he didn't die for nothing, your uncle," he said.

"I wondered whether you might want to know the answer to that. No, he didn't. The accident changed everything eventually. A breakthrough. An amazing breakthrough."

'Lenica' slipped gently out of the lock. A bit more clambering to close the gate, and she was underway.

"Mark...," Marcelle began to say, taking his hand,"...But Mark, how...?"

"Oh come on, Marcie," he said. "First I thought you were fooling *me* about all this business. Well now I am telling *you* there's no fooling."

The captain waved. "God bless you, both of you." he shouted.

"I suppose we must assume they will all be all right now, where Lexin is.," Marcelle said, returning the wave, "whoever 'they' are."

"I think we should," he said, and they exchanged a big long hug.

"We'd better get back now, hadn't we?"

"Yes, I think we'd better," he replied, releasing her and taking her hand again as they turned to go. By the way, have you ever questioned how it is that boats come sailing along just as we pass, even though the canal has been derelict for donkey's years?"

"I suppose it has," she said, dreamily.

"Anyway, the point is that Ida needn't be anxious about Lenica any more now."

*   *   *

Big Nose and Shining Face had remained at Red Hair's shelter for nearly two moons after finding her. They had extended it, drawing down more branches and going a distance to find evergreen fronds to put over the top. Big Nose managed to catch hares and pigeons, while Shining Face did what she could to make Red Hair comfortable, renewing her bed of leaves regularly and making a pillow of duck feathers, and feeding her ready-chewed scraps of meat and soaked dried fruits. Daily she treated the many cuts and sores on her body with Big Nose's healing ointment. For a long time Red Hair was too weak and ill to respond in any way but to swallow, remaining silent on her deerskin, but after a while it seemed that she began to recognize her. Helped no doubt by the perceptible lengthening of the days and the sun appearing earlier and earlier over the mountainside, despite Red Hair's precarious state Shining Face felt a new hope, sensed a turning point.

One bitterly cold, misty morning when Big Nose was out hunting, and she was trying to light a fire in the clearing, she heard Red Hair struggling to call her name and ran to the shelter.

"How...how did you find me?" Red Hair asked with difficulty.

"It must have been the fir cones," Shining Face replied, getting down and putting her arms around her and her face close to hers. Red Hair responded by passing her hands over her face.

"It really is you, isn't it? I am sorry."

"Sorry? What about?"

To Shining Face's surprise Red Hair had raised herself up on her elbow. With her other arm she tried to draw Shining Face to her, but she fell back, wincing with pain. "Thank you for looking after me," she whispered. "I'm sorry I had to leave you like I did."

Shining Face kissed her. "I came to look for you, and I've found you. That's all that matters." Again she lay down and hugged her. How she had aged compared with what she remembered of her! The deep lines, the fading hair, and those alluring eyes that now harboured such anxiety, such sadness! Red Hair fell asleep and did not wake up again until after the middle of the day – not that there was much difference in the dull light. Shining Face was gathering firewood in the forest when she heard her call again. She gathered up most of the wood, ran to the camp and knelt down by her.

Red Hair gripped her arm with surprising force. "Your father, where is he?"

Shining Face stared at her, questioningly.

A dark shadow crossed Red Hair's face. "Don't tell me it was a dream. Don't tell me that!"

"So he *is* my father?"

There was a long silence. Gradually, Red Hair's face relaxed. "Yes, of course. Surely he told you!" Her voice was fainter now. Shining Face realised what an effort it must have been for her to shout out.

"I did not want...I mean, I did not dare...to believe him. Just now he's hunting."

"And how did you find *him*?"

"He found *me*. He came to a cave where I was trapped by lions."

Red Hair was silent for a while. Then she said, "So he rescued you."

"Yes."

There was another long silence during which Red Hair seemed lost in thought. "He's a good man, such a good man, Shining Face," she said.

"You said you did not care what happened to him," Shining Face said, gently, but saw that she had fallen asleep again. When she had got the fire going, she returned to find her awake and repeated what she had said. Red Hair's eyes filled with tears.

"I didn't really mean it," she said. "Not at all. I was just angry."

"*I* was frightened that he would bring me bad luck and that I would never find *you*. They all said he brought bad luck, didn't they?"

"Your father never brought anybody bad luck. It was just because he was crippled. He saved me like he saved you. I got very weak and ill in the forest like I am now. Then suddenly he was there. He said it was by chance, but I wonder. Then we got separated." Again she fell silent. When she spoke again she said very quietly, "We got separated because when we got to another camp, another people, they made him leave. They saw he would never run with the hunt. It was a terrible place, anyway." Red Hair tried to raise herself up, but gave up and lay back.

Yes, he had told *her* all that and she had only half believed him. Shining Face called to her father as he approached with a duck he had found frozen into a lake. It was mid-afternoon, and the sun was making a last desperate effort to break through the mist. It had taken him most of the day to get one duck. Suddenly she felt very sorry for him. "My mother woke up," she said. "She's able to speak now; asked where you were."

"That's good," he said, "very good. She will get better now," and he went and helped her to a sitting position. Shining Face went and tended to the fire.

Later, when he was preparing the duck in the semi-darkness, she said. "My mother said I was wrong to have thought you would bring me bad luck."

"Do you believe her?"

"I think so. I'm sorry."

"She may be wrong. I didn't bring *her* very good luck in the end. That last camp, where the vile headman kept her for himself, it was terrible. I tried to go back, you know, to rescue her, more than once. I think I told you. But I might have tried harder, crept in at night, whisked her away."

Red Hair ate some of the duck, and after that her appetite improved. In a few days she was much better. Another two days, and she was well enough to move, and they headed in the direction she had come from, which Big Nose was sure would soon get them to the sea. He carried everything and pulled the sledge with Red Hair on it most of the time, Shining Face taking over whenever there was a down-slope, when he would walk behind with all their stuff and give the sledge an occasional shove with his foot. For three days they continued thus, spending the nights in makeshift shelters, except that Red Hair, gaining in strength, would increasingly get up and walk alongside for a while.

The weather had let up a bit, and here lower down where the mountains were beginning to change into hills the snow was less deep and the sun shone from time to time. For days it had been melting the top of the snow in the afternoons so that in places Shining Face could almost see the form of herself in its surface. Frozen streams gently thawing seemed to calm the struggle for survival that had gripped them for so long, and warmed a little by the ever strengthening sun it seemed possible to imagine a better, an easier life ahead.

"We will get on better there, by the sea," he said. "It won't be quite as cold, and we can stay there awhile."

"We won't go to that camp, that last camp of yours, will we?" Shining Face exclaimed, alarmed.

"Of course not," Red Hair said.

"Or to our old camp, our real home, I suppose," she said a little wistfully, "even though it may be a better place now." The memory of Toothy had come to her suddenly, Toothy who had saved her more than once.

"It would be better to find a new people, where nobody knows me," Red Hair said. "As for your father, in such a place we will be able to tell his heroic story. Then maybe he won't suffer wrongly any more."

They came to a place where massive holly trees dug into a hollow in the hillside.

"There's something I want you to see," Red hair said, breaking away and going to a space among the trees where the snow had thawed to reveal freshly dug earth. When they were all together there she said, quickly, "I buried my little girl here."

They stood still. Red Hair seemed unable to move, her face full of tears. Shining Face put her arm round her and clasped her tightly, and the two of them remained there until numbness and cold forced them away. Big Nose had wandered on a little way with the sledge and everything on it, and when they emerged from the trees into the sudden sunlight and caught up with him he pointed ahead to where they had just a glimpse of the distant sea beyond the still whiteness, sparkling grey-blue and inviting.

By early evening they were at a cave in the sea cliffs above a shingle beach, and they lit a fire in it and made themselves comfortable, spreading dried seaweed over the floor of the cave, and thickly in a niche in the rock wall to make a bed for Red Hair. They warmed themselves at the fire, and when Big Nose went off to see if he could find food – maybe an unsuspecting hare venturing forth with friends or kin at dusk up on the cliffs – Shining Face took the opportunity to ask Red Hair what she meant exactly by finding a place where no-one knew her.

"The truth is," she replied, "that I find men too attractive, and it has been my undoing. Likewise, men find me attractive – I think I should say, 'found'. Perhaps it was the red hair..." Red Hair's features were dancing, shaping and reshaping themselves in the firelight as her fingers played nervously with the stones of the shingle. "It ends up by me being a slave to one man – the most powerful old man in the camp, so that when he goes and I lose his protection I am hated by everybody. But now I shall be beholden to no man but your father. It is him I have always really wanted."

There was a long silence, except for the sea pulling and pushing.

"I never knew that. How could I know it?"

"I did not want you to know. It would have been too dangerous. If it had got about...if Giant Man had got wind of such things being said, it might have been bad for both of us."

"I thought you had finished with my father. If I had known how you felt..."

"You were very young, Shining Face. And Giant Man's jealous rages were to be feared."

Yes, even now, Shining Face could understand men's attraction for her, scarred, careworn and weary though she was – the generous features of her face and that hair, still thick and flowing, though beginning to lose its deep colour, and just occasionally the suggestion of a full and shapely frame in the changing light and shadow. "I suppose there wasn't much you could do about it," she said, "when Father got turned away at the last camp."

"I could have had a go at escaping. Some women might have helped me."

"Why didn't you?"

"Easier to do nothing, to slip back into old ways? I don't know. I could have refused to have anything to do with Big Bear."

Shining Face went and sat close. "He might have been angry, yes?"

"He was certainly cross when he found out about Mountain Ash."

"Mountain Ash?"

"The baby wasn't Big Bear's, Shining Face. As I say, there are consequences in being attractive. Big Bear might have killed me if I hadn't been with child."

Shining Face thought for a moment. "All the same I wish *I* had my mother's red hair."

They were silent for a while. Then Red Hair said, quietly, "You do indeed have your mother's hair, Shining Face dear: dark, and just as beautiful"

"But your hair..." A sudden doubt overwhelmed her. "You *are* my mother, aren't you?" She asked after a few moments.

"No, I am not your mother. A bear killed Curvy Lips when you were a baby. I looked after you then. And when your father had to go away, through no fault of his own, I cared for you."

Shining Face broke away gently and stood up, staring at Red Hair in amazement. "I always thought...I mean... the cones, the necklace..."

"You will always be my daughter, nevertheless," Red Hair said, gently. "It was no chore. There is only one man I have ever loved, Shining Face, and that is your father. Like I said, he is a very good and a very brave man."

Shining Face went and stood a long time in the mouth of the cave, listening to the waves coming in relentlessly, washing back over the shingle. It was a long time since she had seen the sea, but it was just as she remembered it: something cleansing, making things new, something everlasting... She went back to Red Hair.

"Why did you not tell me before that you were not my mother?"

Red Hair seemed at first unable to say anything. Clearly it was a difficult question, and Shining Face waited, anxiously, not knowing at all what to expect. "I have to confess something," Red Hair said, slowly. "It was because I wanted you for myself, for my own daughter. You might have wanted someone else to take my place. I did not want to lose you. I even warned the women never to tell you I was not your mother. I did have a certain power over them."

"But you did want to go with my father when he left the old camp – and leave me behind. Isn't that so?"

"And I would have lost you for ever!"

"Tell me, Mother, why did Father leave the old camp really?"

"Because the only time I ever lay with him, someone told Giant Man and Giant Man was going to have him killed. It was not long after the bear killed your mother. Sometimes we have no choice. I am glad I did not go now – now that I have got both of you..." She hesitated. "...I *have*, haven't I?"

Shining Face threw herself down and hugged her. "You're the best mum I could have had," she said, "and I shall always be thankful that you gave me the cones. I would never have found you otherwise."

Soon Big Nose returned with a baby seal that had got itself trapped somehow, and they skinned it and cooked it in a hollow in the shingle. in front of the cave under the stars.

* * *

Shining Face was very tired. They had walked for two days by the sea, half mesmerized finally by the incessant loud grating sound of the undertow on the shingle. There was very little snow here, and certainly not enough for the sledge, which they had abandoned back at the cave. As often happened, she and Red Hair were climbing one in the endless chain of headlands, while Big Nose made his way along the difficult, rocky shore, examining tide pools from time to time in the hope of spearing some stranded fish, and clambering over the rocky arms that enclosed each little bay.

Red Hair was setting the pace up the slope, but slipping from time to time because in the afternoon the remaining snow was slushy. She was stronger now, and carrying extra skins that they had had time to prepare in the many days spent in the cave. Shining Face, still in some pain from the wound in her side and even now weak from her long starvation, trapped in that other cave, tagged along behind. Aided by her spear, she carried merely the pouch with her most precious things and a couple of skins.

How she admired the woman who had always been mother to her – and still was, who had cared for her for many years. And how steadfastly Big Nose had remained faithful to Red Hair! How could she, his daughter, have been so unkind to him? So untrusting! But if even *he* said he thought he might be a bringer of bad luck, who was she to argue otherwise? She would not argue; she just knew what she knew! She was determined now always to stand by him, and that nothing would separate the three of them.

"But some man may want to take you to another place, hopefully a good camp where you would come to no harm," Red Hair said when not for the first time Shining Face had voiced her regrets and her resolve concerning her father.

"Maybe I would go, but only if we all go together," she had replied, and she was turning these things over in her mind when without warning, on a stretch of sand far below them, a fearful sight brought them to a sudden halt. Big Nose, on the sand between some rocks, had stopped in his tracks and was being surrounded by many men gesticulating and shouting – though most of the sound was carried away on the wind – before being escorted somewhere down under the cliff. Then everything was as it had been before – just the endlessly repeated crashing and drawing back of the waves, and the sound of the wind blowing the grass. Otherwise – silence. So quickly had it happened that it could almost have been an illusion.

"We have to go down," Shining Face said with a sinking feeling in her stomach and scarcely believing that her loyalty to her father might be tested so soon! "It's no good trying to hide and attempt a rescue. Not in the state we're in." She searched in her pouch for her Toothy knot and kept holding it in her hand. "We'll have to go back down the way we've come."

In the event, they must have been seen, for they had not got very far when four or five men with spears were coming up towards them, and soon they had been escorted by these men in disciplined fashion down a hidden and precipitous path to find Big Nose surrounded by many men in front of an enormous cave. The men turned in curiosity towards the new arrivals, while women standing behind, in the cave mouth, also watched with interest, several feeding babies or gathering older children close to them. Others were tending a lively fire in a hearth of beach boulders to one side of the cave entrance. The large carcase upon it might have smelt very appetising if Shining Face had not felt sick with foreboding.

Clearly, Big Nose was having difficulty in making himself understood, but very soon everybody moved back a bit as the three of them were thrust forward amid nods and grunts of approval from the men as Red Hair came close to them. When one young man close to Shining Face tried to touch her, evidently (as she admitted to herself) because he was not sure whether she was boy or woman, and she shrank back, there was a great roar from a giant wearing a lion's mane skin. As the older men pulled back the young upstart roughly, the headman motioned to the three newcomers to stand before him.

The people around were silent except for an occasional Shsh! Shsh! when some child made a noise, but the headman's questions were incomprehensible, and with no communication possible tempers became slightly raised. The headman motioned most of the people away and went into a discussion with two of the men.

The onlookers dispersed immediately – there was no questioning Lion Man's authority! As the men finished debating, a gangly young fellow, not much more than a boy but quite tall and with long, untidy hair and the beginnings of a beard, stepped forward from the background and spoke to one of them, who then went to the headman again. Evidently the man-boy was requesting permission to communicate with the captives himself, because he came over to Big Nose and, with a worried look on his face, spoke to him in words they all understood:

"Lion man says you may eat with us but then you must go," he said. "He says he has no room for invalids."

Lion Man uttered more words, loudly so that everyone could hear.

"I think he is saying the women will stay," the man-boy explained.

"Tell him we all stay or leave," Shining Face said. At least it made things clear, she thought, but when the translation was passed to Lion Man he erupted into a roar, the meaning of which was not in doubt either, and that seemed to be that. The man-boy disappeared.

"Since they're offering us food, let's eat," Red Hair murmured as they were shown a place to sit a little way from the cave entrance, "and we'll talk about what to do later." There they were brought pieces of meat by the women, and also wooden bowls filled with nuts and dried berries.

Afterwards, the young fellow came to them again and spoke to Big Nose. Shining Face could hardly believe her ears when she heard him ask if it was possible he could be Shining Face's father. She was dumbfounded. Surely it could not be *him*! So tall, and that voice – a man's voice.

"Yes," he replied, "How do you know her name?"

"I was brought up among the same people. She was my friend. It must have been long after you left."

Then she recognized those spindly legs, a bit hairy now, emerging below an elegant apron of well stretched deerskin; those skinny arms likewise from the armholes of a smart bison fur – arms that were nothing much to look at but which could throw a stone and hit a flying bird with deadly accuracy – and were getting a bit hairy too... Of *course* he was tall and sounded different. He was a man.

"So that is how you speak our language," Big Nose said.

"Yes. And the woman is Red Hair, the mother she went to look for?"

"Yes," he replied for simplicity's sake. "Can you put in a good word for us? What's your name?"

"Toothy."

"So you know Toothy," Big Nose said, turning to Shining Face without waiting for any reply to his first question..

"Yes, without the things I learned from Toothy I would not have survived." She smiled at him, and received in return the same old grin long remembered and long wished for and only then revealing those unforgettable teeth..

But then, turning to Big Nose Toothy said quickly, "Lion Man will be watching us. He has many women, but never enough. It's best we stop talking. Of course, I recognized Shining Face straight away. But," he said, turning to her, "I must not be seen to know you. The chief is a very suspicious man, and very jealous. I have simply told him that it is because I happened to have met others from your people that I understand your language."

"How come that you are here, Toothy?" Shining Face asked him.

"I'll tell you later. Look, we cannot talk more now, but I'll try and persuade him at least to allow your father to stay till tomorrow. If your father agrees, I suggest you and I should meet secretly and decide what to do." Sensing that Big Nose did not disagree, he said, "It would be too dangerous to meet today, but at dawn tomorrow look out for a signal from me near the bottom of the cliff. It will come from that dark clump of bushes right across from the cave," he added without looking round. "Do you see it?" Shining Face nodded. "We must talk. If you walk and scramble slowly over there, the women, if they see you, will just think you have gone to relieve yourself."

Big Nose was allowed to stay the night and went off to find what shelter he could along the shore. Red Hair and Shining Face were taken to sleep with the women in another cave nearby – or was it part of the same cave?

Just before dawn, the camp was already beginning to stir. No sooner had Shining Face made her way among the rocks and taken the opportunity to relieve herself than she caught Toothy's distant arm movement. It was a childhood signal between them. She walked and clambered on without hurrying, another woman crouching among the rocks taking no notice. It took longer than she expected, but once across, she soon found him.

A faint path led steeply up to a concealed gap in the gorse and brambles near the cliff top.

Before she could say anything as they crouched there in the bracken, he said, looking very serious, "Shino, I want to help you. I so much want to help you and your mother escape."

"Wouldn't you be the first suspect?"

"I could risk it. You could both come up this path with me, and your father could be waiting for you both here. Nobody uses this path. I made it."

"It's too dangerous for you. Supposing you were found out."

"I could make a run for it if the worst came to the worst. You know how I can run!"

"But in any case you have found a home here. Wasn't it hard enough getting *here*, never mind risking everything again?"

"Never mind that. Shino, you must not stay here, any of you. They will ill-treat you, especially Lion Man. You *must* let me help you."

Shining Face looked into his eyes. "Toothy, there is another thing: I cannot leave you. I have been holding this for ages," she said, showing him the Toothy knot, "hoping that it would help me find you."

Toothy looked at it. Shining Face suddenly realised he might be thinking it made him look ugly. "Toothy, I think you're beautiful," she said, and kissed him. He hung his head. It was unlike him to be embarrassed... They said nothing for a while, then, seeming to pluck up courage he seized her and kissed her on the lips.

"I could come with you, hunt for you, Shino," he said. "The only thing is..." He hesitated.

"It's Big Nose, isn't it?" He looked shame-faced. "Toothy," she said, taking both his hands in hers, "It's nonsense, all that about him bringing bad luck. Do you believe me? Didn't we always say the truth to each other?"

"Yes," he replied, "but ..."

"Listen! My father is the bravest man. He saved me and Red Hair. By the way, Red Hair was never my mother."

"But I thought... so..."

"She fostered me when my mother was killed. It was before you were born. She has been as good as any mother to me. My father soon had to leave the camp suddenly because Giant Man found out that he had allowed Red Hair – his favourite – to visit him and lie with him. Red Hair wanted my father to take her with him, but his mind was made up to go alone. Then when the chief died Red Hair had to go too, because the women hated her. I think you knew that. But somehow they came together after a long time, only to be separated again. Meantime, as you know, I went in search of her but finished up getting attacked by lions in a cave." Toothy had been casting anxious glances towards the camp, but now he was looking at her questioningly and was very attentive as she went on, "My father found me there, looked after me and nursed and fed me. After journeying together for nearly a year we found Red Hair at death's door. We brought her to the sea with us, and here we are, in more trouble. So are you going to tell me how *you* came here?"

"I was looking for you," he replied. "I left just after you. But look, we must stop talking now. The men are getting ready to go already. I must go and join them, and you must go down to be with the women."

She gripped his hands. "You will come with us, won't you?" she implored him.

He looked hard at her, looked into her eyes. "Do you *really* want me to come, Shining Face? Really?"

"Yes, you know I do," she replied.

He was silent for a moment, looking at her. "I will come," he replied. "And this is how we can do it. The men will soon leave. I have to go too, but we shall all return by nightfall. *We* shall leave tonight," he said. "The best time will be when the men have returned, had their food and drink and got a bit merry and the women are clearing up or have gone to their quarters. Your father will have to leave the camp this morning. Some older men, not hunting, will accompany him a long way to get rid of him, but he must find his way back and wait here, at this spot. I will wait for you at the bottom of the path with as much of all your stuff and mine as I can carry without attracting attention. The men know I often hunt at night and won't think anything of my departure. Get there as best you can, and with any food you can lay your hands on, when I light an ember in a place which can only be seen from the women's quarters. Come separately, the two of you, and join up on the path. Even if the women see you and are suspicious, they won't say anything. They'll be glad to be rid of you both. But I must see your father before he is taken away. tell him how to get back from where I think they will take him. Let's go!" Toothy said, getting up, "and talk later. There are things I want to tell you."

*   *   *

It had seemed a long wait on the cliff top for the three of them to come up. Big Nose had been on his own long enough to be used to watching the stars or listening to the sounds of the forest while waiting, lying and listening for prey, but this was something else, something else altogether, *this* waiting!

At first when Toothy had come and found him and explained his plan for all four of them to escape it had seemed almost too good to be true. Then doubts had begun to assail him. Even supposing he got back all right (and he had!), and the three of them got up the path safely and they all made their escape, what would the coming days bring? How would it be when Toothy warded off the lions, or went hunting with Shining Face and brought back all the food they needed? What use would he be? And would Red Hair really want him now – and for always?

He caught his breath. There had been no alarms sounding down below and yet he could hear hurrying steps on the rocky path. His fingers brushed the ring of acorns.

"Big Nose!" came a whisper. It was Toothy, heavy with skins and slings and bulging pouches.

Big Nose crawled out from the bushes. Red Hair, heavily laden too, grasped his hand, letting Shining Face, carrying a smaller load, go in front a few paces behind Toothy as he hurried forward in the growing light. It was just before moonrise. No words were spoken as they hurried on into the night, more quickly when the moon emerged from behind the clouds, more slowly when it retreated behind them.

Sometimes, now, where the way was easy they walked all together, he with Red Hair, Toothy with Shining Face, but often it was difficult, especially for himself, with sudden precipitous slopes and streams, and rocks ready to break their bones. Here Toothy's knowledge of the terrain and his agile assistance were invaluable. Shining Face told them the women had either not seen or heard anything when they left, or they had pretended not to, yet still the fugitives tried not to reduce their pace, determined to put as great a distance as possible between themselves and Lion Man. Gradually Big Nose's fears began to subside and his hopes increase, especially in the knowledge that the spring season on the verge of appearing would bring more tolerable conditions and an improving food supply. Sometimes in the moonlight he would see Red Hair smiling at him.. If he had had moments when he feared she might not always think the same about him, those fears had already begun to fade when some time after they had found her he had braved the lioness and dared to call her 'My Fairness', and she had clasped him to herself. Now they had all but vanished.

They rested just inside a thick wood near a fast-flowing stream that offered good drinking water, and ate some of the scraps of food that they had managed to bring with them. Big Nose asked Toothy about himself and who his father was.

"My father was a brave man," he replied. "He died when I was very small, saving a man from drowning."

Something came together in Big Nose's mind. "What was his name?"

"It was Strong."

Big Nose caught his breath, but said nothing. How pleased he was to hear that! So he was a son of his best friend now so long passed away. It awakened all the old sadness, but at the same time it seemed in some strange way to be saying that now things were going the right way for all of them. He asked Toothy to tell them how he had got on since leaving the old camp.

Big Nose did not doubt Toothy's word any more than Shining Face did when he came to describe herding mammoths around and driving lions out of a cave in dreams that were more than dreams, or later when he mentioned that once he did not fish a drowning deer out of a flooded river because he felt someone needed it more than he did.

"I knew you were behind all that," Shining Face said.

"You knew?" Toothy looked at her curiously.

"And I was frightened for you."

"I always knew you were different, Shino, so different."

She smiled. "Yes, I knew *you* were, as well." At that, she felt his hand grip hers, and she was happier than she had ever been, especially when he gave her that big smile that was all teeth and Toothy.

Nor, when Shining Face recounted all her experiences, did Big Nose doubt that it was she who had saved Toothy when he turned into a duck and she plucked it from the water with a mind to eat it but then let it fly away.

"Yes, it was a terrible day," Toothy said, "I could never understand why I did not drown unless it was you who came to my rescue."

Things had been hard for Big Nose since the bear that he had angered took Curvy Lips from him. Now, as the first orange streaks began to appear in the eastern sky, he felt that just as long as all of them could be together everything would turn out well wherever they ended up, and when the stars disappeared and another day burst into light he felt content.
